THE SOUND OF ONE HAND CLAPPING

Fay Doxford

Pen Pen Press Publishers Ltd

First published in Great Britain by
Pen Press Publishers Ltd
25 Eastern PLace
Brighton
BN2 1GJ

ISBN 978-1-906206-05-5

Excerpts of lyrics used throughout this book are attributed to:

Romeo & Juliet by Dire Straits, written by Mark Knopfler
Girl by The Beatles, written by Lennon and McCartney
Spanish Harlem by the Mamas and the Papas, written by Lieber-Stoller
In Too Deep by Genesis, written by Genesis (Banks/Collins/Rutherford)
Cardiac Arrest by Madness, written by Chas Smash and Chris Foreman

---

Printed and bound in Great Britain by
Cpod, Trowbridge, Wiltshire

A catalogue record of this book is available from
the British Library

Cover design Eleanor and James Cramphorn

The Sound of One Hand Clapping

This life is far too tough, and there's never quite enough
Love and peace and stuff to go around.
Each day's a constant fight, we're shut off from the light,
We're locked up way too tight to hear the sound.
The sound of one hand clapping,
Spreading hope and harmony,
The one hand of compassion,
Reaching out to you and me.
One hand is all you need for a hand job to succeed,
It's time for us to heed our limitations.
Time for us to see, time the world was free,
Time for unity; accept no imitations.
And hear the sound of one hand clapping,
Spreading hope and harmony,
The one hand of compassion,
Reaching out to you and me.

It was Friday, December the second. The Royal Albert Hall was packed. Everyone was there, all their families and friends, even Coral and Miles. Coral had insisted on coming, although she had given birth only nine days earlier. She'd had a boy, weighing in at six-and-a-half pounds. He had Stephen's black hair, but his eyes were exactly the same colour as hers.

"I begin to think we might get away with it, Coral's father has very dark hair. We can't thank you enough, Stephen," Miles had said when Stephen managed to steal a couple of hours to visit the hospital. They had named him Theodore John – "Theodore because he was a divine gift," Miles explained, "and John because he was *your* gift." He smiled. "We wanted to call him Theodore Stephen, but reluctantly came to the conclusion that your middle name would be more discreet."

"I wanted him to have eyes like yours, Stevie," Coral pouted. "Never mind, I'm sure the next one will have."

"Coral!" Miles exclaimed. "She's incorrigible!"

Stephen kissed her. "I wouldn't have her any other way."

Backstage, they could feel the level of anticipation rising from the audience. The tour had been a huge success.

"I can never get used to playing here, like!" Andy said.

"Yeah, it's amazing," Fin agreed. "Twenty-five years ago I was well chuffed by the thought of playing at UMIST Union!"

"Mind, if someone had told me then we'd still be together in twenty-five years, bonny lad, I'd never have believed them," George smiled.

"We've had some incredible times," Stephen sighed. He looked at Dominic. "It's great having you here, too, Charlie. You're all such good, good friends." His eyes filled with tears.

The others groaned.

"Howay, you lass, pull yourself together," George said affectionately.

Stephen held out his arms. "Time for a group hug, lads?" he asked, grinning.

"As if!"

"Stop being a wimp, like."

"Oh, for fuck's sake, Markham."

"I'm going to have to belt you in a minute, man!"

It was time. The five of them walked out into the lights. A howl went up from the audience; the building rang with cheering and applause.

Stephen stepped forward. "Hi, there!"

"Hi!" they yelled back.

A girl near the front shouted, "I love you, Stephen!"

"Shh!" Stephen feigned alarm. "My wife will hear!"

This got a laugh and a round of applause.

"Well, as you all know," he went on, "twenty-five years ago tonight, Sid's Six played their first ever gig. The venue was a *little* smaller than this." The crowd laughed. "Since then, we've got ourselves a new lead guitar, good old Dominic Chaplin here. He actually played in Sid's Six for a few months in Manchester, although he was only playing rhythm guitar then. He always was pushy!" More laughter. Stephen and Dominic grinned at each other. "OK," Stephen continued. "We'd like to start with a song I wrote a long time ago as a bit of a joke. I never realised how much it would come to mean to me." He held up his right hand and rapidly pressed his fingers up and down into his palm.

The audience immediately followed suit.

Stephen smiled. "Ladies and gentlemen – The Sound Of One Hand Clapping!"

Part One
Tabula Rasa

I'm a blank slate,
Waiting for the chalk you hold in your hand.
Make your mark on me,
Take this darkness from me,
I don't need to talk,
Just understand.

Chapter One
Next of Kin

They make you happy, make you sad,
Keep you sane, drive you mad,
Rescue you, do you in,
Next of kin.

"Steve, I think you know why I want to talk to you, don't you?"

Genuinely puzzled, Stephen shook his head. "No, Dad."

His father looked at him, sighed and polished his reading glasses on his tie – never a good sign. "Are you quite sure there's nothing you want to speak to me about?"

Stephen racked his brain apprehensively. "I don't think so, Dad."

They were sitting in his father's study, a small room crammed with books and papers. The battered old sofa and chair were leather, and redolent of his father; for the rest of Stephen's life, the smell of leather would bring back the picture of John Markham – a tall, thin, patient, quietly spoken man – and with it, a mixed feeling of love and guilt. All his father's triumphs were in this room, including his graduation certificate from Oxford University, and his trophies from St Paul's, an exclusive and excellent grammar school for which he had won a scholarship – the school Stephen now attended. A framed photograph of Stephen himself, at the age of eleven and in school uniform, had a prominent place on the desk.

John sighed again, and handed a letter to Stephen, who read it in horrified silence. He gave it back, unable to look at his father.

"What's it all about, son?"

Stephen dug his nails into his palms. "I just… see Dad, I said we didn't want me to play cricket any more."

"Is that the truth, Stephen?"

"Well, kind of, Dad. *I* don't want me to play it."

"Why not, son?"

"Because of my fingers."

John was startled. "What's wrong with them?" he asked in alarm.

"Nothing, Dad, that's the point. But if I keep on playing cricket there might be. Greg Parrish broke his fielding last month; I didn't think anything of it at the time, but you should see them now, all swollen and twisted. He doesn't care, he loves sport anyway, but supposing it happened to me? I'd never make it as a guitar player!"

There was silence. Stephen could see his father groping for words. Finally John said, "Son, you must understand that the sports you play at school are as important in their own way as the academic subjects. You're getting a fine education that will prepare you for the rest of your life. You're a very competent pianist – you take after your mother – and you play the guitar well, but music can only ever be a hobby. You're old enough now to take control of your life and start shaping it towards the future." His tone changed, and he gave Stephen an exasperated look. "Your marks have been very poor indeed, you're at the bottom of the class in everything except English and history. It's simply not good enough, son, you'll be sixteen in November, and sitting your 'O' Levels next year. And it's not as if this is the first time I've had to speak to you about your attitude to school. You've got to pull yourself together, Stephen. I can't imagine what your next report will say, the last one was atrocious."

Stephen was stung. "But I'm top in music and art, Dad, you know I am! And Mrs Hill says my cello playing is exceptional!"

John raised his eyebrows. "I'm talking about serious subjects, Stephen. Music and art are very well in their way, but academically, they don't count." He shook his head. "Son, I know you think I'm a boring old man who doesn't understand, but I do. Once you get to a certain age, you have to make some changes."

Oh no, thought Stephen, here we go: When I was a child...

"When I was a child, I spake as a child, but when I became a man I put away childish things. Now, when I was your age..."

This homily was as familiar to Stephen as the room in which they were sitting. If his father was struck dumb, Stephen could finish it word for word. He tuned it out, turning up the music that was always playing inside his head. This time it was Paul Simon's 'The Boxer'. He was thinking about Simon's fingerpicking style, and wondering how good the man had been at his age, when he realised his father had stopped speaking and was looking at him quizzically.

"Sorry, Dad, I didn't hear you."

"I asked you to give me your word of honour that your marks will improve. That means less music and more study." John smiled at him. "Let's make a bargain. You make that promise and I'll write to Mr..." he groped for the letter "...Baker, and tell him you won't be playing cricket this term. How's that?"

Stephen sagged with relief. "Thanks, Dad! I promise I'll work really hard, you'll be so proud of me."

John put his arm round his son's shoulder. "I'm so proud of you already! And think how proud I'll be when you go up to university! But, son, a good degree means working, not just at university, but now. You must form the habit of working hard, then by the time you're grown up, it'll be second nature. When you come into the firm I'll expect a good, hard worker, eh, son?" He laughed, but Stephen knew he wasn't joking. His path had been shaped before he was born; he would go up to Oxford, study law, follow in his father's footsteps.

"What a team we'll make, eh, Stevie? Wait till you have a son, you'll want him to join you. It's every father's dream."

Stephen thought of his grandfather, John's father. He could barely remember him, just a strong northern accent and a comfortable, kindly presence. He had been a miner and had died of pneumoconiosis before Stephen was five. "Didn't Grandpa want you to work with him?"

John was silent for so long that Stephen thought he hadn't heard. "Dad?"

"No," John said quietly. "No, he didn't." He smiled at Stephen. "Well, off you go, son. It's a lovely day, you should be outside with your friends."

Stephen shut the door quietly behind him, sighing with relief. He'd got off lightly, considering. God! He'd never dreamed that bastard Baker would send a letter home. Bloody teachers! He made his way to the kitchen to get a drink. The radio was on, and his mother was ironing, and singing along to 'Mamma Mia'.

"Hello, Mum." He poured himself a glass of lemonade. "Mum, why didn't Dad become a miner like Grandpa?"

Sian stopped ironing. What a very good-looking boy he is, she thought with pride. He had thick, silky black hair and her warm, creamy complexion; a firm, square jaw, and John's rather tough-looking mouth, which could relax into a charming smile. But his most striking feature was the unique colour of his eyes. They were a very pale blue; ice blue was how Sian always thought of them. She had no idea who he'd got them from; her family were Welsh and their eyes were all very dark. John had blue eyes, but they were a bright blue, not the fascinating colour his son's were. People looked twice at Stephen.

"What a strange question! What on earth put that into your head?"

"He said it's every father's dream to have his son going to work with him."

Sian sighed. "For him it is. I'm not sure about other dads. I know your grandpa was very proud of him. See, Stevie, parents always want their children to do well. And to be happy," she added.

"So if I didn't want to do law," Stephen said slowly, "Dad wouldn't mind as long as I was happy?"

Sian busied herself with the ironing. This had become a very difficult conversation. She knew John had set his heart on Stephen studying law, but she also knew Stephen wasn't like his father. Not at all. He was an intelligent boy but he had no interest in learning for its own sake. He would work at what interested him: English, history and art had always been his favourite subjects. She didn't include music; to Stephen, music wasn't work. He loved music, he sang all the time, often without realising he was doing it, and he could lose himself playing the piano. He had been composing music for it for the last couple of years, and Sian was very impressed by what she'd heard. Her father had given him an acoustic guitar when he was thirteen, and he'd taught himself to play it very well, very quickly. He was having cello lessons at school and they were the highlight of his week, even though he didn't much like the theory that went with it, preferring to feel the music through the instrument and his voice. Sian didn't believe he'd ever be happy in a legal career and had recently attempted to point this out to John, who'd looked at her, amused, and shaken his head. "Of course he will, Sian, whatever are you thinking? It's all planned. By the time he's finished at Oxford, I'll be nearly ready to retire. I can show him the ropes for a couple of years, then he can strike out into his career without the old man breathing down his neck!"

"But he has to be able to choose what *he* wants to do with his life, John, like we did."

"Oh, Sian, as if I'd force him to do something he didn't want to! It *is* his choice, he wants it as much as I do, we've discussed it so many times!"

You've told him what you want him to do, you mean, Sian thought. "But John—"

"Sian, Sian! Whatever are you worrying about? I know my son. He's just like me."

Sian didn't answer. How could so intelligent a man be so blind?

"Do you think you might not want to do law, then?" she asked Stephen.

He looked at her, trying to gauge her attitude to the subject. She'd never said she thought he should be a solicitor, but she'd been there when his father had talked about it, and she'd said nothing then either. "I don't know, Mum," he said finally. "The thing is, I might, but I might not. I don't want to let Dad down though."

He looked so wretched that she felt a flash of anger towards John. *He* had done what he wanted with his life; Stephen should have that choice. She hugged him. "Don't worry, cariad, it'll all come out in the wash. As I said, we just want you to be happy."

Stephen and his sisters, Kathy and Rebecca, spent the long, unexpectedly hot and dry summer with their grandmother on the Isle of Wight. Gwen Hughes – Mam, as her children and grandchildren called her – had a large old house at the bottom of Dover Street in Ryde, overlooking the sea. The front garden was a fragrant mass of roses, and their scent filled the house, mingling with the smell of dog. Nesta, Sian's elder sister, had never married, and lived at home breeding pugs.

Sian was the youngest of six. She'd been born in Cardiff, but had suffered bronchitis very badly as a child, and her mother, fearing that the smoky, polluted air was damaging her lungs, had taken the drastic step – for a Welshwoman – of leaving Wales. Sian's father, Rhodri, known to the entire family as Dada, had died the summer before, leaving a void in all their lives. Stephen had been very close to Dada, who had shared and encouraged his love of music. As a young man, Rhodri had trained as an opera singer, although he had eventually chosen a career as an accountant. "See, son, numbers are my passion," he'd told Stephen, "and you should always follow your passion." He had left his records to Stephen, but the pleasure of owning such a large and eclectic collection was overshadowed by the loss of Dada.

The children spent every summer in Ryde, with Sian and John coming down from York for two weeks in August. This year, however, John didn't come, and when the children asked where he was, Sian told them vaguely that he was too busy. Stephen thought this odd; John was permanently busy, but this had never stopped him before. He missed his father; the two of them always went fishing together. It wasn't the same without him. But then, nothing's been the same since Dada died, Stephen reflected sadly.

When they got home, it was only a week until the beginning of school, and the rest of the holiday was taken up with shopping for sports kit and various items of uniform. John had kissed them when they got back, and asked if they'd had a good time, and said he was sure they'd grown, like he always did. But Stephen sensed a certain coolness, not exactly towards himself, just around everything. He pushed it to the very back of his mind. He'd promised he would continue to work after trying very hard last term and getting a decent report. He somehow felt it was extremely important this year to show his father how well he could do.

"What do you think Hardy meant by that line, Markham?"

Stephen jumped. He had no idea what poem the teacher was referring to, let alone what line. It was nearly three-thirty, it had been a long, dull day, and although he enjoyed English, this teacher, Colin Ferry, somehow managed to make it as boring as maths. "Um… sorry, sir, which one?"

Ferry gave him a dark look. "I don't care what time it is, Markham. I'm in no hurry to leave, I've got a staff meeting tonight, and I'm quite happy to sit here until you start paying attention. I shouldn't think your classmates are keen though."

Stephen felt himself going red. Why did the man have to be such a bastard?

"'*When you had changed*'," his best friend, Ray Wallace, muttered from the seat next to him.

At that moment, the bell rang, and Stephen breathed a sigh of relief. There was a general buzz of conversation, and chairs were scraped back noisily. The teacher raised his voice. "All right, that'll do. I want your essays on my desk first thing Friday morning and I want at least four sides *neatly* written. Is that clear?"

Ray turned to Stephen. "Saved by the bell, you jammy sod! You going down the chippy?"

Stephen nodded. "Yeah, all right. Let's go to the one off Gillygate, we can have a look at the guitars in Walkers on the way." He was saving hard for an electric guitar, but as John already thought he spent far too much time on his music, he hadn't mentioned this. He would be sitting his 'O' levels the following summer and was determined to do well, but he also felt he was entitled to a spend a little time doing things he liked.

On the way home from the chip shop, he bought a local paper. The weather had turned cold, and he hurried into the house. "Hello, Mum. It's freezing outside! Do you want a cup of tea?" He put the kettle on and fetched the teapot. "Shall I make Dad one?"

Sian was washing up. "I'd love one, cariad, and I'm sure Dad would. You're late, have you been to Ray's?"

"Yeah, we got chips," he said, fetching mugs. He sat down and studied the paper, suddenly breathing in sharply.

Sian looked at him, her curiosity piqued. What could he have seen that had made him so excited? His normally pale skin was flushed, and he was lost in concentration. She went and read over his shoulder. He was looking at the For Sale section. "What is it?" she asked.

He looked up in surprise. He'd been miles away, completely absorbed in the adverts. "Oh, nothing you'd be interested in, Mum."

"Come on, Stevie!"

"This, here, look, a Fender Strat for sale – *'as new, unwanted gift'*," he read. He looked at her. "Unwanted gift! Who in their right minds wouldn't want a Strat?"

Sian was bemused. "What's a Strat?"

"Mum! You must have heard of Fender Stratocasters! They're electric guitars. Jimi Hendrix played one – and Hank Marvin," he added, remembering that Sian liked the Shadows.

"Oh." She looked at the advert again. "Gosh, it's expensive!"

"Yes, but much cheaper than new. They make such an incredible noise, Mum, so mellow, so…" He shook his head. "I can't describe it; you know that turquoisey colour that tropical seas are? That's what they sound like."

She nodded. She didn't know what he meant, but she was used to him describing sensations in this peculiar way, he'd done it since he was small. "So this is what you're saving your pay for, is it?"

Stephen and Ray had Saturday jobs at Maurice Braithwaites, Gentleman's Outfitters, in the centre of York. He glanced warily up at her. "Um…"

"Stevie, it's your money, you work for it. You can do what you want with it."

He grinned. "Yeah, this sort of thing. This one's far too much, but I'll get one eventually." The kettle boiled and he poured the water into the teapot, whistling.

She studied him, thinking. Of course John wouldn't like it, but he'd simply have to live with it. Stephen was working so hard at school for him, and now he had a job, he was no longer given any pocket money. "It'll teach him the value of money," John had said.

"He's not sixteen yet!" Sian had protested.

"You can't learn too young, Sian, and it won't hurt him, do him good, in fact. I started working part-time when I was only fourteen."

"But, John, your family needed the money."

John shook his head. "That's not the point, Sian. You'll see, he'll thank us for it when he's older."

Us! Sian thought resentfully. Stephen hadn't seemed to mind, but she did. Very much.

Stephen picked up his mug of tea. "I better go, I've got an essay to write," he sighed. "What time's tea?"

"I thought you said you'd had chips?"

"That was ages ago! I'm starving!"

Sian smiled. "So what's new? It'll be about an hour – and no, you can't take those upstairs!" she said, slapping his hand as he reached over for the biscuit barrel. "Go and get on with your essay. Oh, and leave the paper, would you? I'd like to look at it."

"Stevie! Happy birthday! Where have you been? Kath and I have been down here for *hours*! We've got you great presents, haven't we, Mum?" Rebecca wriggled around on her chair in excitement

Sian smiled. "Yes, Becks, we have." She kissed Stephen. "Happy birthday, cariad." She turned back to the frying pan. "Dad'll be in any second."

Stephen sat down and sniffed appreciatively. Sian always made a cooked breakfast on birthdays. The door opened and John peered round it. "Shall I bring it in, Sian?"

Sian nodded. She bit her lip, her eyes glowing. John opened the door wide, and produced a long rectangular case and an amplifier. "Happy birthday, son. This is from your mother and me."

Stephen stared at the case, stunned. His heart was racing. "Oh, my God, is that a…? It can't be a..?"

"Open it, open it!" Rebecca yelled.

His hands trembling, Stephen opened the case. "A Strat," he whispered. "It's a Fender Strat! Oh, Mum and Dad! I don't know how to thank you!" He lifted the guitar reverently from the case. "It's so beautiful! How did you ever find one in ocean turquoise?"

"It wasn't easy," Sian admitted. "But I wanted it to make the right sound!"

They smiled at each other.

"What on earth are you are talking about?" John asked, mystified.

Sian shook her head. "Nothing. Come on, Stevie, play us something!"

They watched while he plugged the guitar in and adjusted the amplifier. "What shall I play?" he asked, his right hand softly stroking the guitar.

"Anything you want," Sian smiled.

He shut his eyes and picked out a tune. The guitar felt as if it had been made for him. He could see the lithe turquoise bands of music snaking sinuously around him, he was lost in it, there was nothing but the music, the sound he was making. It was all that existed.

When he finished there was silence.

Finally Sian said, "What's that called, Stevie? I don't think I've heard it before."

"I haven't played it to you before. It hasn't really got a name. Maybe 'Rhodri's Land'. I wrote it for Dada after he died."

"*You* wrote it?" John stared at him.

"It's lovely, Stevie." Sian was crying. "Dada would be so proud of you!"

John took her hand. "Wherever he is, he *is* proud of you, son," he said, quietly. "But not as proud as I am."

Stephen broke into a huge grin. "Thanks, Dad!" He strummed the guitar softly, and began picking out another tune.

Sian squeezed John's hand, unable to speak. She pulled herself together. "Come on, Stevie, open your presents from the girls and then we must have breakfast, or everyone will be late."

To Stephen's surprise, John met him at the door when he got in from school that afternoon. "Dad! You're home early!"

John smiled. "It's your birthday, Stevie, I thought it would be nice to be here when you got home. Did you have a good day?"

Stephen screwed up his face. "It was OK. Double maths this afternoon. I don't think I'm going to do very well in the exam, Dad, I'm not much good at it," he said, seriously.

"Come in here and talk to me." John held the study door open.

Stephen's heart sank. He went in, thinking: Oh, no, on my birthday?

John cleared his throat self-consciously. "This morning, Steve, when you played that tune, I was… well, amazed is the only word. I hadn't realised you wrote music, but your mother tells me you've been writing tunes for years. I had a long talk with her when I got home this afternoon and I accept that you don't want to study law. Why didn't you tell me, son? Am I so hard to talk to?"

"No, Dad, of course not. It's… well, I didn't really realise it myself till recently, and then I didn't want to hurt you." He felt tremendous relief, but also a huge sense of guilt. "I do want to go to university though," he added quickly. He couldn't disappoint this man any more. Besides, he couldn't imagine *not* going to university, however much he wanted to make music.

John was pleased. "To study what?"

"English lit, I think. Then I could always teach if…" He stopped.

"If?" John prompted.

Stephen bit his lip. "If what I really want to do doesn't work out."

"And what *do* you want to do?" John asked gently.

"I want to have a band. I want to write and play my own stuff, music and lyrics."

Despite being really appalled that Stephen should choose to waste his brain like this, John was interested. "Do you write lyrics?"

Stephen grinned. "Some. They're mostly rubbish at the moment, but I'm hoping I'll get better at it. I dream about being able to write like Dylan –"

"Ah, yes, Bob Dylan." John nodded sagely, anxious to prove that he was abreast of popular culture.

Stephen laughed. "Well, him too, but I was going to say Dylan Thomas."

"Oh." John was pleasantly surprised. He disliked Bob Dylan immensely – whiny, weasely little man, urging youngsters to rebel against their parents. Dylan wasn't even his real name, he understood. But Dylan Thomas was quite different. If Stephen wanted to write like that, there might be some hope for the boy. "Dylan Thomas, interesting man."

Stephen agreed. "Reading his prose is like reading poetry, he uses words in such an extraordinary way. We're doing *Under Milkwood* at school, it's brilliant."

From the ashes of John's dream of Stephen qualifying as a solicitor, a new one arose; Stephen gaining a first in literature at Oxford, becoming a Don, and publishing his poetry. He smiled at him. "I'm *so* glad we had this talk, Stephen!"

Stephen beamed back. "So am I, Dad." A huge weight had lifted from his shoulders. He'd told his father he was going to try and make it as guitarist and not only did John not mind, he actually seemed pleased about it.

The only trouble with the new guitar was that he wanted to play it continually. He couldn't practise into the night because he disturbed the others, so his only option was to move bedrooms. He decided to check out the attic, which had several rooms leading off a thin passage that ran the length of the house, and the one at the end was perfect. It was spacious, with a large window that overlooked the garden; its only drawback was that it was above the central heating boiler and very hot. He tried to open the window, but it was painted shut. The room itself was filthy, there were dead flies all over the floor, and the walls were covered with dust and cobwebs. But it had electricity and plenty of sockets. All it needed was cleaning and painting.

He tackled his mother that afternoon. "Mum, you know that big room in the roof, can I have it?"

Sian looked up from her book. "What do you mean, can you have it?"

"Can I have it as a bedroom?"

"What are you talking about? You've got a perfectly good bedroom, it was only redecorated in the summer."

"Yes, but I can't practise in it without disturbing everyone."

"All those rooms in the attic are filthy, Stephen," she said impatiently.

"I'll clean and paint it."

She burst out laughing. "This I would like to see. You wouldn't even clean your shoes if I didn't make you!"

"Really, Mum, I mean it."

She looked at him consideringly. "All right. But you *will* have to do it on your own, you're the one who wants to move. What about getting your furniture up the attic stairs?"

He hadn't thought of that. "It should go up there," he said hopefully.

"Well, you ought to look into that first. If there *is* enough room, how will you get it up there?"

He shrugged airily. "I'll sort something out."

She smiled at him. "All right, cariad, it's fine with me."

"What about Dad?"

"Oh, your father won't mind. He likes you children to show a bit of initiative."

Children! thought Stephen indignantly. He went off to find a tape measure. Sian smiled to herself. She could see this idea fizzling out within a few days.

She was wrong. Stephen spent his weekends cleaning and decorating the room. The only thing that defeated him was getting his furniture up there. He rang Ray Wallace. "Ray, you know how you said you want to learn to play guitar?"

There was a grunt from the other end of the phone, which he took as a yes.

"I'll teach you if you like."

"On your Strat?" Ray sounded enthusiastic.

"Well – on the acoustic, to start with. But if you get on OK with that we could move on to the Strat," Stephen temporised.

There was a pause. "What do you want in exchange?" Ray asked warily.

"What makes you think I want anything?"

"Fuck off, Markham!"

"Yeah, OK, there *is* a little something you could help me with, as it happens."

"What?"

"Just moving a bit of stuff in my bedroom."

He could practically hear Ray thinking about it. "That doesn't sound too bad. Yeah, OK, when?"

Stephen grinned to himself. Poor, simple Ray. "How about tomorrow? If you come round in the morning you can stay to lunch and I can give you a lesson in the afternoon."

"OK. I'll be there about eleven."

"Make it ten-thirty."

Ray stood in Stephen's old bedroom. "OK, Steve, what do you want me to push round?"

"It's not so much pushing. What we've got to do is get this stuff up to the attic."

Ray stared at him. "What are you talking about? You said move some stuff in your bedroom."

"Yeah, but this isn't my bedroom any more."

"Well, where the hell *is* your bedroom?"

"I just told you. In the attic."

"You bastard!"

"Come on, Ray, you said you'd help!"

Ray paced up and down the room. Finally, he said, "On one condition. I get to have a go on your Strat."

Stephen nodded resignedly. "OK, OK. Let's get on with it then."

Once they had finally got everything into Stephen's new room and arranged to his satisfaction, they were totally exhausted. "Don't you ever try anything like this again, Markham!" Ray warned from Stephen's bed, where he had collapsed with a groan.

"Raymond, did I lie to you?" Stephen asked reasonably.

Ray craned his head round to look at him. "I just finished rearranging your bedroom. Don't make me rearrange your face. What's for lunch?"

"Sausages and chips. But you'll have to use a knife and fork because my sisters'll be there and they're not used to watching animals eat."

"You're really asking for it, aren't you, Markham?" said Ray, without heat. "If I wasn't so fucking knackered, you'd be sorry."

Ray turned out to be easier to teach than Stephen had feared. They carried on with the lessons for several months, by which time he'd become reasonably good. They started to talk about forming a band after they'd finished their 'O' Levels, which were looming on the horizon.

"After all, once we're in the Lower Sixth, we can piss about as much as we want," Ray said, idly strumming Stephen's Stratocaster. "Why's it this colour?"

"Why are you so ugly? We'll have to do *some* work though, Ray."

"God, you're such a fucking swot. Yeah, all right, teacher's pet, *you* can work. *I'll* have a band and pull all the birds."

"I didn't say we couldn't have a band," Stephen objected. "I was just saying."

"Yeah, well, don't. I've got a low enough opinion of you as it is."

The 'O' Levels were hard. Stephen hadn't done too badly in the Mocks, but he hadn't bothered too much about them, they weren't the real thing. These were, and he started to worry about letting his father down. He got through them by revising very hard, getting lots of sleep, and promising himself he'd spend every spare moment of the summer holidays playing guitar. After the final exam, everyone went to the pub. When the landlord called time, they reeled into the street.

"What shall we do now?" someone asked.

"Carole and me are going home." Ray took his girlfriend's hand. "See you."

Angie Cartwright touched Stephen's arm. "Are *you* coming, Steve?"

He hadn't really noticed before how pretty she was. "Coming where?" He felt slightly unsteady on his feet.

"We're going round to Craig Broomall's. His mum and dad are on holiday."

"OK."

She smiled and took his arm. "Good."

At Craig's, someone gave Stephen a joint. He took a long drag and passed it to Angie.

She giggled. "I've never done this before!"

He smiled at her, his head spinning. "It's fun."

She put it in her mouth hesitantly, inhaled, and began to cough.

Stephen grinned. He patted her back and took the joint. "Like this."

She tried again. This time she managed without choking. "It tastes odd."

"Mmm," he said. She really was very pretty. He kissed her.

She responded instantly, pressing herself into his body. This, of course, had an immediate physical effect on him. He gave the joint to someone else, and pulled her closer.

The next day he had an appalling hangover. He also had a date with Angie.

He and Ray still had their jobs in Braithwaites. It was a small shop, old-fashioned, dimly lit and smelling faintly of mothballs, but always surprisingly busy. During the summer, the first he didn't spend on the Isle of Wight, they worked every day except Sunday and Wednesday afternoon, and Stephen discovered he had a flair for selling. He was polite and good-looking with barely a trace of an accent apart from a slight Welsh lilt that he had picked up from Sian and Rhodri and never lost.

The job didn't take much mental effort and paid reasonably well. Ray was saving for an electric guitar, and they spent a lot of time discussing the idea of a band. They needed a bass player and a drummer. Stephen was quite keen on a keyboard player, but Ray disagreed. "We'll have enough trouble finding a bass and a drummer. We don't want to complicate things."

"They've got to be decent players."

"Yeah, course. How are we going to find anyone?"

"We can put something up on the notice board when we're back at school."

Ray's face fell. "That's not for weeks!"

"Yeah, but you haven't got your guitar yet, and we're going to have to practise."

"I suppose. OK, what shall we call it?"

"How about 'The Brigands'?"

Ray thought about it. "The Brigands. The Brigands. Yeah, OK. Why?"

"A band of brigands, you know, like dear Lady Marchmain."

"What the fuck are you on about?"

"*Brideshead Revisited*. Don't you ever read anything?"

"*Playboy*."

"That doesn't count, you just look at the pictures."

The 'O' Level results came out at the end of August. Stephen picked up the envelope by his plate with trepidation.

"It won't bite!" Sian laughed.

"It might," he said seriously.

His parents were watching him. He swallowed and tore it open. As he read, he began to relax.

"Well?" asked Sian. "Come on, Stephen, did you pass?"

He handed her the slip. "Yep! Even maths!"

"Stevie! You've done really well! Five As!"

"Yes, you've done extremely well," agreed John. "If you carry on like this you should get very good results indeed when you sit your 'A' Levels." He beamed at

Stephen, imagining him graduating from Oxford. "Well done, son."

"I'm not even going to start thinking about any more exams yet," Stephen groaned.

Sian laughed and leant over to kiss him. "I can't say I blame you."

"It's never too early—" John began, breaking off at the look on Stephen's face. "Well, all right. It's only that I want the best for you, son."

"I know." Stephen smiled at him. "I'm going to ring Angie."

"What about breakfast?" Sian asked.

He picked up a piece of toast as he went out.

Angie had passed all her exams, getting mostly Cs. She was happy; she had no desire to go to university, although she was going to take a couple of 'A' Levels, mainly to please her parents. She wanted to take a shorthand and typing course after she finished school. "I can't see the point in all this studying," she told Stephen. "I'd rather be earning money. Being at school is like marking time, I want real life. Still, if I left now, I'd hardly ever see you, so it's worth it."

Stephen kissed her. "School would be unbearable without you."

She smiled at him. "That's how I feel. And I don't intend to work very hard either!"

He agreed with her, he was really only staying on for John. Despite discussing university with his father, he'd realised that all he really wanted to do was form a band and make a go of it.

Ray had done very well in the exams, getting six A grades and four Bs.

"And you call *me* a swot!" Stephen said. They were counting the stock at the end of the day.

Ray had the grace to look embarrassed. "Yeah, well, I did work quite a lot really," he admitted. "Actually, I'm looking forward to going back to school," he confided. "I'm getting a bit bored working here."

"Yeah, it's not very stimulating. How's the saving going?"

"Pretty good. My dad said he'd put something towards it since I did OK in the exams. I was going to have a look in that music shop in Stonegate at lunchtime, see what they've got. You coming?"

Stephen nodded. "Well, course. I mean, you'll need my expert advice, won't you?"

As soon as term started they put a card on the notice board in the entrance hall asking for drummers and bassists to contact them.

"You ought to know people really, Steve. You have cello lessons."

"Not any more. I think the cello and me have come to a parting of the ways."

"Yeah, but you must know other people who take lessons."

"In violin, piano and cello," Stephen retorted. "It may have escaped your notice, Raymond, but they don't give guitar or drum lessons here."

"Stupid, really, isn't it?" mused Ray. "Loads of us would take them if they did."

Harry Taylor stopped at the noticeboard as she always did when she arrived at school. She wasn't looking for anything in particular, but you just never knew. There might be something that would make life a little more fun. She didn't particularly want to still be at school, would much rather have left after 'O' levels, but her father wanted her to stay on. She'd done very well in the exams, and he wanted her to go to university, she knew, although he never said. Her two brothers had left school as soon as they could, Will at fifteen with no qualifications at all. She knew Dad hated that, like he hated the fact Will and Nick never came near him. They'd stayed down in London when she and Dad had moved up to York, lucky things. Nick had been eighteen, and Will twenty-two. She'd been thirteen, and had loathed it, missing everyone, particularly Nick, to whom she was very close. Her mother had died when she was born, but there was Nan and Gramps, her mum's parents, and Gran, her dad's mum, and aunts, uncles and cousins. And all her school friends. But they'd had no choice except to move after what Dad had done. She sighed.

And then, just as the bell went, she saw it: *Drummer and bassist wanted for band. If you are interested – AND CAN PLAY! – please see Ray Wallace or Stephen Markham, Sixth Form Common Room, any lunchtime.* She breathed in sharply. Bassist wanted! She played bass. But even better, *Stephen Markham* wanted a bassist! He was so incredibly gorgeous, with that sexy mouth and those curious, fascinating eyes. And he always smelled nice, not only clean, but *nice* as well, a sort of lemony smell. She'd fancied him for ages. They had English literature, music and history together, although he'd never noticed her. There were always girls after him, he could have his pick, but he'd split up with his girlfriend at Easter and she'd dreamed that maybe she could get talking to him after a lesson or something; if she could get his attention, he might ask her out. Then, to her disappointment, she'd heard he'd started going out with Angie Cartwright. Apparently the lucky cow had got off with him at Craig Broomall's party. Harry hadn't been able to go, Dad had been short handed in the pub. God, how she hated that bloody pub! Anyway, stuff all that, Steve wanted a bassist and she was determined it was going to be her.

She ran to the common room as soon as the lunch bell went. He wasn't there. Damn. She pulled a comb out of her bag and dragged it through her short, dark hair, studying her reflection in the mirror. Heart-shaped face, dark eyes – smallish, but an interesting almond shape – slim nose, wide, full lips, hmm, not too bad... And a spot like Mount Vesuvius on her chin. Shit! Why hadn't she put some makeup on that morning?

The door opened, and she moved quickly away from the mirror as Stephen came in with Angie, Ray and Carole. Her heart started to perform a tap dance against her ribs. She walked towards them. "Steve?"

He smiled. "That's me."

"You want a bassist for your band."

He was interested. "Yeah! Do you know one?"

"I *am* one!" she said indignantly. What a sexist bastard!

He'd gone red. "God, I'm sorry!"

Ray was laughing. "And you call me a tactless oaf, Markham!"

"Really," Stephen said earnestly. "I'm really sorry. It's Harriet, isn't it? We have quite a lot of lessons together, don't we?" He felt terrible, and the poor girl was red with annoyance. He didn't blame her.

God! He *has* noticed me! Harry thought, wishing she wasn't blushing. It was so mortifying. "Oh, well, never mind," she said awkwardly. "Anyway, about this band..."

"Yeah, when can you play for us?" Stephen asked, anxious to atone for his mistake.

"Oh, any time! This evening if you like."

He smiled at her, and she felt faint. "That's great! Where? You could come round to my house, or we could come to you. Where do you live?"

God! She didn't want them coming to the pub! If two boys showed up asking for her, Dad would have a fit! And besides, she'd love to see his house, she sometimes walked past it, it was a big, posh-looking one in Clifton. "It's probably easier if I come to you, I'm having some problems with my amp," she lied.

"OK, I'll give you my address." He hoped she was good, he liked her, there was something straightforward and refreshing about her. She didn't play games. He had this weird feeling about her, that she'd be a very good friend. "About five-thirty be OK?"

As soon as she started playing, he knew she was good, exceedingly so. She was very pretty too; full figured with dark hair and lovely sexy eyes, a deep, almost hot, brown colour with gold flecks around the iris. If I wasn't dating Angie, he thought, I'd ask her out, although she doesn't seem in the least interested in me – the opposite, if anything. Hardly surprising after the way I put my foot in it today.

When she finished, she looked at him questioningly. "Well?"

"We'd love to have you in the band, Harriet, you play brilliantly!"

She grinned with pleasure, feeling as if her heart was going to burst. "My brother taught me. Oh, and please don't call me Harriet, I hate it, it's so old-fashioned! Call me Harry. When do we start rehearsing?"

Stephen smiled at her. "As soon as we've got a drummer."

Ray wasn't too keen on the idea of a girl playing for them. "We can't have a girl in the band. It would cause too many problems," he commented after Harry had gone home.

"Why? Loads of bands have women in. Fleetwood Mac, for example. There's two in that."

"We're hardly Fleetwood Mac, are we?" Ray was scathing.

"I didn't say we were. I just said they've got girls."

Ray changed tack. "Yeah, but we're going to be playing in pubs and stuff. You know, what about getting changed, all lads together and so on?"

"I don't know where you think we'll be playing, Raymond. We're just going to turn up, play, get paid and go home. You can change if you want to, but you'll be on your own."

Ray muttered something that Stephen didn't catch.

"What?"

"I said, what about Angie and Carole?"

Stephen stared at him. "Neither of them can play anything. What the fuck are you talking about?"

"God, you're dense sometimes, Markham. I mean they're not going to like it if we've got a girl in the band."

"Jesus Christ, Raymond. That's your real objection, isn't it? I can't see Angie caring. Carole knew about the band when you started going out with her, I don't see how she can complain, but if she does, just tell her to shut up."

"Oh, yeah, and I can see you saying the same to Angie if *she* doesn't like it."

Stephen shrugged. "Certainly would. This is important, Ray."

Ray looked at him curiously. "You really mean that, don't you?"

"Certainly do."

They eventually found their drummer, a boy called Graham Lucas. He was tall, thin, and quiet, with thick Joe Ninety glasses and a friendly grin.

Next, they needed to find somewhere to rehearse. Stephen broached the subject with his parents. Their garage wasn't very big but it had a light and a couple of electric sockets. He asked if they could use it. Sian said she couldn't see it would be a problem as long as they didn't expect to be out there till the early hours of the morning.

John had no objection as long as Stephen's work didn't take second place. "After all, Stephen, you're working on a Saturday at Braithwaites, you've got the clubs you belong to at school, and you'll be taking your driving test shortly." John was teaching him to drive.

"Don't worry, Dad, I'll make sure I don't fall behind."

Stephen had been thinking a great deal about the whole concept of the band, not just from the point of view of the music, but presentation as well. During the holidays he'd gone to see as many live acts as he could, and noticed that the ones that had a bit of showmanship (for want of a better word), who looked clean, who came on with a bit of panache, who actually looked at the audience and mixed with them afterwards, were far better received than the other sort, who shuffled in, stared down at their guitars or shut their eyes while performing, and shuffled off again. He was going to make sure that The Brigands were among the former.

He also had definite ideas about the songs the band should perform. He'd been listening to Dada's records, and he'd become fascinated by the blues players. Rhodri had often played his blues records to him, particularly Stanton Crawford, B. B. King, and Tampa Red. The sound that the National Steel guitars made had fascinated and stirred him, he thought they sounded like gigantic sparklers, and he longed to play one. Rhodri had explained that, back in those days, there was no electrical amplification of sound and the places where the blues singers played were noisy and often dangerous. The National guitars were about four times louder than wooden guitars – with the added advantage that they could stop a bullet.

Stephen was amazed and enthralled to think of these artists playing their music and dodging bullets at the same time. "But Dada, who would be shooting at them? People who didn't like their playing?"

This had made Rhodri roar with laughter. "Music critics were tough in those days," he said, wiping his eyes. "No, Stevie, they were often singing in places where bootleg liquor was sold. See, in those days in America, alcohol was against the law but people still wanted to drink it, so it was made illegally and sold by gangsters to clubs and what have you. Course, then you got rival gangsters and shootouts. They weren't actually shooting *at* the performers, but they didn't care who got hit just so long as they won."

"Oh," said Stephen, awed. What an amazing place America must have been, he thought. It combined the best of both worlds, music and Cowboys and Indians! Something occurred to him – maybe it still did! "Is alcohol still against the law in America, Dada?" he asked hopefully.

Rhodri smiled and shook his head. "Would have been exciting to have been there, wouldn't it, Stevie?"

Stephen grew to love the songs as much as the sound of the National guitars and now that he was older, he was beginning to appreciate the dedication and the hard work, the truth behind the music. The blues men sang about the grinding poverty and incredible hardships faced by black people of the USA in the early years of the century. It made him feel humble and elated in equal measures. It also made him evaluate how he played, listen to the sound he was making, and think about the sound he wanted to achieve. He wanted to be in a band – no, he wanted to have his *own* band; he thought he'd like to be rich and famous – but most of all he wanted to be the best guitarist he could be. This began to change the way he looked at his music and, to an extent, the way he looked at his life.

The band's first rehearsal turned out to be not so much a rehearsal as a thrashing out of what they were going to rehearse. Stephen told them the sort of things he thought they ought to play and, to his relief, no one argued. They discussed the songs, and he played them any they didn't know.

To his surprise, Harry was very enthusiastic about blues music. "Do you like John Lee Hooker and Stanton Crawford?"

"Very much." There was no one who played and sang like Stanton Crawford as far as he was concerned.

"Yeah, so do I. Perhaps we could do some of their stuff?"

"Sure, Harry," he said happily. "Anyone else got anything else they want?"

"Who's going to sing?" Graham asked.

"Not me," said Harry. "I don't mind backing, but I don't want to be lead singer."

"Me, I suppose, then," Stephen shrugged. "I like singing anyway."

"Can you sing though?" Graham asked.

"Yes."

"Go on then," said Harry.

He played the introduction to 'Peace Like A River', and started to sing. When he'd finished there was a silence.

"I think it's safe to say he can sing," said Graham.

"God, Steve! I've never heard you sing like that before!" Ray was amazed.

Stephen was embarrassed. "It's only like you being able to do maths. I can just sing, that's all." He changed the subject. "OK, so we're all happy with the songs?"

They nodded.

"Right. Well, I reckon we'll need to do about fifteen songs a gig, so we need a basic core, but then we can add things if we want. What we need to do is get really good at about twenty or so, and then go on from there. I also think that we should always start with the same song."

"Why?" Ray asked.

He explained his concept to them. "We want people to remember and recognize us. If we make sure they know our name – put a banner up or something – and always play the same song first every time, people will know it's us when they hear the introduction. It's the same with clothes, really. I'm not saying that we have to dress up, but looking clean and eager can't hurt. We want our image to say we're good, we work at being good, and we want our audience to have a good time."

The others were impressed.

"What should we start with, then?" Harry asked.

"Let's try some songs, see what we like, what we're good at."

They did some Paul Simon first, and then went on to the Hollies and the Kinks.

"Let's do some blues," Harry suggested.

She and Stephen had a lot of fun, playing their favourites back and forth, and choosing which to put in.

At eight-thirty, they trooped over to the house for a cup of coffee.

"I think we should always start with 'Peace Like A River'," Harry said. "It's got a great sound, kind of dramatic, and Steve sings it really well."

Graham and Ray nodded agreement.

"OK," Stephen smiled. "I love Paul Simon, I think he's a genius."

"Why don't you all come to the pub later?" Harry invited.

"I said I'd go round to Carole's," Ray said apologetically.

"Bring her as well," Harry suggested.

"OK, thanks, Harry. I'll ask her. Can I use your phone, Steve?"

"Go ahead."

"What time shall I tell her to come round?"

"I don't know – about an hour?" Stephen looked at the others, who nodded. "I'll ring Angie, we can all go together."

As they walked to the pub, Angie hung on Stephen's arm and asked about the rehearsal. "I wish I was musical."

Stephen kissed her. "You're perfect as you are."

"Excuse me while I vomit!" groaned Ray.

"Come on, you lot," Harry said impatiently. "My Dad wants to meet you!"

"Why?" asked Stephen.

"He said if we were any good, we could do our first gig there."

Stephen stopped dead. This was seriously good news. "Why didn't you say before?"

"You might all have been crap. Come *on*!"

The Angel was an old, rambling building, backing onto the river. It was very busy, with people spilling out into the small beer garden at the side. One of the barmaids waved to Harry when they went in. "Hello, love. Your dad's in the cellar putting on a fresh barrel. He said to go upstairs, he'll be up in a while."

They followed Harry through a passage to the back. She took them upstairs into a long, low living room, with cream walls and a floor of warm, golden pine boards. There was a huge ginger cat asleep on the sofa. Stephen stroked it and it purred loudly. "Nice cat. What's its name?"

Harry flashed him a smile. "Thanks! He's mine, he's called Longfellow. Sit down, I'll get you a drink. Oh, hello, Dad."

A very tall, powerfully built man stood in the doorway. He had thinning brown hair, cut very short, and his eyes were darker than Harry's. There was something almost menacing about him until he smiled. "Hello, Princess." He had a strong cockney accent. "They're OK then, are they?"

"Yeah, and you should hear Steve sing!" Harry enthused.

Ted Taylor looked pleased. "You got to be able to sing. I was in a group when I was about your age, down in London, that's where I met Harriet's mum, her brother was in the band. There wasn't none of us could sing, I sound like a frog croaking and Harriet's uncle's even worse, ain't he, Princess?"

Harry smiled. "You're not that bad, Dad."

"What about doing your stuff here, then?"

"That'd be really great, Mr Taylor—" Stephen began, but Ted interrupted.

"Ted, son, call me Ted."

"Thank you, Ted, that'd be really great."

Ted smiled. "Right, then, we'd best sort out some details."

They were ready for their first gig by Christmas. Ted was very supportive, helping them get their gear to the Angel and setting up for the evening in the function room. "I love a bit of live music," he explained, "and who knows? If you're any good it might even help with the takings. We can always use a few more quid."

They'd stuck with the songs they'd originally practised, but added Bobby Vee's 'The Night Has A Thousand Eyes', because it was one of Ted's favourites, and some Christmas numbers.

They were all nervous.

"Suppose they don't like us?" Ray kept saying.

"If they don't, they don't." Stephen shrugged fatalistically.

"We'll just have to be fantastic," said Harry.

"I don't feel fantastic, I feel sick," Graham said.

"Let's go home!" Ray was only half-joking.

"Too late," Stephen said. "Ted's introducing us." His fingers felt like a bunch of bananas and he was afraid he wouldn't be able to speak, let alone sing, but as soon as they played the opening bars of 'Peace Like A River', he knew he was going to be all right. He grinned over at Ray, who managed to grimace back. Harry was playing brilliantly, and although Graham still looked a little green, he wasn't having any trouble. When they stopped for a break, they were all buzzing.

Angie was beaming with excitement and pride. "You were really, really, really *great*! Everyone loved you!"

Stephen pulled her onto his lap. She nuzzled his neck. "Yuck! You're all sweaty!"

Harry lit a cigarette and offered them round, trying not to look at Angie on Stephen's lap. Ray, Carole and Graham took one; Angie and Stephen shook their heads.

Stephen could barely wait until the others had finished, he just wanted to get back up there, he loved playing to the audience, loved the feedback and the sense of rapport he felt with them. And he was enjoying singing almost as much as playing guitar, it made him feel as if he was flying. He was fronting his own band – well, technically his and Ray's – and they were playing somewhere where they didn't have to worry about being treated badly or not being paid. He could see the others felt the same, especially Harry. It seemed to finish far too quickly.

Harry voiced his thoughts as they relaxed afterwards. "It went much too fast. I could've played all night!"

Ted was well pleased with them. "This'll get around and next week we might double the takings," he said with satisfaction as he handed them their money.

Stephen stared at him. "Next week?"

"Yeah." Ted's face fell. "You're not booked anywhere else, are you?" He looked over at Harry.

She shrugged. "Ask Steve, Dad. He's in charge."

Stephen was elated. Another gig already! He shook his head. "No, we wanted to see how it went here first."

"Excellent, my son! You can consider yourselves booked here every Friday until further notice. And if the takings do go up, you might even get a raise!"

Right at the end of the Christmas holidays, Stephen passed his driving test, which meant, theoretically, that the band could start playing gigs further afield. However, they needed a reliable vehicle, big enough to carry them and all their instruments and equipment. He'd been saving his pay steadily and had got some money for his birthday, but he only had enough to buy an old banger.

John, who knew his way around an engine, went with him to look at a few old cars that were up for sale, and they settled on an eleven-year-old dark blue Mini, which was in reasonable condition, considering its age. "I'd buy it if I were you, son," John said. "For the price they're asking, it's quite a bargain. The body needs some attention, but the engine is fine."

It was exciting, having a car of his own, but it didn't solve the problem of transport for the band. Stephen discussed it with the others in the common room at lunchtime when they were back at school.

Harry had an idea. "Dad's got an old van he uses to go to the cash and carry. He might let us borrow that."

"Do you think he'd let me drive it?" Stephen asked dubiously.

"I can ask him. The worst that can happen is he'll say no."

A pair of socks rolled together to form a makeshift rugby ball hit Ray on the shoulder. "Chuck it back!" someone shouted.

"It's getting ridiculous in here," snorted Harry.

Angie appeared in the doorway, looking for them. Stephen waved, and she weaved her way across the crowded room, fell onto his lap and kissed him.

"Hello, sexy," he said, smiling at her. She was so pretty, he thought, with her big baby blue eyes and short, tousled blonde hair. He sighed with happiness.

That evening, Harry rang Stephen. "I've spoken to Dad and he says we can use the van as long as we pay for our own petrol and keep it clean," she reported.

"Brill! Well done, Harry! Thank your dad for me – for us, I mean. We'll have to sort out some sort of petrol money fund at the next rehearsal."

The band started playing at other pubs and occasionally they were booked for a function, although they always played at the Angel on Friday night. It was good to have a regular venue, it gave them a certain cachet. Because they often played to the same crowd, Stephen made sure they varied their material, and added their own style to it. That May, he heard 'Because The Night' by Patti Smith. He immediately bought it and learned how to play it. "Listen," he told the others at rehearsal, "we're doing this."

"I love this song!" exclaimed Harry. "I was going to suggest we did it!"

"It's not a bit punky for us though, is it?" asked Ray dubiously.

"It's no more punk than 'All Day and All of the Night' or 'You Really Got Me' or 'Stop Your Sobbing' is it, and they were written in the Sixties," Stephen pointed out. "It's just got a rawness to it and so have we, mostly. We're not a smooth band, are we?"

"We do Paul Simon and the Beatles," Ray pointed out.

"Yeah, but Steve's right," said Graham. "We don't do the smooth numbers. Look at 'Stranded In A Limousine'. You wouldn't think that was Paul Simon, would you?"

"Specially not the way you lot do it," put in Angie.

"But that's what makes us good," said Harry. "We're different. It's the way Steve arranges our songs; we're not punk, but we're not just rock and roll or pop or folk. We mix up rough and smooth, rock and roll and blues, and then we play them our way, sort of raw and Country and Western. We've kind of got our own sound, even though we're doing other people's songs."

"I think the way you all play is *fantastic*!" Angie enthused.

"It's great having a fan club!" Graham teased.

After Stephen had taken Angie home, he made a cup of tea for Sian, John and himself, and they watched the news. It was very depressing, with reports on the rising number of unemployed in Britain, the famine in Ethiopia, and a rare species of butterfly that had become extinct. It made him sad and angry. He went to his room and began to play his Strat, his mind still on the news and the shocking state of the world. As he played, he began to hear lyrics forming in his mind. He stopped playing and wrote. When he was satisfied with it, he went back to the music. He called it 'Eye Witness'. He thought they might be able to play it at the Angel, but wasn't sure it was good enough. When he sang it to Angie, she was very enthusiastic, but he wondered if she mostly liked it because he'd written it and she liked him. He knew he was a good singer and a reasonable guitarist – 'adequate' was the way he described his playing to himself – but he had little faith in his abilities as a songwriter. He *liked* writing songs, and often found it a useful way of crystallising his feelings, but whether the songs were good or not was something he found impossible to judge. Although he was not the least bit shy in any other way, he found saying 'I've written a song' very difficult. He decided not to tell the rest of the band that he'd written 'Eye Witness' until he'd played it to them. That way, he was more likely to get their honest opinion.

"Listen," he said at the next rehearsal, "I was thinking of putting this in." He played the song. The riff was fairly simple, powerful and urgent with a good beat, but the melody that he'd built around it was haunting and compelling and slightly melancholy. "What do you think? Should we do it?"

"Definitely," said Graham. "I like it."

"So do I," agreed Harry. "I like it a lot. Who's it by?"

Stephen didn't answer. He looked at Ray. "What do you think, Ray?"

Ray nodded slowly. "I like it. Although it's a bit different from our usual sort of thing."

"It is," agreed Harry. "It sounds like our kind of song though. You know, what I was saying the other day about our raw rock'n'blues'n'folk sound. I really love the music, it's… um…" She cast around for a word.

"Stirring," suggested Graham.

"Yeah, *stirring*. It makes you feel – odd."

Odd, thought Stephen. Is that good or bad?

"So who's it by?" Harry asked again.

"Whoever it's by, it's better than a lot of the stuff we play," Ray said unexpectedly.

Stephen relaxed. He breathed in deeply, suddenly aware he'd been holding his breath. "The sound *is* ours. *I* wrote it."

They stared at him in silence.

Ray was the first to speak. "Bollocks!"

"I *did*," Stephen protested. "You can ask Angie. I kept changing the words and making her listen to each version."

"Bloody hell!" said Graham.

"Well, why didn't you just say straight away then?" asked Harry.

He grinned sheepishly. "I don't know. In case you lot didn't like it."

"No wonder it sounds odd, you're a really odd boy. What else have you written?"

"Oh, you know. Just bits and pieces."

"Get them sorted out into songs, then. This could be a really big thing for the band, Steve."

Stephen pushed his hair back off his forehead. "I'll try. But I can't just sit down and say I'm going to write a song. Something happens and then…" He shrugged helplessly, unable to articulate the weird way that music and lyrics would jumble about in his brain until they finally coalesced into a song. Sometimes he'd write a few words, a phrase; sometimes it would be something he saw or heard that would spark off the lyrics. Then he'd fit them to some music he'd been playing around with and keep worrying at it until it was right. 'Eye Witness' had been different in that the music hadn't needed working on at all. "I will try," he promised.

They didn't play 'Eye Witness' in public for a few weeks. It was harder than Stephen had expected to arrange it for the others to play. With the songs they covered it was easy, really just a matter of *re*arranging them for the band's style. 'Eye Witness' needed a lot more work. Finally, he felt they were ready to perform it. He decided to put it into the set about halfway through, before they took a break. Harry wanted him to say he'd written it himself, and although he thought it was unnecessary, she bullied him until he agreed.

He was more nervous than he had ever been before. After they'd finished 'Days', he swallowed and said, "We'd like to play you a new song, it's one we've written ourselves, 'Eye Witness'." He looked down at his guitar and concentrated on the intro. He was afraid he wouldn't be able to sing, but as he played and the others joined in, the nerves and doubts fell away. It felt so right. He couldn't understand why he'd been so hesitant about his writing. He scanned the room for Angie. When their eyes met, she gave him a smile so full of love it made him feel weak. He smiled back. They finished the song and the audience burst into applause.

The success of 'Eye Witness' inspired him to finish another song he'd been playing around with for a while, 'Something Like Love'. Having arranged 'Eye Witness', he found it much easier to arrange this one. As he was writing it, he heard in his head where he wanted the other instruments.

The band was enthusiastic. "I knew you could write another one," Harry said approvingly. "All that stuff about you can't just sit down and write them, you need inspiration! You've rattled this one off in less than a week!"

"Doesn't mean I can do it again though," he warned her.

She gave him an old fashioned look. "Sure. Oh, and this time, Steve, don't say *we* wrote it. *We* didn't, *you* did. Is that clear?"

"Have you ever thought of becoming a teacher, Harry?"

She frowned. "No, why are you asking?"

"No reason."

He started writing songs in earnest. Their Friday night residency at the Angel became the showcase for the new material he'd written and, to his amazed delight and excitement, they began to acquire a following.

Back at school after the summer holidays, everyone was talking about university. "Where are you applying, Steve?" someone asked him.

"Oxford," Ray grinned.

"Are you?" Harry asked with interest.

Stephen shook his head. "My Dad'd like me to go there, but it's not my sort of place."

"Nottingham looks good." Ray wanted to study metallurgy. "It's going to be my first choice. Why don't we go together, Steve?"

"Yeah, maybe," Stephen said offhandedly. He'd decided over the summer he wasn't going to university. Harry and Graham weren't either, and the band was doing so well he thought they could maybe go down to London, make a demo. They'd have to replace Ray, although they could possibly manage without a rhythm guitar – after all, The Jimi Hendrix Experience hadn't had one, nor did Genesis. He knew he should tell Ray, but he didn't want to do it in front of everyone else. He hadn't told his parents and he didn't want there to be any chance, however remote, of them finding out beforehand. He knew Angie would be pleased. On the way home he explained his decision to her and Ray.

She gasped and squeezed his arm. "Stevie! How exciting! Can I come?"

He kissed her. "Certainly can!"

Ray wasn't happy. "But, Steve, I'm in the band too! You can't make a demo without me!"

"What are we supposed to do, Ray? Wait three years till you've finished?"

They walked on in silence.

Ray said slowly, "You know, you're a bit of a bastard, aren't you?"

Stephen shrugged. "It's what I want to do with my life. If I'm really serious about it, I've got to go for it. You don't have to go to university. Stay with the band, see what happens. But if you do go, remember it's your decision, same as not going is mine. I've got to tell my dad I'm not going and that's not going to be fun." God, what an understatement! The very thought of telling John made him feel almost sick with apprehension.

Ray sighed. "Yeah, I guess you're right, Steve. Sorry I said you were a bastard."

"No, it's OK, you're right in a way. It was *our* band. But I kind of took it over."

"I let you," Ray admitted. "I love being in it, but I didn't want the hassle. And I couldn't arrange the songs like you do and I sure as hell couldn't write any. Someone's got to be in charge. Anyway, when are you going to tell your dad?"

Stephen swallowed. "Oh, you know. Soon."

It was his eighteenth birthday on the fourth of November. There was a lot of discussion about it: what did he want, where would he like to go for a meal?

"Or would you rather have a party, Steve?" Sian wondered. "We could hire the church hall. We could get a band to play for the evening," she joked.

"But who would you get?" Stephen asked, trying to join in the fun. "The only decent band in the area would be busy that night!"

The guilt that he wasn't going to university and that he still hadn't told his parents was beginning to make him feel physically ill. The trouble was, the longer he put it off, the harder it became. The idea of telling Sian first and asking her – not to tell John for him, exactly, but just to be there with him – had occurred to him but he knew that was the coward's way out. He had to do it himself. Like a man. Unfortunately, he felt more like a mouse.

Mr Grainger, his English teacher, asked him to stay behind after the lesson on Wednesday afternoon. Stephen wasn't worried, his work was well up to standard, and even if it hadn't been, Rick Grainger was one of those teachers – rare in Stephen's experience – who not only knew his subject, but was able to teach it with enthusiasm whilst treating his class as likeable human beings; unlike some of the other members of staff, particularly the head of the English Department, Colin Ferry, known throughout the school as the Ferret. Stephen had been very relieved, when he started his 'A' levels, to find that he was no longer in Ferry's class. "Steve, I think you're going to do extremely well in the exams," Grainger started. "I've talked to your other subject teachers and they all say the same thing. I would predict an 'A' for you in English if you keep on working. I understand you haven't applied to university yet. Is there a problem? The grant, something like that?"

Stephen tried to think of a way to answer noncommittally. The silence lengthened.

"Steve?" Mr Grainger said finally.

"I'm not applying," Stephen said in a rush.

Grainger walked over and sat on the edge of his desk. "Why not?"

Stephen bit his lip. "Well, I play in a band," he explained. "With Ray Wallace, Harry Taylor and Graham Lucas."

Grainger nodded "I know. My girlfriend and I have seen you perform. My girlfriend's a music teacher; she thinks you're excellent."

Stephen flushed with pleasure. "Thanks! I'll tell the others."

"Well, yes, she thinks the band is good, we both do, but I meant she thinks *you* are excellent, Steve. She says your voice and playing are exceptional, and the songs you write are getting better and better."

Stephen didn't know what to say. But here was vindication, if he needed it. He could have kissed Mr Grainger. Well, Mr Grainger's girlfriend, anyway.

"So. What's this got to do with university?"

"Everything. That's what I want to do, make a go of the band."

"I see. What about the others? Won't they be going to university?"

"Only Ray. It's a shame, but we can get someone else to play rhythm."

"Sue plays the guitar – my girlfriend," Grainger said, slowly.

Stephen was amazed. "Would she be interested? I mean, we're school kids."

"Well, you won't be next year," retorted Grainger. "Anyway, how old do you think I am? Neither Sue nor I are much older than you! Just because we're teachers, it doesn't mean we're decrepit. Don't lump us all in with Colin Ferry," he grinned. "You didn't hear that! So your parents are all right with you not going to uni, then?"

Stephen shut his eyes. "No."

"What did they say?"

"Nothing. That is, I haven't told them yet."

Grainger looked concerned. "You'd better do it soon then, before the school writes to express disappointment that you've not applied."

Stephen was appalled. "Does that really happen?"

Grainger nodded. "I'd tell them tonight, if I was you." He looked at Stephen with sympathy and amusement. "Come on, Steve, you've gone green! It won't be that bad!"

"You don't know my dad."

Grainger's expression changed. "He's not likely to get violent, is he?"

The thought of John being violent brought an involuntary smile to Stephen's face. "No, not at all." He sighed. "It's – he's going to be so disappointed."

Grainger squeezed his shoulder. "Nobody said life was easy, Steve. I've got to go, I've got a staff meeting. Good luck!"

Stephen sat in the classroom after Grainger had gone. He couldn't put it off any longer. He had to tell them now. He trudged home through the darkening twilight, feeling as if he were on his way to his own execution.

Sian was in the kitchen. "Hello, Stevie!" she called as he let himself in.

"Hi, Mum." He felt terrible, guilty and sick. It was very cold outside but the room was as warm as toast. It was a cosy, inviting room, Sian had seen to that. It always smelled deliciously of good food, and there was a large table in the middle, where they usually ate, only using the rather gloomy dining room for special occasions. The walls were pale primrose, with a huge corkboard on one of them, which was always crammed with reminders and adverts, and the recipes that Sian cut out of magazines. She was at the Aga, stirring something in a saucepan.

"You're late! Is everything all right, cariad?"

"Fine. What time will Dad be home?"

"The usual. Why?"

"I want to talk to you both."

She turned to face him, perturbed by his tone. "What is it, Stevie? What's happened?"

"Nothing's happened. I just need to talk to you."

"All right." She squinted up at the clock. "Well, he shouldn't be long now. Look, get changed, then come and lay the table. We'll eat first and send the girls off to do their homework while we talk. Steve, you're not in trouble at school, are you?"

He gave a half-grin. "Not exactly."

As he put out the cutlery and fetched the dishes, he realised he wouldn't be able to eat a thing. He'd rehearsed this conversation over and over again in his head, but he knew it made no difference. Sian would understand, he was sure of that. But his father? He felt sick and his hands were cold and clammy. He felt like Judas. The front door banged and his heart lurched.

John came in and Sian hurried into his arms, as she always did. The girls ran in to kiss him and he beamed round at them all. "How was school?"

Please let him not ask about university. "Fine thanks, Dad."

The girls started to talk about lessons and friends, much to Stephen's relief.

The meal seemed to take forever. Stephen pushed his food around his plate, thankful for once for his sisters' continual chatter. His father didn't notice that he wasn't eating, but Sian did. She took his plate away with her own. He shot her a grateful look.

"Have you finished, girls?" she asked finally. "Go and do your homework, then."

"Oh, Mum!" wailed Rebecca. "What about Steve's homework?"

"Stephen will be eighteen next month. He can do his homework when he wants to. Go on, off you go. And shut the door." She put the kettle on. "Would either of you like a cup of tea?"

"Yes please, love," John said. "Let's take it into the sitting room and have a look at what's on the television."

Stephen swallowed. "Dad, I need to talk to you first."

John looked over at him, smiling, eyebrows raised in inquiry. His smile faded as he saw Stephen's expression. "Are you all right, Stevie?"

Stephen took a deep breath. "Dad, I'm sorry, but I've decided not to go to university when I finish 'A' Levels – not for a year at least, anyway."

Sian left the tea and came over to the table. She sat down next to John. "Why, Stephen?"

He looked at them both earnestly. "I've thought about this really hard. I know we talked about university, Dad, but the band's doing really well, we're good, and we might be able to make it. I really want to give it a try. Everything I said about going to university – I thought I meant it, Dad, but I don't want any career except music."

John was staring at him, stunned.

"I just want to give it one more year, Dad. If it doesn't work out, I'll go to university then, but if it does…" He looked over at Sian pleadingly. "Remember how Dada used to say you should always follow your passion? Well, see, music is my passion."

"Oh, Stephen." She took his hand. "But surely Ray is going to university, isn't he? He was talking about Nottingham last time he was here. And what about Harry and Graham?"

"Yes, Ray is going. We'll probably have to replace him, but we could manage without him. Harry and Graham want to get jobs."

"Wait a minute," John said. "Wait a minute. Just supposing for one moment that we are even entertaining this ludicrous idea. How do you propose to support yourself?"

Sian looked at him in surprise. "Surely—" she began, but Stephen interrupted.

"I'll get a job."

"Doing what?" John asked coldly.

Stephen flushed. "Braithwaites would take me on full-time. Colin, the assistant manager, is leaving after Easter. Mr. Carlton said they might be able to keep the post open for me if I want it."

John's face darkened. "So you've talked about it to him but not us?"

"No, no, I haven't. He asked me and Ray what we were going to do after our 'A' Levels. I just said I wasn't sure and then he said they'd be glad to have me full-time if I decided not to go to university."

"So you intend to work in a shop by day and play the guitar by night?" John asked tartly.

"Well – yes."

John was getting angry. "We discussed this, Stephen. I accept that you don't want to read law, although I cannot see why not, you've a perfectly good brain. But we agreed that you would be going to university."

"Yes, I will. Probably… maybe… just not yet," said Stephen desperately.

"For God's sake!" John exploded. "You're talking complete rubbish, boy! This *band* is nothing more than a ridiculous, adolescent daydream! We discussed this music business, it was agreed you would go up to Oxford first."

"We didn't actually agree that, Dad. I mean, I've got nothing against Oxford, I just – I don't want to go there."

"Why ever not? What is wrong with going to Oxford?"

"'*Very nice sort of place, Oxford, I should think, for people that like that sort of place*'," quoted Stephen, trying to lighten the atmosphere.

It had the opposite effect.

"How dare you!" John shouted. "How dare you sit there and quote George Bernard Shaw at me and expect me to put up with you wasting your mind in order to play a guitar in a *band*?" He brought his fist down on the table, making Stephen and Sian jump. "It's time you grew up!"

"John!" Sian was distressed.

"Be quiet, Sian! He's behaving like a child and you know it!"

Stephen lost his temper. "So what do you want me to do? Put away childish things? I'm sorry, Dad, but it's not just an adolescent daydream. We're good, we're really good. People like us, they like my songs, and they're willing to pay to see us."

John gave a scornful laugh. "People will pay to see animals in the zoo."

Stephen stood up. He was shaking with anger. "We're getting paid for what we do and that's what I want to do with my life. Be in a band, writing my own songs and performing them, and I'm not going to let anything stop me!"

Sian grabbed his wrist. "Stephen—" she started, but John stood up at that moment and faced his son. He was taller than Stephen by at least five inches. Stephen wasn't quite five foot eight, but Sian noticed that he'd filled out; his shoulders were broader than John's. The look in their eyes was identical.

"Not under my roof," John said quietly.

Sian's hand went to her mouth. "John!"

Stephen felt numb. "I'll make a phone call and then I'll pack. Excuse me." He walked blindly from the room.

"Stephen!" cried Sian. She turned to John. "Stop him!"

John sat down. "He's eighteen next month, as you yourself pointed out. The choice is his," he said distantly.

"If you don't stop him, I'll never forgive you," Sian said, her voice unsteady.

In the sitting room, Stephen picked up the phone and dialled the Angel. He felt peculiar, unable to take in the enormity of what had happened. When Harry came to the phone, he calmly asked her if he could stay at the pub for the night.

"Why, Steve?" she asked, surprised.

"My father's kicked me out. Can I explain when I see you?"

"God!" She was stunned. "Yes, of course. I know Dad'll say yes. Come whenever you're ready."

"Thank you, Harry," he said politely. He hung up and ran upstairs. He was experiencing a strange out-of-body sensation, and no emotion at all. It must be shock, he thought as he threw some clothes and toiletries into a rucksack. He put on his coat, carefully placed his Stratocaster into its case and slung the acoustic and his rucksack over his shoulder. With his amp in one hand and his Strat in the other, he walked to the door.

Sian burst in. She stopped at the sight of him. "Stephen!" she gasped. "He didn't mean it! Please come down and talk to him!"

Stephen shook his head. The numb feeling was wearing off and he was starting to feel terrible. "If he doesn't mean it why isn't *he* here telling me?"

Sian wrung her hands. "Stephen, you know what he's like! But I *know* he doesn't mean it!"

Stephen kissed her. "Bye bye, Mum." His voice wobbled and he bit his lip.

"Wait! Where are you going?"

"The Angel." He went swiftly down the stairs, afraid he might bump into one of his sisters, but they were obviously in their rooms, oblivious to what was happening. John was nowhere to be seen either. He flung his stuff into the Mini.

When he got to the pub he went round to the back and knocked at the door. Harry opened it straight away. "Come in, Steve." She stood back to let him pass.

He walked in and put his bags on the ground. She took one look at him and hugged him fiercely. How could anyone be mean to him?

He held onto her gratefully. Thoughts were chasing round and round in his head. Should he have left? But what choice did he have? John would never forgive him. But Sian. He didn't want to leave her or the girls. He pulled away from Harry, covered his face with his hands and wept.

"I'm getting Dad," Harry said, dismayed. She didn't know what to do. She was afraid that if she stayed there with him, she'd put her arms round him again and blurt out how much she loved him.

Ted didn't waste time asking questions. He put his hand on Stephen's shoulder. "Stop it, Stephen. Princess, we need to get the spare bed made up."

"I've already done that, Dad."

"Good girl. All right then, put the kettle on and make a hot water bottle. Come on, Steve."

"Is he going to bed?" Harry asked.

Ted nodded. He was shepherding Stephen out of the door.

"But it's only half past eight," protested Harry.

"He's in a real state, Princess, it's the best place for him." He followed Stephen out. A few seconds later he looked back round the door at her. "Do you know his parents' phone number?"

She nodded.

"Good. I want to have words with them."

After Stephen left, Sian sat on his bed, appalled. She couldn't believe what John had done. How could he? she asked herself. How could he do this to me, to Stephen, to us all? The door opened slightly and the cat came in. She wandered around the room, sniffing at Stephen's things, finally jumping onto the bed and turning around several times before she settled down. Sian stroked her and the animal purred like an engine. "Oh, Mitten, what am I going to do?" Sian started to cry, the tears dripping down onto Mitten's back. The cat's fur rippled indignantly and she moved away. Sian wiped her eyes.

Kathy appeared at the door. "There you are! I've been looking for you everywhere, didn't you hear me calling? There's a Mr Taylor on the phone for you." She stared at Sian. "What's the matter, Mum?"

Sian stood up. "Not now, Kath, I can't explain now. Later, I promise."

"Is it bad?" Kathy asked fearfully.

Sian nodded. "Please keep Becks busy for the time being. Play a board game with her or something." She ran down to the phone.

"Sian Markham," she said, her heart thumping.

"Mrs Markham, this is Ted Taylor, Harriet's Dad. I've got your Steve here."

"Can I speak to him? Please?"

"Well, he's in bed, asleep. I gave him two aspirin and he went straight off. He was in a right state."

"Yes," said Sian faintly.

"He told Harriet his dad's kicked him out."

"Yes," was all Sian could answer.

"Well, if you don't mind me saying so, I think we need to talk. Don't get me wrong, I've got no objections to Steve being here, he's a great kid, but I really think he should be in his own home."

"Yes," Sian said again.

Ted's voice changed. "Are you all right, Mrs Markham? Steve's Dad – he's not violent, is he?"

"Oh, no, *no*! But… well, it's very complicated."

"I see." He clearly didn't. "That's why I say we need to talk. Can you and Mr Markham get round here tomorrow?"

"Oh, yes, yes, we can," Sian said eagerly. "What time?"

"When Steve gets back from school. About four-thirty suit you?"

"Could we make it a little later, please? John – my husband – doesn't usually get in until later. Could we make it five-thirty?"

"Suits me. I'll see you then. Goodbye, Mrs Markham." He hung up.

"Goodbye," Sian whispered. She heard a movement behind her and looked round. John was standing in the doorway.

"Who was that?"

"Ted Taylor. Harry's father."

"What the hell did he want? Not to talk about that bloody band?"

Sian stood up. "No, to talk about your son. He wants us to go there tomorrow evening and sort it out."

"Sort what out?"

"He's gone there. Stevie's gone there."

John frowned. "Gone there?"

"He's left home, John. What did you think he was going to do? I *told* you to stop him!"

John took the whisky bottle from the drinks tray and poured himself a glass. His hands weren't steady, Sian noticed. "I didn't think he'd *leave*," he muttered.

"Give me a drink. What are you talking about, John? I *told* you to stop him, to tell him you didn't mean it! Why didn't you come upstairs with me and *tell* him?"

John handed her her drink. "But I *did* mean it, Sian. If Stephen is old enough to make up his mind to pursue this… this foolish daydream, he's old enough to take the consequences."

Sian sat down abruptly, spilling her whisky. "I don't know you at all."

"I think you do, Sian. And I think you know I'm right. I'm not going anywhere tomorrow. When Stephen realises how stupid he's been, he'll be back. And when he's apologised, we'll talk."

"You're *mad*," Sian whispered. "Stephen has *nothing* to apologise for. It's *his* life. He can choose to do whatever he wants with it!"

"He's made his choice then." John walked from the room.

The girls were in Rebecca's room, playing KerPlunk. Sian sat on the bed. "Stephen and Daddy have had a row," she began.

"What about?" Kathy asked

"The band. Stephen doesn't want to go to university yet and Daddy is… he's very angry." She bit her lip. The girls looked at her expectantly. "Stephen's gone to stay with Harry for a while."

"He's *left home?*" Kathy asked.

Sian nodded.

Rebecca began to cry.

"But he'll be back soon, won't he, Mum?" said Kathy. "I mean, Dad's just cross now. It'll be all right tomorrow, won't it?"

Sian had her arm round Rebecca. She held her other hand out to Kathy. "I don't know, darling. Your father is acting… he's acting… very strangely."

"Do you mean he's gone mad?" asked Rebecca, horrified.

Yes, thought Sian. "No, of course not, Becks, he's just…" She swallowed and took a deep breath. "It might take a while to sort everything out, that's all."

"So Stephen will come back?" Kathy asked.

Sian hesitated.

"Mum!" wailed Kathy.

"I want my brother!" Rebecca sobbed.

John opened the door. "Stop crying, Rebecca, please."

Sian stood up. "Go away."

He came into the room. "Sian—"

"GO AWAY!" she shouted. "GET OUT!"

John stepped back. "Sian, you're upsetting the girls—"

"It's YOUR fault," she screamed. "YOU did this. Get out, I never want to see you again!"

He stared at her, appalled. "Sian, we have to talk."

"Mummy! Please don't shout at Daddy, *please!*" Kathy begged.

Sian pulled herself together. "Yes. We have to talk. But not now. I can't talk to you now. Please go away now." She was shaking violently. She waited until the door closed behind him, and then turned back to the girls. "It's all right, it's all right, calm down, calm down. I just got cross with Daddy. But it's all right. He and I will talk later and I promise it'll be all right. Calm down. Calm down. I want you to be very grown up and get ready for bed so that Daddy and I can talk." She put her arms round them and they huddled against her.

"You won't shout at each other any more?" whispered Rebecca through her sobs.

"I promise," said Sian.

"And Stevie will come home?" Kathy asked.

"I'm sure he will." Sian tried to smile. "He has to."

She walked into their bedroom and was startled to see John there, sitting in the armchair that she'd sat in to feed the children when they were babies. The thought brought tears to her eyes, and she brushed them angrily away. She'd expected him to be downstairs and had wanted a few moments alone. He'd obviously felt the same.

She sat on the bed. "What do you want to talk about, John? As far as I can see, there's nothing to say."

"Don't be hostile, Sian," he said quietly, sitting next to her.

She gave a hollow laugh. "I'm sorry, John; how do you expect me to feel? My son has left home because his father can't accept him as he is. My God, that makes it sound as if he's some kind of criminal instead of a very talented musician!"

John clenched his fists. "But Sian, surely you can see how *foolish* this is? It's a child's *dream*. Do you honestly want to see your son wasting his life playing a guitar in a pub?"

"I want him to be happy, and if that makes him happy, then yes, yes I do. And besides, why shouldn't he make it?"

"*Make it*? Oh, for God's sake, Sian! I want him to be happy too, of course I do, and I've accepted he won't be happy studying law, and my God, if you only knew how hard *that* was!"

"Yes, that was *your* dream, wasn't it?" she said slowly.

John nodded, his face sombre. "Since the day he was born – oh, no, long before that! Sian, it was all I wanted."

"And all Stevie wants is to make music, but you want to take that dream away from him."

He opened his mouth to speak, but shut it again and took her hand. "Sian, surely you can understand that I just want the best for him? He's my son too, and I love him…"

"You've got a funny way of showing it!"

"Just because my way isn't yours doesn't make it any less valid. I will not sit idly by and watch him ruin his life. If he has to learn the lesson the hard way, so be it."

"John, you don't know the first thing about him!" She pulled her hand away and got up. "He won't come back. He won't fit into the plan you have for his life. Why can't you see that?"

He shook his head. "I don't accept that, Sian. I can't."

She stared at him. "Then I don't know what we're going to do, John. I don't see how I can live with you any more."

"Sian! You don't mean that? Not really?"

"I don't know," she said slowly. "I just don't know." She walked to the door.

"Where are you going?" he asked in consternation, getting up.

"To put Rebecca to bed." She slammed the door behind her.

John sat back down. The dull, constricting pain in his chest was spreading to his throat. He reached across to his nightstand for his pills and opened the bottle labelled 'aspirin', where he kept them concealed from Sian. He put a tablet under his tongue and let it dissolve. He knew his head would start to ache shortly, but the chest pain would go. He lay back with his eyes shut and thought about his son. All the dreams he'd had, all the things he thought they'd share – gone, *gone*. How could this have happened? How was he going to bear it? He thought of Stephen saying 'music is my passion'. *You* are my passion, he thought. He felt the beginning of the dull ache in his temples and his eyes filled with tears.

Sian put the girls to bed earlier than usual but they didn't complain. She went down to the kitchen with the intention of making a cup of tea, but when she got there she realised she didn't want one. All she wanted was Stephen to be at home. She sat at the table. She didn't know what to do. She didn't know what to do about Stephen, she didn't know what to do about John. She didn't even know what she felt about John any more. At the moment it was close to hatred, but surely that would pass? She suddenly felt very scared. Supposing it didn't? They'd been married for more than thirty years. She knew she couldn't sleep in the same bed as him that night. She had a mad impulse to sleep in Stephen's room, but she managed to suppress it. They had two perfectly adequate spare rooms (the smallest was Stephen's once, a little voice whispered). She went to her bedroom to get her night things. To her surprise, John was asleep on the bed, a bottle of aspirin next to him.

He woke when she opened the door. "Sian?" His voice was thick with sleep.

How could he possibly be sleeping at a time like this?

He sat up. "What are you doing?"

"I can't sleep here with you tonight," she said distantly. "I'm going to the spare room."

He was distressed. "Sian, we've never slept apart before, except when you went into hospital to have the children."

"You never threw my son out of his home before."

"Sian!" It was a cry of pain.

She gathered her things together. "Goodnight, John."

The next morning she got the girls up for breakfast as usual, and they straggled downstairs. John was already at the table. He greeted them as though nothing was different.

"Are you and Mummy friends, now, Daddy?" Rebecca asked, her voice trembling.

"Of course we are, Becks. Aren't we, Sian?"

Sian was at the work surface, her back to them. She didn't turn round, couldn't. One look at her face would have told the girls everything. "Of course," she agreed.

Rebecca let out a sigh of relief. "Steve will be home tonight then?"

Sian froze. Her mouth was so dry she couldn't answer.

John said easily, "Maybe not tonight, he's having fun at his friend's."

Sian couldn't believe he'd said that. There was a bread knife lying on the counter; with horror, she found her fingers curling around the handle. All she had to do was take a couple of steps across the room and plunge it into his heart. The strength of her desire to do so frightened her more than anything had ever done before. She put it carefully down and dug her nails into the palms of her hands.

"Are you all right, Mum?" Kathy asked.

"Fine," she heard herself say without even a tremor. "I've just got a bit of a headache."

"Oh dear, can I get you some aspirin?" John asked solicitously.

"No." She turned and looked at him and he recoiled at the expression in her eyes.

The girls finished breakfast and went upstairs to clean their teeth and get their school bags.

"And how long do you think we can keep up the fiction of Stephen 'having fun' at the Angel?" she spat at John.

"That's really up to Stephen."

"I am going round tonight to talk to Mr Taylor. He wants us both to be there, as I told you yesterday."

"Then want will have to be his master," John replied, getting up. "I've got an early meeting, Sian, I'm going to work now."

"You are a heartless bastard," she said and swept from the room.

After the girls had left for school, she fetched the telephone book and dialled the Angel. A woman answered.

"Please may I speak to Ted Taylor?" she asked politely.

"I'm afraid he's out. Could I take your name and number and ask him to phone you back?"

Damn! "Yes, certainly. My name is Sian Markham, I'm Stephen's mother."

"Steve's mum! Why didn't you say? Hang on, I'll get Ted for you. He's upstairs, it's his day off."

She waited.

"Mrs Markham?"

"Yes."

"How can I help you? Steve's left for school, I'm afraid."

"It was you I wanted to talk to. My husband – he won't be able to come tonight. Could I come earlier, when Stevie gets home from school?"

"You can come whenever you like, Mrs Markham."

Sian began to cry. She tried to stop herself, but she couldn't.

"Is your husband home, Mrs Markham?"

"No," she managed to say.

"All right, just you sit tight. I'll be there in a jiffy. We'll sort this out."

The line went dead.

She did as she was told. She was incapable of doing anything else. She'd hardly slept the night before, she'd not been able to eat anything that morning. She sat as if carved in stone. She could barely manage to get up to answer the door.

The man on the doorstep was about her age, very tall, very big, but not fat. He had sinister dark eyes, and he looked as if he had seen everything and done everything and nothing would shock him. And then he smiled and he looked totally different.

"I'm Ted, Ted Taylor. Come on, I'm taking you back to the Angel. You look like death warmed up. Get yourself some shoes and a cardy."

"Oh – they said… they told me it was your day off. I don't want to be a nuisance."

Ted smiled. "I'll be glad of the company." He waited while she got her shoes, her bag and a sweater. "Got your door key?"

She nodded.

"Come on then." He helped her into his car. At the pub, he led her through a back door into a well-appointed and spotless kitchen. "Sit down. I'm going to get you a cup of tea and some grub. Scrambled eggs do you?" He cooked the eggs, whistling cheerfully, and put the plate down in front of Sian, along with a steaming mug of tea. "Get that lot down you, and then we'll talk."

"I don't think—" Sian began.

"No, that's right, you don't want to think. Just eat up and you'll feel better. Come on." He stood over her as though he might force-feed her. She ate. It was delicious and to her surprise, she cleared the plate.

"That's better," Ted said with satisfaction. He took her plate, and, pouring himself a mug of tea, sat down opposite her. "Can I call you Sian?"

She nodded.

He smiled. "Excellent. And I'm Ted." He stuck his hand out and she shook it. "Pleased to meet you, Sian."

Despite herself, she smiled. "I'm pleased to meet you too, Ted."

"There you are, see, you're looking almost human now. What are we going to do, Sian?"

She shook her head.

"I imagine the fact that your husband won't come here and talk means he hasn't changed his mind?"

"He hasn't."

"We've got a problem, then. Like I said to you last night, I don't mind Steve being here, he's a lovely boy, polite and respectful and a real character. And talented! Well, you'll know about that better than what I do. But the fact remains that this ain't his home, is it?"

Sian shook her head again.

"What I don't understand," said Ted after a minute, "is what he's done that's upset your husband so much. I mean, like I said, he's a nice, polite boy, and Harriet says he's always getting 'A's at school."

"Yes," Sian sighed. "That's part of the problem. That and music."

Ted looked at her as if she was mad. "Music? How do you mean, music?"

And Sian found herself telling him everything, from the moment she and John had first met. "We were married within a few months of meeting, even though I was only just seventeen, and he was nearly thirty. And we were so happy, Ted, everything was perfect. Until we tried to have children. I... we... well, we had a lot of problems. And John so wanted a son to follow in his footsteps."

Ted frowned. "Why?"

Sian shrugged. "I don't really know. Partly, I think, because he and his father... well, Norman was a miner, and he and John never really had anything in common, even though they loved each other. John was so intelligent, and Norman was very proud of him, and I think a little in awe of him – but maybe a little contemptuous too. Physically, John would never have been strong enough to work at the coal face as Norman did. And then, I don't know, I think it's just something in John, this yearning for Stevie to be like him. Who knows what goes on in someone else's head? I thought we were so close and yet..." She bit her lip, her eyes filling with tears.

Ted squeezed her hand. "So what happened next?"

She pulled herself together. "Well, eventually, we had Stephen. We'd been married for twelve years, and it was like a miracle." Her face lit up at the memory. "And he was a lovely baby, very small, but healthy; oh, he was perfect, so pretty with his amazing eyes, and then I'd always thought babies were born bald, but he had lots of hair and it sort of stood up from his head, and he was so good, sleeping through the night from a couple of months – and very clever. He was talking by the time he was nine months old. His first word was 'cow', there was a picture of one in one of his rag books, he pointed it out to us. John was apoplectic, he was so proud. And Stevie was talking in sentences by the time he was a year old, and he sang all the time." She sighed. "Although John didn't like that much, didn't think it was normal. But, see, Ted, I sing all the time too, all my family do. And I taught Stevie to play the piano before he started school, not that he needed many lessons. But John was teaching him to read and write, so what was the difference?" She looked appealingly at Ted.

He shook his head. "None as far as I can see."

"No. But there was for John. Don't get me wrong, Ted, he loved Stephen to distraction, he spent so much time with him, reading to him, telling him tales of his father's whippet, Glover – the worst dog in the world, according to John – helping him with his homework. He still *does* love him, Ted, but he can't let go of this dream Stephen. Why can't he see Stevie as he really is? There's so much to be proud of!"

As the morning became the afternoon, Ted made sandwiches and fetched whisky from the bar. They shared it, Ted drinking several glasses to each one of Sian's. She went on talking, telling him how she and John had given Stephen his Strat, how John had seemed comfortable with Stephen having the band.

"But he thought it was just a hobby, apparently he thought Stevie would still go to Oxford, but study literature instead of law. He only hears what he wants to hear and I just don't know what to do!" She looked at Ted. She felt as if she had been carrying a very heavy burden for a long, long time, and had finally found someone who was strong enough to help her bear it.

"Well," he said.

She was starting to feel the effects of the whisky, but he was acting as if he had been drinking water.

"It seems to me that Steve and his father need to talk. I mean really talk, not just skirt around the subject, and that John has to listen, has to be made to listen. Your husband is obviously very unhappy, but Steve has to do what he wants with his life." Ted ran his hand through his thinning hair. "I'm trying to think if there's some sort of compromise that could be reached, but I'm blowed if I can." He sighed. "Would you like some coffee?"

While he put the kettle on, Sian wandered rather unsteadily around the room. She stopped at the welsh dresser. "I'm Welsh, you know,"

Ted grinned to himself. "You told me."

She picked up a photo. "She's such a pretty girl, your Harry." She peered at the picture. "She's sensational with her hair long like this." She stared at it, puzzled. "Wait a minute. This doesn't make sense. How can she have long hair here and short hair not in the picture? I mean, at the same time?"

"That's not my *daughter* Harriet, that's my *wife* Harriet. She died when my daughter was a baby."

"I'm so sorry," Sian stammered.

"Why?" He put the coffee pot on the table. "Stands to reason, if I didn't want to remember her, I wouldn't have the picture there. And you just said lovely things about her and my little Princess. Come and sit down and drink this coffee, Sian. You're a little drunk and the kids will be in from school soon."

Sian was amazed. "What's the time?"

"Just after three o'clock."

They drank their coffee in silence, Sian absorbed with the thought that at any time Stephen would come in through the door, and Ted watching her with amusement and affection. It was obvious that she was Steve's mother, and not just because of the physical resemblance. Steve had all her warmth and charm. He wondered what the husband was like that made her stay with him despite the way he behaved over Steve. She's a looker too, he thought.

They heard a car pull up outside. The back door opened and Harry came in, followed by Stephen. His face lit up like a Christmas tree. "Mum!"

Sian stood up and Stephen fell into her arms. They hugged fiercely, Sian repeating 'cariad' over and over again.

When they let go of each other, Harry said, "What does that mean?"

"Hmmm? Oh, hello, Harry! I'm sorry, what did you say?"

"Are you drunk, Mum?" asked Stephen with amusement.

Sian waved her hand at him as if she was swatting away a troublesome fly.

Stephen looked at Ted, who nodded.

"I asked what that word means, Mrs Markham," Harry said.

"Cariad? It's Welsh. It means love. We use it as a term of affection, like darling."

"It would be a beautiful name for a baby," said Harry. She dropped a kiss on Ted's head. "I'm off to get changed."

"OK, love," Ted smiled. He turned to Stephen. "Sian's told me all about problem, Steve, but we ain't cracked it yet, have we, Sian?"

Sian shook her head. "Nope."

"I think you and your Dad need to talk, Steve." Stephen opened his mouth to protest, but Ted went on, "I mean really *talk*. It seems to me that you've both got a lot to get off your chests. The difficulty is, your Dad don't seem to want to. You can stay here as long as you want, Steve; as long as it takes to get it sorted. How's that with you, Sian?"

"I'm really grateful to you, Ted – well, both Stevie and I are. But I don't see how we can impose on your hospitality."

"Don't talk rubbish, Sian, it's no imposition! Really, he's company for Harry. Her brothers are a lot older than her – Nick's twenty-two and William's nearly twenty-seven. Besides, they both live in London so we don't hardly ever see them."

Sian gave a forlorn smile. "Thank you, Ted. Apart from home, I can't think of anywhere I'd rather Stephen stayed."

Ted smiled. "That's one of the nicest compliments I've had for a long time. What you ought to do, Sian, is go and see where Steve is sleeping, make sure you approve. Take as long as you want. When you're ready, I'll drive you home."

The room Ted had given Stephen was big, with a comfortable double bed, dark, heavy furniture, and a washbasin. Stephen had stacked the few things he'd brought with him neatly in the corner.

Sian sat on the bed. "Are you OK, Stevie?"

He shrugged. "Yeah." He sat next to her and leant against her, the way he always had when he was unhappy.

Her eyes filled with tears and she fought to control herself. "Listen, darling, Ted's right. All of us – you, me and Dad – we need to talk. You know, I don't think we've ever had one honest discussion about your music. I don't mean you and I," she added. "I mean Dad and I. I'm going home now, he and the girls will be home soon, and I'm going to try to talk to him. We'll sort it out, cariad, don't you worry. Give me a kiss. I'll see you tomorrow one way or the other." She left the room without looking back.

Ted was in the bar. He looked up when she came through. "You ready to go?" She nodded. "Come on then, I'll get my jacket and we'll be off."

They drove in silence. Ted pulled up at the gates of the house. "Do you want me to come in with you?"

She shook her head. "Thank you for everything, Ted. For listening to me, for looking after Stephen, for everything."

"You know where I am if you need me. I mean it, Sian – any hour of the day or night."

She got out of the car and he watched her walk into her house. He was startled by the strength of his feelings for her.

Sian let herself in. It was quiet, the girls had dance lessons on Thursdays, and John picked them up on his way home. She looked at her watch. They'd be in in about ten minutes. She went into the kitchen to warm up a casserole. As she got it out of the fridge, she heard John's key in the door, and the girls' chatter. She went out into the hall.

"How was ballet?"

"Brill!"

She smiled. "Go and get changed then, tea in a minute."

John had gone into the sitting room. She followed him in and took a deep breath. "John, we need to talk."

He seemed smaller somehow, and frail. "I know. But not now. I'm very tired, Sian. And I need time."

Her heart turned over. He looked ill and old. "The girls are getting changed for tea. Just sit here until it's ready. But afterwards, John, we *have* to talk. I can't go on like this."

"Now then, girls," Sian said, when they had finished, "Daddy and I want to have a talk, a private talk, in the sitting room. I want you to tidy up in here and then go and do your homework, all right?"

"You're not going to argue, are you?" Rebecca asked with alarm.

"No." Sian was emphatic. "Absolutely not. But we do have some things to sort out." She smiled at them. "You be good girls for us."

"Mum! I'm not Becks's age!" Kathy protested. "Honestly," Sian heard her mutter as she and John went out. "Grown ups!"

John sat down and looked at Sian. "Where do we start?"

"With complete honesty. That's how we used to talk to each other, John. These days we only seem to manage platitudes."

There was silence.

"I do agree with you," John said at last. "I just can't see how to begin."

Sian smiled. "Who was it said, '*Begin at the beginning and go on to the end*'?"

"Stephen would know. Oh, Sian! That's just it, isn't it? Stephen *would* know and he's throwing it all away for a dream!"

"Why?" Sian asked. "Why is it a dream? See, John, it's not as if he's the only boy in the world to want to do this. You only have to turn on the wireless!"

"Yes, but for every group that becomes famous... And that's another thing, Sian, do you really want Stephen to be *famous*?"

"Well, never mind that now. What were you going to say?"

"I don't know – oh, yes, for every group that becomes famous there must be countless others that don't."

"Yes, I agree. I agree completely. And I also think, that as well as talent and determination – both of which Stephen has – luck plays a large part in it. But, John, that's for him to discover on his own. Whatever we think, however you might feel he's ruining his life, it's *his life* to ruin, to do what he wants with."

"I had so many dreams and plans for him," he whispered. "And he took them all, all my dreams, and crushed them. I don't know if I can ever forgive him."

Sian was appalled. "But, John, he's your *son*."

"I know that, Sian. But I can't change the way I feel any more than you or he can."

Her heart was thumping in her chest. How could he be saying this? How could he possibly feel like this about his own son? Her marriage, which she had thought so strong, so solid, was nothing. *Nothing*.

He stood up. "I'm sorry, Sian. I don't feel very well. I'm going to lie down."

She watched him as he walked slowly out of the room. I don't think I can take much more of this, she thought. She went upstairs to the girls. "Darlings, I've got to go out. I need to... to take some things to Stevie. Daddy's here, he's lying down. I won't be long."

"Can we come?" asked Rebecca.

"Not now."

"When, then?"

"Soon. Give me a kiss. I'll see you shortly."

She walked briskly to the Angel, knocked at the back door and waited. There was no reply, which meant she'd have to go into the pub and ask for Ted. It was noisy and smoky inside, and very busy. A jukebox was blaring out. She pushed her way to the bar, where Ted was serving a boisterous group. He saw her, and his face lit up. "Sian! This is a nice surprise! Here, come through."

He lifted the counter and ushered her in. "Straight down the corridor, turn left, you'll see the kitchen. I'll be there in a jiffy."

She found her way and stood awkwardly, waiting for him.

He hurried in. "You'll be wanting Steve?"

She nodded.

"Sorted it out then, at home?"
"No."
He went out and she heard him calling Stephen. "He's coming. Sit down, Sian. Can I get you anything? You look frozen!"
"No thanks, Ted. I walked, it's cold tonight."
Ted raised his eyebrows. "It's quite a walk from your place."
"I'm sorry to be such a nuisance."
"It's the last thing you are."
Stephen came in. "Mum! Are you OK?"
Her heart contracted with love and pride. He's so handsome, she thought. She couldn't bear him living here, nice as Ted was. She'd always thought she loved all her children equally, but with a shock she realised that no one in the world meant as much to her as Stephen did. She was so angry with John that she wasn't sure she ever wanted to see him again. Her chest felt tight and she took a deep breath. "Stevie, I tried to talk to Dad—"
Stephen interrupted her. "It doesn't matter what he says, Mum, I'm not coming home."
She stared at him. "What do you mean?"
"What's the point of my saying all that to Dad about wanting to make it with the band and make my own way if I just come running straight home? What would that prove? I've been thinking about this. Dad meant what he said – well, so did I. I'll leave school and get a job and find somewhere to live. But I have to stand up for what I believe in, and show Dad that I can look after myself."
Sian was appalled. "But Stevie, if you decide you do want to go to university, you'll need 'A' Levels."
He shrugged. "I'll cross that bridge when I come to it."
"I can't let you do this, Stephen."
He smiled at her fondly – almost, she thought, as if she were the child. "You can't stop me. I'll be eighteen in less than a month."
"Can I say something?" Ted asked. "Steve, I agree with your Mum. You should get your 'A' Levels. Wait," he said, as Stephen started to speak. "Let me finish. I understand your reasoning, and I tend to agree. So why don't you stay here? You can pay for your keep by working in the pub a couple of nights a week and carry on at school."
"I'd like that. I'd like that very much. Thank you, Ted."
"I don't." Sian was near to tears. "I want you at home."
"But, Mum, if I was going to university next year, I'd be leaving home then. What's the difference?"
"Well, a year, to start with," said Sian tartly. "But it *would* be different. You've *had* to leave. You weren't given a choice."
"These things happen, Mum. And I have been given a choice. I could come home, make it up with Dad, go to university. I choose not to do that."
"It isn't the same, Stevie, whatever you say. It's not that I'm not grateful for your offer, Ted."
He put his hand on her arm. "I know."
"I suppose there's nothing else to say." She sighed. "I've got to go. We're going to have to organise your stuff, Stevie."
"We'll sort that out, Sian. Stop worrying," Ted said.
She gave him a lopsided smile. "I'll try."

Chapter Two
The Cost Of Living

In this life nothing's free, ten losses for each victory,
But if you want to win, you've got to play,
And if there's a price to pay, hey, that's the cost of living.

Stephen didn't find living at the pub too hard to adjust to, but he missed home, Sian especially; they had always been close and she understood him so well. He missed the minutiae of family life, the private jokes and the sense of being around people who cared about him. The Markhams were a close-knit family and he'd always taken that for granted. He particularly missed the evening meal at home, when they'd all gather together, and Sian would serve up something delicious, and everyone would talk, telling each other what they'd done that day, discussing problems, sharing jokes. At the Angel, Harry and Ted would get themselves something to eat when they felt like it; Harry had school dinners, so she'd often just fix herself a sandwich. It wasn't the food Stephen missed, it was the companionship. He didn't see Angie till later, and he found the early evening a depressing time. Normally he'd have played his guitar, but he felt strangely guilty about playing it now; it seemed to have caused so much trouble

One good thing about this new life was that he could spend more time with Angie. They could make love whenever they wanted, his bedroom door had a lock, and as far as Ted was concerned, Stephen's private life was his own affair. Being with Angie, holding her, making love to her helped enormously. Especially making love. He could lose himself, forget everything but Angie. It was like being in another world. He hated it when she went home.

After taking her home one night, he went into the kitchen to make a hot drink. It was the middle of October and very cold. He was sitting on the table, half-heartedly reading the paper and waiting for the kettle to boil, when Harry came in. "Oh, hello, Steve. What are you doing?"

"Getting a cup of coffee. D'you want one?"

"Yeah, and I'm starving too." She fetched a packet of biscuits and offered him one. "You look a bit miserable."

He sighed. "I suppose I am. It's not that I don't like it here, Harry. It's just that I miss my family."

"Even your dad?"

Stephen smiled. "He's not an ogre, you know. He's just doesn't understand."

"Hmm," said Harry noncommittally. She ate another biscuit.

Stephen tried to explain his father's obsession with academic success. "It was my fault in a way," he sighed. "When he realised I didn't want to do law, I felt so guilty I had to say I still intended to go to university, even though I knew all I really wanted to do was have a band. And then when he asked me about my lyrics, I said I dreamt about being able to write like Dylan Thomas, which I do, but he immediately thought I'd go to Oxford and study literature! I'm a wimp, Harry, I should have just told him what I was going to do. After all, it's my life!" He narrowed his eyes. "I won't make that mistake again."

"Fathers are a pain," Harry agreed.

"Ted's OK though, isn't he?"

"I suppose so, but you've seen how overprotective he is."

"He just looks out for you," Stephen grinned.

"Is that what you call it? He chucked a customer out of the pub yesterday because he was chatting me up!"

Stephen was surprised. "Ted? He's so laid back!"

Harry gave a hollow laugh. "Laid back? I don't think so! Why do you think my brothers never come here? You've never seen Dad lose his temper, Steve, it's frightening. It's the reason we moved. He got into a fight with some bloke in London and beat him up so badly he nearly died. He's never touched me or Will or Nick, but Nicky told me that they were always scared to death of him."

Stephen stared at her, chilled. The kettle boiled and he made the coffee. "I can't imagine what that must be like," he said slowly.

"Most of the time, he's great, and if I was ever in any sort of trouble, he'd sort it out." She grinned at Stephen's sombre expression. "Don't worry, Steve, he likes you. And he thinks the world of your mum."

"Yeah, well, I can understand that," Stephen smiled. He reached out and ruffled Harry's hair. "Thanks for telling me about your dad."

"Why?" she asked.

"I don't know," he shrugged. "It just makes me feel less of an outsider, I suppose." He went off to his room.

Harry stayed in the kitchen, sipping her coffee. She loved Stephen being there, she'd never dreamed this would happen. She'd been in love with him since she was fifteen, but he'd never thought of her as anything other than a friend, so to be able to see him, talk to him every day, even occasionally hold his hand, was more than she'd ever expected. On the Saturday after he'd moved in, while he was at work, she'd sneaked into his bedroom and had a look in his wash bag. Pears soap, Vosene shampoo. She knew that, his hair always smelt of it. She'd opened the bottle and breathed in, shutting her eyes. It was Stephen, but it wasn't the smell she was after. She rummaged through the bag and found, right at the bottom, underneath his razor and a flannel, a bottle of aftershave, Blenheim Bouquet, by Penhaligon's. She sniffed it: yes, that was it, Steve's smell. It was delicious. She knew the shop that sold it, it was in the centre. She put everything back as she'd found it and went out into York. She wandered round the shop, trying all the fragrances. She liked Bluebell best. She bought a small bottle of it and wore it the following Monday morning.

As they walked out to his car, Stephen sniffed appreciatively. "You smell nice, Harry."

"Oh, thanks," she said in an offhand way. "I haven't worn this for ages, it got knocked to the back of my dressing table. It's called Bluebell, it's made by Penhaligon's, they've got a shop in the centre."

"I know!" he exclaimed. "I use their stuff, too! Isn't it great we've got the same tastes?"

Of course, in her dreams, he fell in love with her, but she couldn't have everything. She sighed. Maybe one day. She let her imagination run riot for a minute, then pulled herself together, washed up her coffee mug and went to bed.

Stephen organised as many gigs as possible. It was now more important to him than ever to make the band as good as he could. He'd left home, caused untold problems; he had to put all his energy into the band. And more than that, he wanted to. It was all he wanted to do, he loved playing to a live audience, loved the interaction and the sense of connection he got from them.

At the end of October, he got them a gig at Tiffany's, a big venue in Hull. After school, they loaded up Ted's van. Ted came out to give them a hand. "Keep an eye on Harriet, you lot, won't you?"

Stephen rubbed his back. He'd hurt it playing rugby a few months ago, and lifting anything was still painful. "Course we will, Ted. We always do, wherever we're playing."

"You're good boys. When are you taking your test again, Ray?"

Ray looked sheepish. "I just did."

"Failed *again*? That was your third time wasn't it?"

"Don't rub it in."

"Well, what about you, Graham? It seems a bit unfair that Steve always has to drive."

"I'm saving up for lessons. My mum can't drive and I hardly ever see Dad now he's moved to Bristol."

"You should've said. I'm teaching Harriet, I can teach you too if you want," Ted offered.

"That'd be brill! Thanks, Ted!"

Harry came out.

"What on earth do you think you're wearing?" Ted demanded.

"Oh, Dad! Give it a rest!" groaned Harry. Why did he always do this? As if she was a kid! It was so embarrassing! "Are we ready, Steve?"

"You've got far too much make up on," Ted continued.

"Well, compared to the boys, I suppose so. Look, Dad, I've got the same amount of make up on that I always have." She kissed him. "I'll see you later. I expect you've already asked them to look after me, so you know I'll be all right." They climbed into the van, and drove off, leaving Ted shaking his head.

Harry raised an eyebrow at Stephen. "See what I mean? Thank God we didn't tell him Tiffany's is a punk venue! He'd never have let me go!"

Stephen nodded. He could see that Ted was very protective of Harry, but in some ways he didn't blame him. If he had a daughter, especially one as pretty as Harry, he'd worry about her. He thought maybe she exaggerated just a little.

Sian and John's relationship had deteriorated into a distant, uneasy routine. Sian was still sleeping in the spare room, and was now beginning to think of it as *hers*, adding bits and pieces from the room she used to share with John. They were polite to each other and behaved as normally as possible in front of the girls, but privately they were estranged. John started to stay later at work, and Stephen called in for an hour or so most evenings before his father got home.

Sian had taken to dropping in to the Angel during the day. Ted always made her feel welcome and she found herself confiding in him. He was so easy to talk to and, compared to John, very tolerant, so it was a shock to her to discover he wasn't as easygoing as she'd thought. They were talking about Stephen and Angie's relationship.

"She's a lovely girl," Sian smiled.

Ted nodded. "Yes, she's a knockout." His face darkened. "I don't get her parents though. Nothing against Steve, Sian, but I wouldn't let Harriet stay out till all hours with some boy."

"Stevie isn't 'some boy'!"

Ted wasn't joking. "I mean it, Sian. No boy touches my Harriet until he's married to her."

"But, Ted, they're all nearly eighteen. It may not be the way we behaved, but that was then! Times have changed."

"Not as far as I'm concerned," Ted said, grimly. "I've told Harriet. If anyone lays a finger on her, I'll knock his block off."

Sian was alarmed. It was a side of Ted she'd never seen before and she didn't know what to say. He looked the way he'd done when she'd first met him; sinister, his eyes so dark they were like pitch, dead and expressionless. "Ted?" she said hesitantly.

He smiled, and he was his usual self again, and she wondered if she'd imagined the look in his eyes. She changed the subject and pushed the incident to the back of her mind.

On the Monday before Stephen's eighteenth birthday, Sian decided she'd be damned if she was going to let John's attitude ruin everything. The fourth fell on a Saturday that year. When Stephen came in after school, she tackled him about it. "You're taking the day off work, aren't you?"

He nodded, his mouth full of fruitcake. "This is delicious, Mum," he mumbled.

"Mmm," she said vaguely. "Stevie, I want you to spend the day here."

He looked dubious. "Is that a good idea though, Mum? I don't want to argue with Dad."

"Yes, it bloody well is!"

Stephen was taken aback. Sian never swore. "OK, OK!"

She smiled. "Sorry, Stevie. I'm just so fed up with everyone tiptoeing round your father. I'll cook whatever you want and we'll have a lovely day. Bring Angie if you like. I expect you were going to spend the day with her, weren't you?"

A small secret smile curled round his lips and she remembered the conversation she'd had with Ted.

"Stevie, you and Angie – you are *careful*, aren't you?"

He coloured. "Of course," he said with embarrassment.

"Anyway, about your birthday," she said quickly. "I've got something for you from Dada."

"From Dada?" He stared at her. "How could you possibly?"

"He got it a long time ago, when you were about fourteen. He wanted you to have it for your coming of age."

Stephen stared down at the table. "I miss him all the time," he said quietly. "I know I didn't see him all that much, but just knowing he was there if you needed him made all the difference."

"I feel the same, cariad." She realised with a shock that this was how she was beginning to feel about Ted too. It was something she didn't want to pursue. She switched her thoughts with a slight effort. "I told you because I wondered if you'd like to have it before your birthday. I know we don't usually do this, but being as it's from Dada… There's a letter with it too, it might get a bit emotional."

"I'd love to have it! I'm really excited, but do you think Dada would mind?"

"Not Dada. He'd understand. Do you want it now?"

Stephen nodded.

She got up. "Come on, then. It's in my room."

Upstairs, he went to the room she and John had always shared.

She shook her head. "In here." She indicated the spare room.

He was shocked. "Are things that bad between you and Dad?"

"Oh, Steve, what do you think?"

"Are you going to split up?" He felt cold.

"I don't know, I honestly don't. We're coping at the moment and I don't want to upset the girls, specially not Becks, you know how she hated St Paul's at first and was so unhappy. She seems to have settled down now, and I don't want to unsettle her all over again." She gave a half-shrug. "I'm just taking each day as it comes. Anyway, Stevie, that's not why we're here."

They went into her room, and she opened the cupboard and handed him a guitar case.

"What is it?" he asked, bewildered.

"A pair of socks! Just open it, Steve!"

He opened the case. It was a National Steel guitar.

"Oh, my God!" He looked at Sian. "Oh my God, Mum! Did you know?" He picked it up reverently. "It's a Style Three Tricone! Tampa Red played one like this. Look at the engraving! Isn't it beautiful?"

The guitar was engraved with a delicate lily of the valley pattern, and the solid steel body shone like silver.

She nodded. "Yes it is. I'd heard Dada talking about National Steel guitars to you, but I always thought they looked like your acoustic. Play it, Stevie."

He played the tune he'd written after Dada died. The rich music rang out, cascading from his rapidly moving fingers, smooth and sweet and clear.

Sian shut her eyes and let it wash over her. "Dada would have loved that, cariad," she said, her voice not quite steady. She handed him an envelope.

His face changed. He put the guitar back in its case, sat down on Sian's bed and opened it slowly.

Dear Son, he read.

If you are reading this it means I'm not around any more. Stevie, as your Mam will tell you, I bought you this guitar a while ago because I could see, even then, what a very fine musician you would be. I hope I will be there to hear you play it, son, but if I'm not, remember I am so proud of you and I love you so very much and nothing can ever change that.

Happy birthday, Stevie,

Dada.

Stephen handed the letter to Sian. "I wish he *was* my father," he muttered, blinking back tears. Sian put her arms around him. "Stevie, your father does love you, he really does," she said desperately.

He hugged her tightly and stood up. "Let's go and show this to Kath and Becks."

At the Angel, Harry went into ecstasies over the guitar. "It's the most fantastic thing I've ever seen! And the sound! God, Steve, you're so lucky! Are you going to play it on Friday?"

"What do you think?"

He was really looking forward to Friday. Angie had somehow managed to persuade her parents to let her stay the night at the Angel. She told them she'd be sleeping in the spare room. "After all," she said to a delighted Stephen, "it's not a lie, is it?"

And then he had his National guitar. He'd completely forgotten his feeling that playing the guitar had caused the row with his father, and he was spending all his free time perfecting his style. He and Harry sat in the kitchen every night after school, practicing. The National was a joy, and he let Harry play it too. They became very close, and Stephen began to talk to her in much the same way as Sian did to Ted. She had her father's way of cutting through to the heart of an issue.

The gig that Friday seemed to him to be the best they'd ever done. They were all very comfortable with each other's playing by now and Stephen and Harry, in particular, had a great on-stage relationship. By the end of the evening, he felt elated. Even without Ray, he thought that they really stood a chance of going places. And Angie was staying all night. The thought of waking up next to her was intoxicating.

When Ray and Graham had gone home, he took her hand and they went up to his room. He put his arms round her. "This is the best birthday present I've ever had."

"Better than the guitar?"

He pretended to think about it, and she pulled his hair, giggling.

He started to undress her.

"No." She shook her head.

"Why not?"

"Because. I've got a surprise. You get undressed, then get into bed and get right under the covers. I'll tell you when you can come out."

He did as he was told. "Can I come out yet?"

"No."

"It's hot under here. I can't breathe."

"Tough."

"I could die in here!"

"If you don't shut up, I'll kill you anyway. OK, I'm ready."

He threw the covers back. "Wow! Angie!"

She was wearing a silky, clinging nightgown. It was sapphire blue, and made her eyes look almost purple.

He leapt out of bed and pulled her against him. "You look gorgeous! You *feel* gorgeous!" He ran his hands over the silk covering her body. "God, Angie, let's go to bed!"

She slipped out of his grasp. "Not yet."

He groaned. "I'm going to explode!"

She turned her back on him and bent over her bag.

"Jesus! Are you doing this deliberately?"

She straightened up and grinned at him. "Maybe a bit. Here, Stevie, happy birthday." She gave him a small, beautifully wrapped box.

"Angie! I thought you were my present! I was going to unwrap you in a minute!"

"This is a bonus then. Open it!"

He unwrapped it carefully and opened the box. Inside, nestled in tissue, was an antique tortoiseshell guitar pick, a thin, silver edging, as delicate as lace, around the top. "Oh, Angie!" He took her in his arms.

The next morning, she woke first. He was still sleeping, tangled up in the covers. She looked at the clock. It was just before ten. She slipped out of bed, pulled on his dressing gown, and went for a shower. Afterwards, she sat on the edge of the bed. "Stevie! Happy birthday!"

"Mmmm." He rolled away from her.

"Steve! Wake up! It's late!"

He opened one eye. "What time is it?"

"Quarter past ten. Get up. We've got to have breakfast and go to your house. We said we'd be there by about eleven."

He rolled out of bed. "You look sexy in that towel." He started to unwrap it.

She slapped his hand. "Stop it! We haven't got time! Go and have a shower." She kissed him. "Happy birthday," she said again.

He pulled her into bed and reached for a condom. "I can shower really quickly," he grinned.

Later, they went downstairs to the kitchen for coffee. Harry came in as they were drinking it. She'd agonised for a long time over what to get Stephen – it couldn't be anything too much, he would think that was odd, but she wanted to get him something special. He was a big fan of Stanton Crawford, the blues singer, and he'd always wanted his first album, 'Backwoods Man', but had never been able to find it anywhere, so she'd asked her brother Nick, who was still living in London, to look out for it. To her delight, he'd found a copy.

"I thought I heard you! Don't go out yet, Steve, I've got something for you!" She fetched the present. "Happy birthday!"

"Thanks, Harry!" He was touched. He hugged her and kissed her cheek. To his surprise, she held onto him for a minute.

"What is it?" Angie asked.

"Give us a chance!" he laughed. He pulled the paper off and stared at the album. "Harry! Oh, my God, how did you get hold of this? I've wanted it for ages!"

She was hot with pleasure. "Oh, you know… it was just, I just saw it," she said, trying to sound casual. "Anyway, have a great day."

He glanced at her quickly. She almost sounded… what? Sad? She grinned at him, and he ruffled her hair, strangely relieved. "When I get back this evening we'll listen to this," he promised.

"It's a date," she said, almost breathless with anticipation.

The Christmas holidays sped by. Stephen had meant to play more guitar and spend more time writing songs, but between studying, working at Braithwaites and the Angel, and playing gigs around York, there wasn't much spare time. He'd written a song for Angie for her eighteenth birthday called 'High On You'. The others were sworn to secrecy and they could only rehearse it when she wasn't there.

At school, there was a feeling of being on the last leg of a long journey. This was their last proper term. The summer term would be made up of the exams and then that would be it. School would be out forever and they'd all be scattered into their own lives and futures.

The day before Angie's birthday, her mother collapsed and was rushed into hospital, where she was diagnosed with acute pancreatitis caused by gallstones. Angie was distraught. Her birthday was on Sunday and Stephen spent the day with her, driving her to the hospital at visiting time.

"My poor little baby. It's your birthday and you've had a miserable time!"

"Not as miserable as Mum," Angie replied wanly. "And you sang me my lovely song on Friday night, and you gave me this." She fingered the necklace he'd given her, a garnet in a silver setting that matched the earrings he'd given her the year before.

They pulled up outside her house. "What would you like to do tonight?" he asked.

"Go to bed with you."

"We can't, not here."

"Let's go to the Angel then. I'll leave a note for Dad to say where we are and that I won't be home late."

They drove to the pub and went straight to Stephen's room. He undressed her gently and lifted her into bed.

"Can we just cuddle?" she asked, her face pressed against his chest.

"Of *course*." He realised she was crying. "What's the matter, Angie?" he asked in alarm. "Is it your Mum? Is there something else wrong with her?"

"No." She moved away from him a little so she could see his face. "Before you came round this morning, Dad said—" She stopped and drew in a ragged breath.

"What?" he prompted. He was really worried.

"He said he'd decided to move to Scarborough. The doctors say Mum's going to need lots of looking after and both her sisters live there."

Stephen was stunned. "When?"

"As soon as possible. He even said we might rent somewhere and look for a house to buy later."

"But – what about school? It's the exams soon!"

"I can do them anywhere. Let's face it, Stevie, I'm only doing general studies and art. It's not like moving school will make much difference."

"You can't go, Angie! I can't do without you!"

"I know! I know, Stevie!" She drew in a long breath. "It's not far to Scarborough," she said, trying to smile. "You've got your car, we could see each other at the weekends."

"I have to work on Saturdays, so it would only be Sundays. One day!" he said savagely. "We see each other all the time now and it's not enough!"

"There's nothing else we can do." She was crying hard.

He felt as if his heart was breaking. "Don't cry, Angie! Please, I can't bear to see you so sad. We'll think of something." He wiped her face with the edge of the sheet. Gradually, she stopped crying. He stroked her taut little body and she began to relax.

Within a month, her father found them somewhere to live, and the removal of her mother's gall bladder was scheduled at the hospital in Scarborough. They were due to move at the beginning of March.

Stephen couldn't believe it. It was as if some malignant deity waited until he was happy and then snatched it all from him. He and Angie spent every moment they could together. They cut lessons so that they could go to bed. Often they just held each other and when they did make love, it was with a kind of desperation. Stephen kept telling himself it wouldn't happen, *couldn't* happen, something would turn up at the last minute, so it was with absolute desolation that he watched them drive away forever. He went back to the Angel, locked himself in his room and cried.

After she'd gone, nothing seemed to matter. The band rehearsed, he played, they did their regular gigs at the Angel. He couldn't be bothered to arrange any elsewhere or write any new songs. He didn't do any schoolwork, didn't bother with homework, was moody and sullen. He lived for Sundays and hated them at the same time because they went so quickly.

Angie wasn't happy at her new school. She talked of leaving and getting a job.

"In York?" Stephen asked hopefully.

She shook her head. "Mum needs me here."

Just before the Easter holidays, Rick Grainger, Stephen's English teacher, asked him to stay behind after class. "What's wrong, Steve? Your work has been non-existent this term. Apparently, the same goes for all your lessons. If you carry on like this you'll fail your 'A' Levels."

Stephen shrugged.

"Don't you shrug at me like that! I asked you a question. What's the matter with you?"

"Nothing."

"Stephen, if you don't pull yourself together, your head of year will send a letter home asking your parents to come up to the school and discuss the problem."

"Big deal," muttered Stephen.

Grainger stared at him. "I don't understand you."

"Can I go?"

"No, you bloody well can't!" Grainger shouted. "You can't throw this away, Stephen. What happened to you? Just tell me, just make me understand, and you can go and ruin your life in any way you see fit."

"Angie."

"What?"

"Angie. Angie Cartwright, my girlfriend. She's moved to Scarborough because her mum's been ill."

Grainger ran his hand through his hair. "Stephen, I know how you feel—"

"How can you possibly know how I feel?" Stephen demanded.

"Oh, Steve, grow up! Do you think you're the only man in the world who's lost a girlfriend?"

"This is different."

"It's different for everyone. Is behaving like a two-year-old going to bring her back here? Is failing your exams going to make her feel better? She's probably having enough trouble adjusting to a new place, a new school and a sick mother without you acting like this. You're lucky she hasn't dumped you. I can't believe that a few months ago you sat in this room and told me you were serious about your band and I believed you!"

"I am serious about it!" Stephen was annoyed and hurt.

"And supposing you make it and you're on tour and your girlfriend leaves you. Are you going to run home crying? Judging from the way you're behaving now, I'd say the answer would be yes."

Stephen stared at him. Grainger was right. He was behaving like a child. And he hadn't looked at it from Angie's point of view at all. How could he have been so selfish? "You're right," he muttered. "I've been behaving like a tosser."

"You'll get no argument from me. Write it down, Steve. Turn it into a song. It's what songwriters do. And pull yourself together. No one ever died from a broken heart."

He did as Grainger suggested. He saw his other teachers and made up the work. He organised gigs for the band. He wrote new songs. And he never whined to Angie. He took her flowers and silly little presents. He listened to her troubles and tried to help. But inside he felt as if something had died. There was no joy, no spark. He went for a run every night before bed to exhaust himself so that he would fall straight into a dreamless sleep. He loathed running, but it worked. And he got fit.

He saw as much of Angie as he could during the Easter holidays. He had to work and he had to revise, but he drove over whenever he had time. She managed to stay at the Angel for a weekend. He took the Saturday off work and they spent the entire two days in bed, only emerging to use the bathroom or make sandwiches. They couldn't get enough of each other. After she went home, he thought of the song he'd written for her, 'High On You'. It was true, she was his drug. His body craved her.

One Sunday at the end of April, they drove to Whitby. It was a beautiful day, and the little seaside town was drenched in spring sunshine. They wandered around, hand in hand, looking at the shops. Stephen bought her some little jet earrings. They got fish and chips, and climbed up the steps to the Abbey.

"I'm leaving school," Angie told him.

"Why?"

"I've applied to the hospital to train as a nurse. I've been accepted."

"That's a really good idea, Angie. You'll be a wonderful nurse."

She looked relieved. "I thought you'd be cross."

"What right have I got to be cross?"

"Well, we won't be able to see so much of each other."

He stared at her. "Why?"

"I'll have to work some Sundays."

He hardly ever saw her as it was. How could he bear to see less of her? He looked out at the amethyst sea. How beautiful it was, how deceptively smooth and calm and beautiful.

"Now you're cross with me, aren't you?" she asked in a small voice.

He turned to her. Her sweet, rather childlike face was troubled, her brow furrowed. He wanted to break down and cry – for himself, for the forlorn little girl beside him, for everyone who had ever cared about another human being. He wanted to walk away, to never see Angie again, to armour himself forever against love and pain and heartbreak. Instead, he carefully folded the remains of his food in the paper, put it under the bench, and took her in his arms. "I'm not cross, Ange. I'm… well, I suppose I'm sad because I want to be with you all the time, and that's not going to happen, but if being a nurse is what you want to do, then I'd never try to stop you. What I *really* want is just for you to be happy."

She clung to him. "Thank you, Stevie."

If he'd thought it was bad when he only saw her once a week, it was purgatory now. He flung himself into revision as if his life depended on it. To make matters worse, Harry, who he'd come to rely on as a confidante, had fallen violently in love with a plumber called Jason Howarth, who'd come to the pub to install a new boiler. Stephen didn't like him. He could see the attraction for Harry, Jason was good-looking in a flash kind of way, and he always seemed to have plenty of money, a lot of which he spent on her. He was nine years older than she was, and Stephen felt there was something untrustworthy about him. Ted agreed. The two of them were united in their dislike. Stephen didn't tell Harry; he didn't want to upset her. Ted had no such scruples.

Harry didn't care. She knew Stephen didn't like Jason, but she went on seeing him. She had to. He was her way out, her lifeline. When she'd complained to Stephen about Ted, she'd known he thought she was exaggerating. If only she had been! Instead of getting better as she got older, her father was getting worse. He was obsessed with the idea of protecting her from men, who, according to him, were 'only after one thing'.

"Even a boy like Steve," he said, darkly. "Nice, polite, respectful, but all he wants to do with that Angie is get her knickers off! If I was Angie's dad I'd give him what for!"

"For God sake, Dad, he's in love with Angie!" Harry retorted.

"Then why don't he ask her to marry him? Because he can get what he wants without marriage. Nobody's going to hold you cheap like that!"

She was afraid that one day Ted would really lose his temper and hurt someone badly, like he had in London. However he behaved, he was her father, and she loved him, and she didn't want him getting into trouble because of her.

And Jason had asked her to marry him. He was good-looking and funny and doing well in his job. Of course, she didn't love him – how could she? She'd never love anyone but Steve, but that was hopeless, she had to get away from him, make a life for herself. He was talking of going to London, making a demo, trying to make it with the band, but she couldn't, she couldn't do that. She couldn't live in the same house as him any more. She told Jason yes.

"Steve, can I talk to you?" She put her head round Stephen's door.

He was trying to commit to memory all the salient details of the Corn Laws and Peel's repeal of them. "I could use a break." He turned off his record player. He'd been playing Dire Straits.

"You can leave it on, I love 'Sultans Of Swing'."

"It's OK, I wasn't listening exactly. I just find it easier to study with music on. What do you want to talk about?"

She held out her left hand. A diamond ring sparkled on her finger.

"You're engaged!" He was amazed. He'd never have put Jason down as the marrying type.

She smiled shyly. "You're the first person I've told."

"Ted'll go through the roof! Congratulations," he added quickly.

"Thank you. Dad won't. He won't mind me being engaged. If me and Jace are getting married, he won't be worrying that I'm being 'trifled with'. When he knows Jason's intentions are honourable, he'll fall over himself to welcome him into the family! We thought September. Jason's just been accepted for a job with a big firm in Sheffield and he'll be starting in July. He can find us somewhere to live and then I can move down there."

"But, Harry, the band!" Stephen said, horrified. "You can't chuck it, Harry, you're too good! We're going to London when we've finished school, remember?"

She looked apologetic and guilty. "I'm really sorry, Steve. But you can understand how I feel. Think of Angie. If it was a choice between the band and her, you'd choose her."

Stephen considered this for a minute. "You know, Harry, I'm not sure I would. And even if I did, we've been going out for two years! You barely know Jason. Do you really love him that much?"

She looked stubborn. "I do love him, yes. And you don't know what it's like with Dad, Steve! He seems great to you and your mum, good old Ted, always reliable, laid back. He'll hardly let me do anything!"

"Then come to London with me!"

"And if it doesn't work out? I come crawling back here. Anyway, I wouldn't put it past him to refuse to let me go."

"Don't be silly, Harry," Stephen said with exasperation. "It's 1979, not the Dark Ages! And, anyway, you'll be eighteen next month."

"You don't know Dad," she said grimly. She leant over and kissed him on the cheek. "Thanks for listening."

"Hey, any time. You've listened to me often enough!"

"I'm sorry about the band, Steve."

"Harry doesn't mind if she doesn't make the scene," he said, trying to look pleased for her and not as bleak as he felt. After she'd gone, he sat staring at nothing. Ray was off to university in September, so they'd need someone to replace him. They'd known that, and Mr Grainger's girlfriend might just be interested. But another bassist of Harry's calibre? It seemed to be one thing after another. It was all falling apart. He might as well have applied to university last year and spared everyone the hell of his estrangement from John. And he hadn't seen Angie for ages, she'd been too busy. He had to admit, if only to himself, that Grainger had been right about that too. The ache was fading. He couldn't understand it. Wasn't absence supposed to make the heart grow fonder? He'd been out to a couple of parties lately and found himself dancing and flirting with other girls. Of course, it hadn't gone any further and he didn't want it to, but all the same… He felt disgusted with himself.

And then they were into the exams and all he did was revise, eat, sleep and sit in the hall at school writing essay after essay. Harry had her eighteenth birthday and Ted organised a party at the pub. Stephen wanted Angie to be there, but she was on duty. She seemed to be continually on duty. He bought Harry some Penhaligon's Bluebell scent and body lotion from them both, and a very pretty and expensive little gold and pearl necklace (pearls being Harry's birthstone) with matching earrings from himself.

And finally the exams were finished and that was it. All those years of hard work and learning dates and quotes and theorem were over. They all went to the Nag's Head and got smashed. Stephen went back to the Angel, rolled into bed and slept until late in the evening.

In July, he started working full-time at Braithwaites as assistant manager. Angie was becoming simply a nostalgic memory. He fought against it, went over and over all the things they'd done together, conjured up images of her naked body. She wrote and he wrote back, but it wasn't the same. He confided this to Harry who was moping around the pub, at a loose end without Jason, who'd gone to Sheffield to start his new job.

"I know what you mean," she nodded. "I feel the same way about Jason."

Stephen was appalled. "Don't marry him then!"

"I've got to, Dad's got it all arranged." She giggled. "He'd kill me if I called it off now. Anyway, once I see Jace again it'll be fine."

Stephen was doubtful, but didn't pursue it.

The 'A' Level results came out in the middle of August. Ray was in a state of anxiety over his, terrified he wouldn't have done well enough to get in to university.

"Of course you'll pass," Stephen said for the fiftieth time as they counted stock at work.

"Yeah, but suppose I don't? What'll I do then?"

"Get a job, I guess," Stephen shrugged.

"It's all right for you! I'm talking about my future here, Markham!"

"Oh, suck it up, Raymond! You've taken four 'A' Levels and you only need two 'B's and a 'C'. Of course you'll get them!"

Sian came round to the Angel early the next morning with Stephen's results. He was finishing breakfast when he heard the back door open. "Hi, Ted."

"It's not Ted, it's me. I can't stay, cariad, I've got the girls in the car. I've just brought this." She waved the envelope.

"Oh. OK. What does it say?"

She stared at him. "I haven't opened it."

He shrugged. "I don't mind."

"You are the most peculiar boy! Here, open it!"

He tore it open and pulled out the slip. "I passed." He handed it to Sian.

"Stevie! You've got four 'A's! Well done!"

"Dad'll be pleased."

She looked at him curiously. "Aren't you?"

"Yeah, I suppose. It doesn't really seem to mean anything. If I apply to university for next year it'll be helpful."

"Are you going to?"

"I don't know. Didn't you say you'd got the girls in the car?"

"Oh God, yes I have! They've got dental appointments!" She gave him a kiss. "Well, I'm *really* pleased, cariad. Really proud of you!"

Ted came in from the cash and carry as she was driving off. "Was that Sian?"

"Mmmhmm."

"Oh." Ted was disappointed to have missed her. "What did she want?"

"Just my results. I better go, I'll be late."

"Wait up, Steve, what did you get?"

Stephen passed him the slip. "'A's. See you this evening."

Ray was already in the shop when he arrived. The look on his face told Stephen all he needed to know. "You passed then?"

"Yeah, three 'A's and a 'B'. I'm so relieved! I'm going to the pub at lunchtime. You coming?"

"Sure," Stephen shrugged. "Congratulations."

Ray glanced at him. "Didn't you do well, Steve?"

"I did fine. Why is everyone so worried about my results? Like you said yesterday, it doesn't matter for me."

"I didn't say *that*," Ray objected. "Did you fail?"

"No, I got four fucking 'A's," Stephen said in exasperation. "I'm just not too bothered about the whole thing, OK?"

"Sorry for breathing," Ray muttered.

Stephen sighed. "I'm sorry, Ray. It's just… well, maybe Dad was right. I caused all this fuss by not going to university, and you're leaving the band, and now Harry. What was it all for? If I'd done badly it wouldn't have mattered, but I've done really well and it's just going to cause more trouble between my mum and dad. He'll be unbearable."

Ray stared at him. "You really do know how to complicate your life, Steve."

"Yeah," Stephen said bitterly. "I can always be relied on to fuck a good thing up."

At the beginning of September, Angie rang to say she was coming to York for the day. Stephen was ecstatic. He met her from the train and they walked up through the city. Angie smiled and kissed him, but more like a sister than a lover. "We need to talk, Steve."

He stopped dead, his heart sinking. "Go on, then."

"We can't talk here." It was a glorious day, and York was still heaving with tourists.

He grabbed her hand, and ran as fast as he could to the Museum Gardens.

"Steve! Slow down!" she pleaded.

He took no notice, dragging her through the crowds to a secluded part of the old Abbey, where he pulled her down onto the grass. "OK, let's talk."

"Let me catch my breath!" she panted reproachfully.

He scowled at her. "You said you wanted to talk."

She sighed. "Oh, Steve. If only my mum hadn't been ill!"

"If only. I *hate* those words."

"I just think…" Angie faltered. "I just think we should stop seeing each other."

Stephen laughed bitterly. "I thought we had! This is the first time we've seen each other for ages. You're always busy!"

Her lips trembled. "You know what I mean. Oh, Stevie, don't be angry. We've had so many good times!"

He could feel a lump forming in his throat. How could he have thought he was over her? He only had to see her again. She smelt exactly the way she always had, clean and fresh and *Angie*. Like spring flowers. "You're going to say it's over, that we've both changed and grown up and can we always be friends," he said flatly.

She stared at him. "How did you know? How did you know I was going to say those things?"

"Because you're Angie and they're Angie things. What can I say? I don't think I've changed, but maybe I have. And if you've changed, it doesn't make any difference whether I have or not." He had to stop for a minute to control himself. He was *not* going to cry in public. "Yes, we can always be friends. I'll always be your friend, Angie, always."

She burst into tears and threw herself into his arms. "I'm so, so sorry," she sobbed. "I still love you, I'll always love you. I'm just not *in* love with you any more." She got up. "I'm going back to Scarborough."

"But…" He was bewildered. "What time's your train? I thought you weren't going for ages."

"There'll be one along. I'll just wait."

He stood up. "I'll come with you."

She shook her head frantically. "No! No, I couldn't cope with that. Goodbye, Stevie." She ran down the grass to the path.

He got back to the pub and slipped quietly in, hoping that no one would hear him. No such luck.

Ted came out of the kitchen. "Steve! Where's the lovely Angie?" He saw Stephen's face. "What's happened?"

"We've split up." His voice shook and he clenched his teeth.

Ted was shocked. "I'm really sorry, Steve. Shall I get us a drink?"

What the hell. Why not? "Yeah, OK."

Ted fetched the whisky. They didn't bother with glasses, just drank from the bottle.

"The thing is, Ted, I was starting to get over her. Kind of. Not seeing her, it made it harder to remember stuff, you know?" He paused for a swig of whisky. He was feeling blurry and had to concentrate on what he was saying. "If she hadn't come today, if it had been in a few months' time, I think I could have beared it." He stopped. That wasn't right. "Borne it. But as soon as I saw her – I just remembered everything, everything… You know what I mean, don't you?"

"Yeah, I know what you mean." Ted gulped a mouthful of whisky, wiped the top of the bottle and passed it to Stephen.

He finished it and pushed the bottle away. "I'm going to lie down."

He woke several hours later with a splitting headache. He sat up and groaned. Why had he drunk all that whisky? The very thought of it made him heave. He ran into the bathroom and threw up. He sat on the floor by the toilet for a while, and when he was sure he wasn't going to be sick again, he fetched a towel and had a shower. He felt better when he'd finished. He took two paracetamol, cleaned his teeth, got into his pyjamas, and went back to bed and dozed. Eventually, he got up and looked at his watch. It was nearly ten o'clock. The whole day gone. He had to get up for work in the morning and he wasn't in the least bit tired now. And all he could think of was Angie. When he shut his eyes he could see her as if she was standing in front of him.

A knock on the door made him jump. He ignored it, he didn't want to talk to anyone. Another knock, and the door slowly opened. Harry, wearing a short nightgown, stood in the doorway. "I saw your light was on. Can I come in?"

He shrugged. "I'd say you just about are. Why bother to ask? I'm sorry," he added. "But I'm not good company, Harry."

She sat on the bed and took his hand. "I know what happened, Dad told me. I'm so sorry you're sad, Steve." She stroked his face. "I wish I could help. It's what friends are for." She wanted him so much, wanted to help him, wanted to hold him. She couldn't bear to see him so sad, she'd give her life to make him happy. She leant forward and brushed his lips with hers.

He started.

She let go of his hand and put her arms round his neck. "I could make you feel better."

"Harry." He tried to move her arms, but she kissed him, opening her mouth.

Despite himself, he was becoming aroused. He pulled away. "Harry, stop it! You're getting married in a few weeks!"

"Forget that, Steve, it doesn't matter. It's not real. You and me, we're all that's real. We're on an island, outside time. You need someone to care for you right now, and I need *you*. I've wanted you for such a long, long time. No one will ever know." She unbuttoned his pyjama jacket and kissed him again.

This time he responded, cupping her face in his hands.

She wriggled out of her nightgown, and he took off his pyjama trousers, staring at her body. She had a lovely figure, rounded and voluptuous. Her breasts were full and heavy, her nipples hard. He stroked them and, leaning forward, took one in his mouth, sucking it. She reached down and caressed him, rubbing up and down.

"Oh, God! Harry, we *can't* do this! Anyway, I haven't got any condoms."

"It's OK, I'm on the pill." She pushed him down and straddled him. He drew in a ragged breath. She began to ride him, moving harder and faster. He moved under her, thrusting upwards. He had his hands round her breasts but as they moved furiously together, he slipped them down around her waist.

She came, and cried out. He gave a last convulsive thrust and she fell against him. He put his arms round her, rubbing her back. She wriggled off him and lay next to him and he turned towards her, pulling her against him and kissing her very tenderly. "I'm so sorry, Harry, I shouldn't have done that." He felt terrible. He felt he'd used her, his good, good friend; he felt, however irrationally, that he'd betrayed Angie. And then there was Jason.

"Steve, lovely Steve, please don't feel guilty. I don't. No one will ever know, no one will get hurt. It'll be our lovely secret forever. It *was* lovely, wasn't it?"

"Yes, it was," he said, stroking her hair back off her face.

She sighed happily and put her head on his shoulder. He kissed her cheek. Eventually, he heard her breathing change as she slept. He lay awake until early morning, when he fell into a dreamless sleep.

Chapter Three
Someone Who Loved Me

You gave me everything, gave me your life with arms outstretched and heart breaking,
And I just took, and kept on taking, like a blind man, like the fool I am,
I couldn't see someone who loved me.

He wrote a song, 'Madonna of the Seven Hills', for Harry. He felt both responsible for and tremendously close to her. The guilt he felt for what had happened between them was monumental. He wasn't in love with her and couldn't shake the feeling that he'd used her. She told him the next morning she'd fancied him for ages, and reiterated what she'd said before they'd made love, but it made no difference.

He went to the staff room at school on Wednesday afternoon and asked for Rick Grainger.

"Steve! I didn't think I'd see you here again! I always got the distinct impression with you that you loathed school. Hey, congratulations on your results!"

"Yeah, thanks. Mr Grainger."

"Rick."

Stephen smiled at him. "Rick. You know you said your girlfriend plays guitar? Does she play bass?"

"She can. I don't think she's particularly keen. Why?"

"Harry Taylor's getting married in a couple of weeks. We wanted to play at the reception, but she's our bassist."

"Look, I'll ask Sue and get back to you. Can I reach you at home?"

He shook his head. "Here." He wrote down the pub's number. "Thanks, Rick."

Later that evening, Grainger's girlfriend rang him. "Hi, Steve, it's Sue, Rick Grainger's girlfriend. You want a bass player for a wedding?"

"Yes. Rick said you might be interested."

"I might. Look, we need to get together. When's the wedding?"

"Three weeks."

"Doesn't give us long. Do you want to meet up now?"

"Sure. Can you come round here?"

"Where's here?"

He gave her directions.

"OK. See you in half an hour."

Stephen privately thought that Harry's wedding was turning into a circus, but both she and Ted were more than happy with it. Ted was holding the reception at the pub and becoming increasingly wound up about the arrangements.

"God," Stephen said to Ray at their next rehearsal. "I'm never getting married. It's appalling. Everything gets sorted, then they find something they don't like, they spend the whole day arguing and obsessing over it and then change it back to how it was in the first place!"

Sue laughed. "For God's sake don't say that to Rick! I've been working on him and I think he's just about ready to pop the question."

Stephen was glad he'd asked Grainger about her, she fitted in with the others and while she didn't have Harry's talent or instinctive feel, she was good. She was very complimentary about 'Madonna of the Seven Hills'. "The melody is beautiful, Steve, and the guitar solo will blow them away."

"Why's it called 'Madonna of the Seven Hills'?" Ray wanted to know.

"Well, because they're going to live in Sheffield."

"So?"

"God, Ray, how do you manage to even dress yourself? Four 'A' Levels and you don't know anything! Sheffield's got seven hills, like Rome. Rome's known as the City of Seven Hills. It's kind of a play on that."

"OK. And Madonna's an Italian word. Yeah." He thought about it.

"Come on, Ray, I can see the wheels turning. What?"

"Well, why Madonna? Isn't that what they call Mary?"

"Yes, but it means 'my lady' and anyway, Harry's going to be all virginal and Madonna-like in her wedding dress."

"Oh, yeah, right, I get it! D'you suppose she is?"

"What?"

"A virgin?"

Stephen felt the colour rising in his cheeks. He bent down and fiddled with the amp. "No idea."

Harry told Ted that Stephen was her honorary brother, and as such he was sitting at the front of the church with the bride's family, including her brothers, Will and Nick. Will looked exactly like a younger version of Ted, but Nick was slighter, more like Harry. They were both very quiet and detached. Harry had said that they'd been scared of Ted when they lived at home, and they certainly didn't seem to have a lot of time for him. But they were friendly enough to Stephen and obviously very fond of Harry.

Stephen was unprepared for the way he felt when Harry came up the aisle on Ted's arm. He suddenly understood Ted's protectiveness of her, he found himself thinking that Jason had better cherish her or else. She looked very young and innocent with her veil covering her face, not a bit like the devil-may-care tomboy he knew. He got a lump in his throat and had to blink back tears as he listened to her clear voice making her marriage vows. And then she was walking back down the aisle, this time with Jason, her veil off her face, and the organ playing 'The Wedding March'.

The Angel was crammed with guests. The breakfast was a buffet rather than a sit-down meal, and people were wandering around with plates of food. Sian and the girls were looking smart and pretty, particularly Kathy, Stephen thought. She had fairer hair than the rest of the family, a kind of toffee colour, and she was wearing it piled high on her head.

John was standing alone. Stephen took a deep breath, and walked over to him. "Hello, Dad."

John smiled. "Hello, son."

"Dad..." Stephen paused. John waited politely. "I was going to say you were right, but thinking about it, I'm not absolutely sure you were. This year has done me good, I've grown up. But anyway, I thought you'd like to know. I've applied to Manchester University."

John stared at him, his face transformed. "Stephen! This is marvellous news!"

"They haven't accepted me yet."

"With your 'A' Level results? It's a foregone conclusion!" He looked over at Sian, catching her eye. "Does your mother know?"

Stephen shook his head. "You're the first person I've told."

John was enormously touched.

Sian joined them." You look happy, John! Enjoying yourself?"

"I am now. Stephen's just told me he's applied to university next year."

"Have you, Stevie? Which one?"

"Manchester. The course looks really good."

"Ted was just telling me his manageress is leaving," Sian said slowly. "He said he'd spoken to you about it because he wants to get a couple who'll live in."

"Yes, we talked about it yesterday. I knew Liz was leaving, she's pregnant. If she doesn't go soon, we'll be delivering her baby with the drinks!"

Sian smiled. "The thing is, Steve, what about you? Ted said Harry said you could have her room."

"I'm moving out. I thought about it last night and it's time for me to move on. The Angel's a great transitional kind of place, not home, but not on my own. It'd be different without Harry, anyway. I'm going to get a flat. Graham's got one up by the hospital. I know he earns more than me, but I could afford to rent a smaller one. I thought I'd sell the car, I don't really need it."

Sian was stricken. "But now you've applied to university and everything's like it used to be, I thought you'd be coming home!"

He put his arm round her. "I'm sorry, Mum. But don't you see, I couldn't. I've got used to living alone, doing what I want when I want. If I came back home now, it'd be like a butterfly trying to crawl back into its chrysalis."

"Come on, you lot." Ted walked over to them. "You can't stand here in the corner with long faces, this is a wedding, not a wake! Come and circulate!" He turned to John. "I wonder if I could ask your professional advice?" The pair of them walked into the centre of the room, lost in conversation.

Sian and Stephen followed them, Sian smiling fondly. "He's really good at that."

Stephen wasn't sure whether she meant John or Ted, but he had a worrying suspicion that she meant the latter. Harry and Jason came over, and Harry took Stephen's arm. He smiled at her. "Happy?"

She nodded enthusiastically.

A young, dark-haired woman, looking as if she was at least eleven months pregnant, bore down on them. "Congratulations, you two! Eeeh, Harry, you do look beautiful! Ted must be dead proud!" She gave Harry a smacking kiss.

Harry hugged her. "Thanks, Liz. And thank you for the present. It's lovely, isn't it, Jason?" Jason looked blank. Harry elbowed him in the ribs. "Isn't it, Jason?"

"Oh, er, yeah, thanks," he said.

Liz beamed. "I made it myself! Now, then, Steve, I've been meaning to speak to you for ages. You're dead clever. What shall I call Junior?" She pointed to her huge bump.

Stephen was taken aback. "Um, I don't know."

"I had a scan the other day and they said they thought it were a boy," Liz continued, as if he hadn't spoken. "Now, I'd expected a girl so I'd got a name all picked out, Gypsophila, what do you think?"

"Lovely," murmured Stephen.

"Yeah, dead pretty, i'n't it? Anyway, I haven't got any boys' names."

"Well, I like Robert," Stephen said. "You can shorten it to Rob, it's a great name for a little boy, you can imagine him stumping up and down the stairs."

Liz wrinkled up her face. "Not *Robert*. There's hundreds of *Roberts*! No, you know, Steve, I were thinking of something like a name from Shakespeare."

"Oh, I see! OK, let me think. Well, there's Sebastian, Angelo, Orlando… um… Antonio, Valentine…"

"Wait on – did you say Orlando?"

"Mmmhmm."

"What play's he from?"

"*As You Like It*."

"*As You Like It*. I *do* like it, I like it a lot! Orlando! Thanks Steve." She wandered off.

"What's Liz's surname?" Stephen asked Harry.

She gave him a quizzical look. "Spivey, as you very well know."

"Just making sure it wasn't Florida," he grinned. Harry and Sian burst out laughing.

"What's so funny?" Jason asked.

"Orlando Florida, you know!" Harry said.

"Oh, yeah." Jason looked at Stephen with dislike. He'd never been happy with Harry and Stephen's friendship, and the little tosser was a right know-it-all.

When The Brigands started to play, Stephen saw Kathy dancing with a tall, red-haired boy, and when the band took a break, she was still with him. He went over to Rebecca. "Who's Kath dancing with?"

"Nice, isn't he? He's called Paul, he's at the university."

"How does she know him?"

"I don't know, I expect he asked her to dance."

"Hmm."

"God, Steve, you sound like Dad! She's sixteen, you know!"

"OK, OK, sheesh! I only asked!"

"It was the *way* you asked. Just go and play something people have heard of."

"Like what?"

"I don't know, Boomtown Rats or Blondie or something!"

Harry and Jason left just after ten, and gradually everyone started to drift away. The band stopped playing and they sat around with beers.

Rick joined them. "You lot were great. Did you have a good time, Sue?"

"Fantastic! When are we going to do it again, Steve?"

"I don't know." He was surprised; he hadn't thought she was that interested. "We've got our regular spot at the Angel. We'll have to get another rhythm guitar."

"I know people," Sue said. "I'll ask around. Rick said you were serious enough last year to think of going to London, trying to make it. Is that still on?"

Stephen laughed. "Ironic, isn't it? If only we'd met a month ago! I've just applied to Manchester University."

"No! What course?" Rick asked with interest.

"English and American Literature."

"My old university, my old course! You'll have a brilliant time, Steve!"

Shortly before Christmas, Stephen moved into his new flat. It was tiny, no room to swing a cat, but it was all he needed. He felt he was marking time. He missed Ray and his friends from school, and he missed Angie very much, although he didn't feel the same anguish. He was seeing girls, but there was no one special. He didn't want to get heavily involved with anyone. He saw Harry occasionally; she was pregnant now and came to stay with Ted from time to time. Everyone seemed to be getting on with their lives. He played at the Angel on a Friday night, but didn't organise any other gigs, there didn't seem to be much point. His musical career seemed to be going nowhere fast. Maybe he was going to end up like the Sultans of Swing, a daytime job and saving it up for Friday night.

Harry lay in the hospital bed staring into the crib. She was breathless, literally overcome with love for the tiny little boy lying there. She felt he was still joined to her, that the umbilical cord was still attaching them. He was so incredibly precious to her. Nothing else mattered, not even the fact that her marriage was over, had been since it began. Jason had another woman, he'd known her long before he met Harry, and he had no intention of giving her up.

"Why the fuck did you ask me to marry you, then?" she'd screamed at him when she found out.

"Because I fancied you rotten and a quick fuck in the back of the van once in a blue moon wasn't enough! I knew the only way I could have you properly, without that fucker of a father of yours killing me, was to marry you! But I wish to God I'd never bothered! You were such fun in York! What happened to you? It's not even like we do it much, is it? Christ only knows how you got pregnant!"

Harry was speechless. Finally she said, "Well, if it's so bloody awful with me, why do you stay?"

"Don't worry, I'm not going to! This was the worst mistake of my life, and God knows that's saying something!"

She didn't try to stop him leaving. She didn't want him, had never really loved him; he'd simply been her escape, her way out. But marrying him hadn't stopped her loving Stephen; if anything, it had made the longing worse. She was glad Jason had never really loved her. It meant she didn't have to feel guilty.

"Sian, can I come round? I really need to talk."

"Of course you can, Ted, you know that! After all the times I've bent your ear!" Sian put away the ironing and got out mugs. She couldn't imagine what he could possibly want. When he arrived, looking tired and anxious, she made them both tea. "What's wrong, Ted?"

"Harriet's had the baby."

A delighted smile spread over her face. "Oh, Ted! It's nearly a month early! What is it? What did it weigh?" A horrible thought struck her. "There's nothing wrong with it, is there? Or Harry?"

"As far as I can make out, they're both fine. Apparently she had it a week ago. I wouldn't have known at all only I phoned her to see how she was feeling and heard it crying. It's a boy, he weighs six pounds three ounces."

"Gosh, he's tiny! Although, being early, I suppose he would be. Oh, Ted, a grandson! Congratulations, you must be over the moon! When are you going to see them?"

"That's just it. She don't want me to."

"Why ever not?"

"Search me. She says her and Jason are having some problems and she don't think it'll be a good idea for me to go down there right now. Well I know I don't like Jason much, but he's my son-in-law, and she's my daughter, and I want to help, Sian."

Sian drew in a breath. "I don't know what to say, Ted. Maybe Harry feels you being there might intimidate Jason. Young couples do have these problems, especially when it's the first baby. You can't imagine how much your life is going to change, can you?"

"Yeah, I know, but I know Harriet, Sian, and I'm afraid there's something seriously wrong."

"Then go, Ted. That's what I'd do."

Ted smiled with relief. "Sian, you're a little darling. I don't know what I'd do without you."

"Steve! There was a phone call for you."

Stephen turned on the stairs. "Hi, Val. Who from?"

"I don't know, Dud took it before he went to work. He wrote it down." She handed him a grubby piece of paper.

He peered at it. "What does it say?"

Val shrugged. "I couldn't make it out either. Sorry, love. But you can see the number."

"Yeah. It looks familiar. At least, I think."

"You could try ringing it."

"That's a good idea."

He ran downstairs, pulling change from his pocket and dialled the number. It rang and rang. Shrugging, he hung up, pocketing the piece of paper. He let himself into the flat. I'm knackered, he thought, making himself some tea. Thank God I'm off tomorrow. He sank onto the sofa and started playing guitar.

There was a thunderous knocking on the door. He sighed. "Yeah, all right!" He turned the amp down and started to play again.

The banging got louder.

"Bloody hell!" He walked over and wrenched the door open.

Ted stood there, his face dark with emotion. He pushed Stephen back into the room and slammed the door shut. Stephen opened his mouth to speak and Ted hit him. He fell back onto the flimsy little coffee table, which collapsed. "What the hell?" he gasped, pulling himself up.

Ted grabbed him by his tee shirt. "You're coming with me, you little fucker."

Stephen broke away, and stepped back, wiping blood from his lip. "Have you gone mad?"

Ted lunged for him again and Stephen ducked, came back up, and swung a punch at him. Ted barely noticed. He grabbed Stephen and shoved him against the wall.

Stephen fought back. He was younger and fitter than Ted, but Ted had the advantage of size and experience. Stephen twisted and kicked out, catching Ted on his knee. The older man shouted in pain and relaxed his grip. Stephen tried to pull free, but Ted grabbed his jaw and a handful of his hair. "I don't think you got the message. I said you're coming with me. I'm really angry with you, Stephen, and you're pissing me off even more."

"Just tell me what the fuck I'm supposed to have done!" Stephen shouted furiously.

Ted sighed. "It would be so easy to break your neck, so just do what you're told, OK?"

Stephen remembered what Harry had told him about Ted when he'd first moved into the Angel. He was suddenly very scared. "OK."

Ted took his hand from Stephen's chin. He was still holding him by the hair, and he pulled it viciously, cracking Stephen's head hard against the wall. He let go, and Stephen staggered sideways, dazed.

Ted pulled him upright. "Come on, get up. The car's outside."

Stephen glanced at him as he drove. Ted looked murderous, his jaw was clenched and his face set. Stephen was more scared now than he'd been earlier. He didn't know what the hell he'd done, he didn't know where they were going or why. If Ted wants to kill me – and why the hell should he, anyway? But then, why burst into my flat and beat me up? – he could have broken my neck earlier. But if he isn't going to kill me, what is he going to do?

"Ted, you've got to tell me what's wrong." Ted ignored him. "At least tell me where we're going."

They drove on in silence.

Stephen couldn't stand it. "If you don't fucking tell me what's going on, I'm going to open the fucking door and jump out!"

Ted braked hard, and Stephen jerked forward, despite his seatbelt. There was a tremendous blast from the horn of the car behind as the driver swerved to avoid hitting them.

"For Christ's sake!" Stephen said faintly. He was shaking. "Are you trying to kill us?"

Ted put his foot down on the accelerator. "Just sit there and shut up."

They drove down to the M1.

"Are we going to Sheffield?" Stephen asked hesitantly.

"Yep."

"To see Harry?"

Ted didn't answer.

Stephen sighed. His head was aching, and his jaw and ribs hurt. He shut his eyes. Eventually they pulled up outside a row of terraced houses.

"Get out," Ted ordered. He hammered on one of the doors. They heard footsteps, and Harry opened it a fraction.

Ted dragged Stephen forward and thrust him in.

Harry gasped. "Steve! Jesus Christ, Dad, who the hell do you think you are? What have you done to him? Oh, God, Steve, are you all right?" She stared at Stephen, stunned and horrified.

"Where's the baby?" Ted demanded.

"He's upstairs asleep. How could you hurt Stephen, how could you? I told you not to come, I told you not to interfere, it's none of your fucking business!"

"Don't you dare speak to me like that! Get the baby." She started to argue, but he was adamant. "I said, get the baby," he shouted, his fist raised. He pulled Stephen through into a tiny sitting room. "Sit down."

Stephen sat nervously on the edge of the sofa. Harry came in, holding a sleepy baby. He was tiny and very pretty, with a shock of black hair standing up from his head.

"Tell him," Ted said.

Harry gave him an angry look. She sat down next to Stephen. "He's yours, Steve."

He stared at her. "What do you mean, mine?"

"She means you're his father, and her husband isn't."

"That's impossible," Stephen stammered.

"No. Remember that night, Steve?" She looked at him with love.

"But that was—" he stopped.

"Nine months ago," Harry agreed.

"B-but Mum came into the shop this morning and told me about him. She said he was premature. I got you a card. It's at home."

"I told people he was early. He's so small."

"Wait a minute. I don't understand. You were on the pill. What on earth makes you think he's mine?"

Ted crossed the room, grabbed Stephen's jacket and shook him like a terrier with a rat. Harry was terrified. She screamed at him. The baby started to cry.

Ted dropped Stephen back onto the sofa. "First you seduce my daughter under my own roof, and now you're calling her a liar! You're not going to wriggle out of this! Her husband's left her because of you. You're going to marry her, do you hear me?"

"Dad!" Harry shouted. She was crying now too. "Leave him alone and shut up! I asked you not to interfere!" She rocked the baby, trying to soothe him. "He is yours, Steve. Look." She handed him to Stephen, who took him gingerly. He looked down into the baby's eyes and gasped. It was like looking into a mirror. They were exactly the same colour as his own.

"That was my reaction too," Harry said. "I'm so sorry, Steve."

"*You're* sorry?" Ted interrupted.

"Shut up, Dad, just *shut up*, will you, and let me talk to Steve." She was furious with Ted, so angry at the way he'd hurt Stephen and the way he was trying to bully her now. Well, she wasn't going to let him. She realised that, deep down, she'd been scared of him all her life, but something had changed. She had Stephen's son, and she wasn't frightened any more. "I said we were on an island, didn't I, Steve? Outside time, and no one would ever know. I'm so sorry."

"And Jason's left you? God, Harry, I'm sorry." He looked down at the baby again. My *son*. My son.

"He didn't leave because of this. I told you that, Dad," she spat at Ted. "You were right about him, Steve. He wasn't even there when Rob was born."

"You called him Rob!"

She nodded. "I remembered you saying you liked it."

"Yeah. Yeah, I do. I always thought if I have a son, I'll call him Rob."

"You do have a son."

"Yeah." He looked up at Ted. "Of *course* I'll marry her. How come you've got such a low opinion of me, Ted? All you had to do was tell me."

Ted sat down, the anger draining out of him. "Steve." He shook his head. "Forgive me."

"Why should he?" Harry demanded. "I wouldn't. And I'm not marrying you, Stephen."

"Why?" Stephen looked down at Rob. My son. He had never felt such love and tenderness before. A wave of fierce protectiveness swept over him. This boy would *never* have to conform to someone else's expectations. But then he couldn't prevent the thought, I wonder if he'll be musical, creeping into his head. "He's our son, Harry."

"Well, that's no basis for a marriage, we'd drive each other nuts in a week. Rob's your son, he'll always be your son, and I'll never stop you seeing him, but I'm not marrying you."

"You have to, Harry. I'll get a job, a real job. You need someone to support you." She shook her head. "All right, *he* needs someone to support *him*. You can't do that, you've got to look after him. You should have just told me, Ted. I would have come. You know I would have. But I do forgive you. I understand how you feel, I'd be angry if someone messed with Rob. I think I'd kill anyone who hurt a hair on his head. God, what a cliché! It's true though."

"I'm not marrying you, Steve," Harry repeated.

He breathed in despairingly. "Well, what *are* you going to do?"

"Come back home," Ted offered quietly.

"Oh, no." She gave him a contemptuous smile. "Do you honestly think I could live with you breathing down my neck, beating up anyone you thought was taking advantage of me? I'm not letting you mess up my life any more."

"Princess, I won't, I swear. You can live your own life, this won't never happen again."

"You always say that, Dad. But when you lose your temper you're like another person."

"I'll get help."

She stared at him. "Do you mean that? Do you really mean that?"

He nodded.

She leant back and shut her eyes. "OK. I'll come home." Tears trickled down her face. "I've wanted to for ages."

"Why didn't you?" Ted was appalled.

She shrugged. Rob started to grizzle. "He wants feeding, I expect." She leant over and kissed Stephen's cheek. "I meant it, Steve. He's your son and I want you to see him. A lot. I want him to grow up knowing who his daddy is."

"Well then—" Stephen started, but she cut him off. "I'm not marrying you. Dad, make Steve a drink. When I've fed Rob and put him in his cot, we can talk."

Stephen and Ted were drinking tea in silence, each preoccupied with his own thoughts, when Harry came back. "You can both stay here tonight. You can have the couch, Dad."

Ted looked at the sofa. It was at least six inches shorter than he was. "OK, Princess."

"Then tomorrow, you take Steve back home and you go and see Sian and tell her everything. And I mean everything, Dad. London, the lot."

Ted stared at her. "But, Princess—"

"If you're serious about me and Rob coming home, you'll do it." She stared at him challengingly.

He looked away first. "OK, Princess."

Harry knocked on the bedroom door and walked in without waiting for an answer.

"Harry!" Stephen was standing in his underpants. He grabbed his shirt and pulled it on.

Harry leant against the door, appalled. Stephen's upper body was a mass of ugly bruises. "Those are *awful*," she said, really shocked. "Dad did *that*?"

"Yeah." He buttoned the shirt up. "What do you want, Harry? You can't just come in like that."

"Why? It's not like I haven't seen it all before."

"That's not the point." He was annoyed.

"Sorry," she said contritely. She sat on the bed. He stood looking down at her. "Why don't you come and sit down?" she asked, patting the bed.

He sat right at the end. She burst out laughing. "Don't worry, I haven't come to launch an assault on your virtue! I wanted to talk to you about your mum and dad."

He was mystified. "What about them?"

"Well, they're Rob's grandparents."

He stared at her. "God. I hadn't thought of that."

"Neither had I. I mean, I told Dad to go and talk to Sian – but she doesn't know about any of this. It'll be a bit of a shock."

"I can't imagine what Dad'll say. Oh, well, I should think they're used to me messing up by now."

"Don't say that!"

"Why not?" He grinned at her. "It's true, you of all people know that!"

"What do you mean?"

"Well… Rob!"

She looked at him earnestly. "Steve, Rob is the best thing that's ever happened to me. I was really pleased to be pregnant, even though Jason wasn't… well, what I wanted him to be. But once I knew Rob was yours, it made him even more precious." She paused and said shyly, "Will you cuddle me, just for a minute? I've missed you very much!"

He held out his arms and she snuggled against him. He winced.

"Sorry," she said, moving. "Is it very painful?"

"Yep."

"He can't… he didn't mean it, Steve."

"I think he did."

"Yes. I mean – he's really sorry."

"I know." He kissed the top of her head.

She moved away from him. "I'll bring you in some paracetamol. Is there anything else you want?"

He shook his head.

She fetched him the pills and a glass of water. "Goodnight, Steve."

"Goodnight, Harry."

Stephen and Ted drove back to York in silence. Ted glanced over at Stephen's closed face several times during the journey. Finally, as they were approaching Clifton, he couldn't stand it any longer. He pulled over and stopped the car. "Steve."

Stephen looked up at him. "Hmm?" He frowned, puzzled. "Why have we stopped here?"

"Look, Steve, I'm really sorry about yesterday. I didn't mean it to happen. I was just going to talk to you, but as I was driving up from Harriet's, I started thinking about you and her together and something just snapped. I've never been able to control it, but it's been so long since it's been like that that I thought… well, that it wouldn't never happen again. I don't know what else I can say, Steve, except I'm sorry." He stared at Stephen earnestly.

"I know," said Stephen, bewildered. "You said that yesterday and I understood, remember? When I was holding Rob." His mouth curved into an involuntary smile as he thought about his son. He'd held him for a while that morning before he and Ted set off.

"Oh." Ted was taken aback. "Why are you angry, then?"

"I'm not." Stephen looked at him in surprise. "What makes you think I am?"

"You've looked it all the way here."

"Oh!" Stephen's face cleared. "No, I've been wondering how to tell Mum and Dad they're grandparents. I can't even think how to begin. And if you're going to talk to Mum, I'll have to tell them first. When are you going to talk to Mum? You can't do it while Dad's there." He looked at Ted, his eyes narrowed. "What exactly is the relationship between you two, anyway?"

"We are really, really good friends, Steve, and that is it, I swear to you. Your mother is a wonderful woman, and I'd be a liar if I said I don't find her attractive, and if she wasn't married to your Dad I might even let myself think of her in a different way. But she is, so I don't. I don't know why we have such a deep connection – it was there when we first met. Harriet's quite right. If – when – I talk to her, she'll make sure I sort myself out. I suppose I'll have to wait till next week before I see her. What about you?"

Stephen grimaced. "Things only get worse if you leave them. I was supposed to be going to a wedding today, but I think these bruises would clash with my suit." He gave Ted an exasperated look. "So you might as well drop me off there now."

He let himself into the house as John was collecting the newspaper. He recoiled at the sight of Stephen's face. "Steve! What on earth happened? Come in!"

It dawned on Stephen that this was a huge mistake. If he told his parents about Ted, it might prejudice Sian against him before he'd had a chance to explain. He felt infuriated that he was looking out for Ted after the way he'd behaved, but he understood him. Especially now he had Rob. Rob! Whenever he thought of his son, he felt invincible, the luckiest man in the world. What did anything matter compared to that little boy? "I was mugged," he lied, following his father to the kitchen.

John was horrified. "Have you reported it?"

"Yes. I don't think they'll get anyone, I didn't see what they looked like."

Sian was making breakfast. "Stevie, how lovely, I thought you were going—" She saw his face and gasped.

"He was mugged," John said heavily. "Shocking, isn't it, not even safe on the streets of York."

"When did it happen?" Sian asked, kissing him carefully. "Have you seen a doctor?"

Stephen sat down and poured himself a cup of tea. "No. Don't worry, Mum, it's not as bad as it looks. It happened last night. I'd… um… been for a drink with… er… with a couple from my building. They've just moved in," he said, rather desperately. Why, when you were lying, he thought, did you always give far too much information? "Anyway, I'm fine, it looks worse than it is."

"Oh, I wish you hadn't moved out of the Angel!" Sian exclaimed, distressed. "I never had a moment's worry about you when Ted was looking after you!"

Stephen wanted to laugh at the irony of this. "Um… no, I guess not. Really, Mum, forget it, I'm OK, honestly. Listen, where are the girls?"

"Still in bed, of course!" Sian smiled. "Toast, Steve?"

Stephen took a deep breath and stood up. They stared at him, surprised.

"OK. You're used to me doing… well, things you find hard to understand."

They were beginning to look alarmed.

"Harry's baby. He's mine."

His parents sat frozen.

Sian was the first to recover. "But, Stephen, how?"

"The usual way, I imagine," John said acidly.

"It was an accident. I mean, it was just after Angie split up with me. I was… unhappy. Harry came to my room to see if I wanted anything—"

"And you took advantage of her," said John.

"No! What is it with you and Ted?"

"Ted?" asked Sian quickly. "What about Ted?"

"Nothing. I didn't take advantage of her, Dad. She wanted… she was determined… I said it wasn't a good idea, but… well, anyway, it happened, it wasn't anyone's fault, it was both of us. We're both responsible. Harry was even on the pill." He shook his head. "It was meant to happen."

"Wait a minute," John said. "How do you know it's yours? And legally—"

"He's mine. Wait till you see his eyes. Harry's are dark and Jason's are hazel. Rob's are exactly the same colour as mine."

"You've seen him?" Sian asked.

Stephen nodded. "He's amazing."

Sian looked at John. "Our first grandchild!"

"What about Harry's husband?" John asked.

"He's left her. He wasn't even there when she went into labour, and no one knew Rob wasn't his then either! Harry said he had other women all the time they were married."

"So they'll be getting a divorce?" John asked, slowly.

"I suppose so. I asked her to marry me, but she said no."

"Why?" Sian was secretly relieved.

Stephen shrugged. "I don't know. She said having Rob wasn't a basis for a marriage. She's coming back to live at the Angel though, so we'll be able to see him all the time."

Sian and Ted sat facing each other in the sitting room of the Angel. Ted had made tea, and plied her with cakes and biscuits, and they'd talked about Rob, Sian saying how shocked she and John had been initially, but how delighted she was at the thought of a grandson. Ted noticed that she'd said 'we' were shocked and then 'I' am delighted. John isn't, then? he thought. And then she started to tell him that Stephen had been mugged, and he sat like a stone, filled with shame, unable to look at her. He couldn't imagine how he was even going to begin to tell her what he'd done, but to his horror, she said, her voice almost like a caress, "I can't tell you how much I wish he'd stayed at the Angel, Ted! You always took such good care of him for me—" She broke off at the look on his face. "Ted? What's the matter?"

He was shaking. "Oh, Sian, Sian, oh, Sian…" He couldn't go on.

"Ted! Ted, what is it?" She started to get up. "Are you ill? Shall I call the doctor?"

He caught hold of her hand. Guilt and self-loathing were coursing through him. "No," he croaked. "I'm not ill, Sian, not ill. Oh, Sian, dear, dear Sian, what you think of me means more to me than anything on earth…" He had to stop and take a gulp of air.

She sat back down, astounded. This wasn't what she'd expected. "Ted—"

With an immense effort, he controlled himself. "Sian. I have to… I have to tell you some things about myself that will… will shock you. They shock me – they *horrify* me," he whispered. "They horrify me, but I did them."

Sian was frowning at him in bewilderment. "I don't understand."

"You will. Whether or not you ever speak to me again is another matter."

She was really alarmed. "I'm not sure I want to hear any more."

"Please, Sian." His eyes were impossibly dark, like bottomless pits.

She clasped her hands. "All right."

"I have a temper, Sian. It takes a lot to trigger it, but when I lose it, I lose all control." He swallowed. "Finding out that Steve was Rob's father… I couldn't cope. Harriet is so precious to me, the thought that Steve had taken advantage of her… I drove straight back here to fetch him. That's all I was going to do, I swear, but when I got to his flat the thought of him… the thought of him… touching Harriet…" He stopped to take a breath.

Sian had gone white.

"I just lost it. I started hitting him. I wanted to kill him."

Sian was on her feet, unable to believe her ears. "You d-did *that* to Stevie – to m-my Stevie!" she managed to say. She felt sick and she was shaking violently. "You bastard! You *bastard*! He would *never* take advantage of Harry, of *any* girl!" She could hardly speak, her throat was tight with hatred and distress. "I trusted you! I *trusted* you to look after him! I can't stay here and listen to you, I can't! I hate you, I hate you! I never want to see you again!" She burst into tears and turned blindly away from him, moving towards the door.

"Sian, please!" He caught her arm.

"Let me go!" She hit him, her fists beating against his chest. He stood patiently, waiting until she calmed down.

She stopped hitting him, and he gently wiped the tears from her face. "That's how I felt, Sian, but I'm bigger and stronger than you, and I can do far more damage. It don't matter if you lose your temper like that. It does when I do. *Please* will you stay? I want your help – no, I *need* your help, Sian. I don't want to do nothing like that ever again."

"*I* can't help you. You need to see a… a specialist."

"I know. But I thought if I told you first it'd give me the courage to go and see one."

She sat down again. He sighed with relief. "Thank you, Sian."

"I don't know why I'm doing this."

"Don't you?"

"Ted—"

"I know. You're married. And I'm not going to talk about that. We're friends, that's what matters, now more than ever. What you said about Steve not taking advantage of Harriet… I know. I think I knew then, but I wanted to blame someone and I couldn't blame her. I'm so sorry, Sian. He's a lovely boy, he could have told you and John what I'd done." He couldn't go on.

"That's not Stevie's style. He's incredibly moral. I don't know where he gets it from, but I've no doubt that in some peculiar way, part of him felt he deserved the beating for sleeping with Harry in the first place. He won't hold it against you, Ted. If he's forgiven you, which he must've done, he'll never mention it again."

"What about you, Sian? Will you hold it against me?"

"Yes," she said slowly. He was stricken. "It won't stop me loving you, but I can't promise I'll ever forget it, and I certainly can't promise I'll never bring it up again because I know I will."

"You said you love me," he breathed.

"You knew that," she said steadily, "just as I know you love me. And that we'll do nothing about it and after today we won't mention it again. Did you hear anything else I said or did you stop listening after I said I loved you?"

"I heard it all. I love listening to your voice."

They were silent, staring at one another. There was so much they wanted to say, so many things that couldn't be said. Sian was the first to recover. "Tell me about your temper. Tell me everything."

She listened while he told her about growing up in the slums of the East End. About his father – or the man he'd called his father, the man he later discovered had killed his father in a drunken brawl and had moved in with his mother when Ted was two. "Violence didn't mean nothing to him, no more than a form of currency, no different from a handshake. He used to beat us kids and my mum regularly, until my big brother grew up and gave him a taste of his own medicine. I wished so much that I'd been the one to do it!"

"Lots of people come from violent backgrounds, Ted. It doesn't necessarily make them violent."

"Due respect, Sian, you don't know what you're talking about. You can control it a lot of the time – my God, do you think I don't?" he burst out suddenly. "If I didn't, I'd be behind bars for murder by now! I really wanted to kill Steve, I could have broken his neck, no problem at all." He hated himself for the pain he saw in her face. "I'm so sorry, Sian."

"But you didn't break his neck. Yes, I see what you mean. Have you ever… ever…"

"Killed anyone? No. I came close once. I got into a fight in a pub with some bloke and nearly beat him to death. That's why we moved up here, a new start. It scared me and for a long time I thought it had cured me." He looked away from her. "I was wrong."

She put her hand on his. "Thank you for telling me, Ted. I can't absolve you, but I can tell you that although I can't even begin to imagine what your childhood was like, I understand." A thought struck her. "You told me when I first knew you that you didn't get on with your sons, and I saw that at Harry's wedding. Did you ever hit them?"

He shook his head. "No. But they was scared of me. I wasn't a good father to them. I wasn't a good husband to Harriet. I never hit her, neither," he said quickly, "but I did bully them. When she died, I couldn't believe it. I thought it was divine retribution, although why she should suffer and not me was something I didn't consider at the time. It was all about me, my loss. I promised myself that at least I could be a good father to little Harriet."

"You are."

"No. She only married that rat Jason to get away from me."

Sian was shocked. "How do you know?"

"She told me. And you know, Sian, I loved my sons and my wife so much, but they never knew and I threw it all away. And I've done the same with Harriet."

"With your wife, yes, but not with the others. You've never told them about your childhood, have you?"

"Of course not!" He was shocked.

She laughed. "You are an idiot! How do you expect them to understand, much less forgive you, if you don't?"

"But do I *deserve* to be forgiven?"

"Oh, yes."

He stared at her. "I love you so much, Sian. You're the most incredible woman I've ever known."

"I've loved you since we first met," she admitted. "But I love John too," she murmured, her face troubled. "If only I was two people! I'm sorry, Ted."

"I'm not, I wouldn't want you any different. I know how much you love John." Lucky bastard doesn't deserve you, he thought. But then, neither do I. He sighed. "I'm just grateful you love me too. You're perfect, Sian."

She was very moved. She took his hand and they sat in silence for a minute. "I've got to go," she said, pulling herself together. "There's a limit to the amount of emotion I can cope with and we're so far over it now I can't even remember where it is!" She paused. "Oh, Ted, can I have Harry's phone number? I want to go and see little Rob."

He smiled. "Sure. He's a real star. Spit of Steve. You know I'm taking the van on Saturday to bring her back here though, don't you? You could save yourself a journey."

She smiled. "I'm longing to see him! And Harry must be feeling a bit stressed on her own. I bet neither you nor Stephen so much as changed a nappy for her while you were there!" She kissed his cheek. "Go to your GP. Find a specialist."

After he'd gone, she rang Harry, who sounded surprised and slightly apprehensive.

"I'm coming back to Dad's at the weekend. Are you sure you don't want to wait, Mrs Markham?"

Sian repeated what she'd said to Ted. "And please call me Sian, Harry," she added.

Sian went into York and bought toys for Rob and toiletries for Harry and arrived at the house shortly after ten the following day. Harry was still in her dressing gown, tired and exasperated.

"All I've done since five o'clock this morning is feed and change him! He just won't settle. I can't see how he can be hungry, but listen to him!" They could hear him from the door. She took Sian through to the sitting room. The baby was in his Moses basket, screaming, his face scarlet with rage, his back arched.

Sian smiled. "Can I hold him?"

"Be my guest!" Harry collapsed onto the sofa.

"I bought these for you both." Sian handed Harry a carrier bag and then picked up the furious, squirming baby.

"Oh, Sian, thank you!" Harry's eyes filled with tears. "It's not that I don't love him, I do, I adore him, but I'm so tired! And feeding him is so painful! The midwife said it would get better, but it's getting worse."

Sian held Rob against her and began walking briskly, rocking him as she went. "You poor thing!" she said to Harry. "It's a terrible pain, isn't it? Everyone tells you how much you'll love breastfeeding and how rewarding it is, and it's true, but to start with it's pure torture and no one tells you that! If you look in that bag you'll see some cream, it's so soothing. I wasn't sure they'd still make it. I found it really good, especially for Stephen. He was such a glutton, never stopped feeding! I honestly started to think there was something wrong with him, but no! He was just a pig!"

Harry laughed. "That sounds familiar!"

"Rob takes after him in that too, then?"

"He looks just like him, doesn't he? Oh, Sian, you're wonderful! How did you do that?"

Rob had stopped crying and was gazing at the collar of Sian's dress with total absorption. "It's only because I'm walking around. If I stopped, he'd be howling again in seconds. Look, Harry, why don't you go and have a long, relaxing bath while I look after him?"

"Sian you are *so* kind!"

"Go on, off you go!" After Harry had gone upstairs, Sian carried on walking around the room, making soothing noises. Rob's head began to nod and his eyes kept closing and jerking open again.

"Fighting it, eh?" whispered Sian. She kissed his soft little forehead. "You smell delicious." She took his tiny fist and manoeuvred his miniscule thumb into his mouth. He moved his head indignantly, but she persevered. On the fourth attempt he suddenly grasped the idea and started sucking fiercely. His eyes closed and his body became floppy and heavy with sleep. "You're cleverer than your daddy," Sian said softly as she tucked him tightly into his basket. "It took him ages to get the idea." She went into the kitchen and filled the kettle.

Harry came in behind her. She was dressed and looking much better. "I feel like a human being again! Sian, you're a miracle worker! And he's sucking his thumb!"

"You don't mind, do you?" Sian asked anxiously.

"Mind? Of course not! I love it when babies suck their thumbs! Did Steve?"

Sian smiled. "Eventually. I thought he'd never get the hang of it, your Robbie is tons cleverer!"

Harry smiled back at her. "And Sian, thank you so much for all the things! All that gorgeous stuff for me, and the toys for Rob! That lovely rabbit – and the big white bear! It's bigger than he is!"

"Oh!" Sian said guiltily, "That's from Stevie, there's a card too, I think it's in the car. He's got something for you as well, but he wants to give it to you himself."

Harry's face lit up. "I can't wait! Would you like a cup of tea?"

"Yes, please. So… how long have you been in love with him?"

"Ages! Ever since—" She stopped and turned slowly. "How did you guess?" she whispered.

"The way you say his name, the way you look when we talk about him. It's why you won't marry him, isn't it?"

Harry finished making the tea. She carried the teapot to the table. "Yes. He's not in love with me. He's got his whole life in front of him. I love him too much to tie him down." Her chin wobbled and she bit her lip.

"The same is true of you, Harry. You've got your whole life ahead of you and you're even younger than he is."

"Well, yes, but I've got Rob." She looked at Sian indecisively. She was Stephen's mother, but she was so kind, so lovely. If I could choose a mum, I'd choose Sian, she thought. "I lied to Steve," she said in a rush. "I wasn't on the pill. I really wanted to get pregnant, I wanted Steve's baby. It was so lucky that Jason was away – I hadn't been with him for over a month!" Her mouth curved into a joyful smile. "How *lucky* I was! I knew I only had that one chance! If Steve hadn't been so upset about Angie he would never have slept with me, and to get pregnant after just that once!"

Sian was staring at her. Harry's smile faded. "What is it? You're not cross, are you? I said I'm not going to marry him."

"You lied to Stevie, and then you let your father think… and then you let him beat my son?"

Harry was horror-stricken. "Oh, no, Sian, no, it wasn't… I didn't… I *told* Dad not to come, I wanted to see him first, prepare him, but he just showed up here, and when he got so angry and drove off, I tried to ring Steve, I left him a message, but I never thought – I never *dreamed* Dad would hurt him, not Steve!"

"Why didn't you ring me? I would have gone round there."

"Oh *God*, yes, you're right! I didn't even think of that!"

"And the fact still remains that you let Ted think it was Steve's fault, that he seduced you. You *saw* what he did to him!"

Harry started to cry. "I *couldn't* tell him. I wanted to, but… oh, you've never seen him like that, Sian. He gets *so angry*, it's terrifying! I was so afraid of what he might do to me – or even Rob. I've been scared of him all my life, why do you think I married Jason? Yes, I liked him, he was sexy and funny, but he stood up to Dad, really stood up to him, and I thought maybe I did love him, it wasn't simply the need to escape, and Steve was still with Angie, he never looked at me, so I agreed to marry Jason and Dad was so pleased with me, and then Steve and Angie split up—" She stopped. Her nose was running and she looked around for something to wipe it on.

Sian handed her a packet of tissues. She'd just remembered that she'd advised Ted to go to Harry. She should have kept her mouth shut. It was possible that she was as much to blame for Ted's actions as Harry. She looked at Harry's anguished face and her heart turned over. Poor little girl, no mother and Ted for a father. Whatever Sian felt for Ted, and however tough his childhood had been, she couldn't condone the way he'd treated Harry.

She took Harry's hand and stroked it. "It's all right, Harry, it's all right, don't cry. I understand, I do. It's done now anyway, and Stevie doesn't bear any grudges. He's so delighted with Rob. And with you for producing him."

Harry clung onto her hand.

"I'm sorry I was angry," Sian said. She couldn't imagine her girls getting in a mess like this because of John. And yet look at what had happened in Stephen's life because of him. She sighed. "You can pick your friends, Harry, but you're stuck with your family. I know we're sort of family now, but let's be friends anyway. You'll always be so special to Steve, you know."

Harry gave her a watery smile. "I'd love to be your friend. And we are sort of family, aren't we? Because you're Rob's grandmother. It's almost like having a mother!"

Sian felt a surge of love for her. "It can be exactly like having a mother if you'd like, Harry," she said gently.

Harry's grasp on her hand tightened. "I would," she whispered, her lips trembling. "Thank you, Sian. Did Dad talk to you?" Sian nodded. Harry heaved a sigh of relief. "So he was serious. He really is going to do something about it!"

"Yes, he is. And he's going to talk to you and your brothers, Harry, explain about his childhood. He should have done it a long time ago."

"Was it bad?"

"It sounded appalling," Sian said grimly. "God, Harry, life can be wretched!"

As if on cue, Rob started to cry. The two women smiled at each other.

"Yeah, wretched," Harry agreed. "But it has its good points, and he's definitely one of them!"

As she drove home, Sian brooded over the situation. There was no one with whom she could discuss it, certainly not Ted, and not Stephen either. And John? She sighed. Maybe John. Or maybe it would be best to forget the whole thing. What was done was done; Rob existed, but she wished in some ways that Harry hadn't confided in her. She felt tremendously maternal towards her, couldn't help loving her, she was a lovely girl, and she was an excellent mother to Rob, obviously adored him. But she'd caused so much trouble. If she *had* been on the pill, and Rob *had* been an accident, it would have been different, but to set out deliberately to have a child, to unilaterally make a decision that had the potential to upset so many lives, not least that of the child himself! Sian found it difficult not to blame her. Stephen would now have the responsibility of this son for the rest of his life and he had been allowed no say in the matter whatsoever. Then she reminded herself that he hadn't been obliged to have sex with Harry, whether he believed her to be on the pill or not.

As she pulled into the drive, she noticed an envelope sticking out of the glove compartment. Damn! She'd forgotten to give Harry Stephen's card. She decided she'd walk down to Braithwaites at closing time and give it to him to give her at the weekend, and then she could tell him how adorable his son was. And after all, it was impossible to wish that Rob hadn't been conceived.

Stephen invited Harry to spend Sunday with him. "You ring me when you're ready and I'll borrow Mum's car and come and get you and Rob, and we can spend the day together. I'll cook you a meal and we can take Rob to the park or whatever you want."

Harry was delighted. She'd never spent any time alone with Stephen and the prospect of a whole day with him was intoxicating.

While he was sitting on the sofa holding his son, she wandered round his flat. It was so typical of him. Like Sian, he had a flair for making places his, and making them comfortable. There were bright posters and prints on the wall, and he'd bought rugs to cover the faded carpet. One wall had a vast corkboard, like the one at Sian's, and Harry felt choked when she saw that a picture of her holding Rob had pride of place. There was a big jug of fresh, aromatic lavender on a shelf, books everywhere and, of course, his guitars. He'd recently bought a twelve-string acoustic. Harry picked it up and strummed.

Stephen was smiling down at his son, who was lying lengthways on his knees. The baby was staring intently up at him. Harry suddenly felt breathless with love for both of them. She thought how brilliant it would be if the three of them lived in this flat together. If only Steve was in love with her! It seemed so unfair that he wasn't. They were both musical, and shared the same tastes. They were good in bed together. She remembered that night in every detail, how loving he'd been, how he'd held her afterwards, and how sweet he'd been the next morning, kissing her when his alarm woke them, and making her breakfast while she had a shower.

He looked up and smiled at her. "I've got something for you. It's to thank you for Rob. Here, you take him and I'll get it."

She opened the jewellers box he gave her and stared down at a gold ring with an orangey red stone surrounded by little seed pearls. She took it out, hardly breathing. The stone had gold flecks in it.

"It's a fire opal. It reminded me of you, all warm and glowing, and the gold flecks are like your eyes. I hope it fits. Ted found a ring that you'd left when you moved out, so I used that as a guide. I can always have it altered if it doesn't. Hey, don't cry!" He sat down next to her and wiped her cheek with his thumb. "Let's see if it fits." He slid it onto the third finger of her right hand. "It looks lovely on you! You've got really nice hands."

"It's such a beautiful present. I don't deserve it!" She cried harder.

Stephen fished around in his pocket for a tissue, couldn't find one and fetched the toilet paper out of the bathroom. "Course you do!" he said, wiping her face. "The miserable time with Jason, then having Rob." He put his arm around her, looking earnestly at her. "If you knew how guilty I feel about the way things have turned out for you. I mean, I know you love Rob, but if it hadn't been for me, you and Jason would probably still be together." He sighed.

Harry was horrified. "Don't *ever* say that!" she said fiercely, startling him. "I'm really glad Rob is yours, not Jason's. There's *no* comparison between the two of you! There's no need to feel guilty, you're not to, do you hear me?" She couldn't bear the thought of him feeling guilty when the pregnancy had been exactly what she'd wanted.

"That's better," he said, grinning. "That's the Harry I know and love."

"Thank you so much – Stevie." She'd never called him Stevie before, never dared to.

He made lasagne and salad for lunch. She was impressed.

"I got bored with takeaways so I bought a cookery book," he said simply.

"Are you looking forward to university?" she asked. She was dreading him going.

"Yeah," he said thoughtfully, "in some ways. It'll be weird though. I've got used to living alone and being at work. It'll be odd to live in a Hall of Residence and go back to studying." He smiled at her. "You'll have to come and stay for weekends. Mum'll look after Robbie for you."

"Maybe." She was torn between the anxiety of leaving Rob for longer than an hour and the joy of spending an entire weekend with Stephen.

He smiled at her uncertainly. She was a lot different from the Harry he'd known a year ago. That one was so carefree and insouciant. Today's Harry was hesitant and emotional. He put that down to her hormones, but there was something else too: she seemed… not older exactly, but somehow subdued, as if she'd put her youth behind her. He hoped that was just a side-effect of pregnancy too. He missed the old, sparky Harry.

"Will you come with me to register the birth?" she asked. "I want your name to be on it as Rob's father."

"Of course I will, but are you sure, Harry?"

She stared at him anxiously. "Don't you want to be down as his father?"

"It's not really about what I want," he said gently. "It's about what's best for Rob. If you put me down, then he'll officially be illegitimate. If you put Jason down then nobody will know unless you or Rob want them to."

She thought about this. "I think it would be better if he had his real father on his birth certificate," she said finally.

"OK. When do you want to go?"

"You still have Wednesday afternoon off, don't you?"

"Yes. Shall I pick you up?"

She shook her head. "I'll meet you at the shop."

They walked to the Register Office together, Stephen holding her hand. Harry gave Rob's details, and Stephen confirmed that he was the baby's father, and they both signed the certificate. When the registrar asked father's occupation, Harry said 'musician' before Stephen could speak. The registrar gave them an odd look. Stephen grinned at Harry. Outside, he said, "I think she thought we were hippies or something!"

"Who cares?" Harry said. Stephen had taken her hand again and nothing else in the world mattered.

"Let's go and have a cup of coffee, unless you have to get back to Rob?" She'd left him with Ted.

"No, it does Granddad good to look after him once in a while," she laughed.

They went to Betty's and he bought them coffee and rich cream cakes.

"I can't eat this, Steve, I put on far too much weight when I was pregnant, I've got loads to lose!"

"Rubbish! You've got a fantastic figure, Harry, all curvy and voluptuous."

"You mean fat! Really, Steve, I can't," she said, pushing the plate away.

He ate his, and eyed her plate. "Are you sure you don't want it?"

She laughed. "I'd forgotten what a pig you are! Do you remember the time I made that chocolate cake and you ate it all in one evening? Poor Dad didn't get any!"

He grinned. "I'm a growing boy."

They finished their coffee and he walked her home. He came in and helped her bath Rob, and then he put a nappy on the baby and dressed him.

"You're really good at this now," she said approvingly.

"Only the best is good enough for my son." He kissed the sleepy baby and handed him to Harry. "I'd better go, Mum's cooking me tea tonight and I'm starving! Oh, hey, Harry, I nearly forgot, let's take Robbie swimming."

"Swimming? Isn't he a bit young?"

"No, that's the point. I was reading about it in the paper. The younger they are, the better. You just chuck 'em in and they swim!"

"That doesn't sound like a very good idea!" Harry was shocked. Whatever her feelings for Stephen, she wasn't about to let him chuck Rob into a swimming pool.

"Yeah!" Stephen was saying. "I'll show you the article. Next Wednesday, then? I'll pick you up." He leant over and kissed her.

She watched him walk down the road. She could see he was singing. She suddenly felt overwhelmed with the thought that she was going to love him forever and all she could hope for was occasionally holding his hand and the odd peck on the cheek. Like he'd kiss one of his sisters, she thought. And one day he'll get married and I'll never have him again. She leant her head against the window and cried till she felt sick.

She spent the rest of the week dieting and exercising feverishly. If she was going to be wearing a swimming costume, she at least wanted to look halfway decent. On Tuesday she bought the most flattering one she could find and practised sucking her tummy in. She was dreading wearing it in front of Stephen.

He picked her up in Sian's car. He was in an exceedingly good mood. "I'm really looking forward to this," he said, kissing her and Rob. "It's ages since I've been swimming."

She remembered what a good swimmer he was. "You were in the team at school, weren't you?" He nodded. "I'm not a brilliant swimmer," she said, rather anxiously.

He flashed her a reassuring smile. "You don't have to be. We're teaching Rob, remember?"

He was waiting in the pool when she came out of the changing room. He climbed out and took Rob. She walked towards the baby pool.

"Where are you going?" he asked. He was carrying Rob to the deep end. "We're going to chuck him in here."

"Stephen, no!" she cried, distressed.

He turned contritely. "Sorry, Harry! I was only teasing."

Rob loved the pool. They didn't throw him in, but let him slide down into it, Stephen supporting him. The baby's fluid movements, which looked so odd on dry land, were exactly right in the water.

"God, he's loving it! This was a great idea, Stevie."

"I don't think I said earlier, but you look fantastic, Harry! No one would think you'd given birth less than a month ago."

She blushed. "Thanks," she said shyly.

Stephen stayed with Rob while she got dressed. He loved holding him as he wriggled around in the water, and was sorry when Harry came to fetch him.

As she took Rob into the changing room, one of the other mothers joined her. "You're really lucky to have such a great husband, catch mine coming down here to take this one in the pool! How did you persuade him?"

"It was his idea," Harry said, drying the squirming Rob.

"Wow! You want to hold on to that one. He's gorgeous too, you lucky thing!"

"I know," Harry agreed with a sigh.

They took Rob every Wednesday afternoon. By the time Stephen left for Manchester, his son was practically swimming.

Part Two
Nets Of Gold

Never knew I was lost until you found me,
Couldn't see I was alone and cold,
Until you bound me in your nets of gold,
And wound your love around me.

Chapter Four
Such A Candle

Such a candle you've lit, such a bright flame of love.

Stephen's room in Grosvenor Place Hall of Residence was square and basic, with a tiled floor, a bed, a wardrobe, a desk and chair, and a washbasin. It had a large window overlooking a side street and the residence bar.

The Hall, which was self-catering, was made up of interconnecting corridors, each with twelve study-bedrooms, a communal kitchen and communal lavatories and bathrooms. It was purpose built, practical and ugly, but it had a kind of shabby charm. Stephen felt at home immediately.

John drove him over, and helped him move his stuff in. They were both still a little uneasy with each other, and after telling him to ring if he needed anything, John patted him awkwardly on the shoulder. "Take care then, son."

"You too, Dad."

The door of the room opposite Stephen's was open and when John had gone, the occupant came over to introduce himself. "Hi, Finbar Harper. Call me Fin." He had a strong Northern Irish accent.

"Stephen Markham."

Fin was a friendly looking boy, with curly, sandy hair and very bright blue eyes. He peered into Stephen's room. "Wow! Four guitars! I play keyboard, but I've only got the one."

"Come in," Stephen invited.

Fin sat on Stephen's bed. "Why do you need four?"

"They're different." He got them out of their cases.

"Wow! A Strat! Have you got an amp?"

Stephen lugged his amp out from under a pile of clothes.

"Play it, then. Let's see how good you are!"

Stephen plugged it in and played 'Hey, Joe'.

"Wow!" It seemed to be Fin's favourite word. "You're brill! Have you played in public?"

"Yeah, I used to have a band. We were quite good."

"What happened to it?"

Stephen shrugged. "The bass player got married and moved away, the rhythm guitar went to university. There was only me and the drummer left."

Fin helped him sort out his belongings. When they'd finished, he looked at his watch. "It'll be opening time in a minute. Will we get a pint?"

"Sure. I'll have to make a phone call first."

Fin grinned. "Girlfriend?"

Stephen shook his head. "Just a friend."

The phones were in the big hall, next to the porter's lodge and the pigeonholes for mail. Fin hung around, waiting for Stephen to finish.

"Hi, Harry… Yeah, it's great. How's Rob?… Did he?… Oh, that's cute, I wish I'd been there!… Listen, Harry, I've got to go, I'm out of change, I just wanted to let you know I got here OK. I'll ring tomorrow. Have you thought any more about coming over for the weekend?.. Well, let me know. Give Rob a big kiss from me, and there's one for you too. Bye, Harry."

He hung up, and turned to Fin, who was looking distinctly uncomfortable. "Shall we get that drink?"

"I've got a girlfriend, so I have," Fin blurted out.

"Where?" Stephen asked, looking round.

"In Belfast."

Stephen was beginning to wonder if Fin was a bit unhinged. "That's nice," he said, cautiously. Then he suddenly realised what was wrong with the other boy, and started to laugh. "Harry is short for Harriet," he explained. "Rob is our son."

Fin stared at him. "Your son?"

"It's complicated. Let's get a drink and I'll explain."

"Honestly, Stephen, I sometimes think I'll go mad if I have to put up with another oily little northerner trying to make a pass at me! Talk about being transported beyond the sea for the term of your natural life! I can't believe I'm stuck up here with these hideous northern oiks – oh, present company excepted."

Stephen grinned. "Thanks, Vanessa."

"Well, York is a kind of no man's land, isn't it, so cosmopolitan, and your mother's Welsh. And your father *is* a lawyer."

"He got a first from Oxford, too," Stephen said naughtily, egging her on.

She opened her eyes at him. "Well, there you are then!"

Stephen had been going out with Vanessa Dane since meeting her at one of the Freshers' balls that were held all over the university in the first week of term. She came from Surrey, her father was a stockbroker, and she was a spoiled bitch. She loathed northerners and made sure everyone knew it. She hadn't realised Stephen was from Yorkshire when he'd asked her out, and by the time she found out, she was enjoying his company and the fact that, owing to a combination of his good looks and guitar-playing prowess, he was very much in demand with other girls, making her position as his girlfriend a highly desirable one. Stephen knew very well that this relationship was not going to be a permanent one, but she made him laugh, often unintentionally, and she was dynamite in bed. They were on their way up the stairs to his room.

Fin came racing up behind them. "Hey, Stevie boy!"

Stephen turned and didn't see the girl coming round the bend at the top of the stairs until too late. "God, I'm so sorry!" he apologised, helping her up. He knew her, Lynn something; she was in the room directly below his. She was small and slim with superb legs. Her shoulder-length hair was pale gold with a slight curl, and her eyes were almost the colour of violets. She had a kind of fragile loveliness, he thought, and beautiful lips, full and rose tinted; the most kissable mouth he'd ever seen. He'd fancied her since he'd first seen her in the bar, but she was going out with a boy called Chris Wilby, who lived in the neighbouring hall, Bowden Court. He was a prize jerk, tall and skinny, the type who took an umbrella out with him if it looked as if it might rain. Stephen couldn't understand what she saw in him.

Lynn gave him a funny little smile. "I'm fine." She patted his outstretched arm and walked past him.

Paul Simon's 'Late In The Evening' began to play in his head. While he and Vanessa waited for Fin, he watched the other girl disappear down the stairs.

He bumped into her again a few days later. It was a miserable day, pouring with rain, and he was half-heartedly working on an essay, and had wandered to the kitchen to get a cup of coffee. As he came out with it, Lynn, her hair dripping and her jacket wet, hurried through the doors at the entrance to the corridor, walking directly into him. He cried out as the hot coffee spilled down his front.

"Oh my God, are you all right? Quick, you need to get that shirt off!" She took the mug from him, deposited it on the floor, and started to pull off his tee shirt.

"Hey, I'm OK," he protested, pulling it back down. "I'll take it off in my room."

"Can I come with you? If you're burned you might need some help."

Stephen grinned. "I'm sure I'm not, but be my guest." Great way to pick her up, he thought.

They went to his room and he stripped off the sodden tee shirt, dumping it in the sink.

"Your chest's a bit red. Have you got a flannel? You should put cold water on it until the pain and the redness go."

"It doesn't hurt," he assured her, pulling on a clean tee shirt. "Look, I'm getting another cup of coffee, would you like one?"

"Oh, well – I was on my way to see a friend in the next corridor." She bit her lip. "She's probably gone out now though, I was late back." She smiled at him. "I'd like some coffee."

Yes! he thought jubilantly.

They listened to music and talked in a desultory way, and he began to feel very comfortable with her. Something about her, some sort of inner serenity, reminded him of Sian.

His Strat was propped up against the bed. "Your guitar is lovely, I've never seen one this colour before," Lynn said admiringly. "What made you choose it?"

Stephen hesitated. This was something only his family and Harry knew, he'd always told everyone else that his parents had chosen the colour, but he had the strangest feeling about Lynn, that he could tell her anything. "Whenever I hear the Strat being played, I see the sound it makes in that colour – like shining turquoise snakes coiling around me. Don't tell anyone," he added quickly.

"Gosh! Of course I won't. Thank you for telling me. Would you play me something?"

He picked up the guitar. "What would you like?"

"Anything. Play me anything." She shut her eyes.

He played 'The Girl From Ipanema'.

When he'd finished, she opened her eyes and sighed. "Oh, that was fantastic, Stephen! I tried to see the turquoise snakes, but I couldn't, all I could do was wallow in the music. I could listen to you play forever. Maybe—" She stopped.

"What?" he asked, delighted by her reaction to his playing.

"Well, I play the flute. Maybe we could play together sometime?"

He was overcome with joy. He'd never expected her to be musical. "Certainly could!" he said enthusiastically.

"Good," she smiled. "I love music. My dad wanted me to study it, he was really disappointed when I decided on speech therapy."

"God, how ironic!" exclaimed Stephen. "My dad hates my music, he wanted me to go to Oxford and study law."

"Like him?" asked Lynn.

"How did you guess?" he grinned. "Hey, Lynn, can I buy you a pizza?" He held his breath. He knew she wasn't going out with Chris Wilby any more, but that didn't mean she'd want to go out with him.

To his relief, she smiled. "Yes, I'd like that, but aren't you going out with that posh girl?"

"No, that was never more than a nine-day wonder. She just wanted a bit of rough."

Lynn raised her eyebrows. "I wouldn't have put you down as that!"

He took her to Pizza Junction on Oxford Road. They talked as if they'd known each other for months rather than hours. He found out that her full name was Cherilynn Eve Jackson and that her parents ran a guesthouse in Hampshire. Her father was nominally Protestant, but didn't believe in God; her mother was a Roman Catholic, and very religious.

"It's the tragedy of her life that I'm an only child," Lynn said, helping herself to a slice of pizza. "She'd envisaged a tribe of little offerings to Our Lady. Course, she's convinced herself it's all Dad's fault." She sighed. "I was baptised a Catholic and I went to Catholic schools, but I don't believe."

Like Stephen, she didn't smoke, although, unlike his parents, her mother and father did. "I tried one when I was twelve, it made me so sick I've never wanted another," she confessed.

He told her about his family and his father and the band. To his delight, when he told her the band was called The Brigands, she cried, "Oh! Like Lady Marchmain!"

"You're the only person who's ever got that. I never thought I'd be pleased someone spilt hot coffee over me," he laughed.

The only thing he didn't tell her about was Harry and Rob. It didn't seem the time, somehow.

When they were leaving, she wanted to pay half, but he wouldn't hear of it. "I offered to buy you a pizza, remember? What do you want to do now?"

She took his arm. He felt as if he'd touched a live electric cable. He couldn't remember when he'd last wanted anyone this much.

"Let's go to the Ducie and have a Guinness," she said. "I'll buy those."

He took her back to her room when the pub closed and she gave him a friendly goodnight kiss at the door. "I've had a lovely time, Stephen. Thank you." She turned to go in.

"Wait! Can I see you tomorrow?"

She nodded. "Come down about four o'clock. Night, Stephen." The door shut.

They went out every night. They found they had the same tastes in music, in literature, in food. They liked the same films, they laughed at the same things, but every night he got the same chaste goodnight kiss. It wasn't that he wasn't allowed into her room; she often made him a drink last thing and they'd listen to records together, but there was no petting. And he didn't exactly know how to initiate it. She was friendly and great fun, she seemed to like spending time with him, but she was very self-contained. He decided to do nothing. Either she'd get more… friendly, or she wouldn't. If she didn't, she didn't. He very much wanted to make love to her, but he didn't want to jeopardize this friendship that he valued very much by rushing her into anything.

"Fin, I haven't seen you for ages!"

Fin grinned. "I've been spending all my time with the most gorgeous woman you've ever seen!"

"That's what you said about the last one."

"Ah, to be sure I did, but she was nothing compared to Roisin! Listen, I wanted to talk to you. Roisin, my wild Irish rose, knows someone who plays bass. Apparently, he's very good. If we find ourselves a drummer we could form that band we're always talking about."

"Who is this bloke?"

"George the Geordie. She doesn't know his surname. He's on her course at the Tech."

Stephen smiled at the use of the nickname. Fin meant UMIST, the University of Manchester Institute of Science and Technology. "Well, I'm game. Perhaps your Irish rose might introduce us?"

"Great minds think alike," Fin grinned. "I've already organised it, he's meeting us for a drink tonight."

"I'll have to check with Lynn."

"Who's this, who's this?" Fin rubbed his hands together eagerly.

"Lynn Jackson, from downstairs."

Fin whistled. "You've got good taste, my boy!" He leant confidentially towards Stephen. "And is *she* good?"

"None of your business!"

Stephen and Lynn met Fin and Roisin at the Church – not a house of God, but a pub not far from Grosvenor. "Hey, you two," Fin called, as they pushed their way across the crowded room. He indicated the pretty, dark-haired girl at his side. "Steve and Lynn, this is Roisin. Roisin, Steve and Lynn. Steve, I took the liberty of getting you a Pils. What can I get you?" he asked Lynn.

"Pils would be great, thanks."

Fin pushed his way up to the bar.

"What course are you on?" Roisin asked Lynn.

"Speech therapy."

Roisin raised her eyebrows. "Speech therapy and pathology?"

"Yes."

"I've a friend on that course, he says it's really hard. You must be brainy!"

"I wish I was," Lynn smiled. "I'm finding it pretty tough, I have to work like anything!"

Fin came back with six bottles of Pils. Lynn gave him an amazed look.

"Don't worry, I'm not trying to get you drunk," he reassured her. "Just stocking up. We don't want to spend the evening queuing at the bar."

"Who's the extra one for?" Stephen asked.

"George the Geordie?" suggested Lynn.

"Beauty *and* brains, well done, Steve!" Fin approved. He grinned. "I can't think what you see in him though, Lynn!"

"Ciggie, anyone?" Roisin offered a packet round. "Oh, here's George."

A huge figure loomed over them. "Hello, Roisin. Sorry I'm late." He took the cigarette she held out. "Thanks, pet." He had a Geordie accent so thick it would have taken a chainsaw to cut it.

"We got you a drink," Fin said.

George looked round the table. "Where?"

Fin proffered the Pils.

George looked at it with disgust. "Howay, bonny lad, call that a drink? We give that stuff to the bairns! I suppose it's all right for the lasses, but it's not a man's drink! Newcastle Brown, that's a drink. I won't be long."

They watched as he cleared a path to the bar.

"It's like the parting of the Red Sea," said Stephen, awed. "Does it matter how well he plays? I mean, he'd be a real asset to a band!"

But he could play. He's almost as good as Harry, Stephen thought. She was coming to stay that weekend. He smiled with pleasure. He was borrowing Fin's room; Fin, of course, would be at Roisin's. The only thing that was worrying him was Lynn. He hadn't told her about Harry or Rob yet, it was a difficult subject to broach. He had a photo of them in his room along with pictures of his family and, as Harry was dark like Sian, and Rob looked like him, he knew she'd assumed they were just part of the family. Had he and she been as physically intimate as they were mentally, he would have told her, but they weren't, and he felt too constrained by the lack of that intimacy to talk about something so personal. Lynn had only just started to french kiss him. Although he had to admit that there was something very erotic about this approach of hers. When she'd opened her mouth to kiss him, he'd practically come. He decided he'd have to tell her that night. She knew he had a friend called Harry coming to stay, but he hadn't even said that Harry was a girl.

He cooked a meal for her and they were lying side by side on the bed in his room, drinking wine and listening to 'Zenyatta Mondatta', which Lynn (who, in Stephen's opinion, was overly fond of Sting) had recently bought.

"That was a delicious meal, Stephen. I wish I could cook."

"Anyone can cook, you just follow the recipe." He poured them more wine.

She shook her head. "Not true, not true. I've tried, it doesn't work. You have to have the knack. And then everything in the kitchen seems to hate me. I tried to make toffee once, I was stirring away at it and there was this peculiar smell and it turned out the spoon I was using was melting into it! Who would've expected that?"

"Was the spoon made of plastic?"

"Well, yes it was," she admitted, "but it didn't say in the recipe you couldn't use a plastic spoon."

"But my little ignoramus, you're a scientist! You *know* plastic melts!" He was starting to laugh.

"Well, yes, but you think cooking utensils will withstand anything. That's what they're for!"

"God, you're adorable!" He kissed her on the nose.

"You're not so bad yourself," she replied. She rolled over and pulled him closer, and their kisses became very intense. Extremely aroused, he began to caress her breasts. She pulled away from him and he groaned.

"Sorry." She sat up.

"Lynn—"

"I'm not ready, Stephen," she interrupted, her face anxious.

He sat up too. "It's OK, there's no pressure. I'm just happy being with you."

She smiled at him. "You're too good to be true, you know that?"

"No, I'm not. I've got something to tell you."

She listened without speaking. When he'd finished, she said, "She must love you an awful lot."

He stared at her. "What do you mean?"

"Not to marry you."

"You're not making sense."

She paused. "You're right. Do you want to finish this wine? I can't drink any more."

"No. Lynn, what do you mean?"

"Nothing, I'm talking rubbish, too much wine. In fact, I think I'd better go." She stood up. "I've got loads of work to do."

"No. Tell me what you meant."

She hesitated. "I don't think…"

"Please, Lynn."

"Look, I can't speak for Harry. I was just putting myself in her place. I'm sure we're totally different."

"So, speaking for yourself..." he said, inexorably.

She sighed. "Speaking for myself. From what you told me, you and she have an awful lot in common. You're both extremely musical, you rate her talent and her friendship very highly. You were in a band together for two years and far from getting on each other's nerves, you were often united against... um... what was his name?"

"Ray."

"Ray. You lived in the same house for a year, went backwards and forwards to school, had classes together. Did you ever drive each other nuts?" He shook his head slowly, stricken. "God, me and my big mouth. I'm really sorry, Stevie."

She'd never called him anything but Stephen before. He realised, even in the middle of his misery and guilt over Harry, that he loved her more than he'd ever loved anyone except Rob, and he'd never stop loving her, no matter what happened.

"What?" she asked, puzzled. "Why are you staring at me like that?"

"You called me Stevie." He took her in his arms. "Cherilynn. My sweet, sweet Cherry."

She leant against him, listening to his heart beating.

"I think you may be right about Harry," he said finally. "I can't think how come I didn't see it. But what shall I do? I can't marry her, I'm not in love with her." I love you, he thought.

"I don't think you should do anything. If she wanted you to know, she'd have told you. And this is just my dumb theory, Stevie. I could be *so* wrong!" She looked at him shyly. "No one's ever called me Cherry before."

"I can't think why, it's so pretty. Everything about you is so incredibly pretty. Your hair is such a beautiful colour, and your eyes! They're like violets! You're the most perfect girl I've ever seen."

She kissed him. They carried on kissing until he couldn't stand it any more and broke away. "I'm sorry, Lynn, I'm not trying to make you do anything, but I can't kiss you like this. I feel like I'm going to explode. We'll have to stop."

"Make love to me, Stevie."

He stared at her, not trusting his hearing. "Are you sure?"

She nodded, blushing. "I've never been so sure of anything. I wanted to go out with you the very first time I saw you, but I've never, you know, made love before. I'm a bit scared."

Stephen held her against him. "Oh, Cherry, I can't tell you how that makes me feel! Don't be scared. We don't have to do anything. We can just cuddle."

She shook her head. "No, Stevie. I love you. I want you to make love to me."

"Oh, God, Cherry, I love you too." Slowly, almost reverently, he undressed her. He was shaking with desire for her, and the sight of her body was almost a torture. Hurriedly, he pulled off his clothes, gazing down at her as she lay waiting for him, her hair a cloud of gold on his pillow. "You're so beautiful," he breathed.

Lynn tried to smile, but she was tense with nerves and anticipation. He got in with her, and she moved awkwardly towards him, bumping his nose with her forehead. "Sorry," she mumbled, mortified. "My body seems to have gone all stiff!"

He smiled at her. "That makes two of us!"

Much later, she fell asleep in his arms, her head on his shoulder. I worship you, he thought, I adore you, I'd die for you, and the only way I can express all these feelings is with one small, inadequate word. Love. "I love you," he whispered. She stirred slightly, and nestled closer to him, and he could feel her breath on his neck. Deeply at peace, deeply happy, his body deliciously sated, he drifted between waking and sleeping, vaguely aware of the wind singing in the telephone wires outside, and the rain soughing against the windowpane. It was getting colder, winter was nipping at autumn's heels, but in that small, square, basic room, on that narrow, hard little bed, he and Lynn slept, warm and safe in each other's arms, the only people in the universe.

He wrote a song for her, 'Sweet Cherry'. He knew, without a shadow of a doubt, that no matter what might happen in the future, he would love her for the rest of his life, world without end.

He watched Harry like a hawk when she arrived on Friday, trying to see if he could spot any signs that she was in love with him. She was her old self, funny, confident, forthright. She got on extremely well with Lynn, and seemed perfectly at ease with her being his girlfriend. He was relieved, he'd hated the idea that Harry was in love with him, he already felt guilty enough about Rob. And after all, he thought, how would Cherry know what Harry's feeling? She doesn't know her like I do.

"So you're forming another band, then," she said to Stephen, late that night as they were drinking tea in his room. "Will it be called The Brigands?"

He shook his head. "There'll only ever be one Band of Brigands. How is everything, Harry?"

"Everything's ace, Stevie. I've going to take a book-keeping course, so I can help Dad out, and he's promised to give up smoking in return." She'd given up when she was expecting Rob, and had been trying to make Ted stop ever since she'd moved back to the pub. "Oh, and he's found a psychiatrist, did I tell you?"

"You said he'd been referred, but he didn't get on with that first one he went to."

"It took him a while to find one he liked, but he's happy with the one he's got now, says he really listens and talks back to him. The first one wouldn't talk, said he was just there to listen. Not Dad's style at all. He likes a bit of interaction."

Stephen smiled. "Yeah. But what about you, Harry? Apart from the book-keeping?"

"Well." She blushed. "I'm seeing someone."

"Harry! I'm so pleased! Is it anyone I know?"

"Not exactly. I met him at your house. He's a solicitor at your Dad's firm; he's only just qualified. His name's Julian Cavendish and he's really nice. He gets on really well with Dad, and he's very good with Robbie."

Stephen felt a pang of jealousy at the thought of another man looking after his son. He stamped on it immediately. "He'd better be nice to you. You deserve it. How's the divorce going?"

"Your dad's being great. And talking of being good with Rob, your dad is amazing with him."

Second chance, thought Stephen. Back off, Dad. "That's great. I was thinking of coming home for the weekend after my birthday; will that be OK?"

"Of course," she said, surprised. "Julian knows all about you."

"Good, because I won't come if it's going to mess things up for you."

"But, Stevie, what about Rob? You want to see him, don't you?"

"Oh, yes." There was no mistaking his sincerity, and Harry relaxed. "But I'd do without seeing him if it meant making things difficult for you."

"Well it doesn't. So come home whenever you want. You've got to come home for your birthday, our son's got you a present and he wants to give it to you himself!"

On Saturday evening they took her to the Highland Fling, a pub that had a dance floor and live music every weekend.

"Hey, Stevie, you could play here when you get a drummer," Harry said. "Have you written any more songs?"

"More than you could shake a stick at," he grinned.

They were holding auditions for a drummer at George's house in Whalley Range the following week. George's father, who owned a large building firm, had bought it for him as an investment. It was a big Victorian detached house with three floors. George rented out the top floor, and used the rest of the house himself.

"What are you calling the band?" Harry asked.

Stephen shook his head. "No idea. Anyone got any suggestions?"

Everyone started to think up stupid names, each more ridiculous than the one before, until they were laughing too much to speak. Stephen particularly liked Harry's suggestion of 'Gay Boys in Bondage'. "You know, it might work!"

"Don't even think about it, bonny lad," George warned. "I'm only in this poncey band for to pick up lasses and make a fortune, and we're not going to do either with a name like that!"

"'This Poncey Band' sounds quite good," laughed Lynn. "Sums you all up nicely."

Sunday was a lovely day, crisp and cold, the leaves a glorious spread of reds, golds and oranges, even stunted by the smoke of the city as they were.

"Let's walk down to Rusholme," Stephen suggested. "We can go to Platt Fields Park; the trees will be beautiful there."

"Oh, yes, and we can go to the Pet's Corner," Lynn enthused. She turned to Harry. "They've got the sweetest animals there!"

"And talking of sweet, we can take Harry into the sweet shops on the way back," Stephen said.

"What's so exciting about sweet shops?" asked Harry, mystified.

Stephen smiled at her. "You've never seen any like these before. They're Indian sweet shops. They're amazing!"

He took her to the station the next morning. She hugged him tearfully as the train drew in. "I've had the most fantastic time, Stevie!"

"Me too. You're going to have to come over a lot, Hal."

Her heart swelled with happiness. I've got a nickname, she thought, and I've got his son as well – so there, Lynn Jackson! Then she felt mean. "Lynn's really nice," she said. "What does she think about you singing all the time?"

"She just thinks I'm weird. Sometimes she says something like, 'It's getting a bit loud' if we're shopping or whatever, but that's all." He carried her bag onto the train, and kissed her. "I'll see you in a couple of weeks, Hal."

She managed to smile brightly. "Yeah, see you, Stevie."

As the train pulled out of the station, she indulged in a flood of tears. Still, she told herself, drying her eyes, she'd always known Stephen would find a girlfriend in Manchester, and at least Lynn was nice, very like Angie, although a bit goody-goody. She imagined she might be rather hard to take in large doses, but obviously Stephen didn't think so. And at least I've got Robbie, so I'll always have a part of him. She sighed. She liked Julian very much, and she knew he was in love with her, but she wasn't going to rush into anything. I've grown up a lot since marrying Jason, she thought, and of course, Dad's so different these days. Even Will and Nick's attitude towards him had changed slightly.

"Lynn, will you come home with me and meet my family – not next weekend, but the one after?"

She kissed him. "I'd love to."

"What did you think of Harry?"

"She's very nice, I like her. She's very pretty too." She'd been taken aback when Harry arrived, she hadn't expected her to be so striking; the picture Stephen had in his room didn't do her justice. She was taller than Lynn, who was five foot three, by a couple of inches, possibly more – she was as tall as Stephen when she wore heels – and again, Lynn hadn't expected that, she'd somehow got the impression from the photo, which was only head and shoulders, that Harry was small and dumpy, when, in fact she had a terrific figure, and her eyes, a coppery brown with gold flecks, were beautiful. And she and Stephen were so close, which was something else Lynn hadn't expected. Her suspicion that Harry was in love with him had been confirmed as soon as she'd seen them together, but she hadn't realised how strongly he felt about her. She glanced up at him from under her lashes. "Do you think she's prettier than me?"

A slow smile spread over Stephen's face. "Jealous?" he teased.

Lynn frowned. She'd never suffered from jealousy before and she found it unpleasantly disconcerting. Stephen was the most handsome man she'd ever seen, with his square jaw and high cheekbones, his tough looking, sexy mouth, and fascinating, aquamarine eyes. And that thick, shiny black hair, you just wanted to run your hands through it, you wanted to touch him. But it was more than that, more than skin deep, more than a matter of bone structure and eye colour and an athletic body; there was something about him that not only drew the attention but held it. Girls swarmed round him like cats with catnip. Catnip for women, she thought, that's what he is. He seemed oblivious to his looks and never flirted with other women, but it was unsettling, and made her feel somewhat insecure.

"No, I'm not jealous. Should I be?" she asked, rather more aggressively than she'd meant to.

He pulled her against him. "Certainly shouldn't! You're the most beautiful woman in the world, and I'm so lucky to have you."

"Oh, Stevie!" She felt supremely happy. "I *was* a little jealous," she confessed. "You and Harry are so close. But I think your son's in very good hands, I'm looking forward to meeting him. You wait till you see what Harry's got you from him for your birthday! Which reminds me, you still haven't told me what you want."

"Othello Gateau, champagne, and you wrapped in a turquoise ribbon!"

"OK, OK," Lynn sighed, "I'll think up some ideas of my own if you're not going to give me anything."

"There are plenty of things I could give you. I can think of something to give you right now!"

"You are *obsessed* with sex," sighed Lynn.

"You're a fine one to talk about being obsessed! I'd barely got back from seeing Harry onto the train before you were ripping my jeans off!" he retorted.

"Oh, well, if you don't like it," she shrugged, grinning.

"I didn't say I didn't like it!"

"Oh come on, Steve, this one looks like a weasel. And that accent! Thick as the wall!"

"*You* don't have an accent at all, of course."

"He's a *Scouser*! Girls like a bit of Irish charm."

"Girls! That's not what this band's about, Fin."

"All bands are about girls, Stevie boy."

"Unless they're girl bands," George put in.

"They might be lesbians," Fin suggested hopefully.

"Canny, man!"

"For Christ's sake, you two! Why don't we just play all our gigs in a brothel?"

"You know, you might have something there."

"Shut up and let's listen to him."

George sniffed. "He smells like the docks, man."

Stephen was listening. "He plays brilliantly! He's in."

His name was Andy Lake and he was ecstatic to be chosen. "Great way to pick up birds, like!"

Stephen groaned."What's it called, then, this band, like?" Andy asked.

"'Gay Boys In Bondage'," Stephen grinned.

"Oh ey, I don't like the sound of that!" Andy said, a worried look increasing his resemblance to a rodent.

"It's a joke," Fin explained.

"Let's go and have a drink to celebrate," Stephen suggested.

They walked to George's local, The Tappit Hen. It was only just opening time and the place was practically empty. They got their drinks and sat at a table for four.

The landlord watched them sit down. "You can't sit there."

"Why not, man?" George asked.

"Saved for Sid's six, isn't it?"

"There's only four chairs," Stephen pointed out.

"Look, if you're going to cause trouble, you can fuck off. I've said you can't sit there, all right?"

"Let's move," Andy said nervously.

They got up. "That's it!" Stephen exclaimed.

"What's what?" Fin asked.

"The name of the band – 'Sid's Six'!"

"But there's only four of us," Fin objected.

"And none of us are called Sid, like," Andy added.

"Exactly!"

Sian was waiting at York Station. She flew into Stephen's arms. "It's *so* lovely to see you!" She turned to Lynn and smiled. "I've been looking forward to meeting you so much, Lynn, we've had glowing reports of you from Harry."

"I'm really pleased to meet you too, Mrs Markham."

"Oh, call me Sian. Come on, let's get in the car quick, or we'll be soaked! Have you got the bags, Stevie?" She chatted all the way home, filling Stephen in on anything new and explaining things to Lynn. "I wasn't sure about sleeping arrangements, cariad," she said to Stephen. "I made up the bed in your attic room, but it's only a single. Would the two of you prefer the double in the guest room?"

"Whatever Lynn wants," Stephen shrugged. "Cherry?"

"Oh, well," Lynn said, flustered, "I'd love to sleep in your attic room, Stevie." She spread her hands. "You know, I could never have this conversation with my mother, not in a million years!"

"Well, you're both adults," Sian smiled. "And it would be ridiculous to be coy about it with Steve," she added wryly. "His son's coming round in half an hour."

Harry arrived with Rob at the same time as the girls got home from school. In the general hubbub and confusion, everyone kissing each other and talking at once, Lynn had a chance to take a look at Stephen's family. He was holding Rob, who was five months old, small and active, and as like Stephen as it was possible to be without actually being him. Kathy was very like Sian, petite and full figured, whereas Rebecca was tall and very slender. Both girls had hazel eyes; neither of them had inherited Sian's very dark brown ones, and only Rob and Stephen had those marvellous ice blue eyes.

The kitchen door opened and John, tall, thin and distinguished, stood there. He was sixty-two, but he didn't look it. He must have been very handsome when he was Stevie's age, Lynn thought, although they weren't particularly alike, apart from their mouths. John's eyes were a brighter blue, and his face was different, longer. He was staring at Stephen and the look on his face made Lynn want to cry; it was like a child looking at something he longs for but knows he'll never have.

Stephen looked up and saw him. For a second, his face was expressionless, and then he smiled. "Dad!" He put the baby over his shoulder and held out his hand to John, who grasped it. "This is Lynn."

John smiled at her as they shook hands. "We've all been looking forward to meeting you. Harry's been singing your praises, haven't you, love?" He turned to Harry, who nodded, giving Lynn a friendly smile.

"I hope I live up to this," Lynn said rather nervously, thinking how good it was of Harry. I'm not sure I could've been so generous in her place, she thought.

While Sian was cooking the evening meal, Stephen and Lynn took their bags upstairs. Lynn had offered Sian a hand, but Stephen advised against it. "She's murder in the kitchen! And if I didn't cook for her she'd exist on dry bread and cottage cheese."

"It's easy and non-fattening," she explained.

"Non-fattening?" John shook his head. "You don't need to worry about that, Lynn, you're all skin and bones. You girls these days! We liked women to have curves when I was young," he said to Stephen. "Like your mother here!" He patted Sian's bottom and she smiled and pretended to hit him with the ladle she was drying.

"Go on, you two," she said. "Take her upstairs and show her your room, Stevie."

"Your family is lovely," Lynn said as they walked upstairs. "And your Dad's charming."

Stephen's smile melted away. "Start talking about Sid's Six at the dinner table later and you'll see just how charming he can be," he said shortly. He was sick of John projecting this 'I'm a wonderful husband and father image'. He opened the door. "Well this is it."

"Stevie, what a lovely room!"

"All done with my own fair hands," he grinned. He looked round the room. "You should have seen it originally! It was filthy, full of spiders."

They both shuddered.

"Stevie said you're a speech therapy student, Lynn." Kathy passed her the gravy. "Do you really have lessons in a room with dead bodies?"

"Kathy!" Sian cut in. "I don't think we want to talk about that when we're eating!" She glanced at Rebecca who had gone white and was looking revolted.

They ate in silence for a while.

"Harry said you've got an Irish friend." Rebecca looked inquiringly at Stephen. She had regained her colour but was picking at her food.

"Yeah, he's called Fin."

"Fin!" It made Rebecca laugh. "Like a fish?"

"It's short for Finbar. It's an Irish name. He's the keyboard player in the band."

There was a silence. John put down his knife and fork.

"Band?" Sian tried to sound casual.

"Didn't Harry tell you?" Stephen inquired blandly.

You know she didn't, Lynn thought furiously, you told her not to! She tried to catch his eye, but he was looking at John.

"Yeah, we've just found a drummer, we'll be doing some gigs soon."

"What about your work?" John asked.

"What about it?" Stephen's voice was cold. He had been getting angrier and angrier since Lynn had commented on how charming John was. We'll see what you think of him now, he thought, waiting for the diatribe. Nothing happened. John picked up his knife and fork and started toying with his food as Rebecca had done.

Lynn turned to Kathy. "Stephen was telling me you're going to catering college next year. It must be great to be able to cook! Are we having anything you've made this weekend?" She was aware of Sian smiling at her warmly. She went on talking as if nothing was wrong, but inside she wanted to kill Stephen.

Stephen, for his part, couldn't understand the lack of response from his father. Nothing had ever surprised him so much. The meal came to an end, and John excused himself from coffee and went out.

Stephen put his hand over Lynn's. She shook it off without looking at him. The girls went off to their rooms, and Sian, Stephen and Lynn went through to the sitting room.

Lynn needed to use the toilet and ran upstairs. A hoarse whisper from the window seat overlooking the front garden made her jump. "Lynn." It was John. He was holding his left arm. His face was grey and there were beads of sweat on his forehead.

"John!"

"Shh," he whispered. "Sian…"

"I'll get her!"

He plucked feebly at her arm. "Not Stephen."

"No." She ran downstairs and looked round the sitting room door. "Sian, can you help me? Female stuff," she explained to Stephen. "It's John," she said to Sian once they were outside.

"Oh, God!" Sian ran upstairs into a bedroom, and came out with a bottle of pills. John opened his mouth and she put one under his tongue. "It's angina," she told Lynn. "Will you help me get him into the bedroom?"

Lynn helped lift him and they got him onto his bed. Sian took off his shoes and Lynn loosened his shirt. His colour was better and he was breathing more easily.

"I'll look in on you later, darling," Sian promised. "Try to sleep now." They tiptoed out.

"Come in here." Sian beckoned Lynn into the guest room.

"How long has he had it?" Lynn asked.

"A while. He doesn't want the children to know. It hasn't been too bad recently, he's so happy now Steve's at university. I could wring that little bastard's neck!"

Lynn was startled.

"He did it deliberately, Lynn. Harry told me about the band. I know he doesn't know about the angina, but why try to provoke a row?"

"I think that's my fault. I said John was charming earlier."

"Oh, for God's sake!" Sian was disgusted. "I'd like to slap his legs hard!"

The absurdity of Sian slapping Stephen's legs hit them at the same time and they became hysterical with laughter.

"*You* could do it later," Sian giggled. "Although he might like that."

That made them worse. Eventually, Sian controlled herself. "I can't really blame Stevie, not entirely. John caused all this. Has Stephen told you?" Lynn nodded. "And he worked so hard for John. He hated school and he had no real interest in academia, but God, did he work." She smiled reminiscently and slightly sadly. "He hated school from his very first day. I remember, when I picked him up, I asked him if he'd enjoyed it, and he said, 'Well, I suppose it was all right, but I don't think I'll go again'. He was horrified when I explained he had to go every day! And he found it so hard not being allowed to sing whenever he wanted to. He was constantly in trouble about it at first. But he desperately wanted to be the son John wanted him to be, so he conformed." She shrugged. "More than conformed, in fact. Did you know he got four A grades at 'A' Level?"

"No, he never said."

"He wanted so much to please John. But he never could because they're different people who want different things. Families, eh?"

"Yes. It was the same at home. Mum wanted me to be a nun, and Dad wanted me to be a music teacher. Needless to say, they were both disappointed!"

Sian shook her head. "What on earth is wrong with 'I want you to be happy, so you do what you want'?"

"Well, I think that's Steve's attitude to Rob, anyway."

Sian smiled at her. "Bless you, I think you're right."

Lynn was still angry with Stephen when they went to bed.

"What's up?" he asked, knowing full well.

"You were despicable tonight. How could you behave like that?"

He flushed. "It's none of your business."

"Yes, it is," she flashed back. "You made it my business by bringing me here, and I was ashamed of you!"

He stared at her, stung. The worst part was, he knew she was right. "If I'm so disgusting to you, perhaps you'd rather sleep in the guest room."

"Perhaps I would!" She picked up her bag and turned to go.

"Cherry!" She stopped. "I'm sorry. You're right. I *was* despicable. I just wanted to show you. But I don't understand. Usually he'd have hit the roof."

"Sian was really cross with you." Lynn put her bag back down. "She said she wanted to slap your legs." Stephen started to grin. "Yeah, it made us laugh too. She said I could do it, but you'd probably like that!"

"I might too. We could try it and see. Or," he said slowly, "I could spank *you*. What do you think?"

"Try it, buster, and you'll be singing falsetto!"

Sid's Six played their first ever gig at the Grovenor bar on the second of December. The bar committee had been let down at the last minute, and the committee chairman asked them if they would play, warning them there was very little money in it. They jumped at the chance.

"It doesn't really matter about the money," Stephen said.

"Speak for yourself, bonny lad!" George retorted.

"Yeah, but it'll get us known. And word'll get around how good we are and it'll be easier to get gigs elsewhere. I've done all this before." He'd discussed his concept of the band's image with them. He was the only one with any real experience; George had been in a band for a few months while he was at school, but they'd only played at their local youth club, and had never been paid for their performances. He felt he should have more input into Sid's Six because of it, however, and tended to resent Stephen's control of the band. For his part, Stephen felt that a few amateur gigs in a youth club didn't amount to much, and, as he considered Sid's Six his band anyway, and Fin and Andy had no problem with him being in charge, George would have to suck it up.

They rehearsed constantly. They would be playing the songs he'd written for The Brigands as well as the ones he'd written recently: 'Sweet Cherry', 'White Heat', 'Tabula Rasa', 'It's All True' and 'Jetsam'.

Fin was impressed. "There's more than enough songs here for an album, Steve, and they're bloody good songs too. 'Sweet Cherry' is brilliant, I love the outro."

"I like 'Kissing in the Crypt," Andy said, referring to a song Stephen had written for The Brigands. "It's just like an Elvis Presley number, isn't it?"

"Yeah, rockabilly," Fin said. "This stuff ought to go down really well."

They were all nervous on the night, except Stephen.

"How can you not be?" Fin asked, watching him calmly eating a bar of chocolate as they waited to go on stage.

"I'm used to it. How bad an audience can they be?" He grinned. "We once played at a punk venue in Hull. It was bloody terrifying, but we lived! They even applauded. And we made seventy-five quid!"

As Stephen and Lynn's relationship deepened, the amount of time he spent on his music came as a surprise to her. When they'd first started going out he'd spent every minute with her, and so she hadn't realised how much music meant to him, how very seriously he took it. He could spend hours playing guitar, immersed in it to the exclusion of all else, even her, and when he was writing a song he'd sometimes work late into the night and fall asleep still holding the guitar. It was disconcerting and occasionally irritating, but she didn't really mind. It was part of who he was.

On the ninth of December, he came stamping in from his lectures. It was freezing outside, and despite his coat, gloves and scarf, he was shivering. All he wanted to do was get to his room and have a hot drink and something to eat before he and Fin headed off to George's for a rehearsal. They were booked for the end of term dance at the bar on Thursday, and he'd written a new song.

"Stephen! Wait!"

He sighed. It was Michaela Kyriakides, also known as Pickles. At the beginning of term she'd come along to the boys' corridor to introduce herself, bringing a jar of pickled walnuts with her. Stephen had christened her Pickles on the spot and it had stuck. He turned back. "I'm freezing, Pickles," he pleaded.

"They've shot John Lennon."

"What?" He stared at her. "Who have? You're joking, aren't you?"

"No! It's been on the radio all morning. Someone's shot him!"

He grinned. "I didn't come down in the last shower, Pickles!"

"It's true! It is! Come in and listen!"

He went into her room. "If this is some sort of ploy to get me in here for nefarious reasons of your own—"

"Listen!"

He sat on the end of her bed. They *were* playing 'Imagine'. It finished and a sombre-voiced announcer corroborated what Pickles had said. Stephen stared at her in shock.

"You see?"

"Jesus," he said. "Jesus." He walked slowly to his room. He had several Beatles

LPs, and 'Double Fantasy', which he'd only just bought. He spread them out on the floor, staring at the photos of John Lennon. It seemed impossible to believe that he was dead, and the words '*Imagine the world without him. The long and winding road leads to another door, a jail cell, woman in hell, and all those diamonds tumble from the sky, dropping like tears from a little boy's eyes...*' leapt into his mind, and he grabbed a piece of paper and a pen and started to write. He called it 'Blown Away'. He read it through and heard the music in his head. Picking up his National guitar, he began to play.

Half an hour later, Fin knocked on the door. "Have you heard about John Lennon?"

Stephen sang 'Blown Away'.

Fin sat and listened. "Christ, Stephen. That's just so fucking sad. It'll go down brilliantly at the gig on Thursday night!"

Chapter Five
Sweet Cherry

And I know I'll never tire of your loving, I just want more,
Sweet, sweet Cherry

Stephen and Lynn spent the Christmas holidays in York. Stephen had bought dozens of presents for Rob.

"He'll never play with them all," Lynn giggled.

"Don't you want to be at home for Christmas Day?" he asked her.

She snuggled up to him. "I'm with you. I *am* home."

On Christmas Eve, Sian shooed them out of the house. Rebecca had gone to see friends, and she and Kathy wanted the kitchen to themselves to cook.

"It's cold outside!" Stephen protested. "Why can't we stay here?"

"Because you keep coming in here and eating mince pies. You're just a pig, Stephen, you always have been, and unfortunately for her, Cherry has to suffer for your gluttony. Now go!"

"Go where?" Stephen whined.

"The pub. Here's a tenner. Have lunch."

"I cannot believe my own mother is *paying* me to go to the pub on Christmas Eve!" Stephen's voice scaled up indignantly. "Have you no shame?"

Sian hit him across the back of the head. "Get out! Take him away, Lynnie!"

They went to the Hansom Cab and sat in front of a roaring fire, eating beef sandwiches. Stephen couldn't choose between treacle tart and sherry trifle for pudding, so he had both.

After they'd finished eating, Lynn dragged him up. "Come on, you've got to walk off that stodge."

"I don't know! You and Mum! Bossiest women in the universe!" he grumbled. He followed her outside. "It's cold out here! I hope you're not going to turn into a nagging wife!"

They stared at each other.

Impulsively, Stephen went down on one knee. "Cherry, darling Cherry, will you do me the honour of becoming my wife?"

Tears welled up in Lynn's eyes. "Stevie! Oh, Stevie, yes, yes, yes!" She pulled him up and threw her arms round him. "I'm so happy!"

He hugged her, his heart singing. "Oh, Cherry, I love you so much! Come on, let's go and buy you a ring."

He took her hand and led her through the busy market to a jeweller's shop in the Shambles that sold antique rings. They peered at the window display.

"They're very expensive," Lynn said doubtfully.

"Not all of them," Stephen replied. "Look, there's a nice one on the tray at the back that's only a hundred and forty pounds, and that one there's a hundred and forty five."

"Stephen, that's far too much!"

"No, it's not. I've got about a hundred and sixty pounds in the bank. I'm sorry it's not more."

"Stevie, you can't spend all your money on a ring!"

"Watch me," he smiled, opening the door.

Lynn chose a Victorian rose diamond solitaire. Almost breathless with joy and excitement, Stephen slipped it on her finger. To their delight, it fitted perfectly. As he wrote a cheque, Lynn stared down at her ring. She hadn't thought it was possible to be so happy.

They wandered idly round the streets, hand in hand. The air was like wine, and Stephen felt intoxicated, drunk with bliss. He thought he'd never seen the old, mellow stones of the city look so beautiful, and Lynn shone like a jewel in the perfect setting. They stood on Lendal Bridge, staring at the chilly water. The pale lemon sun, which had been struggling to break through the overcast sky all day, had finally given up the ghost, and was dissolving in a glow of iced apricot on the horizon. The sullen clouds had taken on a threatening sulphurous hue, and it was very cold.

"'*All will be well, and every kind of thing will be well*'," Lynn murmured.

Stephen looked at her. "What did you say?"

She smiled at him. "It's something we did at school; Dame Julian of Norwich."

"I think I've heard of her."

"She had visions, and she wrote a book called *Revelations of Divine Love*. That '*All will be well*' is in it." She shrugged. "I feel – well, as if I know how she felt."

Stephen put his arm round her, moved. She leant over and kissed him. "Come on, let's go and show your family my ring!"

They started home. Above them a single, frosty star, white as bone, broke through the gloom, and there was a flurry of snowflakes.

Lynn gulped. "If this day gets any more perfect, I'm going to experience a sensory overload!"

Stephen burst out laughing. "Romance is lost on you!" He banged on the door of the house. "Let us in," he shouted through the letterbox. "We're freezing!"

John opened the door. "Where have you been?"

"Didn't she tell you? Mum turned us out."

"That was hours ago," Sian shouted from the kitchen. "We've been getting worried."

"Well, worry no more. Is everybody in? The girls?"

"Yes, upstairs," Sian answered. "Why?"

"We've got an announcement to make. Come on, Cherry, into the kitchen. I'm starting as I mean to go on."

"Suicide, ordering me into the kitchen with my track record!" Lynn laughed.

"Sisters! Get down here!" Stephen shouted as they went through the hall.

The girls came running down. "What's going on?" Rebecca asked.

"In here, in here. OK, everyone, I want you to meet..." He held up Lynn's left hand. "My fiancée!"

Pandemonium in the Markham kitchen.

"What time train are we catching to your Mum's, Cherry?"

Lynn jumped. She was lying on the bed, reading, and Stephen had come upstairs from the sitting room where he'd been watching *Goldfinger* with John.

"Er, not sure now," she said nonchalantly.

He looked at her, puzzled. "What do you mean? I thought you said you were going to ring the station."

She reluctantly put her book down. "I did, but then I thought maybe we wouldn't go. I don't really get on that well with them, Mum's so holy, and Dad and me… well, we've never had much to say to each other."

"Oh." Stephen was taken aback. "So what are you saying? That you don't want anything to do with your parents any more?"

"No, I'm just saying I don't want to go. After all, they weren't very nice when I told them we were engaged."

"I expect they were surprised, it was a bit sudden. Anyway, you can't just pick people up and put them down again when you feel like it, it's not fair."

"Well, you're a fine one to talk!" Lynn snapped. She didn't like being lectured like this.

He stared at her. "What's that supposed to mean?"

"You moved out of your house because you had a row with your Dad!"

"It was much more than a row, you know that. My father made it very clear that he didn't want me here if I wasn't prepared to conform to his wishes."

Lynn snorted.

Stephen was hurt. "Anyway, that's got nothing to do with this. Your parents invited us, we said yes, end of story."

"I don't see why it should upset *you*, they're my parents," she shot back. "We'll see them another time."

"No we won't," he said, beginning to get irritated by her attitude. "We're going now, when we were invited. You agreed to marry me, I'm going to be their son-in-law. I want to meet them and they're entitled to see the sort of man you're going to marry."

"For God's sake stop being so boring, Stephen! It's so much nicer here!"

"Lynn, they're expecting us the day after tomorrow! They'll have made arrangements. If you feel like this, you shouldn't have accepted in the first place. It's too late to cancel now."

She stood up. "I don't want to go, Stephen."

"Well you'll just have to suck it up. Go and ring them and tell them when we're arriving."

"Who the hell do you think you are? Don't you tell me what to do!"

He lost his temper. "If you weren't behaving like a spoilt brat, I wouldn't have to. Go and ring them now!"

She was shaken. She'd never seen Stephen like this. He looked implacable. She wanted to argue with him, ask him how dare he speak to her like that, but something in his eyes stopped her. They'd never had a real row, and on the odd occasions they'd disagreed, Stephen had always given in first. She'd congratulated herself on her ability to manage him, commenting smugly to her friends that you had to know how to handle men. She realised with dismay that she didn't know him half as well as she thought she did and at this moment, she had no idea how to handle him at all. She tossed her head, trying to look as if she'd changed her mind about going. "OK, OK. I don't know why you're making such a fuss!"

He followed her downstairs and pulled his jacket on. "I'm going to the Angel to see Rob." He didn't even say goodbye, let alone kiss her.

She rang her parents, and watched TV with Sian and John, waiting for him to come home and trying to behave as if nothing had happened.

When he got in, he didn't mention the row.

As they undressed for bed, she said, nervously, "I phoned Mum."

"Great," he said agreeably, getting into bed and picking up his book.

She climbed in next to him. "Stevie?"

"Hmmm?"

"I love you."

He smiled at her. "I love you too, Cherry." He threw the book on the floor and took her in his arms. "Let me show you all the bits I specially love..."

They went out for a drink with Harry and Julian the following evening. It was pretty obvious that Julian was deeply in love with Harry, and, although Harry always put up a good shop front however she was feeling, Stephen thought that she seemed genuinely fond of him. He was glad; Julian would take good care of her.

When they were in bed that night, he asked Lynn what she thought of Julian.

"Julian? He's nice."

"How do you think he feels about Harry?"

Lynn rolled over and punched the pillow into a more comfortable shape. "These pillows are horribly hard. I think he's in love with her. And he's very sweet with Rob."

"Hmmm."

She turned the bedside light on and looked at him. "Are you jealous?"

He stirred uncomfortably. "Not as who should say *jealous*."

"Good, because it wouldn't do you any good if you were. If Harry marries Julian, Rob will grow up calling him Daddy."

Stephen's blood ran cold. "No!"

"Of *course*, Stevie, what did you think? He'd be there all the time, you pop in when you feel like it."

"That's not fair!" Stephen was hurt. "I don't pop in when I feel like it. I would have married her but she wouldn't have me!"

"How hard did you try, Stephen? Did you woo her, for want of a better expression? Did you give her flowers, take her out, in short, be as irresistible as you can be when you want to? No. You said, 'Oh, you've spent nine months carrying this baby, who turns out to be someone I fathered in an irresponsible five minutes of lust, I'd better marry you. No? Are you sure? Oh, all right then'."

He sat up and stared at her, his face white. "It wasn't like that."

She sighed. "It was a bit though, wasn't it, Stevie? You would have married her if she'd said yes, but she kind of let you off the hook, didn't she?"

"I can't believe you *think* that!" He was very upset.

"I don't *blame* you. It's natural. And a lot of men wouldn't even offer. But let's be brutally honest, Stephen – can you really see yourself doing a nine to five job for the rest of your life? All you want to do is have a band, write and perform your music. I don't even know what you're doing at university. You say it's to fall back on, you could teach, but you won't. I think you'll make it anyway, but if you don't, you'll spend your life doing temporary jobs to support yourself while you concentrate on your music. You're a musician, Stephen. It's more important to you than anything or anyone. Harry knew that." She looked at him, an odd expression in her eyes. "So do I."

He got out of bed in distress. "How can you say that, Lynn? How can you say that? Don't you believe I love you?"

"Of course I do. I love you too, but that doesn't make me blind. I see you so clearly because I *do* love you. And it doesn't matter. I'm never going to stand in the way of your music – hey, in fact I'd be more than happy to support you when I graduate! I want you to have a band, Stevie, and I want you to get to the top. You've got *so much* talent. It would be a crime to waste it. How did we get on to this anyway?"

"I asked you about Julian."

"Oh yes. Come back to bed, you'll get cold. You've spent so much of your life trying to deny who you are because your father wanted you to be someone different. It's time you put that behind you. You're a musician, Stevie, a musician, and don't you ever let anyone tell you different! Stop apologising for it and start living your dream! And Rob will always be your son even if Harry does marry Julian. When he's old enough to understand, you and Harry will make sure he knows."

He got back into bed. She flinched away. "God, you're freezing!"

"Sorry. Do you think I ought to give up university then?"

"There you go again! It's not what *I* think, or what anyone else thinks! It's what *you* want! I don't want you to drop out, and I don't think Fin, George and Andy would want to drop out, so if you want them you'd have to wait anyway – what course *is* Andy taking? – but it's your choice."

He sighed. "Thanks, Cherry."

"What for? Lecturing you?"

"Yes, because you're completely right. Music is all I want to do. But I'm not going to drop out, because you're right about the others, I do want them for the band, I think we could be really good together." He lay and stared up at the ceiling. "Don't you think it's wrong though, to be wasting grant money and what have you, if I've no intention of doing anything with the degree?"

"For God's sake! If there's nothing to be guilty about, you'll manufacture it! Are you enjoying university?"

"Well, yes…"

"Then there's your answer. What's that bit in the American Constitution? Something about the pursuit of happiness. Most people spend their life pursuing it and never get it. Take it, Stevie, while you can. This isn't a rehearsal, it's all you get."

He pulled her close to him. "You are so amazing. I don't deserve you."

"That's true, that's so true. Just make sure you always remember it."

Next morning, Lynn woke early and couldn't get back to sleep. She lay in the dark for a while, listening to Stephen's regular breathing, and trying to work out why she felt so miserable about going home. She was going to be with him; surely, then, it didn't matter where they went, as long as they were together? She puzzled over it, and it dawned on her that, compared to Sian and John, her parents really had very little interest in her. Which was why she'd been so angry with Stephen for the way he'd goaded John that first weekend she'd spent at the house. John so obviously worshipped Stephen, whatever Stephen believed to the contrary, and she realised she'd been jealous. She got carefully out of bed and tiptoed downstairs to the kitchen to make a drink.

To her surprise, Sian was sitting at the table sipping tea and looking at a cookbook. She smiled at Lynn. "You're up early. Couldn't stand the snoring?"

Lynn smiled back. "He doesn't snore." She poured herself some tea.

Sian raised an eyebrow. "John always did. Mind you, he was twenty-nine when we married."

Lynn laughed "Something to look forward to!"

"So how come you're up so early?"

Lynn shrugged. "I don't know, because we were up till late last night, talking." She sighed.

"Everything all right?" Sian queried.

"I suppose so. We started talking about Julian. I pointed out to Steve that if Harry married him, Rob would probably grow up calling him Daddy."

Sian inhaled sharply. "You're right! I hadn't thought of that. Poor Stevie!"

Lynn stared at her. "But… well, Sian, you know how much I love him, and I'd hate to see him hurt, but I don't see how he could expect anything else. I mean, it was really bad luck, especially as Harry was on the pill, but you know… five minutes of lust! Harry's entitled to her life. It's much worse for her than for Stephen."

She was amazed to see tears in Sian's eyes. "Sian? I'm sorry, I didn't mean to upset you!"

Sian gave her a tight smile. "It's not you, love." She took a deep breath. "Lynn, I'm going to tell you something that you must never tell anyone, especially not Stevie or Ted." She looked at Lynn expectantly.

"I promise," Lynn said, bemused.

"Harry wasn't on the pill. She'd been in love with Stevie for a long time and she hoped she might get pregnant. She knew it was unlikely, just the once, but she tricked Steve. And Rob wasn't premature. Harry knew her baby was his."

Lynn stared at her, appalled. "But you can't do that! You can't make a decision like that! It's not fair, it's not right, not to Stevie *or* Rob!"

"I'm so glad you said that, Lynnie! I thought maybe it was just my generation who thought like that."

"Not at all! Not at *all*! I can't *believe* she would take advantage of Stevie like that! At least she had the decency not to marry him!" A thought struck her. "And she called him Robert too! It's Stevie's favourite name! If we have a son, he won't be able to call him Rob. That's so unfair!" She felt terrible about what she'd said to Stephen the night before.

"Yes," Sian said, "it is. But you see why we can't tell anyone. There's no point in upsetting Stevie. It's done now and nothing can change it. And you know how he loves that baby!" She sighed. "Perhaps I shouldn't have told you, but if Harry were to marry Julian – or anyone – while Rob is so small, Steve will need a lot of support."

"Yes, I do see. I suppose the only thing is, Harry loves him so much. She wouldn't do anything to hurt him."

"For now," Sian said darkly. "People can fall out of love, Lynn."

"How could anyone stop loving Stevie?"

Sian smiled at her. "Well, that's true!"

"Does John know?"

Sian shook her head. "I nearly told him. In some ways I'd like to, because I know he thinks as you did, that Harry is nobly bearing the brunt of all this, but on the other hand, with his angina… well, I didn't want to risk him getting upset. I'm glad I told you, Cherry! And I'm very glad Stevie has got you. I'm going to miss you so much when you go to your parents."

Lynn was very moved. "I really don't want to go," she said in a rush. "If it was up to me we wouldn't bother, but Stephen got incredibly cross with me, and made me say we would. Goodness, you can't *think* how angry he was! I've never seen him angry before, I didn't even really realise he had a temper."

Sian laughed. "Oh, yes! He doesn't lose it very often, but when he feels strongly about something, all hell breaks loose! He's not petty though, and he never holds a grudge. It always reminds me of summer lightning – sudden, spectacular, and then over." She put her hand on Lynn's. "I'm sorry you're going, but I have to say, I do agree with Stevie that you ought to. After all, if he told me he was engaged, I'd want to see the girl who was going to be my daughter-in-law."

"That's more or less what he said. I suppose you're both right. It's just… well, I'd rather stay here with you. You're so much more of a mother than mine."

Sian was touched. "You never know, now that you've left home, she might start seeing you in a different light. Especially now you're engaged. How did she take the news?"

"She said, 'Is he Catholic?'"

"Oh."

"Exactly."

The door opened and John came in. "Hello, you two! Am I interrupting?"

"Course not!" Sian poured him a cup of tea. "I was just telling Cherry how much we're going to miss her."

John smiled at Lynn. "We certainly are! It's a good job it's not long till Easter!"

"They may spend Easter with Lynn's parents, John," Sian warned.

"No, my mother usually goes into retreat at Easter."

"Oh." Sian was taken aback. "Well, you may want to see friends or something – don't feel you have to come here."

"I love coming here," Lynn smiled.

"And your course?" John asked. "Stephen was saying you've got a tremendous amount of work."

"Yes, it's tough, I didn't realise it was so hard. I'm loving it though."

"And Stephen?" John said, casually. "How's his work going?"

Sian and Lynn exchanged glances. "Very well," Lynn said truthfully. "He's getting very good marks. And he told me last night he's enjoying it."

John smiled, relieved. "That's good news."

Sian stood up. "Well, I'm going to get dressed, and then I'll start breakfast." She smiled at Lynn. "You better get that fiancé of yours up, you've got a train to catch!"

Bill and Theresa Jackson were waiting at Southampton station.

They ran a guesthouse in the New Forest, imaginatively named Forest Lodge. Bill was a balding man, running to fat, who looked as if he'd done his best to beat the odds but never quite managed it. He gave off an aura of defeat. Theresa, on the other hand had a strangely martial air about her. Stephen couldn't see how they could possibly have produced Lynn.

"You're not adopted are you?" he whispered as they sat in the back of the car on their way to the guesthouse.

She frowned at him. "Shh!"

He'd never been to the New Forest before, despite spending all those summers on the Isle of Wight, and he was enchanted with it. "It must be so beautiful in the spring and summer!"

"Yes it is, and in the autumn," Lynn replied.

"Pretty awful this time of year," Bill said gloomily.

"Take no notice of him, Stephen," Theresa ordered. "The glory of God is evident all year round. Isn't that so, Lynn?"

Lynn sighed wearily. "Course, Mum."

They drove into the guesthouse car park.

"You're in your old room, Lynn. We've only got one guest staying at present, so I've put Stephen in the Wisteria Room," Theresa said as they went in to the house. "You'll want to unpack, so we'll see you at supper." She swept off down a corridor. Bill gave them an apologetic smile and followed her.

"Blast! The Wisteria Room is miles from mine. I hoped she'd put you in the Rose Room."

"Can't we swap?" Stephen picked up their luggage.

"Yes! Yes, we can!"

Stephen followed her up winding staircases and down narrow passages until he was completely disorientated. "Are we nearly there yet?"

For answer, Lynn opened a door. "The Rose Room."

He put their cases down and looked round. It was a pretty little room, all pink chintz, and the wallpaper had big, very pale golden roses on it. "These roses are the same colour as your hair. Where's your room?"

"Just down the corridor. Come on." She took his hand.

He started to sing 'Stranger In Paradise'.

"That's not quite how I'd describe it, Hammer House of Horror, more like," Lynn said darkly, opening the door to her room. "I can't believe you made us come here, thank God it's only for a few days."

Stephen was thinking the same thing, but he said, "You know it was the right thing to do, Lynn. This is a nice room!" He walked to the window. "What a stunning view!"

"Don't change the subject. They haven't even congratulated us on being engaged."

"Perhaps they're just shy," he suggested, which sent her into fits of laughter. "What time are we expected for supper?" he asked.

"Not for hours yet!" Lynn snorted. "Mum'll be communing away with God. I hope you're not hungry."

"Time for a little war work then, I think." He rubbed his hands together.

"I wish we could share the same room here," Lynn sighed as they lay in bed.

"Me too!" Stephen kissed her shoulder. "Let's get married soon."

"As soon as you like," she smiled, turning towards him.

"It'll take ages to arrange," he said, thinking glumly of Harry's wedding.

"Why? We go to the Register Office, book it, and get married."

He stared at her. "Don't you want… you know… a long white frock and bridesmaids and all that stuff?"

She shuddered. "God, no! Mum would go mental if we didn't get married in a Catholic church and I'm never doing that!"

"Well, she won't like a Register Office! As far as she's concerned you won't be legally married."

"Then let's not invite them."

"We can't do that!" he said in shocked tones.

"Yes, we can. You've seen what they're like, they live in a little world of their own! You shouted at me and made me cry and so we came, but admit it, I was right."

"I didn't make you cry!"

"Yes, you did. After you'd gone to the Angel, I cried."

"Oh, Cherry, I'm sorry! I'm a bad-tempered git!"

"Oh well, sufficient unto the day." She kissed him. "I forgive you. And Sian said the same as you anyway, that they ought to meet you. But really, really Stevie, let's not have them at our wedding."

"I can't not have my family," he said slowly.

"I never thought you wouldn't. As long as no one ever tells my family, it doesn't matter. You'll have to explain that to Sian, Stevie."

"Oh, thanks very much!"

"Well, she is your Mum."

On a seriously cold morning in January, Stephen was sitting in the university library doing research for an essay on a comparative study of Boccaccio's *Decameron* and

Chaucer's *Canterbury Tales*. He was so absorbed that he didn't see a tall, blond boy approach him.

"Steve Markham?"

"Hmm?" he answered vaguely.

The boy leaned over and shut his books.

"Hey!"

"My name's Dominic Chaplin."

"I don't care if it's *Charlie* Chaplin! I'm working!"

"Fuck that, old chap." Dominic had a cut-glass accent. "I want to talk about something important." He sat down at the table. "I play guitar. Extremely well. I'm between bands at the moment and you don't have a rhythm guitar. I can help you out."

Stephen began to grin. "What's in it for you, Charlie?"

Dominic grinned back. "Playing with a good band. I heard you at the Grosvenor Bar last term and I've been asking around. You write good stuff and you play well."

"What do you mean, you're between bands?"

"I had a band, now I don't."

"What happened to it?"

"Creative differences. I wanted to create, they didn't. I told them to fuck off in the end, the constant hassle of trying to get the fuckers to rehearse was getting me down, frankly, old chap. To be honest, it'd be a welcome change not to have to make the decisions for a while."

"OK. How long is a while?"

"Six months. I graduate in July, and then I'll be off to London, to fame and fortune. You won't see my arse for dust."

Stephen shrugged. "I suppose I could audition you."

"*Audition* me? Audition *me*? Listen, Markham, you're not going to get a better fucking offer than this all fucking century, old chap!"

"Do you have to be quite so foul-mouthed?"

"Does it offend your middle-class sensibilities?"

"I suppose you can't help it," Stephen shrugged. "All that inbreeding you Hooray Henrys indulge in must tend to dull the wits. All right. We're rehearsing tonight. Come round to my room at half past six and we'll go together. I'm in Grosvenor, GE 6. Now fuck off, Charlie, old chap, and let me get on with this."

Stephen had finished in the library by lunchtime, and was working on his essay when Lynn got back from her lectures. "God, Stevie, it's freezing out there!" He put his pen down. "Come here, I'll warm you up!" They ended up in bed. Stephen had meant to get up earlier, but they'd both gone to sleep. They were woken by a knock on the door.

"Come in, Fin," Stephen shouted.

"It's not a fin, it's me," said Dominic, walking in. "Hello," he said to Lynn. He gave her a charming smile, and sat at Stephen's desk.

"What are you doing here?" Stephen asked, annoyed. "I said six-thirty."

"Nothing else to do, old chap. Unlike you. Aren't you going to introduce me?"

"Pass me my robe. Cherilynn Jackson, Charlie Chaplin. Charlie Chaplin, Cherilynn Jackson."

"Dominic." He extended a well-manicured hand.

"Stephen told me about you."

"He kept you a secret," Dominic replied. "Not that I blame him." He noticed her ring. "You're engaged!"

She smiled and nodded.

"Does your fiancé know you're here?"

"*I'm* her fiancé, you tosser," Stephen said. He pulled his underpants and jeans on and reached over for a tee shirt.

"Surely a girl like you could do better for yourself than a little runt like him? Me, for instance. Heir to tracts of Northumberland, an historic old pile, and my mother's the daughter of an Earl."

"Really?" Lynn wasn't sure she believed him.

"Absolutely."

"I'll take little Lord Fauntleroy to meet Fin while you get dressed, Cherry," Stephen said.

"Oh, you go, Markham. I'll stay here and chat to Cherry while she dresses."

"No you bloody well won't!" Stephen grabbed him by the collar. "Out, Charlie boy."

He played extremely well. He reminded Stephen of Harry in that he seemed to have that extra something, that intuitive feel for the music. They went to the Tappit Hen afterwards and Fin explained how the band had got its name. "That very table," he said, pointing. "We've never seen anyone sitting there."

Dominic kept staring at Andy. Eventually he asked, "What course are you on?"

"Me? I'm not at the university! All I've got is a C.S.E. in woodwork, me." The others stared at him. "No, I work in Collin's the fishmongers in Rusholme, like."

"Fuck me, I thought it was you!" Dominic said. "I get my kippers from you."

"If you're not at university, how come you knew about the audition?" Stephen asked, puzzled. "I only put the notice up in the Union."

"I go in there all the time, it's a great place to pick up birds. I tell them I'm studying marine biology."

"Does it work?"

"Like a charm," Andy grinned.

Stephen wanted to get married on Valentine's Day, but Lynn wasn't so keen.

"It'd be so romantic, Cherry!"

"Yeah, but… oh, this sounds horrible and not in the least romantic, but I can't help being practical, it's just me!" She looked at him apologetically.

"What?"

"Well, suppose we split up?"

"Cherry!"

"Or even if we don't, when one of us dies, it'll be even sadder for the one left. My dad's parents were married on Christmas Eve and when Grandfer died, Nan found that day really hard to get through… you know, it being so special and everyone being merry and what have you."

Stephen considered this. "I suppose you're right. OK, but let's make it soon."

"First of April?"

He gave her a stern look. "You're not taking this seriously, are you?"

They settled on Saturday the fourteenth of March at ten o'clock.

"I think we should go home this weekend and explain to my mum about your parents," Stephen said.

Lynn noted that he didn't include his father in this conversation. "OK. Let's make a list of who we want to invite."

"I hope Ray can be my best man."

"You'll have to write his speech for him then," Lynn warned, "otherwise he'll manage to offend at least half the guests in his opening sentence!"

Sian was a great deal more difficult about the wedding than Stephen had anticipated. "I don't see how you can even contemplate getting married without your parents being there, Lynn."

"I agree, Sian," John nodded.

"It just wouldn't work," Lynn sighed.

"She's right," Stephen put in. "I've met them."

"And, what's more," Sian went on, as if neither of them had spoken, "you're asking us to lie about it."

"I agree, Sian." John nodded again.

What are you, a fucking parrot? Stephen thought, starting to get irritated.

"We're not asking you to lie, Sian, simply to say nothing," Lynn was explaining. "If they ask you are we married, then obviously you'd say yes, but why would they?"

"And if they do ask us, we'd have to tell them that we knew of and condoned your decision," John said.

"Yes, but…" Lynn looked appealingly at Stephen.

"Look, the bottom line here is that we're not telling them and we're not inviting them," Stephen said, suddenly very tough. He'd had enough of John. "If you two don't feel you can come because of that, fair enough. But we're getting married on the fourteenth of March, and what you do is up to you."

"Don't you speak to us like that, Stephen!" John said sharply.

Lynn looked at him, alarmed. She'd never heard him use that tone of voice before. The anger in Stephen's eyes alarmed her even more. Sian had gone pale.

"Or what, Dad?" Stephen demanded aggressively. "It may have escaped your notice, but I no longer live at home, so you can't chuck me out." Who the hell did John think he was? He was sick of him, he was a useless husband and a worse father. What a pity we can't just have Mum to the wedding, he thought angrily, although even she's pissing me off at the moment.

He got to his feet. "I appreciate we're your guests, but we won't trespass on your hospitality any longer. Come on, Lynn."

Sian stood up, her face white with anger. "Don't you *dare* walk out, Stephen Markham. You came here and you'll listen to our opinion. We think it's a despicable thing to do, not to even inform Lynn's parents, but as you point out, neither of you live at home any more, you're adults, what you do is up to you. Your father and I haven't yet decided whether we wish to attend this wedding. When we have, we'll let you know."

"Oh, yes?" Stephen said, his voice ultra polite. "Well, we haven't yet decided whether we wish to *invite* you to this wedding. When we have, we'll let you know." They stared at each other across the table.

Lynn burst into tears. "Stop it, both of you! I don't want to get married if it's going to cause all this trouble!"

"Cherry! Don't cry, cariad, don't cry!" Stephen took her in his arms. "We should've just eloped," he muttered bitterly.

"Stephen! Stop saying stuff!"

Sian and John were fussing round her. "I'm sorry, Stevie," Sian said. "I hate deceit."

"No, I'm sorry, Mum. I lost my temper."

"Of course we'll come to your wedding," Sian said. "We wouldn't miss it for the world. We've told you what we think; we'll say no more about it. I'll make us another cup of tea."

"How are you going to pay for it all?" John asked.

"It's not going to be fancy. George is letting us hold the reception at his place and he, Fin and Andy are buying the booze as a wedding present. The food'll be homemade – sandwiches and what have you."

"The girls on my corridor are all making something," Lynn said.

"What about a cake?" Sian asked.

"We went into Hagenbachs, they'll ice a sponge cake for us."

"Oh, I think Kathy and I can do better than that." Sian started to laugh. "It's like a wedding during the war! Do you remember, John? At least the cake won't be cardboard!"

On the way back to Manchester, Stephen and Lynn discussed whether they should invite Dominic.

"He's in the band, so we really ought. He's just…" Stephen searched for a word to describe Dominic, couldn't find one, and finished up rather lamely with "…different."

"Yes, but he's funny. And ever so good looking."

"And that's a recommendation how?" Stephen wanted to know.

"Well, it'll be nice for my friends," Lynn said innocently.

He regarded her with narrowed eyes. "Listen, woman, you're marrying me in just over a month. I don't like this interest in other men!"

"No, master. But are we inviting Charlie?"

"Yes."

Dominic seemed genuinely touched to be invited.

"It's not going to be posh. Far from it," warned Stephen.

"Don't worry about it. We aristos have to rub shoulders with the fucking hoi polloi from time to time, noblesse oblige and all that. Where are you going for your honeymoon?"

Stephen shrugged. "Haven't even thought about it. Here, I expect, we're pretty skint. I don't think Cherry cares as long as we're together. I know I don't."

Very briefly, Dominic's face lost its look of world-weary cynicism. "I really envy you," he said sincerely. The mask descended again, and he punched Stephen on the shoulder. "The rest of your life with a woman as gorgeous as Cherry, and me in your band. You're a lucky little fucker, Markham."

The next day he called round to Stephen's room. "Cherry about?"

Stephen looked at his watch. "I'm expecting her any time, she wants to look for a hat for the wedding."

Dominic raised his eyebrows. "Sooner you than me, old chap."

"What do you want her for, Charlie?"

"I want you both," but he refused to say more.

Lynn came bursting in a few minutes later. "I think it's going to rain!" she wailed. "Oh, hello, Charlie."

"God damn it, I have a perfectly good name, you know!"

"Yeah – Charlie," Stephen grinned.

Dominic sighed. "I came here full of kindness and cheer, and like Scrooge's nephew, I'll keep my good humour to the last. Here!" With a flourish, he produced an envelope and gave it to Lynn.

Puzzled, she tore it open, and drew out two train tickets, first class, Manchester to Morpeth for the fourteenth of March, with an open return date.

"Someone will meet you at the station and drive you to Fenroth. It's my parents' house. There's a guest cottage on the estate, I thought you might like to honeymoon there. It's not a bad little place. Stay as long as you like."

They stared at him.

"God," Stephen said, moved. "You really shouldn't have!"

"Can't think why I did," he shrugged. "Not my style at all."

Lynn threw her arms round him and kissed him.

"Oh, yes," he grinned, hugging her. "Now I remember why I did it. Plus, seeing as you'll be staying on the estate that will someday be mine, I claim *droit de seigneur*."

The night before the wedding, Stephen moved into George's house. He awoke the next morning to a churning stomach. He thought he was hungry, but after eating several slices of toast and jam, he realised it was nerves. How could he possibly be nervous? It was Lynn, the woman he loved, the other half of him. It didn't make any difference. He was nervous. He bathed, shaved and dressed with cold, shaky fingers.

"God, Markham, you look as if you're going to a funeral," Ray commented when he saw him.

"Fuck you, Raymond!"

George looked round the door. "Howay, bonny lad, get a move on, or we'll be late. That's the bride's prerogative."

He'd gone to the trouble of cleaning out his van in honour of the day. The ashtray had been emptied and all the old Newcastle Brown tins and bottles had gone, along with the fish and chip papers and pizza boxes, but afterwards, Stephen couldn't remember the journey into Manchester, or going into the Register Office on Jackson's Row. He remembered Ray exclaiming how apt the name of the street was and realised he and Lynn had never noticed it was the same as her surname. It won't be after today, he thought. It was the most amazing feeling. This incredible girl wanted to marry *him*.

The anteroom was filling up with guests. He saw his family: John, very distinguished and formidable, Sian elegant in a soft yellow suit, the girls looking extremely pretty. Rebecca waved to him and he managed to smile back. Harry, holding Rob who was squirming impatiently, was standing with Ted and Julian, looking happy and sad at the same time.

His heart leapt. Lynn was there! She looked stunning. He hadn't seen the outfit she'd chosen until now, but it was perfect – a fitted cream silk dress, with a delicate coffee-coloured pattern. It matched her hat, which was small, with a feather that curled around the side of her face and under her chin, and a veil that came down over her nose. He heard someone breathe in sharply and realised it was him.

"For God's sake, don't start crying," Ray muttered.

The Registrar appeared and invited them all in.

Lynn smiled at Stephen, and his nerves melted away. He reached out and took her hand.

"You're a lucky bastard, Stevie boy!" Fin raised his can of lager in a mock salute. "Out of the two best looking girls at this reception, one of them's your wife and the other's the mother of your son!"

"Don't you wish you were me?" Stephen grinned. He lowered his voice. "But I wouldn't let Roisin hear you say that, Fin. Where is she anyway?"

Fin's mouth turned down at the corners. "She's gone. She said goodbye to Lynn, I don't know where you were. I don't think there's a lot of mileage left in that relationship."

"I'm sorry."

"I'm not. It was getting a bit grim. Sometimes you just have to cut yourself loose. Anyway, there's this little stunner I met at the Union the other day—"

"Stop!" Stephen laughed. "I don't want to hear any more!"

Lynn came over and took his hand. "It's time to cut the cake and Ray's going to make his speech. You checked it over with him, didn't you?"

"Yes, Mrs Markham." He hugged her, elated by the fact that she was his wife. "Don't you worry."

Ray picked up a pint glass and banged a fork against it. "Ladies and gentlemen, as Stephen's best man, I just want to say a few words." He patted his pockets. "I actually had a speech prepared but I seem to have lost it. Oh, well, never mind, I'm sure I can keep you all entertained with some anecdotes about Steve. Like the time…" His eyes rested on Stephen's anguished face. He grinned. "Just kidding, Steve!" He pulled a piece of paper out of his pocket and flourished it, clearing his throat. "Sort out ring, take clean underwear…" His voice trailed off. "Wait a minute, this isn't it. Damn! I *have* lost it!"

Stephen groaned.

Ted got up. "Sit down, Ray. Ladies and Gentlemen, please charge your glasses and let's toast the bride and groom. May they always be as happy as they are today. Steve and Lynn!"

Stephen stood up. "We'd like to say thank you to everyone, it's been fantastic. I can't believe I'm so lucky." He raised his glass. "To good friends!"

"This is the most relaxed wedding I've ever been to," Sian smiled, as slices of cake were passed round. "It's magic!"

Stephen hugged her. "Thanks, Mum." He raised his voice. "Hey, everyone! Charlie's given us a honeymoon in Northumberland; thanks again, Charlie! Charlie? Where is he?"

Dominic's head appeared from the sofa. Lynn's friend Caro was sitting on his lap. She was a big girl and it wasn't possible to see much of him. He waved at them, grinning.

"So we've got a train to catch," Stephen continued. "Thank you all for coming, and for the presents. If Ray and George weren't here, I'd probably be crying by now, so it's definitely time for us to go." He saw George and Ray nod at each other.

"Give Daddy a kiss," Harry told Rob, handing him to Stephen.

"Bye bye, Robbie. I'll see you soon." Stephen kissed Rob on the head, handed him to Sian, and took Harry in his arms. She clung to him like a limpet, her face pressed into his shoulder. Over her head, he saw the look on Julian's face. He gently disengaged himself.

Harry blinked back tears.

"I'll see you soon too, Hal." He was shaken by the look on her face. He had so much wanted to believe she wasn't in love with him; the thought that he was hurting her was very painful indeed.

Everyone crowded out onto the pavement to see them off and throw confetti, waving as the taxi drove away.

Lynn turned to Stephen. "I can't believe we're married!"

"I can't believe Ray lost his speech!"

Stephen had thought a great deal about the conversation he'd had with Lynn. He had spent his life trying to live up to John's expectations, and had never questioned them, only his fitness to achieve his father's goals. He was so used to thinking of himself as a failure that it was difficult to reverse this mindset and start putting music first. It was peculiar not to have to apologise for spending his time playing guitar, writing songs and singing. He began to concentrate on his course less and the band more.

He found that he was starting to like Dominic very much. They had a similar sense of humour, and it seemed to Stephen that the other boy's arrogance, flippant manner and cynicism were a kind of protective shell, which he lost when he felt at ease. He wrote too, and Stephen had been impressed enough for the band to perform some of his songs.

They spent a lot of time rehearsing, and Stephen got them a gig at the Highland Fling.

"That's brilliant, Steve!" Fin was very enthusiastic. "If we play at places other than student bars we can really start to get known!"

"It's what you need to do," Dominic agreed, "create a buzz, and get people talking about you."

"You wouldn't consider staying on with us after you graduate, Charlie?" Stephen asked hopefully.

"Tempting, fucking tempting, old chap," Dominic drawled, downing his pint. "But rhythm guitar in someone else's band isn't really my scene. I want *my* band, playing *my* music." He looked at his watch. "Anyway, I've got a date with a hot little nympho at Owens Park and I don't want to keep her waiting." He stood up. "I tell you what though, Markham, you keep practising, and when my band's world famous, I might just let you play rhythm in it."

Lynn wanted to stay in Manchester over the Easter holidays; her workload was very heavy and she needed to be able to use the library. That suited Stephen. The rest of the band was also staying on, and it meant they could really work on their act and get some more gigs.

He and Lynn spent a couple of days after Easter with Sian and John. Ray was also home. He'd recently split up with his girlfriend and wasn't his usual ebullient self. To cheer him up, Stephen and Lynn borrowed Sian's car with the intention of taking him, Harry and Rob to Helmsley for the day, to a National Trust property, a big old house reputed to be haunted, set in beautiful gardens.

Harry had made other plans but had no objection to them taking Rob. She handed Stephen a large bag. "OK, all his stuff is in here. There's nappies, wipes, cream, a changing mat, plenty of bibs – you'll definitely need those, you know what a messy eater he is, what else?" She rummaged through the bag. "Oh, yes, his blanket, he'll want that when he gets tired, then there's juice and a change of clothes. Don't let him sit on the grass if it's damp, will you? Or eat anything he finds on the ground?"

"Don't worry, Harry, I know what to do."

"You've never actually taken him out anywhere on your own though, have you?"

"No, but I've got Lynn and Ra— I've got Lynn to help, haven't I?"

"Hmm." Harry was unsure.

"Seriously, Hal. You know I'll look after him." He strapped Rob carefully into his car seat. "You have a lovely day, you deserve a bit of time on your own." He felt bad about Harry, especially as she'd recently stopped seeing Julian. He knew she'd taken his marriage hard, and though no one had said anything, he felt that it had something to do with her and Julian splitting up.

Harry sighed. "OK." She kissed the baby and he squirmed away. She watched anxiously as they drove off.

It was a warm day and Nunnington Hall was crowded. Stephen carried Rob in a baby sling and the pretty little boy attracted quite a bit of attention, especially from younger women who thought that Stephen was cute too, and even more so with the baby cuddled against his chest.

"Let me have a go with that," Ray demanded. "I don't see why you should get all the attention."

"He's not a *toy*!" Stephen said, half-exasperated, half-amused. "I feel sorry for any children you might have, Raymond."

Stephen loved having Rob with him. He couldn't think of a better way to spend the day than with his wife and son. They went into the gardens, and he put Rob down on the grass and let him crawl around.

"It won't be long until he's walking," Lynn said, as he held on to Stephen and tried to pull himself up.

Stephen smiled at him. "He's a clever boy, aren't you, Robbie?"

The baby gave him a gummy grin.

Stephen leant over and kissed Lynn. "People think he's ours, you know." She nodded. "I'm really looking forward to that," he went on. "*Our* babies, and we won't have to give them back at the end of the day, either!"

"When we can afford it. That won't be for a while yet."

He put his arm around her. "I know. And by then you'll be an eminent speech therapist." A thought struck him. He knew how serious she was about her career. "You do want children, don't you?"

"Of course! I mean, I want a career, and I'd like to work for a while first, but I do want our babies. Although, don't you want the whole penthouse in London, parties every night, rock and roll lifestyle?" she asked anxiously. "I don't want you to miss out because of me."

"God no, where's the fun in that? I don't know, maybe if I hadn't got you." He squeezed her against him. "Even so, I think that sort of existence would pall very quickly. I suppose we'll have to live in London for a while, but I don't really like city life. No, what I want is to make music and live happily ever after with you and our children in a lovely big house in the countryside. And as much of Rob as we can have."

"It sounds blissful," she laughed, kissing him. "And I'd love a house here in North Yorkshire. Although I don't really care where we live or how rich we are as long as we've got each other."

"Oh, we'll always have each other," he promised.

In the summer, they searched for accommodation for the following year and eventually found a small, furnished flat in Rusholme. It was a cut above the usual student places, all the other tenants had jobs in the city. A BBC reporter lived in the flat below them.

Their flat was on the top floor in what had been attic space, and had big skylight windows. The sitting room overlooked Birchfields Park, and on a hot summer's day, with the windows opened wide, it was like living in a tree house. Their favourite time was the evenings, when they'd curl up together on the tiny sofa, watching TV, listening to music or studying.

Sometimes, when Stephen played the guitar, Lynn would play her flute. He delighted in hearing the sound they made weaving around them. He tried to persuade her to play in the band. "Come on, Cherry, it'd be brilliant! And I'd love to write for the flute."

She wouldn't hear of it. "I'm nowhere near good enough!" she exclaimed. "I just love playing, I feel like I'm flying when I play, like I'm as free and light as the air."

"Well, there you are then." He knew just what she meant. Playing made him feel like that too. As if he *was* the music as it soared around them, multi-coloured.

"But I'd never be able to play if people were watching!"

"*I'm* watching," he said fondly. She was so self-deprecating, he thought. She was amazingly talented, but she didn't see it at all.

"That doesn't count," she smiled. "You're the other half of me, Stevie. You're my life. I meant an audience. I just like playing here, with you."

She took a job in a nursery and crèche for the summer. Stephen was working at their local Kwiksave, but only for a month, as Ray had got him a job in Selby, cleaning out the boiler house in one of the mines. Ray had done it the summer before; it was a hellish job, he said, but the pay was six hundred pounds for two weeks.

"God, I'm going to miss you!" Stephen said. He was going to be living with Sian and John while he was working.

"I'll miss you too. Thank God it's only two weeks! At least I'll be busy during the week – and you'll be home at the weekends."

"Home!" he said, looking round. "It's so lovely having our very own home!"

"I know. We're so lucky."

By the following summer, Sid's Six was making a name for itself in the city. The band was in demand, and Stephen decided not to take the boiler cleaning job in Selby again. Instead he got a job as a delivery driver, which paid reasonably well; and as the hours were seven until two, he had the afternoons free for rehearsals.

He heard from Dominic on a fairly regular basis, which pleased and surprised him. He'd got the impression, from Dominic's manner, that he considered his time with Sid's Six to be nothing more than a bit of fun, and that once he'd gone to London, that would be the last they'd see of him. He was glad that Dominic thought of him as a friend; he'd grown to like the other boy very much, and had always considered his off-hand, arrogant attitude, which so irritated the other three – particularly George – to be a form of defence, and ignored it. It felt good to be vindicated. Stephen also missed Dominic's input into the band; he played well and had been fun to work with. He had a competitive edge, which had sparked a response in Stephen. In the long-term, this might have degenerated into friction, but for the time Dominic was with them it had been exhilarating, and they'd both benefited from it.

Dominic had now put together a band, which he'd called GI Joe. Stephen suggested he rename it GI Tract. "It's more you somehow, Charlie."

Dominic made a predictably obscene reply.

GI Joe had an album out, 'Class Act'. That was Charlie, all right, Stephen thought affectionately. A class act.

"Cherry! Where are you?" Stephen burst into the flat.

Lynn came out of the kitchen. "Where's the fire?"

"Guess what?"

"You've been kicked off your course for non-attendance?"

It was the beginning of the autumn term in their final year and Stephen was putting all his effort into the band, attending very few lectures and doing the minimum amount of work that he could get away with.

"Sid's Six has got a gig at Utopia!"

"Oh, wow!" Lynn hugged him. "Have you told the others?"

"Yeah, I rang on the way home. Let's go to bed and celebrate!"

Utopia was a club that had opened in Manchester at the end of June, and had quickly became a hot-spot for clubbers from all over the area. More importantly, it put on live concerts featuring up-and-coming new bands. Getting a gig at Utopia was the aim of every band in the city. Inside, the décor was Mad Max meets Blade Runner – stark, post-apocalyptic, and entirely unlike anywhere else. Upstairs, the Geisha Bar included sushi and sake and other Japanese delicacies, along with the usual fare.

The club was the brainchild of Nathan Wilde, the DJ, and Taro Watanabe, a former Japanese Idol singer.

"What's an idle singer?" Andy had wanted to know when the club first opened.

"Kind of like David Cassidy – you know, young, good-looking pop singers that girls fancy. Or boys fancy them if they're female singers. They make pots of money, but by the time they're about twenty-five they're over the hill and have to do something else." Stephen had scoured the papers for information about the place.

"Do they sit down to sing or something, then?" Andy asked.

Stephen stared at him. "What are you on about?"

"Well, why are they called idle?"

Stephen rolled his eyes. "Forget it, Andy!"

"So when's the gig?" Lynn asked as they lay entwined.

"Next Friday. This is really big for us, Cherry!"

"I know." She hesitated. "I wish I could be there!"

His face fell. "Can't you?

"You know I can't, Stevie, I've been working flat out all summer, and you know how much work I've got already this term!" Along with her lectures, she had placements in schools, hospitals, clinics and nurseries. "I'm sorry." She kissed him. "But this'll just be the first of many, you know it will! You'll get sick of me tagging along, cramping your style with the groupies!"

He shook his head. "That'll never happen. God, I wish you could come."

"Well, I can't, so it's no good wishing. Don't sulk, Stephen."

Sid's Six rehearsed like demons before the gig.

"We're not nervous are we?" Stephen said, when the others picked him up on the Friday night. Fin and Andy had moved into George's house at the end of the first year.

"Howay, man, are we likely for to be nervous?" George scoffed.

"Why does Andy look so green then?"

"Something I ate," Andy muttered.

"Where's Lynn?" Fin asked, surprised, as Stephen got into the van.

"She can't come. She's got loads of work to do."

Fin glanced at George. "Oh, well," he said heartily, but couldn't think of anything to follow it up with. He lapsed into silence.

Stephen was upset that Lynn hadn't come. He knew she was right; she loved her course, she wanted to do well, and she always had a huge amount of work. He had no right to resent her not coming, but it made no difference. He felt hurt, rejected and angry.

There were lots of girls in the audience – the band had a big female following – but he noticed this one as soon as they started playing. She was standing near the front of the crowd and she was very attractive in a slutty way. She was heavily made up and wearing a vest top, a very short ra-ra skirt and boots, and a wide turquoise ribbon, which appealed to him, tied in a floppy bow around her hair. It was obvious she was interested in him and he felt himself becoming aroused. By the time they finished she was right up against the stage, and he could see she wasn't wearing a bra. Her nipples were hard under the tight vest. His mouth went dry with lust. As they came off-stage, she darted round the security man by the door. He put out his hand to stop her, but Stephen grabbed her wrist. "It's OK, she's with me."

She looked at him in delight.

He pulled her along the corridor and into an empty dressing room. Locking the door behind them, he leant against it, surveying her. She looked about sixteen under the make up. But her body was even better close to. He had to have her. "Take your clothes off."

She was startled. "All of them?"

"Yeah. I want to see your body. Come on."

"You want me to take all my clothes off? Now?"

"Don't piss me around, you little tart! You've been begging for it all evening, and now you're going to get it! Strip!"

Awkwardly, she undressed and stood in front of him, naked.

"Mmmm." He cupped her breasts in his hands. "Nice tits." He rolled and squeezed the nipples between his finger and thumb, making her gasp. Unzipping his jeans, he pushed her head down. She took him in her mouth and he groaned in ecstasy. When he could wait no longer, he pulled her up again and bent her forward over the back of a chair, ramming himself into her and thrusting hard until he came.

She straightened up and he pulled her against him, his mouth curving into a grin. "God, Cherry, that was fantastic." He kissed her passionately. "I couldn't believe it when I saw you out there! You're a terrific groupie! Where did you get the clothes?"

"I borrowed most of them. Was I enough of a slut?"

"Oh, yeah!"

She shivered. "It's cold in here. What was all that take my clothes off bit?"

He helped her dress. "You were my groupie, I wanted to see your body. You're not supposed to argue."

"I thought you'd just… you know, pull my knickers down and… well… you know." She made vague gestures with her hands.

"Fuck you?" asked Stephen, grinning.

She blushed rosily. "Yes."

"Ah, I can see you haven't quite got the point of groupies. They exist to service a rock star's every need. I mean, I might have wanted to…" He whispered in her ear.

She recoiled. "Stephen Markham! You can wash your mouth out with soap when we get home!"

He laughed. They went out into the corridor, and he put his jacket around her shoulders.

"Wow!" she said in a strong Cockney accent, "I'm wearing Stephen Markham's jacket!"

"Shut up, you idiot," he grinned. "Come on, let's get you home before someone recognises you."

Chapter Six
Broken Flower

And all I ask of life is just to stay beside you, to hold you safe in my arms and to lay beside you, the flower that died, it wasn't all that tied you. Don't let go.

Lynn sat on the bus feeling deathly. It wasn't far from the Medical School to the flat and usually she walked, but over the last few days she had been feeling so tired and ill. She'd been snappy with Stephen too, and she felt bad about that, but all she really wanted to do was curl up in bed and sleep. As she got off the bus, she saw Stephen coming out of the little grocery shop opposite.

His face lit up when he saw her. He ran across the road and took her bag. "Hi!" He kissed her cheek. "You look tired, cariad. When we get in, you have a nap while I make you some lunch."

"I can't, I've got a pile of work to do," she said shortly.

"A little nap won't make any difference!"

"Look, just because you don't do any work doesn't mean we're all like that. I've *got* to work this afternoon. Anyway, I know what'll happen if I go and 'take a nap'. You'll be in there expecting sex!"

His face hardened. "You're being an absolute bitch at the moment. It's hardly my fault you have periods. Why don't you go to the doctor and get the pill? Isn't that supposed to help?"

"Well, it would certainly make life easier for you, wouldn't it?"

He unlocked the front door and they started up the stairs. "That wasn't what I was thinking and you know it. But suit yourself. If you want to be a martyr, see if I care." He went into the bedroom and she heard him playing his guitar. She shut the door to the sitting room and started to work.

"Lynn? Lynn!" Stephen was gently shaking her shoulder.

"Hmm?"

"You were asleep. You'll get a stiff neck lying like that. Come on, come and lie on the bed. If you're not feeling better tomorrow, I think you ought to go to Student Health." He settled her on their bed and tucked the duvet round her.

She smiled sleepily up at him. "Thanks, Stevie. I'm sorry I was so mean."

He kissed her. "Forget it! I'll leave you to have a good sleep."

Perversely, now that she was lying comfortably on the bed, she couldn't sleep. The same thought that crept into her brain when she woke at night desperately needing to pee was clamouring to be heard. Her period was nine days late. She hadn't told Stephen because she didn't want to worry him, but she was almost never late, and then only ever by a day. Normally she was early. But she couldn't be pregnant, Stephen was always so careful to use a condom. She froze. Except that night when she had been his groupie. That had been about three weeks ago. But it was only that once, for God's sake! Worry makes your periods late. She'd read that somewhere – worry and stress. Well, she was worried right now and she was finding her course very hard, which was stressful. That was it then. She rolled onto her back and shut her eyes. Her period would probably start any minute now. She wasn't going to worry any more.

Stephen was struggling with a lyric when he heard Lynn open the front door. He braced himself, determined not to row with her, no matter what she said. Lately, she seemed to have been going out of her way to pick quarrels with him, and he was so fed up with it.

She came into the sitting room. "Stephen."

He carried on writing. "Hmm?"

"Can I talk to you?"

"Yeah."

"No, I mean, can you stop doing that and look at me?"

"I'm working."

"Well, stop."

"Why should I? You don't when I want you to."

"Oh, for God's sake! That's different."

"Why?"

"Because it's important. I have to work so I can pass my exams."

He held onto his temper. "And this is important because I haven't written any songs for ages and we need some new material. We've got another gig at Utopia."

"Fuck the gig!" She sank down onto the sofa.

She had his attention. He stared at her. She never swore – not like that, at any rate. "What's up, Lynn?"

"I'm pregnant!"

He was dumbfounded. "Pregnant?"

She nodded.

"What do you mean, you're pregnant? How do you know?"

"I did a test."

"A test?" He was completely astounded. She'd never even hinted that she might be pregnant. "When? Why didn't you tell me?"

"I didn't want to worry you. I wasn't sure, it might have been a false alarm. I did the test at Caro's."

He stood up, hurt and shaken. "At Caro's? You told Caro and not me?" He couldn't believe that she hadn't said anything to him, that she'd told Caro first.

"Of course not, you idiot! She's on that field trip, remember? I've been feeding her fish."

"Oh, yeah. But you could've told me," he said, annoyed. "This really *is* important, Lynn!"

"Oh, Steve, what was the point in worrying you too? And I hoped so much I was wrong!" She burst into tears.

He sat down next to her, and put his arm round her. As the realisation that she was carrying their child sank in, he could feel himself beginning to smile. "Don't cry, Cherry. Why are you crying? You're having our baby!"

"What are we going to do?"

"I don't know, but don't worry. We'll sort it out."

She stared at him. "How?"

"Well, when's it due?"

"I don't know!"

"OK, let's see." He counted on his fingers. "Beginning of July. You'll be able to finish your course, and she can come to our graduation ceremonies!"

"Oh, thank you very much! I really want to sit my finals at seven months pregnant! And what do you mean 'she'?"

He shrugged. "I just get the feeling it's a girl."

"Don't say that! I don't want to think about it being anything! It's a blob. A blob that's going to ruin our lives."

"You don't mean that!" He was shocked.

"Yes I do! Why shouldn't I? For God's sake, Stephen, just for once bury that bloody emotional Welshman and let your English side have a chance! How could we manage if I have a baby now?"

"I don't know, but we'll sort something out."

"The only way would be for you to give up the band and get a job after you graduate. A proper job."

"I know."

"You can't do that, Stevie! I don't want you to do that!"

"If I have to, I have to." He tried to smile reassuringly.

"This is so unfair," she whispered. "We had our future all sorted out."

"I know. But darling Cherry, we can still do everything we said, we're just starting a little early."

"Oh, Stevie! You know we can't. This spoils everything."

He took a deep breath. "Do you want, would you like to have… to have…" His lips were trembling and he couldn't say the words.

But she knew what he was thinking. "An abortion?"

He nodded.

"Yes," she whispered. "But I couldn't, I could never kill our baby. But, oh, Stevie, I wish… If only we could go back!"

"Shhh. It'll be all right, cariad." He took her in his arms as she cried, and thought how brilliantly the band was doing. Well, tough. "These things happen, Lynn," he whispered, kissing her hair. "So it'll be a while before I make it. So what? I'd rather have you and our baby than a band. Any day."

I wouldn't, she thought. Oh, why had this happened? Why hadn't she just gone to the gig with him? Or thought to take a condom? Why was life so unfair?

The next few weeks were a nightmare. She saw her tutors and explained the situation. They were sympathetic and helpful and said that there was no reason why she shouldn't finish the course and graduate, it had been done before, and if she had any problems she should tell them straight away so that they could sort them out. She battled with morning sickness and constant tiredness and Stephen's cheerful acceptance of her pregnancy. She thought of all the men who would have encouraged her to have an abortion, and began to feel a small seed of resentment growing inside her, which she knew was unfair, but she couldn't help it. It was all very well for him to talk about 'our' baby. He didn't have to carry it round, he didn't have to spend half an hour in the bathroom every morning throwing up. He was still rehearsing with the band and playing gigs. And all she wanted was to finish her course and work as a speech therapist and live the life they'd planned. She wanted to be with Stephen and go to gigs with him and watch him become successful. She was only just twenty and she didn't want a child, not for several years. She tried hard not to be cross with him, but pregnancy was making her tired and irritable and she was so unhappy. There was no one she could talk to without feeling she was being disloyal. And she couldn't talk to him. He was as stressed as she was.

"I don't want to tell anyone."

"But if we're going to Mum and Dad for Christmas, we'll have to."

"You haven't told the band."

He was thrown. "How do you know?"

"I saw George yesterday. It was obvious he didn't know."

"Maybe he was just being tactful," Stephen said defensively.

"George? Tactful? That's a contradiction in terms if I ever heard one! *Have* you told them?"

"Well… no."

"Why?"

"Well, what's the point right now? And suppose we got offered a deal? We're doing really well, Lynn, it could happen. Then everything would be OK."

Yes, you wouldn't have to give up your dream, she thought bitterly. She was shocked. How could she feel like that? But I love speech therapy, she thought, I was so looking forward to doing this job, helping people get better. And pregnancy seemed to be turning her into someone else, someone mean, resentful and bitter.

"Well, I don't want to tell anyone, either. How come it's OK for you and not me?"

"It's different."

"Why? It doesn't show and I've stopped being sick! How would they know?"

"Surely they have a right to know? It's their grandchild."

"It's not like it's their first."

"I know, Lynn, but… well, I just think they have a right to know. Why are you so paranoid about it?"

"Look, it's my body and no one has any rights over it, not even you. I don't want to talk about it, OK, I don't want Sian fussing over me and John asking me how I feel every five minutes all because I'm carrying a Markham grandchild!"

"For Christ's sake, Lynn, grow up!"

"No, you grow up! I'm the one who's pregnant and too tired to have fun, or make love to you. You think men miss sex when they're not getting it; well I've got news for you, buster, so do we! I love making love to you, and these days I'm always too bloody tired and uncomfortable!"

"Uncomfortable? How?"

"I don't know. I just feel – *heavy*."

"OK, cariad." He rubbed her back. "I'm sorry. It's up to you who we tell. I mean eventually we'll have to, she'll be too big to hide. But for now, it's your choice."

"Why are you so sure it's a girl?"

"I don't know," he said slowly. "I just… it's like a little flower growing inside you, and I just see it as a girl. A little blossom." He smiled at her. "Cherry blossom. It's called Sakura in Japan. Isn't that lovely? Miyuki, you know, that Japanese girl who works in the Geisha Bar, she was telling me about it after our last gig. If it *is* a girl we could call her Sakura." He sighed. "I don't know why I think it's a girl. Maybe it's just wishful thinking."

"Do you want a girl?" He nodded. "Because you already have a boy?"

"Oh, no!" He was horrified. "No, I love it whatever it is. It's more to do with my father, I think, and the relationship we had."

She stood up restlessly. "Would you mind very much if we didn't go to York for Christmas? Couldn't we stay here? I really don't feel like travelling and we weren't going for long anyway because of the band's gigs."

Stephen thought of Rob and how he'd been looking forward to seeing him open his presents. He had an idea. "Would you mind if Harry brought Robbie over here?"

She smiled wanly. "No."

By the beginning of the spring term, Lynn was feeling a little better physically, which helped her emotionally. Her doctor told her that after the first three months, pregnant women often felt very well indeed and she had to admit that she did. She was a little anaemic, but apart from that she felt fine. She also looked very well, and Stephen kept telling her how gorgeous she was. She'd not really put on any weight, but her breasts and face were fuller and rounder, both of which suited her. She'd finally given in and let Stephen tell his parents, and he'd told Fin, George and Andy, who had been surprised, and made risqué jokes and ribbed him, as he'd expected; but they'd also been tremendously supportive, which he hadn't expected and which had touched him very much.

"Cheer up, mate," Andy had said, over several pints at the Tappit Hen. "It's not the end of the world, like."

"He's right," Fin agreed. "And we're so good, we're bound to get offered a recording deal long before the baby's born."

"Aye, any day now," George laughed. "Seriously though, man, Steve, I'm sure we could manage even after Lynn has the bairn. The three of you can move into the house with us and we'll pool wor money. We'll sort something out, bonny lad."

Apart from her tutors and a couple of close friends, Lynn hadn't told anyone, not even her parents. When she'd told them she and Stephen were married, they'd been shocked, and her mother had been angry that they hadn't had a Catholic wedding, telling her that she wasn't married in the eyes of God.

"As if I give a toss about what some non-existent God might think!" Lynn had said scornfully to Stephen, annoyed and hurt by their attitude, and the way her mother referred to Stephen as 'that boy'. But now she was beginning to think about God. She told herself it was just superstition she'd absorbed from her mother, but she couldn't help wondering if her pregnancy wasn't some sort of retribution for not believing in Him. She knew this was ridiculous and she didn't mention it to Stephen. Pregnancy doesn't agree with me, she thought. She still didn't want the baby, not because she had anything against the child itself, but because it had unwittingly ruined their lives. She tried not to think about it growing inside her. She was dreading the day she first felt it kicking. She sometimes had daydreams of a little dark-haired girl with eyes just like Stephen's. She felt so helpless. If only this hadn't happened, she thought endlessly.

Stephen, meanwhile, was struggling with his own feelings. In his secret heart, he knew he would have supported Lynn if she'd had an abortion – if *she'd* chosen, not him. Then he wouldn't have felt guilty, but things would have been all right again. He despised himself. What kind of a scumbag would behave like that? But it would have solved everything. He didn't want to give up his dreams and get a job – teaching, he supposed. He had the terrible feeling that if he did that, he'd never have a band, a real band. He could imagine himself playing in his local pub on Friday nights, wishing things had been different. He started to run again, as he had after Angie moved away, aiming to tire himself so completely that he fell into bed and slept dreamlessly until the alarm went off. He was working very hard; despite what the lads had said about managing, he thought it was unlikely to happen, and he had to be realistic. He had a wife and child to support and if he was going to have to get a job, he wanted to do as well as he could in his finals. It wasn't that he didn't want the baby, he did; his first reaction had been one of delight. If only it hadn't been *now*. Sometimes, when he ran, he found himself wanting to keep on running and never go back home, and that shocked him more than anything.

"Are you all right, Lynn? You're wriggling around like you've got fleas!"

"My back hurts."

"Do you want to go to bed? I'll make you a hot water bottle."

"Yes please."

He turned off the T.V. It was an old black and white portable, and the reception wasn't very good anyway. "I'll run you a bath, too."

She smiled at him. He was being so good to her. He did all the cooking, cleaning and shopping and looked after her as well, so that all she had to do was concentrate on her work. She stood up and frowned. Her knickers felt odd – wet. She went into the bathroom.

Stephen was just coming out. "It's not ready yet."

"I'll see to it. I need to go to the loo."

She took off her clothes. Her knickers were definitely wet. She felt bloated and heavy. She wondered if she had cystitis, but she had no pain or burning. She turned off the hot tap and got into the bath. It was lovely, relaxing and soothing. She stayed in until it began to get cold.

Stephen looked round the door. "Ready for the hot water bottle?"

They got into bed together.

"Will it disturb you if I read for a while?" he asked. "I've just got to a good bit."

"Be my guest," she yawned. "I could sleep through anything!"

She woke later, needing to use the toilet badly. She got up, and a stab of pain across her lower abdomen made her gasp. She had a strange feeling of fullness in her vagina, and it hurt to pee. *Definitely cystitis*, she thought. She decided to stay home the following morning and get Stephen to ring the doctor. As she got back into bed, she felt another sharp pain. She caught her breath, and lay down carefully. The pain receded and she began to relax. She suddenly became aware of a feeling of warm wetness. She sat up, feeling dizzy.

"Stevie! Stephen, wake up!"

"What is it?" He rolled over and turned on the light.

"I don't know, I— Ow!" More pain, and again the full, almost bulging feeling. She put her hand down into the wetness and her fingers came out smeared pink. "I think I'm having a miscarriage," she said, very frightened.

Stephen leapt out of bed, grabbing his clothes. "Stay still. I'll call an ambulance."

They couldn't afford a phone, but there was a box just across the road. He ran very fast all the way there and all the way back. "They're on their way, darling Cherry. Don't worry, it'll be all right."

She gripped his hand. "I'm scared."

There was a knock at the door. He ran and opened it. "In here."

The ambulance rushed them to A&E, where Lynn was taken away to be examined. Stephen sat tensely in the waiting room, feeling useless and trying not to panic.

Eventually, a doctor came out. "Mr Markham? I'm afraid your wife's lost the baby."

He felt stunned. He'd known she was miscarrying, but hadn't let himself believe it, had told himself they would give her something that would stop it. "Is she all right?"

"We've given her a sedative. She was very distressed, but she's all right. They'll be taking her up to the ward shortly. We want her to stay in tonight." She sighed. "There was nothing anyone could have done. I'm very sorry."

"But why? Why did it happen?"

"From the symptoms your wife described, I would say an incompetent cervix."

Stephen looked at her blankly. "It means that the cervix can't take the weight of the pregnancy and starts to dilate."

"Can I see her?"

"Of course."

Stephen followed her along the corridor. He was sick and tired of life. It was so pointless. All that distress when Lynn had first discovered she was pregnant. What had it all been for?

Lynn was lying on a bed in a small side room. She looked grey and worn out, and she had purple shadows like bruises under her eyes. A tear rolled down her cheek.

Stephen took her hand, and tried to smile at her. "It's all right, Cherry, it's all right." He knew the words were meaningless, but he didn't know what else to say.

"I'm so sorry," she whispered. "It was a little girl, did they tell you? Your little flower. All broken."

A lump formed in his throat and he blinked back tears. "Don't, Cherry, don't be sad, please. We've still got each other."

She moved her head restlessly. "It was my fault. I don't work properly."

"Don't say that," he pleaded. "It'll be all right, it will."

She shook her head.

"I love you," he said.

They took her up to the ward. Stephen went with them and sat in the day room. It was a depressing place; uncomfortable armchairs, faded lino on the floor and uninteresting prints on the walls, but he didn't want to go home, he wanted to be with Lynn in case she disturbed and needed him.

He finally fell asleep in one of the chairs and woke up when the cleaner came in, a cheerful Jamaican lady. "Your wife in labour, lovey?" she asked in her rich, lilting accent.

Stephen shook his head. "She had a miscarriage."

She was deeply sympathetic. She made him a cup of tea and held his hand while he drank it. "You're just a boy yourself. How old are you?"

"Twenty-two."

She made a clucking noise with her tongue. "And your wife?"

"She's twenty."

"It's too bad! You take care of each other when she comes out." She gave him a wide smile. "Long as you love each other it will work out, you see!"

Stephen thanked her. His head was aching and his back hurt from sleeping in the chair. He'd injured it years ago playing rugby and it had never been right since. He went out to the nurse's station. There was one nurse there. She didn't look much older than Lynn. "Could I see my wife?"

"It's not visiting hours yet."

"Please. She's had a miscarriage."

The nurse looked at him properly. "Oh, yes, Mrs Markham. Yes, you can go in, but not for long." She frowned. "Don't I know you?"

He shook his head. "I don't think so."

"Yes! I've seen you at Utopia! You play lead guitar and sing in Sid's Six!"

He nodded.

"Wow! You're really good! Who writes your songs?"

"Me."

"Wow!" she said again. She remembered why he was there. "Go on in. She's down the corridor in a side room, we didn't want to put her in with the ladies who've had their babies. Stay as long as you want."

He tried to smile charmingly. "Thank you. When can I take her home?"

"Have to wait till the doctor's seen her. He's usually round at about ten o'clock." She leaned towards him. "I'll make sure he sees her first. Um… I know it's not really the best of times, but could I have your autograph?"

Lynn was asleep when he went in. He sat on the chair next to her and watched her. She was looking better than she had earlier, there was more colour in her cheeks. He loved her so much it was like a pain around his heart. He thought about the baby. What a waste, what a complete and utter waste. A nurse came in, a different one, older. She asked him to leave. He stood up to go, and Lynn woke. He bent and kissed her.

She clutched his hand. "Don't go!"

He looked at the nurse. "All right. Only five minutes though."

"Thank you," he said gratefully. He sat down beside Lynn again and stroked her hair. "How are you feeling, Cherry?"

"OK." She started to cry. How could she tell him she was glad? How could she admit it to herself? How could she be such a monster? If he knew, he'd stop loving her. He'd wanted it so much. He must never know. "Very sad."

"I know. It *is* sad. It's sad and pointless." His throat tightened. "I love you."

"I love you too."

They sat in silence, neither knowing what to say to comfort the other, both knowing that nothing they said would help. The nurse came back in, and Stephen felt almost glad to go. He hung around until the doctor had seen Lynn.

"We want to keep her in another night," the doctor said. "She lost quite a bit of blood and she has a slight temperature."

Stephen went back in to Lynn. "I'll get some stuff from home and bring it in. Is there anything special you want?"

She shook her head listlessly.

"OK." He kissed her. "You try and rest. I'll be in later."

"Stephen?"

"Yes?"

"I'm sorry."

He went back to the flat and packed a small case for her. He felt terrible. He hadn't wanted her to be pregnant, and now she'd lost their child. It made him feel like it was his fault. He'd caused her all this pain. He supposed he ought to tell Sian. He trudged over to the phone box. Then he remembered he'd scheduled a rehearsal for that afternoon. He fished about in his pocket for change. He had a five pound note and two ten pences. He rang George's house. Fin answered.

"Fin, it's Stephen. I can't make the rehearsal this afternoon."

"Oh, I see. It's one rule for you and one for the rest of us, is it? You'd better have a bloody good excuse, my boy."

"Lynn's had a miscarriage. She's in hospital."

There was a shocked silence from the other end of the phone. "My God, Steve, I'm so sorry," Fin said eventually. "Is there anything we can do?"

The pips went.

"No, I'll be in touch," Stephen said as the line went dead. He rang the operator and made a reverse charges call to Sian.

She was stunned. "I'm coming over."

"Would you bring…" His voice was shaking. He stopped and took a deep breath.

"Would you bring Rob?"

As he started over to the flat he remembered he hadn't notified Lynn's tutor. He turned wearily back to the phone.

"Daddy! Look, Daddy, Thomas!" Rob waved a toy train at him.

"How lovely!" He swung his son into the air.

Rob grabbed his face and gave him a smacking kiss.

"You look awful, cariad," Sian said as he put Rob down. She brushed the hair off his forehead. "You ought to get some sleep."

"Where's Cherry?" Rob demanded, appearing back in the sitting room, having rampaged through the flat.

"She's tired, she's gone to have a rest in a big, quiet house. You can see her next time."

Rob looked mutinous. "I want Cherry."

"How about a chocolate biscuit?" Stephen offered.

Rob brightened. "Choklik bikkit, choklik bikkit, choklik bikkit," he chortled.

"You shouldn't bribe him," Sian said mildly as Stephen gave him a biscuit.

He watched Rob licking off the chocolate. Most of it seemed to go on his face and hands. The little boy nibbled the edge of the biscuit, and handed it to Stephen. "For you," he said kindly, before looking down at his hands, licking off what he could and wiping the rest on Stephen's jeans.

"Rob!" Sian's voice was stern. "That's very naughty!"

He stuck a chocolate-covered tongue out at her and hid behind Stephen's legs.

Stephen picked him up. "Come on, let's wash you off and then we'll take Gran out in the car."

"See how easy it is?" he said, as she pulled up at the hospital. "You'll be able to find your way back, won't you?"

"Oh, yes. But could you draw me a quick map, just in case?" She got a notebook and pen out of the glove compartment.

He smiled and sketched out the route.

She took Lynn's case, kissed him and went into the hospital.

He put Rob in the pushchair.

"I can *walk*!" Rob said crossly, kicking his legs out. "Let me *walk*, Daddy! Walk, walk, *walk*!"

"OK, OK, but you have to hold my hand, and if it starts to rain, you have to get back in, all right?"

Rob nodded enthusiastically.

"Lynnie, how are you, cariad?"

Lynn started to cry. "Oh, Sian, I'm so glad to see you!" She sat up and held out her arms. Sian held her, letting her cry out her misery.

"I didn't want the baby," she sobbed. "I didn't want her and now she's dead and it's all my fault!"

"No, cariad, no it's not."

"Yes it is, my cervix doesn't work properly."

"But that's not your fault! John's heart doesn't work properly, is that his fault? Of course not! It's just the same."

"I hadn't thought of that." Lynn reached for the tissues and blew her nose. "But do you think… do you think God might have been punishing me for wanting an abortion?"

This was the first Sian had heard about an abortion. I need to talk to Stephen, she thought. "Of course not, Cherry! If you believe in God, you can't believe he would kill an innocent child to punish you! But I thought you didn't believe?"

"I don't. It's just… well, you don't know do you? And when I was little, Mum always said that if I behaved badly, God would see and punish me. I know it's not really *true*…" Her voice trailed off.

Bloody religion, Sian thought. It's responsible for more trouble than anything else. "Well, I don't believe that. And anyway, Lynn, you didn't behave badly. All right, you weren't ready for a baby, but that's perfectly reasonable. You're only twenty and you've got your career to look forward to. But you'd have been a wonderful mother, Cherry! You've got nothing to blame yourself for."

Lynn squeezed her hand. "Thank you, Sian," she said gratefully. "I did love it, it was just…"

"Now wasn't the time."

Lynn shook her head. "Please don't tell Stevie, he wanted her so much."

"Don't worry," Sian said, kissing her. "I won't tell anyone."

They talked for a little while longer, and then Sian got up to leave. "You ought to have a nap, cariad, you're looking very tired." She kissed her. "Stephen will be in this evening. You look after yourself, won't you now, and no more of this talk about punishment. You and Stevie have just been really unlucky."

Lynn lay down, feeling a little better. Sian was right, she was so tired. She turned over, shut her eyes and slept.

She came home the next day. She felt weak and shaky and horribly tearful. Stephen had cleaned the flat and made a casserole for lunch. He'd bought fruit and cakes for her, and several Mars Bars, her favourite sweets.

She didn't want anything. "I just feel tired," she told him apologetically.

"God, Cherry, it doesn't matter! You can do whatever you want! Would you like to lie down while I run you a bath?"

She nodded. She simply wanted to be alone. It had been so easy in hospital, she hadn't had to talk to anyone if she hadn't wanted to. She didn't want Stephen fussing around her. She lay on the bed and stared at the ceiling.

He came in. "The bath's ready, Cherry."

She shook her head restlessly. "I don't want it now."

He was at a loss. "Well, I'll leave the water for the time being in case you change your mind. Is there anything you want?"

"To be left alone!" she snapped. He looked as if she'd struck him. For a second, and to her horror, she was pleased she'd hurt him and had the urge to do it again. She felt so raw and unhappy that somehow, seeing him suffer made her feel better. It was a horrible feeling. "I'm sorry. I'm just tired, Stephen." She tried to smile at him.

"It's OK." He sat on the edge of the bed. "I understand."

No, you bloody well don't! she wanted to shout, just leave me alone! She shut her eyes.

He stood up. "I'll leave you to sleep."

She could hear the desolation in his voice. Good, good, said a little voice in her head. Let him see how it feels.

After he'd left the room she cried herself to sleep.

She went back to her lectures the following week. Physically, she felt better. She wasn't bleeding much any more, but she was very tired all the time. She also felt as if she wasn't in control of her life any longer. She had terrifying moments when it seemed as if everything around her had speeded up and was rushing past her and she was helpless. She gritted her teeth and threw herself into her work.

Stephen found it impossible to reach her. She seemed to have withdrawn into herself, retreated from him both physically and emotionally. He missed her all the time. It was as if Lynn had gone into hospital and a stranger with her face had come out. He never saw her body any more. She locked the door to the bathroom and dressed and undressed in there. In bed she wore a long nightgown. She spent her days at lectures, or in the library, or out on placement. In the evenings she worked until bedtime. She was sarcastic and prickly with him. Nothing he said or did pleased her. He found himself spending more and more time with Fin, George and Andy. They were easy to be with and sympathetic in an inarticulate way. They didn't ask him any questions. They took him out to the Tappit Hen and plied him with alcohol.

He could lose himself in his music. He spent most of his time rehearsing, and playing gigs. Sid's Six was in residency at the Highland Fling, and often played at Utopia. When he wasn't playing, he wrote new songs or worked on his dissertation. The topic he'd chosen was Welsh Writing since 1930, concentrating on the English-language writing of Wales, and he found it totally absorbing. He'd always loved Dylan Thomas and R.S. Thomas, and he enjoyed reading the more contemporary poets and novelists with whom he wasn't so familiar.

"Lynn, we're playing at the May Day Ball at the Union. Let's go out and buy you a new frock!"

Lynn glanced up from her books. "No, thanks. I'm busy."

"You're always busy these days! You need to take some time off and enjoy yourself!"

"It may have escaped your notice, Stephen, but we've got exams in a few weeks." She started to write again.

He snatched the pen from her.

Her lips tightened. "Don't be childish, Stephen." She wrinkled up her nose. "You've been drinking!"

"Yeah, I had a few pints with the lads to celebrate getting this gig. Look, Lynn, we have to talk. We should have talked weeks ago, but you wouldn't. I'm fed up of tiptoeing round you, of treating you as if you might break. Have you ever considered how I might be feeling?"

"Oh, poor little Stephen! Well, aren't we all sorry for you? I didn't ask you to treat me like that, in fact, I'm sick to death of you fussing around me!"

He stared at her. "I know you're very unhappy, Cherry. I just want to help. Look, it's been nearly four months since the miscarriage. Perhaps it would be a good idea if you went to see someone – someone you could talk to. God knows you don't want to talk to me," he added bitterly.

"I don't need to talk to anyone. I just want to get on with my work." She held her hand out for her pen.

Stephen ignored it. "You do need to talk to someone. You're not yourself, Lynn."

She sighed. "Don't think I don't know what this is all about. It's sex. You haven't had any since I lost the baby and, being a man, you can't manage for a few months without it. Well, to use your own singularly pertinent phrase: suck it up, Stephen!"

She couldn't believe she was being so horrible to him, but she couldn't seem to stop. And she couldn't talk to him, either. She'd been to see Caro and Pam and they'd both said, talk to Steve. But she couldn't, she was too angry with him. He'd made her pregnant. If she'd never been pregnant she'd never have realised how mean and selfish she was. She couldn't talk to him because she blamed him. And nothing had changed for him. He hadn't had the pain. He didn't feel like she did. He wasn't so tired he could barely think. But she didn't want him to feel those things, so why was she so angry with him? She despised herself. And she was tired all the time. So tired. Too tired for sex and anyway, she didn't feel like it these days. There was no desire for anything except sleep.

He held on to his temper with difficulty. "That's neither true nor fair, Lynn," he said evenly. "I can easily wait till you're better. Although it seems odd that you're well enough to go out with Caro and Pam and stay out till three in the morning, but not well enough to go out with me or let me make love to you."

"Oh, for God's sake!" she sneered. "I knew it was about sex. Anyway, I do go out with you. We went to see that film you liked so much, *Local Hero*."

"We both liked it! And that was in February, you haven't wanted to do anything with me since!"

It had been fun, that evening. They'd got a takeaway afterwards and talked about visiting Scotland one day and finding Ben's beach. He'd thought she was over the miscarriage, and had wanted to make love to her, but that had made her angry and they'd had a ridiculous row and she'd accused him of not understanding – well, all right, maybe he didn't, but she wouldn't explain, and he was trying so hard – and, even more hurtful, of not caring, which was so far from the truth as to be ludicrous. She'd shut him out ever since. She'd got gradually worse over the months and he'd only now realised how bad things had become between them, how much she'd changed.

"Well, how about this," she was saying. "Maybe I just don't fancy you any more! Ever thought of that?"

"No, actually, I hadn't, Lynn. I thought you loved me."

"Think again."

He went white. "You don't mean that?"

She shrugged and stood up. "Believe what you want to believe. I couldn't care less any more. If you won't give me my pen, I'll get another one."

He was suddenly furiously angry. He'd tried so hard, made so many allowances for her, been sympathetic and kind when he just wanted to be comforted himself. "Well, you know what, Lynn? If you don't want me there are plenty of others who do!" He stalked from the room, slamming the door behind him.

He went to the pub and drank steadily. How could she have said those things? How could she? He went over and over the conversation in his mind, fuelling his anger, telling himself she was a bitch, a cold, heartless, evil bitch, and he was better off without her, but all the time he was conscious of a terrible feeling of fear and desolation. Supposing she really had stopped loving him? How could he get through the rest of his life without her? Eventually, he moved away from the bar, and the room swayed. He caught the bus to George's and hammered on the door.

Andy opened it. "Hey, calm down, Steve! You're making enough noise to wake the dead, like!"

"Are they in?" Stephen asked, pushing past him.

"Who? The dead?"

"Fin and George."

"Yeah, they're working. I'm watching the footie. Liverpool's thrashing Everton nil nil. Do you want to watch?"

"I want to go out, get drunk and get laid."

Andy stared at him. "You already are drunk."

"I want to get drunker. And I want a woman."

"Oh, bloody hell! Ey, lads! Get down here!" Andy shouted.

Fin and George appeared on the landing. "What's going on? We're working."

"Steve's pissed. He wants to go out drinking and get laid."

They looked at each other in consternation. "Let's go and sit down," Fin suggested reasonably, starting down the stairs. "We can have a drink here, watch the footie."

"You can come with me or stay here, I don't care. But I'm going."

George looked at the others. "We'll have to go. Someone's got to keep an eye on him."

Stephen woke up and immediately wished he hadn't. His head was hammering and he felt sick. He opened his eyes. The room spun hideously. He shut them again.

"Stephen?" It was a girl's voice, but it wasn't Lynn's. It had an unusual accent. He remembered going out with Andy, Fin and George. Where did they go and where was he now?

"Stephen!"

He cautiously opened one eye. Miyuki was bending over him, wearing a very short, sheer kimono. He shut his eye and moaned as his memory helpfully started to fill in the missing pieces. They'd gone to Utopia. He'd got off with Miyuki, one of the waitresses from the Geisha Bar upstairs, who'd been flirting with him for weeks, and George had ended up with her sister, Kagami. And the four of them had gone back to the girls' flat.

"Drink this, Stephen. It will make you feel better."

He sat up carefully and drank. It would cure or kill him. Either was preferable to the way he was feeling now.

"Lie back down and sleep for a while and you'll feel better when you wake up."

He lay down. He was incapable of doing anything else. He didn't just feel terrible physically. He couldn't believe he'd slept with Miyuki. One tough time with Lynn, one crisis, and he ran out and was unfaithful to her. He knew he wouldn't sleep, couldn't. He'd probably never sleep again. '*Macbeth doth murder sleep, the innocent sleep.*' The quotation hung in his mind. Innocent sleep. He'd never experience it again.

"Steve! Wake up!"

"Go away! Leave me alone!"

"Howay, bonny lad, wake up! It's the middle of the afternoon, the lasses have to go out!"

He sat up. His head still hurt, but not as much, and he no longer felt sick.

"What was that stuff you gave me?" he asked Miyuki. "It's amazing."

"Herbal tea," she smiled.

"Come on, man. Get up and get dressed."

He did as he was told. He wandered out of the bedroom, his face burning with shame. "Miyuki, can I talk to you?"

She smiled. "There's no need to talk, Stephen. I know you're married. We had fun. That's OK with me."

He swallowed. "Thank you."

"There's no need to thank me. You're a nice boy. I like you very much." She gave him a kiss. "I'll see you at the Geisha. If you want to have fun again, maybe we will."

"Howay, Steve, get a move on," George said. He kissed Kagami. "See you tonight, then, pet."

Stephen opened the door of the flat like a burglar. He had a feeling that Lynn would be waiting with a rolling pin. In a way, he wished she was. The flat was empty. He didn't know what to do. He wanted to tell her everything, to confess, to be punished and then absolved. But he knew he couldn't do that. What good would that do her? His punishment would be that he would have to live with what he'd done for the rest of his life and there would be no absolution. He lay on the bed and waited. At five o'clock she came in.

"Stephen?" Her voice was tentative.

He got up and walked to the door. They stared at each other.

"I was worried about you," she said finally.

"I'm sorry. I went out with the lads. We got drunk."

"Where did you sleep?"

He swallowed. He could practically taste the shame. "George's," he mumbled. "Are you all right?" he asked awkwardly.

She nodded.

"I'm sorry I went out. I was... upset."

She shrugged. "I'm sorry we argued."

He waited. She didn't go on. "Lynn. I love you," he said desperately. She didn't answer. "Do you love me?" he whispered, tears starting to his eyes.

"I don't know," she said. His heart turned over. "I don't know anything. Let's get the exams out of the way. Then maybe we can work things out, OK?"

"OK."

By the end of June, their finals were over for better or worse. Stephen didn't really care about the outcome; Lynn cared desperately. She had applied for jobs all over the country, but hadn't told him. She'd had several offers, but had short-listed them to Leeds, Wolverhampton and Edinburgh. She didn't know what to say to him. And, she told herself, she didn't have to take any of them.

They went out with a large group of friends to celebrate the end of the exams, ending up at The Bay Tree, a big pub in Fallowfield with a dance floor. They danced and drank and looked as if they were any other couple. Only they knew how precarious their marriage was and how much they needed to work on it. They came back from the dance floor and he bought her a glass of white wine, and a mineral water for himself.

She raised her eyebrows. "Mineral water?"

He nodded. "I thought we might go home and talk. Cherry, I just want us to be like we were before."

She put her hand on his. "So do I," she whispered. "I feel so awful, Stevie, so unhappy and tired. I can't stand feeling like this any more. Please help me!"

He slumped in his chair with relief. "Oh, Cherry, I love you so much! We can sort it out, I know we can! Let's go now."

"OK, but I need the loo first." She kissed him on the head as she went past.

He felt as if he was flying. She hadn't done anything like that for so long. He started to sing 'I'm Alive'. George, Fin, Andy and a group of girls came and sat down. One of them, a very pretty little brunette, sat next to him.

Lynn had to queue for the toilet. Finally she got into one of the cubicles. As she sat down she heard a voice she recognised, Jean Pritchard, who had been on her corridor in Grosvenor Place in the first year. They saw each other occasionally and chatted politely, but privately, Lynn didn't like her. She had a thin, weedy little boyfriend called Mike, who, she insisted on telling everyone, had a body like whipcord. "More like a whippet," Stephen had said once.

"And you'll never guess who's here!" she heard Jean saying. She decided to wait in the cubicle till Jean had gone, she really didn't want to talk to her now.

"Lynn Jackson, as was," Jean went on, "and Steve Markham. You know him, that dead sexy boy that sings with that group. Course, they're married now, but I heard they'd split up. Carol Johnstone said that Maria told her that Alan said… Alan Kirkbridge, Maria's boyfriend, yes, you've met him, Alan said Steve had been sleeping with a Japanese girl, the sister of George the Geordie's girlfriend. Oh, yeah, it's definitely true, George told Alan himself when…" Her voice trailed off as the door shut behind them.

Lynn sat frozen. How could Stephen have done that? After all they'd been through, after all she'd been through? Her heart was beating so fast she thought she was going to throw up. She got up and leant over the bowl, retching. Eventually, she went out and splashed cold water on her face, oblivious of her make up. Her heart felt like a stone. All this time and he hadn't ever really cared. He'd probably laughed about her behind her back, moaned to George and the others that he wasn't getting any sex. How could he, how *could* he?

She walked like an automaton to their table. Stephen was laughing at something George was saying. She got closer.

The brunette who was sitting next to Stephen turned to him. "It's not just me, Steve! All my friends think you're really hot!"

Something inside Lynn snapped and flooded her with molten rage. She ran across to the table and picked up a pint of beer. "Hot, are you, Stephen? Perhaps this'll cool you down!" She flung the beer in his face.

He gasped and stood up. The beer trickled down his neck and stained his tee shirt. Everyone sat in stunned silence.

She turned and walked away.

Stephen started after her. "Lynn!"

She ignored him, walked out of the pub and down the street.

He caught up with her. "Lynn!" He grabbed her arm.

She shook him off. "Don't you ever touch me again, you adulterous bastard!" she hissed.

"Oh God!" he said, horrified.

"Yeah. Oh God. You bastard, you *bastard!*"

"Lynn, I'm so sorry, please, you've got to believe me, it was just once, that night you said you didn't love me, I got drunk and I'm so, so sorry."

"Do you really expect me to believe that?" she demanded.

"It's the truth. How did you—"

"Find out? I overheard Jean Pritchard telling someone while I was in the loo. George told some friend who told someone else who told someone else. I'm sure you get the idea. I think I must be the only person not to know!"

He shut his eyes. "God, Lynn! Oh God, I'm so sorry! It was only that once, I swear, I swear on anything you like, I don't know what else I can say!"

"How about goodbye? It's over, Stephen. Don't come back to the flat tonight. I'll pack and be gone by tomorrow evening." She turned away.

"Let me come back with you, let me explain, Lynn," he pleaded.

She shook her head.

"At least let me take you home." He felt numb.

"I'll call a taxi from that phone box. Just go away, Stephen. I don't want you any more."

He waited until a cab picked her up, and then he walked back into the pub and pushed his way across the dance floor. They were playing 'The Birdie Song' and Kagami was dancing with a group of other girls. She smiled and waved. He managed to smile back. He was going to kill George. He walked to their table. Fin, Andy, and George were drinking and laughing, watching the girls dancing.

"Lynn got a bit carried away about something, Steve!" Andy said.

Stephen didn't even hear him. "You fucking moron!" he shouted at George. "Why the fuck did you tell anyone I'd slept with Miyuki?"

George's mouth dropped open. "It was a good story, man. The two hard rockers and these two gorgeous oriental lasses!"

"Lynn overheard someone talking about it when she was in the lavatory," Stephen went on furiously. "Why the hell can't you keep your fucking mouth shut? Talk about who *you* fuck as much as you want, I couldn't give a toss, but who said you could talk about me? I ought to smash your fucking head in!"

George stood up, unfolding himself to his full six foot three inches.

"Perhaps you ought to temper justice with mercy, Steve," Andy suggested.

Stephen sat down and put his head in his hands. "She's left me," he said in desolation. "Our marriage is over."

They gaped at him.

"Come on, Steve, she's just upset, you know what women are like. You need to talk to her," Fin said at last.

Stephen shook his head. "Things have been bad between us since she lost the baby. We had a huge row the night – the night I slept with Miyuki. That's why I did it. Well, kind of. I mean, I wasn't actually going to..." He stopped and looked at George. "Sorry, George. If I hadn't slept with her, you couldn't have said anything. It's my fault."

George shook his head. "If I hadn't said anything..."

Stephen shrugged. "It happened," he said, his voice full of pain. "She could have found out about it at any time."

"Look, go after her," Fin urged again.

"She said not to go back to the flat tonight, she'd be gone by tomorrow."

"Why, bollocks, man!" George said. "Women never mean that stuff! Go after her!"

Stephen looked at them, undecided. "Should I? I don't want to make things worse."

"Well, if you ask me," Andy said, "I don't think they could get much worse. I mean, she's left you, hasn't she?"

"I didn't think I'd ever say this," said Fin, "but Andy's right. For God's sake, Steve, get over there and talk to her!"

"Lynn?"

He let himself into the flat. There was a light on in the bedroom. He opened the door. Lynn was standing by the bed, wearing only a tiny pair of knickers. He drew in a painful breath. He hadn't seen her naked since February. He hadn't forgotten how beautiful her body was, he spent a lot of time thinking about it, but to see it without warning was unbelievably arousing.

"What are you doing here?" she demanded, pulling her nightgown on. She got into bed and sat against the headboard, the covers pulled up to her chin.

"I live here." Bad start. He tried again. "Lynn, please can we talk?"

"There's nothing to talk about."

"How can you say that?" he demanded. "There's *everything* to talk about! Things have gone so badly wrong between us since February, we've got to sort it out! I love you, Lynn!"

"And sleeping with someone else is your way of showing it?" She couldn't seem to unfreeze her feelings. She had locked herself away from him, she didn't think she could stand the pain otherwise.

"No!" He was close to tears. "That happened because we had that row, remember, when you said you didn't love me—"

"Oh, of course! It's all my fault!"

"That's not what I'm saying! It was all my fault, I'm just trying to explain. Please, Lynn, please let me explain!"

"Go on then."

"I was really upset that night. I'd tried so hard to help you by not pushing you or making demands on you. I was sad too, I wanted her just as much as you did, I know losing her wasn't the same for me, I didn't have all the physical pain, but I wanted her too." He stopped to compose himself. "And you kept pushing me away when all I wanted was… you know, just to comfort you and be comforted, and then you said you didn't want me and you didn't love me. I went to the pub and got drunk, I didn't really realise how drunk till I got to George's and by then it was too late." He paused and took a deep breath. "This is really hard to tell you, Lynn, because I have to be honest, you've always been so honest with me. By the time I got to George's I wanted to have sex with someone else. Partly because I wanted sex and you weren't ready, partly – partly to hurt you," he faltered. He started to cry. "And I'm so, so sorry, Lynn, I can't ever tell you how sorry I am. There's no excuse for how I hurt you. But Lynn, you've got to forgive me, I can't live without you, you're my world, you're all I ever wanted, just to be with you, Cherry, please, *please* forgive me!"

Tears welled up in Lynn's eyes. If he knew! If he only knew how very, very much she hadn't wanted the baby, how relieved she'd been when she lost it and how guilty she felt. And yet, how could he betray her like that? She would never do that! But then, he would never lie to her like she had about the baby. But to sleep with someone else! That was much worse that omitting to mention the way you felt about something. It was the worst kind of betrayal as far as she was concerned. How could she forgive him? If something like this happened in the future, how could she ever trust him again? And I'm so tired, she thought. I'm so tired all the time, tired and lost and there's no one I can trust.

"I can't trust you any more, Stephen. It's like you're a stranger."

He sat on the edge of the bed. "How can I be a stranger when I know every inch of you? I know that funny little scar you've got on your bottom where you sat on some broken glass at the beach when you were twelve. I know that little cry you make when you come. I know how you like your tea, your favourite food, your politics, what makes you sad, what makes you laugh; I'm not a stranger, Cherry! I'm just Stephen, who's human, who made such a stupid mistake and who is so, so, *so* sorry."

"The Stephen I knew wouldn't have ever done that to me. It's over." Very deliberately, she took her rings off and handed them to him.

He stared down at them in disbelief. "Cherry! Oh, Cherry, oh no, oh, please, Cherry, please, *please* don't do this, *please*! I love you so much," he begged.

She climbed out of bed. "If you won't go, I'll have to." She reached for her clothes.

"You really mean it, don't you?" He was shaking.

"Yes."

He shut his eyes, trying to control his breathing, which seemed to have stopped working properly. He was still holding her rings tightly in his hand. Crossing to her jewellery box, he took out a little silver heart necklace he had given her for her birthday the year before.

"What are you doing?"

He didn't answer. He slipped the heart off the chain, and put the rings on it. He turned back to her, his eyes full of tears. "It's not too late, Cherry."

"It was too late the moment you climbed into her bed."

His face changed. She'd never seen him look like that before. It was as if something inside him had died, the happy boy she'd loved had gone completely. The tears spilled unheeded down his cheeks as he fastened the chain round his neck

She watched him with despair. She'd loved him so much. Why couldn't she feel that any more? Why couldn't she feel anything? What was the point of being alive?

He grabbed her arm and pulled her to him. "I'll never stop loving you, Cherry, never," he whispered desperately.

She stood stiffly against him, her eyes shut. When she opened them again he'd gone, and she was alone in the silent room.

Part Three
Real Life

So this is reality, this is daylight,
This is what people call normality, it's too harsh too bright.
Being grown up is a tough game to play,
And I don't think I can bluff the same way I did when I was a kid,
And I'm just trying to find a little peace of mind
In the midst of all the strife,
Looking for someone to love in this real life.

Chapter Seven
Lost Souls

Lost souls, we're bleeding on the ground,
Lost souls and no help here to be found.

He walked to George's house. It was only a couple of miles and he didn't want to talk to anyone, not even a bus conductor. It started to rain and he got soaked, but he hardly noticed. He felt ill with grief, and every so often the misery inside him became so strong that he was afraid he'd be physically sick, and he had to stop until it passed.

When he got to the house, the others were still out, having obviously assumed he would make it up with Lynn. He sat on the doorstep for a while before he realised where he really wanted to be. He wanted to be with Rob. He got up wearily and trudged to the station. There wasn't a train for several hours, so he bought a ticket, sat on a bench and waited.

The Angel was in darkness. He looked at his watch; it was just after six. He couldn't wake Rob this early, it wasn't fair. He carefully moved the milk bottles and sat on the doorstep. Within five minutes, he was asleep.

Ted's alarm went off at six-fifty-five. He showered and went downstairs to make breakfast. He opened the back door to fetch the milk, and Stephen fell in.

"Steve! What the hell are you doing? God, you look terrible! And you smell like a brewery! What's happened?"

"I want Rob."

"You want a hot bath and something to eat, by the look of it."

"I just want Rob. Please can I see him?"

"He's still asleep, Steve. You wouldn't want to wake him up, would you? How about I make you some toast and you eat it while I run you a bath? You ain't got any luggage with you, have you?"

Stephen looked around blankly.

"No, of course not," Ted said. "Stupid of me! Come on then, come and have breakfast." He sat Stephen down at the table and made him some toast.

Stephen looked at it. "I don't want any."

"You do what you're told." Ted's voice was cheerful, but there was an implacable look in his eyes.

Stephen picked up a piece of toast.

"Good boy!" Ted patted his shoulder. "Sometimes it's easier doing what you're told, you don't have to make no decisions that way. Now, you eat that and I'll run a bath."

Upstairs he started the bath and rang Sian. Rebecca answered.

"Becks, it's Ted, could I have a word with your Mum, please?" He heard her shouting to Sian, and a few moments later, she answered. "I can't have him this morning, Ted, I've got to go to the dentist, and John's got an early meeting."

"It's not your grandson, it's your son."

"Stephen?" she exclaimed.

"He's here and in a state."

"What's happened?"

"I don't know. I opened the door this morning and he was asleep on the doorstep. He fell in. It would've been comical if it hadn't been worrying. He wants Rob, but he's eating toast right now and I've got a bath running for him. Sian, he's got no luggage and he looks like he's been wearing the same clothes for a couple of days."

Harry came in with Rob, who ran to Ted and clambered onto his lap. "Hello, Granddad!"

Harry took him away. "Shhh! Granddad's on the phone."

"Can I talk? Is it Daddy?" he asked hopefully. Stephen had been over a few weeks earlier for his third birthday, with a huge assortment of presents, and Rob was hoping the experience would be repeated soon.

Ted waved to Harry and carried on talking. "Can you come round? And bring some clothes?"

"Of course," Sian said, all thoughts of the dentist forgotten. "I'll drop Becks off at school and be straight round. Ted – thank you."

"What's going on, Dad?" Harry asked.

Ted got up. "Steve's here."

"Daddy's here!" she told Rob, who capered around the room in delight. She took his hand. "Come on, let's go and see him!"

"Harriet! There's something wrong." She looked at him, puzzled. "Go and see him. He might talk to you."

"Daddy!"

Stephen turned, and his face lit up. "Hi, Robbie!" He held out his arms and Rob ran to him.

"What's going on, Stevie?" Harry asked, shocked by his appearance.

He was cuddling Rob close. "Lynn's left me," he said into the child's shoulder.

Harry stared at him in horror.

"Where's Lynn?" Rob asked, looking round. "I want Cherry!"

Stephen started to cry. "So do I."

Rob stared at him uncertainly for a minute, and then he reached out and touched the tears on Stephen's face. "Daddy's crying!" he said to Harry in alarm. His own face puckered.

"It's OK, Rob." Stephen pulled himself together. "I… um… I had a pain, that's all."

"Poor Daddy!" Rob said, concerned. "I'll kiss you better!"

Stephen kissed him. "There, you did. Thank you, Robbie." He put the little boy down as Ted came in.

"Bath's ready. Did you eat that toast?"

Stephen shook his head.

"Granddad'll be cross with you now," Rob said sympathetically, taking his hand. "No *Mop and Smiff* if you don't finish every mouthful!" *Mop And Smiff* was one of his favourite TV shows. He sounded exactly like Ted, and Stephen couldn't help laughing.

Ted smiled. "I'll let him off this once, Robbie. But he'd better eat his dinner, eh, kiddo?"

While Stephen was in the bath, Sian arrived, bringing him a change of clothes.

"Lynn's left him," Harry told her. "That's all we know."

They were upstairs in the sitting room. Rob was watching *Rainbow* avidly, face close to the screen, chuckling at Zippy's bad behaviour.

"Why would she leave?" Sian asked, horrified. "I know they were having a few problems because of the miscarriage, but… " She shrugged helplessly.

The door opened and Stephen came in, swamped in Ted's bathrobe. "Hello, Mum."

"Cariad." It was Sian's natural inclination to hug him, but something in his face stopped her, a look she'd never seen before. "Oh, Stephen," she cried, distressed. "What's she done to you?" She wanted to kill Lynn. When your children are little, she thought, you would do anything, anything, to protect them from harm. And then they grow up and walk out into heartbreak, and there's nothing you can do.

Stephen shook his head. "I can't talk about that now," he said politely, as if she'd asked him about the weather. "I don't want to think about it. Did you bring some clothes?"

Silently, she handed him the carrier bag. He thanked her and wandered back to the bathroom.

She looked at Ted.

"Denial," he said.

"Should I *make* him talk to me?"

"I don't see how you could," Harry said. "I should think it would only antagonize him. It would me if I really didn't want to talk about something." I'd like to tear that bitch's head off, she thought viciously.

"Yeah, I'd leave him," Ted agreed. "He knows you're here, Sian, whenever he's ready."

Rainbow finished. "Where's my Daddy?" Rob demanded.

"Here I am. How was *Rainbow*?"

Rob laughed. "Zippy was *so* naughty!"

"He's a bad boy, that Zippy!" Stephen picked Rob up and swung him in the air. "Just like you!" He looked at Harry. "Can I take him home?"

She stared at him, aghast.

"I mean to Mum's, not Manchester."

"Oh! Yes, of course."

Sian drove them home. "How long are you staying?"

"I'll have to go back tonight, we've got a gig tomorrow and we've got to rehearse. Damn!"

"What?"

"I should've rung the lads. Can I ring from home?"

"Of course! You don't even have to ask, cariad."

"Grandpa!" Rob called, running into the house.

"He's not home yet, Robbie. He comes home after lunch these days," Sian told Stephen. He was surprised. "He *is* sixty-five," she reminded him and was alarmed to see his eyes fill with tears.

The notion of John ageing upset Stephen. Everything had gone so wrong in his life that he couldn't bear the thought of anything changing at home "I suppose he is," he muttered.

"Stevie—"

"I can't, Mum. I'm sorry."

She hugged him, wanting to break down and cry herself, but she sensed this would be the worst thing she could do.

He pulled away and picked up Rob. "I'm sorry," he repeated.

She shook her head. "Whatever helps you cope."

He smiled in relief. "You always understand. I don't know what I'd do without you."

Rob took his father's face in his hands and turned it so that they were staring into each other's eyes. "Let's go into Grandpa's sweetie room," he said in a confidential whisper.

"Which room?" Stephen asked, confused.

"His study," Sian explained. "He hides sweets in there for Rob to find, and gives him clues. Robbie loves it!"

"Yes, I imagine he would. Teaching him to think logically, eh?"

"He loves Rob, Stevie," Sian said uneasily.

To her relief, he smiled. "I know."

He and Rob played hide and seek and rough and tumble in the garden. Rob loved rough and tumble. It was a game in which Stephen lay on the ground and Rob leapt on him and they rolled around, fighting. Stephen would pick Rob up and swing him round, pretending he'd won, and he was going to eat Rob, who would squeal in genuine terror, but somehow manage to end up the victor, stamping on Stephen's prone and defeated body in triumph.

Sian called them in for lunch. "You'll have to read to him afterwards, quieten him down a bit," she commented.

"We're going to play the piano when we've eaten up all our lunch, aren't we, Rob?"

He clapped his hands. "Yes, Gran, and the guitart!" Stephen's very first guitar, the acoustic that Dada had given him, was still at home, and Rob was fascinated by the sound it made, especially when Stephen played it. "Now me!" he'd demand, sometimes getting cross when he couldn't coax the same noises out of it.

He was sitting on Stephen's lap at the piano and picking out a tune with one finger while Stephen filled in with his left hand when John came home. He stood and watched them unobserved for a while until Rob caught sight of him. "Grandpa! Listen to me play!"

"It's lovely, Robbie." John looked at Stephen. "What are you going to do if he doesn't want to do music though, Stephen?"

He was taken aback by the fury in Stephen's voice. "As long as it makes him happy, he can sweep the road if he wants to!"

Rob glanced from Stephen to John anxiously, aware of the tension. "Daddy? Are you cross?"

Stephen smiled at him. "Of course not."

Sian looked in. "John! I didn't hear you come in. Have you told him, Stevie?"

Stephen looked down at the piano and shook his head.

"Told me what?"

Sian held out her hand. "Robbie! Come and help me make a cup of tea for Grandpa."

Rob slid off Stephen's lap. "And biscuits?" he asked, hopefully.

"And biscuits," Sian agreed.

"Chocolate?"

"Chocolate," Sian promised, taking his hand. They went out, and she shut the door quietly behind them.

"This isn't just a social visit, then?" John asked.

"Actually, I came to see Rob." Stephen stood up. "Lynn and I have split up."

John stared at him. "Stephen! My God, I'm so sorry! What happened?"

"Too much. I'll tell you soon, Dad. I… I can't…" He couldn't go on.

John hugged him.

After an initial moment of amazement, Stephen relaxed against him. All the love he'd had as a little boy for his father came flooding back. He remembered how John had solved any problem he'd ever had, how he'd been a rock, a tower of strength, always there for him. He cried as if his heart would break. And through it all, John held him, rubbing his back, as he had when Stephen had been Rob's age.

Finally, Stephen stopped. He was hollow inside and his head ached, but he felt better. "Thank you, Dad," he whispered.

John let him go. "I'm your father, Stevie and you are my beloved son. Whatever our differences, don't you ever forget that."

Stephen went up to the bathroom and washed his face. He stared at himself in the mirror. His eyes looked curiously colourless. His skin was usually a warm cream colour, but today it was pale and washed out. He looked almost featureless under the black hair that was falling over his eyes. He pushed it impatiently back. Who am I, he wondered, and what is the point of it all? He went downstairs to the kitchen. The scene made him smile, despite his misery. Sian and John were talking seriously, and John had taken his jacket off and hung it over the back of his chair. Rob was on his lap, holding a chocolate digestive. He had licked the chocolate off it and was now busily crumbling the base into the breast pocket of John's jacket. He looked up and saw Stephen and his eyes widened. He looked down at John's pocket and back over at Stephen.

Stephen shook his head, but was unable to resist grinning. Rob grinned back, relieved.

I'm Rob's father and John and Sian's son, Stephen thought. Surely that's enough?

"Cariad! Would you like a cup of tea?"

He shook his head and fetched himself a glass of water. "I've got a bit of a headache," he said, taking a paracetamol.

"Stevie, I've been thinking. You said you have to be back for rehearsals tomorrow. If you like, you could stay here tonight and I could drive you over tomorrow morning. Becks would love to see you," Sian suggested.

Rebecca was the only one still at home. Kathy was at a catering college in London. She was engaged to Paul Lightfoot, the boy she'd met at Harry's wedding, and they were getting married that summer. He had joined the RAF and was stationed at Brize Norton in Oxfordshire.

"Are you sure?" He wanted to stay more than anything. He wasn't looking forward to going back to that empty flat.

"Of course! And I know Harry will let Robbie stay if you'd like him to. We often have him overnight, it gives her a break, and he's no trouble, is he, John?"

"No trouble at all," John agreed.

"He's a darling, aren't you, Robbie?" Sian continued.

"I'm a blewser," Rob said, taking another biscuit. Stephen looked at him, eyebrows raised. "I'm going to eat this," he said with dignity, biting into it.

"You're a what?" John asked.

"A blewser," Rob said indistinctly.

"What's a blewser?" Sian asked.

"It's the goodest fighter," Rob explained. "*You* know, Grandpa," he said, turning to look up at John and smearing his chocolaty face across John's shirt. He looked back at Stephen and nodded gravely. "Grandpa knows everything."

"That's true." Stephen smiled at John. "Who says you're a blewser, Rob?"

"Granddad!" Rob was starting to get impatient. "When I fight him I always win!"

"A *bruiser*!" Stephen said. "Yes, that's true! I've got a terrific bruise on my leg from where you kicked me this morning."

Rob smirked. "I'm a blewser, a blewser, a blewser. May I get down?" he asked, wriggling off John.

"Go on then," said John.

Rob ran out into the garden. "Can't catch me, Daddy!"

"I'll catch you in a minute. Go and see how fast you can pedal your trike and then I'll come and race you."

"Come now!" Rob shouted, putting his head round the door. "Now, now, now! Or I'll blewser you!"

"Practise first or I'm not coming at all!"

Rob stumped off, muttering.

"God!" Stephen groaned. "He's remorseless!"

That night he bathed Rob and read to him. He'd never done this on his own before. He'd helped Harry, but to be totally responsible for Rob was a new experience and one he enjoyed very much. Rob, warm and fragrant and sucking his thumb, leant sleepily against him while he read *Thomas the Tank Engine* and sang *Rainbow* several times. At last, he kissed Rob and tiptoed out, leaving the door slightly open and the light on in the hall.

He went down to dinner, and afterwards, when Rebecca – who'd been as shocked as her parents at his news, and very sympathetic – had gone out with her boyfriend, he told Sian and John what had happened. He tried to be as honest as he could and he found it very hard to tell them about Miyuki. "I tried to talk to Lynn – God, was it only last night? It seems like years ago! – but she says she can't trust me any more, which is fair enough."

"What a load of absolute fucking rubbish!" John exploded.

Stephen nearly fell out of his chair with shock. He had never heard his father use language like that before; indeed, if asked, he would have been reasonably certain John didn't even *know* language like that. He looked at Sian for her reaction.

She was nodding agreement. "He's right, Stevie." She laughed. "Look at his face, John! Did you think old fuddy duddies like us didn't know words like that, Stephen?"

"Yes, I shouldn't have sworn, but it made me angry," John said. "Of course sleeping with another woman was wrong in the context of your marriage, Stephen, but then again, Lynn was hardly living up to her marriage vows, was she? I'd say very little cherishing was forthcoming from her, never mind the carnal side of the relationship."

"Well, yes," Stephen stammered. Again, he was embarrassed. He hadn't expected to be talking about sex with his parents. He'd thought they'd say it was a terrible shame and he shouldn't have slept with Miyuki, but what was done was done and he was their son, even if he was, as usual, a big disappointment.

"We're not blaming Lynn," Sian said gently. "From what you've told us, Stevie, she was terribly depressed – possibly she still is. That being tired all the time, that's a classic symptom."

"You got tremendously depressed, didn't you?" John said to her.

She nodded and sighed. "Yes."

Stephen frowned. "When was this?"

"I had three miscarriages before you were born. And then a stillborn baby." She smiled at him. "You were so precious to us, Stevie. We thought we'd never have children!"

Stephen was appalled. He remembered that Sian had mentioned a miscarriage when Lynn lost the baby, and he'd meant to ask her about it, but his deteriorating relationship with Lynn had driven it from his mind. To find out that his parents had gone through not one but *three* miscarriages, and then the unimaginable hell of a stillborn child, chilled and awed him. He finally understood his father's obsession with him. If I'd known this earlier, he thought, how much of a difference would it have made? I could at least have been kinder to him. He felt a huge surge of pity and respect for them both.

"I was angry too," Sian was saying. "With myself, especially with you, John—"

"Why?" Stephen interrupted. "Lynn was angry with me. Why?"

"I don't know. The need to apportion blame, I suppose. I really don't know. It happened to me, but I don't understand it. It's all chemicals, isn't it, a chemical imbalance in the brain. So they give you pills to try to balance it up again. Sometimes it works, sometimes it doesn't, so don't blame yourself for not insisting she saw a doctor."

"Don't anyway," said John. "I'm not blaming Lynn, Steve, but she's an adult. She could have gone to see a doctor when she started to feel so bad."

"It is difficult though," Sian said. "Often, by the time you feel that bad it's too late, you think the way you're feeling is normal and everyone else is wrong. Stevie, what I don't understand is why you told her about this other girl."

"I didn't! God, I wanted to, just to make myself feel better, but I knew it wouldn't do any good. George told one of his mates. He thought it was a good story, the two of us with these Japanese sisters. Word got around and Lynn overheard someone talking about it at the pub last night."

"My God, what appalling luck!" exclaimed John.

"But it's not just luck! I have to take the blame for that!"

"Maybe, in a way," John said. "But don't you think an awful lot of life is about luck or the lack of it? Bad luck, you might think at first, for Harry to become pregnant after one night, but such terrific luck for the baby to turn out like he has." He fixed Stephen with a stern eye. "Did you know about my jacket pocket?"

Stephen grinned. "I couldn't grass him up, Dad! You should have seen his worried little face."

"What vulgar expressions you use, Stephen. To continue – good luck you met Lynn, bad luck she became pregnant when she did. And then tremendously bad luck that you'd already drunk so much the night… the night…" He struggled to find a neutral way of expressing it.

"The night I was unfaithful," Stephen said bluntly.

John inclined his head. "Do you see what I mean?"

Stephen nodded.

"Dad's right. If you two hadn't gone to that pub last night you'd probably still be together."

"Yes, but people have to take responsibility for their actions, surely?" Stephen said, confused.

"Of course they do, and it was wrong of you to sleep with someone else, whatever the provocation," agreed Sian. "Dad didn't, and I was just as bad as Lynn."

"It wasn't so easy in those days," John remarked.

They both stared at him.

"*Would* you have done?" asked Sian, really shocked.

"I don't know. It's lucky I was never put to the test, isn't it? There you are, you see, luck again. I know I was desperately unhappy, and I missed making love to you, Sian." Sian blushed. "We've been married for… how long is it?" He stopped to think. "Thirty-five years! Good Lord! – and there are areas I can't experience and vice versa, Sian, but I've always believed it's easier for a man to separate love and sex. When you were so unhappy after the baby died, I was very sorry for you, but also for myself, and I know that, after a while, not having access to the physical love I'd become used to was very, very difficult indeed. And if I'd been in Steve's place and been told I wasn't loved or physically desired any more, I think I may well have done the same thing."

Stephen was staring at him. He couldn't believe this was John talking, his reserved, unemotional father.

John smiled at him. "Not like me, this, is it, Stephen? There's something I should have told you a while ago. I couldn't bear you to think of me as an old man, though. I've got angina, Steve, and it's getting worse. I could go on for years, but then again, I could have a heart attack at any time."

Stephen was aghast. His heart began to pound and he felt cold. Tears started to his eyes.

"Don't get all emotional on me," John said testily. "That's one thing I never could like in you, Stephen, this sentimentality and tears everywhere! I know you get it from your mother, but it's acceptable in a woman!"

"Take no notice of him, grumpy old thing!" Sian said. Tears shone in her eyes too. "There's nothing wrong with expressing your feelings, Stevie. These buttoned-up English, it does them no good at all!"

John reached out and squeezed Stephen's hand. "I just wanted us to have an honest conversation at last. I don't approve of this band rubbish, I think it's a waste of a very good brain, I think you're throwing everything away, but if you are going to do it, son, you'd better be a damned success, because if you're not, I shall want to know the reason why!" He stood up. "I'm going to bed, I'm not feeling a hundred per cent." He patted Stephen's shoulder and kissed Sian. "I'll see you both in the morning."

"What are you going to do now, Stevie?" Sian asked, after John had gone.

"Go to bed. I didn't really get any sleep last night." He yawned hugely.

"No, I mean with the band. Now you've finished at university."

Stephen stared into the fire. It was a chilly night, despite being mid-June, and John had lit it earlier. He watched the flames pouring round the logs like molten gold. "We'll have to find part-time jobs, I suppose; you know, building sites, that kind of thing."

"Don't be silly, with your back?"

He smiled. "Well, something. Andy hasn't given up his job, and George always seems to have cash. We've been talking about going down to London, making a demo tape, I don't know. Mum, how long has Dad been ill?"

"About five years."

"Five years!" He was appalled. "Why didn't you tell me?"

"He didn't want you to know. I had to respect his wishes, Stephen. I didn't know for a long time, and the girls still don't. I'm surprised Lynn didn't tell you."

"Lynn knew?"

Sian nodded. "When you were here – one Christmas, I think – he had an attack and couldn't get to his pills. She came and got me. He asked her not to tell you, but I thought she would."

"No. Not if he'd asked her not to."

She looked at him curiously. "Would you have, Stevie?"

"Yes," he said slowly. "It was hell not telling her about Miyuki. After I told her about Harry, there was nothing I didn't tell her until that." He sighed. "I'm going to bed, before I fall asleep down here. Goodnight, Mum. And thanks."

"What on earth for, cariad?"

He kissed her. "Everything."

He was sleeping in the guest room. Sian and John had long been reconciled and once again shared the same room. His old room had become Rob's bedroom and he didn't want to sleep in his attic room, it reminded him too much of Lynn, and besides, he wanted to be near Rob in case his son needed anything.

Sure enough, he was woken in the early hours of the morning by the door opening and a little voice whispering, "Daddy?" It wobbled upwards and ended on a sob. He turned the light on. "Robbie! I'm here, cariad."

Rob shot into his bed and burrowed under the covers, clutching at him.

"What's the matter, little boy?" Stephen asked, holding him.

"Had a bad dream," Rob murmured fearfully, nestling against him.

"Well don't you worry about it. It wasn't real, it can't hurt you. You stay here with me and I'll look after you."

"Can we leave the light on?"

"Of course we can!" He cuddled Rob, stroking his head and singing quietly in Welsh to him; the same songs Rhodri had sung to him when he was Rob's age. Rob drifted off to sleep. Stephen held the warm little body close to him and wished he didn't have to give him back.

In Manchester, he tried to submerge his pain. He ran every afternoon after rehearsals. He got a job as a cashier at a petrol station from six in the morning until one in the afternoon. It was a boring job, but it gave him the chance to write, and left the afternoons free for rehearsals. While he was working there he wrote several songs: 'Broken Flower', 'Lost Souls', 'Just Hanging On', 'The End of the Day' and 'This Northern Sky'. He tried to fill every moment so that there was no time to think. Sometimes, he'd realise that someone had been talking to him but he had no memory of it. Some part of his mind must have been paying attention because he'd obviously answered rationally and to the other's satisfaction. The words from the Dire Straits song 'Romeo And Juliet', '*And all I do is miss you, and the way we used to be*', kept bouncing around in his brain. He and Lynn had liked that song; when it first came out, one of Lynn's friends had said, "Romeo and Juliet, that's you two", and they'd laughed and agreed, but he'd never really listened to it before. He knew the song, had sung it more times than he could remember, but it'd just been words then, he'd never heard the suffering in it, the pain. And he'd never stopped to think what had happened to those two. When he was fifteen, his class had been taken to the Theatre Royal in York to see a production of the play. He remembered thinking it ludicrous – nobody would behave like that. He and Ray had discussed it afterwards and laughed to scorn the idea that anyone would be suicidal about love. How could he have *ever* been so naïve? He had never known such pain.

He couldn't listen to that song any more, couldn't listen to a lot of songs. Nothing made any sense to him, except Rob. Rob was his talisman, the only reason he could see for existing. He went back to York as often as he could, even if it was only for a few hours, and carried a small photo of his son with him all the time.

He graduated from university with a first-class honours degree. It was like some sort of cosmic joke at his expense, he thought bitterly. Still, at least John was proud. He didn't want to know what Lynn had got, didn't want to think about her, couldn't even say or hear her name without wanting to chuck himself off the top of the Refuge Assurance building, but he bumped into Caro in the Precinct Centre one day, and she told him Lynn had got a 2.1. He was barely polite, walking away before she'd finished speaking. Afterwards, he cursed himself for not asking for Lynn's address. He hadn't even let Caro finish telling him where Lynn was working, and he had no idea where Caro or indeed any of Lynn's friends were now. He went to the houses where they'd lived, asked around, haunted the pubs and clubs they'd gone to, but to no avail. Finally, in desperation, he rang her parents.

Theresa answered the phone. She listened in silence. "I think you've caused more than enough trouble in this family," she said coldly, and hung up.

He'd moved into George's house, which made it much easier from the point of view of rehearsing and going to gigs, although he found the squalor in which they lived deeply depressing, and they vigorously objected to his efforts to make them clean the place up.

"What are you, a lass or something?" George said one morning when he came downstairs and found Stephen cleaning out the inside of the kettle. "I'll get me Mam to send you one of her pinnys!"

"There was something green growing in there," Stephen said faintly. It made him feel sick to think about it.

"Could've been some sort of fantastic new drug, like penicillin, bonny lad," said George, making himself some toast. "And you got rid of it. Did we tell you about the time we found a dead mouse in wor toaster?"

"I really don't want to know."

"We could never get the bread in properly, and one day Andy got fed up, so he poked it with a screwdriver and skewered this dead mouse. Its head had all rotted away – pass the marmalade, man." He smothered his toast in marmalade. "Which explained why wor toast had always come out with these kind of smears all over it." He looked at Stephen's horrified face. "There's nothing in there now, man. We turn it upside down and shake it from time to time."

"I can't believe you didn't chuck it out!" Stephen said, looking at the toaster with horror. He'd had toast out of that machine.

"Howay, man, none of us have died!" George scoffed.

"Telling him about the toaster?" Fin came in to the kitchen. "You'd have laughed if you'd been here, Steve! The look on Andy's face!"

Kathy's wedding was the first Saturday in August. Stephen didn't want to go, but, of course, there was no way out. He travelled over very late on Friday night after a gig at Utopia. Sian had asked him if he'd stay at the Angel, as the house was full of relatives, and he was more than happy to spend time with Rob. He'd bought some sticker books and a fuzzy felt set to keep him amused at the reception.

Harry was waiting up for him.

"You shouldn't have bothered. Ted gave me a spare key after I turned up here when—" He couldn't finish the sentence.

Harry hugged him. "I know. I wanted to. You're in my flat."

After she'd moved back in with Ted, he'd had an extension built onto the living quarters of the pub, a self-contained flat for her and Rob. It had three bedrooms: one for her, one for Rob and a very small guest bedroom, a bathroom, a sitting room and a large kitchen diner. There was a door connecting it to the main part of the house, but it also had its own entrance.

Stephen's face lit up. "Great!"

Harry smiled. "I'm glad you think so! The spare bedroom is tiny."

"I know, I don't care, it's lovely being with you and Rob. And if you could see the conditions I'm living in at George's! They don't know the meaning of the word clean. Has Mum foisted some relatives on Ted?"

Harry nodded. "Some Welsh cousins of yours, I think. Come on, we'd better get some sleep. Big day tomorrow!"

His face changed. "I'm dreading it."

She took his hand. "Rob and I'll look after you, Stevie."

He sat right at the far end of the front pew, with Rob on his lap and Harry pressed close to him. She was looking very pretty in a red frock with a tiny boxy black jacket, very high-heeled black shoes and an elegant little Fifties-style hat. Sian leant forward from the other end of the pew and smiled at them both. There was an air of suppressed excitement in the church. Paul was standing at the front with his best man, both of them in uniform, both of them nervous. Stephen remembered Ray losing the speech. Don't think about it! he told himself. He looked down at Rob. Harry had bought him a little sailor suit, and he looked angelic in it.

"You all right, Blewser?"

"It's bording, isn't it, Daddy?"

"Yes, but don't worry, there's singing later and I've got some presents for you to play with at the party if you're good."

Rob made a loud whooping noise.

"Shh! You'll get me shot!"

The organist began to play 'Here Comes The Bride', and everyone stood up. Stephen lifted Rob onto his shoulders so that he could see what was happening.

"Grandpa!" Rob shouted, as John came up the aisle with Kathy, who was looking beautiful in white tulle. John turned and smiled.

Stephen didn't have to see Kathy's expression to know how she was feeling; she was incandescent with happiness, lighting up the church. She practically danced up the aisle on John's arm, and, as Paul turned to her, his face was shining with joy. Stephen fought back tears, and begged the God he didn't believe in that the marriage would last and that Kathy and Paul would always feel this way about each other.

The wedding breakfast was the same as all wedding breakfasts. People ate and drank and talked and laughed. The women cooed over Rob in his sailor suit, wanting to pick him up and kiss him. He squirmed away from them, wiping his face distastefully. Toasts and speeches were made and the bride and groom cut the cake. Stephen drank far too much champagne, which seemed to be flowing like water, and wondered how much this wedding had cost. As everyone got up and trickled through into the lounge for coffee and more alcohol, he and Rob fetched the carrier bag he'd left in Ted's car and took the contents to the far side of the room, where, unobserved, he pushed a small sofa across a corner, leaving enough of a gap for the pair of them to sit on the floor behind it, against cushions he took from the surrounding chairs.

They were completely absorbed in the fuzzy felt, Stephen making up ridiculous stories as Rob put the figures on the board.

"What did the raddit do then?"

"He said, 'If you don't give my carrot back straight away I shall have to blewser you'."

"And what did the fox say?"

"The fox didn't believe him. He said, 'You can't blewser me!'"

"And did the raddit blewser him?"

"Certainly did. The raddit had secret powers from eating carrots that made him much stronger than the fox. He blewsered him like anything."

Rob chortled with glee.

"Go on, make him blewser the fox."

There was a movement above them. Stephen looked up. Sian and Harry were kneeling on the sofa peering at them.

"We've been looking everywhere for you two," Harry said.

"Mummy, the raddit blewsered the fox with his special powers from eating the carrots! Can I have carrots and blewser Granddad?"

Harry raised her eyebrows. "Thank you, Stephen."

"Well, at least he'll eat carrots now," Stephen grinned.

"Come on out, the pair of you," Sian said. "It's time the Blewser went home to tea."

"Carrots?" asked Rob eagerly.

Stephen lifted Rob over the sofa and picked up the fuzzy felt.

"You really should have mingled a bit, Steve," Sian said reproachfully. "Kathy is your sister, after all!"

"Sorry. It's difficult not to think about… my wedding. When I'm with Rob it's easier."

"I know, but you're an adult, Stevie. You can't keep running away. These things happen, you've got to face the truth sometime." She squeezed his arm. "Lecture over! Anyway, Rob won't be at the disco tonight, so you can mix then."

Stephen stared at her, horrified. "I wasn't going."

"Well, now you are," Sian said in a voice of steel.

Harry looked round at them. "Come on, Steve, we've got to get Rob sorted and get changed."

Ted was babysitting Rob. "Wedding discos aren't my scene," he told Stephen as they sat in the sitting room of the Angel, drinking whisky.

"Mum's making me go," Stephen said gloomily, pouring himself another glass.

"Have you eaten anything?" Ted watched him down the whisky in one.

"Yeah, the breakfast."

"Since then?"

"Not hungry."

Ted picked the bottle up. "I don't think you ought to have any more of this then."

Stephen shrugged. "I'm not really thirsty either, just keeping you company."

Ted gave him an old fashioned look, but before he could say anything, Harry appeared at the door. "I'm ready."

Both men gaped at her. She was wearing a strappy little gold dress, very short, and high-heeled gold sandals. Her legs were bare and tanned, and her hair, which she had grown, was rippling down her back.

Stephen recovered first. "You look amazing, Harry, really…" He wanted to say 'sexy', but was afraid that Ted might take it the wrong way, so ended feebly with "nice."

It was obvious from Ted's face what he was thinking, but he managed to smile and say, "Very pretty, Princess."

"Rob's sound, he was out like a light. We won't be late back, Dad." She kissed him. "Come on, Stevie."

Mindful of Sian's words, Stephen mingled, dancing with Kathy, Rebecca and several of his cousins. He talked to Paul and made polite conversation with the relatives. He also drank steadily.

Towards midnight, the DJ started playing slow, smoochy dances. Stephen took Harry's arm. "Dance with me, lovely Harry?"

She could tell he was drunk, but she didn't realise how drunk. They moved out onto the floor together and he pulled her close. "I've never seen you look so gorgeous," he whispered.

She didn't answer, she was too busy enjoying dancing with him. He'd always been her friend, since she first joined The Brigands, but apart from that night she'd slept with him, he'd never shown any desire for her and he certainly hadn't instigated it then.

His hands moved down from her waist to her bottom and stroked it. "You're so sexy, Harry. You were always pretty, but these days you're beautiful."

She moved his hands back up, stepping away from him slightly as she did so. He stumbled.

"I think we ought to go home," she said regretfully. She didn't want him falling over.

"Whatever you want," he shrugged, unconcerned. They said their goodbyes, and Harry loaded him into her car, a soft top Triumph Spitfire Ted had bought her for her twenty-first birthday. They drove back to the Angel, Stephen singing loudly.

"Hush," Harry whispered as she parked. "Rob's asleep!"

He put his finger to his lips. "Not another sound," he said, unsteadily.

"Good." She helped him up the stairs. "Go to bed, Stephen. I'll tell Dad we're home." She disappeared through the connecting door. When she came back, he was sitting on the sofa. "Come on," she sighed, hauling him up.

He put his arm round her and she guided him to the spare room. "There you are, Steve." She turned to go, but he moved quickly and shut the door. He pushed her gently back against the wall and began to kiss her, his tongue making long, slow, serpentine movements that melted her very bones. He peeled the straps of her dress down over her shoulders and caressed her breasts. "You're *so* beautiful, Harry. You're like a sky full of summer stars. My beautiful summer star."

"Stevie," she breathed, unzipping his trousers.

Somehow, they got to the bed, both of them naked.

"Have you got a condom?" she whispered.

"Let's have a baby, a little girl, a daughter, Sakura."

Harry started to wriggle away from under him, but he caught her wrists and held them above her head.

"Steve, stop it!" she said sharply. "I don't want a baby!"

"You're skin's so soft," he said, stroking her inner thigh.

"Let me go, Stephen!"

He ignored her, and tried to open her legs.

She resisted and struggled to free her wrists. "Stephen!" she said desperately. "Let me go!" She got one hand free and, pushing him away, tried to sit up.

He forced her down onto the bed again, and lay on top of her. He was heavy, and very fit from all the running he'd done in the past few weeks.

Scared, she started to cry. "Stephen, please stop, you're hurting me."

"Why won't you let me make love to you, Cherry?" he whispered, kissing her throat. "I love you so much."

Her blood ran cold. "Stephen, I'm not Lynn!"

He parted her legs with his knee. In desperation, she bit him very hard on the shoulder, drawing blood. He shouted with pain and she shoved him, pushing him off her. She sat up, still crying, and shaking with fear and shock.

"Why did you do that?" he asked in confusion.

She could barely speak. "Look at me, Stephen!" she managed to say finally. "I'm not bloody Lynn, I'm Harry! I thought you wanted *me*!"

"I know, I did, I do." He sat up.

"No, you don't!" She thumped his chest. "You just want a girl's body, *any* girl's body, so you can pretend it's Lynn! Well, you're not using me!"

The door opened and Rob stood blinking in the light. "Mummy? Wossamatter?"

She threw Stephen a look of hatred and swept Rob up. "Nothing, darling, nothing. Come on back to bed."

Stephen got up and fumbled around, trying to find his pyjamas. Pulling them on, he went into Harry's room to wait for her. His head began to ache and he lay on the bed. He had just started to doze off when she opened the door.

She stopped in the doorway. "Get out." She was wearing an old towelling robe and her make up was all smeared. She looked very young and vulnerable.

His heart contracted with guilt. "I'm sorry. I'm really, really sorry. What did I do?"

She shut the door and stood in front of it. "Oh, you only called me Cherry and tried to rape me."

"Harry! I'm so, so sorry." His voice was full of pain. "I'll get my stuff and go." He stood up unsteadily.

"No. You're too drunk, Stephen. Sit down."

He sat back down and she sat next to him. "It was horrible, Stephen. *You* were horrible."

He gazed at her, his eyes full of remorse. She put her arm around him and he nestled against her as if he was Rob's age.

"Poor little Stevie," she whispered, starting to cry.

"Oh, please don't cry, Harry," he said in consternation. "I'm so sorry."

"You're so mixed up and miserable. What are you going to do?"

"I don't know," he whispered, despairingly. "I miss her all the time, I miss her so much it hurts. I can't stop thinking about her, remembering. How can she be gone? How *can* she? We shared everything, we were part of each other, we'd finish each other's sentences, she always knew what I was thinking and feeling, even when I didn't. I can't manage without her, it's like losing a limb. I don't know how I can live with this pain." He suddenly realised what he was saying and to whom. "When I first told her about you and me and Rob, she said you were in love with me. Are you?"

She didn't answer.

"Harry?"

"Yes," she murmured, so quietly he could barely hear her. "I was. So I know exactly how you're feeling." She bit her lip and looked away from him. "I wasn't on the pill that night, Stevie. I was marrying Jason to get away from Dad, you knew that, didn't you? But it was to get away from you, too. And then you split up with Angie, and I couldn't believe it had happened when I was so nearly married to someone else and then I thought, I can comfort him, and make love to him and maybe…"

He tilted her face so that she had to look at him. "You tried to have Rob?" he asked gently.

Her lips trembled. "Yes. So how can I stay mad at you, when I used you too? I do know how you feel, Stevie. I'm sorry."

To her surprise, he was smiling at her. "Oh, Hal, my lovely, lovely Hal, I'm so pleased!"

She stared at him, amazed. "What?"

"That you wanted Rob to be mine." He hugged her. "You're my best friend, Harry."

"W-what about Lynn?" she stammered.

"That's entirely different. I love Lynn, I'll never stop loving her, even when I get over this – this, what I feel now. I'll always want her, but you're my best friend. I think you always have been," he said slowly, "right from the beginning. When Dad kicked me out, it was you I turned to, not Angie. I mean, it made sense - I'm pretty sure her mum and dad wouldn't have let me stay there, but I wasn't thinking rationally at the time. I just thought of you. Are you still in love with me?"

She shook her head. "No. I don't yearn for you any more. I love seeing you and being with you." She stopped and began to blush. "And I'd love to make love to you again, but I'm not *in* love with you."

"Would you like to go to bed with me now?"

"Not if you'd be going to bed with Lynn."

"No. With you. Beautiful, loyal, kind Harry. But I don't want to spoil our friendship."

"Do you really want *me?*"

"Very much."

She kissed him. "I don't think it would spoil our friendship. If what happened earlier and me telling you about Rob didn't, I don't think anything can. But there's still the problem of the condom."

He was surprised. "What problem?"

"I thought you didn't have any!"

"There's a packet in my washbag. It's been there for ages. Do they have sell-by dates?"

She giggled. "Let's check!"

The condoms were still usable.

"Are you sure you want to do this, Harry?"

"Shut up and get into bed!"

The next morning he had a monumental hangover. He managed to get to the bathroom before he was sick.

As he heaved, Rob stood beside him, rubbing his back, and eating a piece of toast. "Poor likkle Daddy! Are you coming to live with us, now?"

Stephen couldn't answer. He was sick again.

Rob wandered out and he heard him asking Harry the same question.

"No," she laughed. He was relieved not to hear any regret in her voice. "He's got to go back to Manchester and do his singing and guitar work."

Later, she drove him to the station. As his train pulled in, she took him in her arms. "I meant it, you know, and last night proved it. Sex with you is tremendous, and really fun, but that's all it is. And you're still my best friend."

He hugged her. "You're still mine. I really love you, Harry."

He went back to Manchester feeling better than he'd done for a long time. The heavy pain around his heart had lightened a little. He loved knowing that Rob hadn't been just a happy accident.

Fin heard him whistling as he unpacked. "You sound happier."

"I am, a bit."

"Good. It's been a tough time for you, Steve. You know the reason we haven't said anything isn't because we don't care. It's just hard to know what to say."

Stephen smiled at him. "I know. I'm lucky to have such good friends."

They were doing a gig that night at a big pub in Salford and on Monday they had another spot at Utopia. George was still seeing Kagami and Stephen had been dating Miyuki on a casual but carnal basis over the previous month and had only just discovered that she and Kagami were Taro Watanabe's sisters-in-law. He wondered if that was why they had been playing at Utopia so often lately. He asked Miyuki before the gig.

She laughed. "Taro would never let that affect his business! He likes that you're nice boys, but if you were crap you wouldn't be playing here. He thinks you're very good! He has someone here tonight to see you."

"Someone here? Who?" Miyuki smiled teasingly. "Who, Miyuki?"

"Maybe you'll see. You better play well!"

"Great! I'm guaranteed to be shit, now!"

He tried to put her words out of his head as they waited backstage. One of the lighting crew had a joint and he asked for a drag.

"You can finish it, I gotta get back to work."

"Is that a good idea, Steve?" George asked.

"It helps my asthma," Stephen replied. He'd never had asthma in his life, but it was the first thing that came into his head. He didn't want to tell them what Miyuki had said, bad enough he was nervous.

"Oh." George was perplexed.

"I didn't know you had asthma," Andy said, surprised.

"I'm a complex guy," Stephen grinned. They were on. He ground it out and took a deep breath.

"Stephen, do you know what time it is?"

"Sorry, Mum, I didn't think. I need to talk to Dad." He was gripping the phone so tightly his knuckles shone white.

"Well, you're lucky, the phone woke him up, too. Are you in trouble?"

"No; Mum, please!"

"Stephen?" John's voice was anxious. "Are you in trouble?"

"How come my family's got such a low opinion of me?" he demanded. "No, Dad, I'm not in trouble."

Andy and George hooted with laughter. Fin opened another can of lager and offered it to him. He took a swig and swallowed quickly. "At the gig… um… an A & R man – Euterpe – a record company – they want to sign the band! We need a lawyer, one who deals with this sort of thing. I hoped you might know one."

"Stephen! That's terrific news! Hold on, son." Stephen heard him telling Sian, who squealed loudly. "I'm back, son. Now, let me see. Off the top of my head I would say possibly Nigel Pearson's son, Alan. Steve, I'll do some telephoning first thing in the morning and get back to you. Your mother has your number, doesn't she?"

"Yes, yes she does. Thanks, Dad!"

"Very well, I'll speak to you tomorrow. Well done, son! Your mother wants to talk to you. Goodnight, son."

"Stevie? Oh, cariad, I'm so pleased!" Sian made a spluttering sound.

"Don't cry Mum, or you'll start me off!"

George hit him on the back of the head. "Don't be a big lass, man!"

"Ouch! Mum, I've got to go and kill George, he's pushed it once too often. I'll speak to you tomorrow, bye, Mum." He hung up. "Right, you big Geordie bastard!"

George pushed Miyuki in front of him. "Don't let the hobbit hurt me, Miyuki, man!"

Stephen picked Miyuki up and swung her round. As usual, he was bowled over by how tiny she was. She was less than five foot tall and impossibly slender, with delicate, rounded little breasts. The first time he'd made love to her, drunk as he was, he had been afraid she might break, and even though he'd grown more used to her body over time, there was still the feeling that he had to be very gentle. They went up to his room – an oasis of clean in a desert of grime, he'd described it to her the first time he'd taken her there – and he undressed her carefully and laid her on the bed.

"You ought to have 'Fragile, handle with care' tattooed on your bottom," he said, kissing it.

She grabbed him. "You talk too much!"

He started to make love to her. He had found that sex was almost a narcotic. When he was making love he could forget who he was, forget Lynn, become nothing more than a body experiencing a sense of bliss and wellbeing. It was like being given a shot of oblivion. It was a much better way of getting to sleep than running. Unfortunately, sex didn't happen nearly as often as running.

John rang him late the next morning. "Alan Pearson, Steve, he's the man you want." He gave Stephen a phone number. "Ring him today, I've already spoken to him, he wants to see you all as soon as possible."

"Thanks, Dad," Stephen said, gratefully. "I'll ring him now." He hung up and stared at the paper in his hand. This is where it all changes, he thought. For a second he almost considered tearing it up and running away, but sanity – or was it insanity? – prevented him. His fingers shaking, he dialled the number.

"That your last one for the day, Lynn?"

Lynn looked up. Diana, the community midwife, was standing in the doorway.

"Yes. I should've had one more, but they cancelled."

"I'm done too. Just sent my last mum-to-be home to enjoy the bank holiday weekend." She looked at Lynn keenly. "What will you be doing?"

"Sleeping. I always seem to be tired. I even wake up tired."

Diana ran a professional eye over her. "You are pale. You might be anaemic. You should get it checked out. Look! Come out for a drink tonight, there's a crowd of us going, I guarantee you a good time!"

"I don't know," Lynn said reluctantly. "I wouldn't be good company."

"Course you would! Do come, Lynn, I know you'd have a good time, and you never go anywhere. It's probably boredom that's making you tired! If you're not having fun, you can always go home."

"Who's going?"

"Well… me, some of the other midwives, Andrea from reception, Dr Abbot's secretary, Zeno, the nurses from ENT, Tim Franklin—"

"The Senior Registrar?" Lynn was surprised. "I wouldn't have thought he'd have mixed with the likes of us!"

"Don't let that grave and aloof air fool you, Lynn. He's great fun! Oh, do come."

"Oh, OK, just to shut you up!"

"Good girl! We're meeting at the Barley Mow in Burmantofts. I'll tell you what, I'll pick you up, shall I?"

"Afraid I'll chicken out?"

"Afraid you'll get lost!"

Lynn drove home through the heavy traffic. It was only just after four, but it was the Friday before the late August Bank Holiday, and everyone wanted to get out of the city early. She was working in Leeds, at the Child Development Clinic at St. James's University Hospital, affectionately known throughout the area as Jimmy's. She'd taken the job after graduating, nearly two months ago. She'd heard from Caro that Stephen had got a first. It won't mean anything to him now, she thought sadly. She had to stop thinking about him, it was the only way she could survive. Sometimes at night she'd lie awake going over and over it, wondering if she had done the right thing. But it seemed to her she'd had no choice. How could he have done that to her? And then she'd start thinking: if only. If only Stephen and she hadn't had that row. If only she'd gone to the loo ten minutes earlier or later and not heard Jean Pritchard. If only she'd never got pregnant in the first place. And then she'd start to cry and be unable to stop and have to go downstairs and have a large whisky. Or two.

She'd bought a small house in Saxton, a village to the east of the city. Belsay Crescent was a quiet little street within walking distance of the local shops. Her neighbours were a garrulous widower in his eighties on one side, and a young female opera singer who was very friendly, but rarely there, on the other.

She made herself a sandwich and ran a bath. She couldn't think why she'd agreed to go out, all she wanted to do was sleep. She dragged herself out of the bath, dressed, and put on a minimal amount of make up. The doorbell rang.

"Hi, Lynn. You look nice."

"Wow, so do you, Diana! I hadn't realised it was going to be dressy. Had I better change?"

"No, you look good. Stylish. And no one else will be wearing anything like this, I just like getting dressed up. I suppose it comes of having to wear a uniform for work. Come on, let's go."

The Barley Mow was crowded, noisy, and smoky. Diana pushed her way in and headed for a large group sitting at two tables at the back, Lynn following her rather reluctantly.

A voice behind her said, "I didn't know you were coming!"

It was Tim Franklin. He was beaming at her as if her being there was the highlight of his day. She couldn't help smiling back.

"Let me get you a drink," he offered.

She looked over at Diana, who quickly looked away and became deeply involved in a conversation. A suspicion that she'd set this up entered Lynn's head. Oh, what the hell! She was here anyway, she might as well enjoy herself. "Thank you, I'd love a whisky."

His eyebrows rose very slightly. "Back in a sec."

She sat down and chatted to Andrea, half her mind on Tim Franklin. He was the only man she'd seen who could even begin to hold a candle to Stephen. She watched him walking back from the bar. He was almost as attractive as Stevie, she thought, although physically he wasn't in Stephen's league. Stephen was only five foot eight, but he was well proportioned with a lithe, muscular physique and broad shoulders. Tim was tall and very thin; his arms and legs reminded her of a newborn foal, just that bit too long and skinny. It was rather endearing though.

He put the whisky down in front of her and smiled.

She took a sip. It was strong and warming. Since she'd left Stephen, she'd had to limit herself, she'd started to drink far too much. It blurred the edges of the pain, but she'd found recently that she needed more and more to do that, and she was afraid of becoming dependent on it.

"I'm jolly glad you could come," Tim said, taking a mouthful of beer.

He had an olive complexion, rather bushy brown hair, and beautiful eyes, thickly lashed and a smoky amber colour. He didn't look very English. She wondered if that's what she found so attractive about him. Stephen didn't look English, either, you could tell he was Celtic immediately, that silky, lustrous black hair, his warm, creamy skin. She couldn't place Tim. Just not English.

Without thinking, she asked, "Where are you from?"

"Surrey," he replied, bemused.

"Oh, Surrey," she blushed. "I just… um… I didn't think you could be from the north, you don't have any accent. Not everyone does, of course," she babbled.

"Where are you from? You don't have an accent either."

"Hampshire."

"Oh, beautiful countryside."

"Have you seen North Yorkshire? That's fantastic."

"Perhaps you could show me sometime?"

"Oh, well—"

"How about next weekend?"

"I don't—"

"Oh, do say yes, it's my birthday," he said disarmingly. "I'd love to spend it seeing the delights of North Yorkshire!"

So she felt she had to say yes.

Alan Pearson negotiated a four-album deal for Sid's Six with the record company Euterpe UK, a subsidiary of Muse International, the media giant. Stephen also got a publishing deal for his songs. Pearson was a short, stout man in his forties, with a wry sense of humour. Stephen liked him immediately. He was prepared to listen to them.

"I take it you don't have a manager?"

Stephen shook his head. "I've been kind of managing us."

"You need a manager. Can I recommend someone? You might have heard of her, Steve – Janice Ellery."

"The jazz singer? Yes, I have," Stephen replied. "She was very good, I've got a couple of her albums."

"She's currently managing The Silver Spiders, Stiff Upper Lip, The Martyrs and Guttersnipes." He laughed at their expressions. "Yeah, I know what you're thinking. Why would she bother with the likes of you? Three good reasons: one, she wants to take on a new, young band. She wanted GI Joe, but just missed out on them. From what I've heard about you four, you could be as big as or bigger than them. Two, she likes a challenge, and three – the best reason of all – she's my wife."

The boys began to grin.

Alan held up his hand. "That doesn't mean she'll take you just because I'm your solicitor, but it does mean she's more likely to be favourably disposed towards you. I'll set up a meeting. When are you next playing at Utopia?"

Three pairs of eyes turned expectantly to Stephen. His brain had turned to mush. "Um… um… um… Sunday."

Alan Pearson grinned. "See you on um… um… um… Sunday, then."

They went out into the street, feeling like kids let loose in a sweet factory.

"Thank God you said Janice Ellery was a good singer, Steve," Andy said. "Suppose you'd said she was crap!"

"I'm hungry," George announced. "How much money have we got?"

They checked wallets and pockets. Added together it came to three pounds and fifty-three pence.

"We've got a four-album deal, a hot-shot manager, hopefully, and we can barely afford a burger!" Fin said ruefully.

Stephen shut his eyes. He'd just realised once again that Lynn was gone forever, and he wasn't going to be bursting into the flat that night to tell her the good news and take her to bed to celebrate. Why hadn't this happened last year? He kicked the side of the building and leant his head against it.

"Have you gone mental, like, Steve?" Andy inquired.

"Shut the fuck up, Lake! What's wrong, Steve?" Fin asked.

"Nothing. Andy's right. Just being mental." He pulled himself together. It wasn't fair to spoil this for the others. "Fuck our lack of funds. None of us have had anything to eat since breakfast, our train doesn't go for..." he checked his watch "...four hours, we're going somewhere good, we're going to have a great meal, with wine *and* pudding, and I'm paying by cheque!"

"Have you got enough money in the bank though, bonny lad?"

"Well if I haven't, the cheque'll bounce, but if I can't take my band out to celebrate when we've just got an ace deal, life isn't worth living!" He waited for someone to deny it was his band.

They just grinned at him.

He grinned back. "Come on, then! I'm starving!"

"So, where are you taking me?" Tim asked.

Lynn had packed a picnic and a map book. "Castle Bolton." It was somewhere she'd never been with Stephen. "Oh, and happy birthday. Is it today?"

"Tomorrow." He glanced at her. "I was hoping I could take you out to dinner."

"Thank you. I'd like that." She felt very at ease with him, he didn't seem to expect anything of her apart from her company.

It was a lovely day, and he enjoyed Bolton castle immensely, especially the view. "It's absolutely stunning!" he said, as they gazed from the castle at the bleak, beautiful scenery. "Look at those drystone walls! And that sky, it's such a perfect blue!"

Lynn nodded. "I know, it's so... so wild, isn't it? I grew up in the New Forest, and that's lovely, but this is just so *primeval*, I suppose, although that isn't really the word I want. And as for that sky – I've seen it change from this to black and threatening in an instant, and hurl rain down!" She smiled, and Tim, watching her face as she stared into the distance, was struck by how happy she looked. "I remember once, at Fountains Abbey, we—" She stopped. "Never mind. Shall we go and look at the gardens?"

She didn't look happy now, he thought. Why? And who did she go to that Abbey with? but he merely said, "Splendid, yes, let's."

His accent was very posh, very upper-class. He reminded her of Dominic Chaplin, but without the obscenity or the cynicism; on the contrary, he didn't swear once, and it was refreshingly easy to engage his enthusiasm.

They wandered around the grounds. He was interested in the herb garden. "My mother's trying to establish one, but unfortunately she hasn't got green fingers, although she's convinced she has. She drives the gardeners to distraction."

"Gardeners?"

He blushed slightly. It made his already warm colouring irresistible.

"My parents are quite well-to-do. Well, rich, actually. My stepfather's in banking."

"What about your real father?"

"He was in the army. Killed in Korea a month before I was born."

"I'm so sorry!"

He smiled at her. "I never knew him. He's just a photo, I don't even look like him, I take after my mother's side of the family – she's half-Italian. Actually, I'm a lot darker than she is!"

That explained the un-Englishness.

"Anyway, tell me about you. I've waffled on about myself quite long enough."

Lynn sat on the grass and leaned back against the wall. He sat next to her.

"Nothing to tell, really," she said. "I'm not posh. My parents run a guesthouse in the New Forest. I suppose we're estranged, I hardly ever see or hear from them. I studied speech therapy at Manchester University and this is my first job. That's about it."

"Is it?" he asked, gently. "What about the love affair that went wrong?"

"I don't know what do you mean," she said stiffly.

"I'm sorry." He was contrite. "I… it seems to me you're not very happy. And that makes me sad, although as you quite rightly point out, albeit in a very nice way, it's none of my business."

She bit her lip. "I'm sorry, I didn't mean to snap. There is… there *was* someone. We were married but—"

"Oh," he interrupted, thoroughly surprised. "You're so young to be divorced!"

She coloured. "I'm not. I don't wear a wedding ring because…" Because Stevie has it, she thought, her heart aching. She had nothing of him, nothing, only a few old photographs. "Because there's no point. I loved him very much, but it went wrong. And please don't ask," she added quickly. "Because I really don't want to talk about it. Maybe not ever."

He put his hand on hers. It made her start. It felt warm and capable and she had an urge to throw herself into his arms and say, sort me out, take all my problems away! Instead, she said, "Shall we get the picnic?"

The following night, he took her to Corleigh Manor, an opulent hotel towards Keighley. She wanted to get him something for his birthday, but as it was Sunday, she was limited for choice. She settled on a bottle of Bollinger champagne.

He was delighted. "I feel like James Bond, although I'm shaken *and* stirred! Thank you, Lynn!" He kissed her on the cheek.

For a mad moment she expected him to call her Cherry. She swallowed hard. He noticed. He noticed everything. She suddenly realised he was very keen on her and felt flattered and panicky at the same time.

"Are you all right?" he was asking.

"Fine." She managed to smile at him. "A goose walked over my grave, that's all."

There was no expense spared at dinner. Lynn let herself off her self-imposed rein and drank a great deal more than she'd meant to. She was shocked by how much she liked him, and felt off-balance. Alcohol made her feel in control, dulling the edge of the panic.

They had coffee and liqueurs afterwards in a very plush lounge.

Tim leant towards her. "Thank you, Lynn. I've had a terrific birthday." He opened his mouth to say something else but closed it again.

She had a feeling she knew exactly what he was going to say. "What?" she asked.

He shook his head, smiling. "It'll keep."

"Were you going to ask me to go to bed with you?"

He was taken aback. "How did you know?"

She shrugged. "I don't know. Ask me."

He looked at her, unsure.

"Ask me."

He put his hand on hers. "Dear Lynn, would you do me the honour of staying here with me tonight? I haven't got a room booked or anything," he added hurriedly.

"But my mother always stays here when she comes to see me and I'm sure they could find one."

She believed him. He'd told her a little about his family. His stepfather owned a lot of property, and she imagined he could buy this place for cash if he wanted. A thought occurred to her. "Does your stepfather own the hotel?"

He went red. "Well, yes, actually. But I pay my own way – on my wages, I don't get an allowance or anything. I've never brought anyone here before. I can't believe you came here with me. I'm... well, I'm not very good at relationships. A bit, you know, shy and awkward." His face was like a beetroot. "I'm all right with my patients, get on fine with them, especially children, but when I've not got my 'doctor's head' on, well..."

Suddenly she liked him immensely, and it was so lovely to be wanted again. As she'd started to feel better, she'd thought Stephen would come and find her. She hadn't expected this silence from him, and now she felt it had gone on too long for her to initiate contact between them. She cursed herself for not trying to reach him earlier; but it was too late now, he obviously no longer wanted her. She'd felt as if she'd died inside when Caro told her how uninterested he'd been in news of her. She was so grateful to Tim for making her feel human again, and a worm of sexual desire for him was stirring inside her. Tim wanted her. And he was good-looking and kind and *so* nice.

"I'll stay here with you," she said.

"I hear you boys are looking for a manager?"

Alan Pearson was waiting for them in the dressing room with a petite, slender but somehow formidable woman, who stared at them appraisingly. They nodded.

She ground out her cigarette and lit another. "Looks like you've got one, then. I'm Cell, also known as Hard Cell. Comes from running my names together, JaniceEllery."

"Overpowering, isn't she?" Alan grinned. "Get used to it."

Like Shirley Bassey, Cell hailed from Tiger Bay in Cardiff. Stephen didn't find her overpowering in the least; on the contrary, her forthright manner reminded him very much of his aunt Mabli, and her warm, Welsh accent made him feel instantly at home.

"All right then," she said, "if we're all happy, I'll liaise with your solicitor later, see if there's anything I need to know." She leered at Alan suggestively. "In the meantime, boys, you need to tour. What you need is to open for someone hot. That'll get you into the public eye. I'll sort something out. Next, we've got to find a producer and get this album going. Why are we standing in here? Isn't there a bar in this place?"

To Stephen's delight, she managed to book them as the supporting act for GI Joe's forthcoming tour of England.

Tim came back into the lounge and smiled at Lynn. Suddenly her mouth felt dry. She stood up and tried to smile back at him.

"Lynn, I can just drive you home if you want."

"I don't have a change of clothes," she said, idiotically.

He looked relieved. "I'll take you home first thing in the morning, wait while you get ready and drive you in to Jimmy's."

"What about you?"

"I'm not on duty till the afternoon."

He held out his hand and she took it hesitantly. She couldn't put it off any longer.

"What a cold little hand," he said, rubbing it.

They climbed the stairs to their room. Tim opened the door and stood back to let her in.

It was a big room, beautifully decorated and appointed. The bed was a large four-poster. Lynn stared at it. It was too late to wonder if she was doing the right thing, Tim was taking her in his arms and kissing her. After a second of near outrage, she relaxed and kissed him back. He smelt wonderful, she didn't recognise his aftershave, but it was certainly enticing. Stephen had always smelled delicious too – oh, God, no, don't think about him, she told herself feverishly, don't think! Tim was unzipping her dress and she felt panicky again. He didn't notice this time. The dress fell to the floor. She wasn't wearing a bra and he drew in his breath sharply as he looked at her. Picking her up, he carried her to the bed, where he carefully took off her knickers, and stroked her body. "You're so beautiful, Lynn. But your hands are still so cold!" He peeled his clothes off and chucked them on the floor. Climbing into bed with her, he took her hands. "I'll warm them against my heart," he smiled, holding them to his chest.

Afterwards she cried, and he held her, stroking her hair.

"I'm sorry," she sobbed. "I did enjoy it, Tim, very much, but it's the first time I've been with anyone since my husband. I haven't made love for a long time."

He kissed her. "It's OK, I understand."

She held him gratefully, drifting off to sleep in his arms. She woke a few hours later to his caresses.

"I'd like to make love to you again, Lynn," he said, kissing her.

"I'd like that, too."

"Charlie!"

"Markham, you fucker! I can't believe you're opening for us!"

"Yeah, and just think, you wouldn't be where you are today if I hadn't let you play rhythm guitar in my band!"

"Hey, Steve, I'm really sorry about Lynn."

Stephen looked away. "Yeah."

"Anyway." Dominic changed the subject. "Touring. Right, well, we're the fucking stars, I'm the biggest, of course—"

"The biggest fucker?" Stephen inquired.

Dominic ignored him. "So you have to do what I say. Apart from that, it's a fucking doddle, old chap. Fun on stage every night and totty coming out of your ears. You never had any trouble getting girls in Manchester – fuck knows why, frankly – so I can't see you having any problems. Hell, even Andy'll probably get some. That should be a new experience for him!"

Dominic advised them to work out in preparation for the tour – behind the banter, he'd been very helpful. They'd all be staying in the same hotels, using the same bus and the same equipment. Stephen could hardly believe it was happening, and to open for Charlie's band was the icing on the cake.

Harry was tremendously enthusiastic. "This is just what you deserve, Stevie," she said, kissing him on the mouth. "Did you say you were touring with GI Joe?"

"Yeah."

"That Dominic Chaplin is *so* gorgeous," she sighed. "He's got such a sexy voice, and his hair's like burnished gold. He's even more handsome than Sting!"

Stephen was amused. "Charlie? I can introduce you if you like."

"Oh, do you know him, then?"

"Yeah. He was at… at my wedding."

Harry smiled at him kindly. "I'm talking about Dominic Chaplin, the lead guitar and singer with GI Joe."

"Yeah, Charlie."

"Is Charlie his real name?" she asked, confused. "And how was he at your wedding? And why didn't I see him?"

"Whoa! Slow down, Harry! What's his surname?"

"Chaplin. Oh, I *see*, Charlie Chaplin!"

"He was at the wedding because he was at uni with me, and he was playing rhythm guitar with Sid's Six. He spent most of his time with Caro on his lap. He gave us the honeymoon on his parents' estate in Northumberland."

"Oh. I never noticed him."

"Shows you how attractive fame can make you," Stephen grinned. "It's like: what's the definition of charisma? A fat, bald, old man with ten million pounds!"

She thumped him. "I was wrapped up in you at the time, if you remember! I couldn't believe you were getting married! I thought I'd never see you again!"

"Yeah, well, you needn't have worried. It didn't last very long, did it?"

"Don't be sad, you're going to be a star! Fancy a little romp, Mr Guitar Man?"

"Harry, we can't keep doing this," he said, laughing.

"Why not?" she asked, unbuttoning his shirt. "I love your smooth chest," she said, nuzzling against him. "Anyway, we're consenting adults with a son, we can do whatever makes us happy."

"Talking of our son, where is he?"

"He's out with Becks. She's taken him to the fair."

"What a good girl that Becks is! Come on, then." He slapped her bottom. "Let's romp."

Stephen loved touring. It was everything he'd hoped it would be and more. He got such a huge high from playing to an audience, especially one that was there to listen to the music, not just to dance and drink, with a band playing in the background. He didn't care that they were doing the same thing over and over again, it felt different every time.

While they were away, they locked their stuff up in George's room, and he let out the rest of the house. "I'll put it on the market when we get back," he said. "I expect we'll be living in London soon."

The tour had three nights at the Manchester Apollo. Stephen booked a room at the hotel for Harry. She arrived in her Triumph, looking very pretty, very nervous, and very thin.

"Jesus!" Stephen exclaimed, as she got out of the car. "Has Ted lost all his money or something?"

"What do you mean?"

"Well you obviously can't afford food any more! I hope you haven't eaten Rob!"

"No, he's our emergency food supply. Good eating on Rob! Don't I look nice then, Stevie?"

"You look lovely, more beautiful than ever," he said, kissing her. "Come and meet Charlie."

"Wait!" She handed him a large parcel. "For your birthday. You're going to be in Birmingham, aren't you? I wanted you to have this to open. There's something from Rob in there too."

"Thank you, Hal!" He was touched.

Dominic was in his room.

Stephen banged on the door.

"Unless you're a gorgeous groupie, fuck off."

Stephen rolled his eyes. "Groupies don't even look at you any more now I'm on tour. Open the door, you moron."

Dominic appeared in the doorway, wearing a red and yellow striped silk dressing gown and sipping champagne. His eyes widened with appreciation when he saw Harry. "You bring gifts, Markham. Come in."

Stephen turned to Harry. "Don't expect too much in the way of brains, Hal. In fact, in the way of anything."

"Fuck off, Markham." Dominic held out his hand to Harry. "Dominic Chaplin. Any friend of Markham's is in need of sympathy. Have some Krug."

Harry smiled delightedly.

"This is Harry Taylor, best bass player I've ever heard or worked with," Stephen said. "Harry, this is Charlie, absolute moron and big-head."

"Yes, well, thank you, Markham, I think your work here is done. Fuck off, there's a good chap." Dominic turned to Harry. "You were the bass player in Markham's first band, The Village Idiots or something, wasn't it? I'd love to play with you sometime."

"No suggestive remarks, please," Stephen sniggered. Dominic took him by the ear. "Ow! That hurts!"

Dominic marched him to the door. "I know you're a complete and utter retard, Markham, but I'd've thought even you couldn't fail to understand 'fuck off'. How wrong I was." He propelled Stephen out of the door and leant against it, smiling at Harry. "I remember you from Steve's wedding."

She felt breathless. He's even more handsome in real life, she thought. "Yes… um… m-me too, I remember you too," she stammered.

His smile deepened. "Rot! You never even saw me. You spent the entire day staring at Markham, no eyes even for that self-effacing chap who was trailing in your wake."

"How do you know I was staring at Stevie the whole time?"

"Because I was staring at you! Until that huge, jolly girl carried me off to the sofa. You not noticing me was a considerable blow to my ego, I can tell you!"

She was overwhelmed. Dominic Chaplin – *Dominic Chaplin!* – was telling her he fancied her. Her nerves vanished. An intoxicating warmth and happiness stole over her. "Well, I'm noticing you now," she smiled.

He took her out to dinner and told her ridiculous stories about the music business, swearing they were all true. She was dizzy with emotion, a strange, wild elation unlike anything she'd ever known before. Even with Stephen, she'd never felt like this.

She spent the next day with him and Stephen, and went to the concert. She was enormously pleased and touched by the fact that Sid's Six not only ended their set with '(Like A) Sky Full Of Summer Stars', a song Stephen had written for her after Kathy's wedding, but that Stephen introduced it first.

"We'd like to finish with a song I wrote a little while ago for a very special friend, an incredibly beautiful girl who happens to be in the audience right now. Harry, thank you for everything."

On the last night, after the concert, the three of them shared a bottle of champagne, and then Stephen, yawning tactfully, went off to bed.

Dominic insisted on walking Harry back to her room.

"Because I might get lost otherwise," she giggled.

"Well, you *are* inebriated," he pointed out. "It doesn't take much, does it? Still, why the fuck am I complaining? You're a cheap date!"

They stopped at her door and she wound her arms around his neck. "Take that back!"

Dominic bent his head and kissed her.

"Dom," she whispered, when the kiss finished. "Do you want to come in?"

He nodded. When the door closed behind them, he took her in his arms. "God, Harry, you're so beautiful, I want you so much."

Afterwards, they lay and talked for a long time. The conversation turned to drugs. Harry had only ever smoked pot. Dominic asked if she wanted to try anything else. "It's so easy to get hold of everything."

"What have you tried?"

"Everything. I like coke best, but smack's fun."

"You've actually shot up?" Harry was shocked.

He shrugged. "It's no big deal. Do you want to try?"

She shook her head. "No. I'm too much of a coward. Suppose I got hooked? Suppose you do? Is it worth it?"

"Well, making music on smack is incredible. Getting hooked?" He shrugged again. "Can't see it matters. Who'd care?"

She was even more shocked. "Dominic! Stevie would! *I* would!"

He was taken aback by her vehemence. "Would you?"

"Very much."

He pulled her against him, and kissed her. "OK. I won't do it any more."

She was surprised. "Just like that? For me?"

"I like you. I like you a lot, beautiful baby." He started to make love to her again.

Later, she remembered something she'd meant to ask him. "You know we were talking about drugs earlier?"

He grunted, half-asleep.

"Dom. Does Stevie do all those drugs? Does he shoot up?"

He opened his eyes. "Stephen's a good boy. Mostly. He won't shoot up, but he's done coke a few times." He grinned.

"What are you laughing at?" she asked, curious.

"Just thinking about something that happened earlier in the tour. It was fucking mind-blowing, I've never seen him so high. But he doesn't do much in the way of drugs usually," he added, before she could speak. "It must be my bad influence." He laughed rather guiltily. "Or Fin's. Whatever. It's such a shame he and Lynn split. They were ideally suited, both so fucking holy."

Harry giggled. "Yes, she was very goody-goody wasn't she? Although I liked her. Until she left him, the total bloody bitch."

"What about you and Markham?" Dominic's voice was very casual.

She shrugged. "He's my best friend. I was in love with him for a long time, since I was fifteen. But now I'm not."

"Why?"

"God, I don't know. I just got over him, I suppose. I'm glad I did, it was hell, wanting him when he didn't want me."

"He must have done at one point; after all, you had his son."

She explained how Rob came about. "And then Dad nearly beat him to death. Poor Stevie!"

Dominic was startled. He remembered Ted from the wedding, he was the only man he'd ever seen who made George look short. "Does your father make a habit of beating up men you go to bed with?"

Harry grinned. "Scared?"

"No, of course not!" He saw the look on her face. "Well, *uneasy*, perhaps."

"And aren't I worth it?" she teased.

Dominic looked at her for a long minute. "You are," he said slowly.

"Oh, Dom, that's lovely! Thank you!" Harry was touched and pleased. "He doesn't, anyway. Not any more."

"Thank God for that! So it was just that once then, you and Markham?"

"Um… yeah. Look, why are we talking about this?"

Dominic rolled over and looked into her eyes. "Because I like you. I fancied you the first time I saw you, and I've thought about you on and off since then. But now we've met and made love, I… I find I really like you, Harry."

A warm glow spread through Harry's body. "I like you very much too, Dominic."

"Good." He started to stroke her. She shivered with delight. "You're skin's so *soft*," he whispered. "Like velvet. And you smell and taste so delicious. I'd really rather like *us* to be… to be best friends."

"Mmm," Harry breathed. "Oh, me too, Dom. I'd like that very, very much."

Lynn found she was becoming more and more involved with Tim. She'd thought at first it was simply a mad love affair, it had moved so fast that she'd been sure it would burn itself out, but they just seemed to get closer. She began to think that maybe she ought to slow down a little. She'd been feeling so much better, no longer tired and washed out, but the way she used to before she got pregnant, and she was beginning to see how very depressed she'd been, and had started to feel terrible about Stephen. There was still no real excuse for him to have slept with someone else, but she could certainly understand it now. She almost talked to Tim about it on several occasions, but could never quite bring herself to.

At the beginning of November, he asked her to spend Christmas with his family. "There's no pressure, Lynn. It's not so that they can vet you, or anything. They're not like that anyway. If you come, they'll be pleased to meet you, but they're so wrapped up in themselves that they won't bother you."

"Can I think about it, Tim? I really need to sort some stuff out, about my marriage."

"Of course." He tried not to look disappointed.

That night she rang George's house. A girl answered. She could have been Andy, George or Fin's of course, Lynn told herself. "Can I speak to Stephen Markham?"

"He's not here. None of them are."

"Oh. When will he be back?"

"Dunno."

Lynn sighed. Most likely Andy's, this one. "Please could I leave a message for Stephen?"

"All right. I'll get a pen." There was a long pause. "OK."

"Could you please say his wife, Lynn, phoned and could he phone me on this number as soon as he gets home." She gave her number. "Could you read that back to me?"

The girl obligingly read the message back, including the number.

"Thank you," said Lynn, heartened by this. "Could you also say I've been thinking about him and I'd like to see him again?"

"Yep. Bye then." The girl hung up and put the note on the table by the door. The next time the door was opened the wind blew it into the street.

By mid-November, the house in Manchester was sold and the boys were renting a flat in South London. They were about to record their first album, 'Tabula Rasa'. Fin, Andy and George wanted 'Market Town', a song Stephen had written when he and Lynn got engaged, and 'Sweet Cherry' on it.

Stephen categorically refused to use them. "They're too personal."

"Howay, man, Steve, you're thinking like a lass again," George said in disgust.

"Yeah, come on, Steve, 'Broken Flower' is about you and Lynn splitting up!" Andy pointed out. "How much more personal can the others be? And if they're so bloody personal, like, why did you write them as songs in the first place? They weren't too personal for Utopia, were they, or when we did them in pubs?"

They stared at him. It was the longest speech any of them had ever heard him make.

"Yeah, he's right," Fin agreed, still staring at him.

"I don't care," Stephen said stubbornly. "All right, we sang them at Utopia, but that was before I lost Lynn. If they go in the album, the words'll be written down and anyone will be able to read them and anyone will be able to sing them. I'm not ready for that. They can go on the next one. Not this." He gave them a hostile stare. "Or I won't sing any of them."

"I could crack his head against the wall a few times," George said reflectively. "For to knock a bit of sense into it, man."

"I'd like to see you try," Stephen said furiously, squaring up to him.

"Yeah?" George pushed him.

"Yeah!" Stephen pushed back harder.

"For Christ's sake, stop it!" shouted Fin. "You're not helping, George! Steve, come on. Reconsider? 'Sweet Cherry' could be a single."

"No. I can't do 'Sweet Cherry'. We'll do 'Market Town', but not 'Sweet Cherry'." There were tears in his eyes. "Please, lads. I honestly can't. I'm sorry, I just can't."

"OK, OK," Fin sighed, shaking his head at the other two.

George couldn't resist giving Stephen a last push. Stephen's temper flared up out of control and he hit George hard on the nose. George went reeling backwards in shock. He, Fin and Andy were used to Stephen's brief outbursts of temper, they were sudden and vocal, but never violent.

Stephen didn't even give him time to get up. He hurled himself on the big Geordie, yelling and punching. George hit back at him, knocking him sideways. Andy and Fin recovered their wits at the same time and grabbed Stephen, who struggled aggressively. "Let me go! I'm going to kill the bastard!"

George leant against the wall, laughing until his eyes watered. The other three stared at him, astounded. His laughter was infectious, and they found themselves joining in.

Stephen offered George his hand. "Sorry, George. I lost my temper."

"Aye, I noticed! Howay, bonny lad, forget it! I'll not call you a lass again. Not tonight, anyway. That was a canny punch, man."

Stephen grinned. "Let's have a drink."

They started with beer. When that was gone, they drank wine, and then moved on to whisky, gin, and finally vodka.

"Now we're going to be famous, I'm changing my name," Andy announced.

"Why?" Stephen asked.

"Andy Lake's a crap name. I want a cool name."

"Like what?"

"I don't know; something Rock."

"Something Rock is even crapper."

"Not *Something* Rock, something *Rock*. Where d'you come from, Steve?"

"York."

"York Rock. Nah."

"My Mum and Dad live in Clifton," Stephen said, trying to be helpful.

"Clifton. Yeah, Clifton. Clifton Rock. It's the name of a superstar."

"It's the name of a prat," George scoffed.

"What shall we drink now?" Fin asked. He could barely stand.

Andy managed to get up and look. "There's nothing left in the crupboard. In the crum... um... in the place where we keep the... um... the stuff."

"George drank it all," Stephen said, staring accusingly at George, who was stretched out on the floor. "Listen, I wanna get my... um... my..." He couldn't remember the word, and pulled at his ear lobe. "What's this called?"

Andy peered at him. "Ear."

"Ear." He nodded. "Yeah, ear. Thanks, Andy."

"What about your ear?" Andy asked.

"I just told you. I wanna get it pierced."

"Why?" asked Fin.

"Because I'm a rock star and they have it pierced."

"Don't be a lass, man," said George from the floor.

Stephen blinked at him. "You said you weren't calling me a lass tonight."

"I didn't call you one. I said don't be one. It's different."

"I'm going out to get my ear pierced." Stephen stood up and fell over him. "Sorry, George. I didn't see you lying there."

"There'll be nowhere open now, Stevie boy," Fin said. "Do it tomorrow."

Stephen stared at him owlishly. "We're recording tomorrow. I want it done now."

"All right, all right, I'll do it," Andy announced in a martyred tone.

"You?" queried Fin.

"Yeah, it's easy, our Mum did our kid's, both ears. I need a needle, a cork and some ice."

"We've got all that. Do it now, Andy," Stephen urged.

"Wait," said Andy. "We've got to be sterilized."

"How?" asked Stephen.

"I think you boil everything," Fin said.

"Is that why we need the ice?"

"We can use alcohol. Our Mum used gin," Andy stated.

"We haven't got any," Stephen reminded him.

George stared at him. "We've got buckets of it, man."

"You drank it," Stephen said.

"Did I?"

"There may be enough in the bottom of the bottles, we don't need much, like," Andy said. "Fin, you get it. In a cup. George, you get the ice. Where's the needle, Steve?"

Stephen found the sewing kit he'd bought when they moved in. Andy selected the thickest needle. George and Fin came back with the ice and a small amount of unpleasantly bitty-looking liquid.

"There wasn't much, so I added some Coke and the beer George spilled in the ashtray," Fin said.

Andy put the needle in it. "We've got to hold the ice on his ear. Sit down here, Steve."

Stephen obediently sat on the floor and Andy put a cube of ice on his ear lobe. Stephen yelped.

"It'll freeze your ear, and you won't feel anything, like," Andy reassured him.

"How long does it take? Because I can feel it now and it hurts!"

"When you can't feel it, it'll be ready," Andy said, sagely.

They knelt round him.

"Is it ready yet?" Fin asked.

"No," Stephen said.

They waited.

"It must be ready now," said Fin, impatiently.

"Maybe." Stephen was doubtful.

"That'll do," George said.

Andy took the needle out of the cup, dried it on his tee shirt and rubbed the rest of the liquid on Stephen's ear. He held out his hand. "Cork!"

There was a slight delay while Fin got a cork out of the bin. He slapped it into Andy's hand.

"Right. Hold his head."

George caught Stephen's head in a vice-like grip. Andy put the cork behind his ear and stabbed the needle through the lobe. Stephen screamed.

"What's the matter, needle not sharp enough?" George asked, still holding his head.

"Not enough ice," Stephen said faintly.

"Howay, you're not crying are you, man?"

"No! My eyes are watering with pain," Stephen replied with dignity.

"Where's the earring, Andy?" Fin inquired.

"Shit," said Andy. He and Fin looked at each other in consternation.

"I know," George said. "There's a group of lasses living across the hall, one of them's bound to have one we can borrow. I'll knock them up."

"How will that help, like?" Andy grinned.

"Howay, man, you know what I mean."

He came back with two girls. "They're nurses, man," he said with a leer. "This is Yvonne and this little cracker's Suzy."

Stephen didn't care. The pain was quite extraordinary. His ear was throbbing.

"Oh, my God!" said Yvonne.

"I didn't take the needle out because I don't want it to close up and have to do it again, like," Andy explained.

"Oh no, please don't," Stephen said desperately.

"Do you really want an earring?" Suzy asked him. She was small and blonde and reminded him of Angie.

"Yes, please."

She smiled at her friend. "He's cute! I've got a spare pair of sleepers I've never opened; he can have one of those. What's your name?"

"Stephen."

"OK, Stephen, but we'll have to clean you up. The bacteria on that needle alone…!"

"We were sterilized first!" Andy was indignant.

"You should be," Yvonne grinned. "Those are genes you definitely don't want to pass on!"

Andy looked down at his trousers in bewilderment. "I wasn't going to."

The girls cleaned up Stephen's ear and put the sleeper in.

"It's not a bad job really, considering," Suzy commented.

"We'll give you some paracetamol," Yvonne said. "And we'll look at it tomorrow.

But if you think it's getting infected, see a doctor straight away."

"How will I know if it's infected?"

"It'll hurt."

"More than this?" Stephen was horrified.

Yvonne grinned. "You'll see pus round it."

"Great!"

"You ought to go to bed," Yvonne said. "All of you. And drink plenty of water before you do. It'll help lessen your hangovers."

"We're not drunk," Andy said truculently.

The girls looked at each other. "If you say so," Yvonne shrugged. "Come on, Suze."

Stephen staggered off to the room he shared with Fin.

"Which one will he be shagging by the end of the week, do you think?" Fin asked.

"Both of them," Andy said, gloomily.

"Better not be, man, the blonde's mine!" George objected.

Suzy looked in the next day to tell Stephen to clean round the earring twice a day with surgical spirit and turn it at the same time. "But don't take it out," she warned. "You can't take it out for about six months or the hole will close up." She looked at his Strat. "That your guitar?"

"Yeah."

George came out of his room, with his bass. "Come on, bonny lad, we'll be late. Hello, pet!"

"We're recording an album today," Stephen told her.

"Come on, I wasn't born yesterday," she grinned.

Stephen shrugged. "Well, whenever, that's what we're doing."

"Wow! You really mean it, don't you? What's your group called?"

"Sid's Six. We're going to be phenomenal."

"Where are the rest of them? I only saw four of you last night."

"That's us, just the four of us."

"Oh. That's a bit weird."

Stephen grinned. "Thanks. Would you like to go out for a drink tonight?"

She smiled. "I'd love to!"

Lynn waited to hear from Stephen with barely suppressed excitement. She realised how much she'd missed him, how much she still loved him. The thought of speaking to him again, hearing his voice, was intoxicating. The first thing she did when she got home from work was check her answer machine. Every time the phone rang her heart leapt, but as time went on and she heard nothing from him, she became puzzled and rather annoyed by his silence. Why would he ignore her? He wasn't petty, he never held grudges. She came to the conclusion that he hadn't got her message and rang again, picking mid-afternoon as the time he was most likely to be in; after rehearsals and before a gig. This time a foreign girl answered. She sounded Japanese. Lynn's heart stood still. The girl Stephen had slept with? Could she have moved in? Was that why he hadn't phoned?

"Could I speak to Stephen, please?" she asked coldly.

"Steven? Hang on." There was a lengthy pause. Finally, the girl came back on the line. "Sorry, Steven's out."

"Please could you tell him his wife phoned?"

"His wife?" The girl was incredulous. "Oh. Well, he's at his girlfriend's, he won't be back till tomorrow."

Lynn hung up, shaking with anger, hurt and humiliation. So this was why he hadn't got back to her. He had a girlfriend, he didn't want a wife any more. OK, that was fine with her. She rang Tim. "Is the invitation for Christmas still open?"

She could hear the smile in his voice. "It most definitely is!"

The next day she saw a solicitor and started divorce proceedings.

It took them just over a month to record the album. Afterwards they held a celebratory party at a small pub down the road from the studio. They were all wired and everyone drank too much. They drifted back to the flat, and Fin produced some cocaine.

Stephen was sure the album would be a success. "It's such a good omen that Mal's surname is Crawford," he kept saying. Their producer's name was Malcolm Crawford.

"Why?" Andy asked.

"Because of Stanton Crawford. You know Stanton Crawford? The blues singer? Oh, come on, you *must* have heard of him! 'Lost And Low'? 'One More Time'? God, you lot! I can't believe you've never heard of him! He's a huge hero of mine! I'd love to work with him!"

"You say that about everyone," Fin said. He was smoking a joint, which he offered to Stephen.

Stephen took a puff. He was feeling peculiar, as if his head was only attached to his body by a string, and it was floating away. "Well, I'd like to work with everyone," he said, flinging his arms wide.

"Even Des O'Connor?" Andy inquired.

Stephen ignored him. "I'd especially like to work with Stanton Crawford. I can't believe you lot have never heard of him! You're all so unhip that when I say Dylan, you probably think I'm talking about Dylan Thomas, whoever he is."

"What the fuck are you talking about, man?" George demanded.

"Misquoting 'A Simple Desultory Philippic', which is what this is! Paul Simon, you know? You must have heard of *him*!"

"He another hero?" Fin inquired.

"Oh, certainly is!"

"Erm, Steve – who *is* Dylan Thomas?" Andy asked.

"Jesus Christ!"

It was nearly Christmas, and Stephen went home for a few days.He hadn't been back for over a month, the longest he'd ever gone without seeing Rob. The day after he arrived, he was served with divorce papers. He was devastated. He couldn't believe that Lynn would take a step like that without at least writing to him first. He gave them to John, who glanced through them.

"I take it you won't be contesting?"

Stephen shook his head. "Can you sort it for me, Dad?"

John nodded. "Don't worry about it, son. Divorce is pretty straightforward these days. I'll pass it on to Julian, it's his field." He looked at Stephen with concern. "I can't do anything about the way you're feeling, Stevie, but at least I can make sure this goes smoothly for you. It should all be over in about six months."

Stephen was grateful. He was sick of the whole thing. If that was what Lynn wanted, then let them get on with it. He just wanted to be free of it. If this was love, he was better off without it. He spent lots of time with Rob.

"I started divorce proceedings before we came away," Lynn said, staring into the fire.

"You've never told me anything about your marriage," Tim said.

"What is there to tell? We were happy at first and then... then things went wrong."

"What things?" Lynn bit her lip. "It's all right, forget I asked."

"I got pregnant. Autumn last year. It was a disaster. A baby would have ruined everything for us. I lost it anyway. And it did ruin everything."

"Oh, Lynn. I'm so sorry."

She looked at him. "I was glad. Not that the baby died, that was terrible. But so glad that it was over, that I could finish my course and get a job. And then... well... then I was very depressed. I didn't realise how depressed until recently. And that's when everything fell apart."

"He didn't understand?"

Lynn's lips trembled. "He was marvellous. He would have done anything for me. And he was so sad and I never comforted him, I wouldn't let him near me. I drove him away, but even then he would have stayed. He wanted us to stay together more than anything. I told him... I told him I didn't want him any more."

Tim put his arm around her. He didn't know what to say.

"So, after you invited me to come here, I didn't know what to do. I wanted to talk to him, but he never got back to me." She gave a bitter little smile. "Giving me a taste of my own medicine."

"What do you mean, never got back to you?"

"I left a message for him at his house."

"Maybe he didn't get it."

"I phoned again. Apparently he was at his girlfriend's. Anyway, I think it's obvious he's over me."

Tim looked dubious. "Can't you ring him at work?"

"I don't know what he does." Tim raised his eyebrows. "He was in a band, I don't think he got a job after he graduated. They wanted to make a demo or something, he's probably working in McDonalds in Manchester. Anyway, he's never contacted me. He's obviously not interested any more. I should have known, he never had any trouble getting girls." This was said with such venom that Tim was taken aback. "Sorry. I shouldn't be involving you in this."

"Lynn." He took her hand. "I want to be involved in everything in your life. But have you thought? You left him. Maybe he thinks you still don't want him."

"I phoned him! Twice!"

"But you don't know that he got the message."

"Why are you on *his* side?"

"Darling, I'm *not*. I'm on *your* side, completely. I just want you to be absolutely sure you're doing the right thing."

She smiled at him. "You're so nice to me! I don't know. I think I'm doing the right thing, but... oh, Tim, I can't stand feeling like this! I want to forget it ever happened and get on with my life. I just want to forget him!"

It was only much later, when she was asleep in his arms, that Tim realised that she hadn't once called her husband by his name.

The album was released in the early spring, along with a single, 'Lost Souls'. Sid's Six was in residence at the Portico, a popular and prestigious London club, a significant engagement for them. They were due to make a headlining tour of Britain after the album came out, and they awaited the releases with a mixture of excitement and trepidation.

The single went into the charts at sixteen; by the following week it was up to two. The boys couldn't believe it. Stephen was elated. *He'd* written this song; these were *his* lyrics, it was *his* music playing in pubs, clubs, on the radio, in passing cars. The four of them went into HMV and stared at copies of the album and the single, watched people actually buying them. They grinned at each other like idiots, unable to take it in. Suddenly, they were in huge demand. Overnight, they went from being four talented nobodies to a commodity. And everyone wanted a piece of them. When they filmed the video for 'Lost Souls', Fin spoke for them all: "Someone pinch me, I think I'm dreaming!"

"Lynn! I didn't expect to see you tonight!" Tim held the door open.

Lynn handed him a bottle of wine and hurried in. It was raining, and cold for the time of year, and Tim's house was, as usual, like Tim himself, warm and welcoming. "The meeting was cancelled at the last minute. I'm not disturbing you, am I?"

"You always disturb me," he smiled. "Come on through."

They went into the sitting room, and Lynn stopped dead. 'Blown Away' was playing. She went white. "Where did you get this?" she whispered.

"HMV. Why?"

"HMV? What is it?"

"Are you all right, Lynn?"

"What is it?"

He handed her the record sleeve. 'Tabula Rasa: Sid's Six' leapt out at her. Slowly, she turned it over. There was a photograph of them all on the back, grinning. Stephen was looking impossibly handsome; she'd never seen a bad photo of him, but this one was phenomenal.

"It's just come out," Tim was saying as he poured them a drink. "Michael Carruth had the tape on last night, I had to get it! Apparently, there was a single, but I never heard it. It's an amazing album, their lead guitarist and singer is so talented. He writes their songs too, which are superb." He turned round with the drinks.

Lynn was reading the lyrics and crying silently, her tears dripping down onto the sleeve.

"Lynn! What's the matter?" He put the drinks down and hurried to her side.

"Look what he's put," she said, pointing. There was a dedication at the bottom, which he hadn't noticed: *'For Cherry, who showed me how to live the dream.'*

"I don't understand," he said, confused. "Who's Cherry? Why are you crying?"

Lynn's finger caressed the photo. "I'm Cherry. He's my husband. Stephen Markham is my husband."

Tim stared at her.

"You're right," she said. "He *is* superb. He really deserves this. Oh, God." 'Broken Flower' began to play. "Turn it off, Tim!" Her voice rose. "Turn it off, turn it off!"

He turned it off and took her in his arms. "Is that you?" he asked.

"Me and the baby. Stevie was sure it was a girl. He said it was a little flower blossoming inside me. I lost it at twenty weeks, and it *was* a girl. I said… I said his little flower was all broken, I remember saying it to him. All broken." She was crying so hard he could barely hear her. "Oh God, oh God, I loved him so much!"

At least Tim hoped she said 'loved' and not 'love'. Stevie, she'd called him. How could he hope to compete with someone who looked like Stephen Markham? Who wrote and performed like he did? And who was now a household name?

Lynn went out the next day and bought the album. She listened to it continually when she was alone, hearing only Stephen's voice. She spent a long time looking at the picture of him. It must have been taken recently, his hair was different. It was still untidy, and fell down over his eyes, but it was short at the back and the sides. It suited him very much, she thought. As she pored over it some more she noticed he had an earring. At least, it looked as if he did. Maybe it was a mark on the photo. She became obsessed with finding out. She went into the big branch of WH Smith in the city centre and searched the shelves. Most of the music papers had articles or interviews with the band. Some had both. She bought them all.

"Big fan, eh?" smiled the girl on the till. "That Steve Markham, he's gorgeous, isn't he? Did you know there's an article about the band in *Scarlet*, and an interview and a poster in *Hot Date*? They're on the shelf over there, look." She pointed to the teen magazines. Sure enough, there was Stephen's face plastered across the front of the magazines. And yes, he had an earring. Lynn hadn't thought to look in teen magazines, although they were an obvious choice. She picked up a copy of each, despising herself.

She devoured them all evening, staring at the pictures. It was so odd to be looking at her husband like this. It was as if he'd become someone else, the way a familiar landscape becomes distorted and frightening in a dream. He belonged to everyone now, the assistant in Smiths, the girls who read the teen magazines, bored housewives, everyone. The reporter from *Scarlet* described him as *'sex on legs'*, which had stuck and was repeated in several other articles.

There was a big interview with the band in *Melody Maker*. George and Fin had done most of the talking; Stephen came across as very quiet, almost wary. She noticed that he wasn't smiling in any of the pictures, just staring out at the camera. He looked moody; it was sexy, but she had the feeling it wasn't a pose. She remembered what an intensely private person he was, despite his warm, affectionate personality, and wondered how he was feeling about being famous like this. He'd said years ago that he didn't want to live a rock and roll lifestyle. Maybe he'd changed, but looking at these pictures and reading the interviews, she didn't think so.

All the reviews said much the same things; they were complimentary about the band, they enthused over Stephen's voice and playing, and they liked the songs. *'Country Meets Blues in the Valleys'*, one headline read; *'Exhilarating Raw Talent'* was another. *'The Band With The Perfect Sound'*; *'Superb Playing, Sublime Music'*, *'Emotive, Evocative Lyrics'* – the praise was endless.

The reviewers were very taken with Stephen's playing, declaring him a *'new young guitar hero'*, a *'virtuoso'*, *'the most exciting guitarist to emerge for several years'*. They went into ecstasies over his *'sinuous, stinging, vibrant playing'*, talking of *'shimmering, phosphorescent phrases'* and *'gleaming, serpentine, impressionistic guitar lines'*. *'His notes are like taffy for the ears, the way he bends and pulls them,'* one music critic said. *'He manages to wring the smallest nuance of feeling, colour and tone out of every note'*. Another, rather grandiosely, likened his playing to *'shining bullets shot from a silver bell'*. Yet another, having recently seen the band play, raved about Stephen's *'astonishing, lightning-speed finger picking'*, and commented on the *'tremendous energy the band generates'* and Stephen's *'sheer joy in what he does'*. The reviewer's comment about his *'overwhelming drive not only to entertain the audience but to involve them in his performance, at which he succeeds admirably'* touched Lynn, who knew that that would probably please Stephen more than anything else they'd said. And they'd all been enormously impressed with his singing, talking about his *'operatic range'* and the way he used his *'effortlessly powerful, flexible voice like another instrument, sometimes smooth and mellow, sometimes rough and edgy'*. The general consensus of opinion was that Stephen's place in music history was assured and that Sid's Six had a very bright future indeed.

Most of the interviewers had asked, "*Why Sid's Six?*" They'll get tired of explaining that, she thought, grinning.

Lastly, she looked at the interview in *Hot Date*. It was entitled *Stevie Wonderful*, which she thought rather sickly. She wondered briefly how George, Fin and Andy felt about him getting so much attention. It was inevitable; he wrote their songs, he played the guitar and sang superbly, and he was so very good-looking, but still. She was pretty sure Fin and Andy wouldn't mind, but George was a different proposition.

She read the article. It was obvious that he'd charmed the female interviewer, who had clearly fallen for him in a big way, raving about his *'intriguingly mesmerising silvery blue eyes, sexy mouth, and fit body'*, but he had actually said nothing, albeit in a polite way. Sure enough, he'd been asked about the band's name. They'd got his birthday wrong, and in the poster he was wearing a tee shirt she'd bought for him just before she lost the baby. She felt as if someone was cutting her heart out, bit by bit. Judging by some of his songs, 'Lost Souls', 'Broken Flower' 'Just Hanging On' and 'This Northern Sky', he felt the same. So why were they apart? But she'd tried. And he'd received the divorce papers; she'd spoken to her solicitor who'd said everything was going very well and she should have the decree nisi within the month. He hadn't contested it, hadn't got in touch. The only logical conclusion was that he no longer felt like that about her. After all, he'd moved on, he had another woman, he was getting on with his life. Those songs must have been written a while ago; 'Market Town' was about the two of them getting engaged, and he'd written that over three years ago. It was a lovely song and in a way, the one she found the most difficult to listen to. They had been so happy then. 'This Northern Sky' had just been released as a single and had gone straight to number one. All the articles and reviews she'd read had picked this one as the album's best. It was about York, and Stephen missing her, and it made her cry, especially the lines, 'All our tomorrows, where did they go?'

One of the music papers had a list of the venues where Sid's Six would be appearing during their forthcoming tour, and the dates. She seriously debated buying a ticket to the one in Leeds. When she was fourteen, she'd had a crush on Woody from the Bay City Rollers. It had been incredibly intense and passionate while it lasted, she would have died for him. That was how she felt now for Stephen, only worse. She didn't know what to do, how to get over him.

She began to spend more and more time with Tim, practically moving into his house. He was so kind, so gentle, so loving. He was fun too, he made her laugh. And he could cope. Strangely, considering his mother was half-Italian, he was very English, very phlegmatic, in contrast with Stephen's emotional Welshness. He was so different to Stephen. Being with him assuaged her aching sense of loss.

At Stephen's request, Cell hired the band an experienced tour manager, Dave Mitchell. Stephen had quickly realised that touring as the headlining band was totally different to being the supporting act. The concerts were still magic to him, even more so now, as the audience came to see *them,* to hear the band, listen to his songs. It created a relationship between them that he cherished. But the media circus was something else. He didn't like it. He didn't like having to explain what his songs meant to him, how they made him feel, what made him tick. As far as he was concerned, he was an ordinary man who wrote and played and sang. He was pleased and grateful that people liked the noise he made, and he didn't mind explaining what his songs were about in a general sense, and talking about his playing and singing – it was what he was doing, after all. He couldn't see that anything else was relevant. He rang Rob every day. The press, and missing his son, were the only drawbacks to this new life.

Halfway through the tour, '(Like A) Sky Full Of Summer Stars' was released as a single, and reporters turned up at the Angel, taking photos of Harry and Rob.

Harry phoned him, distressed. "It's horrendous, Stevie, they won't go away. I feel like a criminal or something!"

"Bloody hell! Sorry, Hal. God, I hate journalists! Look, don't talk to them, whatever you say they'll twist it."

"I know, I rang Dom, he said the same."

"Dom? What's wrong with Charlie?"

"I'm not calling him Charlie! And don't you go encouraging Rob to call him that either!"

"Is it serious, Harry?"

There was a pause. "I don't know. I think it might be."

Stephen felt a sense of desolation. He didn't want to lose Harry, even to Dominic. Which made no sense, he'd introduced them in the hope that this might happen. He was ashamed of himself. "He doesn't deserve you, Hal."

"Oh, I know that," she laughed. As if she'd read his mind, she added, "No matter what happens, Stevie, it won't make any difference to how I feel about you."

The papers printed pictures of a bewildered-looking Rob and a grim-looking Harry, and followed up with salacious articles about Stephen and Harry entitled *Sid's Sex Life* and *Sid's Sizzler*. It made his blood boil and his dislike of journalists increased.

"I'm legally a single woman again, Tim."

"And how do you feel about that?"

She shrugged. "You know, I don't feel anything. Just empty."

He rested his chin on his hands and looked at her.

She smiled at him. "What?"

"I was thinking. You wouldn't want to repeat the experience?"

"Divorce? No thanks!"

"No, Lynn, marriage. I suppose you wouldn't consider marrying me?" She burst out laughing. "Oh, thank you very much!"

"Sorry, Timmy, I wasn't laughing at the proposal. You just sounded so apologetic!"

"It's my way. But seriously, Lynn, might you feel like marrying me sometime? I'm clean, I'm house trained, I'm sound in wind and limb and I've got all my own teeth. I feel sure I'd give satisfaction."

Lynn stared at him. The ache she felt for Stephen had not gone, but it had become muted, dull, chronic rather than acute. She'd got used to it. The only time it ever receded was when she was with Tim. Perhaps this was the answer. To marry him and be with him forever. He'd protect her from her pain and eventually she'd get over it entirely. They'd have a family and she wouldn't ever think of Stephen again except as a kind of bittersweet dream.

"Yes, Tim, I might feel like marrying you."

He gave an enormous grin. "Oh, I was hoping you'd say that!" He fumbled in his pocket and drew out a small leather box. "I've been carrying this around for days, but I haven't had the nerve to ask. Will you marry me, Lynn?"

She opened it in astonishment and gasped. It was a ring, a huge ruby surrounded by diamonds.

"Try it on. It should fit, I used that little turquoise ring you've got as a guide."

She slid it onto her finger, trying not to think of Stephen spending all his money on her engagement ring. This one must have cost ten times the amount. "Oh, Tim, it's beautiful! It fits perfectly." She leant across the table and kissed him. "How soon can we be married?"

He blinked. "As soon as you like, it's entirely up to you."

"I don't want a big wedding. I wish we could simply run away and get married!"

"Would you really like that?"

"Yes. I just want to be married to you, Tim. I don't want any fuss. I don't think I could cope with it. Do you think your family would mind a very quiet wedding?"

"My darling, my family won't mind what we do." He thought for a minute. "You can get something called a registrar's licence which authorises a marriage after one working day."

Lynn's mouth curved into a smile. "Timmy! Can we really do that?"

"Of course we can! But are you quite sure, Lynn?"

She nodded. "I just want to be your wife, Tim, I want to be Mrs. Franklin." I'm not Lynn Markham any more, she thought sadly, and I'll never have Stevie ever again. I want a new me.

Chapter Eight
The Dying Of The Light

Darkness shrouds me, clouds my sight,
Losing you forever with the dying of the light.

Stephen had been buying property. The success of 'Tabula Rasa' had made him a great deal of money, and he'd bought a flat in London and an apartment in Venice for himself, and a house in the West Highlands for Sian and John. They'd spent their honeymoon near Ullapool, and had taken several holidays there since, and John loved fishing, so Stephen bought them a lodge, Drumduart House, with three miles of double bank fishing on the Kirkaig. John was overwhelmed. He and Sian had spent two weeks there in May and they planned to go up for a month at the beginning of October.

Stephen's flat was a four-bedroomed place in Knightsbridge with its own front door and a porter. It was behind a private courtyard and had a pretty little garden. That had been important – to find somewhere he and Rob could play, and Rob could have his trike and his pedal car, in complete privacy.

He had an Aga installed in the kitchen, and the entire flat redecorated in warm colours. He bought paintings from art galleries and junk shops, not caring whether they cost a lot of money or just a few pounds, as long as he liked them. He bought comfortable furniture, and splashed out on a king-sized bed that didn't hurt his back no matter how long he spent in it. The second largest room became Rob's. He put Rob's name on the door, and filled it with new toys, a desk, a train set and a rocking horse. He had one of the smaller bedrooms soundproofed and converted into a music room, so that he could play whenever he wanted without worrying about disturbing the other residents. All the rooms had under-floor central heating, and he had an open fire in his bedroom and the sitting room. He thought, his heart heavy, how much fun it would have been if he and Lynn had been decorating it together. He had enough money now to buy her all the lovely things he'd always dreamed of giving her. But what was the point of even thinking about it?

He tried to put her out of his mind, and bought the apartment in Venice almost as an act of defiance, to prove to himself, and everyone else, that he was better off single, and that he didn't want or need to be tied to one woman. The place was exquisite, a first floor *piano nobile* in San Marco, with a private water gate entrance and a street entrance through the garden. It had a master bedroom and two guest suites, and a huge drawing room with a balcony overlooking the Grand Canal. Stephen bought it with the express intention of throwing seriously decadent parties, and the first he held there was the reception for Andy's wedding to Giovanna da Mosto, a voluptuous and predatory Italian actress at least fifteen years Andy's senior. Stephen couldn't see the marriage lasting; they'd only known each other a matter of weeks, and Andy spoke no Italian, and Giovanna very little English. During the reception, she made a determined pass at Stephen. He managed to fend her off with as much charm and tact as he could muster, and heaved an enormous sigh of relief when Andy, his weasely face blissful, carried her off to their hotel.

At the end of June, Sid's Six went back into the studio to record the band's second album, 'Nets Of Gold'. Once again, Malcolm Crawford was their producer, but Stephen had been learning and had more of an idea of what he wanted, the sound he wanted the band to make and the direction he wanted it to take. He liked having more input into the album very much.

It took longer to record than 'Tabula Rasa', and they weren't finished with it until the beginning of September. They were all tired, and irritable with each other, and things that wouldn't have bothered them at all under normal circumstances became major grievances. Tempers flared. The trouble was mostly between Stephen and George, who wound each other up very easily. Stephen's control of the band, his perfectionism and refusal to compromise, coupled with the amount of attention he received – far more than the rest of them – annoyed George, who felt that, in spite of the fact that Stephen wrote, sang and played lead guitar on all their songs, they were a team, and as such, were equally important. He'd never been able to resist taunting Stephen and calling him a lass, but now there was a real edge to the teasing. Normally Stephen would have taken it in good part and either ignored him or returned the banter, playing down George's simmering resentment and making him laugh. But towards the end of the recording he lost his sense of humour, and it took the combined efforts of Andy, Fin and Mal Crawford to prevent the pair of them from coming to blows.

Then, in mid-August, Stephen received a letter telling him that his decree nisi had been converted into a decree absolute. His marriage to Lynn was over. George, Andy and Fin took him to the pub and he got very drunk. There was no more trouble between him and George. They finished recording and took a break.

Stephen decided to take Rob to the Caribbean for a couple of weeks. He'd never had a holiday alone with his son and he wanted to go somewhere hot, where he and Rob could swim and sail and enjoy themselves, away from the glare of publicity.

Harry brought Rob down to the flat and Stephen invited Dominic to dinner the night they arrived. Harry and Dominic had been seeing a lot of each other and he wanted to see them both.

He kissed Harry when she arrived. "You're looking more beautiful than ever, Hal."

She returned the kiss. "Thanks. How does it feel to be rich and famous?"

He grimaced. "Rich is great – famous I'm not so sure about!"

"You and Dom are so different," she said, wandering around the flat. It was the first time she'd been since he'd moved in a few weeks earlier. "He loves the fame."

"Well, that's Charlie for you. I always said superficial was his middle name!"

Rob had been exploring the flat too. He was very impressed with the fact that he had his own room with his name on the door. "Mummy! Come and see my room! It's got new toys in it!"

Harry frowned at Stephen. "You shouldn't keep buying him new stuff, Steve. You'll spoil him!"

"Not Rob. He's a good boy, aren't you, Blewser?"

The doorbell buzzed. At precisely the same moment, the phone rang.

"Can you get the door, Hal? It'll be Charlie, hours early as usual. Hasn't he got any other friends? Stephen Markham?" he said into the phone. "Hello, Mum." Dominic was being his usual boisterous self in the background. Stephen listened to Sian speaking. He saw Dominic kissing Harry, noticed the way he kept his arm around her waist afterwards, the way he held out his hand to Rob and swung the little boy up onto his shoulders. The way he and Harry were looking at him… He shut his eyes. Sian stopped talking. He answered her and hung up.

"What is it, Stephen? What's happened?"

"It's Dad. He's seriously ill."

They stared at him. "Stevie! What's wrong? What did Sian say?" Harry was breathless with shock.

"Um…" He was having trouble thinking. "He's… um… he's got leukaemia, some sort of leukaemia. He's in hospital."

"But surely they can treat it?" Dominic asked.

"Well, apparently he's had it for a while, but he didn't realise, he just thought he was… um… tired and run down. I said… um… I said I'd go home."

"I'll take you," Dominic said. "You can't drive."

Stephen shook his head. "I couldn't… couldn't just sit in the car, thinking about him. I'll be OK to drive. It's not that I'm not grateful for the offer, Charlie," he added.

"Steve, no, I understand completely."

Stephen hugged Rob and Harry. "Robbie, Grandpa's not well, I've got to go and see him. I'll be back soon. Look after him for me, Hal."

"Can I come?" Rob asked.

"Not this time, darling," Harry said. She kissed Stephen. "Phone us when you can."

Ted was waiting for Stephen in the hospital lobby. "Steve." He gave him a brief hug. "Sian and Rebecca will be so glad to see you."

"What happened, Ted?" Stephen asked, as Ted guided him through the maze of corridors.

"He's not been well for a few weeks, tired and short of breath, but your mum put that down to his angina, although she's been on at him to see the doctor. Anyway, he collapsed at work this morning and they called an ambulance. They got him in here and did tests and stuff, but… I'm so sorry, Steve."

Stephen couldn't take it in. "You mean… you can't mean… there must be *something* they can do?"

"They've given him blood transfusions and steroids and antibiotics, but he's so weak and it's very advanced."

"But he was fine, *fine* at Rob's birthday, Ted. I don't understand. How could he be…" He swallowed. "*Dying?*" It was hot in the hospital, but he was numb, frozen, even his bones felt cold.

Ted shook his head helplessly. "I don't know, Steve. The doctors told Sian it's usually people your Dad's age that get it, and sometimes it can kill them in days." He led Stephen through a swing door. "Here we are."

"Oh, Stevie, I'm so glad you're here!" Rebecca, tears running down her cheeks, hurried out of the day room and fell into his arms. "We haven't been able to get hold of Kathy yet." Paul had been posted to Germany, and he and Kathy and their first child, Ceridwen, had been living there for the last six months.

"Can I see him?" Stephen asked.

"Of course. He wants to see you. He's been asking for you. Mum's in with him at the moment. Listen, Steve…"

"Yes?"

"He looks… he looks terrible. Try not to be shocked."

John was in a side room along the corridor. Sian was coming out as Stephen made his way to it. "Stevie. Dad was asking for you, I was just coming to see if you were here yet." She clutched him tightly. "Oh, Stevie. The doctors are lovely, really kind, but they don't think… they say…" She couldn't go on.

He nodded, his teeth clenched.

She kissed him. "Go on in."

John was surrounded by drips and, as Rebecca had warned, he looked ghastly, his face shrunken and yellowish. Stephen had only seen him a couple of months ago, on Rob's birthday. He couldn't believe the difference. He remembered Rebecca's words, and tried to change his expression, willing himself not to break down and cry.

John smiled at him. "Stevie."

Stephen sat next to the bed, and very carefully took his hand. "Dad." He couldn't say anything else.

"I thought it'd be the old ticker that got me." John's voice was little more than a dry whisper.

Stephen tried to swallow the lump in his throat. "Oh, Dad."

John squeezed his hand. "I've not had a bad innings, son. Remember, it's all luck, blind chance, spinning in a vacuum. Such luck I had you."

Stephen's heart was breaking. "I'm the lucky one," he managed to say. "You're the best father anyone ever had."

John shook his head. "I've watched you with Rob. You're the one, Stephen."

"No. Oh, no. It's easy to be a good father when it's only part-time. You were always there for me, always. I love you, Dad."

John was too tired to talk any more. "Give me a kiss, Stevie."

Stephen bent and gently kissed him, trying to will his own youth and strength and health into his father. He wanted to hold the wasted body to him and never let go.

John stroked his hair. "I'm so proud of you, son. Always been so proud, no matter what I said or did. So lucky to have had you. Send Sian in. Goodbye, son."

Stephen walked blindly from the room. "He wants you," he said to Sian.

He walked over to the window and stared out. He wasn't seeing the view, he was seeing a kaleidoscope of memories: his father reading to him, playing with him, helping him with his maths homework, making up ridiculous stories about Glover, the whippet… so many memories. The times they'd disagreed, the time spent living at Ted's, that didn't matter. All that mattered was the love, all the love his father had always given him.

"Stevie." It was Ted. Ted had never called him Stevie before.

He turned slowly. Sian was coming towards him, crying.

The following day, Stephen went to John's office to see Julian.

"Steve!" Julian gave him his hand. He was very distressed. "I'm so sorry! We're all so very sorry! John was such a wonderful man."

Stephen was proud that so many people thought so highly of John. "Thank you." He felt tears prickling under his eyelids, and he swallowed hard. When he had his emotions under control again, he said, "Julian, I want Lynn to come to the funeral. She loved Dad and he thought the world of her, but I haven't got her address."

Julian nodded. "I'll get the file for you. Ah, yes, here we are. There's a phone number too." He wrote them down and gave them to Stephen. "Steve, if there's anything I can do, anything at all. Tell Sian… tell her… well, we're all so sorry."

"Yes. Thank you, Julian."

He looked at the address as he walked back to the house. Leeds. Hardly any distance away. They'd played in Leeds when they were touring, and he hadn't known how close she was. That evening he rang the number. An unfamiliar female voice answered.

“Can I speak to Lynn…” What would she be? He remembered her joking once in Manchester that she’d work under her maiden name. “After all, you’ll be so famous by then, my patients will be forever asking me for your autograph otherwise!” she’d laughed, but he’d never thought any more about it, never dreamed that they wouldn’t always be together. He didn’t have to finish anyway.

“Lynn Jackson? She doesn’t live here any more.”

“Oh.” He hadn’t foreseen that. “Do you have an address or phone number for her? It’s urgent.”

“’Fraid not. But she works at Jimmy’s.”

“Jimmy’s?” It sounded like a wine bar.

“St. James’s Hospital. In Leeds. She’s a speech therapist in the child development clinic. Do you want the number? There’ll be no one there now, of course.”

He thanked her and took the number.

First thing next morning, he rang the hospital. They told him Lynn didn’t have a clinic until that afternoon, but she’d be in at two o’clock. He made Sian a cup of tea and took it up to her and let her talk about John.

Finally she gave him a small smile. “I’m sorry, Stevie.”

He shook his head. “It’s important to talk about him. So often people don’t.”

She squeezed his arm. “I’m going to have a bath.”

“Can I borrow the car, Mum?” He hadn’t told her he was going to ask Lynn to come to the funeral, he felt that if he talked about it, it wouldn’t happen.

She opened her mouth to ask him why he wanted it, but something in his face stopped her. “Course you can, Stevie.” She gave him a kiss.

He went downstairs and tried to read the paper, but he couldn’t, he couldn’t just wait around. He was too restless and unhappy, he’d never felt so alone. Maybe when he saw her… maybe they could get back together. She might still love him. Maybe. He got into the car and drove to Leeds. He was there much too early.

It was a huge hospital. He had a couple of hours to wait, so he bought a newspaper and went to the cafeteria for a cup of coffee. The girl at the till stared at him, but didn’t say anything. He sat down with his back to the room and tried to concentrate on the news. Time seemed to crawl past. His heart was hammering in his chest and he felt sick. He couldn’t manage more than a sip of the coffee. At one-fifty he went and sat in the waiting area of the clinic with several worried-looking parents who were surrounded by unconcerned children.

He stared at the door. There she was! He caught his breath, and his heart lurched in excitement and trepidation. She was wearing a coat that matched her violet eyes, and she’d had her hair cut into a pageboy style, which curved under at the edges like a bell. She’s so heartstoppingly lovely, he thought. She looked very happy; she was laughing, and talking to a tall, dark-haired man who stopped and fiddled with his briefcase, but she carried on, pushing the door open.

Stephen stood up, and she saw him and stopped dead. He held out his arms and she fell into them.

He shut his eyes. “Cherry.” She still smelt the same, she still felt the same. It had all been a dream and when he opened his eyes again they would be lying together in their bedroom in Manchester.

“Stevie!” she said against his shoulder. “What are you doing here?”

It was real. “Dad’s dead.”

Her eyes widened in shock. She stepped back out of his arms. “When? How? Was it his heart?”

“Leukaemia.”

"Lynn?" Tim had joined them.

"Oh." She looked at Stephen. It was so obvious that he was still in love with her. She couldn't possibly tell him that she had remarried, not now, but...

"Hello, I'm Tim Franklin, Lynn's husband," Tim said, holding out his hand. "You must be Stephen."

The blood drained from Stephen's face. There was a rushing in his ears and the room tilted. He stared at Tim. "What?"

People were beginning to look.

"Let's go into my office," Lynn said. She was furious with Tim. "Haven't you got a clinic now?" she asked pointedly, glaring at him.

He looked steadily back at her. "I'll see you at five-thirty, then."

She ignored him and led Stephen into an office off the waiting area. It was large but somehow cosy, with a comfortable sofa and several easy chairs, as well as her desk. There was a well-appointed play area in one corner, with a box of toys and dressing up clothes, and a little desk, equipped with paper and pencils, rather like the one he'd bought for Rob when he'd moved into his new flat. God, that seemed light years ago.

"Sit down, Stephen." She pressed the intercom on her desk. "Andrea, please could you bring in a cup of tea, four sugars. Yes, four." She went and sat next to him, taking his hand. "Stevie…"

"How can you be?" he burst out. "How can you be married?"

She sighed. "I tried to contact you, Stephen. You never phoned me."

He frowned. "When? I don't remember. I would've remembered."

"I phoned George's. Last year. November. I left a message."

"We were touring. George sold the house."

"I thought you didn't want me any more."

He stood up in distress. "I always wanted you! I've never stopped wanting you! I tried to find you, I even rang your mum, but she wouldn't tell me where you were. You're all I want, nothing else matters, I'd give it all up tomorrow, I'd lose it all for you!"

Andrea came in with the tea. "Your first appointment's here, Lynn." She stared at Stephen. "Aren't you…"

Lynn remembered that there was a Sid's Six poster on the wall in the secretaries' office. She took the tea from Andrea and gave it to Stephen. "Yes, he is," she said crisply. "Thank you, Andrea." She held the door open for Andrea, who backed out, still staring at Stephen.

"Listen, Stevie, I've got a clinic now. I finish at five. Can you wait?"

"Yeah," he said listlessly. He felt numb. It didn't seem to matter what he did now.

She dug into her bag. "Look. Here are my house keys. You can go there if you like, I'll draw you a map." She pulled some paper towards her.

Stephen carefully put the still full teacup down. "You seriously expect me to go to the house that you share with *him*?" He was shaking – with hurt, with shock, with anger. "I don't need to wait, Lynn. I came to ask you to go with me to Dad's funeral, but it couldn't matter less. I don't think you're the Lynn he knew. You're not the Lynn I knew."

And he walked out of her life.

"I've never been further west than Anglesey before!"

"Will you shut the fuck up, Andy! That's the fiftieth time you've said that!"

"Yeah, but I'm in Boston, like!"

"Mind, it's the arsehole end of the city, man," remarked George, staring out of the window.

"What are you complaining about, for Christ's sake, you can see the fucking Charles River!" Stephen pointed to a shining ribbon in the distance.

"Yeah, man, look – along with gasometers, a storage depot, a garage, a coach park, and a six lane highway," George retorted.

"Can't really call the accommodation first-class, either," Fin grinned.

Stephen stared miserably round the room. Fin was right. It looked as bleak as he felt. Everything was beige; walls, curtains, carpet, bed covers. "That mirror's not straight," he muttered.

"Stop being a fucking lass!" George groaned.

"Oh ey, what's wrong with you lot? Me, I'm chuffed, like! I'm in America!"

"We're all in fucking America, Andy. Why you're all in my fucking room, I don't know." Stephen went and lay on his bed, rolling over so that his back was towards them.

"Just keeping you company," Fin shrugged.

"I'm not going to get drunk if you go away. We've got a sound check later."

"It didn't make any difference the other day, like," Andy said.

"For Christ's sake! It happened once on this miserable fucking tour! At least I'm not snorting enough coke to fill the fucking Grand Canyon before every fucking concert!"

Fin glared at him. "It doesn't impair my performance, in fact it enhances it. You, on the other hand, you could hardly stand."

"Well, I've fucking said I'm not going to do it again, OK? So fuck off, the lot of you. I want to sleep."

"What are we going to do, man, Fin?" George asked, as they walked down the corridor.

Fin shrugged. "I don't know. I don't even know why he's like this. He won't talk to me. I know his Dad died, but…" He shrugged. "It seems like more than that."

Stephen lay on the bed and stared at the wall. He didn't think he could stand much more of life. It was all so pointless. Last time he'd rung Rob, Harry told him she and Dominic were getting married in the new year. He was pleased for her, he was pleased for Charlie. But it meant that Rob would now be living in a family unit. He'd never call Dominic Daddy, but that's in effect what he would be. It would be great for Rob, but he hated the idea of anyone, even Charlie, having that relationship with his son. He reached for a tissue and wiped his eyes. He couldn't stop crying either, it was embarrassing. He'd be in the middle of talking to someone or they'd be doing a sound check or something, and he'd suddenly think of Lynn and Tim Franklin together. He'd never lost it at a concert, but it was unnerving to think that he might.

They were on the first leg of their North American tour. He'd been looking forward to it so much, but now it had all turned to ashes. He knew he should tell the others about Lynn, but he wasn't sure he could get the words out without crying.

He had arranged, before his father died – it seemed like years ago, now, a different lifetime – to see Ray, who'd got a job in Boston last year and had decided to apply for American citizenship. He was dating an American girl and bringing her to the concert tomorrow and backstage afterwards. Stephen knew he'd have to pull himself together before that. He'd have to go and see the others. Explain what was going on.

He rang room service and ordered a bottle of whisky. When it arrived, he had a glass. He was tempted to go on drinking to oblivion. Alcohol and sex were the only things that seemed to help and even they were only temporary. Sex was easy to come by, there were girls everywhere, eager to do anything he wanted. Drugs too – as usual, there were dealers available at any hour of the day or night. He didn't want drugs. The odd joint, maybe, but he didn't much like the way coke made him feel, and although he wasn't squeamish – was, in fact, a blood donor – he didn't fancy the idea of injecting himself. He screwed the lid back on the bottle. Later, after the concert, he'd choose the girls he wanted and come back here and finish it.

"...so Lynn's remarried."

He looked down at the floor. Please don't let them be too sympathetic or I won't be able to control myself, he thought. He dreaded breaking down in front of them.

"What a bitch!"

They looked at Andy in surprise. None of them had ever heard such venom in his voice, he was usually the most easy going of them all.

Fin cleared his throat. "At the risk of upsetting you, Steve, I have to say I agree with Andy. I can't see how she could possibly have done that."

Stephen looked up. "I suppose the only explanation is that she didn't really love me." He was glad he'd told them. He'd constantly denied to himself that it was over, but now he had to believe it. It was finished, Lynn was with someone else. She *hadn't* loved him the way she'd said she did. He had his life to get on with. "Thanks, Andy." He smiled painfully. "I'm sorry I've been such a tosser. It won't happen again."

Lynn couldn't forget Stephen's words, 'You're not the Lynn I knew.' She'd wake in the morning with them going round in her head. That day after he left, she'd had no choice but to get on with her clinic, to put him out of her head and concentrate on the children. They had enough problems without an inattentive speech therapist who thought her troubles were worse than theirs. And in a way, it put her life into perspective. The little Down's syndrome girl, Dora, who was so gorgeous – she was easily Lynn's favourite patient. And her mother, Claire, whose husband had left after Dora was born because he couldn't stand the baby's disability – she never complained, was constantly cheerful. Lynn felt humbled by them all.

After the clinic, she thought about her mother. How could she have refused to give Stephen her address? It was wrong to hate your parents, she knew, but she did. She never wanted to see them again.

She and Tim drove home that evening in silence, Lynn refusing to speak to him until they were in the house. Then she rounded on him.

"How could you do that?"

"What? See, I don't see what I did! I come in and find my wife of less than three weeks in the arms of her ex-husband, the man she once described to me in a drunken moment as the love of her life. Not just *any* old ex-husband, may I point out, but a bloody heart throb, who writes and sings hit records and whose picture is every bloody where I look!"

She had never seen him so angry. "But you must have heard what he said!"

"I didn't hear him say anything!"

"Oh." She wandered into the sitting room and sat down. "Oh, what a mess!"

Tim followed her in. "Well, what did he say?"

"His father just died of leukaemia. He wanted me to go to the funeral with him. I liked John a lot, but he and Stevie... well, he loved Steve very much but he didn't approve of his music. He wanted him to go to Oxford, become a lawyer like he was. The pity of it was that Stevie is more than capable of doing that. He's very clever and he works. He got a first from Manchester. It was all such a waste as far as John was concerned. And Steve is half-Welsh, very emotional. I remember saying to him once that if there was nothing for him to feel guilty about, he'd have to manufacture something. He must be feeling guilty as hell now." She started to cry.

Tim sat next to her and took her hand. "I honestly didn't hear. I... well, I saw him with his arms round you, and I know how you felt about him. Lynn – you aren't still in love with him, are you?"

"It wouldn't make any difference if I was. He said I wasn't the Lynn he knew. I'm never going to see him again." She found a tissue and blew her nose. "I've got to shower. We're out with the Carruths tonight, aren't we?"

Much later, it occurred to him that she hadn't answered his question, merely sidestepped it. He didn't ask again. Stephen Markham was out of her life and she was with him, Tim. She was his wife. She seemed happy, she was always saying how much she loved him, and she was loving and eager in bed. She was his bird in the hand. Why rock the boat?

He had no idea about her ever-growing collection of 'Stephen' magazines. It was an obsession with her. Every time she bought a magazine with Stephen in it, she felt slightly ashamed, as if she was doing something morally wrong. She also got a similar feeling to the one a child gets when it eats too much cake or chocolate – an unpleasant nausea. She always resolved she wouldn't look for them any more, but gradually she'd feel the craving growing and find herself haunting newsagents and bookshops. She found a little book on a bookstall in Birmingham when she went to a conference there in the New Year, '*The Unofficial Stephen Markham*'. There were a lot of photos of Stephen in it but no new information, and several inaccuracies; their marriage, for instance, wasn't mentioned. As far as she was aware, there had never been anything written about her and Stephen. She found it hard to believe he could be so petty. I didn't really know him at all, she thought with sadness and resentment. It was a tiny book, pocket-sized, and she kept it at the bottom of her handbag, wrapped in an old silk scarf. Another time, she hit the jackpot and found an exclusive interview with him in an imported American magazine when she was in London for the day visiting Caro, who'd married a very successful cosmetic surgeon twenty years her senior, and actually bumped into Stephen occasionally at parties.

Lynn pumped her casually for information.

"Oh, I don't see him often," Caro said. "Donald and I went to a charity do the other day and he was there with a stunning girl on his arm. It's always someone different with him, isn't it? Quite the Romeo." She gave a little shiver. "You're well out of that, Lynn! I read he'd been seeing that gorgeous American actress with the funny name... you know, Michelle whatever it is."

"I don't think she's that great," Lynn said sourly. She'd read the article, in which Stephen had been quoted as saying that the actress was the most beautiful woman in the world. That had hurt. He'd always told her *she* was the most beautiful woman in the world. "Did you speak to him at the party?"

"Yes I did, and he was very nice, I must say. He didn't pretend not to know me, like some people would. Actually, he asked if I ever saw you and how were you and Tim, which I thought was quite sweet. It's nice that you're both on such good terms."

Clever, thought Lynn admiringly. "Did he say anything else?"

Caro thought. "Not really. He looked a bit odd though. More handsome than ever, but odd."

"What do you mean, odd?"

"I don't know. Wild. I wouldn't be surprised if he was doing drugs."

Lynn felt a coldness round her heart. Surely he wouldn't be that stupid? On her way home, she found the American magazine at the station. She settled down in the train to read it.

'We're sitting in the Cocktail Terrace at the Waldorf-Astoria. I'm drinking one of their famous champagne cocktails. Stephen Markham is drinking Coca Cola with a twist of lemon, and looking serene and unruffled in a white linen jacket over a pink t-shirt, white jeans and his trademark kickers.

"Stephen, how would you describe your music, and what are your influences?"

Stephen nursed his Coke and wished he'd never agreed to this interview. The band had played Madison Square Garden the previous evening and he'd spent the rest of the night partying. He hadn't been to bed – well, not to sleep, anyway – so he was dog tired, and the mere sight of alcohol made him wince.

"Um... my music. Well, it's just stuff I hear in my head. I'm not really conscious of any particular influences, basically, I suppose, because there are so many!" He laughed.

"Like what?"

"Well, blues, particularly Stanton Crawford; I'd love to work with him, I'm a huge fan of his. I actually met him while we were touring, he actually shook my hand and said he liked my music!"

Stephen looked down at his hand, remembering that moment. He hadn't even known Stanton Crawford was at the concert, and when Crawford had come into the dressing room afterwards, Stephen had been as tongue-tied as a small child. He'd managed to stammer out what a fan he was. Crawford had smiled and said they'd have to do something together sometime and he'd practically passed out.

"Who else?"

"Oh... um... BB King, Tampa Red, I love blues music. The Kinks – I think Ray Davies had a huge influence on so many people, he's just amazing. I heard 'Come Dancing' recently, it's phenomenal. And Mark Knopfler, what an incredible guitarist, he's superb, I'll never forget the first time I heard 'Sultans Of Swing', it blew me away. Then a lot of folk influences, Paul Simon particularly, I love his music, I'd love to work with him too. I think he and Stanton Crawford are the greatest musicians of the century. When you think that Paul Simon wrote 'The Sound of Silence' when he was only twenty-two! Most musicians, myself definitely included, would count themselves lucky ever to write a song like that! My other big influence is Welsh music. My grandfather was Welsh and he sang all these Welsh songs to me from the time I was a baby, so there's all that inside me too."

"Welsh, huh? So do you speak Welsh?" Stephen shakes his head, looking amused.

Stephen was unable to suppress a grin. I wonder if you even know where Wales is? he thought.

"No. I sing the songs in Welsh because I picked them up, and I know a little bit of the language but I can't speak it. I ought to learn, but I'm lazy!"

"Most people would call it busy."

"Yeah, but think of people who really are busy, doing real, grown-up stuff, brain surgeons and the rest of it, who still find time to do other things!"

"So you don't count what you do as real, grown-up stuff?"

Stephen laughs incredulously. "No! Are you kidding? I travel round, singing and playing the guitar! An interviewer asked me the other day which of my songs am I most proud of? I ask you! I'm proud of my son, I'm proud of my family. I'm not proud of my songs!"

"You and the band have a very squeaky clean image,"

Stephen smiled to himself. If you only knew, mate! He sipped his Coke.

"Do we?"

"Sure. Well, look what you're drinking! And you don't do drugs, you don't have messy affairs."

"Well, personally, I don't want to do drugs. Ultimately they're bad for you. Same with messy affairs. If they don't screw up your body, they'll screw up your mind. What's the point? If other people want that, it's up to them, I'm not about to interfere or preach, but I'd rather be thought of as square, as boring. I think the others feel the same."

"You've been described as 'sex on legs'. How do you feel about that, and about being a heartthrob?"

Oh, come on, how do you think?

"Well, obviously, I'm very flattered," he grins. "Who wouldn't like it?"

"You don't feel it will stop you from being taken seriously, detract from your career?"

"If it does, it does, there's nothing I can do about it," he shrugs. "Although I don't see why it should, I imagine that people who like my music will still like it, no matter what the press label me."

"So, then, we know that women find you irresistible, but what about you? Tell us about your perfect woman."

At this point Stephen looks pensive.

Stephen's mind instantly filled with images of Lynn. He had never talked to the press about her, and he never intended to. For a start, he considered it to be none of their business, and secondly he didn't want to put her through the whole publicity nightmare. And, anyway, he couldn't talk about her. It hurt too much. He remembered the first time he'd seen her, in the bar at Grosvenor Place, looking exquisitely beautiful, the only woman in the world. At their wedding, alluring and mysterious behind the veil of her hat. Playing her flute while he played guitar. Holding her against his heart, the softness of her skin, the scent of her, the weight and warmth of her in his arms. And through it all, mocking him, on a continual loop, he could hear Franklin's voice: "I'm Lynn's husband." He flinched away from the memory.

"My perfect woman? Um, I won't know till I've found her."

Lynn's heart lurched. Had she meant so little to him?

"Oh, come on, blonde, brunette, tall, small, what?"

Stephen smiles. "Hey, there are thousands of women out there, I'm not about to alienate a huge section of them by picking one particular type! They're all gorgeous in their own way!"

"What about girlfriends? Anyone ever come close to being 'the one'?"

Stephen shrugs. "I don't kiss and tell."

"OK, OK. Let's talk about your career, then. What's your long-term plan?"

Stephen raises his eyebrows. "My long term plan? I don't have one. I mean, I've never sat down and thought out any specific plan. As long as people want to keep on listening to my music, I intend to carry on writing and performing."

"What about a solo career?"

"I don't know. At the moment, I'm more than happy being with the band."

"One last thing. Do you have any advice for the readers?

Stephen looks thoughtful.

Stephen considered the question. How idiotic! Advice about what? Being in a band? Playing guitar? Eating pancakes? Life, the universe, everything?

"Never stir hot toffee with a plastic spoon," he says finally. He leans forward earnestly. "It will always *melt. That bit of advice was for one special person, although it's advice everyone should take on board."*

"One special person? Who would that be?"
"If she ever reads this, she'll know who she is."

Lynn stared down at the magazine. She'd forgotten she'd told him that she'd melted a plastic spoon making toffee. So she *was* still special to him. How could she ever get over him? She had to stop buying these magazines and start living her own life.

That night, as they went upstairs to bed, she said to Tim, "Let's have a baby."

Chapter Nine
Amité Amoureuse

Amité amoureuse, the line between friend and lover blurs.

"Touring's pretty lonely, isn't it?"

Stephen was not long back from the band's tour of the U.S. He drained his glass and stared into the fire. "Don't get me wrong, I love it, I love playing to the fans, it's terrific, the best part of what we do." He smiled to himself, thinking back over the tour. He always joked around with the audience, was usually able to establish a rapport with them very quickly, and he revelled in the feeling. "It's just the actual touring – bus, gig, hotel, night after night – that I don't relish."

"Frankly, old chap, I've always found plenty to do. Plenty of groupies," Dominic grinned.

"Don't you get bored with that? I mean, you can't really talk to them, can you?"

"Well, that's not why I seek them out, Markham. But I know what you mean. Still, I'll be taking Harry with me next time."

That made Stephen even gloomier. "And my Blewser, too."

"Look, why don't we organise it so we go at the same fucking time? You speak to Cell, I'll speak to Jimmy and we'll sort something out. It'll be fun!"

'Nets Of Gold' shot up to number one in the album charts, and the first single released, 'If I'd Known', reached number three. In the early spring, Euterpe released a second single, 'I've Got Your Number', which went straight in at number one. Sid's Six was in huge demand, with continual interviews and TV appearances.

Dominic's band, GI Joe, had just released a fourth album, 'It's Nice, But is it Art?', and a hit single, 'Whisper my Name'. Their third album, 'Looking Glass', had been certified multi-platinum, but Dominic was more concerned with his and Harry's forthcoming wedding, which was being held on the third Saturday in March. Stephen wished they'd chosen another month – his own marriage to Lynn had taken place almost exactly four years earlier.

"I'm really sorry, Stevie," Harry had said, looking at him anxiously when she'd told him the date. "It's ridiculous, I don't have any say in my own wedding, it all seems to be about what Susan and Angus want. It's driving me mad! I just don't understand Dom's attitude. I've said to him several times let's just elope, but for some reason, he's really keen on doing what his parents want." She frowned. "I mean, it's not like they're particularly close or anything, in fact sometimes it's almost as if he deliberately winds Susan up."

"Oh, you know Charlie," Stephen shrugged. "Likes everyone to think he's a rebel, but he always ends up doing the done thing, it's his upbringing. And don't worry about me, Hal, I can cope. I'm over Lynn now. Well, almost," he added, at the look on Harry's face.

He was to be Dominic's best man. They had been watching football at Dominic's beautiful and exceedingly expensive house in Cheyne Walk, Chelsea, one Saturday, when Dominic asked him.

"After all, you know us both so well, Markham, you fucker. It's a little incestuous, really, isn't it? Harry tells me Ted and your mother are getting hitched later in the year, which will make her your sister as well as the mother of your child. Still, I suppose coming from fucking Wales, you'll be used to that kind of relationship, old chap."

Stephen stared at him. "Mum's going to marry Ted? It's the first I've heard of it!"

"Fuck. You're right, old chap. Now I come to think of it, she did mutter something about not mentioning it to anyone. Fact is, she was just about to go down on me – something she's exceptional at, as you probably know – and I clean forgot. Most distracting when she's chatting to me at the same time. Odd creatures, women. I mean, do you think about anything but fucking when you're fucking?"

"Look, Charlie, I don't mind you telling me in precise and graphic detail what you do to and with groupies, although it does get a little tedious—"

"It's the sheer volume of numbers you can't cope with, old chap," Dominic interrupted, grinning.

"—but you and Harry together, it's kind of… well, voyeuristic."

"Really? Can't see why, we're practically brothers."

"I don't think that makes any difference. Dominic?"

Dominic looked at him, surprised. Stephen never called him anything but Charlie. "Yes?"

"If you ever hurt Harry in any way at all, I'll disembowel you."

Dominic was silent for a few minutes. The two of them stared at each other. Finally he said, "I really fucking resent that, Markham."

Stephen shrugged. "So would I in your place. But Harry is very special to me."

Dominic wandered over to the drinks cabinet and poured himself a whisky. He held up the bottle enquiringly. Stephen nodded. He knew he was drinking far too much and partying far too hard, but he couldn't make himself care. He was still running every day, even though he was having a great deal of casual sex. Running had become a habit, almost a comfort; much as he hated the thought of it, once he started he found he could think of anything or nothing. No one was asking him anything, no one wanted anything from him. Even with groupies, there was constant pressure to perform, he could never simply say, "Shall we just cuddle?" And he couldn't be bothered with the rituals of establishing a proper relationship with a girl. His original squeaky clean image had tarnished, and he was getting a reputation in the press as a hell-raiser, constantly partying and moving from girl to girl. He didn't care; as long as he and the woman he was briefly involved with knew the score and no one got hurt, he had no interest in what outsiders thought of him.

The Tony Banks song 'Lucky Me' was constantly playing in his head these days. It reminded him of Manchester, warm summer days in the flat in Rusholme, the windows wide open in the sitting room, the only things visible through them the sky and the treetops, Lynn leaning against him as they held hands and listened to that album.

"Markham? What the fuck's up?" Dominic was standing over him, holding his drink.

"Sorry, Charlie."

"Anyway, as I was saying, if Harry is so fucking special to you, why didn't you marry her?"

"You and she must have talked about this."

"Yes, but I want to hear your version."

"I'd really rather not. Let's just watch the footer. I want to see Man U thrash Newcastle."

"In your fucking dreams, old chap! Harry said she'd always been in love with you but you weren't in love with her."

"Yes, but I would have married her! She refused! I offered twice. I didn't know she was in love with me, for Christ's sake, I'm not a fucking mind reader, and when I finally did find out, she wasn't in love with me any more. Which is probably a good thing or I might have married her and then we'd both have been miserable."

Dominic looked down into his drink. "Are you in love with her then?" he asked tensely.

Stephen shook his head. "No. But it was just after Lynn left me. I wanted… I don't know. I wanted someone to care for me, I suppose."

Dominic relaxed. "I *am* in love with her. Very much so. I won't deny I'm fucking jealous of you, Markham."

Stephen was amazed. "Me? Why?"

"You're such a fucking paragon in her eyes. Can do no fucking wrong. Specially where your Blewser's concerned. It's always, 'Stevie says this, Stevie does that'. Frankly, old chap, it's a fucking pain."

Stephen grinned. "I can't help being perfect. Shall I have a word with her?"

"I wish you would. If I say anything she just smirks. I threatened to spank her the other day, but she just said, 'Yes please'. So of course, then I had to. She's such a bitch."

"I told you, I don't want to hear about your sex life— Yes!" he shouted, as Manchester United scored.

"Harry, can I talk to you?"

Harry was dropping Rob off for the weekend. "Can it wait, Stevie? I'm in a bit of a hurry."

"It won't take long. First, will you *not* say to Charlie 'Stevie' says or does the opposite of whatever he's saying or doing?"

Harry grinned. "Oh, come on, Steve, it keeps him in his place."

"Well, find some other way of doing that. Second, what's this about my mum and Ted?"

"Oh, shit! See, he can't keep his mouth shut! You'd never have done that!"

"Harry!"

"OK, OK." She sighed. "Dad told me he'd asked Sian to marry him and she said yes. No one else knows, they've not made any plans, but when they do, Sian is going to tell you and the girls first."

Stephen thought about it. "Tell Ted to make her get on with it, Hal. She's like me, she'll start feeling guilty about Dad and she won't do it. He'll have to be a bit bossy."

Harry grinned. "Bossy? Dad? He's like me, Stevie. Hasn't got a bossy bone in his body!"

The wedding was going to be a huge affair. "Jesus, Charlie, you've got more relatives than the Royal Family!" Stephen said when he saw the guest list.

"Bunch of fucking German upstarts!" Dominic replied. "My family came over with the fucking Conqueror!"

The Chaplin family had enough influence to arrange for Dominic and Harry to be married at St. Margaret's, Westminster, even though Harry was divorced. Dominic claimed that his mother, Lady Susan, was related to most of the noble houses in Britain and Stephen believed him. She and Dominic's father, Sir Angus, were holding a dinner party for Harry and Dominic at their London house the evening before the wedding.

"This is why I wanted the fucking stag party tonight, this dinner is going to be the posh equivalent of watching fucking paint dry. Oh, well, at least they'll be serving vintage champagne." They were dressing for the dinner party on the Friday night, and Dominic had already downed a large brandy. True to form, he'd got extremely drunk at his stag party the night before. He was staying with Stephen, who'd finally got him home at six in the morning and dumped him on the bed in the guest room before falling into his own bed. He'd got him up at midday and made Dominic shower and drink pints of orange juice. Then he'd made him a hot water bottle and let him go back to bed, while he learnt his speech.

Now Stephen was looking at him in alarm. "You're not to get drunk, Charlie."

"Jesus Christ, are you my fucking mother?"

Stephen suddenly realised that cool, unflappable Dominic was extremely nervous. "Yeah, until the vicar says, 'You may kiss the bride', I'm your mother. And you better bloody well do what you're told, OK?"

"OK, OK, OK!"

"Just think of Harry. Think how very, very pleased she'll be with you if you behave."

"I said OK! Help me with this fucking bow tie, I'm all thumbs."

He managed to get Dominic dressed and ready with the help of a couple more brandies, and they actually arrived at Leezance House, the Chaplins' elegant Georgian mansion near St James's Park, slightly early.

"It's a strange name for a house," Harry had said, when she'd first heard it.

"It's built on the site of an old shrine to some martyr or something," Dominic had explained. "It's a corruption of some fucking French word, I can never remember what. Why the fuckers couldn't have given it a decent Anglo-Saxon name I'll never know."

"Saxons being wonderfully English, of course," Stephen put in.

"Fuck off, Markham, what do you know about anything?"

"I know that the name of your parents' house is a corruption of the words 'Lieu Saint', holy place," Stephen retorted. "It's like Charing Cross, a corruption of Chère Reine cross."

"Shall I put him out of his fucking misery now?" Dominic asked Harry.

"Strewth, Charlie, you lot are really rolling in it, aren't you?" Stephen said, somewhat awed, as they were shown into the drawing room.

Lady Susan, Dominic's mother, came over to them, her eyebrows raised. "You managed to get here on time and looking presentable, Dominic. Well done!" She offered him a skilfully made up cheek.

He kissed her, and turned to the girl standing next to her. "Sophy!" He embraced his sister, who was absurdly like him.

Lady Susan, an attractive woman in her early forties, tall, slim and elegant, was also very like him, although her expertly styled hair was ash blonde rather than his rich gold. There was something rather glacial about her though, Stephen thought, like the ice queen. Her smile never quite seemed to reach her eyes. She extended a beautifully manicured hand to him. "It's really you I should be thanking." She sighed. "I can see he's not going to introduce us. You must be Stephen. I'm Susan." She turned and gestured at a thickset man with muddy brown hair and a choleric expression, who was talking to an elderly couple. "Angus, Dominic's arrived." She introduced him to Stephen, and they shook hands.

Angus turned to Dominic. "Well, Dominic, you're early. When can we expect Harriet?"

Dominic shrugged. "When she gets here, I suppose. Markham, this is Sophy."

"Hello." Sophy smiled at Stephen. "I love your music."

Stephen smiled back. Sophy was very pretty, small and slender, with long, pale gold hair that reminded him of Lynn's, and eyes exactly the same clear dark grey as Dominic's, but a different shape. "Thank you," he said, holding on to her hand. "Charlie tells me you're a medical student."

She looked confused. "Charlie?"

"Poor Markham's a bit simple. He thinks it's funny to call me Charlie because of our surname."

"Oh, I see, Charlie Chaplin!"

"The first time I met him he was being obnoxious," Stephen explained. "I did it to annoy him."

"And you haven't stopped annoying me since. Yes, she's a medic, aren't you, Soph? Wants to be a neurosurgeon."

"Really?" Stephen looked at Sophy with awe.

"Thank you, Dom," Sophy sighed.

"Don't worry, Markham won't be put off. He's a bloody know-all too. He got a first."

Stephen realised that this was the first time Dominic had sworn and it was very mild at that. He can behave then, he thought.

"Really? What subject?" Sophy was asking.

"Literature."

"Oh, you've got an earring!" she exclaimed. "It suits you! Very piratical. It's a lovely colour."

"It's Welsh gold," Stephen smiled.

"Pretentious, moi?" muttered Dominic.

Harry arrived with Ted and Sian. She was looking exceedingly pretty in a long, deep blue velvet frock with a tight, low cut bodice and a full skirt. She kissed Susan and Sophy and took Dominic's hand. She had never been so happy.

"You have got the ring, haven't you? I haven't asked you that already, have I?"

"Not above five hundred times," Stephen sighed. "Yes, I've got the ring, Charlie. For goodness sake, calm down."

"I am fucking calm, God damn you!"

"Keep your voice down and stop swearing," Stephen hissed, as several pairs of eyes turned in their direction. I hope to God Harry isn't too late, he thought, I can't cope with this lunatic much longer.

He glanced round the church. It was packed, mostly with people he didn't know. He saw Sian and the girls, looking very pretty, on the bride's side; further down on the groom's side he saw Fin, George and Andy. George was with Kagami; they'd just got engaged and were talking about getting married in Japan. Fin was with his girlfriend, Shelagh, and Andy, looking subdued in a dark suit, and strangely pink, as if the other two had held him down and scrubbed him raw, was with his latest girlfriend, a very tall, blonde model who was busily painting her fingernails. As Stephen – and indeed all Andy's friends – had predicted, his marriage to Giovanna, the Italian actress, hadn't lasted longer than six months. "But what an incredible six months, like!" Andy had declared with satisfaction.

Dominic muttered something.

"What?"

"I said, is it too late to cancel?"

The reception was held at Leezance House. It made sense, and Ted wasn't the man to make a fuss about image. He was comfortable with himself and didn't care what other people thought. He was paying for the food and drink, including all the champagne, and he'd been delighted rather than otherwise, brimming with pride and pleasure at the thought that Harry's wedding was going to be a society event. His satisfaction had known no bounds when he discovered that Prince Philip's third cousin, the Duke of Mercia, was on the guest list along with his family.

"God! We don't have to invite *them*, do we?" Dominic had groaned. "They can barely string two words together!"

The wedding breakfast went without a hitch. Stephen's speech was witty and to the point, and a huge amount of vintage Veuve Clicquot, Ted's favourite champagne, was poured down appreciative throats. Even Rob, who hated wearing his pageboy costume, behaved.

After the breakfast, the day became far less formal. Ties and tongues were loosened, and the guests roamed around, chatting casually.

Stephen wandered into the drawing room, looking for Sophy. She waved to him from a secluded window seat, and he sat down next to her. "Mmmm," he said appreciatively. "Is that Penhaligon's you're wearing?"

She was delighted. "Not many men would know that! Not many women either, come to that."

"I love Penhaligon's. Harry wears Bluebell, and the first present I ever bought my wife was their Violetta scent and body lotion. Plus, they don't test on animals."

"Are you married?" she asked in disappointment, looking at his ringless finger.

He coloured slightly. "Ex-wife. We're divorced."

Rob came running in. He was still dressed in his page's costume, a little Highland outfit, complete with jacket, kilt and sporran.

"Doesn't he look cute?" Sophy smiled.

"He looks ridiculous," Stephen said crossly. "He even had a real… what do you call it, Skean Dhu knife thing. I had to confiscate it, he nearly had my eye out earlier. I can't think what possessed Harry. She found out there's a Taylor tartan. Honestly!"

Sophy laughed. "That's Harry though," she said fondly.

Stephen liked her even more. Dominic had told him, in the strictest confidence, that Susan and Angus, while not exactly disliking Harry, considered her to be an unsuitable wife for their son. Sophy obviously didn't feel that way.

He sighed. "Yes, that's Harry all right. She wants him to start school next term, but I don't think he's ready. And so much has changed in his life – he and Harry moving away from York, my father dying, Harry marrying Charlie. I think he's had enough, I don't think he should start till September. God, you spend enough of your life at school as it is without starting before you have to!"

He'd had endless arguments about this with Harry, the most recent only a few weeks ago. They were at Dominic's house, and Rob had a cardboard box and was pretending it was a tank, from which he would periodically leap out and try to kill Stephen and Dominic.

"He should be at school," Harry said, darkly, as he launched an assault on Dominic.

"For Gods sake, give it a rest, Harriet!" Stephen snapped. "He's too young!"

"Bloody rubbish! He's well ready for it, you just don't want him to go because you didn't like school!"

"You're talking bollocks." Stephen turned to Dominic. "Don't you agree, Charlie?"

"Hey, don't involve me, he's your kid," Dominic shrugged.

"Don't call him a 'kid'," said Stephen, exasperated. "Come on, Charlie, what do you think?"

"Convoluted and devious thoughts about being best at everything," Dominic grinned.

"Charlie! Stop being a pain. What do you think?"

"Listen, Markham, when I try to give an opinion on anything to do with Rob, I get told he's not my son, OK, so sort it out yourselves." He turned the TV on.

"That's not very fair, Harry."

"He's exaggerating as usual. I didn't say that, Dominic."

"Yes you bloody did," Dominic said, quietly and without heat.

"Anyway, that's not the point. I refuse to let you push my son into school before he has to go!"

Harry stared at him. "And just how will you stop me?"

"My name's on his birth certificate!"

"Yeah, like that gives you any rights!"

"Harry!" He was really hurt.

"Sorry. But, Stephen, I honestly think it would be good for him. He's really eager to learn stuff."

"I'll teach him!"

"When? You're never here."

"I'm here now."

"In a month you'll be on tour."

"Well, I'll teach him before I go… oh, I don't know Harry, but please!"

"OK. I'll think about it."

"Have you considered a Montessori school?" Sophy suggested now. "He'd probably only go in the mornings until he was five. There's a very good one in Hampstead."

"Thanks!" Stephen said gratefully. "That's a good idea. I'll look into it."

"Pleased to be able to help."

"Could I take you to dinner later?" he asked.

She smiled widely. "I'd love that."

"Lynn?"

"Hmmm?" Lynn looked up from her book.

"We've been trying for a baby for a while now. We don't seem to be getting anywhere."

"We're having fun though aren't we?" She threw her book onto the floor and plumped up her pillow. "Shall we try now?"

Tim smiled and kissed her. "Yes, that'd be lovely, but my point is, should we see someone about it?"

"I read it can take the average couple up to a year to conceive."

"I don't like to think of myself as average," he joked, but spoiled it by adding bitterly, "Guess I'm not like super-stud Steve, hitting the jackpot first go, twice!" Lynn had told him about Harry and Rob.

She didn't know what to say. "Darling, sometimes it just happens! Anyway, it's probably me; my cervix doesn't work properly, perhaps the rest of me is a bit defective too."

She succeeded in diverting his thoughts. "Don't ever say that, Lynn! You're perfect, inside and out!"

The next day she made an appointment with a specialist who did some tests and gave her the all clear. She didn't tell Tim, just hoped she would get pregnant very soon. She'd been disturbed by the bitterness in his voice when he'd mentioned Stephen, and the fact that she spent a great deal of her time dreaming about her ex-husband made her feel even worse.

Dominic and Harry's wedding had been in all the papers, along with pictures of Stephen looking stunning in morning dress. Then there were follow-up articles about him dating Dominic's sister, Sophy, and photos of them together on a beach in France. Apparently, Sid's Six was touring Europe and Sophy had flown out for a weekend. Lynn remembered Caro saying once that she'd met Stephen at a party, and that he looked wild, out of control. Well, his behaviour these days certainly justified her opinion. He was always being photographed with different women, and reports of the band's excessive drink, drug, and girl-fuelled after-show parties were constantly in the papers. Much as she couldn't bear the thought of Stephen belonging to anyone other than her, she hoped that this relationship would last for a while.

There was a double-page spread, entitled *Sid's Sixpack*, in Lynn and Tim's Sunday supplement, of Stephen in a pair of swimming trunks, looking very fit, and romping in the surf with Sophy. Tim screwed it up and chucked it in the bin. Later, Lynn got it out, smoothed out the creases and put it with her secret stash. Occasionally, when she was driving to work she'd think: what if I crashed and was killed and Tim found my Stevie stuff when he was clearing out my effects? But she went on buying it.

Sid's Six finished the European tour at the beginning of June. It had gone extremely well, they were hugely popular on the continent, especially in Scandinavia, where Stephen was mobbed. The Swedes particularly liked his 'Nordic eyes', as the papers called them. He could hardly move for girls.

The only time they had a problem was in Spain. Stephen hadn't realised some of the venues for the concerts were bullfighting rings. He flatly refused to play in them. The others exchanged exasperated looks. They were used to him being a perfectionist about the band and respected him for it, even though they grumbled, but he was usually willing to listen to suggestions. Occasionally, though, they came up against something like this and it was like walking into a brick wall. He wouldn't budge an inch.

"Why not, for fuck's sake?" Fin demanded.

"They're evil places! They're places of suffering and death!"

"According to some of the papers then, they'd be the perfect place to hold our concerts, like," Andy grinned.

They all turned on him. "Shut up, Andy!"

George turned back to Stephen. "Howay, man, Steve, don't be a lass!"

"OK, when we get home, I'll get Cell to book a load of abattoirs, we'll give concerts from those."

"Don't be stupid, Steve, it's not the same thing!"

"No, it's not, they actually torture bulls in bullrings!"

"He's got a point, like," said Andy.

Stephen smiled at him warmly.

"It's not as if you're a vegetarian though, is it, Steve?" Fin pointed out reasonably.

The other two grinned. There was a silence. Stephen knew they'd backed him into a corner and there was only one way out. "Yes I am."

"Since when?" scoffed Fin. "We all saw you troughing down that burger yesterday, you hypocrite!"

"Since right now," Stephen retorted. "I'm never going to eat meat again. Or fish," he added. "Nothing with a face."

"How about your shoes, man?" George put in, sceptically, looking down at Stephen's red Kickers. "They're leather."

"Well, OK, I'll have to find an alternative. There must be an alternative to leather."

"What about suede?" suggested Andy.

Stephen sighed. "Thanks, Andy."

"But anyway, Steve," Andy went on, "I'm not sure about vegetarianism, like. After all, man is coniferous."

Stephen burst out laughing. "Yeah, well, maybe you are, Andy. Listen, I'm not playing in a bullring. If they want us, they'll have to find us somewhere else, like Nou Camp stadium."

"You big lass!" George mocked.

Stephen looked at him with such contempt that George began to get uneasy. "Look, man..." he started.

"If caring about the suffering of other creatures is behaving like a lass," Stephen interrupted, "then I'm happy to be a lass along with the likes of Greenpeace, who put themselves in front of whaling boats and their harpoons. I'm *not* playing in bullrings."

They didn't.

On the second Saturday in June, Sian and Ted were married very quietly on the Isle of Wight. Sid's Six and GI Joe were due to start their two-month tour of North America the following week, and Stephen and Dominic had snatched a few days' break to attend the wedding. Stephen took Rob down with him.

It was a bittersweet feeling, being back on the Isle of Wight, back in the house at the bottom of Dover Street. So many memories, the place seemed to echo with them. He'd never realised before what a strange household it had been. He remembered Rhodri and Gwen arguing, shouting at each other in Welsh, Gwen from the door of her bedroom at the top of the house, Rhodri from his on the ground floor. And no one had ever commented on the fact that not only did they not share a bedroom, they didn't even sleep in the same part of the house. It had all seemed perfectly normal to Stephen, they were just Mam and Dada, and that was how they lived. He wondered if they'd always been like that; surely they must have shared a room when they were younger? He could ask Sian, but did he really want to know? If he started asking questions, he'd never see his childhood in the same way again. Let sleeping dogs lie. He simply wanted to remember things the way they'd been. Dada's singing rang in his ears as he climbed the stairs, he could hear the giggling of his sisters, his attempts to master the guitar Dada had given him when he was thirteen. He half-thought if he turned round his father would be coming up the stairs behind him, carrying the small brown leather suitcase he always used when he came to the house.

Nesta's pugs were still barking in the kennels behind the house, and Mam and Nesta were both still there, much older, and only really using the ground floor of the house now, but otherwise exactly the same; talking in Welsh to each other, exclaiming over him, Mam grumbling that he ought to be ashamed of himself, appearing on the BBC dressed in jeans and a tee shirt with half-naked girls cavorting around him.

"What's wrong with a suit?" she demanded. "And getting your hair cut smartly?"

"It was Top Of The Pops, Mam, and they were dancers," Stephen explained.

"Dancers, is it?" she said acidly. "We had another name for them when I was young!"

"She was so proud of you, love!" Nesta ruffled his hair as if he was Rob's age.

"Stop mumbling, Nesta, speak up!" Mam said irritably.

Rob ran in from the garden where he'd been playing with King George, one of Nesta's pugs. "King George is the bestest dog in the world!" he said, grabbing Nesta's hand.

She kissed him. "There's lovely you are, Robbie! And aren't you the living image of your Dada?"

They thought Rob was the best thing since sliced bread. They hadn't seen him for several years and Stephen felt bad about not bringing him more often. He resolved to try to take him at least once a year.

"Stevie, can I have a quick word?" Sian was looking round the sitting room door.

"Sure." Stephen stood up. "You go and play with King George, Rob, and don't bother Mam and Auntie Nesta."

Nesta smiled at him. "He's fine, Stevie, aren't you, cariad?"

"What can I do for you, Mum?" Stephen asked.

"I wanted to talk to you about Ted. Let's go down to the front."

Stephen raised his eyebrows. "OK."

They walked down to the sea wall together and gazed out at the restless sea.

Stephen filled his lungs with the fresh, salty air and sighed. "I love it here. It reminds me so much of the old days."

"That's kind of what I want to talk to you about," Sian said hesitantly. "I've already spoken to the girls, but you've been away so much recently…"

"What is it, Mum?" Stephen was concerned.

Sian twisted her hands nervously. "Well, the thing is, see, love, I know your father hasn't been dead for a year yet, and it's not that I didn't love him, Stevie – I did, so much!" Her eyes filled with tears. "I miss him all the time, but… well, I love Ted too, and neither of us are getting any younger, and well… we could wait for a year, maybe we *should* wait for a year, but…"

"Mum!" Stephen interrupted in amazement. "I know you loved Dad, everyone knew!" He remembered the way Sian would rush into John's arms when he came home from work, and the look of love on his father's face as he held her. Their relationship had always been like that, ever since he could remember – until he'd refused to go to university. The familiar dull, heavy feeling of guilt enveloped him, and he pushed the memory aside. "What difference does it make how long he's been dead? He'd want you to be happy, Mum, you know he would! He'd be so glad you've got Ted." He sighed. "And you should never let love go."

Sian smiled in relief. "Thank you, cariad. I didn't want you to think… well, that anything had been going on between Ted and me before Dad died."

Stephen took her hand. "I didn't." He kissed her cheek. "You worry too much, Mum. This is the only life we have, and if there's a chance of happiness, grab it with both hands!"

They walked back to the house, where Kathy and Paul had arrived with Ceridwen. She had Paul's red hair and green eyes and a huge grin that was all her own. She loved Rob and crawled round after him, offering him half-eaten bits of Rusk, and anything she found on the floor.

He played with her occasionally, but found her very boring. "She can't do *anything*, Daddy," he said to Stephen.

"She's only a baby, Rob. You were like that when you were her age."

Rob looked at him witheringly. "No fucking way!"

Stephen was speechless with horror. "Robert!" he managed to gasp. "If I ever hear you saying that again I will spank you, do you hear me?"

Rob was startled. Stephen had never smacked him. "Dom said it," he explained in subdued tones.

Stephen struggled to contain his anger. "Dominic *shouldn't* say it, it is very, very bad, do you understand?" I'll kill the pair of them, he thought, I'll bloody well *kill* them!

Harry and Dominic didn't arrive until Saturday morning, and he didn't have time to speak to them before the ceremony, which took place at St Olave's Church in Gatcombe, just outside Newport. Sian was wearing a creamy tweed suit with a thin leaf green check and her pearl necklace, and looked blissfully happy.

After the reception, which was really just tea at Mam's, Ted took her away to Venice for a long honeymoon and Stephen finally managed to get a private word with Harry and Dominic before they left. "I hate to sound like a pompous git—"

"You do it very well though, Markham," Dominic interrupted admiringly.

"—but I really don't want Rob hearing that kind of language."

Harry glared at Dominic, who had the grace to look ashamed. "Yes, I'm sorry, I was on the phone in the office. I didn't realise the pair of you were back," he said to Harry. "I'll be more fuck— I'll be more careful in future."

"Rob knows he's not supposed to be in the office!" Harry turned to Stephen. "Course, I blame you, really."

Stephen was stung by the injustice of this. "That is *so* unfair!" he spluttered. "How can it *possibly* be my fault?"

"If he was at school full-time, he wouldn't be there when Dom was making business calls," she said, watching his face. She dug Dominic in the ribs. "See, I told you. He's so easy!"

"Oh, very funny. He didn't have asthma till he started school though, did he?" Rob had had an asthma attack shortly after starting at the Montessori school in Hampstead. Harry's doctor had told her that asthma was common amongst western schoolchildren and not to worry. Rob now had inhalers, to prevent attacks and to control it. Stephen had been horrified and felt that starting school, added to John's death and the move to London, had contributed to the condition.

Harry hadn't agreed. "He's only going in the mornings for God's sake!" she'd snapped. "Shut up about school! He's got to go eventually, it's the law, so get used to it!"

Now she just said, mildly, "He hasn't had an attack for ages, Stevie. You worry too much."

Stephen enjoyed this tour of North America very much. Somehow, having Harry there made all the difference. He envied her and Dominic but was glad they were so happy together. They had such an easy relationship, both friends *and* lovers. *But then,* he reflected sadly, Lynn and I were like that.

When they were appearing at Radio City Music Hall in New York, Dominic took them out to eat at Serendipity 3. It was a strange place, very small inside, and a cross between a general store, ice cream parlour, and casual restaurant.

"This is different," Stephen said, looking round at the marble topped tables, the white on white décor, and the Tiffany lamps.

"Just wait," Dominic said.

Stephen's eyes widened as the couple at the table next to them were served with colossal chocolate sundaes. He grinned. "I see what you mean!"

Dominic and Harry watched indulgently as he and Rob tucked in.

"You're such a pig, Stevie," Harry said fondly, when he ordered a second helping of banana split.

"I wouldn't have thought it was your kind of place, Charlie," Stephen said later, as they were relaxing over a drink in his suite while Harry put Rob to bed.

Dominic took a sip of his whisky and smiled. "Mick and I took a couple of girls there when we were playing those concerts at Madison Square Garden. As soon as we sat down I thought of you."

Stephen grinned. "Yeah, well, it's certainly my sort of…" His expression changed. "Wait a minute. Those concerts were last month. What do you mean 'girls'?"

"They were just a couple of groupies. They were fun, so we took them out. It was Mick's idea really."

"But, Charlie, I don't understand. What were you doing with groupies?"

Dominic raised his eyebrows. "What does one usually do with groupies, Markham?" he drawled.

"But… but… Harry. You mean you still have groupies now you and Harry are married? Does she know?"

Dominic shrugged uncomfortably and rather evasively.

Stephen stared at him. "Are you serious?"

Dominic grinned. "Yes, but listen, Steve, I'm thinking of Harry while I'm fucking them."

Stephen went white. "This is no laughing matter, Dominic! How can you? How can you be unfaithful to her?"

Dominic frowned. "Grow up, Markham. This is the real world, not a mediaeval romance. I love Harry with all my heart, but groupies don't count, as you very well know."

"Of course they fucking count!" Stephen was beginning to get angry. "You're having sex with another woman, for God's sake! How would you like it if Harry was sleeping with, er…" He cast around for an example. "Your gardeners."

Dominic shook his head impatiently. "Don't be fucking dense, Markham, it's not the same. Groupies are… well, they're a convenience."

Stephen lost his temper. "I'm pretty damn sure Harry wouldn't see it that way, and you bloody well know that, Dominic, since you haven't told her. I think your behaviour is despicable!"

Dominic flushed with annoyance and resentment. "How dare you lecture me? It's none of your fucking business!"

"No, it's not, except that I care tremendously for Harry, and I've already told you I won't stand to see her hurt. For God's sake, I care about both of you! What do you suppose will happen if – or more likely when – Hal finds out? Don't throw your marriage away. Believe me, I know what it's like."

As Dominic opened his mouth to speak, the phone rang.

Stephen picked it up. "Hi, Harry… yeah, OK, I'll tell him… Um, no, I'm still really full… yes, I know, I'm a pig. Hey, Hal; I love you." He hung up. "Harry says Rob's asleep. She wanted to know are we having dinner." He paused. "I said no. I can't eat with you both tonight, Dominic, I'm too angry, and Hal would notice." He stood up. "I'll see you tomorrow," he said distantly, staring out of the window.

Dominic left without a word.

Neither of them mentioned the subject again. Harry teased Stephen about groupies sometime later when they were all having a drink together after a concert.

"I'm going out with Sophy," he said. "I wouldn't do that to her." He saw Dominic look at him, but he changed the subject. He just hoped with all his heart that Dominic had taken heed of his advice.

Both bands appeared at the Live Aid Concert at JFK stadium in Philadelphia on the thirteenth of July. It was an incredible experience and Stephen felt profoundly grateful to be involved in it. He was disgusted by Bob Dylan's comment that some of the money should be given to American farmers.

"Fucking unbelievable," was Dominic's observation.

"How could he have said that?" Stephen agreed. "You know, when I was younger, I thought that man was amazing!"

"I never rated him much," Dominic shrugged.

"How right you were!"

"Lovely Bob Geldof should be sainted," Harry put in. "And he's so sexy too!"

"Bob Geldof?" Stephen and Dominic were united in disbelief.

"He's fucking brilliant," Dominic said. " But sexy?" He shook his head. "You are sick, woman. When you've got me! I mean, even fucking Markham, poor little specimen that he is, is sexier than Geldof!"

Harry just smiled annoyingly. "Ask any woman."

When they got home, Sid's Six recorded their third album, 'The Moth Signal'. Stephen had been inspired by a Thomas Hardy poem of the same name, which tells of an unfaithful wife and her lover, who uses a moth as a signal to tell her he's waiting for her. It was one of his favourite poems, and he loved the imagery in it. The first single released was 'Circle Of Lies (The Moth Signal)'. Both album and single reached number one, as did the second single, 'The Dying Of The Light', which Stephen wrote in memory of John. It had also been inspired by a poem, this time by Dylan Thomas.

Stephen couldn't sing it without crying, so they never sang it live.

"Lynn, do you want to go to my family for Christmas, or would you rather stay here, just us this year?"

Lynn looked up from the paper. "Sorry?"

Tim waved a sheet of writing paper at her. "Letter from my mother inviting us for Christmas. Do you want to go, or would you rather stay here?"

"I don't mind, whatever you want to do. Although it might be nice, just you and me."

Tim smiled. "Yes, that's what I thought. Would you like another cup of coffee?"

"Mmm, yes please."

He got up to fetch the coffee pot. His back to her, he said, "Lynn. I've got some bad news."

She looked up, alarmed. "What?"

"I went to see Adrian Martin. I had the results back the other day." He turned round to face her. "About our baby. Thing is, I've apparently got a low-ish sperm count. Well, very low, really. So it looks as if there might not be one, after all." His voice was full of pain.

Lynn didn't know what to say. She got up and put her arms round him. "Pair of crocks, aren't we? Tim, it would be fun to have a baby, but that's not why I married you. I married you because I love you very much. If we have children, then that's just so much velvet. If we don't, I'll have what I want anyway. You."

Tim buried his face in her shoulder. "I love you, Lynn."

"I love you too, Timmy, more than anything."

"More than anyone?"

"More than anyone," she lied.

In April, the band's fourth album, 'Real Life', was released and the single, 'Postmodern Romance', was a huge hit, going straight to the top of the charts and staying there for several weeks. They filmed the video in Sweden, spending two weeks there, and once again, Stephen was besieged by girls. This time he didn't resist. He'd split up with Sophy just after he got back from America and then had had a very intense relationship with a model, Coral Mathieu, who was half-French, half-English, and very beautiful. They had lived together for several months, and he'd begun to get serious about her, but she wanted to break into acting and had gone to LA in February. He was missing her very much, and regretting the break-up, and he indulged himself in Sweden, taking out a different girl every night. He liked women, especially making love to them, but he also liked them as people; he liked talking to them, flirting with them, just being in their company.

Sid's Six was in massive demand and he could hardly get out of his front door without being mobbed.

"Kathy! It's lovely to have you back." He held her at arm's length. "You're looking beautiful. Very fat though!"

Kathy thumped him. "I'm not fat, I'm pregnant, as you very well know." She looked round his flat. "God, Steve, this is amazing! You're doing so well! I can't believe my brother is Stephen Markham, superstar!"

"And heart throb," put in Paul.

"Stop it, you're making me blush. Anyway, look at you, Paul. Squadron Leader Lightfoot! Working in the Ministry Of Defence, no less!"

Paul grinned. "Not exactly the same as winning Grammys and having platinum discs to my name though, is it?"

"No," Stephen said seriously, "it's far more important. What I do is nothing, Paul."

"Oh, come on, Stevie!" Kathy put in. "You're not going to say 'anyone could do it', are you? The way you play the guitar… well, you're brilliant, and you know how well you sing! And, Steve, at the risk of really making you blush, you're very handsome – and sexy. God, I'm your sister and I can see that! You *are* blushing! How sweet!"

"Thank you, Kath." He kissed her. "But what I do is hardly world-shattering, is it? I'm not saving lives, or defending the country like Paul is."

"You're bringing people an awful lot of pleasure, Stephen," Paul said. "Why do you think concert parties and the like are organised during wars? Look at ENSA. Morale and keeping spirits high are very important."

"Well, thank you both. We'll have to agree to differ, won't we, cutie?" He lifted Ceridwen onto his lap. She was eighteen months old, and very well behaved, Stephen thought, compared to the tearaway Rob had been at the same age. "You're a lovely little girl, you're so good," he said, kissing her soft little head. "Rob was a terror at that age," he went on. "Still is, come to think of it."

"Mum says he's just like you were," Kathy said.

"She means he looks like me."

"I don't think so!" Kathy grinned.

"Listen, he's going to be staying here for a few days during the Easter holidays, why don't we take him and Ceri to the zoo? He's been agitating to see some big, fierce, man-eating snakes."

"Do they have those?"

"I'm sure they have something similar. Even if they don't, it'll be fun. How about it?"

"What do you think, Ceri?" Kathy asked. "Would you like to go and see some animals with Uncle Stevie?"

Ceridwen stared at Stephen. "Dog."

"I think that means yes," Kathy smiled.

"Please can we see the snakes first, Daddy?" Rob bent down to Ceridwen in her pushchair. "You want to see the snakes, don't you, Ceri?"

"Ess." Ceridwen nodded vigorously.

"Come on, then," Rob said happily, pulling on the pushchair.

"Wait, Rob," Stephen said. "Kath, what do you want to do?"

"Ceri's too little to care what we do first." Kathy smiled down at Rob. "Snakes'll be lovely. But I can't walk as fast as you, Robbie."

"Yes, you are very fat." Rob looked at her appraisingly. "Mummy's always having diets. Then she gets thin and Dom says, 'Time for a little fun'. You could have one of her diets, Auntie Kath."

Stephen and Kathy exchanged smiles. "I'm not really fat, Rob, I've got a baby in my tummy."

"Why?"

"Um… well, I don't know, I just wanted one."

"Does the daddy want one too?"

"Uncle Paul, you mean, Rob," Stephen said. "Yes, he does."

"Mummy doesn't. She says 'no fear' to babies."

"Well, good," said Stephen, not wanting to hear any more about Harry and Dominic's private life. He looked at the guidebook. "It's… er… this way to the snakes." He took the pushchair from Kathy. "I'll push this. Anytime you want to stop and sit down, you just say."

Rob took her hand. "You don't want to stop, Auntie Kath! Let's run!" He tried to pull her along.

"Rob! Any more of that and we do *not* see the snakes," Stephen threatened. "OK?"

"OK." Rob gave him a wide, innocent grin.

They wandered around the reptile house.

"Ghastly, aren't they?" Kathy shuddered.

"I can't say I'm that keen," Stephen agreed. "But then really, I'm not that keen on zoos."

Rob was thrilled by it. He pressed his face up against the glass at each exhibit and asked Stephen questions he had no idea how to answer. He was struggling with the Latin pronunciation of the name of a snake from Australia, when an Australian accented voice behind him said, "I've been watching you."

Stephen and Rob turned round.

A young woman was smiling at Rob, a very pretty woman, Stephen thought, looking at her with interest. She was about his height, with long hair the colour of conkers, done up in a plait down her back. She was wearing combat trousers and a vest top, which accentuated her toned, curvaceous figure, but it was her eyes that caught his attention; they were beautiful, a lustrous golden green, very long lashed, with heavy, curving lids.

"You love the snakes, don't you, little mate?" she said to Rob.

He nodded. "Daddy doesn't know anything about them."

The girl glanced at Stephen and looked back at Rob, about to speak. She turned to Stephen again, puzzled. "Do we know each other? You look really familiar."

"He's famous," Rob said, bored. "Do you know about the snakes?"

"Famous? Er… yes, I do."

"Can this one kill you?" Rob pointed to the nondescript looking brown snake that Stephen had been trying to pronounce.

"Yep, that little fella'd kill you soon as look at you," the woman said cheerfully. "He's from Australia, like me, but I'm not so poisonous! He's a Common Brown, also known as the Eastern Brown Snake, and more people are killed in Australia by snakes like him than by any other."

"Cool!" Rob breathed.

"What's your name?" she asked.

"Rob."

"OK, Rob, well, I'm giving a demonstration later. I'll tell you about the snakes, and you can hold one."

"Him?" asked Rob excitedly, pointing to the Eastern Brown.

The girl grinned at the horrified expression on Stephen's face. "No, you're too young, I'm afraid, Robbie." She glanced at Stephen, who was relaxing. "Your dad'll be holding him."

"What?" exclaimed Stephen in alarm.

"Just joking! No, sorry, little bloke, it won't be one of these, it'll be Bertha the boa. I'm Antonia Standish – Toni to my mates," she said to Stephen, holding out her hand.

"Stephen Markham. Hello, Toni." She had a strong handshake.

"Yeah, course, I know who you are! You sing with that pop group, don't you?"

Stephen grinned. "Yeah, that's me."

"You're not bad."

"Thanks. You're not bad yourself."

"Well, that wasn't what I meant, but now you mention it…" She looked him over slowly. "You're a bit of a tiddler, but I wouldn't say no."

"Dinner sometime, then?" he challenged.

"Whoa, what about your wife?" Toni indicated Kathy, who was listening to Rob telling Ceridwen about the Common Brown.

"She's my sister. I'm not married."

"Good oh! When, then?"

He had Rob until Thursday, and concerts on Friday, Saturday and Sunday. It would have to be Thursday. "How about Thursday?" he asked, mentally crossing his fingers. He really liked this girl.

"Yeah, Thursday's good for me." She turned to Rob. "I'll see you later, then, Robbie."

He nodded vigorously. "And I can really hold a snake?"

"For sure, it's here at twelve-fifteen. It's always busy, so seeing as we're mates, turn up at twelve, and you can have a quick hold first."

Rob was in seventh heaven. "Feel her, Daddy, she's lovely!"

Stephen touched the boa gingerly. "Very nice."

"An' me!" Ceri demanded. Kathy helped her put her hand on the snake's back. "Dog!" the little girl said happily.

Kathy took her off to change her and get her an ice cream, while Stephen and Rob stayed to listen to Toni talking about Bertha. She began by explaining that all species of boas are either endangered or protected. She told them about the boas' habitat, their hunting behaviour, their diet and their anatomy. When she informed them that boas give birth to live young, and that up to sixty-four two-foot long baby snakes are born at a time, Stephen stopped listening, and watched her hands stroking the snake. He was trying not to think about them stroking bits of his anatomy when he became aware of a hostile silence, and the fact that everyone was staring at him.

"Is it true?" Toni demanded.

"What?" he asked in confusion.

"I told Toni you've got boots like Bertha's back," Rob explained.

Stephen went bright red. He'd forgotten all about those boots. He'd bought them years ago. How could he ever have worn snakeskin boots? And how could Rob possibly remember them? As soon as he got home he was going to chuck them out. "They're not real snakeskin," he lied. "I'm a vegetarian!"

Toni was a stimulating companion. He took her to the Savoy Grill, and they had pre-dinner cocktails in the American Bar. She wasn't the least bit interested in his fame, which he found refreshing and unusual. Most women he took out ended up wanting to talk about Sid's Six, or asking him if he knew Paul McCartney or Princess Diana. Toni talked about everything and anything. At twenty-six, she was nine months older than he was; her birthday was the twenty-ninth of February, but she always celebrated it on the first of March. She'd come to Britain after graduating from university with a degree in zoology. Her parents had split up when she was sixteen, and her mother had married an Englishman and moved to Chester with him. Toni hadn't wanted to leave school or Australia and had stayed with her father in Queensland. While she was at university, her father had remarried. Toni hadn't got on with her stepmother, and had come to England. She had a younger brother, Murray – Muzza – who was living with her mother, and an older sister, Emma, who was still in Australia.

"She's in the police, like Dad. So, you're a vegetarian?" she said, eating a succulent piece of steak.

"Yes. I won't eat anything with a face any more."

She looked at him reflectively. "I suppose you're against animal testing and so on?"

"Certainly am!"

"Hmm. Your little bloke, Rob, he's adorable."

He smiled. "Thank you."

"You'd do anything for him, right?"

"Of course!"

"So, if he's ill and the doctor tells you he has to have a certain drug to get better, you make sure he gets it, yeah?" Stephen nodded. He wasn't sure where this was going. "And, of course, the drug is tested on animals. What do you do?"

He stared at her. She looked back inquiringly.

Finally he said, quietly, "Make sure he gets it."

"Hmm. You having pudding?"

"No," he said flatly. Forget what she did with snakes. He didn't like her at all.

She flashed him a charming smile. "I'm not trying to put you down, I agree with you about the cruelty and so on, I don't buy cosmetics that are tested on animals, for instance, and I'd never wear fur. But I wanted to see how committed you are. Some animal rights types are really, really mental, mate. If you were, I was going to dump you."

"Oh, great, thanks. You've exposed me as a complete hypocrite so that you can decide whether or not you want to go out with me! Well, supposing I don't want to go out with you?"

"I think you do. I saw the way you were looking at me when I was holding Bertha."

"You were stroking her like that deliberately!"

Toni's smile deepened. "I thought you'd like it."

Stephen burst out laughing. "OK. What do you want for pudding?"

She cooked him a meal the following week. When he'd taken her out she'd told him about her pet, Bunyip. "You'll have to meet my Bunyip," she'd said. "He's gorgeous, all furry and cuddly, and quite clever too. You'll love him!"

When he got to her flat, he looked around for a dog. "Where's Bunyip?"

"In his tank."

He stared at her. "What kind of dog is he?"

She laughed. "He's not a dog! I'll fetch him." She came back with a large tarantula spider. "Here," she said, offering him to Stephen. "Isn't he a beaut? He's a Mexican Redknee."

Stephen leapt backwards, shuddering. "Put it away, for Christ's sake!"

"So much for the bloke who loves all living things!"

Dating Toni was like riding a roller coaster. She was loud, outspoken and opinionated, she argued with him about almost everything, nothing was ever easy with her, but she had a terrific sense of humour, and laughed at the same things he did. She was selfish and outrageous; the things she said and did often took his breath away, but they had the same tastes. She was very good in bed, very inventive; he found her lithe, fit body extremely arousing, and she took as much satisfaction in him as he did in her. She liked the fact that so many women wanted him, and enjoyed the envious glances she got when they were out together. She told him he was the prettiest man she'd ever dated.

"I'm not sure I like being called pretty," he objected.

They were out shopping; she wanted a formal dress for an awards ceremony they were due to attend.

"Look, Stevo, you're not clever and you're not good – in a moral sense, I mean," she leered. "So you might as well accept that you're pretty." She wrapped her arms around him and started to rub her body against his. "In some ways you're very good indeed!" she whispered in his ear.

"Stop it! People are looking!"

She let him go, laughing. "Got you going, didn't I?" she said, looking pointedly at his groin.

"Just choose a frock, you bitch."

"Lynn, I've been thinking," Tim said as they were driving home from work one day at the end of June. "We've both got leave due. Instead of decorating the house, let's have a really expensive holiday. I don't think we're going to have children, so there's no point saying we're saving for their education. Let's do something for us." He pulled into their driveway.

"OK," Lynn agreed. "Where shall we go?"

"Where would you like to go?"

"Somewhere neither of us has ever been. Let's get some brochures."

Tim leant over and kissed her. "OK, we'll go into town tomorrow."

They went into several travel agencies the next day and took a stack of brochures home. After their meal that night, they curled up together on the sofa and leafed through them. They'd had wine with the meal and Tim had had a couple of whiskies afterwards. He got up to pour another one.

"Is that a good idea?" Lynn asked hesitantly. "They said at the fertility clinic too much alcohol can have an effect on sperm production."

"Oh, for God's sake!" he snapped. "I can't even have a drink now! Well, I'm sorry I'm not Mr Fertile, like Stephen perfect bloody Markham! No doubt he could drink himself into a stupor and still manage to impregnate you!" He stormed out of the room.

She was stunned. He'd seemed so happy earlier when they were talking about the holiday. She went after him.

He was lying on their bed staring at the ceiling. She could see he was crying.

"I'm sorry, Lynn," he said. "In vino veritas. I've tried so hard to keep up a cheerful appearance, you've been so good about it. I can't earn the money he does, I'm nearly ten years older than he is, I don't have his looks or talent, but I thought I could at least give you children."

"Oh, Tim!" She couldn't bear to see him so unhappy. "Oh, my lovely, beloved Tim. Stephen Markham means *nothing* to me! I left him, remember? If I'd wanted him, I could've got him back at any time. I *don't* want him! I want you, please can you get that into your head? I chose *you*. I'm not even sure I want a baby, to be totally honest, but my darling, I do want you and if you don't forget Stephen we'll never be really happy. Don't let him ruin our marriage!"

Tim looked at her. "Do you really mean that, Lynn? About having children as well?"

She nodded. Because I don't want anyone's children except Stephen's, she thought. Until now she'd always half-expected him to come and claim her as his, but she'd finally realised that this was never going to happen. She'd bought a magazine that very week containing an article entitled *Sid's Six Year Old*. It was about Rob's sixth birthday party, which had been held at London Zoo. There were pictures of Stephen and Harry, of course, but there were also several of pictures of Stephen with a very pretty brunette, Antonia something, a zoologist who worked at the zoo, and it was suggested in the article that he and she were very close, possibly on the brink of marriage. Of course, the press had said the same thing when Stephen was living with that model, Coral Mathieu, but there was something about these pictures of Stephen and Antonia together that made Lynn wonder. They did look extremely close, holding hands in every photo and mirroring each other's body language, as lovers do, and the woman was obviously part of Stephen's inner circle, and accepted as such by not only Harry and Dominic but also Stephen's family – Sian and his sisters – and Rob too. It was over, her secret dream of getting back with Stephen. He had his own life. And so had she. She was married to Tim, Tim who would do anything for her, who loved her like she loved Stephen. Well, her stupidity had lost her Stephen. She wasn't going to lose Tim or let him suffer like she had done. She'd married him for the wrong reasons. She'd put him through this children issue for the wrong reasons. Now she was finally going to do something right. She got onto the bed next to him and kissed him. "Let's make love."

She lay awake for a long time after he had gone to sleep, crying very quietly, saying goodbye to Stephen. Finally, she made a pact with God, the God she didn't believe in, the God who had betrayed her. "Please, Lord," she whispered. "I promise I'll never buy another Stevie magazine again. Please let me get pregnant for Tim."

If asked to describe his relationship with Toni, Stephen would have said 'tempestuous'. If he said black, she'd say white. Sometimes he thought she did it deliberately. She was queen of the put-down, always able to come up with some amusing and seemingly innocent remark to make him look small. He couldn't get the lyrics from the Beatles song 'Girl' out of his head: '*She's the kind of girl who puts you down when friends are there, she makes you feel a fool.*'

"Why do you do it, Toni?" he asked her when he was driving her home late one night after a dinner party.

"Do what?" she yawned.

"Make me look a fool."

"You don't need any help with that, Stevo, you do it beautifully all on your own."

"See, that's the kind of thing I mean."

"It's a joke. Don't turn into a whinging Pom, for God's sake!"

He dropped her off at her building.

"Coming in?" He shook his head and she stared at him. "You always come in!"

"Not tonight."

"Don't be childish, Stephen."

He shrugged. "Goodnight then, Toni."

She leant over and kissed his cheek. "It's a sexy act," she whispered.

"It's not an act, I'm upset."

"Whatever. I'll see you Saturday, then."

"I thought we were going out on Friday?"

"No, I'm busy Friday. Saturday OK for you?"

He frowned. "I suppose so."

"I'll phone you anyway. 'Night."

He waited until she was safely in, and then he drove home, singing, '*She's the kind of girl you want so much it makes you sorry, still you don't regret a single day.*' He wasn't sure what was going to happen with this relationship. He liked her very much, but he couldn't get a grip on her, couldn't seem to adhere to her – not in the physical sense, there was plenty of adhering going on there – but mentally. It was as if she had some sort of hard, veneered finish that he couldn't break through. He liked to feel joined to people with whom he had a relationship, bonded, so that there was a give and take, almost like a bridge across the sea of their separate personalities. He couldn't find that bridge with Toni.

The telephone rang. He picked it up, thinking it would be her, but it was Dominic. He'd been away on tour and Stephen hadn't seen him for a while.

"Markham, old man, I'm forming a fucking band. Like you to be in it."

"You've already got a band, Charlie, remember? GI Tract?"

"A different band, obviously. You're fucking dense, old chap, must be the Welsh blood."

"OK, let's cut the crap, what are you on about?"

"Harry and me. We're forming a band, Tantony Pig. We want you in it."

Stephen was taken aback. "I don't know what to say."

"Think about it. Let's get together and talk. Is Friday any good for you?"

"Yeah, turns out it is."

"Good, we'll see you Friday." The line went dead.

"OK, tell me about this band."

Harry poured him a whisky. "It was my idea. I loved being in The Brigands and I wanted to play in something like that. Just a little band, you know, not circuses like GI Joe and Sid's Six."

"What do you want me to do?"

"Sing, definitely," Dominic said. "And then, well, we're pretty flexible, sometimes lead, sometimes rhythm, depending on the song."

"Hmm. You having keyboard and drums?"

"Just drums."

"Who's your drummer?"

"Not got one yet. We want to know if you're in first."

"Why don't you sing, Charlie?"

Dominic shrugged. "I'm not that bothered about singing, and anyway, I don't have anything like your range."

"What kind of music will we do?"

"Stuff we write. Harry and I have been writing together. If you want to write for the band, we'll do that too. Or whatever we all want. We're easy."

"Yeah, I heard that," Stephen grinned. "OK. It sounds fun."

Harry and Dominic smiled at each other.

"Let's go out for a drink to celebrate," Dominic suggested.

Harry shook her head. "You two go, I don't feel like it."

"It's not Pilar's night off is it?" Dominic asked. "New au pair," he explained to Stephen.

"What happened to Ingrid?" Stephen had liked Ingrid, she was good with Rob.

"Pining for the fucking fjords, apparently," Dominic shrugged. He grinned. "Shame though, she had beautiful plumage."

Harry thumped him. "You shouldn't have been looking! No, it's not Pilar's night off, I just want a nice hot bath and an early night. Go on, the pair of you. Go and play pool or something and talk about whatever it is men talk about."

They went to what Dominic called his local. They ordered two beers and walked towards a corner table. Stephen stopped suddenly.

"What the fuck are you doing?" Dominic demanded furiously, as he stopped too so as not to walk into Stephen, and spilt beer down himself in the process. He followed Stephen's gaze. Toni was sitting at a table with a man. He took Stephen's arm. "Steve."

Stephen shook him off. He walked over to Toni.

"Busy, Toni?"

She looked up and smiled. "Hi, Stevo! Danny, this is Steve. Steve, Danny."

This wasn't what Stephen had expected.

"Hi." Danny was American. He shook hands with Stephen. "Nice to meet you. Any friend of Toni's is a preferred acquaintance of mine." He turned back to her.

"Bye, Steve," she said.

Somewhat stunned, Stephen walked back to Dominic. "I think I've just been dumped."

The next day, Toni rang. "OK for this evening, Stevo?"

"We need to talk. I'm coming round."

"We're not exclusive, Stephen."

He stared at her. "Well, where I come from, when you're sleeping with someone on a regular basis, you're exclusive."

"Danny could say the same thing then."

Stephen couldn't believe his ears. "Say that again?"

"You heard. We're not married, Stephen. I never said don't do other women, did I? What are you complaining about? I never lied to you, I never said you were the only one. You just assumed it because you were sleeping with me, like I'm your property or something."

"Everything you say is right, Toni, but somehow it's also so wrong! I don't think I can have that kind of relationship."

She shrugged. "That's a real shame, Stevo, because I like you heaps."

"Yeah, well, I like you."

"I could be in love with you if I let myself," she said slowly.

They stared at each other. Stephen knew he was falling for her too, but he didn't want to get into that sort of relationship again. He wanted fun, not commitment. Didn't he?

"You couldn't try it?" she went on. "Because somehow I get the impression with you that you don't want to settle down. If I was to say to you now, 'OK, we'll be exclusive, we'll get serious, maybe think about marriage, or at least moving in together', I don't think you'd be up for it, mate."

He looked away.

"Would you?" she persisted.

He shrugged.

"None of your relationships have lasted longer than a few months since your wife left you. I can't believe it was always bad luck, Stephen. I don't want to wake up one day and find you can't commit to me, I'm not going to be the loser here. If you want a relationship with me, that's fine, you've got one. On my terms. I don't want to get hurt, Stephen, and I think I could get quite badly hurt over you."

"Toni, I don't think..."

"Hush. You've got your concerts in Birmingham. Go to them. Phone me when you get back. If you want to. If I don't hear from you in a month, well..." She shrugged.

He thought about what she'd said, turned it over and over. It made him angry and sad by turns. He *had* been unlucky. Lots of relationships didn't work out. Or had he? Was Toni right?

On the last night of the concert, he got drunk afterwards and he and Fin, who was high on some drug, he didn't ask what, shared three groupies. The next day he had a hangover and felt totally ashamed. When he remembered what he'd done with those girls he was disgusted with himself. At home, he found he was out of milk. Cursing, he went out to his local shop. As he queued, a song came on that he hadn't heard before. It was Genesis, he knew that. He stood and listened to it. The lyrics spoke to him.

"What are you playing, Nitin?" he asked the owner.

"It's Genesis, innit, Steve."

"Yeah, I know that, but what album?"

"Hang on." He went into the back of the shop. "Asha!"

"What?" Asha, Nitin's wife came out of the storeroom. Her face lit up when she saw Stephen. "Hello, Steve. How did the concerts go?"

Stephen smiled at her. He was always taken aback by her beauty, whenever he saw her, the song 'Spanish Harlem' began to play in his head: *'There is a rose in Spanish Harlem... it's growing in the street, right up through the concrete, but soft and sweet.'* She was tiny and very slender, with enormous dark eyes. She looked about sixteen; it seemed impossible she could have a son of that age, Chandra. Stephen was giving him guitar lessons.

“Steve wants to know what we’re playing,” Nitin said.

“I’ll get it.” She hurried off and came back with the tape in her hands. “Here you go, Steve, you can borrow it.” She handed it to him and took Nitin’s arm. He looked down at her and smiled, and she looked back at him with such love that Stephen’s heart ached with longing. That was how Cherry used to look at him. “Thanks, Asha,” he said. “Is it OK if I bring it back this afternoon?”

She smiled. “When you’re ready, Steve, we’re in no hurry.”

The album was called ‘Invisible Touch’. He took it home and put it on, searching for the song he’d heard. Eventually, he found it at the end of side one. It was called ‘In Too Deep’, and it described everything he was feeling. What could he make of his life? And who was waiting for him? He was sick of being alone, crying for Cherry. That was over, done with long ago. What was it they said? The past is another country. *‘All this time, I still remember everything you said, there’s so much you promised, how could I ever forget?’* Phil Collins sang. How could he ever forget her? He was in too deep. He remembered writing ‘Broken Flower’. *‘I never thought I could ever doubt you,’* he’d written, *‘You said you’d never go.’* She’d promised to stay, promised she’d never leave, promised to love him forever. But she had gone. She’d run to someone else.

He listened to the song over and over again, and cried. He’d lost Lynn. He’d let Coral slip away from him. He didn’t want to spend his life alone, he wanted children, children who would live with him twenty-four hours a day, every day. He wanted someone to love, someone who loved him. He washed his face and drove to the zoo. Toni was doing her ‘snake talk’, as Rob called it. He waited impatiently until everyone had gone.

“Didn’t expect to see you here, Stevo,” she smiled.

“Will you marry me, Toni?” he asked.

Chapter Ten
High On You

Spaced out and flying, crying out in bliss,
No trace of doubt that this is all I want to do.
Can't get enough of your love, cos you're my drug, it's true,
And girl I'm high on you.

They planned their wedding for the following April, a big civil affair with a huge reception. It was all going to be very showbizzy, very glitzy, for Toni. Stephen felt that if he couldn't give her a big church wedding, not having the Chaplin family influence, the least he could do was give her a good party. He invited Sir Angus and Lady Susan, Dominic's parents, and a sprinkling of Dominic's titled friends.

Dominic was indignant. "Invite who the fuck you want, Markham, but don't introduce them to anyone as *my* friends!"

"But, Dom, they were at Eton with you," Harry pointed out.

"Exactly!"

Toni loved the glamour of Stephen's world, even though she wasn't impressed by it. To Toni, it was fun and that was her favourite thing. "Except you," she told Stephen.

Her family came to stay. They looked Stephen over as if he was a horse. He half-expected them to check his teeth to make sure he wasn't lying about his age.

Toni's father, Jacko, flew in with his wife, Kay, and his eldest daughter, Emma. Jacko was a huge man, as tall as Ted, but several times wider. As soon as he arrived, he clasped Stephen to him in a suffocating embrace. "You little beauty, I've heard all about you. Let's have a look at you. Strike me handsome, you're a bit on the meagre side, son, bit of a taddie! You'll have to feed him up, Tones. Feed him some of those recipes out of *The Weekly*."

He was referring to *The Australian Women's Weekly*, which was, rather confusingly, a monthly publication. When Stephen asked why it was called 'Weekly' instead of 'Monthly', Toni looked at him as if he was stupid. "Don't be an imbo, mate! *The Australian Women's Monthly*! What does that sound like?"

Stephen hadn't liked to ask what an imbo was. He later found out it was an imbecile.

Toni loved *The Weekly*. Her stepmother sent her each copy as soon as it came out, and she devoured it. Stephen had been very impressed by it, surprised by how serious many of the articles were. It had long been a daydream of Toni's to be in *The Weekly*, so she was overjoyed when the magazine wanted to do a feature on them and the wedding.

Stephen loathed the idea. "Come on, Daisy, do we really want a load of journalists hanging round?"

(Toni's middle name was Marguerite. As soon as Stephen had discovered this, he had taken to calling her Daisy. She wasn't sure whether she liked it or not. "You can sympathise with me then, Toni," Dominic said.)

"They're not journos, they're from *The Weekly*, mate!"

In the end, Stephen had given in, on the understanding that they only talked about the wedding, but somehow he found himself giving an exclusive interview and being photographed, with Toni and without her, in his flat.

Toni's mother, Sandy, arrived from Chester, where she lived with Martin, her second husband, and Murray, Toni's brother.

"I was saying to Tones, love, he's a bit of a taddie!" Jacko said.

"You're right, he is." Sandy leant down to kiss Stephen. "But if our Toni's happy, I don't mind having a taddie for a son-in-law."

They all called him the Taddie after that.

"What's a taddie?" he asked Toni.

"Tadpole," she told him, and laughed at his expression. "It could have been worse, mate. Could've been bludger or hoon or drongo or galah—"

"All right, all right, I get the idea."

"You know, I like hoon, myself. The Hoon. It's got a nice ring to it."

"It's making my head spin, and there's nearly a month until the wedding! Thank God they're not staying with me!" Stephen, Dominic and Harry were rehearsing for a gig. He was enjoying Tantony Pig. They did his songs, Dominic and Harry's, and occasionally covers. Stephen and Dominic had started to write together. Stephen had never written with anyone before and he found, to his surprise, that he liked writing with Dominic very much.

Dominic wanted them to make an album, Harry didn't and Stephen and Keith Newbrook, their drummer, didn't care either way.

"If we do record one, let's produce it ourselves," Dominic said. They were having a drink after the rehearsal. Harry had left them to it and gone shopping.

"Why is Harry so against it?"

"She thinks it'll get too big. She says she likes it this way. What she needs is a baby," Dominic said darkly.

Stephen was surprised. He'd always got the impression that neither Harry nor Dominic wanted children. "A baby?"

"Keep her occupied. She's so fucking bossy, on at me day and night, always wants her own way."

"You knew what she was like when you married her, Charlie," Stephen grinned. "She's always been like that. Be assertive! Put your foot down! Tell her you're lord and master of the household."

"Like you did with Toni over that fucking magazine article?"

"Nobody said it was easy!"

Dominic stared gloomily into his beer. "I'd really like my own offspring. I wanted to start as soon as we were married, but Harry said she wanted to have fun first. I don't see why we can't do both."

Stephen was astounded. Dominic, flippant, I-don't-give-a-fuck-about-anyone-Dominic, wanted a child! He felt very sorry for him. "Tell her it'd be good for Rob to have a sibling," he said slowly. "If you leave it much longer, he'll be too old to play with it and neither of them will get any benefit from it. He's six-and-a-half now."

"You know, Markham, sometimes there is a flicker of life in that thick, fucking Welsh skull of yours. I'll give it a try."

"Don't tell her I had anything to do with it though," Stephen said anxiously.

"I'll just say, 'Stevie says'. That's bound to work!"

To Stephen's disappointment, Toni and Harry didn't get on very well. Harry had become friends with Lynn almost immediately and Stephen hadn't even considered that she and Toni wouldn't. It wasn't that they disliked each other, it was simply that they were too alike in many ways, both of them being rather bossy and liking their own way, although the difference between them was that while Toni could be very selfish, Harry was the least selfish person Stephen knew.

"I don't think she's right for Stevie," Harry worried. "She's too bossy."

"Pot calling the fucking kettle black," Dominic muttered.

Harry hit him.

Toni liked Sian and Ted very much. "Your mum's a lovely person," she said to Stephen when she first met them.

Sian liked Toni too, but she had reservations about the marriage, although she didn't voice them to Stephen. "Why on earth didn't he marry Coral?" she said to Ted after Stephen and Toni had announced their engagement. "She was desperate to marry him, she only talked about going to Hollywood to try to force the issue! Although I told her that wouldn't work. *She* thought he'd come after her, *he* thought she'd had enough of the relationship. Oh, Stevie! For such an intelligent boy, he can be really thick sometimes, and yet in his professional life he can do no wrong!"

"Yes, the band's going from strength to strength, isn't it? I suppose that's something, anyway." Ted took a sip of tea and added, "I think he's marrying Toni on the rebound."

"Yes, I agree," Sian worried. "And she's a charming girl, obviously very maternal, she said to me she wanted to start a family straight away. Well, I know Stevie'll love that, and she's so full of beans, she makes him laugh all the time, it's lovely to see him like that again, it's just..." She stopped and bit her lip. "I just hope it lasts. I feel she needs someone who'll concentrate solely on her, and Stevie's so wrapped up in his music. I hope she can cope with him. And she's a handful, always wants her own way." She sighed again. "I hope he can cope with her."

"Steve could cope with anything," Ted said, trying to reassure her.

"Hmm. I don't know, Ted. I don't want him to just cope, I don't want either of them to. I want them to make each other happy. She likes the bright lights and parties too. They're not really Stephen's style."

Ted sighed. "That's marriage though, isn't it? One long compromise."

"You take that back, Ted Taylor!"

Stephen and Toni were married on the ninth of April. It was as different from Stephen's first wedding as it was possible to be. Then, he'd had no money at all, the reception was held in a grotty little house in Whalley Range, the food was homemade, and they drank beer from cans because there weren't enough glasses to go round. This time, money was no object, the reception was held at the Ritz, the food was gourmet, and they drank vintage champagne from expensive crystal flutes.

Toni loved every moment of it. One of the photographers from *The Weekly* attended the reception and they were photographed from all angles. Stephen managed to have a word with Ray, who had flown in from Boston that morning, but it was difficult to talk to anyone for long.

"It's like a three-ring circus," he complained to Sian.

"Toni's enjoying it though, and that's the main thing," she smiled.

Stephen and Toni were spending a month in Australia after the wedding, staying in Brisbane with Jacko and Kay for a few days, and then going to a small island on the Barrier Reef. They were taking Rob with them. When Stephen had tentatively raised the subject, Toni had been enthusiastic, more than happy for Rob to come. Stephen felt that he could have loved her for that alone.

Andy had found them an unusual wedding present. It was a first edition of a book called *Most Deadly: Australia's Poisonous Creatures*, the most gruesome, grotesque book Stephen had ever seen.

The blurb said: *'The most venomous creatures in Australia. What they look like, where to find them, what they can do to you and, most importantly, what to do if you are bitten or stung.'*

It was packed with colourful pictures of insects, reptiles and sea creatures, and descriptions of the agony they could cause. To his horror, Stephen discovered that even some of the sharks were poisonous. "As if sharks aren't deadly enough," he said faintly.

The book showed where each creature could be found. Andy produced a notebook from which he read a list of the ones that lived around Brisbane and the Reef. It was a long list. "Listen to this one," he said, taking the book. "Butterfly Cod. Sounds lovely, doesn't it? Look what it says. *'Take great care when you spot these inquisitive fish,'* " Andy read, " *'which will move towards divers, usually in pairs, with their thirteen stinging spines'*..."

"Thirteen!" echoed Stephen.

"...*'thrust forward in defence. For a person stung by these spines, severe and instantaneous pain occurs, increasing in severity over a very short time. It has been known to become so severe that that the casualty feels agonising distress, and weeps. This can last for several days'.* "

"Several *days?*"

"Listen to this, these are shells, Steve, *shells*. They're really beautiful, like, so people pick them up, but then they shoot out darts, and when they hit you, you feel this unbearable pain, then numbness. And if you've been injected with a lot of the poison, you get tingling round your lips, like..."

Stephen involuntarily rubbed his mouth.

"...and then you're paralysed and unless someone gives you the kiss of life, you can die. And listen to this, Steve – there's no antivenom available."

"Oh, my God!" Stephen was horrified. How could he possibly take Rob to this country?

"Here, I'll leave you the book, you can have a good read of it."

"Thanks, Andy." He flicked through the book. He discovered there was a sea creature called the Glaucus that didn't have any venom of its own. Instead, it recycled other creatures' stinging capsules. So you could be stung by anything, he thought in panic. How could they give you antivenom if they didn't know what you'd been stung by? Sweating with horror, he went to find Toni.

"We can't go!"

"What are you talking about, Stevo?"

He gave her the book. She was furious. "Where did you get this?"

"Andy. It was a wedding present."

"My God! I'm going to kill the little bastard! Stephen, it's not like this!"

"You mean these creatures don't exist?"

"Well, they exist, but hardly anyone ever gets hurt by them."

"But it says in here..."

"Yeah, but that's telling the worst that could happen! It's like the statistics for plane crashes! Trust me, Stevo, I grew up there. I never got bitten and neither did anyone I knew."

"But Rob! Suppose something gets him?"

"Yeah, but Steve, there's an antivenom for just about anything, and people hardly ever die."

"I should think dying is the least of your worries! There's a fish that makes Australians – *Australians*, mark you, and you know how you lot don't make a fuss – weep with agony for days! Death'd be a merciful release! Please can we go to Scarborough?"

"No, we bloody well can't! You've been to Australia before, Stephen, you've given concerts there!"

"Yes – we saw the airport, the hotels and the concert venues, then we flew home! It's not the same!"

"Darling, it's all arranged. Please believe me, we'll be fine. Dad and Kay regularly go out to the Reef with friends. Nothing has ever bitten or stung any of them."

They spent two nights alone at the Ritz before leaving for Brisbane. Stephen spent the journey – the very long journey – in a state of abject terror. As soon as the plane landed he bought a mosquito net and insect repellent and insisted on the net being around Rob's bed wherever they went.

They stayed with Jacko and Kay for three nights. Stephen was surprised by how English it was; apart from the heat and the swimming pool in the garden, it could've been Cornwall. Jacko's house was an attractive brick building, with a veranda, and creeper growing up the wall. Stephen shuddered at the thought of what that creeper might be harbouring, and he was amazed that he didn't turn grey at the sight of Rob careering about in the garden.

The Reef was breathtaking, miles of unspoilt beauty, and the coral island on which they were staying was like nothing Stephen had ever seen. The sea surrounding it was the colour of his first Strat, a beautiful sun warmed turquoise. However, he made sure that he and Rob wore wet suits and trainers on the beach and in the water, despite Toni's pleading.

"When we get home," she said grimly, "I'm going to cut Andy's balls off – very slowly, I really want him to suffer – then I'm going to make him eat them."

The last few days they spent at Cape Tribulation, which was up above Cairns and was unbelievably beautiful. Toni told Stephen it was famed for its superb scenery, and he could see why. Long silky beaches stretched north and south of the lush, forest covered cape. The sunsets were stunning, their colours spectacular; glowing fiery reds melding with the intense lavender blue of the sky, all of it barred with gold. They took photographs, but none of them did it justice.

On the last night, Stephen admitted that he had possibly been wrong.

"Not seen anything frightening, have we, mate?" Toni asked.

"Not as who should say frightening," he allowed.

"And we've not been stung or bitten?"

"Well… no."

"You should be ashamed of yourself!"

"You're right. You're right, and Australia is a beautiful country – no, it's absolutely breathtaking, and next time we come I promise I won't behave like this. But I tell you what, my little Glaucus, Australia is proof positive of extra-terrestrials."

"How do you reckon that?"

"Well, think of dumping grounds for nuclear waste; you get designated ones."

Toni nodded warily.

"Well, I think Australia is a designated dumping ground for alien poison and weird alien creatures. I mean, there's New Zealand, hardly any distance away – why isn't it crawling with poison? Egg-laying mammals – not found anywhere else. Has to be aliens." He grinned. "Then there's the Australian people themselves— Ow, Toni, get off, you're killing me!"

At home, they found the press had been having a field day in their absence. They hadn't bothered with papers in Australia, they had shut out the world, and so it was a shock to find that there'd been articles about Harry, Dominic and Stephen. It was as if the press had just woken up to the fact that Harry was the mother of his son and married to his best friend. There were all kinds of salacious articles, even ones suggesting that the three of them had had a ménage a trois and that now Stephen was married they'd be 'swinging', in other words, wife-swapping. Toni was distressed.

"Fuck them," Stephen said. He was very angry. "They're the lowest of the low, Toni, total fucking scum. Ignore the shits."

They'd been back for a week and there were still reporters camped outside the flat.

"Yes, but Stevo, I think I'm pregnant."

"What?" He stared at her. "Are you sure?"

"No, but my period is late."

"Sit down, sit down." He hustled her to a chair. "How late?"

"Five days."

"Five days. Is that unusual for you?"

Toni nodded. "For sure. And I feel pregnant. I've been feeling queasy in the mornings."

Stephen beamed. He felt as if his world had been flooded with brilliant sunshine. "You little ripper! Oh, Toni, I couldn't be happier! You brilliant, beautiful wife, you!"

"I take it you're pleased?" she asked demurely.

"Pleased? Pleased ain't in it! I'm ecstatic! You'll have to be careful though, Toni," he added seriously. "Rest as much as you can, no heavy lifting..."

"Stevo, I'm just pregnant. It's a perfectly natural state of affairs! I'm fine."

"You just don't know – as Fin would say, you never know the day or the hour."

"I think that's referring to dying."

"Yes, but..." He stopped.

"Stephen, this baby is not going to die. I'm not going to miscarry. You'll see. I'm very strong and very healthy."

She was right. She thrived on being pregnant, enjoying every minute of it, it was the biggest high she'd ever experienced. Even morning sickness didn't faze her. When she first felt the baby kick, she was walking on air. Stephen came home from a rehearsal and found she was lying down. He started to panic. She was eighteen weeks pregnant, just around the time Lynn had lost Sakura.

"I'm fine. He's kicking me. Oh, Stevo, I can't tell you how wonderful it is! I have to lie here so I don't miss any of it. Oh!" She smiled mistily up at him. "He did it again!"

Stephen sat on the bed beside her. "What does it feel like?"

"Like..." She bit her lip, trying to think of a way to describe it. "I don't know. The books say like a butterfly's wing – have you ever caught a butterfly in your hands to let it outside?"

"Yes."

"It's kind of like that, only inside me. Or like a bubble rising up and bursting. Oh!" She caught her breath. "He's really throwing himself around!"

"How do you know it's not a girl?"

"Oh, I don't, but I don't like to say 'it', he's never been an 'it' to me, not since I first thought I might be pregnant, and saying 'she' sounds a bit feminist."

Stephen laughed. "Well, you're hardly the little woman type. I'd have thought you'd have gone for the feminist bit."

"I'm not militant though, am I, mate? I just think everyone should have a fair crack of the whip, male and female, every colour and all species."

Stephen looked fondly at her. Pregnancy had certainly softened her. True, she wanted everyone to have a fair crack of the whip, but the non-pregnant Toni would have added 'especially the females' and only been half-joking. "Oh, Toni, I love you."

She twined her arms around his neck. "Let's make love."

"Should we?" He very much wanted to. Like Lynn, she hadn't put on any weight, but had become softer and rounder all over. Her breasts were magnificent.

"Yes, we should. I'm gagging for it, Stevo. You go out running every night to exhaust yourself, kidding yourself you're doing me a favour. Well, you're not. I spoke to Heather, you know, my obstetrician, about it again today, and she said it's fine to be making love. She also said my cervix couldn't be any more shut if it tried. Come on, Stevie, all that running has made you so fit! You're looking more gorgeous than ever and that's saying something! You're my husband and I want you to pleasure me!"

"What a lovely expression," he said, peeling off his clothes. He gently undressed her and she lay limply and let him stroke and fondle and suck her. He kissed her all over until she felt as if she was melting. He made love to her very gently, very tenderly.

"That was wonderful," she breathed afterwards. "God, Stevo, we're so lucky."

He remembered Lynn saying those words and shivered.

"Are you cold?" she asked, drowsily.

"No." He stroked the rich chestnut hair off her face. "You doze off, Daisy."

She drifted off to sleep. Stephen lay and held her, and allowed himself to think about his first marriage. He knew he'd never love Toni the way he loved Lynn. He'd never love anyone the way he loved Lynn, she had something for him that no other woman in the word did. But that was over, it was all done with long ago, and no one would ever know he felt like this, least of all Toni. He promised himself that.

Trying to assuage his feelings of guilt, he took her away to Paris for a few weeks. They stayed in the Imperial suite at the Ritz, and she enjoyed herself immensely, shopping and sightseeing. He had reluctantly sold his place in Venice, Toni hadn't liked it, and it seemed pointless to keep it if they weren't going to use it. She was the first woman he'd met who hadn't fallen in love with Venice at first sight. "It's damp and smelly," she'd said distastefully, pulling her cashmere cardigan protectively round her shoulders. She grudgingly admitted that the apartment was beautiful, but "It's not exactly cosy, is it?" she commented, and objected volubly to the master bedroom, which had mirrored walls and a huge four poster bed. "I'm not sleeping in a room where you bedded streams of women," she said frostily.

Stephen forbore to mention that their bedroom in the Knightsbridge flat had seen considerably more in the way of amorous encounters than this one had. "Hardly streams," he murmured, kissing her, "and none of them were half as beautiful or sexy as you."

Stephen's marriage had been headline news, and Lynn had read about it with a feeling of sick misery, trying to convince herself that it didn't matter, he meant nothing to her. She had her job, she had Tim – what more could she possibly want? But life seemed drearier, greyer somehow, the days just that bit harder and more tiring, and she longed for a change of scene. She and Tim hadn't even been going out much of late, Tim wanted to become a consultant, but that meant exams, and he'd been studying hard and was tired.

When she got home one evening in June, he was waiting for her, clutching a letter, which he waved triumphantly. "I passed! You're looking at Timothy Joseph Franklin, MRCPCH!"

"Tim! Oh, Timmy, well done!" She hugged him delightedly.

"It means a new job though," he said.

"Well, we knew that, didn't we? I wonder who'll offer you a place first? They'll all want you!"

He kissed her. "God, you're so good to me, Lynn! I couldn't have done it without you!"

To his incredulous delight, he was offered a place at Great Ormond Street. He accepted straight away. They put the house on the market and started to look for somewhere in London.

Lynn had mixed feelings. She didn't think she'd have any trouble finding a job, and anyway, she could always work privately, but she wasn't sure about living in London. The chances of bumping into Stephen were slim, but they were there. She squared her shoulders. It was what Tim wanted and she wanted to make him happy. Anyway, so she bumped into Stephen, so what? He was happily married and his wife was expecting a baby, according to the papers. There was an interview with the pair of them in *Juliette*, a new women's magazine. *'I must have conceived on our honeymoon,'* Toni had gushed. Silly bitch, thought Lynn. She hoped Tim hadn't seen it. He didn't mention it, but all the papers had picked up the interview. Sid's Six was big news these days, and Stephen hardly ever spoke to the press unless it was with the band, to promote an album.

Lynn tried to convince herself that buying a copy of *Vogue* and swapping it for the *Juliette* in the hospital waiting room wasn't breaking her pact – she hadn't bought a Stevie magazine, after all. She pored over the pictures, studying Toni, trying to see what it was about her that had captivated Stephen. She was very pretty and her eyes were beautiful, large and lustrous, and the way the lids curved over them made her look as if she was always smiling, but Lynn felt there was something hard about her mouth. Or was that simply jealousy? The picture she treasured most showed Stephen in his flat, a lollipop in his mouth, putting a load of washing in his washing machine. She kept it in the back of her wallet.

Like Lynn before her, Toni had been surprised by the amount of time Stephen spent working and playing guitar. Unlike Lynn, she did mind. She'd known, of course, that he was a musician, but she hadn't thought much about what that entailed, hadn't looked beyond the tours, concerts and making records, and she'd expected him to feel the way she did about it, that it was a bit of fun, something he did now and again to keep the money coming in. She wouldn't have minded quite so much if he'd kept regular hours; her father was a policeman and worked long hours, but when he was at home, all his attention was given to his family. When Stephen wasn't touring or giving concerts or recording, he still worked a great deal, often at odd hours; he was immersed in his music – almost, she thought, to the point of obsession. Physically, he could be in the same room as she was, but mentally he'd be miles away. She hated that, just as she hated the amount of time he spent playing the guitar. She tried not to be resentful, but she sometimes felt cheated, as though he'd married her under false pretences.

Sid's Six had started rehearsing the new album, 'The Man and His Rice Bowl Have Gone Out of Sight'. It was a collection of songs Stephen had written since meeting and marrying Toni, and it marked a change of direction for the band. The four previous albums had been very personal, many of the songs coloured by Stephen's turbulent emotions in the wake of his break up with Lynn. This one had a much lighter feel, and the element of soul-searching that had characterised the earlier albums had gone.

The only bone of contention had been 'Sweet Cherry'. Fin, George and Andy had wanted it on the band's first album, and Stephen had adamantly refused to include it, promising it could go on the next one. Now they were demanding that the song go on this, their fifth.

"It's exactly the right album for it," Fin enthused. "It'll fit in really well with 'Never A Moment', both of them love songs."

Stephen had written 'Never A Moment' for Toni, when they got engaged.

Andy agreed. "They complement each other, Steve, what with 'Sweet Cherry' being so upbeat, and 'Never A Moment' a ballad."

"Why aye," George nodded. "It'll round the album off nicely. I think it'll be a huge hit, bonny lad."

Stephen had given in. He couldn't think of any plausible reason not to – what could he say? He was married to Toni, he loved her, and she was expecting their child. She knew the song was about Lynn, but she didn't know how much Lynn still meant to him; as far as she was concerned, it was just another song. And how could he voice the thought he tried never to acknowledge? That he loved Lynn best.

Later that summer, he was asked to write the score for a new film, *With Giants Fight*. The Oscar-winning British director Miles Tindall, who would, of course, be directing, had written it, which was enough for it to appeal very strongly to Stephen. When he read the script he knew he wanted to do it, and accepted immediately. It was about the Pilgrimage of Grace, the uprising that took place in northern England after Henry the Eighth's dissolution of the monasteries. Filming was just about to start.

Having accepted, he began to get nervous. "I'm not sure I can do it. Peter O'Toole's in it! It's a big film, Toni, and I've never done this before!"

"Of course you can," she scoffed. "You can do anything, Stevo!"

"I love you being pregnant, Daisy, you're so nice to me! Let's have enough for a football team!"

"Slow down, mate, I haven't had this one yet! And supposing we have girls?"

"Hey, I'm an equal opportunities employer," he grinned, kissing her. "After my meeting, how about I take you to San Lorenzo for lunch?" San Lorenzo was her favourite restaurant.

He was discussing the score with Miles, when the phone rang.

"Excuse me, dear boy. Yes?" Miles listened and then, grinning at Stephen, held the phone away from his ear slightly. Stephen could hear an angry voice on the other end. Miles grimaced. "Always something," he mouthed at Stephen. "Well, all right, dear boy, it's not the end of the world! Just find someone else…as quickly as possible…. Yes, well most scenes, I know… oh, for fuck's sake!" He looked at Stephen and shook his head.

Stephen grinned.

Miles's eyes widened. "Wait a minute, I've got an idea," he said into the phone. "Ever done any acting, dear boy?" he asked Stephen.

Stephen shook his head. "Only at school."

"Excellent!" Miles spoke into the phone again. "Well, do you know, I've got someone here… Stephen Markham, the musician… yes, that's right… Well, absolutely… yes, I'm relying on you to sort the whole thing out." He put the phone down. "Problem solved. The actor who was to play George Saville has apparently been offered something more to his liking, so you're our new George."

Stephen knew the part vaguely from the script. George was one of the rebels, a minstrel, and Stephen was writing a song for him. "Oh, no, Miles, I honestly don't think I could possibly—"

"Dear boy, of course you can. He sings a lot, hardly says anything and gets hanged, drawn and quartered at the end. Just grow your hair a little, and you'll be wonderful. Right then, let's get back to business."

The following week, Toni had an appointment with her obstetrician for an ultrasound. Stephen went with her. They were both transfixed by the image of their baby on the screen.

"Can you see what sex it is, Heather?" Toni asked.

Heather Donaldson smiled. "Possibly. It's not a hundred per cent accurate though."

Toni looked up at Stephen. "Do you want to know?"

He smiled. "I can see you do. All right, then."

They both looked expectantly at Heather.

"I think it might be a boy." Toni clutched Stephen's hand. "Don't take that as gospel though," Heather warned.

"What about names, then, mate?" Toni asked on the way back to the flat.

"What do we both like?"

"Let's make a list when we get home. I'd like John as a middle name; it's your middle name, as well as Dad's name. Oh, and your Dad too," she remembered.

"What a lovely idea," Stephen said. John would have been so happy to see him settled, happily married again, his wife expecting a child. "Yes, Toni," he repeated. "It's a lovely idea."

After a tremendous amount of spirited discussion, they settled on Alexander John.

"But supposing it's a girl?" Stephen asked.

"Strewth, I don't know! I haven't got the strength to go through that again. Alexandra Sian."

"I don't really like Alexandra."

Toni hit him with a cushion. "Well, let's hope it's a boy!"

Stephen discovered that the character he was playing, George Saville, had a small son, who appeared in a couple of scenes at the beginning of the film. He asked Miles if Rob could play him.

"How old is he?" Miles asked.

"Seven. He's small for his age, about the size of a five-year-old."

"I don't see why not, bring him along, we'll have a look at him. No, dear boy, not like that!" he shouted over to one of the actors.

Most of Stephen's scenes were with an Irish actor he'd never heard of, Des Wolfe, who took him under his wing. He was about Stephen's age, but seemed much older. He was playing the part of a tearaway called Ninian Staveley. "Sure, it's a great part, so it is," he enthused. "I egg all the peasants on to rape and pillage and get away with it – unlike you, you poor bastard, who just does a bit of marching and singing and gets hanged, drawn and quartered. Mind you," he added reflectively, "I've heard your band. Perhaps you deserve it after all!"

Rob was a hit on set. Like Stephen, he was very photogenic, and the pair of them were so alike that it made sense to cast him as Stephen's son. He loved every minute of it, and was spoilt outrageously by the female members of the cast and crew. Stephen, meanwhile, was also getting plenty of female attention. He'd grown his hair longer, as Miles had suggested, and someone in the make up department had decided that it would look better curly, so they'd put a light perm in it, giving it a wild, tousled look. In the opinion of most of his female fans, it only served to enhance his looks.

Toni liked it very much. "You should keep it like that, Stevo, you look so romantic, all brooding and poetic, like Lord Byron or something."

His band mates didn't agree. Andy and Fin fell about laughing when they saw him.

"Howay, you nancy boy," George said in disgust. "I always said you were a lass and now you even look like one."

Toni had developed a craving for Celebration Pancakes, a dessert served at a chain of roadside cafes. Stephen had tried making them at home for her, but they weren't what she wanted. She'd drag him out, eat five or six pancakes, and then complain about how full she was for the next few hours.

They'd gone to bed early one night; Toni because she was more comfortable propped up in bed with pillows, and Stephen because he had to be on set at four-thirty the next morning. At nine-fifteen, after they'd undressed and settled down with their books, Toni announced she wanted pancakes.

"Have a packet of Tim Tams," Stephen pleaded. "Or how about those lamingtons I made for you yesterday?"

"No. I want pancakes," she said stubbornly.

Stephen sighed. "Come on then, we'll have to be quick or they'll be closed."

He ordered six portions and watched her eat them.

When she'd finished, she sat back and groaned. "I'm so full!"

"Why did you eat so many then?" Stephen snapped as he was paying.

She burst into tears. "How could you be so mean?" she sobbed. "My poor stomach is squashed by your huge baby and I can't even enjoy a small treat any more!"

The staff stared at Stephen as if he was a wife beater. The woman on the till took his money coldly and handed him his change with contempt. "They're all the same, love," she said to Toni. "Bastards, the lot of them." She looked at Stephen. "You should be ashamed of yourself."

Stephen, his face burning with embarrassment, hurried Toni out.

"Don't push me, I can't walk fast any more," she said plaintively.

He heard a sharp intake of breath from the staff. "Thank you so much!" he said furiously as they drove home.

Toni was still sniffing. "It's the last time I ask you for anything," she said pathetically.

"If only I could believe that! Do you know what time I've got to be up in the morning?"

"Well, I didn't ask you to be in this film!"

"God, I'll be glad when this bloody baby is born," he said savagely as they walked into their bedroom.

That made her cry harder than ever. "First you don't want me, now you don't want my baby!"

"Come on Toni, you know that's not true!"

"I'm so tired," she complained. "And I'll be awake heaps in the night, what with my back hurting and the baby bouncing on my bladder!"

Stephen sighed. She was enormous now, she seemed to be all bump. "Come on. Sit down and I'll undress you."

Strangely, she looked even bigger naked. He could see the baby moving around. A heel appeared where her rib cage would normally be. He put his hand on the little foot and it moved instantly. "Toni, it's amazing!" he said in awe.

"You didn't really mean it when you said 'bloody baby' did you? I know I won't be the first to give you a son."

He took her in his arms; not an easy task any more. "Of course I didn't, Daisy!" He stroked the bump. "This baby is just as important to me as Robbie, it doesn't matter what sex it is. It's our child, Toni! You can't imagine how much I love it!"

"And me? Even though I'm so fat?"

"You are absolutely beautiful like this," he said sincerely.

She smiled. "Let's make love."

He glanced at the clock. It was eleven-twenty-five. The car from Pinewood studios would be picking him up at three-forty-five in the morning. Ah, what the hell. Toni slipped her hand down his body and started to stroke him. She positioned herself over him and took him in her mouth. He stroked her bottom and his hand moved between her legs. Who needed sleep anyway?

On New Year's Eve, Sid's Six was performing at a concert in aid of Have A Heart, the charity for children born with heart defects. The band had become involved with it after their tour manager's daughter had been born with a congenital heart problem. When Stephen got home and tiptoed into the bedroom, Toni was still awake, writhing around, trying to get comfortable.

"Happy New Year to the two of you," he said, kissing Toni and the bump. "Are you all right, darling?"

"My back feels like someone's taking a chainsaw to it!"

"Shall I run you a bath?"

"Please," she said gratefully. "Oh! Stevo! My waters have broken!"

He froze. "Surely not! It's not due till the fourteenth!"

"First babies are often a little early, they said that at the classes, remember? Come on, Steve, get my stuff and phone the Lindo Wing."

Her room at the hospital was like a suite in a luxury hotel, with a large en-suite bathroom, TV, radio, fridge and telephone. The staff made a huge fuss of her. She was undressed and examined.

"You're already four centimetres dilated, but you've got a way to go yet," said her midwife, Liz. "How's the pain?"

"Not too bad, it's just my back."

"Well, if you want anything, just shout, OK? You've had the pain relief explained to you?"

Toni nodded. "I'd rather not have anything if…" She stopped and caught her breath, gripping Stephen's hand as she had a contraction.

"Well, you let us know," Liz said. "I'll be back in a while to check on you. Is there anything you want?"

Toni shook her head. Within twenty minutes, she was having very strong contractions every two minutes. Stephen pressed the call bell.

Liz examined her again, which brought on another intense contraction, making her groan. "Well done, you're fully dilated, Toni! You're going to want to push soon."

"I do," gasped Toni. "Can I kneel up?"

"Of course you can." They helped her up. Stephen massaged her back.

"Come on, Toni, breathe, now! Stephen, help her breathe."

Stephen puffed and panted away.

Toni took no notice whatsoever.

"It's crowning!" Liz cried. "Look, Stephen!"

Stephen never forgot the sight of the crown of the baby's head appearing.

"Another big push now, Toni, here it comes, oh, it's a little boy! He's gorgeous!"

Both Stephen and Toni were crying, the baby was shouting his head off and Liz was beaming from ear to ear. She cut the cord, weighed him, wrapped him in a blanket and handed him to Toni. "Seven pounds, two ounces. Not bad for thirty-eight weeks! What's his name?"

"Alexander," Stephen said, gazing at the little boy.

"Happy birthday, Alexander," Liz smiled. "You're our first baby of 1988! I think he's hungry, Toni." She helped Toni put Alexander to her breast. The baby nuzzled angrily before he finally got the idea and began to suckle.

Toni gazed at Stephen over his head. "Oh, Stevo, isn't he unbelievable?"

"So are you, Toni!"

Alexander stopped sucking and Toni's nipple slipped out of his mouth. He gazed round. He was a very pretty baby, not in the least red or crumpled.

"He hasn't got your eyes," Toni said, disappointed. "His hair's like yours though. He's like Sian, isn't he?"

The baby's hair was as black as Stephen's, but his eyes were a rich dark brown. "He's like Dada," Stephen said quietly, taking him from Toni. "Hello, Alex," he said, looking down into his son's eyes.

"You're very good with him," Liz approved.

"Stevo's got another little boy," Toni told her.

"Oh, yes," Liz said, "I remember reading that somewhere." It was the first time she'd even given a hint that she knew who Stephen was. He was impressed by her professionalism.

"Is there anything you want?" she asked.

They shook their heads, absorbed in Alex.

Liz smiled. This was the very best part of her job. "The phone's right there when you're ready to spread the joy. I'll organise some tea and so on."

They rang their families. "Dad wants us to take Alex over as soon as possible," Toni said when she hung up.

"Don't you think he's a bit young to be exposed to all that p—" Stephen started but shut up at the look on Toni's face. "All right, in a couple of months, maybe," he conceded. "When you're both ready. You're going to have to rest up, my little Glaucus."

"I feel like I could run a marathon," she beamed. "I come from hardy stock, Steve!"

Stephen wanted Rob to see his new brother as soon as possible. He'd bought a load of presents for him from Alex, and, even though Toni wasn't his mother, they were going to make sure that the baby was in the cot next to the bed and not in her arms when Rob arrived.

Someone on the staff at the hospital hadn't been as professional as Liz. There were a crowd of reporters hanging round the entrance waiting for him. "Steve! Congratulations!"

These are the same shit-eating scum who accused me, Harry and Charlie of unnatural sexual practices last year, he thought. He put on his 'rock star' persona and waved.

"What is it?"

"A baby."

"Ha, ha! Boy or girl?"

"A boy, seven pounds, two ounces, Alexander," Stephen said, making for his Porsche.

"How's the missus?"

"The missus is fantastic!" He got into his car and drove away.

When he came back later with Rob, he went in through the back.

The Missus is Fantastic! ran the headline. Tim looked over at Lynn and pulled a face. "The man's insatiable!"

Lynn felt like cheering. Not long ago Tim would have reacted very badly to the news of the birth of Stephen's son. Since they'd moved to London, he seemed to have put all that behind him.

Lynn, having made her pact, had not bought any more magazines, but she didn't think it prohibited her from reading articles or listening to Stephen's music. The band had released another album recently, 'The Man and His Rice Bowl Have Gone Out of Sight'. She'd known it was being released, and had preordered it from HMV, but it had given her a tremendous shock to see 'Sweet Cherry' was on it. He's finally over me then, she thought, sadly. She hadn't been able to listen to it, had skipped on to the next track, aching with pain and longing. But 'Never A Moment' was another shock. She'd known he was married, why had she not realised he'd write a love song for his wife? She listened to him singing *'Hold you forever, that's all I want to do, there's never a moment when I'm not loving you'*, feeling as if the world was coming to an end. How could he be saying those words to another woman? She felt compelled to listen to the track, even though it filled her with sick jealousy. Oh, yes, she thought bitterly, he's certainly over me.

But the rest of the tracks delighted her. The song 'Here's The Thing', which had been the first single, she thought lovely, but her favourite was 'The Sound of One Hand Clapping', which had just been released as a single, along with a video. The lyrics were amusing, but also perceptive and the tune was deceptively simple, very compelling. Stephen's voice was as fine as ever, she never tired of hearing it, and he was playing his Strat. She thought she'd never heard him play it so well. She kept the CD hidden from Tim, could only play it when he was out, and never left it in her CD player, just in case. It was ridiculous that she had to resort to this kind of subterfuge to listen to an album, she thought.

At work, she'd started to specialise in the autistic spectrum; having attended some seminars on the subject, she'd become extremely interested in the whole area. She was doing a lot of work for ASUK, the Autistic Society of the United Kingdom, as well as some private work from home, and working part time at a Health Centre. People were always leaving newspapers or magazines lying around at the Health Centre and so she read several reviews of the album. Unlike the first four, which had been universally acclaimed, this one had provoked mixed reactions. Some reviewers liked it very much, some loathed it and accused Stephen of being pretentious.

There was an interview with the band in a woman's magazine that one of the receptionists was reading one day, and Lynn borrowed it over her lunch hour. There were several pictures of the band looking happy and relaxed, and the interviewer quizzed Stephen on the differences between composing songs and a film soundtrack.

"Well, there are differences and similarities, of course. I would say the biggest difference – for me – is that when I'm writing a song, the inspiration can come from anywhere – a soundtrack obviously has to relate to what the film is about. Also, the way I write songs –" He stops, groping for words. "When I write a soundtrack, I tend to write music, rather than play it. I'll use the piano sometimes, and very occasionally the guitar, but mostly I sit at a desk and write. With songs, I use the guitar all the time, I'll just sit with a guitar, kind of playing with a song I hear in my head, and worrying at it on the guitar until I get what I want." He shrugs and grins. "Sorry, I'm not being very clear, am I? I think you have to be there!"

Lynn couldn't imagine him not sitting with his guitar to write, he'd always used it in Manchester, it had been part of him, almost like another limb. He had often worked late into the night and then she'd find him asleep on the sofa, his guitar across his waist. He's matured a lot, musically, she thought, and felt like weeping at how much of him she'd missed. She would only experience these new sides of him at second hand now. She envied and hated his wife with equal measure.

The interviewer mentioned the mixed reviews the album had received and asked them how they felt about the negative ones.

"As long as it's getting noticed and the fans like it, that's all that matters to us," Fin Harper, the band's keyboard player, says.

"Yeah," George Ferguson, the bassist, elaborates. "We don't expect everybody to like what we do. You have to be realistic. There's always going to be mixed opinions, man, and as it went into the album charts here and in the States at number one, it's pretty obvious wor fans like it!"

"How would you answer the suggestion that this album is pretentious?"

"It certainly wasn't intended to be pretentious," says Stephen. "Really, it was a bit of a joke. Our last four albums have been pretty serious. 'The Man and His Rice Bowl' isn't."

"So why the change of direction?"

Stephen smiles. "I guess we're feeling happy!"

You're feeling happy, you mean, Lynn thought forlornly. Happy with your new wife, happy with your new son. Her heart aching, she read on.

"Tell me about 'The Sound Of One Hand Clapping', Stephen. I understand it wasn't considered as a single originally, yet it's the song that has had the most attention. What's it about?"

Stephen pushes his hair back off his forehead. "Yeah, we didn't really see it as a single, but people seem to like it! What's it about? OK, well, the idea, as I understand it, is that clapping with two hands is a metaphor for dualistic functioning. So the sound of one hand clapping is… well, it's supposed to symbolise oneness. Then that – the hand of oneness – has to reach out and become the hand of compassion, it can't be a private experience, and it has to make us accept our human limitations so that we can reconcile ourselves to the natural world and live in harmony with the universe."

"And if that doesn't sound pretentious, like, I don't know what would," puts in Andy Lake, the band's drummer.

Stephen grins. "Yes, but I didn't study it or anything. I was on a train, a while ago now, and I had nothing to read, and someone had left a magazine, so I read that, and there was this thing in there about Zen. That reminded me of a book where one of the characters is into Zen, and the whole thing came from there."

They discussed some of the other songs, and then the interviewer asked Stephen about playing the harp on the instrumental track 'Rhodri's Land', and whether he'd learnt it specifically for the album.

"Yes. I wrote the music years ago after my grandfather died but I never did anything with it. Then when my son, Alex, was born, I found myself thinking about Dada a lot, and the tune just kind of evolved. And as it's a tribute to him, I wanted to be the one who played the harp, so I had to learn."

"The instrument most people associate you with is, of course, your Ocean Turquoise Fender Stratocaster, which you play on 'The Sound Of One Hand Clapping', but I understand you also play the cello, the piano – and the bass guitar, too?'

Stephen nods, but before he can speak, George interjects, "Aye, he has a go, but the thing about the bass guitar is that it's much harder to master than people realise. They tend to think it's easy to play because it's got fewer strings, but it's not, man! No way! You've got to have a bit of a talent for it."

Stephen raises his eyebrows. "I was about to say that the reason I don't play bass very often is because it's so simple. I like a challenge."

George flushes and Stephen smiles blandly at him. "Just kidding, George."

Lynn remembered wondering, when the band had first become famous, whether there'd be friction between Stephen and George, and felt that the exchange pretty much confirmed her suspicions – Stephen had deliberately made George look small, and that was unlike him, but the interviewer had taken it for light hearted banter.

"You seem, as a band, to get on well with each other. Is this just an image you project?"

"Not at all. We're lucky in that we get on very well, mostly," says Fin.

Andy agrees. "We have our ups and downs, like, but basically, we're mates."

"And we work together well too," adds Stephen. "That's really important. We respect each other as musicians. Everyone's opinion matters."

"Course, we have to keep an eye on Steve, make sure he doesn't get too big headed," Fin jokes. "All this appearing in movies, being told he's a heart throb. It's not good for him."

"Yeah, we're having a tee shirt printed for him, 'Don't Feed The Ego' it's going to say on it," Andy nods.

Stephen grins and refuses to rise to the bait. "Take no notice, they're not very bright."

"So, do you socialise? See each other when you're not working?"

Fin nods. "Oh, yeah, quite a bit, which is actually pretty surprising when you think that we spend a lot of time rehearsing and recording, and of course, when we're on tour, we're together all the time."

"Aye, and it's a very insular world, touring," George adds. "There's not even time for to see the places where we're playing; it's bus, gig, hotel, so there certainly isn't time to mix with anyone except each other."

"Stephen, where would you say most of your inspiration comes from? You're very much a romantic, aren't you?"

"That's one word for him!" George puts in.

"Rack off, George," Stephen says, without heat. "Yeah, I'm a romantic. Isn't everyone? Otherwise, how could we keep believing that things are going to get better? There's so much suffering in the world."

The other three groan good naturedly.

"Where do I get inspiration from? Anywhere and everywhere. There's no formula for it."

"What comes first, the music or the lyrics?"

Stephen shakes his head. "Either. Sometimes I'll hear something, some tune in my head that l worry at for a while; sometimes it's a lyric. Again, there's no formula."

"How do you see the band developing in the future?"

They look at each other. "Impossible to say," Stephen says, eventually.

"We'll let you know when we find out, like," Andy adds.

"Well, thank you all for taking the time to talk to me. Can I just ask you, Stephen, do

you have any advice for the aspiring bands, songwriters and guitarists out there?"

Stephen raises his eyebrows. "My advice? God, I hate this question! Is anyone really interested? OK, let's see, um, believe in yourself, no matter what anyone says, keep playing, and don't give up if things don't seem to be happening for you. Unless you're very lucky, it's not going to be easy, and you've got to really want it, really go for it, and be prepared to put up with all the bad things; grotty hotels, being away from your family all the time, continual travelling. I think, most of all, you've got to love playing to a live audience – that's what it's all about." He grins. "For me, anyway!"

Lynn put the magazine down and rubbed her eyes. Why had she read it? The yearning for Stephen was an actual pain in her stomach. For Stevie and that old life. She remembered the friendship they had had with Fin, Andy and George, the friendship he so obviously still had with them, however much he and George might bicker. Looking back, it seemed all she could remember was laughing, laughing all the time. And loving and being loved by Stephen. How could she have thrown all that away for another woman to pick up? She felt raw with bitterness and longing. She gave the magazine back to its owner after lunch, wishing she'd never borrowed it.

She had to train herself not to think about Stephen all over again. It was the only way; the craving for him was like a mosquito bite, the more you scratched it, the more it itched. What a fool she'd been to succumb to temptation! The only way to get rid of it was to forget it, no matter how strong the provocation. At least Tim was happy and settled, she thought thankfully. He'd recently said how much he was enjoying working at Great Ormond Street. "I love feeling I'm making a difference," he'd enthused.

Then one morning he looked at her over the top of the paper. "Have you ever thought about Africa, Lynn?"

She assumed he was talking about holidays. "No, but now you mention it I'd love to see Kenya. Caro and Donald went there last year…"

"I meant working in Africa, somewhere like Nuranda. Look." He passed her the paper. There were the usual horrific pictures of starving children and war victims.

"It's appalling!" She looked up at him. "But you love it at the hospital."

"I had a word with someone the other day. I could take a year's sabbatical. Come with me?"

"Now wait a minute! This is the first time you've ever mentioned this! I've got my practice, my work with ASUK. I *am* doing something to help, Tim, and so are you!"

"Not these children though," he said quietly.

"Well, they're not going to need a speech therapist, are they?"

"They need administrators and aid workers. I've looked into this, Lynn. We could go together."

"I can't believe you've never mentioned it to me when you've obviously spent a lot of time and thought on it! I don't know, Tim, is the bottom line. I love you and I want to be with you, but I'm helping so many children here. I know they're not starving or getting their legs blown off, but they need a different kind of help just as badly."

Tim nodded. "I agree, but the fact is, if you didn't do it they could find another therapist. Not as good as you, maybe, but someone could do it. In Africa they can't just interview someone for this job. They have to rely on people like us going out there because we want to help."

Lynn sighed. "Oh, Tim. I need to think about it. I'm not sure if I could do it – if I could cope."

Tim smiled. "You think about it. But I know you *could* cope, Lynn. You'd be fantastic."

"What do you think you're doing, Rob?"

It was the Easter holidays and Rob was spending a few days at Stephen and Toni's. Stephen had been out when Harry dropped him off, and when he got back, Toni told him she was worried about Rob. "I think he's unhappy about Alex, Stevo."

Stephen had gone to look for him and found him in Alex's room, kicking the cot.

"Rob! I asked you a question! Why are you doing that? If Alex had been in there you'd have woken him up."

"Good," Rob muttered, kicking it again. "He's stupid."

Stephen knelt down and took him in his arms. "What's the matter, Blue?" Rob's old name for himself, the Blewser, had become shortened to Blews and then simply Blue.

Rob cuddled against him. "Why does *he* live here with you? Why can't *he* live with Mum and Dom and *I* can live with you?"

Stephen didn't know what to say. "Aren't you happy with Mummy and Dom?"

Rob shook his head.

Stephen felt chilled. "Why not?"

Rob shrugged. "Mummy's always cross. It's more fun here. Toni says I'm her little bloke and she lets me hold Bunyip."

Stephen shuddered at the thought of the tarantula. There'd been some heated discussions on the desirability of him moving into the flat. Toni had won, as she usually did.

"Listen, Robbie, how about I speak to Mummy and Dom and we'll find out if you can come and stay here more often? How's that?"

Rob nodded. "Can I stay here forever?"

Stephen hesitated. If it was up to him, Rob could move in immediately, but he didn't want to cause problems for Harry and Dominic. "Well, I don't know, Rob. That's why I have to speak to Mummy. She's in charge, you see."

Rob looked miserable. "Dom says 'bloody women', and sometimes I agree."

Stephen hugged him but he couldn't resist grinning. "I bet he doesn't say it when Mummy's in the room! Don't worry, cariad. I'll sort it out."

Rob clung to him. "Daddy, you do still love me, now you've got Alex, don't you?"

Stephen was stricken. What kind of a louse was he that his son should feel like that?

"Robbie, of course I do! I love you best in all the world! After all, I've had you the longest."

Rob turned this over in his mind. "You have!" He gave Stephen a gap-toothed smile and a smacking kiss. "Let's play fighting, Daddy. I'll be Leonardo and you can be the Shredder."

"How come I'm always the baddie?"

"Oh, Daddy! Because I'm the bestest fighter, remember?"

Stephen spoke to Dominic the following week. They were discussing the possibility of Tantony Pig recording an album.

Harry had finally given in. "OK, but just one," she'd said, staring at Stephen and Dominic with hostile eyes.

"Well, we can only do one at a fucking time," Dominic had said later to Stephen. "Harry and I are 'trying for a baby'," he added.

"Oh, great," Stephen said, taken aback.

"Just thought I'd let you know why she's so fucking bad-tempered, old chap. Once she's made up her mind, she wants everything to happen instantly."

"Well, strangely, I wanted to talk to you about that. Rob's not very happy at the moment. He asked me last week if I still loved him now we've had Alex. He's very jealous."

"Poor little sod," Dominic sympathised.

"Thing is, Charlie, he says he wants to come and live with us. We'll, I've got no objection and Toni hasn't, she's interviewing nannies at the moment, and we're going to start looking for a house, but it's really up to Harry."

"There's a house for sale just down the road from us. It might be a bit bigger than you wanted, but if you lived that close, Rob could come and go as he pleased."

"That's a good idea," Stephen said, much struck. "I'll get the details."

Although the house was larger than the ones they'd been looking at, it was perfect, with spectacular views over the River Thames, and a beautiful walled garden. The previous owners had not been particularly keen gardeners, merely keeping the grass cut, but this only added to the garden's charm, giving it a wild beauty. Rose trees ran riot in the flower beds, sweet scented honeysuckle festooned itself over trees and shrubbery, and the lawn was rich with daisies and buttercups. Stephen and Toni put in an offer, which was accepted immediately, and Stephen put his flat on the market.

Shortly after they moved in, they went to the premiere of *With Giants Fight*, Toni looking stunningly voluptuous in a tight scarlet satin frock with a plunging neckline and a large bow at the back, emphasising the curve of her bottom.

Stephen had had his hair cut short again, much to the disappointment of Toni and his fans, and the relief of the band. His soundtrack had gone into the album charts at number three and the single, 'Forget Me Not', the love theme, which he sang in the film, went in at number seven. After the film went on nationwide release, it went up to number one and stayed there for two weeks, until 'Never A Moment' was released, knocking it off the top spot.

"I told you this album would be a huge hit, bonny lad," George said with smug satisfaction.

"I'm the luckiest man in the world," Stephen sighed as he and Toni lay curled up in bed. "Another best selling album, a beautiful house, two beautiful boys, and you, my beautiful, delectable, adorable wife." He caressed her breasts. "These are even nicer since you've been feeding Ally."

She wriggled with pleasure. "Glad you like them, because they'll be like this for a while. I'm preggers again, mate!"

He stared at her. "Bloody hell! How did that happen?"

"Well, Stephen, when a mummy and a daddy love each other very much…"

"You know what I mean! You had that cap fitted!"

She looked sheepish. "Sometimes I couldn't be bothered with it. Anyway, I thought you couldn't conceive when you were breastfeeding. I'm happy as Larry though, it'll be lovely for Alex."

"When's it due?"

"Next January, mate!" She was grinning all over her face. "Try and tell me you're not pleased!"

He grinned back. "Course I'm pleased! It's you I'm thinking of. Will you be OK? I thought you needed a break after you'd had a baby."

"Well, with a nanny, it's not exactly as if I'm rushed off my feet, is it?"

"You were talking about going back to work part-time though."

"I'd rather have another baby."

There were mixed reactions to the pregnancy.

Sian and Sandy, Toni's mother, were pleased, but concerned about Toni.

Ted commented that Stephen and Toni were like the Larkins. "Steve's only got to look at her across the room and she starts wondering if it's triplets or twins!"

Andy was enthusiastic. "Keep them barefoot and pregnant, like, Steve. That was my mistake, I was never dominant enough." He was in the middle of his third divorce, and had recently started to date a children's TV presenter, Holly Havergill, known by children all over Britain as Havago Holly, due to her propensity for saying, when faced with any difficult challenge, 'OK, I'll have a go!'

Dominic sighed. "You're so fucking tactless, Markham. This is really going to make Harry a joy to live with."

In June, Stephen and Toni flew out to visit Jacko. He'd been over to them a couple of times, but after the second visit, Stephen remarked to Toni that, poison or not, it was much less stressful seeing him in his natural habitat. "It's like having a cross between Crocodile Dundee and Dame Edna Everage staying with you!"

Jacko was delighted with the pregnancy. He fussed around, worrying whether Toni should be flying in her condition. "Why don't you stay on a bit, love, when the Taddie's gone back home?" he suggested when they got to Brisbane.

Stephen knew Toni was very tempted. He didn't really want her to, but he could see the logic of it. She needed a rest, the weather would agree with her and she could spend time on one of her favourite occupations, shopping, with her sister Emma. Stephen had commitments that summer; he had concerts with Sid's Six and Tantony Pig, and he was going to be working on an album with the celebrated British folk singer, Jenny Coleman. He'd been trying to set this up for a while, and their schedules had finally enabled them to do it. He was excited about it, he'd been a fan of hers since his teens. He considered her voice to be second to none, and he was thrilled that she wanted to work with him.

"What do you think, Stevo?" Toni asked.

He could see she was longing to stay. "You do whatever you want, Daisy. If I was you, I'd stay and have a good rest."

Toni sighed with relief. She was feeling tired, much more so than she'd admitted to him. Emma, her sister, was great company, and Jacko and Kay could think of nothing they'd rather do than look after Alex.

Before Stephen went home, he flew to Japan for George and Kagami's wedding. Toni wanted to go very much; she liked George best among Stephen's friends, and she loved parties, but she reluctantly decided against it. She didn't feel up to the plane journey, and her blood pressure was slightly raised.

Andy had brought Holly Havergill with him and confided to Stephen, "This is it, Steve, true love."

Stephen wrung his hand. "I'm so pleased, Andy! Rob'd love to be here," he added. "He loves Havago, thinks she's the best thing since sliced bread. You'll have to bring her round when we get home."

Andy beamed, his weasely little face looking almost human.

"Isn't she a lot younger than you though?"

"No, she's nearly four years older, she's twenty-eight," Andy said. He was the youngest member of the band. He'd been only just seventeen when he'd auditioned, much to the amazement of the other three – he'd looked about thirty.

"Blimey! She doesn't look old enough to have left school!"

Andy's face cracked into an evil grin. "I know. You should see her in a gym slip!"

Fin was there with Shelagh, and they all had a drink together at the hotel before the ceremony, but Fin had been out of it, obviously high on some drug. It worried Stephen; Fin seemed to have got much worse. He'd always drunk a great deal, and smoked, both cigarettes and marijuana, even before they'd formed Sid's Six, and he'd always taken drugs when they toured, but he'd never been like this. Stephen tried to speak to Shelagh, but it was as if she was avoiding him, he wasn't sure whether by accident or design.

"This is a bit different, like, eh, Steve?" Andy said at the reception.

Stephen realised he'd never really talked to Andy on his own before, didn't know him like he knew Fin and George. Andy had always been the quiet one. "Yeah, I've not been to anything like it."

"You ought to get a picture of George in that dress," Andy went on, referring to the kimono George was wearing. "Next time he calls you a lass, you could whip it out and give him a taste of his own medicine."

Stephen started to laugh. "What a bloody good idea! Come on, Andy, let's get stuck into the champagne, before George drinks it all. I don't think he likes the Sake that much."

"You know, Steve, weddings aren't much different wherever you go, are they? Everyone wears their best clothes and gets pissed and that's about it. Not much point, really."

Stephen nodded. "I know exactly what you mean."

"It's all for the girls, really," Andy said sagely.

"So, what about you and Holly? Are you thinking of marriage?"

Andy shrugged. "I'm not sure. Maybe. I think we'd both like to, but she's divorced too, and we don't want to rush into anything. And you know how things change when you get hitched. Usually for the worse," he added gloomily.

Stephen was amused. "Why do you say that?"

"Well, you know. Once they've got a ring on their finger, they change, like. Nothing you do is ever good enough for them. Before you're married, they treat you like someone special, afterwards... well, they might just as well put a ring through our noses."

Stephen was struck by this. "Yeah, you're right," he said, thinking of Toni. She'd always been demanding, but since they'd got married she'd become very much more imperious, despite the softening effect of pregnancy. She'd recently moved Bunyip's tank into their ensuite bathroom, on the grounds that it was warmer for him there. Stephen had objected volubly, but Toni had somehow managed to steal the moral high ground, and accused him of not caring about Bunyip or her – 'Surely you can't want him to be cold? I thought you were against animals suffering? And do you really want me to have to trail all the way down to the utility room, in *my* condition, every time I want to see him?' – and had dissolved into heartbroken tears. Needless to say, Bunyip's tank now resided in their bathroom, and Stephen had started using one of the guest ones.

"Lynn wasn't like that though," he said, sadly.

Andy gave him a pitying look. "You know what, Steve? Considering how clever you are, you can be really thick sometimes. I know how much you loved Lynn and everything, but she didn't exactly treat you well."

Stephen frowned. "What do you mean?"

"Well, come on, Steve! After she lost the baby she treated you like dirt and then she married someone else."

"It wasn't like that!" Stephen started. He saw the expression on Andy's face. "Maybe a bit," he conceded.

"I've always thought of you as my big brother, Steve."

Stephen was surprised and touched. "Thanks, Andy," he said awkwardly. "But why?"

Andy shrugged. "I don't know. You always looked out for us all in Manchester – you still do really, look how worried you are about Fin, and it's not just because he could fuck up the band, is it?"

"Of course not! He's my friend – you all are."

"That's what I mean. No one ever looked out for me before. My dad left home when I was ten, and my mum never gave a shit about any of us." Stephen knew that Andy had moved from Liverpool to Manchester with a girlfriend after he'd left school, but he'd always been reticent about details. "That's one of the reasons it's so great being in the band," Andy continued. "It's like having a family."

Stephen was moved and saddened. He couldn't imagine what it would be like not to have a close family, and Andy was a really nice bloke.

They drained their glasses, and, almost immediately, they were unobtrusively refilled.

"You and Holly ought to get married and have children, Andy. Once you've got children… well, there's nothing like it. That really is family." He thought of Rob and Alex and the baby Toni was expecting. He smiled at Andy. "Nothing like it," he said again.

In Australia, Toni was enchanted to be asked to show off Alex to *The Weekly*. She gave a long interview, during which she mentioned that Stephen had been married before, unaware that he'd deliberately never done so, had been careful to gloss over his time in Manchester, not wanting Lynn to be bothered by reporters. His friends had colluded in this and none of them had ever talked about her to the press. Unfortunately, Euterpe released Sweet Cherry as the next single from 'The Man and His Rice Bowl'. It was very catchy and went straight to number one. The press, armed with the fact that Stephen had been married to a girl called Cherilynn, did some digging and found Lynn. Articles appeared about them in the papers: *The Girl Who Broke Stephen Markham's Heart*; *Sid's Sob Story*. Interest in Stephen was intense. Reporters camped outside his house. One of the tabloids had found someone who had vaguely known them at university, and ran an 'exclusive eye-witness account' of Stephen's 'affair' with Miyuki.

Neither Tim nor Lynn could go out without being photographed. Their pictures were splashed all over the papers, and Lynn's miscarriage was dragged up and written about *ad nauseam*. She'd always felt rather piqued in the past because Stephen never mentioned her when he was interviewed. I'm not important enough to you any more, huh? she'd thought. Now she realised why he hadn't.

Tim went ballistic. He rang the police, his MP and finally his stepfather, who pulled some strings and the reporters left. "It's ridiculous!" he raged. "We can't even get away from that man in our own home!"

"Tim, I was married to someone who's very famous. I think we've got off lightly, I've seen some of the things that have been written about him…" She trailed off at the look on his face.

"Have you? *Have* you? Well, you can do what you like, Lynn," he said, his face set. "I'm going to Africa."

Lynn felt she had no choice. They made their preparations, sorted out their affairs and left for Nuranda.

Toni came home at the beginning of October, bringing the infamous copy of *The Weekly* with her, unaware of the storm she had unleashed. Stephen picked her up at the airport on a cold autumnal evening.

The house in Cheyne Walk had been decorated and furnished to her instructions while she was away. "It's lovely," she said, looking round. They went into the drawing room, where a cheerful log fire was burning.

"Sit down, darling, you look very tired. Here, give me Ally. Would you like a drink? Or some coffee or something?"

Toni shook her head, kicking off her shoes. "No, I'll feed Al in a minute and then have a lovely hot bath and go to bed." She smiled at him suggestively. "You could join me."

"I can't think of anything nicer."

"Look at this, I don't suppose you've seen it," she said proudly, holding up the magazine.

He smiled at the picture of her and Alex on the front. *'Toni Markham shows off her little angel and tells us, 'Stephen is a wonderful father', before confessing 'I'm expecting again!'* "It's a good picture of you both." He dropped a kiss on his son's head. "He's grown since then!"

Alex poked a fat little finger into Stephen's ear and gurgled happily to himself. Stephen gave him back to Toni and took the magazine. "Jesus Christ!" he said abruptly.

"What?"

"It was your fault! It was all your fault! You bloody silly bitch!"

"What the hell are you talking about?"

"This, about Lynn: My *husband's ex wife, Cherilynn*! Why didn't you just give them her married name and full address while you were at it, you stupid tart?"

Toni started to cry.

He ignored her. "I've been so careful never to mention her, the press never had a clue! You go and open your big mouth and we're knee deep in the fucking bastards dragging it all up. It was hell here, God knows what it must have been like for poor Cherry!" He stopped.

Toni had gone very white. She put Alex down on the floor and blundered out of the room.

"Toni!" Stephen scooped Alex up, dumped him in his playpen, and went after her.

She ran into the bathroom and locked the door. He hammered on it. "Toni, I'm sorry! Please open the door!"

"Go away," she said in a high little voice.

"Toni, open this door."

There was no answer. He put his foot against the door and pushed hard. It gave a splintering shriek and burst open.

Toni cowered back, her arms protectively over her stomach. "Go away!" she said again. "Don't touch me!"

"Don't be stupid, Toni, I'm not going to hurt you. I just want to talk to you and I can't do that through the locked door. Come into the bedroom and sit down. I'm sorry I shouted and upset you, it was a despicable thing to do. Come on." He held his hand out encouragingly as if to a frightened animal.

Tentatively, Toni took it.

He pulled her as close to him as her bump would allow, and stroked her hair. "I mean it, my darling. I can't apologise enough. It's just… well, it wasn't fun here for a while. They dragged everything up, Lynn's miscarriage, everything."

"You called her Cherry. You still love her don't you?"

"Of course not, I love you," he said heartily – too heartily, Toni caught the false note. She pulled away from him. "You never got over her. I was always second best. That's why you don't care if my children are boys or girls, you've got no preference because they're not hers."

"That's not true!" said Stephen. It wasn't. "I have no preference because I love them for who they are, not what they are. I love our children and I love you, Toni. You're not second best. Yes, I still love Lynn, I'm sorry, but I do, but it's… oh, how can I explain? It's like a memory, or a dream that made a tremendous impression. The Lynn who's walking around now isn't the one I love. The Lynn I love doesn't exist any more. Can't you see, Toni?" he said desperately. "It's like when someone dies. You can't stop loving them just because they're dead. You don't mind me loving my father or Dada. *You're* my wife, *you're* the mother of my children. I love *you*!"

Toni stared at him. "I'm very tired. My baby is tired," she said politely, rubbing her bump. "I'm going to feed Alex and put him to bed, then I'm going to bed. On my own. Goodnight, Stephen." She gave him a small kiss on the cheek.

The next day she was still polite and distant.

"Toni, when are you going to forgive me?" he asked frantically.

"I forgive you, Stephen."

"Darling girl, I'm going away on tour tomorrow. You can't stay angry with me!"

"Why not?" Before he could answer, she asked, "Why have you never called me cariad?"

"What?" He was caught off balance.

"Why have you never called me cariad?" Sian used the word constantly, and occasionally Stephen said it to Rob. With a leap of intuition, Toni knew he'd called Lynn cariad. "You used to call Lynn it."

"What makes you think that?"

"Sian told me," she lied, holding her breath. Let him say she's wrong, she thought desperately.

Stephen's shoulders sagged. "I don't know, Toni. But if that's your case against me, I don't know what I can do. All I can do is say this: I chose to marry you. I didn't have to. I loved you and I wanted to marry you and I still love you. Very much indeed. I'm going to rehearsal." He went to kiss her and she turned her head slightly, presenting him with a cold cheek.

She was no more responsive that night. He didn't know what to do. He could only hope that she would get over it while he was away.

He spoke to Dominic and Harry and asked them to keep an eye on her. To his surprise, Harry was very sympathetic.

"Poor Toni! And poor you too, Stevie." She kissed him. "But sometimes things seem harder to cope with when you're pregnant." She blushed. "Did Dom tell you? *I'm* pregnant!"

"I'm so pleased! When's it due?"

"April," Dominic said, happily.

Stephen punched him on the arm. "Well done, Charlie!"

"What about me?" Harry pouted. "He had thirty seconds of bliss! I've got to do all the hard work!"

"Thirty seconds? Thirty fucking seconds? It was more like thirty fucking minutes!"

"In your dreams!" Harry retorted.

"Well, I'm going home," Stephen said.

He set off on the tour, feeling tense and worried. Fin didn't help. He was stuffed to the eyeballs with drugs, completely out of it.

"Jesus," Stephen said to Andy. "He's never been this bad before! It's like trying to communicate with the fucking space shuttle! What are we going to do?"

"Fuck knows," said Andy miserably. "And it's no good talking to him, like. I've tried."

"When he comes down we'll have to try again."

Fin took no notice. He was very hostile, and adamant that he could give up drugs whenever he wanted. "And it's none of your fucking business," he said angrily to Stephen. "You're not my fucking boss. The day I can't play, that's the time you can say something, but until then you can stuff your fucking advice up your fucking arse."

"Not exactly successful were we, Steve?" Andy said.

Stephen shrugged. "I don't see what else we can do."

He had problems of his own. The longing for Lynn that he'd told himself he'd get over once he was married and settled was as bad as ever, and the pictures of her in the papers had stirred those feelings to fever pitch. He'd thought that by marrying Toni he would immunise himself against Lynn, but he hadn't, he'd just acquired a similar longing for Toni. He was missing her tremendously. He hadn't realised how much she meant to him, and he was very angry with himself for the way he'd behaved. If only he could make her see how sorry he was! He missed her upbeat outlook on life, her caustic wit, her abrasive but stimulating personality, and he missed her body enormously. He was surrounded by pretty, scantily clad Scandinavian girls who were willing to do anything he wanted. It was torture. The other three were at it all the time; even George, with Kagami expecting twins, didn't look on it as infidelity. "Howay, bonny lad, they're just conveniences! We've got to relieve the stress and tension somehow!"

But Stephen couldn't do that. It frustrated him and annoyed him that he couldn't, but he knew he'd never be able to live with himself if he did. He ran, he drank a little more than usual, he took a lot of tepid showers. The beds in the hotels made his back ache and Toni never seemed happy to hear from him when he rang. Their conversations were short and stilted and seemed to consist of 'how are you?', 'how's Alex?' and 'I love you'. She always said 'how's the tour going?', and 'me too' when he said he loved her. He thought about not saying it to see if *she* would, but then was afraid not to, in case she didn't.

And at every new town he got up on the stage and played and sang as if it was the first time. Which was the easiest part of the tour. Once he had the guitar in his hands and started to play, he forgot Lynn and Toni and everything else. All that mattered was the music.

While Stephen was away, Dominic and Harry kept an eye on Toni. They had her round for meals, Harry spent time with her and they took her out, but she continued to behave sweetly and sadly, like a poor little martyr. At the end of November, Harry took Rob up to stay with Sian and Ted, and Dominic called round to see Toni.

"Dom! Hi! Come in! I'm not dressed for visitors though." She was wearing an old pair of flowery trousers with an elasticated waist that was so loose it tended to slip below her bump, and a long pink tee shirt.

"I'm more than a visitor, aren't I?"

She flashed him a smile. "I guess you are, Dom," she said, her voice sugary. "Come and have a drink."

They went through to the drawing room and Toni poured them drinks. She brought them over and sat on the sofa next to him. "Where's Harry?"

"She's taken Rob up to Yorkshire for the weekend."

"Oh, yeah, I remember."

"So I'm all alone."

"Just like me, though I've got Ally, of course."

"Hardly a fount of stimulating conversation though, cute as he is," Dominic drawled. He put his arm round her. "Still sad?"

She nestled close to him. "Mmmhmm. Did Steve tell you what happened?"

"Yes, he… fuck me, was that your sprog?"

Toni moved slightly. "He's really active tonight."

"He's got a kick like a mule! May I feel?"

"Course."

He put his hand on her bump and she blushed prettily.

His face lit up as he felt the baby move. "That's fucking amazing!"

"You've got bigger hands than Stephen," she said, putting her hand over his and shifting a little so that she was looking into his eyes. Hers were wide and limpid.

He grinned at her. "My motto has always been 'fuck the moral high ground', but do you know what? In this instance I'm not going to give in to temptation. You're luscious, Toni – very, very fanciable – but poor pathetic old Markham is my best friend." He took his hand away. "Anyway, you're vulnerable at the moment, aren't you? Alone, very pregnant, and mixed up."

"Stephen didn't have to go away," Toni pouted. "If he's going to go off, why shouldn't I have some fun?"

"Don't be silly, of course he had to go! It takes a lot of juice to fuel this lifestyle, young Antonia! You love this life and you love Stephen. You're just angry with him because of Lynn."

"Maybe I am," she said, giving him a sideways glance. "But that doesn't mean I don't fancy you too."

He sat back and looked at her. "You know, I take great pleasure in being sordid, perverted, the lowest of the low, totally fucking debauched, but I find I can't be as bad as I thought I was. If only Harry could see this, she might regard me in a new light. Don't be mixed up and angry about Lynn. Steve loves you, you know."

"Not as much as her," Toni said, expecting to be contradicted.

"No, not as much as her," Dominic agreed.

She moved indignantly and he held her against him, stopping her from getting up. "Toni, you're a big girl now, sit still and listen. Stephen loved Lynn to distraction – fuck knows why, frankly. She was pretty and nice and sexy and the rest of it, but she was always a bit too good, too holier than thou, if you know what I mean. And that stupid fucking sap fell for the whole package hook, line and sinker. But then, he's a bit of a Holy Joe himself isn't he? Vegetarianism, thou shalt not fuck groupies when you're married etc, etc. Can't think why I like him so fucking much, really.

'Then of course, she gets pregnant. They can't afford a baby, neither of them are ready for a child, it'll fuck up their lives, and anyone else – me for example – would have marched her straight to a clinic, and voilà, no baby. But no, we know how much the boy loves his kids and can't make tough decisions, so he welcomes the pregnancy with open arms. His perfect girl has now become the fucking Virgin Mary incarnate. He hangs around her with a face like a wet week and waits for the fucking messiah to pop out.

'But then it all goes horribly wrong. And he's left with mostly perfect memories of a mostly perfect romance; the star-crossed lovers, Romeo and Juliet, Abelard and Heloise – you get my drift. Literature-loving little Markham is starring in his own doomed love affair. I'm not saying it wasn't serious and he wasn't heart-broken, but his Welsh temperament elevates the simplest occurrence to epic proportions. You've also got to remember, little Toni, that all this happened at university, that magical fucking place, where for three or four years you live in a world of make-believe. It's not reality, no nine-to-five, no rat race. They had a three-year holiday romance, if you like. How can his memories be anything but golden? And that's all they are, Toni. Memories. He dreams of her, but it's you he lives with, laughs with and makes love to. He hasn't seen her since his father died and that was more than four years ago. He doesn't even know her any more, if he ever really did. But if you keep on behaving like this, all hurt about something that was over years before he met you, you'll lose him. Sometimes he opens up the photo album and takes a little peep, but the bottom line here is, Lynn is dead and buried. Take my advice and don't fucking dig her up again."

"He was horrible to me, Dominic."

"Yes, and that was deplorable, and I'm certainly not excusing him. It was very wrong of him, but Toni, we all behave badly sometimes, you can't go on punishing him for ever."

She leant against him. "I always thought you were a bit of a bastard, Dom. Didn't care about any one except yourself. Charming, handsome, very shaggable, but basically just a bastard. But you're not, are you?"

He shrugged uncomfortably. "I like you and Markham. He's my best friend, for fuck's sake!"

"Pity *we* aren't on holiday."

"Yes, well if you mean what I think you mean, forget it. I'd never be able to look Steve in the face again."

"Well, he's having fun, touring! All those girls! And anyway, what about looking Harry in the face?"

"Ah, Harry and me, that's another story. We understand each other very well. And Toni, Stephen doesn't have groupies when he's in a relationship. I'm going home now." He got up. "Remember what I said. You love each other. Don't throw it away."

Toni stood up too, and leant against him, her right hand tracing the shape of his lips, her left playing with the soft hair at the nape of his neck.

He grinned and caught hold of her hands. "You just can't help it, can you? Stop being a prick-tease, Toni. You're too pregnant and you're too married to my best friend." His grin widened. "Life's a game to you, isn't it? That's fine with me, but be careful with Markham. He always plays by the rules and he never cheats." He kissed her on the nose and left.

Outside, he leant against the door. How the fuck he'd kept his hands off her, he didn't know, but he felt quite proud of himself. Sorry for Stephen though. He was pretty sure she wouldn't be unfaithful – but my God, she pushes it to the limits, he thought. He definitely foresaw trouble ahead in that marriage. He went home and had a very cold shower.

Stephen was due back on the sixteenth of December. On the afternoon of the fifteenth, Toni went shopping with Harry. She'd thought very hard about what Dominic had said. He was right, she did love Stephen and she wanted them to stay together. It didn't excuse the way Stephen had behaved, but he had apologised, profusely and often. She decided to forgive him, and wanted something new and pretty to wear for him. She hadn't told Harry about Dominic's visit; if he'd mentioned it to Harry, she hadn't said anything. Toni rather liked sharing a secret with Dominic, it made her feel special. After all, she thought, Stephen and Harry have so much history, it's only fair.

They were in Selfridges when she became aware of a feeling of warm wetness. "Harry, I think my waters have broken!"

"Oh, my God!" Harry helped her to a chair by the changing rooms and spoke urgently to the assistant. "They're calling an ambulance, Toni. Don't worry!"

Toni started to cry. "It's too early!"

Harry took her hand. "It'll be OK, Toni, it's only a few weeks, and you weren't sure of your dates, were you? Don't worry, it'll be fine." Please God, she thought.

"Stay with me?"

"Course I will!"

"I want Stephen!"

"I know, I know."

She started to have strong contractions in the ambulance; on examination, she was already six centimetres dilated. Harry phoned Dominic when they arrived at the hospital. He got hold of Sian, but couldn't reach Stephen.

He rang Harry back. "He must be on his way home by now. How's Toni?"

"Well, she's certainly in labour. I don't know if they'll be able to stop it."

"Poor little girl! Give her my love."

Toni's baby, another boy, was born three hours later, her usual easy labour. She was tremendously relieved he was all right, and kept asking them to check him just to make sure.

"Toni, he's fine. If he'd gone to term he couldn't be any healthier," Heather Donaldson assured her. "Honestly. He's a lovely wee boy!"

Stephen arrived home late on Friday afternoon, and let himself into the house. Ted came to the door as he shut it behind him.

"Ted! What's happened?"

"Toni had the baby yesterday. Don't worry, they're both fine. Karen's here, she's putting Alex to bed." Karen was Alex's nanny. "Sian's at the hospital."

Stephen slumped into a chair. "Fin overdosed on heroin this morning, that's why I'm late. I tried to ring but I couldn't get through."

"Jesus, Stephen. How is he?"

"Alive." He got up. "I'd better go and see Toni and the baby. What is it? It's not that I don't care, Ted, I do, I just feel shell-shocked."

"I know. It's a boy."

"A boy. And he's OK?"

"He's beautiful. Tiny, but beautiful. He weighs just over six pounds."

"I'll go and see Ally, and change, I feel like I've been wearing these clothes for a week! Then I'll go and see Toni – and Philip."

"Stevo! I thought you'd be here hours ago!" Toni held out her arms to him.

He sat on the edge of the bed and held her, relieved that she was pleased to see him, revelling in her and their new son. "I... um... I got delayed. How are you, Daisy? You look tired."

"I'm fine. Anaemic, Heather says, but apart from that, fine. What do you think of him? He's much quieter than Al."

Stephen looked at the tiny boy lying in the crib next to the bed. He was awake, gazing up at the ceiling.

"He's OK, isn't he?" he asked anxiously.

"Oh, for sure, they've checked him a million times. He's just good. Philip, say hello to your Daddy."

Stephen picked him up. "Philip Stephen Markham! That's a long name for such a little boy! I think we better call you Pip. God, he's like Alex, isn't he?"

"He is, except his eyes are black. So are you pleased?"

"Certainly am! You could have waited for me though!" He kissed her. "Well done, my little Glaucus. No more babies for a while though, I think," he said, looking at her searchingly. "You look washed out."

"I lost quite a bit of blood, but honestly, I'm OK. But you're right, we'll have a bit of a break. I *am* tired." She nestled against him. "Stevie?"

"Yeah?" He was staring down into his son's eyes.

"I'm sorry I wasn't your friend before. Dom came over and had a word to me while you were away."

He looked up at her. "Are you my friend now?"

"Mmmhmm," she nodded, smiling at him.

"Thank God for that! I was really lonely without you, my Toni."

Chapter Eleven
Eye Witness

And this is what we've made, sadness, death, last gasp, last breath,
And I am an eye witness to all these crimes, and no one cares,
Lost under an indifferent sky, a million grains of sand,
And I am an eye witness to the blood on all our hands.

Nothing had prepared Lynn for Africa. She couldn't believe the poverty and despair; it just wasn't feasible that people could live in conditions like these, and that the West did nothing about it. She felt raw with shock. All her problems, and what she had thought of as her suffering, were as nothing beside this. OK, she had miscarried her baby. Well, there were parents here who had watched their children die, one by one. There were children whose parents had died from AIDS or starvation, or been massacred by rebel forces. The toll of misery was appalling, and happening in a heat that amazed Lynn. It even smelt hot, she thought, like the blast you get when the oven is up to temperature and you open the door. She couldn't see how anyone managed to work in this heat, let alone fight.

Nuranda was a small country on the east coast of Africa, just south of the Equator, which had been ravaged by prolonged drought and a bloody and bitter civil war. There was an uneasy ceasefire at present, and the two warring factions were said to be in negotiations, but no one in Djari, the capital, seemed to feel that anything would come of it, there had been fresh outbreaks of fighting in the north already. The country wasn't really a great deal more than a stone's throw from the lush, green Rift Valley, almost close enough to see the fertile plains, but too far to get any benefit from them.

And yet, despite the dust and the heat and the blazing sun, the place had a stark, primal beauty. The sky was vast, always so blue, and at night it was a huge expanse of diamond spattered velvet. Even the stars were different here, strange constellations that awed and moved her. From the camp, she could just see Mount Mwale, whose summit, even in this burning heat, was always covered in snow, and the pearly sheen of the River Tigos. It reminded her of Stephen's guitar, a huge Fender Strat in Ocean Turquoise snaking through an alien land.

The camp was similar to the other refugee camps dotted all over the south of this country, although it was the largest in the area. It was a huge compound containing refugees from the north of Nuranda, victims of the war and the drought. They lived in huts, the refugees and the workers alike, but the hospital, the toilet and shower block, the canteen and the office had all been purpose built.

Lynn had been horrified when she'd first seen their hut. She'd accepted that it would be basic, but she hadn't expected this. It had an earth floor, covered in a worn jute mat. The bed had a metal base and looked supremely uncomfortable, and it was small, not much bigger than a single. We'll *melt*, lying squashed up together in that, she thought in dismay. There was an old filing cabinet for their clothes, a couple of folding chairs of the sort that campers use, three camp stools and a wooden table that had definitely seen better days.

At first she had been terrified of all the insects, had made Tim search their hut every night and kill any he found, although, as he pointed out, it was a drop in the ocean, and for every one he killed, there were ten more to take its place. These days she couldn't bear the thought of killing anything, there was so much death here. She just made sure she kept the mosquito net tucked tightly around the bed, which had turned out to be even more uncomfortable than it looked, although they were both so tired by bedtime that they were asleep almost before they'd finished making love.

Many of their co-workers were very religious. "How could anyone believe in God when there's such wicked suffering here – suffering that could so easily be prevented?" she asked Tim angrily, soon after they'd arrived.

He shook his head. "I don't know, Lynn. I can only suppose it sustains them in some way." He sighed. "At least they're here."

"Yes, that's true." I wish *I* wasn't, she thought. I don't know how much of this I can take. But she knew she couldn't leave.

The first time she saw a guinea worm being extracted from someone's leg she had to go and throw up. The thought of something like that living inside you! And it could so easily be prevented. It was obscene. All that was needed was clean drinking water, as the worm's larvae lived inside a water flea, which in turn lived in contaminated water. Which these people were forced to drink, because no one gave a toss about them. The thought of the outcry there'd be in Britain or the United States if even one person became infected made her burn with anger. She'd been told about the guinea worm, how the larvae broke through the lining of the stomach and settled just under the skin, usually around the ankle; how, maybe a year later, the pregnant female worm would release millions of larvae which would burst through the skin in the presence of water, leaving an opening in the leg. That alone had made Lynn shudder with horror, but even worse was the way the worm had to be wound out of the opening round a stick, a job that took several days and infinite patience, because if the worm broke it caused a severe and sometimes dangerous allergic reaction. And even after it was out, an abscess could form. The thought of it was horrific and nauseating, but actually seeing it was grotesque. She thought she'd never get over it, felt sick and shaky for hours afterwards, but now it had become commonplace, another of the many hideous things she just seemed to get used to.

She was working as an assistant administrator; Tim, of course, was one of the doctors. They had become very efficient, both at their jobs and at keeping their emotions under control. Strangely, their relationship was far better here than it had ever been. Tim was, if not happy, at least fulfilled, and she stayed because he was there and because she wouldn't have been able to stand knowing she had let these courageous, stoic, desperate people down.

"But that's what being brave is all about, Lynn," Tim had said to her once when she'd broken down and told him how she felt and how pathetic and spineless she was. "If it didn't affect you, staying would be easy. You stay despite the way you feel, don't you see?"

She did, and felt a little better. But she knew too that if it did become too much for her, she could run back to England at any time, she could escape if things got too rough. The refugees couldn't. There was nowhere they could go.

She was amazed at first to hear the other Westerners laughing and joking, sometimes even about the conditions at the camp. *How could they?* she thought, but within weeks she and Tim were doing the same. Silly little things still irritated her – having spots and then finding fine lines around her eyes. "It's so unfair," she grumbled to Tim, as they were getting ready for bed. "I thought there was supposed to be a gap after spots and before wrinkles when your skin was fantastic."

"Your skin *is* fantastic," Tim said, fondling her. "Your whole body is exceptionally amazing, even if you do taste of insect repellent."

And, as if to compensate in some obscure way for the carnage around them, their sex life was marvellous. Lynn wrote to Caro, asking her to send some sexy underwear, and she wore it for Tim.

The days fell into a pattern. This was their life, it was normality. One day she heard herself refer to their hut as home and realised that that's what it had become, this was home. "I thought of the hut as home today."

Tim looked up from a chart. He was on his way to the therapeutic feeding centre, where the malnourished babies were cared for. "It is home. We share it, it's our home. Wherever you are, that's home for me."

Lynn was touched. "We ought to name it."

"Hmm," Tim said. "You mean like Thisbeus?"

"Yeah, or Seaview."

They played this game for a several days. Tim suggested Black beri beri Cottage or Guinea Worms R Us, but they decided on Monsoon Blister.

"It's got a French quality to it," Tim said. "We could get deckchairs and sit out of an evening."

"Drinking cocktails and smoking Sobranie Black Russian cigarettes," Lynn agreed.

"If only we smoked!" he grinned.

On their wedding anniversary, they managed to get a weekend in Djari, the capital. Obviously people were better off here, they had homes, businesses, jobs, but it had a weary, defeated air, and the inhabitants lived in conditions that would never be tolerated in the West.

Tim and Lynn went out to the beach. The area had once been a colonial playground, and it was beautiful, the sand a stunning, dazzling white, with palm trees and coral islands out at sea.

"The Seychelles are over there." Tim pointed eastwards. "Seems unbelievable, doesn't it?"

Lynn nodded. "Yes," she agreed soberly. "It's like this place is on another planet, it's so far away from everything we know."

They went to a concert at the British Consulate on Saturday afternoon. People were standing around making polite conservation and sipping very alcoholic punch. It all had a strange air of unreality.

"Did you ever see that Peter Sellers film, *The Party*?" Lynn asked Tim quietly.

He raised his eyebrows. "Yes, I did. Why?"

"That's what this reminds me of. We'll be offered birdynumnums to eat any minute now."

Someone – an American ex-pat – gave them a joint. They took it back to their hotel and smoked it.

"Why is the sky so big here?" Lynn asked, watching the sun, a huge blood orange, melting into the far horizon.

"I don't know," Tim said. "But look at it though. Isn't it magnificent?"

"Do you miss England?" she wondered, idly. She didn't much at all.

"God, yes, all the time," he said fervently.

"Do you?" She was surprised. "Do you really, Tim? I thought you loved being here."

"I love the fact that we're trying to make a difference, but apart from that, no. It's too hot, too dry, too dusty and too foreign."

"Gosh!" Lynn didn't know what to say.

"Funny, isn't it, when it was me who wanted to come."

"Do you want to go back?"

"To England or to Monsoon Blister?"

"England."

"Yes, but I'm not going to. Not yet, anyway. What about you?"

"I'm happy wherever you are."

Tim took her in his arms. "You are so perfect."

Stephen and Toni spent the Christmas after Pip's birth with Sian and Ted, taking Rob with them.

"This is the best thing about what I do," Stephen said to Sian one afternoon. Ted had taken Rob and Alex out for a walk and Toni and Pip were asleep upstairs. Sian was cooking and Stephen was theoretically helping her. In fact, he was drinking lager and eating coffee creams.

"What is?" Sian asked. "Stuffing your face? You've always done that."

"No. *Not* doing it sometimes. I mean, I can choose what I want to do. I am so obscenely rich that I can do whatever I want. It's not right, is it?"

"Well, you've worked for it, cariad."

"Oh, Mum, come on! I've played my guitar and sung!"

"You write your songs too."

"Oh, yeah, course. And there's always the danger of writer's cramp. Any minute now, you'll be telling me there's nothing wrong with gala luncheons."

Sian smiled. "OK, you're a lazy little slob."

"That's better." He fiddled with his beer bottle.

"What is it, cariad?"

"What?"

"Come on, I know you. What's on your mind?"

"Do you remember Lynn's friend, Caro?"

"I don't think so."

"Well, it doesn't matter. It's just that I bumped into her before we came up here. Lynn and her husband are working in Africa."

Sian looked over at him. He was staring into the distance.

"That's… commendable."

"Yeah. It makes me realise how useless my life is. I mean, what is the point of what I do?"

"You make lots of people happy," Sian said sharply. "These days, that's important. Don't start soul-searching, Stephen, you've got a wife and three sons. They all depend on you."

"*What about the wife and kids, they all depend on me*," he sang.

Sian heard Ted come back with Rob and Alex. "Go and watch your video with Ted."

Toni had bought him a copy of *Local Hero* for Christmas. He'd go on and on about how great it was and Ted had expressed an interest in seeing it.

"OK. I'll ring Shelagh first and find out how Fin's getting on."

Fin had gone into a residential rehab programme after he came out of hospital.

Ted put the tape in and poured Stephen and himself a beer. Sian heard them laughing and sighed with relief. Bloody Lynn, she thought. Why can't she and her friends go and live in Outer Mongolia and never ever come back?

In the New Year, Stephen was asked to write the soundtrack for a new TV series, *Cambria's Chieftain*, based on the Welsh prince, Owain Glyndwr.

"Will there be acting to do?" Rob asked hopefully. He'd thoroughly enjoyed playing the child in *With Giants Fight*.

"No, Rob, no acting," It had been an experience, but not one Stephen wanted to repeat. He'd been offered a small recurring role in *Emmerdale Farm*, that of a singer, a recovering alcoholic, who buys a house in the area. He'd turned it down immediately, much to Toni's disappointment.

Cambria's Chieftain was set in the early 1400s in the Welsh Marches. He took Toni there at the end of January, ignoring her argument that Pip needed her. She wasn't breastfeeding him as she'd had mastitis twice and their doctor had advised her to bottle feed and take it easy.

"This is why we have a full-time, live-in nanny, Toni, so that we can go away on our own when we want and you can get some rest." Alex had just turned one and was walking, leaving trails of devastation in his wake. Stephen had taken to calling him the Hoon, a nickname Toni had threatened him with when they first got married. "Both Pip and that damned Hoon can manage without you for two weeks and we can always go home if we're needed."

Toni gave in and they had a marvellous time, despite the weather being cold and wet.

"It always rains in Wales," Stephen said. "That's part of its charm."

They stayed in Snowdonia for several days, but couldn't get to the top of Snowdon because of the weather. While they were in the area, he took her to Portmeirion, where *The Prisoner* had been filmed, and dragged her to the Lloyd George memorial just outside Criccieth, boring her almost to tears enthusing over the man. They went to Betws-y-Coed and saw the falls, and to Caernarfon castle.

"But I warn you, Stevo, any more Welsh history and I'm starting divorce proceedings on the grounds of cruelty," she told him. "And no more bloody singing!" She'd always found his habit of singing aloud, no matter where he was, embarrassing and irritating; in Wales it became unbearable. He was constantly singing, either in Welsh, which made her cringe, or some sort of patriotic song: 'Cwm Rhondda', 'Land Of My Fathers', 'Men Of Harlech'. She wasn't sure which was worse.

At the end of the two weeks they crossed the border and stayed with Toni's mother, Sandy, in Chester.

"Will you be normal again, now we've left Wales?" Toni asked as they were undressing.

"What do you mean?" he responded, amused.

"No more of this Welsh national stuff, stirring poetry and battle songs?"

"Don't you like it?" Stephen grinned, getting into bed.

"You know I bloody well don't!" she retorted. "Hey, stop hogging the hot water bottle!"

"This one's mine," he teased. "First come, first served."

"Talking of first come," she said, reaching for him. They caressed each other for a while and then he got out of bed.

"Where are you going?" Toni demanded.

"To get a condom. Damn! We've used them all."

"Oh, well, never mind, we'll be all right."

"No, we won't. I'm not risking you getting pregnant again."

"But, Stevo! I really want it!"

"Well, we'll just have to manage with fingers and tongues."

"It's not the same, mate!"

"Even so." He was adamant.

"Well, all right, if you're going to be mean, we won't bother at all!"

"Toni, don't be silly. You can't have your own way all the time."

"Oh, come on, Stephen, what are the chances of me getting pregnant?"

"Fucking high, judging by the fact you've had two babies in less than a year!" He was starting to get annoyed. "Be a good girl, Toni, and see sense."

"How dare you talk to me as if I'm a child!"

"Well, stop behaving like one."

"You bastard!"

"Oh, suck it up, Toni. I'm going to sleep." He lay down, his back to her.

"Don't you dare turn your back on me!" He ignored her. "Stephen!"

He didn't answer.

She picked up the glass of water from her bedside table and emptied it over his head.

"Bloody hell!" He leapt out of bed, dripping.

Toni started to laugh.

"You bloody bitch! The pillow's soaking wet! I can't sleep on that!"

"You should have thought of that before you ignored me. Goodnight." She lay down and turned off her bedside light.

Stephen stared at her. He picked up her towelling robe, dried himself on it and threw it at her, put his pyjamas on and opened the door.

"Where are you going?"

"I'm sleeping on the sofa."

Toni grinned to herself. Sandy had a large bull terrier who slept on the sofa at night. "Gwen'll be pleased to have some company."

He'd forgotten Gwen. "Christ on fucking crutches!"

"Come back to bed, Stephen."

"No fucking way."

He slept on an armchair in the sitting room and the next day his back hurt more than it ever had before.

Toni was completely unsympathetic. "And you accused *me* of being childish!" was all she said.

Harry and Dominic's baby was due at the beginning of April. Harry couldn't think why she'd waited so long before having another one, all the emotions she'd felt when she was expecting Rob came rushing back. Apart from a few miserable weeks when she couldn't seem to stop being sick, she was feeling so well.

Dominic was delighted, enjoying her pregnancy almost as much as she was. He loved feeling the baby kick.

They lay on the bed together at the beginning of February, his hand on her bump, a rapt expression on his face. "I love this little bairn so much," he said. "You wait, Harry, I'm going to be such a good father."

She thought he was being flippant at first, as he so often was, but caught a note in his voice that she'd never heard before. She shifted position, and saw that he had tears in his eyes. She was astounded; she knew how much he loved her, but he wasn't a very demonstrative man, and he never cried.

"Dominic! Of course you'll be a good father, you'll be the best! How could you be anything else?" She stroked his hair.

He smiled at her and was silent for a few seconds, his hand caressing her stomach. When he spoke again, he was his usual self. "Too fucking right, Harry, how could I possibly be anything but the best?" He leant over and kissed her.

At the end of the month, she and Toni went shopping for baby clothes. Dominic stayed at home and watched football with Stephen.

"Is there anything to eat?" Stephen asked.

"We're having fucking dinner later!"

"That's not for hours!" Stephen protested. "I'm starving, Charlie."

"How about a Mars Bar?" Dominic asked, coming back from the kitchen. "I don't want to touch anything else without asking Harry."

Stephen made a mewing noise and mimed cracking a whip.

"Do you want this fucking Mars or not?" Dominic chucked the sweet over to him. "Did you ever do that thing with a Mars Bar? You know, like… like someone and someone… Mick Jagger and Marianne Faithfull, I think. " Stephen nodded, his mouth full. "What did you think?"

"It was all right. Lynn thought it was a waste of a good Mars Bar."

"You did it with *Lynn*?"

"Yes, with Lynn. Why do you say it like that?"

Dominic shrugged. "I just can't imagine Lynn in any position except missionary, frankly, old chap. No offence."

Stephen was annoyed. "I hope you don't imagine Toni in sexual positions!"

"Well, fuck you. My imagination is my own business. And considering you've had my wife anyway, I don't see that you can object."

"That's totally different! It was in the past, before you two even met!"

"Well, so's Lynn."

"Yeah, Lynn is, but not Ton—"

"Hello, you, two." Harry came in before Stephen finished speaking, and dropped a kiss on Dominic's head. "Come and see what we bought."

Over dessert, Dominic grinned at Stephen. "Who would you most like to be stuck in a lift with, Markham?"

"What do you mean?" Toni asked before Stephen could answer. She'd been in a strange mood all evening, he thought, very animated, but barbed with it. She'd drunk a considerable amount, as they all had, apart from Harry.

"Dominic, is this a good idea?" Harry asked.

He threw her a look Stephen couldn't interpret, and smiled at Toni. "Harry and I were watching *What's New Pussycat* the other day, and there's that scene where Peter O'Toole and Capucine get stuck in the lift and have sex, and we got talking about who we'd like to get stuck in a lift with."

"Who did you choose?" Toni asked, looking up at him from under her lashes.

His smile deepened. "Who would *you* choose?"

"I'm not sure this is a good idea, Dom," Harry repeated uneasily.

"It's just a bit of fun, Harry. Come on then, young Antonia."

"I asked first." Toni smiled coquettishly.

Stephen frowned. What the fuck is the matter with her tonight? he wondered. He knew that she and Dominic found each other attractive, but she'd never behaved like this with him before. He was annoyed with both of them. It wasn't fair to upset Harry in her condition, and he could see she was perturbed.

"I love that film," he said, hoping to change the subject. "Romy Schneider always reminds me of you, Hal. I wonder what happened to her? I've never seen her in anything else."

"Who did you choose, Harry?" Toni queried, ignoring him.

"Peter Davison."

Stephen tried again. "Oh, yes, you've always liked him, I remember watching *All Creatures Great And Small* and you drooling over Tristan! Have you seen *Campion*?"

"Yes, excellent, isn't it?" Harry replied. "Talking of detectives, did you see—"

"Never mind that," Toni interrupted rudely. "What about you, Dom?"

"Marilyn Monroe, Chrissie Hynde, and Tegan from *Dr Who*."

Toni put her hand on his arm and stroked it with her thumb. "Three's greedy," she said suggestively.

"He's always been a bit of a pig, haven't you, Dominic?" Harry was still smiling, but it no longer quite reached her eyes.

Dominic shrugged. "I couldn't choose between them. Come on then, Toni."

"It'll be Mel Gibson," grinned Stephen.

"Wrong," Toni said, not looking at him. "It's you, Dom."

Stephen went white. Harry looked astonished and then furious.

"What about you, Stephen?" Toni asked, staring challengingly at him.

"Lynn."

There was a horrified silence.

"You bastard!" Toni hissed. "I'm going home!"

Stephen shrugged. "You know where it is."

She swept angrily from the room and they heard the front door slam.

"God, Stephen!" Dominic was shocked.

Stephen turned on him. "You and Toni seem very close all of a sudden. She said you had a word with her while I was away. Are you sure that's all you had?"

"Stephen!" Harry exclaimed. "I asked Dom to speak to her!"

"Yes, don't be fucking stupid, Markham," Dominic said, annoyed.

"Well, you made it pretty clear earlier that you resent those times Harry and I slept together."

"Times?" Dominic frowned, puzzled. "But Harry said—"

Stephen didn't even hear him speak. "Perhaps you thought you were owed Toni," he went on furiously.

Dominic lost his temper. "I think you'd better go home before I punch your fucking lights out, old chap."

"You and whose army?"

Dominic leapt at him. They were pretty evenly matched; Dominic was taller, with a longer reach, but Stephen was fitter.

"Stop it!" Harry screamed at them.

They took no notice.

"I'm in labour!" she yelled at the top of her voice.

"What?" Dominic exclaimed in panic. "Sit down, Harry, no lie down! Stephen, you've been through this, what do we do?"

"Ring the car and get the hospital… no, I mean…"

"I'm not actually in labour," Harry admitted. She sank down onto the sofa and started to cry. "I didn't know how else to stop you."

Dominic squatted down next to her, appalled. "Harry, we're so sorry."

"We are," Stephen nodded. "It was all my fault."

"It was all fucking Toni's fault," Dominic said savagely. "You ought to take your belt to her, Stephen."

"I'm inclined to agree," Stephen said.

"Don't hit her!" Harry cried in alarm.

"Don't worry, Harry; I couldn't. I couldn't hit a woman."

"I might make an exception in her case," Dominic muttered. "Stephen, I give you my word, nothing has ever happened between us." Not for want of trying on her part, he thought.

"I know. I was angry with her and I took it out on you, Dominic. Are you sure you're all right, Hal?"

Harry nodded shakily. "I'd like to go to bed."

"Yeah, I'm going home." He kissed Harry and offered Dominic his hand. "Sorry, Dominic."

Dominic shook it. "For fuck's sake stop calling me Dominic. It makes me nervous."

Stephen couldn't face sleeping with Toni that night, he was too angry, and he was very tempted by Dominic's advice. He slept in one of the guest rooms.

The next morning he went through to their dressing room to get a pair of jeans.

Toni had just woken up. "Is that you, Stevo? Can you get me some aspirin? I've got a thumping headache."

"Good," he said, but he fetched the aspirin. He went on into the dressing room and stopped dead in the doorway. "What the fuck?" Every pair of trousers he possessed was strewn around the room, the crutch cut out. He turned to Toni. "What the fuck have you done?"

"Oh. Oh, yeah. I remember. I was as mad as a cut snake last night. I wanted to cut your balls off. That was the next best thing."

"Jesus!" He sat on the bed. "Why, Toni? You were funny with me all evening. What did I do? Or do you just want a divorce so you can go after Charlie? But I'll tell you something. After last night, I don't think you'll get very far with him."

"No, of course I don't want a divorce! I don't want Dom." She started to cry. "How could you say that? How could you even think it? How could you be so mean?"

"Me?" Stephen asked incredulously.

"Yes, you. You were talking to Dom about Lynn yesterday when me and Harry got home."

"For God's sake, Toni! For a start, how did you know it was Lynn my ex we were talking about? There's a Lynne who works for Cell, you know that! I might have been talking about her!"

"Were you?"

"No, but—"

"There you are then!" Toni interrupted triumphantly.

"Let me finish, Toni. Lynn was my wife. Now, I've told you, and apparently Charlie's told you, that's over, she's in the past, you're my wife now and I love you. But for Christ's sake, Charlie was at university with us, sometimes we're going to talk about those days and we might mention Lynn! If you can't accept that she was a part of my life, then I don't see how we can have a future. Come on, stop crying."

"I'm sorry," she sobbed. "I was upset."

He sighed. "All right. But please, Toni, let this be the last time!"

"OK." She peered at him. "Where did you get that bruise on your cheek from?"

"I had a fight with Charlie after you'd gone home."

A smile tugged at the corners of her mouth. "Over me?" she asked archly.

He scowled. "Because of you, not over you. I told you, Charlie's pretty disgusted with you, Toni. For one thing, he loves Harry very much, and you upset her yesterday. I think you should apologize."

She was indignant. "Mate!"

"I mean it, Toni."

"Can't you? You know her better than me. I was drunk and my hormones are still messed up."

"No. This is your fault, you'll have to talk to her. Knowing Hal, she'll say forget it."

Toni started to cry again. "I don't think I can, I'm too ashamed. Supposing they don't want to be my friend?"

"OK, OK, I'll come with you," Stephen said resignedly.

She stopped crying. "Thanks, mate."

After a very long and difficult labour, Harry gave birth to a girl.

"How are you?" Stephen asked with concern, when he and Toni went in to see them.

Dominic was holding the baby, who they'd named Amabel. "Absolutely fucking shattered, old man. It was hell. I understand why husbands always used to go to the pub. Can't think why it's not fucking compulsory!"

"I meant Harry, you tosser!"

Harry smiled up at him. She was so tired she could barely move, he noticed.

"I'm fine, very happy. Do you think your mum would mind if we had Sian as her middle name? She's like a mother to me."

Stephen kissed her. "I think she'd be overjoyed."

As well as the soundtrack, Stephen had been doing sessions, which he enjoyed tremendously and for which he was in great demand. His superb playing enhanced a lot of albums and he prized the experience of working with other musicians. To his surprise, he found he rather valued this enforced time out from the world of touring and recording. Until Fin was ready, Sid's Six was on the sidelines.

He thought seriously about buying a house outside London. He didn't much like living in London, couldn't see the appeal of city life; as far as he was concerned, cities were dirty, noisy, soulless places. People talked of them having energy, a buzz, but he couldn't see it. Most of the inhabitants seemed to him to be to be tired and grey, moving and living like automatons. And then there was Rob's asthma. It wasn't really any worse, but it worried him. He had grown up so close to the countryside, the beautiful Yorkshire Dales, and York, although technically a city, was nothing like London. It was small and beautiful, and he wanted Rob, Alex and Pip to have the same sort of environment. He started to look at houses near Oxford, and finally found what he wanted just outside the village of Burford, in West Oxfordshire.

Ingleston Old Priory was a Tudor manor house, which had actually been a Priory before the dissolution of the monasteries. Shortly before her death, Elizabeth Tudor granted the land and ruined building to a favourite courtier, Edmund Gascoyne, who had reconstructed it on typically Tudor lines; a hall block with a central porch flanked by two gabled wings. It had come onto the market after the death of the last member of the family.

Toni was very resistant to the idea. "I like it in London," she protested when Stephen showed her the details. "I love this house. I don't want to move."

"Well, we don't have to sell this house, we'll still need a place in London, but it would be so good for us all to live somewhere clean and unpolluted. Come on, Toni, you're a country girl! At least come and look at it," Stephen implored. "It's brilliant, Daisy, it's got, um..." He took the brochure from her. "'*Seven reception rooms and twelve bedrooms suites, all with ensuite bathrooms*'," he read, "'*three house bathrooms, a stillroom, a large, walk in pantry with marble counters to keep the food cool, a warren of attic rooms, and cellars. The house is set in forty acres, and the river Windrush runs through the grounds*'. " He looked up at Toni. "The agent told me that the same family have lived there for nearly four hundred years. Four hundred years! Imagine that!"

Toni raised her eyebrows. "They must be old! What are they, vampires or something?" she asked flippantly. "Stop trying to engage my enthusiasm, Stephen!"

"Oh, Toni, please come and look at it! Pretty please? Pretty please with sugar on? Pretty please with sugar on and..."

"All right, all right! Anything to shut you up!"

They met the agent in Oxford and followed him out to the house.

"Beautiful countryside," Stephen commented, glancing at Toni, who gave him a jaundiced look. Five miles out of Burford, they turned right through large, wrought iron gates, and up a long, curving avenue lined with huge old chestnut trees, their branches heavy with candle blossom, and bluebells budding in the rough grass around their gnarled roots.

"This is lovely," Toni breathed.

"Told you," Stephen replied, with satisfaction, as they pulled up beside the agent's car.

The house stood before them, solid and imposing. Built from Cotswold stone, which had weathered, as Cotswold stone does, to a beautiful, golden patina, it looked as if it had been dipped in sunshine. Huge Tudor chimneys, Elizabethan status symbols, soared up into the heavens. The steep roofs, gables, and turrets provided a fascinating, variegated skyline, and narrow, mullioned windows marched in rows across the front of the house, their diamond shaped panes of glass – that other emblem of Tudor wealth – catching and reflecting the light with dazzling intensity. Hosts of daffodils grew against the foundations in golden drifts, and the smooth, emerald lawn ran down to the tree-lined banks of the Windrush.

The agent joined them. "Impressive, isn't it? The original building dates from 1140, but most of this was built in 1601 – two years before Elizabeth the First died."

Toni grinned. "If we buy it, we could get one of those half-timbered cars, Stevo!"

"Those what?"

"You know the ones, they're old, and they've got wood round the top half."

"Oh, Morris Minors! Yeah, that'd be fun!"

The agent ushered them into the house, and they wandered from room to room. One of the bedrooms had a priest hole, and the staircases in the east and west wings were reputed to be haunted. The main staircase was massive, made of solid oak, rising uncarpeted from the wooden floor of the entrance hall, the steps worn smooth and uneven over the centuries.

They finished up in the Great Hall.

"This would probably have been the monks' refectory," the agent remarked.

Stephen and Toni stared at the enormous room. It had a high, vaulted ceiling, and the walls were covered with exquisite linenfold panelling. The long, narrow windows had stained glass heraldic shields set in the upper panes, which cast delicate rainbows of azure and argent, vert and violet on the polished flagstones, and there was a raised dais at one end, ornamented by a canopy of elaborately carved wood. At the opposite end of the room was a deep minstrel's gallery.

Toni loved it. "Mate! It's like something out of a film!" She stood on the dais. "We can have thrones put here and dispense justice!" She gazed round the room. "And we can give the most amazing parties!"

Stephen turned to the agent with a grin. "Sold!"

Outside there were formal gardens, a herb garden, a sunken rose garden and a bluebell wood. Stephen found the whole place utterly tranquil, and he felt deeply at peace there.

Rob loved it. "Can we live here every day?"

"Every day in the holidays," Stephen promised rashly. "You can have a puppy. We'll go and choose one next weekend."

Alex, who was now seventeen months old, was enchanted with his new playground. He was a sturdy and determined child, and put Stephen very forcibly in mind of Jacko, although he looked like Sian. He was as imperious as Toni, who utterly adored him and made no secret of the fact. Stephen thought she spoiled him and said so. Toni retorted furiously that considering Stephen spent ninety-nine per cent of the time that Alex was awake rehearsing, recording, touring or just playing guitar, he had absolutely no right to criticise her parenting skills. Stephen coldly replied that she was talking rubbish; he spent masses of time with Alex and he had every right to comment on the way his son was raised. This dispute was never resolved and simmered just below the surface of their marriage, periodically boiling over into a full-scale row.

Stephen took Alex and Rob to see the Windrush. It was June and very hot. Alex started taking his clothes off. "Swim, Daddeee!" he chuckled.

Stephen had been taking him and Pip swimming since they were babies, as he had Rob, and he was in the process of having a swimming pool installed at the Priory. He smiled. "Yes, all right, Ally. Do you want to paddle, Rob?"

Rob had just had his ninth birthday. "Can I get my new water gun, Dad?"

"I suppose so," Stephen said cautiously.

"Great!"

Stephen took off his Kickers and socks and rolled up the legs of his jeans. He undressed Alex, and, holding him under the arms, put the little boy, naked, into the shallows. The water came up over Alex's knees. It was cold, but he laughed with glee, slapping it with his palms.

Rob and Dominic came back with Rob's gun. Dominic filled it up and gave it to him.

"Just don't shoot Alex, Rob," Stephen warned.

Rob shot the gun indiscriminately around.

"If only we had more," Dominic said, "we could have a real battle." He took his shoes and socks off, and stood in the water. "God, it's fuc – furiously cold!"

"It's lovely when you get used to it," Stephen said. "You better come out though, Alex, you're getting cold." He picked Alex up.

"No! No!" Alex shouted. "Swim! Lix swim!"

"No more swim," Stephen said firmly, carrying him back to the bank.

Alex went rigid, arching his back. "Lix swim!" he wailed.

"No! Stop being naughty!"

Alex screwed up his face and screamed deafeningly. Then, to Dominic's consternation, he stopped crying and held his breath. His lips went slightly blue.

"God, Stephen, he's dying!" Dominic said in alarm.

Stephen gave Alex a sharp slap on his bottom. The little boy started to breathe again, howling dismally. Stephen dumped him down on the grass, where his crying subsided into hiccups as he was distracted by a caterpillar. He poked at it with a fat little finger, chuckling.

Stephen deftly dressed him. "It's just temper. Horrific, isn't it?"

Dominic nodded, shaken. "Takes after Toni, doesn't he?"

Stephen grinned. "Don't ever let her hear you say that, Charlie! She's convinced he gets it from me."

"I hope Amabel doesn't do it."

"Well, Rob never did, did you, Robbie? Robbie? Where is he?"

Rob was nowhere to be seen.

"Rob!" Stephen called, beginning to get worried. He was answered by loud laughter from above him and a gush of freezing water. Gasping in shock, soaking wet, he looked up to see Rob peering at them from the branches of one of the lovely old chestnut trees that lined the banks. "Rob!" He was furious. "Come down *now*!"

"Got you!" Rob shouted and turned the gun on Dominic.

"You little swine!" Dominic bellowed. He shinned up the tree after Rob, who slid down the other side and ran back to the house, convulsed with mirth.

Toni was very taken with the idea of Alex and Pip eventually attending the Dragon prep school in North Oxford, but Stephen wasn't so keen.

"Oh, come on, Stevo, it's a really good school. It takes day pupils, you know."

"Yes, I know." He smiled at her. "I didn't think you were suggesting we farm them out to boarding school. No, the thing is, do we really want the boys going to that sort of school?"

Toni stared at him. "That's usually what people like us say about state schools!"

He laughed. "I just mean I don't want them growing up different from other children."

"What are you talking about? Think of the sort of people they'd be mixing with!"

"Yes, that's exactly it! I went to ordinary schools and so did you. Obviously we'll make sure that whatever school they go to is academically sound, but, well, I don't want them growing up like Charlie."

Toni was astounded. "He's your best friend!"

"I know, and you know how much I like him, and these days he's atypical of that class, but you know the sort of Sloane Ranger type I mean. And you didn't know Charlie when he was younger, he was pretty obnoxious. I always maintained it was because he wasn't happy, and that was mostly true, but there was an element of that upper class snobbishness in there too."

"Well!" Toni shook her head. "I never realised there was such a socialist streak in you! Dad'll be rapt!"

Stephen shrugged uncomfortably. "I suppose it's something I get from my father."

Toni kissed him. "I think it's sweet."

As promised, Stephen and Toni took Rob to a rescue centre to find a puppy.

He chose a Cairn crossed with a Yorkshire Terrier. The little dog was nine weeks old and looked like a brown furry tennis ball. Rob called him Turtle.

"Why Turtle?" queried Stephen.

"Because *Leonardo* is my favourite turtle," Rob explained.

Stephen waited but Rob didn't elucidate. "Then why not call him Leonardo?" he asked eventually.

Rob sighed. "Does he look like Leonardo, Dad?"

"Well, no."

"Exactly! He looks like Michaelangelo, and I don't like Michaelangelo that much."

Stephen raised his eyebrows. "Of course. Silly me."

Rob gave him an encouraging look and patted his leg. "Never mind, Dad, you can't help it." He took Turtle off to train him.

At the rescue centre, Toni had fallen in love with a tiny Welsh corgi puppy, part of an unwanted litter, and they brought her home, too. Stephen suggested the name Bronwen.

"That's not the name of one of your old girlfriends, is it?" Toni inquired suspiciously.

"Yeah, a bit of a dog!" Stephen joked. "No, Toni, I swear. It's just a Welsh name and it seems to suit her. Bron!" he said to the little creature, who wagged her tail at him. "I'm glad she's not had her tail docked."

"Too right! It's cruel and unnecessary!"

They also adopted a large tabby kitten who'd been abandoned. He'd been brought in on a Tuesday and the staff at the rescue centre had named him Mardi Gras.

"What a great name!" Stephen approved. "Suits him too."

The Priory had become very much Stephen's home. He felt happier there, more at ease than he'd done for a long time.

"I think Dad would have really liked it here," he said to Sian when she and Ted came to stay. "In fact sometimes..." He broke off.

"Sometimes?" Sian prompted.

"Sometimes I feel as if he's here," Stephen finished in a rush. "That's stupid, isn't it?"

Sian shook her head. "It just means you're finally at peace with your memories, cariad," she said gently. "I wondered if you'd chosen Oxford because of John."

"I didn't realise I had. Not until we moved in. Then I suddenly felt terrible for a few days, as if he'd only just died. It was appalling. But lately, I've had the feeling that he's... well, pleased."

Sian took his hand. They sat in silence. "And who knows?" she said. "Maybe he *is* here." Stephen stared at her. "Well, part of him, anyway. You're here, your boys are here. The part of him that's in all of you. You haven't been able to acknowledge that before."

Stephen nodded. "I felt too guilty about him, so I could never think about him properly. Here I can."

Stephen had invited Fin and Shelagh to stay at the Priory for as long as they wanted after Fin left rehab. Fin looked tired, but at peace with himself. He and Shelagh had married the week before, telling no one except their families.

"You don't mind, Steve? And you don't think Andy and George will?" he asked anxiously. "I went to everyone's."

Stephen smiled ruefully. "Several times in my and Andy's case! Of course I don't mind, I think it was a wise thing to do. The last thing you needed was a media circus! How are you, Fin?"

"I'm OK." He nodded and Stephen saw Shelagh's hand slip into his. "Yeah, I'm OK, Steve. I'm so sorry. I nearly ruined everything." Tears shone in his eyes and he wiped them impatiently. "God, I hate that! I'm so emotional all the time these days."

"Now you know how I feel," Stephen joked. "If I wasn't so incredibly nice, I'd be calling you a lass!"

Fin grinned. "Just don't tell George!"

The day after they left, Stephen received a package from Miles Tindall, containing a script for a psychological thriller called *Hoodman Blind*. Miles had written the script and was producing it himself, and wanted Stephen to play one of the leads, David Powell.

Stephen was surprised and flattered. He hadn't considered acting again and wasn't sure he wanted to, but he was tempted. Miles was a hugely talented and respected director. He was even more tempted by the fact that the female lead was to be played by Coral Mathieu, and Des Wolfe, who had been in *With Giants Fight* with him, and had since become a big star, had been offered the part of the other male lead.

He went to find Toni, who was delighted. "You know I want you to do more acting, darling! Take it!"

"Yes, but Toni, there's a love scene in it."

"Naked, you mean?"

"Well, the girl will be."

"But not you?"

He shook his head.

"Who's playing the girl?"

"Coral Mathieu."

"Oh, the girl in *Blaise?*"

Since Stephen and Coral had split up, Coral had co starred in an American TV series set in the Wild West. It was a comedy drama about a gunfighter turned sheriff, known only by his surname, Blaise. Coral played Brianne, the singer at the local saloon, who provided Blaise's love interest.

"Yes." Stephen didn't know if Toni knew he and Coral had been lovers. Their affair had been brief, but very intense. It had been in the papers at the time, and he had been quite serious about her. One of the reasons they had separated was that Coral wanted to break into acting and had gone to Hollywood. The other was that Stephen couldn't quite bring himself to commit to her. After Lynn, he was scared. He'd regretted it very much when she'd gone. He decided to say nothing.

"So you won't be naked?"

"No, Toni."

"Well, then, I can't see why you shouldn't do it, mate! Can I read the script?"

She was rather disappointed that he would be playing the villain.

"Yes, but see, everyone thinks David Powell is the hero, right until the end," he pointed out. He liked the fact that David was an evil character, it made him so much more interesting. "And Des's character, is thought of as the baddie all the way through and then he gets killed."

"Yeah, I suppose. It's exciting, isn't it?"

He smiled. "Yes, Toni, it is. I'll be away on location, you realise that, don't you?"

"Course I do, I read Miles's letter. It's only seven weeks and it's only Scotland. We can come up and stay now and then, can't we? And if you and I want some time alone, Alex and Pip will be fine here with Karen. Just for a few days, of course," she added.

"They will," he said fondly. She was very maternal, and hated leaving the boys; in fact she'd decided not to go back to work. "Children should have one of their parents at home all the time, Stevo, and anyway, I couldn't stand not being with them." She was involved in fundraising for endangered species, but she mostly did that from home.

"Well, then, you better ring Miles and tell him you want to do it."

Filming started on the Isle of Skye towards the end of August.

Coral was overjoyed to see Stephen. "I am *so* glad you're playing David."

They were sitting in his trailer, drinking beer. She hasn't changed at all, he thought, and she's even more alluring. She had long, wavy red hair – coral coloured, which was why her English mother had named her Coral – big, very dark blue eyes, and a superb figure, slim and piquant. He remembered, with pleasure, making love to her.

"I am not looking forward to the nudity, Stevie."

"Why did you agree to it?"

She shrugged. "I really want to be in films. And to work with Miles Tindall! Such an opportunity doesn't come along every day."

"Don't worry about it. Miles promised me it'll be a closed set, and you've got a terrific body, Coco."

"So have you, but you don't have to be naked."

"Well, not on screen, no… but if it'll help, I'll be naked while we film, so you won't be the only one."

"You would really do that, Stevie?"

"Yeah, course."

She sat on his lap and stroked his hair back off his face. "Why don't you get this cut? It's always falling into your eyes!"

He smiled. "I suppose I must like it like this." He tightened his arm around her, pinning her to him.

"I've missed you very much, Stevie," she whispered.

She still smelt the same, a mixture of roses and vanilla. It brought back such a welter of memories. He could feel her breasts pressing against his chest, and couldn't resist caressing them. After all, he soothed his conscience, we were as good as married once, and it's not like anything's going to happen.

Coral leant forward and kissed him, wriggling her tongue against his lips.

He opened his mouth and they french kissed.

She sighed with pleasure. "Shall we rehearse our scene, Stevie?" she asked suggestively.

"I really don't think that'd be a good idea, Coco," he said with regret.

They shared a joint before filming the love scene. It made Coral giggly, much to Miles's disapproval. When he finally called 'cut', Stephen picked up a marker pen that had been left on a table by the bed and rolled Coral over onto her stomach. She had a smattering of freckles at the base of her spine, and he joined them up with the pen so that they formed the shape of an uneven heart. "I always wanted to do that," he grinned, kissing her bottom.

"Wipe that ink off her," Miles ordered. "Stephen, dear boy, do that again when the camera's rolling. We're putting it in!"

Two days later, the tabloids were full of the sex scene stories: *Sid's Sex Shocker! Sizzling Sex Romp! Stephen Markham Bares All!*

"I thought it was a closed set!" Stephen said furiously to Miles.

Miles shrugged. "I'm sorry, Stephen, but these things happen. Any member of the crew could've talked to the press. It's an easy way of earning a few quid."

"Bloody hell! I've had Toni shouting at me on the phone for the last hour!"

Miles grinned. "Think of the publicity though!"

"Yeah," Stephen said sourly. "Hooray."

Miles spoke to the press calmly and prosaically, saying there was nothing romantic or erotic about filming a sex scene. "Shooting these scenes is very technical, almost mechanical; a matter of 'Could you turn this way? Move your leg that way?' It's more a question of choreography than anything else," he said. "I always close the set in order to give the actors privacy, and to make them feel as comfortable as I can. It's certainly not unusual for the actors involved to film naked, even if that does not appear in the final cut. Again, it's a matter of keeping everyone as comfortable and relaxed as possible."

This duly appeared in the papers, and Stephen gave a sigh of relief. Coral, however, with the very best of intentions, then gave an interview explaining that Stephen had only filmed naked because she had been apprehensive about the scene, but she couldn't help adding that they'd relaxed in her trailer first, and smoked a 'herbal cigarette' to calm her nerves, and saying what a great time they'd had shooting, and talking about Stephen's spontaneous dot-to-dot with her freckles. So he wasn't in the least surprised when Toni appeared on the set like one of the Furies.

"Well, Stephen Markham! What have you got to say for yourself?"

"Toni! We're filming!"

"I couldn't give a flying fuck, mate!"

"All right, everyone, let's take a break," Miles said with resignation and amusement. He shot Stephen a look of commiseration.

"Come on, Toni, come and shout at me in the trailer," Stephen said wearily.

"You never told me you lived with her!"

"Toni, it was in all the papers at the time."

"Yeah, well, I don't read that gossip stuff!"

That stunned him. "Don't lie! You love reading the gossip columns!"

She ignored him. "So I suppose you enjoyed yourself then? At my expense!"

Stephen was beginning to get cross. "Actually, yes, I did. It was fun."

She raised her hand to hit him, but he caught her wrist and pulled her against him. "Not nearly so much fun as the real thing is with you, my lovely Toni."

Her eyes filled with tears. "Do you really mean that, Stevo?"

"Of course I do, little Glaucus." He bent his head and kissed her. "Toni, why do you get so jealous? Nothing, absolutely no sex, happened with Coc— Coral. A little caressing and kissing, but that's all."

"I don't know. You're *mine*, Stephen. And she's French, and so pretty, with her long, curly, pink hair and that slim, sexy body! And she's only twenty-three." Toni was going to be thirty the following February, and wasn't looking forward to it.

"She can't hold a candle to you," Stephen said, undressing her. He spent the next hour soothing, stroking, praising and making love to her. Finally, practically purring with pleasure, she was driven to his hotel.

"My dear boy, how did you manage to turn her from devil woman to sweet adoring angel like that?" Miles asked.

"The same way I always do. Told her she's the most breathtakingly beautiful woman in the world and took her to bed." He sighed. "There was a sitcom on in the seventies set in a Welsh village, I can't remember anything about it except that Kenneth Griffith was in it, and someone once said, about a stormy marriage, 'Duw, Duw'—"

"Duw?" queried Miles.

"Welsh for God. 'Duw, what kind of a marriage is this that needs a new engine every few weeks?' That's the way I feel about me and Toni sometimes. She read the script, but she still wanted me to make this film, she wants the glamour and the money…" He broke off, shaking his head.

Miles patted him on the back. "Do you know, they're all the bloody same. Can't live with them, can't live without them! Come on, Stephen, let's get back to work."

For the rest of the film, the press hung annoyingly around, trying to get him to talk to them.

"They wouldn't like what I said," he told Coral.

He went straight into the recording studio when he finished filming, this time to produce Andy's solo album, 'Rock Goes The Weasel'. He also wrote and performed on several of the tracks.

Andy recorded under the name Clifton Rock, and a photo of his weasely little face, grinning hugely, adorned the sleeve. At the end of the recording he and Holly got married, holding the reception at his house in London, where they were living. "I took your advice, Steve," he confided. "Holly's up the spout, she's nearly three months gone. I'm as happy as a pig in clover!"

By Christmas, Fin was well enough for the band to record another album, 'Keeping It Real'. It was their fifth and, as usual, did very well, as did the singles 'Fat Girls', about anorexic girls 'dying to be thin', and 'She'll be Apples', a rockabilly number Stephen wrote for Toni. The band toured Britain and the Continent in the New Year.

Andy's album acquired a cult following, and one of the songs Stephen wrote and performed on 'The Place Behind Your Knee' was released as a single and went to number three in the charts, which pleased Andy very much. His and Holly's baby, a boy, was born at the end of March. They called him Clifton Stephen and asked Stephen and Toni to be godparents.

Tantony Pig finally released an album, 'Stand Up At The Back', which Stephen and Dominic produced. It didn't do as well as 'Keeping It Real' or 'Rock Goes The Weasel', but it was well received, and the critics liked it.

"We're very lucky, Charlie," Stephen said seriously.

"Being so talented?"

Stephen thumped him. "Getting paid enormous sums of money for having fun! Let's give the proceeds from the album to charity."

"Life's never dull here, is it?" Lynn said to Tim as they arrived back at their hut together after a long day. Because of floods in the capital – "Floods!" Matt, the administrator, had said in resignation. "We need rain for months and then we get *floods* and all the crops are ruined! Such as they are," he added darkly – she'd spent all day trying to find some way of getting the food supplies through.

Tim kissed her. "No, dull is a word you certainly couldn't apply to this place." He cupped her face gently in his hands. "Are you all right, my little flower of the desert? You're looking rather thin and tired."

"I suppose that's because I am," Lynn smiled. "So are you, Timmy. We need a bit of a holiday, but I feel so awful saying that when the refugees can't take a break."

"Yes, but we're no good to them if we're not a hundred per cent fit," Tim pointed out. "And as luck would have it, I have a perfect rest lined up for us!" He drew a letter out of his pocket. "It arrived this morning while you and Matt were huddled together in the office and I haven't seen you since."

"What is it?" Lynn asked. She undressed and slid into bed, careful not to disturb the net.

Tim got in next to her. "It's from Oliver. He's getting married and he wants me to be best man."

"Oh, Tim, that's lovely! And you always say you and your family aren't close!"

"I don't mean not close in the sense of not liking each other. I just mean we all respect each other as separate from the family unit, if you see what I mean."

Lynn kissed him. "Well, I'm not surprised your brother wants you to be his best man! You're the best man I know!"

"You say lovely things!" Tim pulled her to him.

"Wait – when's the wedding?" Lynn asked, laughing.

"Um..." Tim reached down for the letter.

"Careful of the net!" Lynn screeched. She still hated the insects.

"End of November. I thought we'd go back for two weeks."

"I'll miss Kentice having her baby! Oh well, it's not like I could do anything to help. I'll bring her some lovely clothes and stuff back."

She had become very close to one of the refugees, Kentice Kinyanyi, an outgoing Nurandan woman of about her age. Before the war, Kentice and her husband Gideon had been lecturers at a college in Ndoro, a city in the north of the country, which had been split by warring factions. They had been caught in the middle of a battle, and Gideon had lost his right leg. Their oldest child, their only son, had been killed and they had escaped with their two remaining children, both girls, Felice and Elizabeth. Kentice had organised a makeshift school for the children in the camp, and Lynn helped out as much as she could. Kentice and Gideon had been overjoyed when Kentice had become pregnant early in the year, and were hoping for a boy. "Although neither of us really cares!" Kentice laughed to Lynn.

Lynn marvelled at how she could stay so cheerful. Sometimes it all made her so incredibly angry. She'd read, in one of the papers that arrived sporadically, about Stephen's film, and felt a flash of anger towards him. The amount of money he would no doubt 'earn' from it would do so much for these people. And then later, she read that he'd donated it all to charity, and also the proceeds from the band he was in with Harry and Dominic, and the old longing swept over her again.

In April, Stephen took Toni, Rob, Alex and Pip to America for two months. Harry wasn't sure Rob ought to have the time off school, but Stephen persuaded her. "It's only four weeks or so of the summer term, and he's only nine, Hal! He's doing so well, he won't fall behind, I promise. And if by some weird chance he did, I can afford the best tutors in the world to help him, you know that! Please, Harry? He'll have such fun, and that's important too."

Harry sighed. "I don't know how you do it, Stephen, but somehow you always manage to talk me round! OK, just this once!"

They spent the first three weeks in Disneyland, and the rest of the time they stayed at a house Stephen rented in Massachusetts. It was on a lake, a typical wooden New England house, the clapboards painted a soft blue. Inside, it was open plan and fairly basic, and the large kitchen, well stocked with gadgets, opened onto a huge room that ran the length of the house. The end nearest the lake, the sitting area, had a patio door leading out onto decking, which, in turn, led down to the lake. The other end of the room, at the front of the house, was the dining area.

A staircase led to the basement, which housed the washing machine and tumble dryer, both of them far bigger than their British counterparts, and the furnace, which supplied the hot water – and heating, if required – and Stephen had to make daily trips to wrestle with the controls. This usually resulted in the furnace making a tremendous banging and roaring noise that he found frankly terrifying.

There were four bedrooms upstairs, the master with an ensuite, and one further, very small bedroom in the roof space, which Rob claimed gleefully as his own.

The house was sparsely but comfortably furnished. It had no TV, which Stephen considered to be a good thing; he privately thought Harry and Dominic let Rob watch far too much television.

Outside, there was a secluded garden with a heated pool, and a boathouse, in which, to his and Rob's delight, were a rowing boat, a canoe, and three kayaks, plus life jackets. Toni and the little boys mostly used the pool, Stephen and Rob swam in the lake, which was freezing but addictive. It was also very beautiful, a pellucid blue, except for the rare occasions when inky clouds would gather and chuck rain furiously down, and the lake would darken and lash angrily at the shoreline. Stephen wasn't sure that he didn't prefer it then, wild and untamed. In the early morning, it was stained a soft pink by the rising sun, and the Canada geese that lived on it would fly over, calling noisily to each other.

They spent all day outside; their neighbours told them they'd been lucky with the weather, it wasn't usually this hot and dry, and they made the most of it. In the afternoons, when Stephen and Rob mucked about on the lake and Alex and Pip napped, Toni sunbathed naked in the enclosed garden. She got brown all over, and every night after the three boys had gone to bed, Stephen went for a swim while she had a long, scented bath, and then they made love. Stephen found himself loving her more than he had ever done, and he was happier than he had been for a long time.

Rob enjoyed himself tremendously. He made friends with the local children and explored the neighbourhood with them. He got very brown and, to Stephen's amusement, picked up a slight American twang.

One weekend, Ray came over from Boston, bringing his fiancée, Shannon, a pretty, quietly spoken, dark-haired girl who was obviously very much in love with him.

Stephen took to her straight away. "So when are you two tying the knot?" he asked as they relaxed on the deck over beers.

"After Christmas," Ray said. "You don't want to rush these things, do you, Shan?"

"Rush things! If you had your way, hon, we'd never get married at all! I've had to railroad him all the way," she told Stephen and Toni. "Your boys are adorable," she added, watching them playing. "They're all so alike!"

"Yeah, which is pretty strange considering Toni isn't Rob's mother!" Ray laughed.

"God, Ray, it's great to see you're still the tactless oaf you always were," Stephen sighed.

"Talking of which, we had a good old chuckle over your nude frolics with that sexy French tart."

"Ray!" Shannon was blushing. "How could you bring that up?" She looked at Toni. "I'm so sorry!"

"So was Stephen when I'd finished with him."

Stephen hauled Ray out of his chair. "Come on, Ray, time for a swim. The lake's heated, you know."

Ray looked at him, surprised. "Really?"

"Of course," Stephen replied, straight-faced. "No point being as rich as me if you can't demand these luxuries."

Ray grinned widely. "Race you then!" He ran down the deck and dived in. Two seconds later his head appeared. "You utter bastard, Markham, it's fucking freezing in here!"

After dinner, they sat with the patio doors open, talking and watching the setting sun turning the lake to liquid gold.

"Shannie's too shy to ask, Steve, but her grandmother's Welsh, and I told her you know a bunch of Welsh songs. Can you play some for her?"

"Ray!" Shannon exclaimed, blushing again.

"Steve doesn't mind, do you, Steve?"

"Certainly don't." Stephen fetched his guitar. "Is there anything special you want to hear?"

Shannon shook her head, her face still scarlet. "Anything, Steve, thanks," she managed to say.

He played 'Llongau Caernarfon', a traditional Welsh song.

Rob drifted down from his room and listened. After a few minutes, he started singing. He had a strong, melodious voice. He's just like me! Stephen thought with a thrill. John's image seemed to appear in front of him. He qualified the thought. He's just like me in some ways.

When the song finished, they all clapped. Stephen was clapping Rob. "That was lovely, Rob," he said.

Rob flushed with pleasure. "I love singing."

"Where are you two spending your honeymoon?" Toni asked later, when Rob was in bed and they were having a nightcap.

Ray shrugged. "We haven't got that far."

"God, no we haven't!" Shannon agreed. "It's as much as I can do to get him to focus on the wedding!"

"I don't know why you bother," Stephen said. "A girl like you could do far better than him!"

"Fuck off, Markham," Ray grinned.

"Listen, if you like, you can spend your honeymoon at Cheyne Walk," Stephen offered. "You can laze around, go sightseeing, come over to the Priory whenever you like – whatever you want to do. You, me and Harry could maybe play some guitar together, Ray. What do you say?"

Shannon gazed at him. "Oh, Steve, thank you! What an amazing wedding present!"

"Hey, that's not our present! That's just an invitation!"

"You know, Markham," Ray said. "Sometimes I can almost believe you're a human being after all! But then I'm not so sure," he added as Stephen hit him across the head.

Before they left, Stephen offered the couple who owned the house an outrageous price for it. He could have bought a much bigger, much more luxurious place, one with a heating system that didn't scare the daylights out of him, but it wouldn't have been the same. This was the first proper family holiday he'd had with Toni and his sons, and he'd fallen in love with it. He wanted to be able to come back here.

They couldn't believe their luck and sold it to him.

During the holiday, Toni discovered she was pregnant. She was delighted. She'd been wanting another baby for a while and, without telling Stephen, had stopped taking the pill after Christmas. She knew he thought they should wait a couple of years before having another child.

When she broke the news, he sighed and shook his head. "Why do I even bother talking to you?"

She sat on his lap. "I thought you wanted a footie team? Come on, Stevie, don't be cross! It's not like we can't afford another one."

"I know. I was just thinking about you. And me, I suppose. I wanted you to myself for a while!"

Toni kissed him. "Well, it's not due till the end of December, mate, plenty of time for making whoopee!"

He grinned. "Hmm. It was making whoopee that got us into this in the first place!"

At the end of June, Sid's Six left for a four-month tour of the Far East. Stephen was tired when he got back, and all he wanted to do was relax at the Priory.

"Oh, I forgot to tell you," Toni said, the day after he got home. "We've been invited to a wedding."

"Yeah? Whose?"

"Dom's sister."

"Sophy? That's nice," Stephen said, pleased. "When is it?"

"The twenty-fourth of November." Toni's mouth turned down at the corners. "Course, I'll be huge by then."

"No you won't, you never get huge when you're pregnant, I don't know how you do it." He gave her a kiss. "I'm going to ring Charlie, see if we can get together when we go over for your scan."

He was taking her to London for a scan later that week. She was hoping very much that this baby would be a girl, and had been talking of nothing else since he'd got home.

"Harry's pregnant too," he told her when he got off the phone. "She's due in June. Neither of you can fly, so I've arranged with Charlie that we'll all drive up to Fenroth in the Espace. Amabel's nanny is taking her to stay with Susan and Angus at the beginning of the month, so there'll be room. Charlie and I can share the driving."

It was bliss to be in London again, sleeping in a huge, soft bed without a net. Lynn felt so grateful for all the luxuries she used to take for granted, and horribly guilty every time she remembered that the Nurandans had never known this kind of life and probably never would.

She and Tim went shopping the day after they arrived. As they wandered round the shops, she realised she knew nothing about the wedding, except that it was being held up north. "Who's Olly marrying?" she asked idly.

"Girl called Sophy Chaplin, she's a doctor."

She stared at him. "Sophy Chaplin? Whereabouts up north, Tim?"

"Northumberland."

"Near Morpeth?"

He looked puzzled "Yes, a place called—"

"—Fenroth Manor," Lynn finished.

"How did you know?"

She felt like Charles Ryder. "I've been there before. Sophy Chaplin is Dominic Chaplin's sister." And Stephen used to date Sophy. They'll all be there, she thought with horror.

"It's a wee boy, Toni."

"Are you sure, Heather?"

"Yes, I am."

"Oh!" Toni's eyes swam with tears and she gripped Stephen's hand.

"Could you be wrong?" As long as the baby was healthy, Stephen didn't care either way, but Toni had set her heart on a girl.

Heather grimaced. "I don't think so. Look." She pointed to the screen.

"Never mind, darling," Stephen said. "I love having boys! We're going to have a footie team, remember?"

But Toni was inconsolable and cried all the way home. She moped around the house, depressed and sulky, until he felt like killing her.

"Come on, Toni, let's go to London for the weekend," he said, just before the wedding. "You've got to get a frock now, and I've booked a table at the Ritz. You can get something new for that too." When there's a problem with Toni, throw money at it, he thought. Or sex. Or both. The sex isn't working. Let's hope the money will.

Toni shrugged. She hadn't bought a dress for the wedding on the grounds that she was getting fatter every day. "Yeah, OK. But I won't enjoy it."

"Course you will! We'll get you some knockout frocks and some new jewellery. You'll look amazing!"

"I'll look fat."

They arrived at Fenroth at five-thirty in the pitch dark and driving rain, and staggered up to their respective rooms, where log fires were burning cosily in the fireplaces.

"You lie down, Daisy, and I'll sort Hoony and Pip out," Stephen said, looking at her with concern. It had been a long, tiring journey.

Toni sank gratefully down on the four poster. "I love staying with Angus and Susan," she murmured sleepily.

Stephen went to find Harry, who had taken Alex and Pip up to the nursery where her nanny, Nanny Davies, Dominic's old nanny, was looking after Amabel.

"They'll be fine here with Nanny, Stevie, their rooms are up here too." She took Stephen's arm and guided him back downstairs. "Ain't it grand being rich?"

The guests had gathered in the drawing room for pre-dinner drinks, and Lynn, sitting close to Tim and drinking cocktails rather fast and nervously, was trying not to stare at the door. Her heart lurched as Stephen and Toni came in. Toni was pregnant! Heavily pregnant, in fact, Lynn saw, although apart from the bulge of her stomach, she didn't seem to have put on weight elsewhere. She was wearing a beautifully cut cream wool dress, and an ornate and elaborate necklace, an emerald surrounded by the biggest diamonds Lynn had ever seen. It must have cost a fortune. She was leaning against Stephen, who had his arm around her protectively. She looked very young and fragile. And fecund. Lynn felt sick with envy.

Toni stopped and looked down at herself. She said something to Stephen who put his hand on her bump. He raised his eyebrows and laughed. He looked so happy. Lynn's heart felt as if it was breaking. But why did that upset her? What kind of a woman was she, who felt miserable because the person she loved best in all the world looked happy? And then he saw her and his face changed. Shock was replaced by joy, and then a realisation of where they were, all in the space of a few seconds.

Susan was leading them over. "This is Tim Franklin, Oliver's brother and best man, and his wife, Lynn..."

Stephen took Lynn's hand. "How are you, Lynn?"

She smiled painfully. "I'm fine, how are you?"

They searched each other's faces for signs of change.

Two more boys and another child on the way. They could have been mine, Lynn thought. And he's more handsome than ever. How will I ever get over him?

She's got so thin, Stephen thought. How can Franklin make her live that kind of life? Doesn't he love her? He certainly doesn't deserve her.

"Hello, Tim," he smiled, shaking hands.

"Here are Sophy and Oliver now," Susan was saying.

Stephen managed to grab Harry and pull her away. "Why didn't you tell me?" he demanded. "I wouldn't have come!"

"I didn't know till now!" She signalled frantically to Dominic.

He came over. "Don't start!" he warned her. "Apparently Tim is Oliver's half-brother. They've got different surnames." He looked anxiously at Stephen. "Will you be all right?"

Stephen shrugged. "No choice. Now I've finally got her here, Toni's looking forward to the wedding. If I drag her away she'll think – rightly – it's because of Lynn. Charlie, do me a favour, explain to Susan, some of it anyway, so that we're not sitting near them?"

He got through the next day by spending his time with the boys. At the dinner party that night, he was seated far enough from Lynn that he couldn't see her without deliberately craning round, which, of course, he didn't do. He was being tremendously attentive and loving to Toni, who'd made a huge scene in their bedroom the night before, accusing him of knowing that Lynn would be there and even of engineering the whole thing. He'd eventually calmed her down and was concentrating on pretending Lynn and Tim didn't exist. He'd hardly slept and felt deathly. He was dreading the reception.

Toni loved the wedding. She'd been immensely upset by the fact that Lynn was there, looking, she thought with envy and hatred, incredibly slim and somehow exotic, a ministering angel taking a well deserved break from caring for sick children in a third world country. She wasn't fat and unattractive and tired, her stomach and breasts weren't scored with stretch marks, she was lissom and vibrant and glamorous, and over two years younger than Toni, who'd been thirty at the beginning of the year. She and Stephen had had a horrible row about her the previous evening, and he'd sworn that he hadn't known she'd been invited and was as surprised as Toni was. She'd watched him closely since then, but he hadn't shown the slightest interest in Lynn and had been in such tremendous spirits that she realised, with enormous relief, that he no longer cared about her.

The wedding breakfast, a buffet, was held at Fenroth.

"I must sit down, Stevo, my back and feet are killing me," Toni said, when they got back from the church.

He settled her in an armchair by the fire. "You take off your shoes and stay put, my darling, and Blue and I'll get you something to eat." He smiled at Rob, who was looking very grown up in a suit. "Come on, Robbie." They disappeared in search of the food.

As Toni kicked off her shoes, and nestled gratefully into the chair, Lynn walked past, looking for Tim. She saw Toni and hesitated.

Toni smiled at her. "Hello," she said, magnanimously, feeling almost sorry for Lynn; after all, Stephen was hers, and it was obvious which of them he loved.

Lynn was surprised. "Oh, hello," she replied awkwardly.

Stephen and Rob came back with champagne and plates of food.

"Lynn." Stephen's heart started to thump wildly.

Rob stared at her. "Cherry?" he asked hesitantly.

Lynn gave him a shaky smile. "Hello, Robbie."

"Cherry!" He flung himself into her arms. "Why did you go away?" A dim memory crept into his head. "Why did you go away?" he asked again. "You made Dad cry."

There was a tense silence. Lynn hugged him.

Stephen recovered first. "Lynn had to go and look after sick people in Africa, Blue," he managed to say.

Lynn let Rob go. "That's right."

"Are you a doctor?" Rob asked.

"No, my husband is. I've got to go and find him. I'll see you later, Robbie." She fled, wishing she could run from the house, from Rob, from Stephen, even from Tim.

Toni was staring at Stephen, her heart leaden. She wanted to scream, to hit him, to wipe the look of longing and desolation off his face. How could he, how *dare* he look like that over another woman? She was trembling in every limb, she felt sick and ill, and her baby was moving restlessly, agitatedly, as if he was aware of, and sharing, her distress.

"You should do more films, Steve, you're a really good actor," she said keeping her voice steady, although the effort nearly killed her. She stood up and tipped her champagne down his front. "Whoops, clumsy me. You'll have to change. I'm going to lie down. Let's go together."

Stephen was furious. If she makes another scene now, I will kill her, so help me God, he thought savagely. Surely she can see how hard this is for me, why is she such a selfish bitch? Why does everything always have to be about her? He turned to Rob. "Silly old Toni!" he said lightly. "Blue, I'll have to go and change. Will you be all right?"

"Course." He nodded emphatically. "I'm going to find Cherry's husband and ask him about Africa."

Stephen and Toni walked to their room in silence.

"I'm not going to argue with you," Stephen said as he closed the door behind them.

Toni peeled her dress off and lay on the bed while he changed. Her heart was racing and she felt drained. The baby had stopped moving and was lying heavily and uncomfortably inside her. She shifted onto her side, and had a sudden stab of pain.

"You really fooled me," she said, fighting back tears. She wasn't going to humiliate herself and let him see how upset she was, not after the way he'd lied. "I actually thought you didn't care about the bitch any more."

His lips tightened. "She's not a bitch, she's just my ex-wife. You, on the other hand, you're being a bitch right now." His voice changed. "Toni," he said pleadingly, "can't you understand? It was a huge shock seeing her, and I do still… still care about her, but it's *you* I love, honestly. Please, please, Toni, please don't go on at me. I can't – I don't want to argue with you."

He looked so lost and unhappy, so like Rob when something had upset him, that her heart contracted with pity. She held out her arms. "Give me a cuddle?"

He got onto the bed and she wrapped her arms around him, stroking his head as if he was a child. She felt his body gradually relax until he was asleep.

Stephen woke with a start. It was dark, except for a small lamp burning at the other side of the room. "What…?" he said, heavily.

Toni got up from an armchair. "You were sleeping like a baby, Stevo, I didn't want to wake you."

"What time is it?"

"Just after nine-thirty," she said reluctantly. She'd hoped he'd sleep all evening.

"God! We'll have to go downstairs! Well, you don't, Daisy, if you're not up to it."

"Don't go, Stephen," she pleaded.

"I have to, I have to explain where we've been."

She stared at him. Did he really believe she'd fall for that? He no longer looked sad and vulnerable, the sleep had refreshed him. He didn't need her any more, he wanted Lynn. How could he treat her like this? She was his wife, she was carrying his child! Just another boy, of course, she thought bitterly. She was suddenly blazingly angry. What was the point in talking to him? He didn't care about her or how she felt, he'd never cared. Nothing she said or did was ever going to make any difference.

"Don't bloody lie. You want to get down to that bitch."

He went white. "Don't be stupid, Toni."

"Yeah, that's me, stupid Toni. Stupid, stupid, stupid. Believing you didn't know *Cherry* would be here. No wonder you were so mad keen to drag me to the back of beyond in this condition, never mind how exhausted I was by the journey! You don't give a shit about me!"

"No, Toni, sometimes I don't, and this is one of those times." He pulled on his jacket. "I'll see you later."

You're not going alone, she thought, dressing. She hurried after him.

When they got downstairs, Sophy and Oliver had left, and most of the guests had moved through to the ballroom. Stephen found Susan and Angus and apologised for missing everything.

"I wasn't feeling really good and Stevo kept me company," Toni explained, hanging grimly onto his arm.

Susan smiled. "Rob told Harry you'd gone to lie down. Don't worry, Sophy understood."

Stephen scanned the room. Lynn was with Tim and a group he assumed were Tim's family. Dominic and Harry were sitting on the other side of the room with some people he didn't know. Harry waved. At that moment, the introduction to 'Market Town' began. Time stood still. Like an automaton, he took Toni's hand off his arm. His music filled his head as the last ten years fell away, and he was back in York, writing these lyrics, the story of his engagement to the woman he loved, had always loved and always would love.

He walked up to her and held out his hand. She stood up and he took her in his arms. Her head stills fits perfectly into the hollow of my shoulder, just like it always did, he thought. She still smells of Penhaligon's Violetta, she's still my Cherry. Mine, mine, mine. He shut his eyes to stop the tears.

And then the music ended and 'Every Breath You Take' was playing and Dominic was taking Lynn from him and dancing with her, flirting outrageously, and Harry had her arms round him, Stephen, and she was stroking his back and whispering, "Oh, Stevie, my poor darling Stevie, that wasn't very clever, was it, never mind, dance with me", and he held onto her and danced with her through several songs. He saw Dominic dancing with Toni and felt such tremendous gratitude to him and Harry. He was raw with emotion, raw with longing for Lynn. Harry was right; it hadn't been clever, it'd been the stupidest thing he'd ever done. Something bouncy came on and he and Harry stopped dancing.

Dominic and Toni came over to them.

"Having fun, Stephen?" Toni asked, her voice shaking with barely suppressed emotion, but the look on his face shocked her into silence.

And then, to his utter disbelief and horror, 'Sweet Cherry' started to play.

Without a word, he walked from the room.

Lynn was dancing with Tim's cousin, Clive. He grinned delightedly. "I love this song!" he exclaimed, whirling her round enthusiastically. She managed to smile at him and, somehow, her body kept on dancing, but she heard the words with her heart breaking:

Sweet Cherry,
You make my head ring,
You make my heart sing,
You take me higher than anything ever did before.
And I'm going to love you my whole life through,

Cos Cherry I knew
It was only ever you
Right from the start,
And if I could, I'd build a palace for you,
Make your dreams come true,
But I guess all I can do
Is give you my heart.
Sweet Cherry,
You light the fire,
Oh, you got me wired,
And I know I'll never tire of your loving, I just want more,
Sweet, sweet Cherry.

Chapter Twelve
Lovesick

I'm lovesick for you, yearning, burning with fever

Stephen had gone to the bedroom and found the little hardback notebook he wrote lyrics in. He was so absorbed, he didn't hear Toni come in.

"What are you doing?"

"Nothing."

She looked at the book and flushed. "You're writing a song for her!" she breathed, hardly able to believe he could do such a thing.

He shook his head. "No, I'm not. I just needed to sort out the way I feel. I'm so miserable." He sighed in despair and held out his hand to her. "Oh, Toni, I'm so sorry I danced wi…" he began, but she wasn't listening.

"Let me see it!"

"It's nothing, Toni, honestly, just private thoughts."

"Private? Oh, I bet!" She snatched the book and rifled through it.

"Toni! Give it back!" He grabbed at it, but she whirled away. "Not till I've seen the song."

"There *is* no song," he said, beginning to get angry.

Toni's self control snapped. The sight of Stephen dancing with Lynn had distressed and hurt her very much. She was tired and overwrought, and her back was aching, an insistent, nagging pain. "You bloody liar!" she shouted, and hit him in the face with the book as hard as she could.

He staggered backwards, his hand over his nose, which had started to bleed.

"I hate your bloody songs, you miserable, bloody little ratbag!" she yelled. She darted to the fireplace. "I hate them, and they're going where they belong!"

He rushed at her. "Toni! Don't be so fucking stupid, give it back!"

She was too quick for him and threw it into the fire. He flung her aside, grabbed the tongs and pulled it out. It was smouldering around the edges. He stamped on it, furiously angry. "God, you bitch, you bitch!"

"Stephen!" Toni gasped.

He looked round. She was crouched on the floor. "Toni! Are you all right? What happened?"

"I fell. You pushed me and I fell." She started to cry. "I'm sorry about your book."

"Doesn't matter. Toni, are you hurt? Is the baby OK?" He lifted her up and got her onto the bed.

"My back hurts," she whimpered. "I'm scared!"

"Tim's a doctor. I'll get him. Hang on." He ran down the stairs.

Harry was coming towards him. "I was just coming to see…" she began. "Stephen!" She stared at him in horror. "What happened? Your poor face!"

"Can you get Tim? Toni fell over."

"Go back to her. I'll bring him up."

Toni was lying on her side. "I'm having pains."

"Oh, my God! Darling, I'm so sorry!" He felt terrible; this was all his fault. He went to take her hand.

She twisted away from him and groaned.

Harry hurried in with Tim and Dominic.

"I think Toni's in labour," Stephen told Tim frantically.

He moved to the bed. "I'm going to examine you, Toni. You tell me how you're feeling."

Harry took Stephen's hand. "Are you all right? What happened to your poor face?"

He shook his head, his eyes on Toni.

"I'll get a flannel." She wiped at the dried blood. It hurt and he winced, pushing her hand away.

"There's nothing to worry about, Toni," Tim was saying. "But I think we'd better get you into hospital, just to make sure. Can I ring from your room, Harry? We'll only be a minute, Toni," he said, reassuringly, motioning to Stephen.

In Harry's room, he dialled 999 and spoke to the ambulance service. Putting the receiver down, he said, "She's three centimetres dilated, but the baby is in the breech position and I think it may be distressed. She might need a caesarean."

Stephen was appalled. He followed Tim back to Toni, cold with fear and shock. Supposing the baby died? Supposing Toni did?

"An ambulance will be here shortly, Toni," Tim said.

"I'll get her some things." Stephen leant down and kissed her head. "It'll be all right, little Daisy."

"Don't touch me!" she cried. "I don't want you with me!"

He was shattered. "Toni!"

"Leave me alone! Harry, will you come with me? I don't want Stephen, I don't want him, I don't want him!" Her voice rose hysterically.

"It's all right, Toni, calm down," Tim soothed. "Stephen won't come in the ambulance if you don't want him to. Think of the baby and calm down. Harry will go with you, won't you, Harry?"

Harry looked at Stephen. She didn't know what was going on, she didn't know what to do. "Um… of course, Toni."

"But darling Toni…" Stephen started, close to tears.

Tim took his arm. "You're distressing her."

Stephen was shaking. "I want to go with her. I *have* to go with her!"

"It might be better if Dominic drives you in behind the ambulance," Tim suggested, looking at Dominic, who nodded immediately. "Could you leave the room, please?" he went on. "For the baby's sake. And it would probably be a good idea to get your face X-rayed at the hospital," he added, sympathetically.

In the car, Dominic asked him what had happened.

"It's just a lousy book, Charlie, why didn't I leave it?" he kept saying.

They took Toni away and performed an emergency caesarean section. She went through the operation with no problems, and the baby, a boy, as Heather had predicted, was born just after one-thirty in the morning, weighing four pounds thirteen ounces, very small, but otherwise perfectly healthy. They put him in the Special Care Baby Unit, but the paediatrician told Stephen that he didn't see any cause to worry. "He's breathing on his own, he's feeding. I don't think there'll be any problems."

Stephen shook his hand gratefully, staring down at his son. Like the others, he was a pretty little baby, but completely different in looks to them. His wispy hair was reddish and his eyes were very like Stephen's. I hope Toni will be pleased, he thought bleakly. She had wanted the others to have his eyes.

"Have you got a name yet, pet?" one of the nurses asked.

"Samuel Rhodri. Sam."

"That's nice," she smiled. "I think someone wants you," she added, indicating Harry and Dominic on the other side of the glass partition.

"Steve, I'm taking Harry home, she's had it," Dominic said.

Stephen hugged Harry and then, to Dominic's surprise, hugged him too. He hugged Stephen back, feeling huge pity for him. "Are you ready to come home yet?" he asked.

Stephen shook his head. "I'll wait till I can see Toni. I'll get a taxi or something."

"Fuck that, old man. I'll come back and wait with you."

Harry felt terrible; tired, aching, and emotionally drained. She lay back in the car and shut her eyes. "I wonder what happened to Stevie's face?" she said idly, not really expecting a reply.

"Fucking Toni hit him with his lyrics book," Dominic said grimly.

She opened her eyes in shock. "Dominic, no! Why?"

"She thought he was writing a song about Lynn."

"God!" Harry breathed. "Was he?"

"I don't think so. I couldn't really get any sense out of him. He said he was scribbling down the way he was feeling, and she came in and thought he was writing something for Lynn. And, of course, the bloody idiot blames himself. It was, 'Oh, Charlie, why am I such a selfish bastard?' all the way to the hospital. I tell you, baby, if I hadn't been so fucking sorry for him, I'd have stopped the car and beaten him to death."

"God, what a mess! Toni said in the ambulance that he pushed her over, but I don't believe that."

"No. As I say, he wasn't making much sense, but I gather she wanted to burn his book, or tried to burn it, and he rushed past her to get it and knocked her over, but again, it was all fucking tears and self-recrimination."

A thought occurred to Harry. "You were sympathetic, weren't you, Dom? You didn't shout at him or anything?"

Dominic shot her an annoyed look. "God, Harriet, you can be a bitch sometimes! Of course I was fucking sympathetic! It nearly fucking killed me though."

Stephen was allowed to look in on Toni a few hours later, after making a nuisance of himself and trading shamelessly on his stardom. She was sleeping peacefully. He kissed her gently.

She stirred. "Stephen?"

"Ssh, I didn't mean to wake you."

"How's my baby?"

"He's right, Toni, a real little beaut. He's got eyes like mine."

She gave a little smile. "I forgive you then," she mumbled, drifting back off to sleep.

He tiptoed out.

Dominic was waiting for him. "Come on, Steve, you need to bathe and sleep. I'll bring you back in later. How is she?"

"She forgives me."

Dominic snorted. "The woman's incorrigible!"

It was nearly breakfast time when they got back to Fenroth. Dominic dropped Stephen at the door. "Go and shower and sleep, Stephen. When you wake up, just ring down to the kitchen for whatever you want." He drove off to the garages.

Stephen started wearily towards the stairs and bumped into Lynn.

Dancing with Stephen had thrown Lynn into utter confusion. Somehow, after he'd gone, she'd managed, with the help of several glasses of champagne, to behave normally, although her mind was racing, torn between longing for him and anger with him. How could he *do* that to her, stir up all those feelings again? And the memory of the love in his beautiful eyes and the way he'd looked at her, almost as if he was caressing her, had kept recurring, making her flinch with pain, but she'd carried on dancing, had laughed and chatted, had had a long talk with Tim's mother about conditions in Africa, and hadn't bombarded Tim with questions when he'd come back from Toni, merely asked if she was all right. When they'd eventually got to bed, she'd made love to him with a kind of desperation, and had fallen into a fitful sleep. She'd woken early, and been unable to go back off. Tim was already up, so she'd dressed and gone downstairs, assuming he'd gone down to breakfast and to ring the hospital to check on Toni.

She was totally unprepared to see Stephen again, and her first emotion was resentment, but the look of desolation on his face, and the bruise around his nose and eyes stopped her in her tracks. "Stephen! What happened to you?" She pulled him into the study to look at him in the light.

Neither of them could possibly know that Tim was sitting in the wing chair by the desk. It was facing away from them, hiding him. He'd been phoning the airport to try to get an earlier flight to London for himself and Lynn; he'd been disturbed by the look of naked longing on Stephen's face when he'd danced with her, and, although she'd so obviously not noticed – indeed, had spent the rest of the evening dancing and laughing, and made love to him, when they finally went up to bed, with more tenderness and love than ever – he thought it would be best for them to get away, to spend the rest of their holiday alone together. He felt tremendously sorry for Stephen, he could only imagine how he would feel if he lost Lynn, but even so, he didn't want Lynn spending any more time with him.

"God, Stephen, that's a terrible bruise!" Lynn was saying. "What happened?"

"Nothing."

"It looks like a very painful nothing. Tell me, Stevie." Her voice cut Tim to the heart, it was so full of love.

Stephen sighed. "I was writing some stuff last night. After we'd danced. I couldn't stay and listen to 'Sweet Cherry'. Toni wanted to see what I'd written. She thought it was for you."

"Was it?"

There was a pause before Stephen said quietly, so quietly Tim could barely hear him, "In a way, I suppose. It was about the way I feel about you, Cherry. I *ache* for you. It's never gone away, but seeing you, *holding* you…" He drew in a ragged breath. "Anyway, Toni demanded to see it. I wouldn't let her, said it was private. I use a hardback notebook to write in…"

"I remember," Lynn murmured.

"Yeah, well, we had a bit of a tussle over it, we were both pulling at it, it hit me, and Toni fell over and went into labour."

"Tim said he'd arranged for her to go into hospital to be on the safe side, I didn't realise she was actually in labour! Is the baby all right? And Toni?"

"Yes, thanks to Tim. But if I'd just let her see that damn book!"

"Stevie, you can't blame yourself."

"Of course I can! She was pregnant, and upset by me dancing with you!"

"Yes, but…"

"There is no 'but'! God, what a mess."

"Stevie," Lynn whispered. "Oh, my beloved Stevie, I can't bear you to be so sad. If only there was something I could do."

"Cherry, sweet, sweet Cherry."

"I wasn't sweet to you." Her voice trembled.

Stephen's voice was rough with emotion. "Always. You were always sweet to me. You always will be…"

There was silence. Tim couldn't bear it. He peered carefully round the edge of the chair. If they saw him, they saw him. Lynn was gently pushing the hair off Stephen's forehead. Tim watched with horror as Stephen wrapped his arms around her, bent forward and kissed her. She melted into his embrace.

Tim's heart was hammering in his chest. He leant back, almost unable to breath. He heard Lynn whisper, "Stevie", and Stephen answer, "I know, I know. I'm sorry. But I need you so much, you're in my blood, I'm ill from missing you, I miss you all the time. All the time. Oh, God, Lynn, I'm so sorry. I shouldn't be saying this. I've got to get to bed, I'm wiped out." There was a brief emotional silence, then, " Oh, Cherry, I love you so much!" he blurted out

"Stop it, Stephen!" Lynn said sharply. "I know exactly how you feel, I feel the same way, but there's nothing we can do and this isn't fair to either of us. Oh, Stevie. Come on, you need some sleep, and I better go and…" Her voice died away as they left the room.

Tim picked up the phone, beside himself with rage and grief. How could she have said those things? All these years! What a travesty it made of their marriage, what a farce! And last night, what an act! Had she been thinking of Markham when they'd made love? Was that why she'd been so very loving? How could he ever have felt sorry for the man? His compassion was washed away in a tidal wave of hatred. He was hurting so badly and he wanted to lash out and hurt Stephen in return. He spoke into the phone. "Craig Ross, please… Tim Franklin… yes, that's right… Craig? Tim… Yes, and you. Craig, I've got something for you, nothing to do with me, of course…"

After he hung up, he sat staring at the receiver. How could he have done that? He must have been mad! The picture of Lynn in Stephen's arms flashed into his head. He wanted to kill Stephen Markham, put his hands round the man's throat and squeeze the life out of him. This was the next best thing. And hurting him will hurt Lynn, he thought with gleeful malice, hurt her like she's hurt me. He shuddered in horror. How could he possibly want to hurt Lynn? Yes, he was mad. Mad with love. It *was* madness, a cancer eating into him, turning him into a monster. He pictured Lynn's face if she ever found out what he'd done, but deep down, he was glad he'd done it. And he despised himself. He put his head in his hands in despair.

Stephen spent the rest of the day at the hospital, relieved that there were no reporters hanging around. He and Dominic took Rob in to see his new brother that afternoon, but they decided to wait until Toni was feeling stronger before taking Alex and Pip.

Rob loved the fact that Sam had eyes like his. "He's like my twin, isn't he, Dad?"

"Yes, I suppose he is," Stephen smiled. Fin had said that Alex and Pip were Irish twins: born in the same year, he'd explained. Rob had wanted to be in on it.

"He's my best brother, but don't tell my siblings."

"Where did you hear that?" Stephen asked, amused.

"Cherry's husband said it. 'Where are your siblings?' he asked me. He's great, Dad, really funny and clever. He's a doctor and he helps starving boys. He hasn't got any boys of his own, but he said if he did have one he'd like him to be like me." Rob was glowing with hero worship. "I might be a doctor when I grow up."

"I don't think there are many better things to be, Blue."

"Jesus Christ!"

"What is it, Dom?"

Dominic and Harry, and Angus, Susan and Tim were eating breakfast the next morning and the papers had just arrived.

Tim and Lynn were due to catch a flight to London after lunch, and Lynn, who felt that the less she and Stephen saw of each other, the better it would be for both of them, was packing.

"Look at this!" Dominic passed the paper to Harry.

"'*Premature Baby For Sid's Six Star's Wife. Toni Markham, wife of rock star Stephen Markham, has had her third child prematurely in Northumberland where they were attending a society wedding,*' " she read out. "'*Sources close to them have revealed that Markham, 30, Sid's Six's frontman, could have caused his wife's premature labour. Apparently, the two clashed over the fact that Markham's ex-wife, Lynn Franklin, 28, who, it is claimed, he is still in love with, was also a guest at the wedding. There is speculation among those close to Markham that he hit his wife during a row, knocking her down. Toni Markham, 30, was rushed to hospital for an emergency caesarean, refusing to let Markham near her. The baby, a boy, is four weeks early.*' " She stared at Dominic. "What can we do?"

Dominic said, slowly, "Be ready to support Steve any way we can. God, this is going to be *hell* for him."

At that moment, Stephen walked in. "What?" he asked, as they all looked at him.

He read the paper in silence and flung it away. "Bloody, *bloody* reporters! I loathe them! I wish they were all dead!"

"Isn't that the paper your stepfather owns, Tim?" Angus asked.

Tim nodded, not looking at him. "Unfortunately. I'm sorry, Stephen. I'll ring him," he said, staring at his plate. "He'll get them to retract, print an apology." He felt appalling, hot and ill. "I'll do it now." He got up.

"Thank you, Tim." Stephen said gratefully. He felt terrible about kissing Lynn, it had been inexcusable, and there were so many people to feel guilty about. "How could this…" Words failed him. "How could it be in the paper?"

Dominic shook his head.

"B-but only people here know about what happened. I don't understand."

Dominic shrugged. "I can only think one of the caterers – or maybe even one of the staff, although I can't imagine they would do something like that! Mama? What do you think?"

"I would hate to think it was anyone from here," Susan said, distressed.

Stephen shrugged despairingly. "It's no one's fault, Charlie. One of the penalties of fame. I'm going to ring Julian."

After speaking to Julian and Alan, he phoned Cell.

"Steve, I'm getting the next plane up. I've drafted a statement, listen." She read it out to him. "Anything you want to add?"

"Yes. I bruised my face playing with Pip and Alex. Pip was chucking his wooden bricks around and one hit me. It's got nothing to do with Toni's labour."

There was a silence. Cell knew Toni well. "If you say so," she said finally. "OK, I'll take care of it."

The hospital grounds were crawling with reporters. Stephen gave them a shorter version of Cell's statement, adding that there was going to be a retraction and an apology the following day, and when asked about his face, told the story of Pip and the brick. "And there's another little tearaway in there," he laughed, indicating the hospital. "So if you'll excuse me, I'll go in and see him and my wife." He went in, relieved to have got away from them so easily.

Toni was pale and listless, and took no interest in Sam. She refused to breastfeed him, claiming she was too tired.

Stephen was riddled with guilt. He'd apologised for his behaviour at the wedding over and over again, but she wouldn't listen.

"I don't want to talk about it, Stephen," she said, turning her face away.

In desperation, he tried everything he could think of to cheer her up, even offering to sort out an interview with *The Weekly*. "We can go out to Jacko and Kay, they'll keep an eye on the boys, and after the interview we can do whatever you want, go wherever you choose. Would you like that, little Glaucus?"

"Maybe," she sighed.

Eventually, he was able to take her and Sam home to the Priory. Sam was delightful. He was a very pretty baby, very lovable, and he reminded Stephen very much of Rob as a baby. But Toni was no happier. She'd lost a lot of weight and looked thin and ill, wilting like a rose at the end of the summer, Stephen thought. He couldn't understand it, it was so unlike her, this silent apathy. Her usual behaviour, if he upset her, was to make her displeasure obvious, do something to hurt or humiliate him. They'd have a furious row, she'd shout and throw things and try to hit him, and then they'd end up in bed, and it would be over, forgotten. He'd never seen her like this before.

"What's the matter, my darling girl?" he asked, taking her in his arms. "Why are you so sad? And why don't you like Sammy? He's a little ripper!"

"He's not a girl." Tears slid down Toni's face.

Stephen stared at her. "But why does that matter? I mean, I can see it would be nice for you to have another female about the place but, Toni, you're such a terrific mother and you get on so well with all of them – look at Rob! He loves you almost as much as Harry, you're a second mother to him."

"I wanted her for you, Stephen."

He shook his head slowly. "I don't understand."

"I love you so much," she said desperately.

"But loving someone should make you happy!" he said, appalled. "If loving me makes you feel like this, is it worth it?"

"When we got married, I didn't even know you called Lynn 'Cherry', she was just your ex."

"And that's all she is."

"Oh, Stephen, don't lie! Dominic said you didn't love me as much as you loved her…"

"How the hell does Charlie know how I feel?" he demanded, incensed. "How dare he say that to you? I'll kill him!"

"No, Stephen, I said it first! He was trying to explain how she was the first girl you really loved, how it was kind of like a three-year holiday romance, you were both at uni, doing just exactly what you wanted, it wasn't real life, so she means – well, all that happy time comes with memories of her. Intellectually, I can accept that, but emotionally…" She stopped.

"Go on."

"Emotionally I can't ever accept it. *I* want to be the one. *I* want to be first with you." She began to cry hard. "I so wanted Sam to be a girl. Harry gave you a boy. I thought if I gave you a girl, a daughter, I'd be special… like Lynn. *She* had a girl."

He was absolutely horrified by these revelations. "Toni, you *are* special! I don't care whether I've got sons or daughters, I couldn't possibly love them more! And what's all this 'giving' me children? How mediaeval! We have our children together, we share them, we don't 'give' them to each other! And isn't it the man who determines the sex of the baby? So it's my fault if we keep having boys! God, it's like being Henry the Eighth in reverse!" He put his hand under her chin and tilted her face so that she was looking at him. "Lynn *didn't* have a daughter, did she? She couldn't even carry the baby to term, it died, remember? You've had three beautiful, wonderful, healthy, *living* children, Toni. I love them so much. And you too, I can't tell you how much I love you."

Toni's lips were trembling. "Do you really mean that, Stevo?"

"Yes, I do," he said. He felt so guilty, so ashamed. He had to put things right. He leant forward and kissed her on the lips, very gently, very tenderly. "You're my heart, Toni. I couldn't live without you."

Ray's wedding was the second Saturday in January. Stephen, who was his best man, flew over for it, accompanied by a fragile Toni, and the four of them flew back. Stephen paid for the flight, despite Ray's objections. "It's part of our wedding present, Raymond, so shut it."

"I've never flown first class before," Shannon said with awe.

Stephen had spoken to Harry and Graham, and arranged for The Brigands to give a concert at York University, much to Ray's delight. Dominic was there, and Stephen called him onstage at the end and they jammed, to the glee of the crowd.

Hoodman Blind premiered at the beginning of May. Stephen and Toni went with Dominic and Harry, who was looking enormous, Fin and Shelagh, George and Kagami, Andy and Holly, and Sian and Ted. Stephen and Toni had attended the premiere of *With Giants Fight*, but then he had written the soundtrack and simply been a glorified extra. Now he had second billing.

"Oh ey, Steve, it's like knowing Mel Gibson!" Andy said, as they walked up the red carpet and the crowd shouted his name.

"I wish!" Toni grinned. She had never regained the weight she'd lost after having Sam, and looked thin and glamorous in a Versace frock.

"Jesus, will you look there, it's Princess Diana!" Shelagh exclaimed as a car drew up. They were all hurried into the cinema.

Stephen was a little embarrassed by the sex scene.

Dominic, who was sitting next to him, dug him in the ribs. "Way to go, Markham!" he whispered.

"God, Stephen, you were amazingly evil," Harry said to him at the party afterwards. "I was so scared of you I nearly went into labour!"

"What was Princess Diana like, Steve? What did she say to you?" Holly asked. "I read she's a big fan of Sid's Six."

"Um… she's tall, blonde, tremendously attractive, she smelt delicious – I can't remember what she said!"

Dominic grinned. "'And what exactly is it that you do?' probably," he mimicked.

The reviews of the film were excellent. They all praised the direction, and the acting of the three principals, particularly Stephen's portrayal of the chillingly mad

David Powell. Only one reviewer hit a sour note, claiming that David Powell was a man who could beat up his pregnant wife without thinking twice.

Stephen was upset.

"He's a small-minded nobody, Steve," Andy consoled. "Take no notice."

Harry's baby was a boy, and Dominic's parents were overjoyed, even more so when Dominic told them he was to be called Angus after his grandfather. "It's the first time they've ever been pleased with me!"

As usual, poor Harry had a bad time. "I really envy you your short labours," she said to Toni when they went to see her and Gus, as Dominic was already calling his son. "Thank God I've produced a son and heir, I might not do this any more!"

Stephen smiled. "I can't imagine you caring, Charlie."

Dominic was staring down into the baby's eyes. "Oh, not me, I don't care about passing on the baronetcy, it's Papa."

"What?" Stephen was startled. He'd known Angus was Sir Angus, but hadn't realised it was a hereditary title. "Do you mean one day you'll be—"

"Sir Dominic, yes," Dominic grinned. "You'd better start practising your bow, Markham!"

The flooding in Nuranda had had a knock-on effect, and early in the New Year they were still coping with the aftermath. The camp had become swollen with refugees, bringing their problems with them. Lynn and Tim had been too busy coping to spend time soul searching, but,although on the surface their relationship seemed to be the same as it had been before the wedding, Lynn sometimes felt uneasy with him. Several times he had been moody and seemed to be on the point of saying something, and she worried that maybe he no longer wanted to be with her, but he still wanted her sexually, and was as loving as ever. She pushed it to the back of her mind.

Life went on. Kentice's baby had been born while they were away, another little girl. They had christened her Julienne. She was absolutely beautiful, Lynn thought, and spent a great deal of her free time with Kentice and Gideon.

"It's terrible, Tim," she said, one evening. They were actually sitting outside Monsoon Blister, although on camp stools, and drinking beer, not cocktails. "They're both far cleverer than me – Gideon's got a PhD – and look at them! Living in a camp, teaching children to read and write."

Tim sighed. "I know, darling. What a world, eh?"

She looked at him. "Tim," she said hesitantly.

He squinted over at her, shielding his eyes from the sun, which was setting dramatically behind her. "Yes?"

"I don't really know how to say this…"

He looked alarmed. "What? You're not ill, are you? Lynn," he added, his voice full of hope. "You're not pregnant?"

She shook her head, feeling awful. "No, Timmy. I'm so sorry."

He gripped her hand. "Never mind, just a thought," he said too heartily. "What did you want to say?"

"I feel stupid now. It's just… I don't know. A few times I've thought… well, it seems you want to say something to me, then you don't. I just wondered… if you were still happy with me," she finished in a rush.

"Oh, darling, of course I am! Come here!" He pulled her onto his lap and the little camp stool he was sitting on collapsed. They burst into peals of laughter.

Fiona, one of the nurses, walked past. She looked down at them, rolling around in the dust, weak from laughing. "Tim and Lynn are pissed again," she commented, walking on.

Andy, Fin and George were very much involved in their own projects for the next few months – Fin was touring with his Irish band, Fodhla; Andy was working in America with Phoebe Storm, the Soul singer, and George was collaborating on an album with singer-songwriter and fellow Geordie, Will Seaton, which suited Stephen, as he wanted to do some writing and spend time with Toni and the boys. Sam was still very small and prone to illness, particularly ear and chest infections. They both tended to worry about him excessively and he was still sleeping in their room. His eyes, which had been almost identical to Stephen's at birth, had changed, to Toni's disappointment, but she had to agree with Stephen that it suited him. They were bright blue and, with his auburn hair, he was a strikingly pretty child.

The two older boys were growing up. Three-and-a-half-year-old Alex attended the village playgroup three mornings a week, and Toni took Pip, who was a year younger, to the mother and toddler club.

Sometimes Stephen took him. At first this had caused a huge commotion. Although it was common knowledge among the locals that Stephen Markham owned the Priory, they hadn't expected to mix with him. Nobody asked for his autograph, but there was a lot of giggling, whispering and nudging the first time he appeared with Pip, and no one spoke to him unless he started the conversation. Within a few weeks, however, they'd become so used to him they were asking him to wash up the paint trays and make coffee.

Toni had made several friends among the other mothers and there always seemed to be swarms of children in the pool and tearing around the house and garden. Stephen had a large part of the attic soundproofed and converted into a music room, where he could practice and write without disturbing or being disturbed by anyone.

Very early one morning at the beginning of the summer holidays, he made his way upstairs, anticipating at least an hour's peace, and was surprised to hear the sound of the piano coming through the open door and then Alex's voice. "Let *me*, Blue!"

"OK, Ally, but not so hard this time!"

There was a terrible discordant noise. Alex chuckled.

"What's going on?" Stephen asked.

"Oh, hello, Dad. I was trying to teach Alex to play the piano, but he just likes making a noise."

"Listen to me, Daddy!" Alex yelled proudly, crashing his hands down on the keys. "Clever old Alex! Now the 'tar." He grabbed Stephen's National steel.

"You put that down!" Stephen exclaimed.

Grinning, Alex let it go and it fell backwards. Stephen picked him up. "You really are a horrible little hoon!"

Alex smirked.

"Sorry, Dad," Rob said. "He followed me upstairs. Pip often comes, and he can nearly play 'Twinkle Twinkle Little Star.' "

"I know." Stephen swung Alex round and the little boy screamed with excitement. "You're just a wrecker, aren't you, Ally?" he said, putting him down.

"I'm clever old Alex. Again, Daddy, swing me again! Pleeeeease!" He caught hold of Stephen's leg.

"Not likely! You weigh a ton, I don't want a broken back!" Stephen took his hand. "Let's find Mummy or Karen. Shall we play together in a minute, Robbie?"

Rob nodded enthusiastically.

"OK, I won't be long." Stephen and Alex started downstairs.

"Sing The Wiggles, Daddy! 'Here Comes a Song'!" The Wiggles were Australian children's entertainers, and Alex and Pip loved them, watching their show avidly when they were in Australia.

Stephen started to sing. They went into the kitchen, both of them singing at the top of their voices.

Toni had Bunyip out. She looked up and smiled at Stephen's expression. "He likes a bit of human company. He needs a mate, really. I might think about getting him one."

"Bunyip!" Alex shouted with glee, diving towards the spider.

"Carefully, Alexander! Look, like this."

Stephen watched, horrified, as Toni put the creature in Alex's outstretched hands. "Be careful, Toni!"

"Don't worry, Alex won't hurt him, will you, little mate?"

"That wasn't what I meant."

Toni gave him a hard stare and he backed out of the room. As he went, he heard Alex say, "Look at his sweet ikkle tummy!" He thought with revulsion of the urticating hairs that could cause a painful rash. How he loathed that spider.

Upstairs, Rob was strumming his acoustic guitar. "What did you do with him?"

"He's playing with Bunyip," Stephen shuddered.

"Oh, is *Bunyip* out?" Rob's face lit up.

"I'm living in a madhouse! How can you like that *thing*?"

"Dad!" Rob was disapproving. "I thought you liked all animals!"

"I'm against cruelty in all its forms, whether towards man or beast, but that doesn't mean I *like* all beasts. I don't like all men much. Anyway, what about cruelty to me? I live in dread that creature will escape, and drop on me when I'm using the lavatory or something! And that mad woman I married is talking about getting a friend to keep it company! Do you want to go and play with it?"

Rob shook his head. "I'd rather make music with you."

Stephen felt choked. He gave Rob a hug. "OK, what would you like to play?"

"I wrote a song," Rob said, shyly. "Shall I play it?"

"Yes, please." Stephen listened as Rob picked out a tune on the guitar and sang. It was a simple little song about Turtle, his dog, but the riff was catchy.

"It's exceedingly good," Stephen said when he'd finished.

Rob blushed. "Oh, Dad," he said, hot with pleasure. "No it isn't!"

"Yes, it is, Robbie," Stephen said seriously. "Ask the lads, I never lie over musical ability. That riff is really good, really catchy."

Rob sighed happily. "Shall I teach it to you?"

Rob wasn't going back to London. There was an extremely good independent Grammar School just outside Burford, and after long drawn out discussions with Harry, who could see the advantages of the school but wanted Rob with her, it was finally agreed that he would live with Stephen and Toni. Every time Stephen remembered that Rob was going to be living with him full-time for at least the next five years, he felt overwhelmed with joy. He smiled at his son. "Yes, please."

At the beginning of August, Stephen drove to London to start recording the band's next album. He was late, the traffic was heavy. He could have gone by train, it was an easy journey, but he loved driving. When the band had become famous, he'd done some racing, entering the Mille Miglia, the four-day Italian road race, dubbed the most beautiful race in the world, and had participated in various celebrity events. He loved it, loved the adrenaline rush and the feeling that nothing else existed, only him and the car and the race, his whole life reduced to this one reality, when all that mattered was winning and staying alive, possibly in that order. And then he was involved in a bad crash; two other drivers died, and although he escaped with only broken ribs and bruises, he was shocked into realising that he'd become hooked on the speed and the danger, and reluctantly came to the conclusion that it was too irresponsible and self-indulgent. He was a father, and it wasn't fair to Rob to take those risks. He contented himself with driving his Porsche 911 far too fast, resulting in depressingly regular speeding fines.

By the time he arrived the other three were already there, playing pool in the Artists' Lounge. The room was fuggy with cigarette smoke. He got himself a Crunchie and a Coke, and coughed pointedly. No one took any notice.

"Howay, man, you decided for to grace us with your presence then?" George inquired sarcastically, lighting another cigarette.

"Shove it up your arse, George," he said shortly. He didn't feel like playing that game.

A very pretty girl smirked at him. She was wearing a low-cut top and a skirt so short it was little more than a belt. She had lovely legs, he noticed.

"Erm, Steve, this is Vivvy, you know, from *Circe*, like," Andy said.

Stephen groaned inwardly. He'd forgotten Cell had set up this interview with *Circe*, the magazine for 'the woman with attitude'. He wasn't sure he wanted anything to do with the woman with attitude, he got enough of that of home and he didn't like giving interviews at the best of times. He smiled and held out his hand. "Hello."

Vivvy took it in hers and smiled back seductively. "I've been longing to meet you," she said, her eyes sliding down to his lips and back up to stare into his. "Your eyes are the most amazing colour." She was still holding his hand, her index finger rubbing the inside of his wrist. He felt himself getting hard. He cleared his throat, removed his hand and sat on the sofa. Bad move. She sat right next to him and put her hand on his knee.

"So, um, Vivvy." He couldn't think of anything else to say. He shifted uncomfortably. The others were grinning.

"Tell me about your new album." She smiled at Andy.

"Well, we haven't started recording it, yet, like," he said, thrown.

Stephen pulled himself together. "It's called 'More Than I Remember'…"

"Interesting title," she interrupted, staring into his eyes again and running her tongue over her lips. "What's it mean?"

"Well." Stephen swallowed. "Disraeli – you've heard of Disraeli?"

She gave him a wide-eyed look. "Benjamin Disraeli, 1804 to 1881, Prime Minister. Twice. Shall I go on?"

"I'm impressed!"

"I've got a degree in History. I wanted to lecture in it."

"So why are you working for *Circe*?"

She moved closer to him. "It has its perks. So, Disraeli."

"Um… well, he's one of my heroes, and he once said, when he was asked about his holiday, 'Like most travellers, I've seen more than I remember, and remember more than I've seen.' "

"Sounds like a barrel of laughs, eh, pet?" George sat down on the other side of her.

"At least he didn't bore everyone to death with his holiday snaps," Stephen retorted. George and Kagami had just got back from India.

"And you know for why, bonny lad? Because cameras weren't invented then!"

Stephen leant forward. "Well, actually, George, the first picture was successfully taken in 1827 by Joseph Niepce. Louis Daguerre was taking—"

"Howay, man, when you're not being a lass, you're being a fucking know-all!"

"Better than being a know nothing," Stephen said, smugly.

"Anyway," Fin put in, quickly. "That's the album. We start recording today."

"Stephen, I understand you've written a song called 'Savages' about the starving millions in Africa?" Vivvy asked.

"Kind of. I've got some friends who work out there. I'm going to donate what I earn from this album to the cause. It's so terrible; I mean, apart from the wars and the famines and what have you, there's AIDS, which is a huge problem. It's appalling. Little children HIV positive, or being orphaned. Or both."

There was a silence. He took a sip of his Coke.

"So," Vivvy said. "Stephen, lads; are you into kinky sex?"

Stephen choked on his drink.

"Is that an invitation, like?" Andy grinned.

When she went to the toilet, George dug Stephen in the ribs. "It's obvious she wants you, so come on, bonny lad, we might all get a bit! Can't you just see her, spread-eagled naked in front of you? Those tits!"

Fin groaned. "Shut up, George, we're married men!"

After the interview, Vivvy took Stephen's hand again. "You know, I'd love to do something special with you, Steve. Here's my card. It's got my work *and* my home number on it. Call me sometime." She kissed him on the cheek, and he watched her wiggle out of the door.

He took a deep breath. "I'm just off to the bathroom, lads."

"You'll go blind," Andy shouted after him.

"Self-abuse, oh dear, oh dear," Fin said.

That autumn, Mam died. She was nearly ninety-four, so it was hardly unexpected except in the way death always is. She'd been there ever since Stephen could remember; he'd thought she always would be.

They all converged on the Isle of Wight for the funeral. It was the end of an era. The house in Dover Street was up for sale; Nesta, who was seventy-five, was moving back to Wales. Stephen had thought of buying it, but it would never be the same. He could hardly bear the thought that it was all over, all those summers when being grown up had seemed light years away, and everything was possible. He wept all through the service, and wasn't alone. And the Welsh voices nearly raised the roof off the little church when they sang Mam's favourite hymn, 'Lord of all Hopefulness'.

At Christmas, he invited all his family to the Priory; Sian and Ted, Dominic and Harry and their children; Kathy, Paul, Ceridwen and Rhiannon, and Rebecca and her partner, Idris Croft, the poet. These two lived in splendid isolation in Pembroke, Rebecca creating abstract and startling sculptures, and Idris writing. Rebecca told Sian she was never going to have children. "How could I inflict childhood on an innocent baby?" she asked with a shudder.

"What was it about being a child that you so hated, cariad?" Sian asked gently.

"Everything!" Rebecca declared.

"It's so sad," Sian said to Stephen later, when she was telling him. "She seemed contented as a child, for the most part, don't you think, Stevie?"

He nodded.

Sian sighed. "It's awful, isn't it? You can live with someone for years and not really know them at all."

Stephen had written lyrics for a song, 'Bara Brith', after Mam died. Bara Brith, literally meaning 'speckled bread', was a kind of fruit bread, a delicacy that Mam used to make for them. The lyrics were unlike any he'd ever written before and he wasn't sure he could write music for them. Nothing seemed right.

"These are good words, Dad. Is it a new song?"

Stephen leaned over. "Which?"

They were in the music room, Rob at the piano, Stephen changing the strings on a Strat. "Oh, 'Bara Brith'. Kind of. I wrote them when Mam died, but I haven't been able to sort out the music." He turned back to the Strat.

Rob read them through again, and quietly began to pick out a tune, a haunting little piece he played several times.

Stephen sat and listened. Reaching for his twelve-string, he began to play with Rob's tune. They carried on together, Rob playing his piece over and over.

Both of them were so absorbed they didn't hear Toni come in. "Steve, I told you it was only half an hour to lunch, what are you up to? Everyone's waiting!"

"Sorry, Daisy, but Rob just wrote the music for Bara Brith!" Stephen's face was alight with excitement and pride.

"No, I didn't!" Rob objected, "I just played this little bit."

"The most important bit! You're a genius, Blue! Let's go and show your Mum and Gran!"

Downstairs, they played Rob's tune, and Stephen sang the lyrics. After they'd finished, there was a silence.

"I'd forgotten that time Nesta accidentally put coffee beans in the Welsh cakes instead of raisins," Sian said, her voice trembling.

Harry threw her arms round Rob and started to cry, which set Toni and Sian off. "You're so *clever*!" she sobbed.

Stephen had tears in his eyes, and even Ted was looking emotional.

Dominic was watching them with growing incredulity. He thought it was time to check the rising tide of hysteria. "Pull yourself together, woman, for God's sake!" he said to Harry. "Jesus Christ, it's like the death of Little Nell all over again, at which, incidentally, only a man with a heart of stone could fail to laugh. I'll get a camera, and we can take a picture of the man and his prodigy with their sweetly matching hair, eyes and guitars, and we can put them on next year's Christmas cards!"

Harry let out an inarticulate bellow of rage and fell on him.

"Ouch, get off, help me someone, she's killing me!" He tickled her and she subsided, half-laughing, half-crying. He pulled her onto his lap and kissed her.

"Yuck! You and Mummy are always doing that!" Rob pulled a face.

"You wait a few years," Dominic grinned.

Stephen hugged Rob. "Blue, you little beaut, this'll be your first song-writing credit. It'll be going on the next album with your name on it!"

Rob stared at him. "Will it, Dad? Really?"

"Certainly will. I'm so proud of you, Rob."

'More Than I Remember' was released at the beginning of January, and resulted in Stephen being asked to write a soundtrack for a film being made about Disraeli's life, *The Vagabond*. He reread the book *Disraeli* by Andre Maurois, and several other biographies, including Kebbel's *Speeches Of Lord Beaconsfield*, and almost drove Toni mad with his constant references to Disraeli's wit and genius. When he started quoting his speeches, she issued an ultimatum: "It's Disraeli or me!" He pretended to consider it, and she thumped him.

The song 'Savages', which he'd written in aid of Africa, was released as a single and got a lot of media attention. The band was asked to sing it at several charity concerts, and, as Stephen had, George, Andy and Fin donated their earnings to third world charities.

The album that George had recorded with the singer-songwriter Will Seaton, 'Newcastle Brawn' was released at the end of March, but by then, George and Seaton were no longer on speaking terms, citing 'creative differences'.

"George would have creative differences with his own reflection," Andy commented.

"Gosh, look at this!" Hazel, one of the health workers, was bending over a magazine she'd received from home that morning. She smiled at Tim and Lynn, who were finishing lunch. "You two are in this article!"

Lynn looked at Tim, who raised his eyebrows.

"Well, tell us more then, Haze," Matt prompted.

"OK. My mum sent it because it's about funds for us. Let's see, hmm, hmm, hmm, yes, here it is – '*Lynn and Tim Franklin, dedicated health workers*'. That's you two!"

Tim was starting to smile. "Why us?"

"I'm not sure, it's really about Steve Markham." She scanned the page.

Tim's smile disappeared.

"Yeah, he's got this new song, it's raised loads of money for Africa. He sounds like a nice man, listen: '"*I feel I'm so lucky, I just want to give something back." Markham, 31, father of four, is a vegetarian and actively involved with several charities, among them Lifeline and Food For All, both of which work for third world countries. Markham and his wife, Antonia, 32, an Australian zoologist, who is also involved in environmentalist issues, sponsor several children around the world. Markham is in the process of setting up a charitable foundation…*"

"Tax dodge, no doubt," Tim muttered.

"Then there's some stuff… um… then he says, '"*I know two people who work in Africa, Lynn and Tim Franklin, dedicated health workers; they make me feel very humble.*"' How come you know him?"

"God, it makes me sick!" Tim exploded. "He gets up on stage and sings a few songs and he's a bloody hero! Never mind us, working right here in the midst of it all!"

Lynn was leaning over Hazel's shoulder, reading the rest of the article. "Well, he says that here, to be fair to him."

"Why the hell should I be fair to him?" Tim shouted.

Matt and Hazel looked at each other, baffled.

Something inside Lynn snapped. "You know what, Tim? I am sick of apologising for having been married to Stevie! He's a lovely man, he was lovely then and he's lovely now! What's he ever done to you?"

"You were married to Stephen Markham?" Hazel asked in amazement.

Neither Lynn nor Tim even heard her.

"You've never got over him!" Tim accused.

"Yes I have—" Lynn started.

"I was in the study," Tim shouted, "when he came back from the hospital and told you, sweet Cherry, how much he still loved you, and you said… you said 'I feel the same way'!"

The colour drained from Lynn's face. She put her hand to her mouth. "It was *you*! You phoned your stepfather's paper! Oh my God, Tim, that's what you never could tell me. Oh, how could you do it? How could you *do* that to him?"

They stared at each other.

Matt cleared his throat, but before he could speak, Fiona burst in. "Tim, all of you, come quickly! There's a bunch of refugees dying at the gates!"

It was cholera. It swept through the camp, despite their best efforts to isolate it. Kentice and Gideon lost all their daughters – the baby, little Julienne, whose first birthday they had not long ago celebrated, was the first to die. Lynn couldn't believe it was happening. How could these people stand any more suffering? The staff struggled on, coping, sharing the grief.

When it was over, Lynn said to Tim, "I can't stand it any more. I know it's pathetic, but that's the way it is. And I can't be here with you. I'm going back to England."

Chapter Thirteen
Storm Warning

We didn't hear the storm warning, too busy having fun,
We didn't see the dark clouds forming, blocking out the sun.
We were standing hand in hand on the edge of bright tomorrow,
We should've turned and run, but we stepped forward into sorrow.

Lynn arrived home in April, and threw herself into her work. ASUK welcomed her back with open arms. She missed Tim enormously and found that, as when she had split up with Stephen, she tended to drink a little too much in the evenings.

"Not thirty yet and two failed relationships behind me!" she said to Caro when they were having a night out.

"Would you go back to Tim?" Caro asked.

"Not in Africa." She shivered. "I couldn't, Caro. When Julienne died…" She stopped and gulped back tears. "I know I'm pathetic," she said, fiercely, "but I just couldn't take it any more."

"You are not pathetic!" Caro exclaimed. "I wouldn't be able to stand four days out there, let alone four years! You're a hero, Lynn! But anyway, about Tim?"

"I don't know. I miss him very much."

"Why did you split up?"

"Oh, you know." Lynn made vague gestures.

"No, I don't, but I can see you're not going to tell me. The thing is, he wrote to Donald."

"What?" Lynn stared at her.

"Yeah. He wanted me to ask you – discreetly, mind you – if you'd have him back. He's coming home."

Lynn burst out laughing. "You? Discreet? Oh, that's marvellous! Poor Tim!"

Caro grinned. "So what do you say?"

"Tell him to stop being a wuss and ask me himself. I will not use a go-between."

Tim took her to lunch a month later. "I couldn't stand it without you. I'm sorry, Lynn, I'm so sorry for what I did to him. I was sorry almost as soon as it was done. But can you imagine how it felt for me to hear the things you said?"

She shook her head. "No, I can't. And I'm so sorry too. Oh, Tim, it's not that I don't love you. I do, tremendously, but…"

"But you love him more," Tim said evenly.

She stared at him. "I'm sorry," she whispered.

He smiled. It didn't reach his eyes. "Right, that's that then. I can't share you, Lynn. Oh, God, I wish I could." He leant over and kissed her.

She watched him walk away, tears dripping unheeded down her face.

Work was the only panacea. She spent her spare time reading, going on courses, and occasionally giving a paper. Freed from her pact, she began to buy magazines with articles about Stephen. There was no need to keep them hidden any more, she could lie in bed on a Sunday morning, eating chocolate and reading her latest stash. She could listen to his albums wherever and whenever she wanted. She bought the videos of *With Giants Fight* and *Hoodman Blind*. *Hoodman Blind* was her favourite, but Rob was adorable in *With Giants Fight*, and she'd always thought Stephen looked impossibly beautiful with his hair longer and tousled, and so sexy in mediaeval costume.

One night after work, she sat down in front of the television with a microwave meal and flicked to MTV. They were about to show a Sid's Six concert that had been held in Sydney the previous month. She scrabbled around for a tape to record it, then sat, transfixed. The band came onstage to huge cheers. Stephen looked exactly the same as he had at the wedding, but far scruffier. He fiddled with his microphone. "G'day, mates!"

The crowd yelled, "G'day, Steve!"

"It's great to see you all, thanks for being here!"

The crowd shouted and whistled.

Stephen shaded his eyes and scanned the audience. "You're all looking fantastic – and it looks like we've got some music lovers here too – no, maybe not, is that a GI Joe tee shirt I see back there?"

The camera panned over to the girl wearing the tee shirt. She promptly peeled it off, revealing her breasts.

Stephen looked pleased. "Bonus! OK, so you wanna hear some tunes?"

"Yeah!" roared the crowd.

"OK – I'm thinking Rolf Harris!" He started to play 'Tie Me Kangaroo Down.'

The crowd screamed, booed and whistled.

Lynn grinned. He'd always joked with the audience like this. He enjoyed interacting with them tremendously.

Stephen stopped. "No?" He sounded amazed. "Really? You don't want that? OK, how about… um… oh, I know, how about Abba? Something to dance to!" He strummed 'Dancing Queen'.

More shouts and whistles.

Stephen looked at George. "What do you think, George?"

"How about 'Cherry'?" George suggested.

The crowd applauded vigorously.

"Oh, right, 'Cherry'! Neil Diamond, isn't it?" He played the introduction to 'Sweet Cherry'.

The crowd went wild.

Stephen stopped. "Wait a minute, that's not Neil Diamond."

The crowd started to stamp and clap.

"You want this anyway? Flaming mental, you lot! Although, didn't we rehearse this?" He looked at the other three.

"Yeah, we did, Steve," Fin nodded.

"Fin says we did! OK!" He started playing again.

Massive applause.

He stopped.

The crowd laughed and catcalled.

"You don't really want this, do you?"

"Yes!"

"Are you sure?"

"YES!"

"Sure you're sure?"

George stepped across and picked him up by the collar of his jacket, so that his feet dangled above the stage. "Howay, man, just play the song!"

"Looks like we're doing this one then," Stephen smiled.

'Sweet Cherry' rang out. Lynn shut her eyes and let the music wash over her. It was her. This lovely man was singing those words to thousands of people and they were about *her*. It was pretty unbelievable, she thought. They played 'Postmodern Romance', which had been an enormous hit in Australia, and 'The Sound of One Hand Clapping' and 'This Northern Sky', and then Stephen said, "This next one's from our new album. Hope you like it." And they played 'Savages'.

God, thought Lynn. If he hadn't written that song, I'd still be in Africa with Tim.

"I'm so worried about him, Steve!"

"I know. I'm ringing Henry again."

"I just did. He can't do anything, it's a virus."

"Is that bath ready yet?"

"Yes, hand him to me." Toni sat in a lukewarm bath with Sam. He had been ill for a couple of days, his temperature getting higher and higher. They bathed him and fed him junior Paracetamol and brought it down, only for it to climb again almost immediately.

"Henry says as long as he's still eating, he'll be OK."

"Thank God he loves his food!"

"Yeah, if it'd been Pip!"

Gradually, over the next few days, Sam began to recover. He remained thin and listless for too long afterwards, Stephen thought, although their GP, Henry, pronounced him to be splendid.

"He doesn't seem to chatter like he used to," Stephen said to Toni.

"I know. He's not nearly so bouncy. Maybe he needs a tonic."

"Will you be all right taking them all to Brisbane on your own?"

Sid's Six was about to tour South America, and Toni was taking the boys to Australia. "I'll have Karen," she said.

"If there's anything, anything at all, I'll fly out," he promised, kissing her.

He rang continually while he was away. He knew he was probably overreacting when he heard Jacko shout, "It's that whinging Pom again, Tones," after the first dozen times.

"He's fine, Stevo, they all are." But something in her voice didn't sound right.

When he saw them again, he was sure. Alex and Pip seemed to have shot up, Sam looked just the same. "He hasn't grown, has he?" he said.

Toni bit her lip. "No. But he's his old self, wolfing down his food, happy as Larry with his action figures."

But Stephen noticed he never played with Alex or Pip, preferring solitary games with the action figures. He didn't talk like the other two did, either; he had a large vocabulary, but his speech was peculiar, idiosyncratic, with strange exclamations and an odd trick of repeating the same word or phrase over and over. He hated anything to change, and when Alex started school a few weeks later, he became distraught, refusing to eat, and hitting Pip with his toys.

Toni got cross with him. "He's so wilful," she said to Stephen, who was spending a lot of time working on the Disraeli soundtrack.

"Not another hoon! Still though, if he hasn't grown by Christmas, perhaps we ought to get Henry to have a look at him."

The following January, they took him to their GP. He hadn't grown at all, and was starting to refuse food. As Toni pointed out, the two older boys had gone through a phase of being fussy eaters; Pip could still be difficult, but they both felt that Sam couldn't afford not to eat well. "Although you're just a tiddler, Stevo, and think how small Rob used to be," she added hopefully.

Rob was nearly thirteen and had grown tremendously in the last few months. He was already five foot five and still growing.

"You'll soon be taller than me," Stephen said, pleased. He'd never lost any sleep over the fact that he wasn't quite five foot eight, but he wouldn't have minded being tall, and he very much hoped his sons would be.

Henry organised a series of blood and urine tests for Sam, which upset the poor little boy very much. They all came back normal, except for the fact that he was slightly anaemic. He had a hearing test, to check whether a hearing loss was responsible for his unusual speech patterns, and it was decided that he was slightly deaf, with fluid in his middle ear, so he had an operation to drain the fluid, and grommets inserted in both ears. By this time, he was thoroughly unhappy, and was refusing to eat most of the foods he used to enjoy, existing mainly on dry bread, which he referred to as 'pizza bread' – he was a big fan of *The Teenage Mutant Hero Turtles* – baby juice, and milk. He had reverted to drinking out of a bottle, refusing to use a cup. Stephen and Toni were so desperate for him to eat and drink that they made no attempt to change his mind. He tended to dribble, and his mouth and chin were always wet and sore.

"I don't know what to do, Steve," Toni said, despairingly. "It doesn't seem to matter how much barrier cream I put on his face, and I don't like using that steroid cream they gave us at the clinic."

Stephen sighed. "I know. He's just not like the others, is he? And have you noticed how much he likes characters who wear masks?"

"What do you mean?"

"Well, the Turtles, Spiderman, Batman. He's not interested in other stuff."

She stared at him. "Yes, you're right. Bedtime stories…"

"I know, I make up stories for him now. He never wants any of the books we've got."

"Why is he so different, Stevie? I'm so worried!"

Then he started to vomit when presented with new food.

"My God, suppose he's got cancer!" Toni wept.

Henry had referred them to a paediatrician but he didn't seem particularly good, and Toni didn't like him. "I'm not really good with hospitals and doctors," she said to Stephen with a shudder.

"Refer us to someone who cares about children, Henry," Stephen snapped.

"Well, as luck would have it, there's a splendid chap I can refer you to who works at Great Ormond Street and has just started to do some private work, name of Tim Franklin."

"Oh, Tim?" Stephen said, surprised. "I thought he was in Africa."

Henry raised his eyebrows. "Oh, you know him? He's been back for several months. Bit sad, really, wasn't it, that crisis out there, then his wife leaving him."

Stephen saw Toni jump. He avoided her eyes. "Yeah… er… please refer us, Henry."

"Sit down, Toni, Stephen." Tim shook hands with them both.

"Thank you for seeing us so quickly," Toni said. She had Sam on her lap.

"Hello, Sam," Tim said.

Sam ignored him.

Tim looked at the notes. "He's been losing weight steadily, he hasn't grown, and now he's vomiting when he eats?"

Toni nodded.

"Well, not exactly," Stephen said. "He's sick if we offer him new food and get him to try it."

"What's the difference?" Toni demanded, angrily.

Tim examined Sam very gently and competently, talking reassuringly to him all the time. "I'll arrange a barium swallow," he said, writing. "I can get it done on Wednesday if that's any good for you?" he asked, looking up.

"Oh, yes," said Toni.

Tim smiled at her. "There is a difference, Toni. It may be that vomiting is his way of telling you he doesn't want the food you're making him eat."

"We don't *make* him eat it!"

"Yes, sorry, I meant encouraging him. *He* might well see it as being made to eat it. Bringing it back up could be his defence mechanism. A little extreme, I grant you! Anyway, having examined him I can't feel any lumps or bumps."

Although the results from the barium swallow were normal, it was a harrowing experience. They gave him the barium meal in a bottle, but it was extremely difficult getting him to swallow it. Eventually, Stephen thought to sing to him in Welsh, as he had when Sam was a baby. Sam became very still and stared up at him. His eyes were red and sore from crying and he was sobbing. Stephen found it very hard to keep singing. He just wanted to pick his son up and cradle him in his arms.

Sam was referred to a dietitian next. He was two and weighed twenty two pounds, which was the average weight of a nine month old. He was given a liquid supplement called Fresubin, which looked and tasted similar to milk, and Denise, the dietitian, suggested mixing it with milk to start with and gradually adding less and less until he was drinking only the Fresubin. This strategy worked very well, and soon he was actually asking for his 'Frezzybin'. He was weighed every week and eventually started to put on a little – a very little – weight. Stephen and Toni were told to let him eat any food he would. "Even chocolate's got iron in it," Denise said.

"I'm going to refer you to a child psychiatrist. There's a very good one in Birmingham, Peter Harmon. I guarantee you'll like him, Toni." Tim smiled at her.

They stared at him.

"Do you mean he's – he's retarded or something?" Toni whispered.

"Not at all, in fact I suspect that he's very intelligent. But it's as if… well… as if the wiring in his brain works differently to ours. But I'm not a specialist in that area."

"That's such a shame," Toni said fervently. "You've been wonderful, Tim!"

He smiled at her. "It's sad really, I only get to see lovely little ones like yours when they're ill! How's Rob?"

"He's fine," Stephen smiled. "He's been asking after you."

Tim flushed. "He still remembers me?"

"God, yes! You made a huge impression on him!" Stephen said. As they drove home, he glanced over at Toni. "I hate the thought of Sam seeing a psychiatrist. Ted had terrible trouble finding one he could get on with, and he said all most of them wanted to talk about was the patient's sex life."

"It's all to do with Freud, isn't it? But Tim said we'd like him."

"He said you'd like him," Stephen said, remembering.

Toni stared at him. "I'm sure he meant both of us."

"Dad! Can Sam play with my Mega Drive?" Rob asked one evening shortly before their appointment with the psychiatrist. He was holding Sam by the hand.

"Your Mega Drive," Stephen repeated. He'd been on the phone to Cell, trying to juggle the band's touring schedule around.

"Yeah. He saw me playing the Spiderman game; he wants to."

Stephen squatted down by Sam. "Sammy."

Sam gazed past him.

Stephen took his son's chin and gently turned his face so that he could look at him. They made eye contact and Sam's eyes slid away. "Do you want to play Spiderman?"

Sam looked at him briefly. He nodded. "In the all-concealing shadows, Dr Venkman," he whispered. The cartoon series of the Ghostbusters had supplanted the Turtles as his favourite programme, refuting Stephen's theory that he only liked masked heroes. He had taken to calling Stephen Dr. Venkman, his favourite character, and Toni was Janine, the Ghostbusters' secretary.

They went up to Rob's room. "You'll have to help him, Blue," Stephen said.

He was wrong. Sam took the controls and played like an expert.

"He's been watching me," Rob said.

The little boy was completely absorbed. He would have gone on playing for hours. The next day, Stephen went out and bought him his own console.

"Is that a good idea, Steve?" Toni asked. "He's so solitary already."

"I know, but I can't see what we can do about that, not letting him have a Mega Drive won't make him play with the others, and it makes him so happy."

Toni started to cry. "It's like he's locked in his own little world," she sobbed, "and there's no way we can reach him."

As soon as they met Peter Harmon, they realised why Tim had predicted that Toni would like him. He was Australian, relaxed and friendly. He smiled at them, shaking hands. "G'day. Tim tells me you're from Brizzie, Toni." He wanted details of Sam's conception, Toni's pregnancy, the labour and birth. He asked at what age Sam had smiled, crawled, pulled himself up, sat up unaided, vocalised, his first word, when he was weaned, when did he first chew, things that neither of them could remember. He also wanted to know about Rob, Alex, and Pip, and Stephen and Toni themselves.

Every time he started a new question, Stephen braced himself, expecting it to be about their sex life.

As Sam played, Harmon watched him through a two-way mirror. "There are a few tests I'd like to do, a few things to rule out," he said, afterwards.

"Not more blood tests?" Toni asked, fearfully. Sam hated them so much.

"I'm afraid so." He smiled apologetically. "I'm sorry, Toni." He stood up.

"But..." Stephen started.

"Sorry, Stephen, did you have any more questions? I should have asked that."

"Aren't you going to ask us about our sex life?" Stephen blurted out.

Harmon grinned. "Well, I'm sorry to disappoint you, Stephen, but I honestly don't think it's relevant, although if you really want to talk about it, don't let me stop you. You might want to get Sam home first though."

"God, Stephen! You imbo!" Toni hissed, very embarrassed.

"B-but I th-thought..." Stephen stammered. He shook his head. "Sorry. I'm being an idiot."

Harmon smiled at him. "No worries! I'll see you when we get the results back." He ushered them to the door. They made another appointment, had the blood tests done, and drove home.

They were tired and worried, and it was difficult to behave normally and respond to the other boys' inconsequential chatter without snapping. Feeling like a traitor, Stephen escaped to the music room and spent a few hours playing guitar, losing himself in the music. When he came downstairs, Karen was bathing Sam, Rob and Alex were watching TV, and Toni was reading to Pip.

"Sorry," he said guiltily.

She gave him a frosty smile.

"I'll put Sammy to bed," he offered.

"OK, I'll get tea. Let's have an early night, I'm tired."

When the boys were in bed, they curled up on the sofa together.

Toni flicked idly through the TV channels. "Oh, good oh, Tom Cruise," she said, pleased.

"Not Tom Cruise, please not Tom Cruise," Stephen protested.

"Shut up! I don't complain when you look at…" She cast around for someone he liked.

"See, who? I only look at you, my darling."

"Kylie."

"Well, OK, Kylie, but she's an Aussie, like you."

"Shut up and let me watch!"

"What is this, anyway?"

"It's a film. Hang on, I'll look. *Rainman*."

They sat and watched the film about the autistic Raymond – Rainman – and his unpleasant younger brother. By the end they were both in tears.

"That's Sam," Toni whispered. "That's Sam, isn't it?"

Stephen could only nod.

Peter Harmon finally confirmed their fears. He thought Sam had Aspergers Syndrome rather than classic autism.

Stephen and Toni sat speechlessly through his explanation of Aspergers, holding hands.

"What causes it?" Toni asked, eventually.

"We just don't know," Harmon told her. "I'm so sorry."

"What can we do?" Stephen asked.

Harmon looked at them with compassion. "I'm afraid – very little," he said quietly. "I think it might be helpful if Sam saw a speech therapist; I'm sure Tim Franklin or your GP will be able to recommend one. Then have you heard of Portage?"

They shook their heads. They'd never been faced with anything like this before, hadn't dreamt they ever would be.

"It's a home visiting educational service for pre-school children with special needs. I'll get Annaliese to sort out the details of the scheme and you can see if you want to use it. I certainly recommend it."

Special needs. The words sent a chill through Stephen. His son had special needs. Poor little Sam had special needs. He wouldn't have the same happy, fun childhood that he, Stephen, had had, that Rob and Alex and Pip were having. Nothing would ever be easy for him, he would always have difficulty understanding the world around him, he would always be an outsider. Stephen wanted to scream, to throw things, to shout and cry and rail against fate. Why Sam? It's not fair, it's not fair!

He lay awake that night going over and over it. How could this be happening to them? He couldn't bear the thought of Sam having this syndrome. All the money he had didn't mean a thing. It couldn't stop this happening. And he'd give it all up tomorrow if only Sam could be like the other three. He got up and made his way up to his music room where he raged and cried. He was so angry, and there was no one he could be angry with, it was no one's fault. He was finally beginning to understand how Lynn had felt when she lost the baby. Angry at the world, angry at life, angry and sad. Devastated, he thought, I'm devastated and desolate. He wondered how many other parents were going through this same thing right now. And then he thought, some parents are facing the fact that their child has a terminal illness. Some parents are grieving for their dead children. And that thought made him cry again and he felt as if he knew all the parents who were suffering this awful dark side of parenthood and that they were all suffering with him. At least Sam is alive, he thought. I've still got him, he's here. So he's different. Well, so what? He's Sam. And he realised he'd been grieving as much for himself as for his son. How selfish can you be? he thought incredulously. Well, no more. He was going to make sure that Sam had the best life he could possibly have. My money can at least do that, he thought. He went downstairs, washed his face and went back to bed.

Toni reached out for him. "Stevie? Where have you been?"

"Crying. Trying to make sense of it. I finally realised there *is* no sense to it, we've just got to accept it and try to make things as easy as possible for Sam."

Toni turned on the light. "What do you mean?"

"Well, nothing's going to be easy for him, Toni. He's not going to be like the other boys."

"But when he gets better…"

"He's not going to get better," Stephen interrupted.

"Yeah, when he has speech therapy and the Portage thing."

"They're not going to make him better. They'll help, but there's no cure. You heard what Dr Harmon said."

Toni stared at him. "I'm not really good with illness, Stephen," she whispered. She was shaking.

He took her in his arms. "It's the shock, Daisy. I know we saw that film and said, oh God, that's Sam, but secretly I thought Harmon was going to say, no, he's fine, it's just a phase…" He clenched his teeth and swallowed hard. "Poor little Sam!"

"I can't, Steve, I can't, I *can't* accept he'll never get better!" Toni's voice rose.

"Oh, my darling, I don't think life has ever looked so bleak." He kissed her. "We're tired, Toni. I know it's not going to look any different in the morning, but at least we might be able to cope a little better." He held her while she cried, rubbing her back and kissing her hair. Eventually, she stopped, and he fetched a cold flannel and bathed her eyes. He turned off the light, and they lay in the dark, holding hands. He heard her breathing change, and her grip on his hand loosened as she drifted off to sleep. He lay awake. At least my money got him seen quickly, he thought. He remembered overhearing a conversation at the mother and toddler group, two women talking about the horrendous amount of time one of them had had to wait for her daughter to see a consultant. And we could choose who he saw.

Eventually, he got up, showered, and went out into the garden. He sat on the terrace and watched the sun come up. It was going to be a lovely day. He must have fallen asleep, because the next thing he knew, Rob was shaking his shoulder.

"Dad! Wake up! What are you doing out here?"

"Robbie." He rubbed his eyes. "I was watching the dawn. Watching the sun being born. Isn't that part of a song?"

Rob shrugged. "Toni says come in to breakfast. Bye, Dad. I'm off to school, I'll see you this evening." He started to walk away, whistling happily.

Stephen stood up. " Rob, wait."

Rob turned back and Stephen hugged him. "Take care, Robbie," he whispered, kissing him.

"Are you all right, Dad?" Rob asked anxiously.

Stephen smiled. "Yeah. Just old and tired. Take no notice."

It was Rob's thirteenth birthday at the beginning of June, and they'd organised a party for him. The family would be there during the day, and in the evening he was having a pool party and disco for his friends.

Stephen and Toni were dreading seeing everyone. They hadn't said much about Sam, only that he wasn't well and was seeing specialists. When people inquired, they had been dismissive, refused invitations, and hadn't asked anyone to the Priory. Without actually saying so to each other, they'd both felt that if they didn't say it out loud it wouldn't happen. The only person Stephen had told was Cell; he felt he owed her an explanation of his behaviour. He'd rearranged the band's schedule with her and they were now due to tour the Far East at the beginning of August.

Harry and Dominic arrived on Friday night. Harry was glowing with health. "I'm expecting another baby," she said as they relaxed over drinks. "It's due just after Christmas."

Toni burst into tears.

Harry and Dominic looked at her in alarm.

"What's wrong, Toni?" Harry asked.

"Sam's autistic," Stephen said.

They stared at him, appalled. Neither of them knew what to say. Harry gripped Dominic's hand. Finally Dominic said, "Tell us."

Stephen told them everything that had happened since they had first seen Henry. "Apparently, Aspergers Syndrome means that he won't have learning difficulties or anything, his intelligence won't be affected. Apparently lots of children with Aspergers are often very gifted in things like maths. It's socially that he's impaired. He can't... he won't be able to make much sense of the world." He could feel his throat tightening. He fetched an information sheet they'd been given.

"The doctor said he'll have trouble making friends," Toni said

"He '*can't interpret body language, can't cope with change, lacks social or emotional reciprocity*'," Stephen read. He gave the sheet to Dominic.

"Why didn't you tell us?" Harry asked. "Every time I asked you how he was you said 'fine'. I feel terrible! I knew there was something wrong, but Toni was so fierce with me last time I asked, that I didn't know what to do. I'm not blaming you, Toni," she added. "Does Rob know? He said last time I spoke to him that Sam was seeing lots of doctors – including Tim."

"Yes, Tim's been wonderful!" Toni said, with feeling.

"Who else have you told?" Dominic asked.

Stephen shook his head. "No one. I was going to ring Mum, but then I thought I'd wait till she and Ted got here. Oh, I told Cell. I've had to keep changing the band's schedule. I just told the lads Sam wasn't well. And we haven't told Blue."

"I'll help you," Harry squeezed his hand. "We're *so* sorry. I can't even begin to imagine how you're feeling."

"Oh, stop it!" Toni cried. "Stop talking about it!" She ran out of the room.

"She's having trouble accepting it," Stephen sighed. "She's angry with me because I have. She needs someone to blame." He started after her.

Dominic took his arm. "Would you like me to go?" he asked quietly.

Stephen stared at him. He nodded slowly.

Dominic found her in the kitchen. "Come here." He held out his arms and Toni snuggled against him.

"I can't stand it, Dom," she said, through her tears. "I can't cope with it, I *hate* illness and disability! I can't *stand* Stephen being so calm about it all, why doesn't he *do* something?"

Dominic held her, letting her cry all her fear and anger and heartbreak out. Who did this for Stephen? he wondered.

Finally she stopped. "I must look terrible, and I've cried all over your tee shirt! Sorry, Dom."

Dominic raised her face to his. "You look beautiful." He kissed her forehead.

She hugged him tightly. "Thanks, Dom. I'm going to wash my face. Tell Stephen I'll be down in ten minutes."

Rob burst into the drawing room before she got back. "Hello," he beamed, kissing Harry and Dominic. "Chocolate biscuit?" He offered the packet round.

"Please." Stephen took several.

"God, you two are such pigs!" Harry exclaimed.

"Dad and Toni gave me a Strat," Rob mumbled, his mouth full. "Candy Apple Red!"

"You've told us," Harry smiled.

"Frequently," Dominic added.

"I'll get it," Rob said.

Stephen held out his hand for the biscuits.

Harry smiled at him. "You were the first person I'd ever seen playing a Strat. You looked *so* sexy! God, I fancied you so much!"

"Hey, woman, stop that," Dominic ordered.

Harry stuck her tongue out at him. She sat on Stephen's lap and brushed his hair off his forehead.

"Why do women always do that to me?" Stephen asked.

"It's a maternal thing," Harry told him, grinning.

Toni came in. She raised her eyebrows at the sight of Harry on Stephen's lap. Dominic patted his invitingly and, after a slight hesitation, she sat down.

Rob appeared at the door. He boggled at the sight of them. "Bloody hell! The papers would have a field day!"

"You have a very vulgar mind, Robert," Dominic drawled. "We're just good friends." He gave Rob an exaggerated wink. "Come along then, musical prodigy, get in here with that guitar and entertain us!"

After the children had finished tea, they all went out to the poolroom. Stephen had had it added to the back of the house, and it had sliding glass doors, so that it was light in the winter, and in the summer, the doors could be opened up, giving free access to the garden. All his boys, even Sam, swam like fish.

Dominic lounged on a deckchair, drinking whisky, and watching Stephen terrifying Alex and Pip by pretending to be a shark.

"Come on in." Stephen climbed out and sat on the edge, his feet dangling in the water.

Dominic shook his head. "The only sport I indulge in involves naked women. Listen, Markham, I wanted to talk to you. GI Joe is officially splitting up, retiring, whatever you like to call it."

"Why?" Stephen asked, surprised. He'd known the band had been having difficulties, but not that things were so bad.

"Gil is leaving to 'pursue a solo career', and frankly, I can't be bothered with replacing him. There's only me and Mick left now from the original line up, the band's had more fucking makeovers than Liz Taylor. We've run out of steam."

"What are you going to do?"

"I don't know, maybe do some solo stuff. Actually, I might do some producing. I really liked producing 'Stand Up At The Back'."

"Well, you've got my business. I want to do a solo album. I've written several songs that aren't Sid's Six material. Will you produce it?"

Dominic grinned widely. "Markham, old chap, you've got yourself a fucking deal!"

They went to the house on the lake in Massachusetts in July, just Stephen, Toni, the four boys and Karen. Stephen hadn't intended taking Karen, but Sam got so upset at the thought of her not being there and so stressed by changes to his routine, that he couldn't see what else to do.

While they were there, Rob fell in love with an American girl, Meredith Siegel. She was fourteen, small and plump, and wore a brace. Rob thought she was the most beautiful girl he'd ever seen. He told her he was sixteen and begged Stephen not to tell her he wasn't.

"OK, Blue," Stephen said, reluctantly. "But behave. You know what I mean."

"Dad!" Rob was shocked. "I *love* Meredith!"

"Exactly, that's what worries me," Stephen retorted.

They spent their every waking hour together. Rob didn't want to leave. "Can she come and stay at the Priory?" he asked on their last evening.

"Um… what do her parents say?" Stephen stalled.

"They say she's too young."

Stephen sighed with relief. "Oh well, sorry, then, Blue. You can see her next time we come over," he added, knowing how inadequate that was.

"She's so beautiful, she'll be going out with someone else by then," Rob said gloomily.

So will you, Stephen thought, but he didn't say it. He remembered the first time he'd fallen for a girl. He was overcome by a wave of nostalgia, and envy of Rob. He's right at the beginning of it all, he thought.

Sam was extremely difficult, throwing tantrums and hurting anyone who tried to calm him. They knew it was because he was stressed, but it was very hard to cope with, hard not to get angry with him. Stephen felt horribly guilty at how much he was looking forward to going on tour and having a break from him.

The week before he went he had a huge row with Toni. Sam had been particularly demanding; he wouldn't let Toni out of his sight for more than two or three minutes, had thrown several tantrums, and had pushed Pip down the steps leading from the terrace to the garden. Luckily, there were only three of them and Pip wasn't hurt.

"Stephen, you can't go away," Toni said.

"I have to, Toni, I can't cancel it now!"

"Why? If you or one of us was ill you would."

"Well, if we were really ill, I suppose, maybe," Stephen said, grudgingly.

"Sam *is*. You going away is going to stress him *so* much! And I can't cope with him on my own."

"Come on, Toni, you've got Karen, and you're hardly struggling in a little two up, two down, are you?"

She flew at him. He caught hold of her wrists.

"Neither are you!" she screamed. "And you're going to be jetting out to do something you love, with all your mates, and sex on offer all the time, while I'm here looking after your handicapped son! It's not fair!"

"Life's not fair," Stephen said, letting her go. "And he's your son too. And it's my job."

"It doesn't have to be."

He stared at her. "What do you mean?"

"We've got heaps of money, more than you could shake a stick at!"

"Yes, and this lifestyle needs it!"

"Well, do more soundtracks! You're always being offered them! You could produce, like Dom."

"Look, I'm in a band, God damn it! I can't just dump them!"

"Yes you can! Surely your family is more important?"

Stephen couldn't answer.

Toni stared at him challengingly.

Finally, he said, "You're right. I suppose I just like being in the band, I like touring and making albums. Soundtracks are fine, but they're not what I want to be doing."

"How can you be so selfish?" Toni demanded.

He shrugged. "I don't know. But I am, Toni. I'm going on this tour."

She looked at him contemptuously for a long moment, before sweeping from the room. He sank down on the bed. He felt awful; guilty, despicable, ashamed. But he was still going.

Toni barely spoke to him before he went. She didn't say goodbye, wasn't even around when he left. Their marriage had never been at such a low ebb.

Toni was furious. She couldn't remember a time when she'd been so angry with Stephen. How could he abandon them to go and enjoy himself? Because that's what he was doing, he'd admitted it to her face. And just when she needed some company, everyone seemed to be unavailable. Her mother went on holiday; Sian and Ted were due to stay at the Priory for a few weeks, but Ted caught a cold which turned to bronchitis, and Harry's blood pressure shot up and she was told by her doctor to go to bed and stay there. Any of them, particularly Sian and Ted, could have probably coaxed her out of the doldrums and made her laugh and look at things from another perspective, but alone, she brooded. She realised how isolated she was, there was no one she could turn to, except maybe Dominic, and she had a sneaking suspicion that if the chips were really down, Dominic would be on Stephen's side. She liked Shelagh, but Shelagh was Fin's wife. She didn't have the kind of relationship with either of her parents where she could discuss her marriage, not more than superficially, and while she got on well with her sister, again, it was a superficial relationship based mainly on shopping and gossip. She had friends in the village, but not close enough to discuss Stephen with, and she'd lost touch with the friends she'd had before she'd married.

She'd never been in this situation before. She and Stephen had always had a stormy relationship, both physically and emotionally; they had frequent, blazing rows, but they always made up – just as passionately. She considered Stephen to be her best friend, and had always thought that no matter what happened, they would face it together. Even when he'd danced with Lynn, and then pushed her so she'd fallen and had Sam early, she'd not felt the same sense of betrayal. After all, Stephen hadn't engineered that situation, deplorable as his behaviour had been. But this! He'd left her when she most needed him, he'd ignored his responsibilities as a husband and father – and as a friend! – and turned his back on her and Sam. She felt utterly alone. And Sam wanted Stephen. He didn't know where he had gone, didn't understand 'Daddy will be back soon.' He was impossibly difficult all day, hurting Pip, scratching at himself until he drew blood, biting and flapping his hands, and throwing continual tantrums. He wouldn't let Toni out of his sight and slept badly, waking several times during the night and very early every morning. She tried putting him into her bed, so that she'd be there when he woke in the night, but he wanted his own bed. The only way she could get him off to sleep in the evening was to lie with him. She couldn't cuddle him, he hated being held or kissed, and screamed and kicked out at her if she touched him. If she didn't stay with him until he was asleep, he ripped the wallpaper from the walls, tore up his bed covers or hurt himself

"Dr Venkman didn't come home again," he'd say, repeating 'come home' over and over again. Karen had tried staying with him, but he wouldn't have her, only 'Janine' or 'Dr Venkman'. Who wasn't there.

He'd started speech therapy, which was a total washout as far as Toni could see. She didn't think the therapist was any good, but Henry said to give it a chance. Yet another thing Stephen could have helped with, she thought angrily. She managed to always be having a bath or seeing to Sam or just out when he rang.

Rob was so apologetic: "Oh, Toni, you just missed Dad! I'm so sorry! He sends his love!" that she couldn't tell him she wouldn't speak to Stephen if he was the last man on earth, simply said, never mind, Blue, he'll be home soon, or words to that effect. She felt Karen was on her side, but again, couldn't discuss Stephen overtly with her.

Then, in the middle of August, Cell rang. *Juliette*, the popular women's magazine, wanted to do a feature on Toni.

"Cell! Really! On *me*!" She couldn't believe it.

"Mmmhmm. I ran it past Steve—"

"And he said no, of course," Toni interrupted bitterly.

"He said it was up to you."

"Oh! Oh, Cell! I'd love to!"

"Toni, hi, I'm Callie Wright. Thanks for agreeing to give us this interview. So, what's it like being married to Stephen Markham?"

Toni smiled. She and Callie were having tea in the Palm Court at the Ritz. Callie was about Toni's age. She wasn't pretty exactly, her nose was too prominent, and her face just a fraction too long, but she was attractive and very smartly dressed. Toni had come over to London for the day, leaving Pip and Sam with Karen. She felt guilty about leaving Sam, but reasoned it was only for a few hours and she had to have *some* time to herself. "Well, I suppose just like being married to anyone."

"Oh, come *on*! He's a huge star and gorgeous to boot!"

"Yeah, well, he is very handsome, and that's nice, but I've been married to him for six years, and I'm used to his stardom. To be honest, it's a bit of a bore."

Callie laughed delightedly. "A bore? Really?"

"Oh, for sure! We can't go out without Stevo being recognised, there's always creepy girls following him around, asking him to kiss them on the street, or phoning up and wanting to speak to him – God knows how they get our number – oh, you name it!"

"Well, but that's the penalty of fame. What about the plus side?"

Toni shrugged. "Is there one? Getting a seat in a restaurant, I suppose. I'm not talking about being rich, the plus side to that is terrific, but fame's different. Like I say, it's boring – and it's also frightening. I mean, we have to live with a much higher level of security than most people do, and there's the constant worry that someone might try to hurt Steve or the children. But that's just my view of it," she added quickly. "I'm not speaking for Steve."

"At the moment he's away on tour. Do you ever go?"

"I used to. It's difficult these days, with schools and stuff. Rob, Stevo's oldest, lives with us now, and my Alex is at school, and Pip will be starting next month."

"So you stay at home with the children while Stephen parties?"

Too bloody right! "Touring's not like that," Toni said, thinking, You owe me, Markham. "It's hard work and a lot of travel. Basically, it's bus, gig, hotel, day after day."

Callie looked sceptical. "What about groupies and those legendary rock and roll parties after the show?"

"Not these days. I'm sure there are groupies available, but since we got married, Stephen doesn't indulge." She laughed. "Well, only in chocolate."

Callie raised her eyebrows. "Chocolate?"

"Yeah. He always had chocolate on the band's rider, but these days I'm surprised they don't need an extra bus for it!"

"Doesn't he worry about putting on weight?"

Toni shook her head. "He eats like a horse and never puts on a pound! And, to be fair, he runs and swims every day, and when he's performing he burns up heaps of calories."

"Before he married you, he had a reputation as... well, as a bit of a bad boy – never seen with the same woman twice, lots of clubbing, those riotous after-show parties and the like. Then he married you and it all stopped. How did you tame him?"

Toni smiled. "I didn't do anything. I think – oh, this is going to sound as if I've got tickets on myself, but I think it was simply that when Stevie fell in love with me he didn't want to do any of the other stuff. He was just happy being with me."

"So you didn't lay down the law?"

"Not at all. Well, not over that sort of thing!"

Callie raised her eyebrows. "Can I ask over what?"

"Oh, you know men, they've got no idea! Steve's not as bad as some, he's a great cook and he knows how to iron a shirt and clean the bath, but, you know, tidiness and remembering birthdays and stuff!" She broke off and shrugged.

Callie grinned. "Yeah, I know, I have the same sort of problems with my boyfriend, and we've been together for nearly as long as you and Stephen!"

"They're all the same, it's a constant battle," Toni agreed, warming to Callie. They talked about shopping and clothes, and discovered they liked the same designers. Toni ordered more tea and they devoured all the cakes.

"I shouldn't have done that," Callie said despondently. "I've been dieting so hard!"

"It kickstarts the metabolism sometimes, having a big meal."

"Is that true?" Callie asked hopefully.

"Yeah, I think. And if it's not, it should be," Toni laughed.

"You're not a bit like I thought you'd be."

"Neither are you," Toni admitted. "I thought you'd be awful, Stevo hates the press. Oh God, please don't print that, Callie, he'd kill me!"

Callie looked at her curiously. "I won't. Are you scared of him, Toni? After you had your last child – is it Sam? – there was a story out that Stephen beat you."

Toni went into peals of laughter. "God, no! The opposite, if anything! My family call him the Taddie – Tadpole. He's shorter than me when I wear heels."

"Yes, so he is. Does he mind?"

"No, he's never been bothered. He told me his Welsh grandfather, who was only five foot two, used to say, 'In Wales, we measure men from the neck up'. And in answer to your original question, no, Stephen has never, ever been violent to me; I don't think he ever could be. I mean, he's been in fights and stuff, I'm not saying he hasn't got a temper, he has, a really shocking one when he loses it, and he gets really mad over weird things, but not violent. No, there was no truth in that story. Stevie is lovely! *All* my boys were born early."

"What kind of weird things?" Callie queried.

"Well, like – I know – years ago, before we got married, the band was doing some concerts in Brighton, and I'd gone with them. It was summer and hot – for this country! – and we went for a walk, and on the way back to the hotel, we passed a charity shop, one of those that work for the third world, and they had a tree in the window they were starving of water, so that people could see the effect it would have on humans, and Stephen went ballistic. He went into the shop and made a huge fuss and said that nothing justified cruelty and demanded they water the tree. The manager was this little bloke, but he wouldn't give in. I could see Fin and Andy cringing. It was really embarrassing."

"What happened?"

"Stephen stormed out, went to the nearest supermarket, bought a large bottle of water, went back and poured it in the bucket the tree was standing in."

Callie grinned. "So then what happened?"

"Oh, the police were called, and Stevo kept saying, 'Yeah, go on, arrest me, I'm famous, I'll tell the papers what you've been doing here!'" She remembered it as clearly as if it had happened yesterday; Stephen squaring aggressively up to the policeman, who was big, like George, far taller than him, the poor man simply trying to defuse the situation, Andy whispering to her, "You know, Toni, I don't think the papers would give a toss", which she thought was quite likely, and Fin practically wringing his hands, and saying quietly and pleadingly, over and over again, "Don't be stupid, Steve, we've got a concert tonight."

"Anyway, the manager didn't press charges, so the policeman told Stephen off and asked for his autograph. We went back to the hotel, and Fin and Andy told George, who said, oh, well, Steve had always been a lass and what else was new, and that was the end of it." She sighed. "I really miss those days! We had such fun! I can't believe the bastard's gone off and left…" She stopped and stared at Callie.

"What?"

"Nothing. Forget that last bit." She thought of Sam, and Stephen leaving them to go on tour. Everything, all the horror of the past year came flooding back. She'd had a good time this afternoon and forgotten it. Her eyes filled with tears.

"Toni! What is it?" Callie seemed genuinely concerned.

Toni hesitated, unsure what to do. Stephen didn't trust journalists, said you had to be on your guard with them, they'll use anything, he always said, they'll twist anything you tell them, but Callie was so nice, so sympathetic, and she so desperately needed someone to talk to. "Sam's autistic. It's just been confirmed," she mumbled.

"On, no!" Callie was stunned. She put her hand over Toni's. "Oh, Toni. I can't say I know how you feel, but my sister's little boy is autistic, so I do have some idea."

Toni stared at her. "How old is he? How does she cope?"

"Six. Just from day to day. She gets a lot of help from ASUK, have you been in touch with them?"

Toni shook her head. "I haven't even heard of them. I got in touch with the National Autistic Society and they were good, sent me lots of information."

"ASUK – it's the Autistic Society of the UK – is more hands on. Look, I'll ring Linda before I go, and get the number for you."

"That'd be great, mate, thanks!"

They chatted a little more. Callie asked her questions about growing up in Australia and being a zoologist, and she and Stephen raising money for charity and sponsoring children in third world countries, and the song 'Savages', and Toni talked about Stephen's vegetarianism and how he couldn't stand cruelty to any species, but how he loathed spiders. She told Callie about Bunyip and how Stephen was terrified of him, although all his boys loved him.

"Oh, so would I! I always wanted a tarantula, but my boyfriend would go berserk."

"Come to the Priory and see Bunyip sometime," Toni offered. "He's gorgeous, he loves a bit of a cuddle."

"Really, Toni?"

"For sure! What about this weekend?"

"Steve! Have you seen this?" Fin, seated in the hotel lounge, looked up as Stephen walked past.

"What?"

"Toni's interview. It's hilarious!"

Stephen grimaced. "What's she said this time?"

"Nothing – well, in fact, everything – but nothing bad." He handed Stephen the magazine. There was a good picture of Toni on the front cover. *'Toni Markham – Not Your Average Plus One'*, it read. Stephen turned to the interview.

'What would you call Stephen Markham?' it started. '*A superstar? A sex symbol? Great guitarist and singer? Well, his Australian wife's family call him the Taddie, short for tadpole, because of his height; and the band's bassist, George Ferguson, frequently refers to him as 'the lass'.*'

Stephen groaned. He read on, cringing at the tree incident and the various other little gems Toni had included. But he noticed how she had been quoted as wistfully saying 'I miss those days! We had such fun!' and how she had totally refuted the wife-beating story and said 'Stevie is lovely!' She hadn't said, 'He's gone off and left me here with our handicapped son' when she'd been given the opportunity. No, she'd loyally stated that touring was hard work. He went up to his room and rang Cell.

The following day, Toni rang Callie. "Mate! Thanks so much for the interview, it's brilliant! Stevo's read it and he's sent me a flower shop!"

"A flower shop?" Callie asked, confused.

Toni giggled. "You've never seen so many flowers."

"I'm so pleased. See, I told you; men need a bit of space, they can't cope with life, it's always left up to us."

She and Toni had become close. She'd got the telephone number of ASUK for Toni and they'd had lunch at the Priory the following Saturday, cementing their friendship with several bottles of very expensive red wine and mutual admiration of Bunyip. It was just what Toni had been missing and needing; frivolous female companionship with another woman who wasn't either related to Stephen, married to one of his friends or, like Harry, his ex-lover; a woman who, in fact, didn't know Stephen at all.

That night, she was waiting by the phone for Stephen's call.

Lynn read the interview too, quite by chance; she found it when she was waiting to see her dentist. She was overcome when she read that Sam had Aspergers Syndrome.

She wanted to ring them up and offer to help, but knew she couldn't. Despite the incident at the wedding, they still seemed to love each other, judging by what Toni said, and the interview came across as truthful. It's time to get on with my life, she thought. The trouble was, she didn't know how. Twice she'd been in love and married, and twice her relationships had failed. She was thirty-one and what had she to show for it? A promising career and job satisfaction, but on a personal level? She hadn't even got a cat. She thought seriously about emigrating.

Stephen and Toni fell back into their old relationship very quickly when he got home. He was glad to be back, the tour hadn't been a success. He could usually forget everything when he was playing, simply become part of the music he was creating, but this time his anguish over Sam and his guilt at leaving him had been too strong. Reviewers called the shows, '*dull*', '*lacklustre*'. One even said '*pathetic*'.

"It's true," he said. "It was my fault."

He was having a drink with Dominic and Andy.

"Trouble is, Steve, I think the others tend to react to you," Dominic said. "If you're not playing as well as usual, they don't." He looked at Andy. "What do you think?"

Andy nodded. "Yeah, kind of. Usually you're so wired, Steve, that it lifts everything. But I think it's only fair to say that none of us were much good."

"It's only fair to say I was rubbish. I forgot the words, didn't always give you lot the cues you needed, and my playing was crappy. I couldn't keep my mind on what I was doing and that's unforgivable."

"Understandable though, given the circumstances," Dominic said.

"Yeah, but the point is, Charlie, those people paid to see us. They've all got their own problems. Christ Almighty, I'm not the only man in the world with a disabled child!"

Andy and Dominic exchanged glances. Dominic was about to make a soothing remark when Andy said, "Yeah, you're right, Steve, you were crap, you were a selfish bastard. Learn from it and move on, like."

Dominic stared at him, appalled, but Stephen nodded. "Yeah." He sighed. "I suppose that's life all over. You just have to learn from your mistakes." He went off to get them another drink.

Andy grinned at Dominic. "Sometimes we just have to be tough with him or we never hear the end of it."

Stephen spent the rest of the month working on his solo album. It was a glorious autumn and he wrote in the study with the French windows thrown open. It overlooked the rose garden, and the scent of the late roses was exquisite.

Toni peered round the door. "I'm making you a quiche for tea." The only full-time help she had was Karen. She had women who came in to clean and iron, and she hired caterers for the frequent, extravagant parties she and Stephen were fond of throwing, but she preferred to cook and care for the family herself.

"I'm writing you a love song," Stephen replied.

She went in and sat on his lap. "What's it called?"

"Its working title is 'Toni's the Best Wife in the World', but I thought I'd refine that a little."

"Am I?" she asked.

"Certainly are," he said, kissing her. The kiss became more and more passionate. They moved from his chair to the sofa. Eventually, he got up and locked the door.

At dinner that evening, he had the quiche with salad, while the rest of them had goulash and rice, apart from Sam, who was wandering around the room in his Spiderman costume, eating a piece of dry bread and drinking Fresubin out of a bottle.

"Dad, why don't you eat the same stuff as us?" Alex asked.

"I don't eat meat because I'm a vegetarian," Stephen explained.

"Is that an alien?" Pip asked hopefully. They'd been watching *Star Trek: The Next Generation*, and he was very taken with Mr Worf.

Alex rolled his eyes theatrically. "God, Pip, you're embarrassingly stupid! I know you're only in Reception, but honestly!"

Stephen and Toni exchanged amused glances.

"Alexander, don't speak to Pip like that, and don't say 'God'," Stephen reproved him.

"Well, what is a veginarian?" Pip asked, looking at Alex.

Alex narrowed his eyes, thinking fast. Everyone waited. Finally, he said, "Someone tell the poor child!"

"Why don't you, seeing as you know all about it?" Toni suggested.

He shovelled a spoonful of goulash into his mouth and pointed at his face. Toni was very strict about good manners and they were not allowed to talk with their mouths full. They'd never forgotten the time she'd rapped Stephen on the knuckles with a ladle, so hard he yelped, for doing it. "Gosh!" she and Stephen had heard Rob saying to the other two afterwards. "If she does that to *Dad*, what would she do to *us?*"

"It's someone who doesn't eat meat," Rob explained, getting himself a third helping. "This is delicious, Toni."

"So's—" Stephen remembered the rule, and swallowed. "So's this quiche. Isn't she amazingly wonderful, boys?"

"But why?" Pip wanted to know.

Stephen frowned at him. "Pip! Because she cooks us lovely food and looks after us!"

"No, why don't you eat meat?" Pip asked.

Stephen looked at Toni for help. They'd decided not to tell the boys he thought it was wrong, Toni wanted them to eat meat until they were at least sixteen. "After that they can decide for themselves, mate, but I think they need it till then."

"Some grown ups don't," she said, serenely.

"Yes, it's a grown up thing," he agreed. He fondled her thigh under the table. "All the best things are," he added, looking at her suggestively.

Rob sighed. "Oh, please! You're too old!"

"Hey!" Stephen objected. "I'm not thirty-three yet!"

He went in the pool with the boys every afternoon after tea, while Toni had some time to herself.

Alex was tall for his age, and plump. Stephen had brought Toni's wrath down on himself earlier in the year by remarking, after putting sunblock on his son, that it was like buttering a porpoise, but he hadn't meant it in a derogatory way, Alex was the picture of health and there was something sleek about him. Pip was small, but Stephen was hoping he'd be like Rob, who'd been the smallest in his class until he was twelve. The boys were completely different in character, although they were very alike to look at, very like Stephen. They both had his thick black hair and warm, creamy complexion; the difference between them was that Pip's eyes were as black as his hair where Alex's were a warm brown.

Sam was more of a mixture. Like Alex and Pip, he was a good looking child, and, like Pip, he was small and slight. His eyes, a bright, clear blue, were very like John's, very arresting, and he had Toni's curving eyelids, which made him look as if he was always smiling. He had Stephen's square jaw and tough looking mouth, and his hair grew like Stephen's, always falling into his eyes, but it was red, and no one knew where it came from.

Sandy, Toni's mother, said, rather doubtfully, that he might have a look of her grandfather, even though his hair had been dark. "He came from Perth, you see, which would explain the red hair."

"Are there a lot of redheads in Western Australia?" Stephen asked.

"Perth, Scotland, Tad."

He was much happier when Stephen was at home, threw fewer tantrums, and slept better. Stephen, who, unlike Toni, never had any trouble sleeping, would read to him, and then lie with him, singing softly in Welsh until they both dropped off. Stephen would wake half an hour or so later, and creep out of the room. He couldn't understand why Toni made such a big deal of it.

"This Portage thing is brilliant, Steve!" Toni said, one evening. Stephen was sitting on the sofa, Bron curled up on his feet, and Toni lying with her head on his lap.

"Yes, you said it was going well, and Sammy certainly seems happier," he said.

"Daphne's so great with him. And his face is so much better."

Daphne, Sam's Portage worker, had shown Toni how to make Sam aware that he was dribbling by very gently tapping round his mouth and chin. "He's so used to it feeling wet that he doesn't even notice it, Toni," she'd said.

"Did I tell you her daughter's got Downs Syndrome?" Toni asked.

Stephen nodded, his face sombre. "That must be so terrible."

"Yes, and she was telling me it took so long for them to get any help for her. Well, that's how come Daphne got involved with Portage. And no one told them about it, either, not their doctor or anyone at all the clinics they took Ava to, Daphne found a leaflet by chance at special needs dentist Ava had to go to!"

"It's bloody appalling," Stephen said, grimly. "When I picked Alex up from Luke's party the other day, his mother was telling me about her friend, whose little boy's got a heart defect. They had to wait months to see a specialist. It made me feel terrible, we never have to wait to see anyone."

"I know. I feel like that when Callie tells me about Martin, you know, her sister's little boy."

"When am I going to meet Callie?" Stephen asked.

"Do you want to?"

"Of course," he said, stroking her face. He'd spoken to Callie on the phone, but Toni had been reticent about inviting her to the Priory, going to London to meet her for lunch instead.

"You might not like her, she's press."

"Some of them must be human," Stephen grinned.

"Hmm, it's that kind of remark that worries me." In fact, it was more that she was afraid that once Callie actually met Stephen in the flesh, she would fall for him and the friendship the two of them had built up would evaporate. Callie had said originally how gorgeous Stephen was – and he was, Toni freely admitted it, and very sexy too. It was something to do with his surprisingly tough-looking mouth, she decided.

"Really, Toni," he was saying. "I promise to be absolutely charming."

God, I'm not sure I want you to be, she thought, but said, "OK, I'll invite her and Fred over for a meal on Friday." Fred was Callie's boyfriend, a physiotherapist who specialised in sports injuries.

"Invite them for the whole weekend. It's a big enough house, and if I genuinely find I can't stand her, there's plenty of places I can hide!"

Callie was excited by the invitation, she was looking forward to meeting Stephen.

As promised, he was charming to her.

"I hear you can't stand the press," she said, grinning at him.

His eyes widened, and then he began to laugh. "Well, I said to Toni, some of you must be human." She laughed with him and introduced him to Fred, a large, confident-looking man, with a receding hairline. "I understand you have back problems," Fred said with professional satisfaction, pumping his hand vigorously. Stephen decided he liked them both very much.

"You choose good friends," he said to Toni in bed that night. They'd had a pleasant evening, drunk a lot of wine, talked about Sam, and played Cluedo. "I always suspected celebrities had rowdy parties like these," Fred had said.

"I know. I chose you, didn't I?"

The following morning, Stephen and Fred went for a swim, leaving the women alone.

"You're *so* lucky, Toni! He's even more gorgeous close to, I had trouble keeping my hands off him last night when I was tipsy," Callie told her.

Toni's heart sank.

"I couldn't live with him though," Callie went on. "All that soul-searching, how do you stand it?"

Toni grinned, partly with relief. "You can see George's point then."

"That he's a lass?"

Toni nodded.

"That's a *bit* unfair, but if I had to spend a lot of time with him, I'd probably agree. I don't mean to be critical," she added anxiously, afraid she'd offended.

"Oh, you're not," Toni assured her. "I was scared you'd fall for him," she admitted.

Callie smiled. "Well, I certainly wouldn't kick him out of bed, but Fred's the man for me. I know lookswise he can't hold a candle to Steve, but… well, he suits me."

"Yes, you two are good together."

Callie smiled. "We are. And he gives the most amazing massage!"

Stephen started recording his solo album, 'Through The Bars', at the beginning of November. Before he went home in the evenings he usually called in to see Harry, who had been admitted to hospital. She was looking extremely pregnant, and not particularly well. Her face and hands were very swollen.

Dominic was very worried about her. "They're going to induce the baby on Monday," he told Stephen one Friday at the beginning of December.

Stephen stared at him, alarmed. "Is it that serious?"

"Yes. They have to get her blood pressure down, it's shot right up to two hundred and ten over a hundred and forty."

"What should it be?" Stephen asked

"About a hundred and twenty over eighty," Dominic said grimly. "The baby's at risk too. I'm sorry, Stephen, but I won't be available next week."

Felicity Cariad Chaplin was born on Monday the sixth of December. She was just over three weeks early, and weighed six pounds three ounces.

"The same as Rob," Harry smiled. "And he was exactly on time. God, that was thirteen-and-a-half years ago!"

"Doesn't seem possible, does it?" Stephen looked over at Rob holding Felicity, the first of Dominic and Harry's babies to be dark. "Especially when you look at the size of him now!"

"I'm being induced again next time," Harry said. "I can't believe how fast the labour was!"

"There's not going to be a next time," Dominic said with feeling, gripping her hand. "I've never been so worried, Hatty. I couldn't live without you." He was looking at Harry with such love that Stephen felt a lump form in his throat. He'd always secretly been a little worried about how much Dominic loved Harry, he was so flippant with her, and Stephen knew that he'd had the occasional groupie right up until GI Joe split up. Now he had no doubts.

Tears welled up in Harry's eyes and she stroked Dominic's hair.

Everyone was silent for an emotional moment.

Toni slipped her hand into Stephen's. "God, this is going to make *me* cry in a minute, I can't think how Stephen's controlling himself!"

"You're fucking right – whoops, sorry, Rob and Felicity," Dominic said. "Let's get some of that champagne this place supplies in here!"

In the Christmas holidays, Stephen took Rob to the studio to record 'Bara Brith'. He thought it would be good for him to get into a recording studio, start learning the ropes. He loved having his son with him.

Rob was fascinated by the whole process. "I wouldn't like to do it for a living though, Dad," he said, on the way back to the Priory.

Stephen glanced at him. "What do you mean?"

"I don't know how you stand it! It's kind of tying music down, isn't it? What's that poem by Rupert Brooke?"

"I don't know," Stephen said, trying to think of a poem about tying music down.

"It's not about music, it's about love. '*Today I have been happy…*' it starts."

"Yeah, I vaguely know it, isn't there something along the lines of the memory of you in the clouds?"

"Yes, about sowing the sky with clouds of love and your memory following the white waves of the sea. I'll find it when we get home. It's in my English book, we did it at the beginning of term."

Stephen was totally confused. "But what's that got to do with the price of fish?"

"Well, it always reminds me of music; when I sing or play, I think of the sound following the white waves of the sea. That recording! Dominic made me do it over and over again!"

Stephen grinned. "Yeah, well, it's got to be right, Blue."

"I know, I didn't mind doing it, I could see what he meant. But I'd loathe it full-time, so frustrating!"

"I suppose so, I never thought of it like that. But how will you get round it? Busk?" Stephen laughed.

"I'm not going to be a *musician*!"

"Oh." Stephen was taken aback.

"I thought about being a doctor for a while, you know, like Tim. But I don't think it's for me. No, what I'm really interested in is the law. I suppose I get it from you, caring about injustice and stuff— Dad, are you all right?"

They were nearly home. Stephen pulled the Porsche into the entrance to a farm field. "Get out," he managed to say.

Rob got out, alarmed. "I'm sorry, Dad, I..." he stammered, and then the breath was knocked out of him as Stephen gripped him in a fierce hug.

"Robbie, Robbie, Robbie," he said, his voice tight with emotion. "Your Grandpa would be *so* proud. No, he *is* so proud! I'm sure he knows. He must know!" He let Rob go and stood looking at him. "You've never looked so much like him before either." It was a perfect end to a perfect afternoon. Dusk was just falling, the sky was a deep, dark blue and the air was still and cold. "Get back in, you'll freeze."

Rob got into the car, dazed.

"Sorry, Blue." Stephen started the engine. "You haven't got a clue what that was about, have you?"

"No. I thought I was in trouble for not wanting to do music!"

Stephen laughed. "If you knew how far from the truth that is!" He told Rob about John, how his ambition for Stephen had nearly caused a permanent rift between the two of them. "Of course I like it – love it – that you're so musical, but I don't want any of you to do music if you don't want to! And besides, we can always share it, we can play together, we can sing together whenever we want." He grinned. "Well, we do! Think how cross Toni was when we went to Waitrose last week and we were all singing carols!"

"I think she particularly disliked the fact that we were all singing different ones though," Rob laughed. Like Stephen, the boys sang continually, wherever they were.

"Dad," Rob went on, his voice ultra casual. "Talking about the olden days – how come you and Mum didn't get married when you had me?"

They had just turned in through the Priory gates. Stephen stopped the car again. "Has Harry ever talked to you about it?"

Rob shook his head.

Stephen didn't know what to say. The truth sounded too brutal: your mother fancied me and I was upset about being dumped, so we made love. It was so much more complex than words could convey. Harry had been in love with him.

"It's very complicated," he said finally.

"Did you love each other?"

That was easy. "Certainly did."

"Then why did Mum marry that other man?"

"Well. I was going out with someone else, I didn't know that your mum loved me."

"But you... you know... slept with her," Rob said, going scarlet.

"Well, obviously, or you wouldn't be here! Rob, I think this is something you, me and Harry need to talk about together. But we did love each other very much, and we still do – in a different way of course – and you were wanted so much. When she and Dominic come and stay next week, we three will talk, OK?"

"OK," Rob agreed.

Stephen rang Harry later.

"I've been dreading him asking," she sighed. "He was bound to one day."

"Yeah, but what are we going to say, Hal? I mean, I've said we loved each other and that he was wanted, but it's kind of bending the truth a little. I did love you, but I wasn't *in* love with you."

"Does that matter? Love is love."

"I suppose so," Stephen said doubtfully. "He's a bit young too."

"They say you should always tell children the truth."

"Who the hell are *they*, anyway?" Stephen demanded. "I fell for that. We were going past the graveyard a couple of months ago, and Pip asked me what graveyards were for, so I said, 'Well, Pipkin, when people die, they put their body in a box and dig a hole in the graveyard and put the box in it', and he went fucking mental. He came into our bed every night for two weeks after having a nightmare, and even now he shudders when we walk past there."

"Well, I don't know! Look, I'll have a word with Dom, you speak to Toni and we'll pool our wisdom when we see you."

"Can't wait."

In the end, they more or less told Rob the truth, stressing how much they loved each other and him.

"Your mother made a huge sacrifice when she said she didn't want to marry me," Stephen said. "That's real love, Rob. And when Cherry left me, you were all that kept me going, you and Harry." He pulled Harry to him. "She's my best friend."

"When you fall in love, Rob, you'll realise how horribly complicated it is," Harry said.

"Yeah," Stephen agreed. "When it works it's the most incredibly wonderful thing in the world, but when it doesn't..." He shook his head.

"Didn't it for you and Cherry?" Rob asked.

Stephen's eyes were dark with pain. "No. Robbie, please can I beg you – don't call her Cherry in front of Toni."

"Why?"

"Because Cherry was my special name for her," Stephen explained. "Jealousy is another terrible downside to love."

"Were you jealous of Tim?"

Stephen drew in a ragged breath. "Yes. Don't let's talk about it any more, it's too painful, Blue." He tried to smile at Rob.

"Can I just ask..." Rob started hesitantly.

"I feel like King Canute. Ask away, Rob."

"You love Toni, don't you, Dad, and Mum, you love Dom?"

Stephen relaxed. "That one's OK. Yes, we do, Blue."

Rob gave a relieved sigh. "So it all ended happily ever after!"

'Through The Bars' was released in March to mixed reviews. Once again, Stephen was accused of being pretentious, but he didn't care. The song writing credits caused a stir: '*All songs by Stephen Markham except 'Bara Brith', words by Stephen Markham, music by Robert Chaplin.*'

He dedicated the album to Toni: 'My Perfect Wife'. The song he wrote for her, 'With All My Heart', went to number three in the charts, and he was immeasurably thrilled when Stanton Crawford, the blues singer, wanted to record one of the other songs, 'Such A Crying Shame'.

Chapter Fourteen
Interesting Times

It's no joke, it's a curse, it's a verse without rhyme,
Immersed in my life in these interesting times.

"This speech therapy isn't doing Sam any good, Steve," Toni said one evening in early April.

Stephen poured them both a drink. He'd just got home from London, where he and the band were recording their latest album, 'Dreaming In Colour'. "Well, his speech certainly doesn't seem any better," he agreed. "What does the therapist say?"

"Nothing useful," Toni snorted. "He's been seeing her for six months now, and she called him Sean today!"

Stephen was shocked. "We've got to get another one! What about that organisation Callie was on about, maybe they can recommend someone?"

Toni turned away. "Mmm. I'll see if I can find out. How did it go today? Did you get a lot done?"

The following week, Stephen bumped into Callie as he was arriving at the studio. "Callie! What brings you to this neck of the woods?" He kissed her cheek.

"Stephen, hi! You know how it is, you've got to go where the job takes you, no matter how seedy," she laughed. "How's the recording going?"

He nodded. "Pretty good, thanks."

"Well, I won't keep you, I'm running late. Oh, how's Sam getting on with the new speech therapist?"

Stephen frowned, mystified. "What new speech therapist?"

"Linda gave Toni the number of this new speech therapist Martin's been referred to, Lynn Jackson. She specialises in autistic children and Linda says she's brilliant. What's wrong, Steve, you look like you've seen a ghost!"

Stephen pulled himself together. "Sorry , Callie, just thinking about the recording. The new therapist, yeah – um, maybe Toni hasn't been able to get hold of her yet. When did Linda give her the number?"

"Beginning of last week, I think. Anyway, I must dash! See you, Steve."

Stephen watched her walk away, his mind racing. Surely it wasn't, surely it couldn't *possibly* be the same Lynn Jackson! After all, it was a common enough name. But both speech therapists? It did seem improbable. Of course, the name would mean nothing to Callie – as far as the press was concerned, Lynn, his Lynn, was Lynn Franklin. He thought about it all day. There seem to be three possiblilities: One; it was a completely different Lynn Jackson. But that was pretty unlikely, and, anyway, if it was, why hadn't Toni got in touch with her? Two: Toni was genuinely trying to get hold of her but had had no luck so far and had forgotten to tell him. Even more unlikely. Three: because it was Lynn, Toni wasn't going to do anything about it. This seemed the most likely of all. He couldn't think about this possibility, it made him too angry. He managed to get through the day and must have seemed his usual self, because nobody, not even Dominic, who was producing the album, asked him what was wrong.

As soon as he walked in through the front door, Sam, dressed in a Batman costume, rushed down the stairs and grabbed his leg. Stephen squatted down next to him. He could see Sam's eyes gleaming with excitement through the little holes in the mask.

"Look, Dr Venkman," Sam shouted, "I've got a, I've got a, I've got a..."

"He's got a Batma—" Pip started to say.

"Pip!" Stephen interrupted sharply. "Let him tell me. What have you got, cariad?" he asked Sam.

"I've got, I've got, I've got..."

Pip rolled his eyes and ran upstairs.

"...a Batman costume!" Sam finished triumphantly. "Costume, costume, costume," he repeated.

"It's fantastic!" Stephen said. "I thought you *were* Batman!"

Sam squealed with laughter and hurried upstairs after Pip, chatting to himself. "Got a Bat, a Bat, a Bat..."

Stephen's heart turned over with pity and love for his son. "Toni!" he shouted.

"In here!" she shouted back.

He went into the kitchen.

Rob was at the table doing homework. "Hi, Dad, how's it going?" he asked, without looking up.

Stephen ruffled his hair. "We're cooking with napalm." He looked over at Toni, who was unloading the dishwasher. "Hi. I thought that was Rob's job?"

She smiled. "Hi yourself. Yes, it is, but he had heaps of homework so I said I'd do it."

"Hmm. When I was your age, Robert, it didn't matter how much homework I had, I still had to do my jobs first."

Rob was interested, Stephen didn't often talk about his childhood. "What jobs?"

"Well, taking the rubbish out was my job, and every night I had to clean everyone's shoes, and on Saturdays I had to wash Dad's car. Then in the winter I had to get the logs in for the fire and light it when I got home from school, and in the summer I had to keep the garden tidy, which included mowing it every week."

"Gosh! What about Auntie Kath and Auntie Becks? What did they do?"

"Oh, you know, girls' stuff, washing up and setting the table and what have you."

"That's a bit sexist, Dad!" Rob was shocked.

Stephen grinned. "This was back in the Seventies, remember, when men were men and women were grateful. They knew their place in those days." He winked at Rob.

"Watch it, mate!" Toni warned. "Anyway, I thought it wouldn't matter just this once, Robbie is such a help to me. Unlike those other little mongrels! Sam decided to empty the contents of his toy chest down the stairs after tea, and Alex and Pip simply stood there giggling, and egging him on!"

That reminded Stephen of Sam's speech therapy. "Any luck with the speech therapist thing?" he asked casually. "Did you get in touch with ASUK?"

Toni bent over the dishwasher. "Oh... um... they said they'd let me know if they could find anyone."

"Hey, what about Callie's sister?" he asked, as if it had just occurred to him. "Maybe Martin's therapist is good."

There was a pause.

"Toni?"

"Um... I don't think he has speech therapy..."

"TONI!" Stephen shouted, bringing his fist down on the table.

Rob jumped, and stared up at him in alarm. "Dad? What's up?"

Stephen took a deep breath. "Rob, I'm sorry, but could you do that in your room?

And shut the door behind you." He turned to Toni. "You lying bitch!" He couldn't remember ever having been so angry. He wanted to smash his fist into her face. He put his hands in his pockets. "I bumped into Callie today. She asked me how we were getting on with the new speech therapist whose number she gave you, the one Martin sees, the one who works for ASUK, who specialises in autistic children, Lynn Jackson."

Toni was ashen. She put her hand on Stephen's arm. He shook it off and walked over to the other side of the room.

"I've been in touch with ASUK and NAS, and I'm looking into it, I really am, but I couldn't take him to *her*, Stephen, you must see that," she pleaded.

"All I can see is a little boy who has so much to say locked inside him and a selfish bitch who always puts herself first."

"Well, what would you have done, St Stephen?" she flashed back.

"I took him to see Tim! I've got far more reason to be jealous of Tim than you have of Lynn, he was married to her for years. Before I met you! How do you think I felt, knowing that she could've had me back, but she chose to marry him? But fuck that, it didn't matter! Getting Sam well, that's what matters! For Christ's sake, Toni, she and Tim have split up! If I'm so desperate to be with her, why aren't I? Because you're my wife and I choose to stay with you. How many fucking times do I have to say it? And what's the good anyway? You never listen, you don't believe me. What's her number?"

"What?" Toni was thrown by the change of subject.

"Lynn. What's her number?"

"I threw it away."

He looked at her with contempt. Fetching the address book, he picked up the phone and dialled. "Callie? Hi, it's Stephen... Listen, Toni lost the number of... yes... would you? Thanks... yeah, I've got a pen... Sorry, four double one...? Thanks, Callie... And the same to Fred! Bye, Call." He dialled again.

Toni stood rooted to the spot.

"Hello? Lynn, it's me." He laughed. "I suppose so. Lynn... Did you? Thanks... no, it's been bad... yes, I was, I mean, we were..." He sighed. "That's what I wanted to talk to you about...that'd be great... no, anytime... Maybe just me... OK. Take care. Yes, so am I... Oh, me too. Bye."

"What did she say?"

Stephen ignored her.

"Stephen! What did she say?"

"You weren't interested before, when you threw her number away." He started towards the door.

"Stephen! Tell me!"

He walked out. She heard him calling the boys for a swim. She sank down onto a chair. What had Lynn said at the end, when Stephen answered, 'Me too'? Had she said 'I love you'?

She went upstairs and ran herself a bath, pouring scented oil in lavishly. When she was dry, she put on matching body lotion, made her face up with care, and slipped into the dark green, wild silk kimono that Stephen had brought her back from Japan. He liked her in green. She heard him bringing the boys upstairs, laughing at something Pip was saying. She positioned herself seductively on the bed and waited for him to come and find her. Instead, he ran back down the stairs and a short while later, she heard the sound of a car roaring off down the drive. She sat stunned. Eventually, she went and found Karen. "Where did Stephen go?"

Karen gave her an odd look. "To London."

"Oh yes. Er… I forgot." She went back to their bedroom. Had he gone to Lynn? Well, where else would he go? OK, let him, she thought angrily. I don't give a damn. She paced around the room, trying to convince herself that she didn't care and that she had a right to be angry, but all she could think of was Sam. So much locked inside him. She knew Stephen was right, and she felt terrible, had done since Callie had told her about Lynn, but she *couldn't* ring her. Why couldn't Stephen see that? She turned the TV on and watched a documentary without taking any of it in. She read to Sam, all the time aware that by now Stephen would be in London, be with Lynn. After Sam was finally asleep, and she'd read to Pip and Alex, and put them to bed, she couldn't stand it any longer. She started to cry. Why hadn't she at least talked to Stephen about it? She didn't want him to leave her. She ran to Rob's room.

"Toni! What's the matter?" He got up from his desk and wrapped his arms around her. He was five foot six now, and it was almost like being held by Stephen. She cried harder. "Has your Dad gone to see Lynn?" she managed to ask.

Rob was astonished. "Gone to see Lynn?" he echoed.

Toni nodded into his shoulder.

"Of course not! He wanted to get an early start tomorrow so he decided to spend the night at Cheyne Walk. Didn't he tell you?"

"No."

"That's really mean!" Rob said hotly. "He shouldn't treat you like that, Toni! Shall I ring him and tell him you're sad? I don't mind."

Toni was sorely tempted. But it was a coward's way out. She kissed him. "No, I'll ring him. Thank you, Rob. You're such a comfort to me."

She went back to her bedroom and rang the London house. The phone rang and rang. Just as she was beginning to think he'd lied to Rob, he answered.

"Stephen Markham."

"Stephen, it's me," she said hesitantly, "I'm sorry, I'm really sorry. You were right. Please come home."

"Toni. Oh, Toni, we can't go on like this."

"Like what?"

He laughed. "Exactly. All right," he said, his tone suddenly very hard and tough. "I'll come back on one condition, and I mean this, Toni. It's over. We had a row and now it's over. I don't want to discuss it or hear your side of the story or any of the things that usually happen. OK?"

"OK," Toni said meekly.

"Plus, Sam is going to see Lynn, and I really, really don't want to hear anything about me and her. This is for Sam, it'll mean seeing Lynn as a health professional and nothing else. Do you understand?"

"Yes, Stephen."

He sighed. "I'll see you in a little while then."

By the time he got home it was late. All the boys except Rob were asleep; he was reading in bed.

Stephen went in to him.

"Oh, hello. You came back." His voice was unfriendly.

"What is it, Rob?"

"You should have told Toni where you were going, Dad, she was really upset! She came in here crying like anything. For some reason, she thought you'd gone to see Cherry."

"You're a good boy, Robbie," was all Stephen said. "Tuck down in half an hour, otherwise you'll be tired tomorrow." He kissed Rob's forehead, and Rob flung his arms round his neck. "Dad! Sorry I was cross!"

"It was good of you to stick up for Toni. Night, Blue."

Steeling himself – despite her meekness on the phone, he didn't trust Toni – he went into their bedroom. Like Rob, she too was reading. She looked up and gave him a slightly uncertain smile.

He didn't smile back. He stood at the door looking at her, his mouth a hard, straight line.

She threw her book onto the floor. "You look really sexy when you're cross."

That was too much for him. He cracked up.

"Why are you laughing?" she asked, mystified.

"You always wrong-foot me." He pulled his clothes off and got into bed with her. "It's like living with a volcano, I never know when you're going to erupt! But I must admit," he added, running his hands over her body, "the eruptions are pretty spectacular. I think I'll start calling you Krakatoa."

"Shut up," Toni murmured, kissing him.

After they'd made love, she cuddled up to him. "What did Lynn say when you spoke to her?"

Stephen looked at her. "I meant what I said, Toni."

"I know. I just want to know what's happening."

"She knew about Sam, she'd seen your interview. She said to tell you she's really sorry."

"Hmm."

"She'll certainly see him. I said we could come any time."

"You're taking him, are you?" Toni inquired, her heart beating faster.

"I don't know, Toni. Can I trust you to keep the appointments?"

She was outraged. "Of course you can! That's really low, Stephen Markham! I might not want to see Lynn – and I *had* asked ASUK and the NAS if there was anyone as good. I thought if there was, he could go there, I was just waiting to see, but if he has to go to her, then of course I would take him."

"But you'd rather not."

"No."

"Then I will."

"I don't want you taking him either."

"For God's sake, Toni! One of us has to."

"Why can't Karen?"

"Antonia! I said I wasn't prepared to argue about this! I'm taking him and that is final, all right? Now shut up, I want to be at the studio early tomorrow and I'm going to sleep."

He rolled away from her, turned off his bedside lamp and shut his eyes. She stared at him. The last thing she wanted was him seeing Lynn again, but she couldn't go and talk to her about Sam as if they were strangers. She could see, as clearly as if she was looking at a TV screen, Stephen dancing with Lynn at that bloody wedding, the way he was holding her, the way he was looking at her. Why couldn't Karen go with Sam for this one thing? She turned off her light and lay staring up into the dark.

"Stephen!" Lynn couldn't think what else to say, there were so many things she wanted to tell him, she wanted to throw her arms around him and say, stay here with me and don't ever go! She looked at Sam, who had moved over to the large box of toys and books. He was dressed in his Batman costume. "You brought Batman to see me."

Sam looked up. "I'm Batman. Batman, Batman."

"Yes, I can see," Lynn agreed. "I've got a toy Batman here somewhere, and a Conan." She rummaged through the toy box. "Yes, and here's a Lion-O. Do you like Lion-O, Batman?"

Sam darted a look at her out of the corner of his eyes and nodded. He took the toys and started to play.

Lynn smiled at Stephen. "Come and sit down. I've had letters from Tim and Peter Harmon. You didn't give me the name of Sam's previous speech therapist, but your GP sent me a copy of the notes. What do you see as his main problems?"

"The way he talks so fast when he's under stress, it's impossible to understand him – and anything can stress him, good things as well as bad."

Lynn nodded. "I know. The slightest change."

"Even Christmas," Stephen said. It seemed so unbearably sad that something other children longed for caused Sam grief.

"I know," Lynn said again. "It's terrible, isn't it?" She put her hand on his.

He jumped as if she'd burnt him. "Please don't. The only way I can do this is from a distance."

Lynn realised he hadn't said her name once. "Yes," she said, briskly. "OK, Ste— Would it help if I called you Mr Markham?"

He smiled. "And I call you Miss Jackson? A bit Victorian! No, Stephen will do – Lynn," he added with difficulty.

"Right, tell me all about Sam."

After they'd talked, Lynn watched Sam play. They sat at a small table and looked at some books. She gave him paper and crayons and asked him to draw her a picture.

"His imaginative play is good," she commented.

"Yes; he's very obsessed with superheroes and masks," Stephen replied.

She nodded. "I noticed. The echolalia – repetition – does he do that all the time or only when he's stressed?"

"Most of the time, although it's much worse when he's stressed."

"OK. Well, there are several areas where he needs help – what we really want is for him to be able to use language socially to communicate. He's very bright, Stephen. That'll be a big help. Do you want me to work with him?"

Stephen was surprised. "Of course. That's why we're here."

"Then let's make him an appointment for some sessions."

He hadn't told Dominic, Andy, Fin or George that he was taking Sam to see Lynn, simply that the little boy had a hospital appointment. He didn't want to talk about it, didn't want to see the pity in their eyes, or have them making allowances for him. He knew there was a certain amount of that attitude anyway and he was so tired of it. And seeing Lynn had made everything worse. He'd managed to form a thin layer of scar tissue over the wound; now it was as if it had been torn away. He felt raw and hopeless. The next day at the studio, he couldn't get into it, couldn't concentrate, didn't really care. It seemed such a pointless thing to be doing.

"Let's do that again, Stephen," Dominic said through the intercom for the fifth time. "This isn't like you," he added. "Are you OK?"

Stephen could see the others exchanging glances. He exploded, threw his guitar across the room, and stormed out.

"What the fuck are you doing?" Dominic demanded, joining him.

"Getting out of here. I'm sick of people asking if I'm all right. Yes, I'm fine, I'm just fed up with you, you're like an old woman. Perhaps we should have stuck with Mal!"

Dominic flushed. "Perhaps you should."

"Steve," Fin said. "Look, if there's a problem—"

"The only fucking problem is you lot asking me if there's a fucking problem!" He pushed past Dominic, who caught his arm. It was the excuse he'd been looking for. He hit Dominic as hard as he could. With a cry of pain, Dominic fell back against the wall. The others were too shocked to move.

Dominic picked himself up, wiping blood from his lip. He glared at Stephen. "Feel better now, do you, you bastard?"

Stephen stared at him, horrified by what he'd done. "Charlie! I'm so sorry! Are you all right?"

"Never felt fucking better!" Dominic said, sarcastically. "What do *you* think? What is it, Stephen? Toni? Sam? Lynn?"

"W-what do you mean, Lynn?" Stephen stammered.

"Toni told Harry you were taking Sam to see her yesterday. When you didn't say anything, I assumed you didn't want to talk about it."

Stephen stared at the floor. "It's – I can't..." He couldn't go on.

"Why don't we go and sit down, have a cup of coffee, like?" Andy suggested.

They went into the Artists' Lounge.

"Do you want to go home, Steve?" Dominic asked.

"That's the last place I want to go! Toni's not exactly a joy to be near at the moment. I swear, if it wasn't for the boys, I'd..." He stopped.

"Perhaps it might help to talk to Harry or someone," Dominic said. "I don't know what you can do, I don't know what I can say to help."

"Why don't you have a few days break?" Fin said.

"But where, man?" George asked. "If he and Toni are having problems..."

"Can't you try talking to Toni?" Andy put in. "Perhaps the two of you should get away on your own for a while. She probably needs a break as much as you do, like. After all, she's at home with Sam all day."

Stephen stared at him. "Yes, you're right. But what about Sam? We can't leave him, he can't cope."

"Would Sian and Ted come down?" Dominic asked.

"Maybe. I could ask. It all seems so pointless!" he burst out. "What is the point of life?"

Dominic put his hand on Stephen's shoulder. "Go home, ring Sian, talk to Toni. I know she can be – difficult, Steve, but I honestly think she feels the way you do at the moment. You need to be able to rely on each other, even if only for Sam's sake. You've got to work it out. And at the risk of getting punched again, old man, I don't think you seeing Lynn on a regular fucking basis is going to be any good for that marriage of yours, frankly."

"Yes, but what can I do? I can't trust Toni to go to the appointments!" He told them what had happened.

"You've got to talk to her," Dominic said again. "You're the strong one in the relationship, Stephen, make her see how hard it is for you."

"It's easy for you to say," Stephen said bitterly. "You're married to Harry."

"Thank God," Dominic said before he could stop himself. "Sorry, Steve."

Stephen shrugged. "At the moment, I agree. OK, I'll go home. I'm no bloody good here, anyway. I'm sorry, lads." He turned to Dominic. "Charlie..."

Dominic grinned lopsidedly. "Forget it, Markham. You owe me though."

Stephen got into his car and sat there. He didn't want to go home. The only place he wanted to be was with Lynn. Her house was so typical of her, the furniture was unfussy and comfortable, and the rooms were decorated very simply, with interesting paintings. Quite a few of them were of Africa. He'd wondered at the time if she'd bought them while she was living there, but had been afraid to initiate any personal conversation for fear of where it might lead. She was still so like she'd been when they were married, still his Cherry, even though she was thinner these days and her hair was shorter, wispier, so she looked slightly elfin. It suited her, with her big violet eyes. And she was still using Penhaligon's Violetta, even the house had smelled faintly of it. He'd taken Sam to the bathroom at one point and it had smelt delicious; Sam had commented on it, saying it smelt nice and loud. Stephen knew exactly what he meant. He wondered if Sam saw music in colour, like he did, and not just music: the seasons, some words, people's names. But he wouldn't be able to ask him that for a long time yet.

Sam. He had to go home. It was the Easter holidays, the other boys would be home. Perhaps they could play football or something. Which would mean that he wouldn't have to talk to Toni. Which was the point of going home. He started the engine and drove off, his mind going back to Lynn. It would be a lie to say she didn't look any older, she did, but only in the sense that she was more mature, not that she looked lined. More confident, maybe. She was still beautiful. He suddenly realised he had taken a wrong turning and instead of heading towards the M40, he was heading towards Lynn's house. Well, it didn't matter. He could get across from there, it wouldn't hurt to drive past. When he got to her road, her drive was empty, which meant she was out. Damn. He parked opposite, telling himself he'd wait half an hour and if she hadn't come back by then, he'd go home. It was a lovely day, and warm in the car. He'd had very little sleep the night before. Gradually, his eyelids drooped and he slept, slumped in the driving seat, his head at an awkward angle against the window.

When Dominic got home, after going for a drink with Fin, George and Andy, a drink that was supposed to be a serious discussion of what they could do to help Stephen, but had deteriorated into hilarity as they'd recalled various incidents from the past, Harry had just got in from dropping Amabel at a birthday party and taking Angus to the park, and she was putting Felicity in her bouncing cradle. She exclaimed at Dominic's face, tilting it to the light. His lip was cut and bruised. "Dominic! What happened?"

"Bloody Stephen punched me."

"Oh, poor Stephen!"

"Poor *Stephen*? Poor fucking *Stephen*? What about *me*? I did nothing to provoke him, he just turned on me! Still, my one satisfaction is *his* face. Can't open his left eye, it's so swollen, and Fin's taken him to have his jaw X-rayed."

Harry had turned pale. "Dominic, how could you?"

"I didn't, you twit, I didn't touch the little runt! I sent him home." He picked up Felicity. "Hello, Fee, you're looking more like your Mama every day!" He kissed her soft little head. "Stephen and Toni really need to talk. I don't know how he copes with that bitch. Frankly, I don't know why he stays with her. However," he added, looking hurt, "I'm very upset by your initial reaction to my injuries."

"Injuries!" Harry snorted. "I'll make you feel better when your bairns are in bed."

Dominic brightened up. "Oh, goody!"

"You should thank your lucky stars you're married to me."

"Yes, I said that."

"Not to Stephen, I hope."

"Um… kind of," he admitted.

"God, you're a tactless oaf! Cup of tea?"

He nodded. "He agreed with me anyway."

"Poor Stevie," Harry said soberly.

"You know, Hatty, when he married Lynn, I was so envious. They seemed to have everything – love, friendship. And then I met you." He put Felicity back in her chair and took Harry in his arms. "Now I'm the lucky one."

"Oh, me too!" Harry said, kissing him. "Poor, *poor* Stevie. And that cow Toni makes every situation difficult for him – unless it already is, of course, then she makes it unbearable." She wrinkled her nose. "You smell horribly smoky, Dom, far worse than usual."

He nodded. "You know how much George and Fin smoke, and we went to the pub after Steve went home. I'll go and shower in a minute."

Angus ran in. "Papa!"

Dominic picked him up. "Hello there, Sir Gus. What have you been doing?" Angus had recently heard his grandfather being called Sir Angus, and had started referring to himself as 'Sir Gus'.

"Mab's gone to a party. I went to the swings. Fee's too little. You smell horrid!" He struggled to get down. "Let's play trains!"

"Stephen! Stephen, wake up!"

"Hmm?" Stephen struggled from a dream in which he was looking for Lynn in a huge, dark forest, but something had hold of his leg and it was twisting his body and hurting his back.

"Stephen!" Lynn was rapping on the window.

He opened the door.

"Stephen, whatever are you doing?"

"Looking for you," he said, still disorientated. He tried to straighten up. "Ouch!" His back was extraordinarily painful.

"You shouldn't have gone to sleep in the car. Come into the house, I'll get you some ibuprofen."

"I didn't mean to go to sleep," he said, walking painfully after her.

She led him into her kitchen and gave him two tablets.

"I always take three."

Lynn frowned. "Is that a good idea?"

"Doctor said it was OK," he mumbled, swallowing them. "Thanks, Lynn." He put down the glass. "I'd better go."

"You've only just got here," she said, beginning to grin. "It's like that joke about pandas – eats, shoots, and leaves."

Stephen shook his head. "I don't know it."

"Why isn't it a good idea to ask a panda for a romantic dinner at your house?" she asked. "Because he just eats, shoots, and leaves."

He laughed. "I haven't eaten yet."

There was a silence.

"Do you want to?" she asked, eventually, her heart pounding.

Very slowly, Stephen nodded.

She didn't know what to make him. She didn't have any vegetarian food. Eventually she decided on pizza with a side salad. She was no better in the kitchen than she'd ever been, and tended to eat microwavable meals. As she made the salad, an idea occurred to her. She'd sent Stephen into the sitting room, where, after doing some stretching exercises that a physiotherapist had given him for his back, he was lying on her sofa. When the meal was ready, she called him through and put the plate in front of him, grinning.

He stared down at the salad. She'd fashioned it into the shape of a face, with cucumber slices for eyes, half a slice of tomato for a mouth, a spring onion for the nose and lettuce for hair. He burst out laughing. "You realise I won't be able to eat this, don't you? How did you know?"

"I've read every article about you and interview with you that's ever been published or recorded. I could nearly tell you the merits of a Les Paul over a superflump GTi analog delay!"

"Same old technically-minded Lynn," he grinned. "A Les Paul is a guitar."

"I don't believe you ever told me that."

"Not above a thousand times, no." He cleared the plate. "What's for pudding?"

"Same old gluttonous Stevie! Do you remember Othello Gateau?"

His face changed. "Oh, Cherry."

"Stephen," she said, distressed. "You shouldn't be here, are we mad?"

He got up and pulled her against him. "Why? You're not married to Tim any more."

"You're married to Toni though! We can't!"

He bent his head and kissed her, his hand caressing her breast.

She gasped and pulled away. "Stephen! We can't!"

"No?" He kissed her again, and went on kissing her until she felt dizzy. She moved her head away. "Stephen! Please don't!"

"Who'd know, Cherry?" he demanded impatiently. "I love you so much!"

"I would! We would! You're not being fair, Stephen! And how could I treat Sam?"

He stared at her. "Cherry. Oh, Cherry, I'm sorry, I'm so sorry. I've just made everything ten times worse. God! What the fuck is the matter with me?" he said, savagely. "I punched Charlie this morning!"

"You punched Charlie?" Lynn was stunned. "Why?"

"Because— Oh, just because. Never mind. I'd better go." He stroked her hair and kissed her once more, very gently. "I really am sorry. Can I still bring Sam to you?"

"Yes. But Stephen – I don't think you'd better come here again without him. I don't think I've got that much willpower."

"It's a good job you've this much," he said, adding bitterly, "I don't seem to have any."

Driving home, he felt better. He couldn't understand why; logically he should be feeling much worse, but he'd decided what he was going to do.

When he got to the Priory, Rob, Alex and Pip, who had been playing in the garden, came running to meet him.

Toni was lying on a lounger, reading. She waved. "You're early," she called, and went back to her book.

"Yeah, good, eh?" he called back cheerfully. "Hi, boys! Let's play footie."

"Great!" Rob said. "I'll get the ball."

"Where's Sam?" Stephen asked.

"Oh, he's not playing, is he?" Alex groaned.

Stephen looked at him sternly. "He is. You know he loves it. He can be on my side. Blue, you choose now."

Before Rob could answer, Alex said, "I don't want to play if Sam is, he ruins it!"

"No, he doesn't. Rob, Pip, are you OK with Sam playing?"

They nodded. "He doesn't ruin it, Alex," Rob said. "Just let him kick the ball and score a couple of times. It's not like we count his goals!"

"Shut up, Rob, you goody-goody!" Alex said. "I'm not playing with Sam, he's a spastic."

There was a shocked silence.

"Alex, that is a horrible word," Stephen said, sternly. "It's a *very* horrible word for someone who is – who can't walk or move properly. I never want to hear you using it again, about Sam or anyone else, do you understand?"

Alex couldn't see why Stephen was making such a fuss. He stared at him mutinously, his mouth turning down at the corners.

Stephen lost his temper. "I mean it, Alexander. If I ever hear you using that word again, I will spank you." He didn't actually have any intention of carrying this out, he was confident that the threat alone would be enough. Despite, or perhaps because of being smacked fairly regularly as a child, he was totally opposed to corporal punishment. The only time any of his sons had ever been smacked was when Alex, as a baby, had held his breath during temper tantrums, and their GP had advised them to slap him sharply on the bottom to make him breathe.

However, Alex had become overexcited and silly, and he hated being told off in front of Pip. "You're a spastic!" he said to Stephen, sticking his tongue out defiantly.

Rob breathed in sharply, and Pip stared at Alex, partly in horror, partly fascination.

Toni, seeing there was a problem, was walking over. "What's the matter?" she called.

Stephen's face was thunderous. He bent Alex over and tapped his bottom. Alex was frozen with amazement for a second, and then he opened his mouth and roared. He threw himself at Toni, bellowing as if he was being killed.

"How *dare* you?" Toni yelled at Stephen. She slapped his face with all the force she could muster.

Rob gasped, and Pip began to cry.

Stephen, furious, his cheek burning, caught Toni's wrist and jerked her arm back. As he did so, Dominic's face appeared in his mind's eye, and he heard his voice saying, 'Feel better now, do you?' He pulled Toni against him. "Do you feel better?"

She started to cry. Alex was still howling.

"Toni, he was really, really naughty," Rob said, the words tumbling out in attempt to make Toni understand. "He called Sam a spastic, and when Dad told him what it meant and that he was never to say it again, he said it to *Dad*!"

"It's all right, Rob." Stephen turned to Alex. "Come here, Al." He let Toni go, and held out his arms. "Things are very hard at the moment aren't they?" he said, cuddling his son. "For everyone. So we're going to Australia to see Gramps and Kay."

The little boys started to dance around in delight, and Rob turned a cartwheel, something he'd just learnt to do, and did as often as he could.

Toni stared at Stephen. "When did you decide this?"

"Earlier, I'll explain in a minute. Boys, go and get your football shorts on, and fetch Sam while I talk to Mummy."

They ran off. Alex had forgotten the incident in his joy. He loved seeing Gramps. As far as he was concerned, Gramps was just about the greatest person in the world, with the possible exception of Granny and Granddad.

Stephen turned back to Toni. "I punched Charlie this morning."

Toni stared at him, open-mouthed. "Why?"

"Absolutely no reason. He annoyed me, so I punched him. Sound familiar?"

She blushed. "Sorry," she said, stroking his face.

"So then I thought, we need a holiday. We'll dump the boys with Jacko, and we'll stay at Brizzie's poshest hotel. You can shop to your hearts content and we'll have time on our own. Then we'll all go out to the Reef for a week or so, Jacko and Kay too, if they want, and the boys can spend all their time swimming. They'll be knackered by bedtime and we can spend our evenings – well, doing whatever we want. How does that sound?"

"Like heaven," Toni said, fervently. "But what about Sam's speech therapy?"

"He'll be OK for a couple of weeks."

"What about the album?"

"Fuck it. It'll have to wait. My family is more important. *You* are more important."

Toni threw herself into his arms, laughing and crying. Lynn was right, he thought. I am married to Toni, and when it's going well, it's a good marriage. I owe it to her and the boys – especially the boys – to try to make it go well again. And to myself. I can't live with this grief. He knew, deep down, that he loved Toni less after the way she'd behaved over Sam's speech therapy. He'd always thought that, despite her sometimes monumental selfishness, the boys would come first with her as they did with him, and when he found out they didn't, something in him changed; he found himself, whilst still loving her, almost despising her at the same time. But in a way, it made things easier, he could step back and look at his marriage objectively. Being with Lynn that afternoon had shown him how much he had to work to get it back together. Well, he was willing to try.

Toni kissed him. "Oh, Stevie," she said, smiling mistily at him. "If you knew how *unhappy* I've been."

Oh, Toni, he thought, so have we all. But he didn't say so, there was no point. "I'm glad you're happy now," was all he said.

Toni was a changed woman in Australia. Stephen gave her all his time and attention, taking her out, and going shopping with her. She spent a small fortune on clothes and accessories, and he bought her jewellery to match. At the Reef, he watched Sam very carefully. He was obviously stressed, but he loved the warm water, and Jacko was marvellous with him. They came home rested and tanned. Stephen went back to recording with renewed vigour, much to Dominic and the band's relief, and Sam began to look forward to his speech therapy sessions, and talked about going to 'Win's' house.

That summer, Stephen was asked to write a soundtrack for a film entitled *First Blood*, a story of a vastly rich, mysterious young woman, Verity Linden, who, with the aid of a hand-picked gang, fought crime. It was hoped that a series of films would be made, very much in the mould of the James Bond films, each one revealing a little more about the enigmatic Verity. *First Blood* was being made at Pinewood studios and was to star Coral Mathieu, who was thrilled to land the part. She rang Stephen up when she heard he was doing the soundtrack and gushed excitedly over the phone.

Toni rolled her eyes disgustedly.

Then, at the end of August, Sid's Six played at the sixtieth birthday party thrown for the head of Muse International.

Stanton Crawford, the blues singer, was at the party, and sought Stephen out; Stephen would never have been able to initiate a conversation with him, in spite of the fact that Crawford had been his hero since he was a teenager. As far as he was concerned, no one, not even BB King or Tampa Red, could hold a candle to him.

Stanton left the party early; he was over seventy – "I ain't no spring chicken no more," he said to Stephen – and Stephen cursed himself for not talking more to him. He'd been as tongue tied as a teenager with a crush, so it was an enormous surprise when Cell rang the next day to say that Crawford's manager had been in touch to arrange for he and Stephen to make an album together. He turned to Toni. "You know Stanton Crawford?"

"That poor old man you frightened so much he had to leave early last night?"

"What do you mean?" Stephen asked, hurt.

"Stephen, you were practically stalking him! And when he finally talked to you, all you did was stand gazing at him with a sloppy grin on your face! He's not dead, is he? You didn't scare him into a heart attack or something?"

"No, I fucking didn't! In fact, he's so unscared, he wants to make an album with me!"

"Pressured into it, eh?" Toni said. "I expect he thinks that if he makes an album with you, you'll never bother him again! Poor man, little does he know…"

"You're just mean! I'm going to ring Harry, she'll be impressed. I might even take her to meet him in Memphis, where we'll be recording."

Toni stuck her tongue out at him.

"God, I see where Alex gets it from now!"

He finally arranged to meet up with Stanton Crawford in the New Year. Sid's Six was due to tour Britain and North America from September, keeping him tied up until Christmas. The new album had been released to good reviews and both it and the first single released, 'Someone In The Crowd', were doing well in the charts. He felt good. He loved touring, he had working with Stanton to look forward to, and his relationship with Toni was better than it had been for a long time. He felt that they were finally beginning to see the light at the end of the tunnel.

Chapter Fifteen
Black Moon

Fear and confusion, diffusion of the light,
Darkness, and evil stalks the restless earth;
Black moon, and no good comes of it.

Working with Stanton Crawford was like a dream come true for Stephen. If he'd ever needed a meaning for what he did, this was it. Because he could play the guitar and sing, he was getting to do what most people could only long for – spend time with his hero. And Stanton thought that he, Stanton, was the lucky one! Stephen couldn't believe it.

Stanton kept complimenting him on his playing and his voice; "You make that guitar sing like you do, and for a man with a voice like yours, that's pretty darn good." When other people complimented him, he was pleased, of course, and liked it, but it never really meant that much to him. But with Stanton! Stephen had always considered him to be the greatest musician alive, and Stanton thinking that he was even halfway decent on the guitar – which was how he saw himself – was amazing. But to have Stanton actually *praise* his playing was something he'd never expected.

He was moved by the fact that Stanton still lived on the street where he had been born.

"It was hard for a black boy growing up in the South in them days, Steve," Stanton said. "The people on this here street was always my friends. Most of 'em are gone now, but the street's still here, and so am I!" He laughed contentedly.

Stephen had written a song especially for the album, 'On Beale Street', Beale Street being the street in Memphis where, at P. Wee's Saloon, W. C. Handy wrote the 'Memphis Blues'. He and Stanton duetted on 'Lost And Low', the song Stanton was famous for, and 'On Beale Street', but Stanton insisted Stephen sing 'Such A Crying Shame' alone. "I'll play on it, but, Steve, this is one of my favourite songs, and I love the way you sing it."

Stephen thought if Stanton kept making these remarks, he wouldn't be able to get his head through the door. He felt he'd learned more in this brief time with Stanton than he'd done in all the time he'd been playing guitar. They became firm friends, and Stephen left, promising to keep in touch, and they made plans to work together again soon.

It was never to be. Stanton Crawford died two months after the album was made. Stephen was the last person he worked with; 'True Blues' was the last album he recorded.

It was Harry and Dominic's tenth wedding anniversary in March, and they gave a party at Fenroth. All the band were there with their wives and offspring. Both Holly and Shelagh were expecting; Holly was enormous, due to have the baby in a couple of weeks, and Shelagh was three months pregnant.

"All these hormones, aren't they making you broody?" Stephen asked Toni as they lay in bed after the party. He propped himself up on his elbow and stroked her breasts. "Why don't we start another one? Maybe a girl this time."

She wriggled her body. "Mmm, that's nice! I thought it didn't matter if it's a boy or a girl."

Stephen paused in his attentions. "It doesn't. I just thought a girl would be nice for you."

"I don't want any more babies."

"I was looking forward to at least two more." He was only half-joking. "What about our footie team?"

"No more," Toni reiterated. "Not after Sam. Suppose there was something wrong with it?"

He hadn't thought of that. "I guess so," he said soberly. "Poor little Sammy! And thinking about it, he might not be able to cope."

Toni wasn't listening. She was thinking how heartbreaking it was with Sam. She and Stephen were extremely tactile people, both of them holding and kissing the children as a matter of course, and Rob, Alex and Pip responded in the same way. Sam didn't. He hated being touched or kissed. He'd throw a tantrum about something and, unlike the other boys, to whom she could explain things, tell them off if need be, and finally cuddle them, she couldn't get through to Sam; he wouldn't look at her, wouldn't let her touch him. She couldn't comfort him when he was sad; she couldn't tell if he *was* sad a lot of the time, couldn't even begin to guess what was going on in his mind, and then she'd feel the most overwhelming sense of failure and despair, and end up shouting at him in frustration, which only increased her guilt and unhappiness, and his alienation. She knew she couldn't go through any of that again.

"I couldn't bear to have another defective child," she said sadly.

Stephen was stunned. "Sam's not defective! He's just different!"

"Yes, that's what I meant, poor little Sam. But, Steve, whatever label you use, it comes down to the same thing. I couldn't stand another one. Why are you looking at me like that?" she asked, puzzled by his expression. He couldn't possibly want another child to go through what Sam had been through.

"We're talking about Sam! Our son! Don't you love him, Toni?"

"Of course I do, Stephen! How can you even ask that? But…" She hesitated. "Don't you ever think it might have been better if he'd never been born?"

Stephen was shocked to the core. He recoiled from her. "No! Absolutely not! How can you say that? He's a darling!" He pictured Sam's thin little face, absorbed in some game, or a book about dinosaurs. He had recently become very interested in them, and devoured information about them. He was still preoccupied with superheroes, spending all day as Batman or Spiderman, wearing the costumes wherever they went. They'd stayed with Toni's mother, Sandy, in Chester for a few days on the way to Fenroth, and taken the boys to Beeston Castle, an old ruin. Sam, wearing his Batman suit, had stood the whole time they were there in a shady area of the walls, claiming he was standing in the all concealing shadows.

"Oh God, I'd forgotten you were due to be canonised any minute now," Toni jeered, suddenly sick of him and his continual sneering and sniping at her. Why did he always twist everything she said? She'd meant better for Sam, and he knew that perfectly well, but as usual, he deliberately misunderstood her.

"Why are you so absolutely vile?" he was asking, shaken. He couldn't believe she could possibly wish that Sam hadn't been born. He got out of bed and pulled on his pyjamas and robe.

"Where are you going?" she demanded.

"Away from you," he retorted.

"Don't be childish!"

"Fuck off, Toni." In the corridor outside, he hesitated, not knowing where to go. Most of the rooms were in darkness. He peered down the hall. There seemed to be a light coming from under Rob's door. He crept down and knocked.

The door opened a crack and Rob's worried face appeared. "Dad!" he said with relief.

"Can I come in? Are you OK, Blue?"

Rob let him in. "I thought you were the ghost."

"The ghost?"

"Yes, Dom was telling me. It's called Black Angus, it was murdered here centuries ago. Every fifty years it roams the corridors and the next morning the youngest person is found to be missing and is never seen again." He lowered his voice. "It's exactly fifty years since it last happened."

"You're not the youngest person," Stephen pointed out.

Rob stared at him fearfully. "I am on this corridor."

"And this ghost politely knocks, does it?" Stephen asked, grinning.

"It might be a trick. I mean you're not going to let it in if it says, 'I'm the ghost, open up, I've come for you', are you?"

"Rob, it's a ghost, it can get through doors and walls and what have you!"

"Oh, God you're right! I'm doomed!"

"It's just Charlie's idea of a joke!" Stephen laughed. "I've never heard any talk of this ghost before, have you?"

"No, but I've always slept up on the nursery floor before. It doesn't go up there, Dom says."

"Perfect place for it, I'd have thought, all those youngsters. Robbie, he's having you on!"

"Do you think so? Really?"

"Yes, I do. Listen, Blue, can I sleep here tonight?"

Rob stared at him. "Why?"

Stephen sighed. "I had a row with Toni."

"Not again!"

"Yeah, again."

"Do you two like arguing or something? It'll be a bit of a squeeze, both of us in here," he added as they got into bed.

"It's like *Withnail And I*," Stephen said. He'd let Rob watch the film last time it was on TV, despite the swearing, because he knew Rob would find it hilarious, as he himself always did, no matter how many times he saw it, and because he knew Rob was sensible and mature enough not to swear like that in front of Toni and the little boys. Personally, he didn't mind Rob swearing; he was nearly fifteen, and Stephen remembered how he and his friends had behaved at that age. Rob had enjoyed the film very much indeed, to Toni's disapproval. She considered him to be too young. "We'll hear Uncle Monty trying to get in any minute now," Stephen added.

"Yes, only we'll think it's the ghost!"

"And it'll be you he wants, so you'll have to offer him yourself!"

They began to laugh, trying to keep it quiet, which made them both worse. Finally, Stephen said, "God, Rob, I don't know what I'd do without you!"

"Sleep on the sofa," Rob said, which started them off again.

"Don't you sometimes wish you were a fantasy character… you know, from a book, or TV, or something?" Stephen asked, when they'd got themselves under control.

Rob thought for a minute. "It'd be fun being Han Solo. Who would you be?"

"Homer Simpson."

"*Homer Simpson*? Why *him*?"

"Oh, you know; he has a fantastic life. He's a lazy slob, but he thinks he's the greatest, and everything always turns out OK for him, and Marge loves him whatever he does or however he looks."

"Hmm, I suppose. But just think, Dad, I bet loads of people wish they were you."

Stephen was staggered by this thought. "God, I suppose so."

"Of course they do, Dad! You're brilliant!"

Stephen hugged him, touched. "I love you, Robbie."

Rob fell asleep, but Stephen's back hurt and he lay awake wondering how much longer he and Toni could stay together. The next day they patched up the quarrel, but the things she'd said lingered in Stephen's mind. He couldn't understand what had happened to her. She'd been so wonderful with Alex and Pip – and Rob too, come to that. She still was, he realised. It was just with Sam that she wasn't. He found it hard to forgive her for that.

He managed to grab a word with Harry before they left. "Listen, you've always liked Lynn, haven't you?"

"Well, except when she left you, yes, I suppose so. Why?"

"I don't know. I get the impression she's short of close friends; she said Caro and Donald had moved to the States. I wouldn't mind if you and she saw each other sometimes."

"Meaning you'd like it if we did."

Stephen tried to shrug nonchalantly. "Whatever."

Harry kissed his cheek. "Give me her number, I'll give her a ring. You're right, I always did like her."

Toni was beginning to feel more and more isolated from Stephen. He wouldn't listen to her, seemed to delight in misunderstanding her, was constantly putting her down and implying she was a bad mother to Sam. And he had a much better relationship with Sam than she did, the little boy responded to him in a way he never did with her. He only had to sing some Welsh song, and Sam calmed down, relaxed, even occasionally asked Stephen to sing again. Toni couldn't make any connection with him. She tried, very hard, but she knew that it was partly her fault. As much as she loved him – and she did, tremendously, with a kind of heart-wrenching pity – she hated his disability, almost feared it. When she was a child, her grandmother, Jacko's mother, had developed dementia and had lived with them, which had given Toni an almost phobic dislike of illness. The old lady had been incontinent and had spent her days sitting in a chair, muttering to herself. She no longer recognised her grandchildren, which had scared Toni. She only lived with them for a few months before going into a home, and Jacko had hired a full-time nurse to help Sandy care for her while they were waiting for a place for her, but that made no difference. Toni had only been seven at the time, and it had affected her profoundly.

Stephen had been impatient with her when she'd explained this to him. "Yes, OK, Toni, I can see that it must have been unpleasant, but it was a long time ago, and Sammy's not like that, anyway. And he's your son!"

She turned away from him in despair. He never gave her the benefit of the doubt, never gave her a chance. Sometimes, she almost hated him.

The director of *First Blood* wanted Coral to sing the title song. She had a pretty singing voice, sweet, but not powerful. Stephen wanted to write something that not only suited Coral's voice but also conveyed Verity's strength of character and skill at all forms of combat, and her strangely naïve, childlike side. Not an easy task. Finally, the song was written and approved. The next step was scheduling a time for Coral to rehearse and record.

"Stevie!" She swept into the studio at the beginning of April, looking and smelling delicious. She had had her long red hair cut short for the part of Verity, and it curled prettily around her face, but otherwise she was exactly the same. She knew Andy, Fin and George from when she and Stephen had been living together, but Dominic had been away touring a lot at the time, and she had only met him very occasionally. She was enchanted when he kissed her hand.

"Oh, for God's sake!" Stephen rolled his eyes. "Take no notice of Charlie, Coco, he's trying to impress you!"

"He's succeeding," she said, her French accent more pronounced than usual.

"Markham just can't seem to take in the fact that people have names they may quite like, can he?" Dominic said to her. "Why Coco?" he asked Stephen.

"When I first saw her, she was wearing a long, dark green frock," Stephen said, smiling reminiscently. "Her hair was all piled up on her head and she was tipsy, so she was swaying slightly as she walked. She looked like a poppy. A beautiful poppy in the moonlight. Then I found out she was French, so it was Coquelicot – French for poppy – and that got shortened to Coco. That song 'The Model' always reminds me of the first time we met; do you remember that party, Coco? I asked you what you were drinking and you just said 'Krug'."

"Yes, and you said I'd had too much alcohol and got me a mineral water!"

Stephen grinned. "I wanted you to remember me. If I'd brought you champagne, I'd have been just another face in the crowd!"

"You could never be just a face in the crowd," Coral smiled. She sighed. "We had such fun, didn't we?"

"Yeah, certainly did. Anyway, better get to work, your time is at a premium, apparently!"

While he was working with Coral, Toni went to London for a few days to shop and have a break. Stephen was at the Priory a great deal; he was there when the boys got up, and usually in by the time the older three came home from school. Karen was there too, of course, and Sam was attending the nursery class at a Montessori school in Oxford three mornings a week. It wasn't the school that Alex and Pip were at, they attended the village school, and Stephen and Toni had worried about the fact that he wouldn't be with them, and that it was further to take him every day, but it seemed the right environment for him. Intellectually, he had no trouble at all, he was far ahead of the other children in his class and could read and write fluently, but socially he had a lot of trouble adapting. He didn't like team work or taking turns. If something interested him, he would pay attention; if it didn't, he tended to be disruptive. Fortunately, he was an amusing child with a quirky sense of humour, and the staff tended to treat him like a lovable eccentric. The education authority was in the process of assessing him in order to issue him with a statement of his educational needs. While accepting the necessity of this, and wanting Sam to have the help he needed, Stephen and Toni found the whole idea of it repugnant. And it was the first situation concerning Sam's autism where Stephen's money meant nothing. The authority moved at its own pace, oblivious to his millions.

Early on in the proceedings, one of the officers had visited him and Toni at home. They offered her a cup of coffee.

She shook her head. "Thank you, no. Now then, I need to fill in a few details. Mr Markham, what's your occupation?"

"Um… musician," Stephen replied, taken aback.

She looked interested. "Indeed. And do you teach music?"

"Er… no, I'm… um… I'm in a band."

"Oh," she said with distaste, and turned to Toni. "And your occupation?"

"Apparently, she's a 'Responsible Officer'," Toni said, after the woman had gone. "God, Sam's doomed!"

Every letter they received told them that they were considered '*an equal partner at all stages of the assessment*', but it didn't seem that way to them. The education department seemed to take very little notice of anything they said.

"Thank goodness the school feels the same way we do!" Toni had said. They were still waiting for the authority's verdict.

As Stephen was at home more at the moment, and Sam seemed to be reasonably settled, Toni felt that she could leave him for a few days. She was staying at the Cheyne Walk house and loved having the time to herself. She met Callie for lunch every day.

"I could get used to this," she said as they studied the menu in a little French restaurant that Callie had discovered. "It's a pity this is my last day."

"Why not stay on?" Callie suggested.

"Stephen's going to be away next week, the band's playing some concerts up North."

"Well, anyway, I've got a proposal for you," Callie said, looking very pleased with herself.

Toni smiled. "What?"

"How would you like to do a spot of modelling?"

"Modelling? Me? How could I? I've never done anything like that."

"Don't worry, it's for charity – celebs and celebs' wives. You'd be perfect! Holly Havergill is going to be there."

"Holly! How lovely! I haven't seen her since she had Primmy."

Holly had had her baby, a girl, which she and Andy had named Primrose, several weeks earlier.

"She's looking fantastic. I asked her what her secret was and she said she's just really lucky and didn't have to work too hard at it. I'm not sure I believe her, she's shorter than me." Callie was five foot two inches tall.

"I think it's true, she eats like a horse and never puts on a pound. She's the only person I know, apart from Rob, who eats like Stephen does."

"How are things going?" Callie asked. Toni had told her about the row at Fenroth.

She shrugged. "OK on the surface, but I know he's judging me. It's so unfair, Cal. I know he's there more at the moment with this soundtrack, but he wasn't there when things were most difficult, and it's not my fault I've got a phobia about illness, is it?"

"Have you told him about your gran?"

"Yes, but it makes no difference. He just won't understand, says it's different, because Sam's my son. I know he is, Cal, and I love him heaps, and I try so hard, but I can't help the way I feel!"

Callie pursed her lips. "If you don't mind my saying so, Stephen's being a bit of a bastard."

Toni didn't mind her saying so at all, it was exactly how she felt herself. "Oh, well," she sighed, "that's the way it is. Cheer me up, Cal, tell me more about this modelling!"

"Well, we're setting it up in aid of the breast cancer foundation. When I suggested you at the meeting they jumped at it – Stephen will come to the event, won't he?"

"Oh, for sure. He's big on charities."

"Great! And we want to do a photo shoot of each of the models for the magazine, if that's OK with you. Will you be able to be here when we need you?"

"Oh, yes," Toni said. Wild horses wouldn't keep her away.

When 'True Blues' was released there was great interest in it. It was Stanton Crawford's last album, and Stephen was interviewed constantly, asked what Stanton had been like and what it had been like to work with him. He got bored saying the same thing over and over, but felt he owed it to Stanton. He wrote a song for him, 'His Place', but then felt it didn't suit his voice and asked Dominic to sing it instead.

"Me?" Dominic was surprised.

"Yeah, your voice is perfect for it, Charlie – in fact, I've got another one that'd be just right for you too. You wouldn't fancy doing them on the next album, would you?"

Dominic grinned. "Well, you know what, Markham, I might consider it!"

At the beginning of May, Toni, feeling as if it was her birthday and Christmas rolled into one, went to London for the photo shoot. She'd been exercising hard, swimming every morning, and she knew she was looking good. Stephen had been very complimentary and amorous, telling her she was seriously sexy.

The photographer, Gavin Leigh, was well known, although she'd never met him. He reminded her of Dominic to look at, although he wasn't as good looking and his hair was darker, a kind of muddy blonde rather than Dominic's rich gold. He had a thick Brummy accent and he was very brusque and, Toni thought, rather rude, calling her 'luv' and grunting directions at her. He was also a hard taskmaster, and she began to get fed up, wishing she had someone to complain to. There was supposed to have been someone there from *Juliette*, but she didn't seem to have turned up.

"I'm not a real model!" she said finally.

"Yeah, that much is certain!" he grimaced.

"What do you mean?" she asked, annoyed. She was used to people treating her with deference because she was Stephen's wife. She could get a seat in practically any restaurant at any time by using his name, same for hotel suites and almost anything else she could think of. The shops where she bought her clothes; the assistants just about had orgasms when she walked in at the thought of the money she was guaranteed to spend.

Gavin's face broke into a broad grin. "Working you too hard, am I? You look like a girl who could take it hard."

Toni stared at him, unsure of what he meant. He came over and straightened the jacket she was wearing, turning her so she faced the camera from a slightly different angle. His hand moved down her back and he rubbed her bottom. "Very nice," he grinned, giving it a sharp slap. "If you're a good girl, you might get a reward after."

Toni swallowed. She was incredibly turned on, almost painfully aware of her body under the thin linen suit. "I'm married," she got out.

"So'm I," Gavin grunted. "Isn't everybody? What's that got to do with anything? I can see you're gagging for it. Hubby too interested in drugs and groupies, is he?"

Toni decided that, however attractive he might be physically, and however turned on she was, she disliked Gavin Leigh immensely. She ignored the question. "Let's just get this finished, shall we? I want to go home."

"I know what you want. All right, there's one more garment. You run along and get changed."

It was a figure-hugging evening gown, very sheer and low cut. Cursing, Toni wriggled into it. Where was that girl from *Juliette*?

She went back out. A slow grin slid over Gavin's face and he whistled. "Even hubby'd get hard if he saw you in that. Come here!"

Toni stood at the door, indignantly. Who the hell did he think he was? "You come here!" she retorted, before she could stop herself.

Gavin's grin got broader. He walked over and pulled her against him. "Ah, the type who likes to pretend she's in charge!" he said, gripping her arms painfully. "Just as long as you know who really is!" He kissed her roughly. "Go and get that dress off. It'll crease something wicked otherwise, and I'll have to do them pictures afterwards." Obediently, Toni went and took the dress off.

"Lovely tits," Gavin leered when she came back. "Come here, darling!"

This time, Toni did as she was told.

She plunged headlong into an intense affair with him. She had to see him, couldn't stay away, and drove to London every day, making an appointment at her favourite salon, and simply having a quick manicure before spending lunchtime and early afternoon in bed with him. She didn't like going to his flat, she had to park her car some distance away, and she was always afraid she'd be seen, but there was nowhere else they could meet; she couldn't go to the house in Cheyne Walk, Harry and Dominic lived just down the road, and Gavin laughed at her when she suggested a hotel.

She'd discovered that his name was really Gary Bewley and that he'd first become interested in cameras at the age of nine, when his older brother's gang had broken into a car one evening. He'd been the look-out, and as a reward, his brother had given him a cheap camera they'd taken. He'd become hooked. "It was a great way of pulling birds too," he told Toni as they lay in bed together one afternoon. "Still is," he gloated, pinching her bottom hard. She had to be very careful with Stephen; she often had bruises on her inner thighs, arms and bottom. She felt tremendously guilty and ashamed, but this somehow added to the feeling of enormous excitement. Gavin was so different from Stephen, who was far better in bed than he was, there was no doubt about that, but Gavin had this roughness that Stephen didn't, a roughness that she found exceedingly arousing. They did what he wanted and he didn't give a damn about her pleasure – if she came, she came, if she didn't, tough. She knew that he was married, and that he had a wife and son and a huge house in Surrey, but he never talked about them, seemed oblivious to their existence. As a person, he half-fascinated, half-repelled her. She was a little scared of him.

One afternoon in late August, she couldn't get to town at her usual time as Pip had toothache and she had to take him to the dentist. She rang Gavin and asked if she could see him around three o'clock.

"Just time for a quick screw, eh? OK, luv, I'll be at the studio. I've got a job on, but I'll be free at half past."

He had another shoot out of the studio at four o'clock, much to Toni's fury. She wanted to storm out, but she was uncertain of his reaction, afraid he wouldn't care, would laugh at her, so she stayed. They left together, and as they got to the street, she looked around quickly to make sure there was no one she knew. Reassured, she reached up and kissed him, and then, out of the corner of her eye she caught sight of Coral Mathieu waiting in her car at a set of traffic lights. She broke away from Gavin with a muttered 'I'll call', and hurried off. She wasn't sure that Coral had seen her, and, even if she had, they didn't know each other very well, so she might not have been recognised. She fervently hoped not.

Coral was re-recording *First Blood*. Stephen wasn't happy with it, and she was meeting him at the studio at four-thirty, the only time she could fit it in. "I saw Toni just now," she said to him as he got them both a Coke.

"You can't have done. She had to take Pip to the dentist." He grinned. "She was really pissed off about it, had to cancel her daily appointment for a facial! Honestly, since she got asked to do this charity modelling thing, it's been nothing but facials and massages and all the rest if it. She's getting obsessed! Do you want a Crunchie?"

They worked on the song. When they were taking a break, Coral asked, casually, "Didn't you say Toni was having some photos taken for the feature? Who's the photographer?"

"Oh, she had those done months ago. It was that Gavin Leigh, you probably know him."

"Only by reputation," Coral said, rather grimly. The reputation for treating women like tissues, she thought. Use them once, throw them away.

"Don't you like him?"

"He's a… a slave driver, so I heard," she said, trying to speak lightly.

"Toni said she didn't like him. Mind you, she hates being told what to do."

Coral didn't know what to do. Eventually, she rang Andy. "I know it was her. They were coming out of his studio together and she kissed him. I mean, I didn't think anything of that, I'm always kissing people, it's like shaking hands, and it was only a kiss on the cheek, but she was holding on to him in a kind of *intimate* way – and when Stevie said she wasn't in London and that she'd finished the photo shoot!"

"Oh ey!"

"What shall we do? I didn't say anything to him."

"Good. I tell you what I'm going to do, Coral, I'm going to talk to Harry. She'll sort it out. She knows Steve best."

"Thank you, Andy. I would so hate to see Stevie hurt."

"I think he's going to be sooner or later, married to that bitch." Andy's voice was glum.

"How are Holly and the children?"

"Wonderful!" She could hear the smile in his voice. "Parenthood's great, you should try it!"

"One day. Salut, Andy."

Harry was almost speechless with rage. "That bitch! That fucking, bloody bitch! I'd like to kill her, Andy, with my bare hands!"

"I know," Andy said gloomily. "Holly couldn't believe it."

Harry pulled herself together. "Thanks for telling me."

"You'll sort it out then?" Andy was relieved.

"How?" Harry demanded. "Wave my magic wand? Sorry, Andy, I'm just so angry." She sighed. "I'll do my best."

"You know Gavin Leigh, don't you, Dom?" she asked when he came in.

Dominic shrugged. "Not very well, thank God. Arrogant bastard, treats his women like dirt; treat 'em mean, keep 'em keen, kind of thing. I don't think he likes women very much, actually. Why?"

"Is he good looking?"

"He's tall, blond hair, regular features. Depends what you call good looking, I suppose." He grinned. "Now, if you were to compare him to me – what's wrong, Harry?"

She sat down, her face serious. "Tall and blond. Like you. Oh, my God!"

"Have you been smoking pot again, woman? Where are my bairns?"

"Your bairns are upstairs in the playroom, glued to the TV screen as usual."

"My God, you're a terrible mother, stoned all the time, the kids brought up on a diet of sex and violence, and that's just our marriage…"

"Toni's having an affair with Gavin Leigh."

Dominic stared at her, his mouth open. "What?"

"You heard."

"How do you know?"

"Coral saw them together, told Andy, he told me."

"The fucking bitch!"

"I know. Stevie's married to a monster, and Andy has this touching belief that I can solve everything."

They talked it over all evening. The next day Dominic rang Stephen and arranged to meet for a drink, ostensibly to discuss the songs Stephen wanted him to sing on the band's next album.

"So, Charlie," Stephen said, as they relaxed over a beer. "The new album! Me and the lads are ready when you are. When can you start rehearsing? When can you *commit* to us, luvvie?"

Dominic smiled. "End of next month."

Stephen rubbed his hands together. "Excellent. I've been thinking of having a studio built at the Priory. It'd be so much easier – well, for me anyway. And I'd be around all the time, Toni could have more time to herself."

"Do it," Dominic encouraged. "Talking of Toni, how is she?"

"Fantastic! Really hyped about this charity modelling thing. She goes to the salon all the time to get a massage, or change her hair. She has different coloured nails just about every day." He smiled fondly. "Actually, I feel really mean, such a simple thing can make all the difference. I should have encouraged her to go back to work. She always said the boys should have a full-time parent and I agreed, but it wasn't me who had to be that parent. Plus…" He stopped and grinned at Dominic. "She's so much more – how can I put it? – *loving* when she's happy. She's all over me, can't get enough!"

Fucking bitch! Hedging her bets in case she gets pregnant, no doubt, Dominic thought. Hope she does and it's blond. He looked at Stephen's happy face. But then Steve would have all that heartache. Bitch! he thought again. "That's nice," he said.

"It's better than nice. We hit a low earlier in the year, but things seem a little better between us now."

Oh, Markham, you poor sod! "How's Sam?"

"You know, not too bad. I've been home a lot, that always helps. That's another reason for recording at home. He'll be going to school every morning in September, instead of three."

"Won't he be starting full-time?"

Stephen looked defiant. "No, he won't. I've had this argument with Toni. Legally, he doesn't have to start full-time until the term after he's five."

Dominic grinned. "I remember you having the same argument with Harry over Blue."

"Yeah, see it didn't do him any harm, he even skipped a year at primary school, he was doing so well, and he's always top of his form."

"OK, OK, it's all the same to me, just as long as Gus doesn't have to go to fucking public school, old chap, I don't mind if he starts the term before or after his birthday." He took a drink of beer. "Is Sam still having speech therapy?"

"Yes. I just drop him off now and pick him up. I don't really see Lynn. She's got herself a bloke anyway." He stared into his beer.

Dominic couldn't believe it. He and Harry had seriously considered telling Stephen about Toni and suggesting that he thought about getting back together with Lynn. No point now, then. It seemed so unfair, the whole world thought he had this fantastic life – a superstar, best-selling albums, films, Grammys, Golden Globes, huge house in the country, but his private life was – and really always had been – a shambles. Dominic wanted to hug him.

Chapter Sixteen
Shadow Of A Woman

Darkness falling, my dreams calling,
Shadow of love, of a woman, hidden from the light.

That autumn, Rob fell in love. The object of his affection couldn't have been more different from his first crush, the American Meredith. This one, Julia Moffatt, was a stunning brunette, tall and statuesque, with a sexy, husky voice.

"Wow!" Stephen said to Toni, when a proud Rob had taken her up to his room to listen to some music after tea. "I may have to have a cold shower!"

"You pervert! She's only fifteen!"

"She reminds me of you. Come here!"

That reminded Toni of Gavin. After the shock of seeing Coral, she'd decided they ought not to meet for a week or two. When she'd rung to tell him, he'd simply said, "Don't worry, luv, plenty more bedwarmers to be had." These words confirmed what she'd already begun to suspect – that he was utterly selfish, thinking only of himself, and no one, not his wife or his mistress, mattered to him, so she finished it, but now she was bitterly regretting the move. She really missed sex with him, it had been so exciting, keeping it a secret from the world. She looked at Stephen. He was gorgeous, no doubt about it, 'sex on legs', as the papers put it, and he was very good in bed, he always made her come, which, surprisingly, considering how excited she'd been about the affair, Gavin hadn't. She couldn't understand why she wasn't content with Stephen. Every other woman in the world would be, she thought, what's wrong with me? She sat on his lap and pushed his hair off his forehead.

He grinned.

"You're not wearing your earring!" she exclaimed.

"I'm too old for earrings now. Talking of which, they're making a new film of *West Side Story* and I've been asked to play Tony."

She gasped. "The lead! Oh, Stevo! That's great!"

He burst out laughing. "I'm nearly forty! Tony's about seventeen!"

"You're not even thirty-five yet, and you don't look thirty. And they can do wonders with make up!"

"They'd need to! And besides, I can't dance. And making films is so boring."

She got off his lap. "Well, why did you tell me if you weren't going to do it?"

"I thought you'd laugh, like I did. Come on, Daisy, do admit! I'm practically old enough to be Tony's father, they'd be much better off with Rob."

"Do you think they'd offer it to him?" she asked hopefully.

"No, and I wouldn't let him if they did. I doubt he'd want to anyway. After 'Bara Brith' there was all that interest in him, he could've done anything, remember?"

"Oh, yes." She was disappointed.

"Hey, cheer up, it's your show in a couple of weeks."

"Yeah." She couldn't work up any enthusiasm.

"Are you OK, my darling?"

"Just a bit tired. Hormones, I expect."

Alex looked round the door. "Come on, Dad, come and swim. Rob and Julia are coming in."

"Oh, God, suppose she's wearing a bikini?" Stephen groaned. "Are you coming, little Glaucus?"

"Maybe in a minute. Stevie?"

"Yes?"

"Don't be too old for your earring, I like you wearing it. It's sexy."

He smiled. "OK. If you like it, I'll put it back in."

He went off to get changed, singing 'Young Girl'.

Toni waited a minute then dialled Gavin's number. A woman answered. She hung up.

"More wine, Lynn?"

"Gosh, I'd better not! I'll be too drunk to move!"

Paul McKenzie laughed. "Don't worry, I'm sure I could carry you to the car."

Lynn and Paul were sitting in a busy, rather posh little restaurant, The Roundhouse, having what Paul termed their first proper date. They'd been out for a drink and for walks, but not to somewhere where they actually had to book.

Lynn had met him when he'd brought his niece, Lizzie, for speech therapy. His sister, Stella, Lizzie's mother, who had recently been widowed, losing her husband to cancer, had broken her leg and couldn't drive. Paul was a driving instructor, so he was able to drop Lizzie off and pick her up. He ran his own driving school, employing three other instructors. He'd been a police driver for four years, but had left the force when he'd married an American girl six years ago and moved to America with her. The marriage had broken up three years later, and Paul had returned to England. He was ten years older than Lynn, but didn't look his age, and she'd been surprised when he'd told her. He looked like a policeman, she thought; he was burly and dependable and tall, well over six foot. He was very Scottish to look at, with thinning dark red hair, warm hazel eyes, and white skin with lots of golden brown freckles. Unlike Stella, he'd lost his accent, apart from a slight burr, which Lynn found very attractive. She liked him very much. This time, she'd been totally upfront about the fact that she'd been married to Stephen.

Paul was surprised and impressed. "Wow! Do you still see him, only Stella's a huge fan and she'd love his autograph!" He reminded Lynn a little of Ray, he had the same somewhat tactless manner, although he was nowhere near Ray's advanced standard.

"Yes I do, he brings his little boy for speech therapy."

"God, that's really nice! Very civilised."

"Yeah, that's us," Lynn laughed.

Next time she saw Stephen, she told him about Paul, and got his autograph for Stella. He wrote 'Hey Stella, hope your leg gets better soon, love from Stephen', and signed 'Stephen Markham' underneath.

"She's having it framed," Paul reported back.

"Apparently Stella's having the autograph framed," Lynn told Stephen, who laughed. "She ought to get out more!"

She'd read that he'd recently bought a new guitar, a 1962 Gibson SG Special, Cherry Red. He'd enthused about it and then remarked that, for various reasons, it was very, very special to him, but didn't elaborate. She'd wondered whether it was because the date, 1962, was her year of birth, and it was cherry red. Cherry, 1962. She wanted to ask him, but was afraid – afraid he'd laugh and say no, even more afraid he'd say yes.

She enjoyed this date with Paul, they'd had fun. He told her amusing stories from his time in the police force and recounted incidents – some of them pretty hair-raising – that had happened when he was teaching people to drive.

"It must be really frightening," Lynn said. "I don't know how you do it."

"I couldn't without dual controls! Seriously, I really admire parents who teach their children in their own cars, it must be absolutely terrifying. Talk about your life in their hands! Who taught you to drive?"

"My dad," she admitted.

"Same here. When I first started as an instructor, I went home and apologised to him!"

He didn't drink any alcohol with the meal. "I never touch it if I'm driving."

"In that case, I'll drive next time," Lynn said.

"I like that there's going to be a next time," Paul said happily.

She invited him in for a cup of coffee, and he accepted and they had coffee and biscuits, and he kissed her before he left but didn't agitate for anything more, which she thought was very nice. They made another date, and she was looking forward to it. Maybe I'm finally over Stevie, she thought.

Toni had not expected to feel so nervous. She saw Holly, looking lovely in a long red dress with a very tight bodice, and she waved, but Holly didn't seem to see her, and she kept missing her in the changing room, Holly was always talking to someone else. When she first walked out in front of the audience she was terrified, but gradually she began to enjoy herself. There was a lot of interest in the clothes, which were all by new, unknown designers. She was going to order some herself, and not only to support the charity; they were very good indeed.

Afterwards, there was a glitzy party, which, like the show, was admittance by ticket only, and buying a ticket to the show didn't entitle the holder to get into the party, a separate ticket had to be purchased, but as it was all in aid of charity, people paid up with good grace. By the time Toni had changed, the party was in full swing and studded with celebrities. She saw Coral Mathieu chatting to Elle MacPherson and Liz Hurley on the other side of the room, and looked quickly away. Dominic and Harry were there, of course, and all the members of Sid's Six and their wives. Holly was talking animatedly to Stephen.

Toni moved to join them. A hand closed round her wrist.

It was Gavin. "Hello, stranger," he grinned.

"Gavin," she said dismissively, looking pointedly at his hand. A feeling of triumph and excitement stole over her. He wanted her back! Well, she wasn't about to make it easy for him. Let him be the supplicant for a change, she could be magnanimous later. She shivered with anticipation and pleasure at the thought of 'later'.

He took his hand away. "Snooty, aren't we, for a tart who's sucked my—"

"For Christ's sake, shut up!" she interrupted in a fierce hiss. "Look, Gavin, it's over, OK, it was fun, but that's it."

"Yeah, course it's over," he said contemptuously. "I've got someone new. But she doesn't like it when you phone up, so stop doing it, there's a good girl." He moved off.

Toni stared after him. She could have wept with humiliation and disappointment.

Stephen came over, carrying two glasses of champagne. "Wow, Daisy, you were the best of the lot. You really walked well!"

"Thanks, darling," she said loudly, kissing him on the mouth. He grinned happily and put his arm round her. Balls to you, Gavin Leigh, she thought, I hope you're watching, because whoever you're fucking now, she won't be as gorgeous or as famous as my husband. She thanked God she hadn't let him see how much she wanted him back.

She took a sip of champagne. "What did Holly want?" she asked, hoping her voice sounded normal. "I've been trying to talk to her all evening, but we keep missing each other."

Stephen smiled. "You know her show? She asked if Rob would like to be on it and take part in that game bit."

Holly was now hosting her own show, *Not Just Kid's Stuff*, a children's entertainment programme, which went out live on Saturday mornings.

"Oh, he'd love that, wouldn't he?"

"Certainly would! So she's going to sort something out and get back to us – hello, Caro!"

"Stephen, how are you? Lovely to see you again! You remember Donald?"

"Of course." Stephen shook hands with him and introduced them to Toni. "Are you over on holiday?" They had moved to the States a few years ago, when Donald had been offered a post in an exclusive clinic in Los Angeles.

"Just a flying visit," Caro smiled. "So, how are things? Have you got a picture of Dorian Grey in your attic, Steve? You never seem to age!"

George was standing near them talking to Helen Mirren, Sting and his wife Trudie Styler, and a very pretty girl Stephen couldn't place, who was holding onto George's arm in a rather proprietorial manner. George grinned at Caro. "A picture of *Doreen* Grey it would have to be in that lass's case, Caro, pet," he said.

"Rack off, George, or I'll find that photo of you in your kimono," Stephen retorted. "I'm good, thanks," he said to Caro. "Everything's right. What about you?"

Toni had never noticed before how many Australianisms Stephen had picked up from her. Suddenly, she felt tremendously homesick. She wanted to go and cry on Jacko's shoulder. Something seemed to have gone very wrong in her life and she didn't know what to do about it.

"Steve, I'm going to see Dad."

"What?" Stephen said, confused. George and Sting had joined them, and they'd been talking about Pinochet.

"I want to go and see Dad. You wouldn't mind if I went for a couple of weeks or so, would you?"

"Well, I'd miss you like crazy, but otherwise, no. We'll be recording the new album in ten days, but now I've got the studio at home it doesn't matter so much."

"Good. I'll book my ticket tomorrow, then."

"Has something upset you, my darling girl?" Stephen's eyes searched her face.

She found to her dismay that hers had filled with tears. "Take me home and make love to me," she whispered.

Holly arranged for Rob to take part in *Not Just Kid's Stuff* while Toni was away, much to Stephen's disappointment. All his boys enjoyed the show, even though it was directed at older children and teenagers. Sam liked it because it showed Batman cartoons. They were thrilled by the fact that their brother was actually going to be on it. Sam, in his Batman costume, sat on Stephen's lap and the other two sat either side of him, practically trembling with excitement.

Rob didn't win the Gunk-Dunk game but did them credit, being the only contestant apart from the winner to get through the maze, answer all his questions and not get gunk-dunked.

"Damn!" Alex whispered. "I hoped he would!"

Stephen suppressed a grin. "Don't swear."

Harry leant over. "If he'd just been quicker through that maze he would have won!"

Stephen nodded. "He's too fat," he said meanly.

"He is not!" Harry objected hotly before she realised he was teasing her.

They had lunch in the canteen after the show.

Holly came and sat with them. "You were great, Rob."

Rob, who had a tremendous crush on her, went scarlet. "Thanks, Holly. It's a pity Toni couldn't be here though."

Holly smiled faintly. "Isn't it?"

The band finished recording the new album, which Stephen called 'The All-Concealing Shadows' for no reason other than that he thought it was a great name, at the end of January. In February, 'True Blues', the album that Stephen and Stanton Crawford had made together, Stanton's last album, won several Grammy awards – Album Of The Year; Song Of The Year – Stephen's 'On Beale Street'; Best Pop Collaboration With Vocal – again for 'On Beale Street', and Best Male Pop Vocal Performance – Stephen for 'Such A Crying Shame'. He and Toni flew to LA. He was elated, but his joy was marred by sorrow that Stanton wouldn't be there.

'The All-Concealing Shadows' was released in May to excellent reviews – words like '*different*' and '*quirky*'. were used. One critic said '*Outstanding music, enjoyable lyrics*'. Another read: '*Although this is not the first time Stephen Markham, 35, and Dominic Chaplin, 37, have worked together – Chaplin played rhythm guitar with Sid's Six for several months in the early Eighties before forming his own band, GI Joe, and the two of them formed the band Tantony Pig several years ago – the song 'She's Mine' is the first time they've sung together. Markham's voice, sounding like raw silk, blends perfectly with Chaplin's sensuous drawl, and the result is a treat of a song. Markham's guitar playing is, as always, a joy to listen to… This is definitely an album to add to your collection, whether you are a Sid's Six fan or not.*'

'She's Mine' was about two men in love with the same girl. Stephen asked for, and got, Coral to play her in the video. The weather over the two-day shoot was superb, and Stephen and Dominic spent most of the time lying in a poppy field with their shirts off, kissing Coral.

During a break in filming, Coral told Stephen she'd like to do more singing. "I'm never going to get the sort of acting parts I want," she sighed.

Stephen was amused. "What sort were you after?"

"Oh, well, Shakespeare or – or Ibsen, you know, like Nora in *A Doll's House*. It's not that I didn't enjoy *First Blood*, I did, and if there are more Verity Linden films I'm up for them, but…" she trailed off, and looked at Stephen sadly. "And it was such fun doing that song with you."

Stephen smiled at her. "You know, Coco, I've been playing around with the idea of another solo album. How would you like to sing on it with me?"

Coral's face lit up. "Stevie! I would love to!"

"OK, well, we'll do it. It'll have to be next year, we start touring soon and we'll be away until Christmas."

"Oh, that suits me!" She flung her arms around his neck and kissed him. He pulled her closer and the kiss became more passionate than she had intended.

"Come on, you two, save it for the fucking camera," Dominic said wryly, thinking: Why the hell didn't he marry Coral when he had the chance?

When Lynn saw the video, she knew she wasn't over Stephen. It was a good video, very funny, especially when Stephen and Dominic, lying on either side of Coral, leaned in to kiss her, and found themselves about to kiss each other. But she couldn't bear to watch it, couldn't get over the sight of him rolling around with the pretty little redhead. It brought back all her memories of being with him, holding him, which she'd managed to bury. She stopped watching the music channels and concentrated on Paul, although she realised now that the relationship wasn't going to lead to anything. She couldn't get into another situation like the one she'd been in with Tim, it wasn't fair.

She'd spoken to Tim not long ago, when he'd referred a little boy with a cleft palate to her. He'd sounded very cheerful, told her he was seeing someone. Lynn was genuinely pleased for him. "So, is it serious?"

Tim hesitated.

"Tim, I really don't mind, you deserve some happiness."

"Yes, yes it is. I'm very much in love with her."

"Oh, Tim, I'm so happy for you. Promise you'll invite me to the wedding?"

Tim laughed. "Steady on, we're nowhere near that stage yet!"

But he hadn't said he didn't see it happening, Lynn thought afterwards, in fact he sounded as if, despite his words, that stage was just around the corner. I *am* pleased for him, she thought, I just wish I could be free to fall in love again. She was seeing Paul that evening. In fairness, he didn't seem particularly serious, and if they could keep it light-hearted, there was no reason why she shouldn't keep on seeing him. And anyway, she thought, brightening, who knows how I might feel about him six months down the line? But at the back of her mind, she knew that her body clock was ticking away like a time bomb, waiting to blow her chances of having children to smithereens. And she wanted Stephen's children. They'd planned them together. She couldn't understand why she had made such a fuss about being pregnant. How could she have been stupid enough to let it destroy her relationship with him? So what if she wouldn't have been able to work for a while? She and Stevie would have been together. And she would have lost it anyway. If only she hadn't got so depressed. If only she'd seen a doctor.

If only. Stephen always hated those words, said they were the saddest words in the world. She got up and went to shower and get ready to meet Paul.

"Alexander! Stop making that flaming racket!" Toni shouted out of the window. Alex ignored her, and continued to run around the garden, screaming, his arms stuck out like aeroplane wings. Pip joined in. Sam, in his Spiderman hood and a pair of shorts, stood staring at them both. Stephen went out and took his hand. Sam looked up into his eyes and Stephen was overwhelmed with gratitude. Thank you, God, or whatever, he thought. They were at the house in Massachusetts, and Sam, who was now five-and-a-half, was obviously not feeling stressed out. If he had been, there would have been no eye contact. This was the first time he hadn't gone to pieces when they'd gone away.

"Why are they doing that?" he asked, watching Alex and Pip. "What are they thinking, Daddy? Thinking, thinking."

Stephen was used to this; Sam found it so difficult to work out what was going on in someone else's head. The only way they'd been able to make him see that he couldn't hurt others was by telling him that people and animals got broken too, like his action figures. He had no empathy, didn't realise they felt pain. Some things were impossibly hard to explain to him.

The previous year he'd spooked Stephen and Toni by announcing he'd seen the 'other Sam' in his bedroom. They'd questioned him casually, not wanting to make a big deal of it. Apparently, he could only see the other Sam upstairs.

"It must be a ghost, Stevo. Maybe Sam can see it because he's different."

"I don't believe in ghosts," Stephen lied. "Anyway, Sam may be different, but he's hardly known for his sympathetic nature! I'd have thought it'd be more likely to be Pip it revealed itself to."

He asked Alex about this 'other Sam' that Sam could see.

"God, how would I know what *Sam* thinks?" Alex said.

"Don't say 'God', Alex!" Stephen said, exasperated. "How many times have I told you?"

"You and Mum do," Alex pointed out.

"Because we're grown ups." Stephen was starting to get annoyed.

"That's not fair," Alex muttered as he turned away.

Stephen caught him by the arm. "No, you're right, it isn't fair, just like it wasn't fair when I was a child and I wasn't allowed to say it. Do *not* answer me back, Alexander, do you understand?"

Alex stared at him defiantly.

"I said, Alexander, do you understand? Do you want to go to bed without any tea?" He knew this threat would hit home. Like Stephen himself, Alex loved food.

"No. I understand." Alex stared at the floor.

"So?"

Silence.

"Alex, I'm waiting and I'm getting very cross."

"Sorry," Alex mumbled.

Stephen knew that was the best he'd get. "OK. Send Pip down here, please."

Alex started up the stairs, yelling "Pip!" at the top of his voice.

"For Christ's sake, I could've done that! Just go and get him!"

He thought he heard Alex mutter "So why don't you?" but he left it.

Pip couldn't help on the 'other Sam' front. "Shall I ask him to show me?" he offered.

God, no, thought Stephen. Suppose it is a fucking ghost? God knows what it might do! "No, don't worry, Pipkin, I'm sure we'll find out soon."

"I don't know what we're going to do with Alexander," he said to Toni that night. He told her what Alex had done.

She grinned.

"Yes, but it's not really funny, Toni. There are only so many threats we can make."

"I told you we should have smacked them." She started to pull off her nightgown and remembered that she had a bruise on her bottom where Gavin had pinched her. "Chilly tonight," she muttered.

"Hmm," Stephen agreed vaguely. "You can't seriously be in favour of slapping children, Daisy?"

"Why not? I was always getting spanked by Dad when I was their age."

"And did you like it?"

"No, of course not! No one likes it, you imbo, that's the point, but whatever it was you did that got you the spanking, you didn't do it again."

"Then why were you always getting spanked?"

She opened her mouth to speak and shut it again.

"Exactly. Mum was always slapping our legs, usually for the same bad behaviour. It just made us devious!"

"Oh, whatever," Toni said, bored with the conversation. "What did Pip say?"

"He doesn't know either." Stephen got into bed and began to undress her.

"Let's do it with the light out."

"Why? I like seeing your sexy body."

She thought fast. "So I can pretend you're a wicked stranger."

"You're nuts," Stephen grinned, turning off the lights.

Toni discovered who the other Sam was a few days later, when she dropped into Habitat after picking Sam up from school. There was a full length mirror by the entrance and Sam stopped in front of it. "There he is! There, there."

"Hmm? Who?"

"The other Sam, other Sam." Sam pointed at the mirror.

Toni stared at him. "That's your reflection," she said, the familiar feeling of sorrow and despair wrenching at her heart. How the hell do you explain a reflection? It's just what you see in the mirror, she thought, forlornly.

"Can you remember a time when you didn't know what your reflection was?" she asked Stephen when she was telling him what had happened.

He shook his head. "Poor little boy. What did you do?"

"I explained as best as I could, but I'm not sure if he took it in."

"Poor little boy," Stephen said again.

Now he said to Sam, "They're excited to be here, Sammy. They're thinking, Hooray! We're so happy!"

Sam watched them for a few more seconds. He looked up at Stephen. "And they say I'm nuts. Say I'm nuts, say I'm nuts. Let's go in the lake."

The weather in Massachusetts was perfect. They all got very brown, and Alex and Pip, like Rob before them, joined the gang of American children. Sam wasn't interested. He stayed close to Stephen, who took him out in the canoe and taught him to dive.

Rowing back to the house one day, Stephen was singing 'Telegraph Road'.

Sam listened carefully. "Was the man a serial killer? Serial killer, serial killer."

Stephen stopped mid-song. "No," he said, starting to grin. "Why do you ask that?"

"Well, because you said other people came down the track, but they never went further and they never went back. So did the man kill them?"

Stephen burst out laughing, becoming almost hysterical at the thought of the sinister slant this put on the song. Sam watched him laughing.

Eventually, Stephen managed to pull himself together. "No, Sammy, he didn't kill them. It just means they stayed there; see, they didn't walk to another place further on and they didn't go back where they came from. They liked it there."

"What did they think?"

"They thought, this is a nice place to live, we'll stay here."

"Why?"

"Um, because the man, he'd made it nice and cosy."

They got to the shore.

"Sam!" Pip shouted. "We've found a cardboard box, we're playing Henry the Eighth! Come on!"

Sam scrambled out of the canoe and ran off. Alex's class had learned about Henry last term and the game consisted of someone – usually Alex – being Henry the Eighth, who had got so fat he had to be dragged about in a cardboard box. This game caused them endless hilarity, and they could play it for hours.

Stephen pulled the canoe up and joined Rob on the deck. They watched the boys for a while.

"I don't remember you ever being as silly as Alex and Pip," he said to Rob.

Sid's Six went on tour at the beginning of August. It was weird having Dominic with them. To Stephen's surprise and pleasure, he showed no inclination to sleep with the groupies who hung around as usual; in fact, it was only George who did.

"Things changed when Harry was so ill with Fee," Dominic shrugged. "I don't know why."

I do, Stephen thought fondly. The same reason Andy and Fin don't sleep around. You're too in love with your wife, that's why. He wasn't sure about George. But then, that's what he'd thought about Dominic. Who knew? And me? he asked himself. He didn't know if he was in love with Toni any more. But she is my wife, he thought. Charlie would probably think I'm mad; George definitely would.

Toni had been very tiresome about the tour, whining about the length of it and muttering about groupies. Stephen didn't bother to say he never had groupies, he'd said it so often in the past. If she didn't believe him, tough. She'd been so loving until the modelling show, he couldn't understand what had happened. And then he'd made that video and she'd become paranoid about him and Coral, making a terrific fuss about the album he was going to make with her, and all but accusing him of having an affair. He'd originally planned to record at the Priory, but Toni had pissed him off so much he decided to use Echelon, the new studio in Fiji. He told Coral they were going and fixed it up.

Toni hit the roof.

He stood impassively while she ranted. Eventually the diatribe reached a halt.

"Blame yourself if you don't like it. I was going to record here but you made such a fucking fuss I decided life would be unbearable while we were working."

They stared at each other.

"You miserable little bastard!" Toni said, finally.

He shrugged. "While I'm touring, perhaps you'd better decide if you want to stay married," he said, and walked out of the room.

She was very subdued after that, and they parted with a show of affection, but he knew that underneath things weren't right.

After the tour, he and Coral met up to rehearse. Coral was like a little girl with a new toy. He found himself enjoying being with her more and more; she never made scenes, she was never difficult. He was getting so tired of Toni's overbearing manner and constant suspicions.

Even Christmas was strained. Alex and Pip were so excited that they didn't notice anything – Alex probably wouldn't have anyway, but Pip was more sensitive. Sam always found Christmas difficult and Rob was wrapped up in Julia, spending all his free time with her. He was taking five 'A' levels and working very hard, so his free time didn't amount to much.

Stephen found a fascinating new book by a Norwegian writer, Jostein Gaarder, called *The Christmas Mystery*, about a little boy with a magic advent calendar. He read a chapter to the boys every day, Sam sitting on his lap and Pip and Alex leaning against him, all three of them sucking their thumbs. Alex had been scathing about the book to start with, claiming he was too old for it, but he soon fell under its spell and was as eager to listen as the other two.

In January, Stephen, Coral, Dominic, who was producing the album, and Andy, who was playing drums on it, flew out to Fiji.

Toni and Holly joined them for the first week and Stephen noticed that Holly was avoiding Toni. It was done very subtly, and Toni didn't realise, merely remarking that Holly always seemed to be talking to someone else. Stephen remembered how Holly had arranged for Rob to be on her show when Toni was away. Had it been a coincidence? And Toni complaining at the charity do that she'd been trying to talk to Holly all evening, without success.

After they'd gone home, he tackled Andy.

"Yeah?" Andy said casually. "I didn't notice. You know what Holl's like, Steve, motor mouth! She's always chatting, even to people she hardly knows."

"So you can't think of any reason why she might not want to see Toni?"

"Wherof one cannot speak, therof one must be silent, like," Andy said carefully.

Stephen stared at him. "Have you been reading Wittgenstein?" he asked, thunderstruck.

"Course." Andy patted him on the shoulder and sauntered off.

"Catching flies, Markham?" Dominic wandered into the hotel lounge.

"Andy just quoted Wittgenstein at me."

Dominic raised his eyebrows. "Good Lord! I didn't know his work was out in comic book format!"

"Look at this!" Toni waved the paper like a flag.

"What is it?" Harry asked. She and Toni had arranged to meet for lunch. "I haven't been here before," she added, looking round.

"It doesn't look like much, but the food's fantastic and it's really quiet. Anyway, listen to this. I'm ropeable, mate!" She read from the paper: *'Guitarist Stephen Markham, 36, seems to be more than fond of French actress Coral Mathieu, 30, with whom he is recording an album at Echelon Studios in Fiji. The pair have been sharing intimate moments on the beach, and it's rumoured that Markham has been seen leaving her room late at night. Markham had an affair with Mathieu, who he calls 'Coco', before he married his current partner, Toni. From the look of things, the affair never ended.'* What do you think of that?"

"Typical press crap," Harry said crisply. "Have you spoken to Stevie?"

"No, it's after midnight there. But I'll bloody well speak to him later! I'll make him sorry he was ever born!"

"I wouldn't make a fuss, if I were you," Harry said evenly. Toni opened her mouth to speak and shut it again. "Because I don't think you've got a leg to stand on," Harry continued in the same tone. "Have you, Toni?"

Toni had gone white. "What do you mean?"

"I mean I wouldn't make a fuss." Harry picked up her bag. "I've changed my mind, I don't think I want lunch."

"Harry, wait!" Toni said, desperately. "How did you know?"

Harry looked at her contemptuously. "Coral saw you. She told Andy and he told me."

"Dominic knows?"

"Of course Dom knows. God almighty, do you think I wouldn't tell him?"

"And Holly. She knows. That's why…" She stopped and stared at Harry, her eyes haunted. "It's over now, Harry, I swear it is. I finished it."

"Want a medal, do you? You should never have started it."

"How dare you lecture me?" Toni stormed, taking refuge in anger. "Who the hell do you think you are, anyway? You were carrying Stephen's baby when you married someone else!"

Harry smiled. "God, you're a bitch. I couldn't give a shit what you think of me." She stood up. "Because I think you're a liar, a cheat and a filthy little tart!" She swept out of the restaurant, practically knocking down the waiter who was bringing their wine.

Dominic struggled to wake up. No, it hadn't been a dream, the phone was ringing. Who the hell? He squinted at the bedside clock. It was nearly one in the morning. "Hello?"

"Dom, it's me."

He sat up. "What's wrong? What's happened? My bairns!"

"Your bairns are fine. Listen, I've done something stupid." Harry recounted her conversation with Toni.

Dominic groaned. "Why did you let her provoke you?"

"Oh, come on, what would you have done?"

"Probably the same. But the thing is, Harry, Stephen's still married to her, he doesn't know about the affair and we've got to act as if we don't either. It's like Holly. I know exactly how she feels, but it doesn't help Steve."

Harry sighed. "I'll make it up with her. Sorry, Dom. God, I miss you!"

"I miss you too, baby."

"Dom – there *isn't* anything going on between Stevie and Coral is there?"

"Of course not! As if. Goodnight, darling. I'll speak to you tomorrow."

Stephen and Coral were drinking cocktails in the hotel bar. Coral was enjoying the recording tremendously. Working with Stephen, Andy and Dominic was fun, and reminded her very much of the time she and Stephen had lived together. She had always regretted leaving him, had only done so in a forlorn attempt to make him propose, and she still had feelings for him. And it seemed to her that he felt the same. She finished her drink. They were the only people left in the bar.

"It must be getting late."

Stephen checked his watch. "It is. We should be in bed."

She looked at him, startled. "Stephen!"

He burst out laughing. "I didn't mean together!" He took her hand. "Come on, I'll walk you to your suite."

"Yes, Papa," she smiled. "Are you coming in for a nightcap?" she asked when they got to her door.

"Coco…"

"Oh, Stevie, do!" she cut in, pleadingly. "Just one drink?"

He hesitated. He very much wanted to. In fact, he very much wanted Coral, and he was finding it hard not to act on the feeling. He knew he was flirting with her far too much, and spending far too much time with her, but she was so easy to be with, so restful, and such fun. Things had been so difficult with Toni recently that he'd forgotten what fun a relationship could be. Not that he was having any sort of relationship with Coral, of course. In which case, one more drink couldn't possibly hurt.

"Yeah, OK, just one."

She poured them both a whisky and sat on the sofa. "Come and join me," she invited.

He sat next to her and she leant against him. "It would be nice to be in bed together, wouldn't it, Stevie?"

"Yes, it would," he admitted. To his horror, he found he was actually considering it. He pulled himself together. "But I couldn't cheat on Toni, Coco. I couldn't."

Coral downed her drink. A sense of recklessness swept over her. It was about time Toni got what she deserved. She stared into his eyes. "What a pity she doesn't seem to have the same scruples."

He blinked. "What?"

She looked away. "Nothing."

"Coral." He was alarmed. "What do you mean?" She shrugged. He grabbed her arm. "Tell me!"

"Toni had an affair!" she blurted out. She started to cry. "Stevie, you're hurting me!"

He let go of her arm. His heart was throwing itself around his chest as if it was trying to escape. "Say that again."

"Oh, Stevie!" Coral was crying hard. "Oh, Stevie, I'm so sorry, I shouldn't have told you, but I care for you so much and I can't stop thinking about it, and…"

"Who with?" he interrupted.

"That photographer, Gavin Leigh."

"I'll break his fucking neck!" He stood up. "I'll break every fucking bone in his fucking body!" He stared at Coral, barely seeing her. "How could she? How *could* she? She never stops doubting me and thinking the worst of me. Because she's such a lying bitch, I suppose. Can't believe everyone isn't like her."

Coral felt terrible. How could she have been so selfish, how could she have hurt him like that? "Oh, Stevie, I'm so sorry."

He sat back down. Very deliberately, he cupped her face in his hands and kissed her.

She moved away. "No, Stephen. Not in revenge."

"No, Coral, not in revenge. I've wanted to do this since *Hoodman Blind*. If you don't want to though…" He shrugged.

Coral pulled him back. "Oh, I want to!"

"Markham?" Dominic rapped on the door harder. "Markham, are you in there?"

Stephen tapped him on the shoulder.

Dominic jumped. "What the fuck are you doing?" He frowned. "Your hair's wet. Have you been swimming?"

Stephen unlocked the door and ushered Dominic in. "Sorry, Charlie. Coco and I are going to be late this morning. She's still in the shower."

"You've been to see Coral? Why?"

"I spent the night with her," Stephen said casually.

Dominic gaped at him.

"Catching flies, Chaplin?" he grinned.

"Oh God, Stephen, why?"

"I think you know why. Whisky?" he asked cheerfully, pouring himself a glass.

Dominic sank down onto the sofa. "Make it a large one."

"Why didn't you tell me Gavin Leigh was fucking Toni?" Stephen inquired as he passed Dominic his drink. "You're my best friend."

"Well, that's why. Why aren't you eaten up with guilt?"

"Why should I be?" Stephen's voice was ultra casual. He held up his glass and looked at it with interest. "Why the fuck should I be?" he yelled, and threw it against the wall. The room filled with an overpowering smell of alcohol.

"Oh, fucking Jesus Christ."

"Why the fuck didn't you tell me?"

"For Christ's sake, Stephen, what did you expect me to do? Waltz in and casually drop the information, oh, by the way, old chap, your wife's having an affair? See sense!"

"Who else knows?" Stephen demanded. "Andy and Holly, obviously."

"Harry. That's it. Unless Toni told anyone, which I would doubt."

"Or that… that *fucker* Leigh."

"Again, I doubt it. Why would he bother to say anything? He's always at it. And he's married too. Look, Steve, we didn't know what to do. After Coral told Andy and Andy told Harry, we just thought, leave it, you were happy and we thought either it would come to a head, in which case you'd find out soon enough, or she'd end it. Which she must have done. And if Coral hadn't told you, you'd have been none the wiser, and you'd have been spared all this. And what would you have done if we *had* told you?"

"I'd have broken his fucking neck."

"Just his?"

Stephen looked at him. His shoulders slumped. "I don't know, Charlie. I don't bloody know anything any more." He bent over the broken glass.

"Leave it. Housekeeping'll do it."

"Why should they? I made the mess. Pass me that newspaper, would you?"

"Fucking leave it!" Dominic said, pulling at Stephen's shoulder.

Stephen shook him off, lost his balance, and put his left hand down hard in the glass. Instantly, there was blood everywhere.

"Jesus Christ, Stephen! Get up, let me see!"

Stephen held up his hand. There was a deepish cut across it, and blood was running down his arm and dripping onto the floor. He grimaced. "I seem to have made the mess worse."

Dominic wrapped a napkin round the wound. "Press down on it as tightly as you can and keep your hand up above your heart."

"Don't fuss, it looks worse than it is."

"What are you, a fucking doctor? I'm calling one, you'll probably need it fucking stitched. Christ, how could you have been so stupid?" he asked, dialling reception.

The doctor stitched the wound, told him the stitches would dissolve in about ten days, bandaged it, and advised him to keep it dry for forty-eight hours. After he'd gone, Stephen winked at Coral, who was sitting anxiously on the sofa. "Day off today, then."

"Cut your fucking vocal chords as well, did you?" Dominic asked sarcastically. "There's nothing to stop you singing."

"Come on, Charlie, I'm suffering from shock! What I really need is to go back to bed with Coral."

Andy, who was sitting quietly in the corner, boggled at him. "What did you say, like?"

"Oh, Andy, I know about Toni, by the way."

"What? How?"

"I told him," Coral sighed. "This is all my fault."

"It's Toni's fault," Stephen said. "Nothing is your fault, Coco. Listen, Toni had a love affair…"

"*Love* affair!" Andy muttered.

"- and if you'll let me, I'd very much like to have one with you, here." He held out his right hand to her.

She took it and held it tightly. "I'd like that, Stevie."

"Clear off, then, you two." Stephen grinned at Andy and Dominic. "Coco's going to administer some tender loving care."

Andy and Dominic headed for the bar.

"What's he playing at, like?"

"I'm not sure, but I think it's something along the line of tit for tat."

"He gets the tits, Toni is the tat, you mean?" Andy grinned.

"I like that. Yes. I think it's the only way he can go back to Toni, Andy. As equals in adultery."

"You think he'll stay with that bitch?"

"Oh, yes. He'll not upset Sam – not any of those boys, but especially Sam – if he can help it. This is his way of saving his marriage."

"God, if only he'd married Coral!"

"Too fucking right," Dominic sighed. "Andrew, that Wittgenstein?"

Andy grinned. "It was 'Quote Of The Week' in the local paper. I thought Wittgenstein was a Danish football team! Don't tell Steve though."

When Stephen spoke to Toni on the phone later, he was breezily dismissive of the stories in the press. "None of that's true. Why are you always ready to believe the worst of me, Toni? We'll have been married for ten years shortly. Have I ever given you cause?"

There was a long pause. "No. I'm sorry," Toni said eventually, in a small voice.

"Good. Course, if you read any more stories about me and Coco, they will be true."

Another silence. He could hear Toni's uneven breathing. "What?" she managed to say at last. She sounded as if she'd been strangled.

"Coco and I are having an affair. It's my turn, Toni."

He heard her gasp. "Did… did Harry tell you?"

"It doesn't matter how I found out. The point is, we're even. One goal each. As far as I'm concerned, there's no recriminations, no blame, it's all over, forgotten. We get on with our marriage. No, don't say anything. Just think about it. If you want to, we'll start again, maybe renew our vows, whatever. If you don't want us to stay together, I'll be sorry, but it's up to you. I think we shouldn't speak to each other again until I get back. Then you can give me your decision. OK?"

"But… but… are you still sleeping with her?"

"Yep. I'll be sleeping – well, not sleeping – with her until we've finished recording. Then it's over, we've agreed that."

"You mean… you expect me…"

"I don't expect anything. And I won't be flaunting Coco or moving into her room. The press has had a go, I imagine they'll soon move on when nothing here changes. The only people who'll know, apart from us, are Coco, Charlie, Harry, Andy and Holly. Sound familiar?"

"My God, you've got it all sewn up, haven't you?"

"Certainly have. Goodbye, Toni." He rang off, and stared at the phone, his heart thumping. It had been a real effort to keep his voice light. He sat for a long time, thinking about his marriage, his life. Everything seemed to be out of control, like a runaway train. Things had been so simple once. What was the point of trying to save this marriage? Toni wasn't going to change. And, to be honest, neither was he. He'd never be what she wanted, although it would help if he knew exactly what she did want. He suspected she didn't really know herself. Perhaps he should just end it now. And then he thought of Sam. He would never cope, moving from one parent to another. Toni wouldn't stay in Oxford, she'd want to be back in London, so it would mean Sam changing schools. It would be bad for all the boys, but catastrophic for Sam. He couldn't do that to him. He had to stay, had to make it work. Oh, Cherry, he thought with despair, why did you leave me?

Chapter Seventeen
Just Hanging On

Just hanging in there, holding on, I need to believe that it's not all gone.

When he got home from Fiji, tired from the long plane journey, Toni met him at the door of the Priory. He'd been unsure of seeing her again, afraid that she might have decided to end their marriage. One look at her face was enough.

"I want us to stay together," she said. "I'm sorry..."

Stephen put his finger on her lips. "No. No discussions, no apologies. That was yesterday, Toni, this is today." He kissed her. "Will you come to bed with me? I'm very tired, so maybe we'll just cuddle, but I want to feel your skin on mine."

In bed, he gazed at her body. "I always forget how incredibly beautiful you are," he said, stroking her. They lay together, her head on his shoulder, and he smiled. "You know, I'm not as tired as I thought I was!"

After they'd made love he fell asleep, and Toni lay and held him, thinking how young and defenceless he looked. She thought back to when she'd first met him eleven years ago, her eyes filling with tears. How wonderful everything had seemed then, when anything was possible, the future stretching out ahead of them, full of fun and excitement. What had gone wrong? And how could they change it? They'd both had affairs, both been unfaithful when they'd sworn they wouldn't. True, Stephen had only had Coral to get even with her, but all the same... If only she could turn back time! Everything had started to go wrong after she'd had Sam, even his birth had been wrong. None of it should have happened like that. If only they hadn't gone to that wedding! Her nose was running and she tried to move to get a tissue without disturbing Stephen, but he woke and smiled at her. His smile faded as he saw her face.

"Toni! What is it?"

"It's no good saying we'll never talk about it!" she wailed. "We have to, I can't bear to think of you with her! I thought you were going to leave me and I couldn't—"

"Well, how do you think I felt?" he interrupted. "I would have sworn, Toni, whatever else you did to me, you would never have been unfaithful: not Toni, I would have said, Toni would never do that." He was shaking and he took a deep breath. "I wanted to kill the pair of you, I wanted to lay waste to the entire world, I didn't see how I could ever forgive you." He sat up and took her by her upper arms. "We have to forget it, because I can't live with you if I'm constantly picturing you... with him. Do you really want us to stay together?" he asked harshly.

She was startled. "Yes."

"Then I forbid you to think about him or Coral, do you understand me, Toni?" He gripped her arms harder and she winced. "We have to put it behind us, or I don't see how we can go on. I never want to hear you mention any of this again. Is that clear?"

She nodded, her eyes wide. He let go of her arms. "Good. Now go and get me some toast and coffee."

She went without a word. He breathed out. Why did he have to lose his temper with her and lay down the law before she'd see sense? This was a fucking marriage, they were equals, he shouldn't have to play the masterful husband. With Lynn I could be me, he thought with a sudden sense of revelation, I never had to pretend to be someone I wasn't. Is that why I can't forget her?

Toni came back with a tray. "I didn't know if you wanted jam or marmalade, so I brought both."

"So what do you think about renewing our vows?" he asked, munching.

"I think it's a good idea." Toni took a slice of toast. "Where would we do it?"

"Wherever you want. I was reading that they do a lot of that sort of thing in Tahiti. Would you like that, Daisy? Like a second honeymoon, but just you and me this time, no children."

Toni leant against him. "I'd like that very much, Stephen."

Tahiti was paradise. They hired a car and explored the island. Stephen bought Toni a necklace of perfectly matched black pearls, incredibly beautiful and incredibly expensive, and she wore them all the time, everywhere they went, even when she was sunbathing naked on the deck outside the bungalow, which was built directly over the pellucid water, so that they could see the fish moving languidly beneath them. They went swimming every day in the warm, sensuous sea.

"I don't want to go home," Toni said on the last day. "I wish we could stay here forever!"

Stephen smiled at her. "I know. But I'm looking forward to seeing the boys and being at home, I seem to have been away for so long recently. I know I was home over Christmas, but only for a couple of weeks. I'm looking forward to spending time with you all. And we can come back again."

"I don't think we should. It might not be as perfect again, and it would be terrible to sully the memory. I've had such a lovely time, Stevo," she said earnestly.

"I know what you mean, Daisy. But we'll come somewhere like this. I was thinking last night, we must have time to ourselves, just you and me. The boys are all old enough now to accept that, even Sam. And he's been fine about Mum and Ted looking after them, hasn't he? Our marriage is important, and we have to take care of it."

For the first time in several years, he had no projects lined up, nothing he had to do. He wanted to spend time with Toni and the boys, even if it was only for a couple of months, doing nothing else, no distractions. He and Toni spent their evenings together watching TV when there was something on that they enjoyed, or listening to music. Sometimes, if he wasn't studying, Rob would join them, usually with Julia.

"They seem quite serious," Toni said one evening, pouring herself and Stephen a glass of wine. Julia had just trounced them all at Scrabble, and Rob was taking her home.

"Yes," Stephen agreed, frowning. Mardi jumped up onto his lap and settled down, purring loudly. "Is it a good thing though?" he asked, stroking the cat's ears. "This cat's getting very thin. Do you suppose he's OK?"

Toni looked at Mardi. "Perhaps it's his thyroid, I'll take him to the vets tomorrow. Don't you like Julia?"

"Oh, I've nothing against Julia, she's a very nice girl. I'm just not sure it's good for them to be so serious at their age. I mean, they're only seventeen. How long have they been going out together?"

"Nearly two years. I wouldn't worry, Stevo, kids fall in and out of love all the time at that age."

"Do they?" Stephen wasn't so sure. Rob was very like Harry. "Terrible worry, children, aren't they?"

"Have you only just realised that?"

That summer they entertained lavishly, holding a succession of riotous and extravagant parties, and filling the house with guests.

Fin and Shelagh came to stay, bringing their son, Ben, twenty months old and very Irish looking, with astonishingly blue eyes and dark hair. "Too pretty to be a boy, isn't he?" Fin laughed.

Harry and Dominic were there at the same time, with their three.

Amabel, who was eight, went into raptures over Ben. "Mama, why can't we have another baby? Ben's *so* sweet!" She gave Ben her favourite toy, a soft Simba from the Disney film *The Lion King*, to look at, while she tried to pick him up, but he wriggled away and tottered off with the wide legged, unstable gait of very small children.

"Why, Mama?" Mab repeated.

"Because we can't, Mab," Dominic said. "Run along and play."

"But, Papa, I want to play with Ben," Mab protested.

"Well, the grown ups want to talk. Go on, take that mangy lion, and off with you," he ordered, clapping his hands.

Mab went slowly out, hugging Simba, who she took everywhere, and casting exaggeratedly longing glances in Ben's direction.

"Catch Alex doing what he was told like that!" Stephen said, admiringly.

Dominic stretched out his long legs and sipped his whisky. "You've got to impose discipline from the very beginning, Markham, like I have," he drawled.

"You! You don't know the meaning of the word discipline!" Harry exclaimed. "It's our nanny, Nanny Davies," she told Stephen. "She's amazing, very strict, but nice with it. Very old fashioned. She was Dominic's nanny." She giggled. "He still jumps to it when she tells him to!"

"Rubbish!" Dominic said indignantly.

"We had a nanny and she was very good," Toni sighed. "I think it's just Alex. He's irredeemable!"

"Military school," Dominic advised. "It's your only option."

"God, we couldn't possibly inflict him on them!" Stephen joked. "Anyway, imagine if they taught him to use a gun!"

Later, they took the children in the pool. After a while, Harry joined Dominic, who was stretched out, half-asleep, on a lounger. She watched Ben splashing in the shallow end, with Shelagh. "Why don't we have another one, Dom?" she said idly. "Ben's so gorgeous, isn't he? I love them at that age."

"Are you mad, woman? You know what the doctors said when you had Fee."

Harry made a dismissive gesture with her hand. "Oh, doctors! What do they know?"

"Considerably more than you do!" Dominic was getting alarmed. "Harriet, as head of the household, I absolutely, categorically forbid you even to think about having any more babies. And, anyway, why would we want more? We've got four splendid children, look at them!"

"Four?"

He was puzzled. "Yes, four. Surely you haven't forgotten any of them?"

"You're counting Rob?"

"Too fucking right I'm counting Rob! Why wouldn't I? I love him just as much as the others. You know how much Gus means to me, Harry, but... well, Rob's my eldest son. I'm just sorry I can't leave him Fenroth and the title, he'd be the perfect lord of the manor, especially now he's going to be studying law."

Harry squeezed his hand, tears in her eyes. "You really mean it, don't you?"

"Really mean what?" Stephen pulled up a chair and sat down, rubbing his hair with a towel. "God, that Alex! Seriously, I don't know how we're going to cope with him much longer. Really mean what?"

"Dominic was just saying he thought of Rob as his own son and wished he could leave Fenroth to him," Harry said, her voice unsteady.

Stephen looked at Dominic, who had flushed slightly. "Charlie." He couldn't find words.

"Oh, for fuck's sake, pull yourself together, Markham," Dominic drawled. "Anyone would feel the same. He's a lovely boy, he always has been."

Stephen took Harry's hand. "This is a very strange relationship, and you'll probably kill me for saying this, Charlie, but I love you two very much."

Harry started to cry.

"Oh, well done, Markham."

"We love you too," Harry said.

Dominic stood up. "Well, I'll leave you two girls to wallow in emotion." He looked at Stephen for a moment. "I've known worse people than you, Markham." He sauntered off into the house.

"He means…"

"I know what he means," Stephen smiled.

Toni was on the phone to Callie. She hadn't seen her since Stephen had gone to Fiji, although she'd spoken to her several times. At Christmas, Callie and Fred had decided to get married, so Callie had been busy with the arrangements, and then her mother had had a mild stroke, and she'd gone down to Cornwall to be with her. She and her sister and mother were very close; her father had treated her mother very badly, had been abusive, had countless affairs, and walked out when Callie was twelve and her sister, Linda, fourteen. "That's why it took me so long to commit to Fred," she'd once told Toni. "I don't really trust men at all."

Toni arranged to meet her mid week for lunch. She hadn't told her about Gavin or Coral, had simply said that she and Stephen had decided to renew their vows because they'd been married for ten years, but she hated hiding anything from Callie, and made up her mind to tell her when she saw her.

They had lunch at Callie and Fred's tiny little house in North London. Callie was absorbed in the final preparations for her wedding. She showed Toni her wedding dress, and over lunch they talked about the hitherto undiscovered difficulties of trying to get all one's relations gathered together in the same place without at least two of them starting some kind of blood feud.

"Talking of weddings, how was Tahiti?" Callie asked. "Have you got any photos?"

Toni shook her head. "No. It wasn't one of those semi-official things, with flower wreaths and dancing girls. We just… it was just us."

"And those ridiculous rumours about Steve and Coral Mathieu seem to have died a natural death. Honestly, sometimes I feel ashamed to be a journalist."

"Well…" Toni started. She'd nerved herself to tell Callie, and had fortified herself with more wine than she usually drank, but now that the opportunity had finally arisen, it was hard to do.

Callie looked inquiringly at her.

Toni swallowed. "You see," she went on, twisting her hands nervously, "Stephen did… um… have an affair with her, because…"

"What?" Callie interrupted, stunned. "Oh, Toni how *could* he?" She was really upset. "The rat, the absolute *rat*! Oh, now I've heard everything! How could he *do* that to you? You would *never* do that to him, I *know* you wouldn't, although when would you get the chance, chained up in Oxford looking after the bastard's children while he's away enjoying himself? It's not even as if Rob is yours! You've been so good all this time, coping with poor little Sammy, while he waltzes off with that French tramp, and this is how he repays you! It's just like my dad; they're all bloody rats! Oh Toni, I'm so sorry!" She got up and hugged Toni, who was amazed to see tears in her eyes.

She swallowed and tried again. "Yes, but, Callie, it wasn't Stephen's fault…"

"I can't believe you're sticking up for him like this, Toni, you're a bloody saint, and he doesn't bloody well deserve you! God, I wish there was something I could do to…" Just then the phone rang. "Drat! I'd better get that, it's probably Fred. Have some more wine, Toni."

Toni could hear her exclaiming over the phone. She didn't know what to do. How could she possibly tell her now, after Callie had said that she wasn't capable of behaving like that? She couldn't bear Callie to think badly of her; if only she'd just come out and said 'I had an affair with Gavin Leigh.'

Callie came back, looking pale. "I'm so sorry, Toni, I've got to go, Fred's had an accident, someone went into the side of his car. He's in casualty."

Toni stood up, all thoughts of her confession driven from her mind. "Callie, no! Is he OK? Would you like me to come with you?"

Callie smiled. "No, it's all right; he hit his head and he's a bit shaky, but otherwise he's OK." She kissed Toni on the cheek. "I'm really sorry to do this! Not very hostessy is it? Listen, I'll ring you tomorrow. Shall I give you a lift to the station?"

"No, no, you go. I'll get a taxi." It was only when she was on the train that she remembered she hadn't told Callie about her and Gavin. Too late now, she thought. Oh, well, what's the hurry? I'll tell her another time.

"Stevo, guess what! Swiggsy wants to come and stay!"

Stephen looked up. He was sitting at his desk in the study on a glorious August morning. "Oh, no, Toni, not Swiggsy!"

Toni bridled. "And why not? He's one of my oldest friends!"

"He drinks us out of house and home!"

"Well, that's how he got his nickname!"

"You don't say! I wouldn't mind if he could hold his drink! Anyway, we've got the charity concert in a couple of weeks, you know how busy we are rehearsing, and next Friday we'll be in London for Coral's film." This was the premiere of the second Verity Linden film, *The Festival Begins*. Stephen had written the soundtrack for this one too "It's not a good time, Toni. Maybe at Christmas."

Toni scowled. "Yeah, and at Christmas, there'll be another excuse." She was fed up with his attitude. The band members and Dominic and Harry were always at the house, she was always entertaining them and cooking meals. And Sian and Ted. She loved Sian, and enjoyed seeing them, but it did seem unfair. And it wasn't as if *her* family were constantly there; Stephen didn't really like having Jacko over, preferring to see him 'in his own habitat', as he put it, as though her father was a zoo exhibit. She opened her mouth to protest as the phone rang.

Stephen picked it up, glad of a reason to end the conversation. "Stephen Markham? Oh, hello, Callie! We haven't seen you for ages… Yes, she's here." He offered the receiver to Toni, his hand over the mouthpiece. "Callie. She doesn't sound very happy."

"I'll take it in the kitchen."

Stephen stared out of the window. Alex, Pip and Sam were playing outside. Pip said something, and Stephen heard Alex hoot with laughter. They came closer to the open French windows.

"I don't see why I can't!" Alex was saying

"You know what Miss Piggott says, Al," Pip said seriously. "Beggars can't be Jesus." They walked on towards the river.

Beggars can't be Jesus, Stephen thought. What a great phrase!

"God, Dad, look at this!" Rob passed the newspaper across the breakfast table to Stephen. Pictures of him and Coral in Fiji, and stills from *Hoodman Blind* and the 'She's Mine' video were splashed across the page. The headline read *'Love Rat!'* and there was a long article claiming that a source in the Markham family had confirmed that Stephen Markham and Coral Mathieu had had an affair while they were recording the album 'Do Let's!', due to be released the following month. Stephen scanned the article grimly and handed it to Toni. The blood drained from her face as she read. It was slanted very strongly in her favour, saying what a loyal and supportive wife she'd always been, even to the extent of giving a home to Stephen's illegitimate son. It dragged up Sam's birth, and hinted that Stephen was violent towards her. *Callie*, she thought, remembering how Callie had called Stephen a rat, and gone on about her looking after Rob. This could only mean that Callie had told someone. Toni felt very sick. She stood up and went quickly out.

"What is it?" Pip asked, scared.

"It's all right, boys, it's just the paper saying mean things," Stephen said. He picked it up and went after Toni.

She was washing her face in the downstairs cloakroom. "I'm all right. It was just a shock." She went upstairs, and Stephen walked slowly back to the kitchen. He couldn't see how this had happened. The press had done some fishing while they'd been in Fiji, but he and Coral been so careful and the reporters had moved on, oblivious. Apart from Dominic, Harry, Andy and Holly, no one had known anything about it. He could hear Alex, Pip and Sam laughing idiotically, which meant they hadn't taken any notice. Good. But Rob was waiting at the door, looking as sick as Toni.

"It's not true though, Dad, is it?"

Stephen licked his lips, wondering desperately what to say. His silence was enough.

Rob went white. "Dad! How could you do that to Toni?"

"You don't understand, Rob…"

"Oh, yes I do! And poor Toni knew, didn't she? That's why you went to Tahiti to renew your vows, wasn't it? You're disgusting!" He turned and walked away.

"Rob! Where are you going?"

"To Julia's. Don't worry; if they've seen it, I'll say it's not true. It's the least I can do for Toni."

Stephen watched him walk out. He didn't know what to do. He checked on the three little boys. They were finishing their breakfasts.

"I ate your toast, Dad," Alex said apologetically. "Sorry! I thought you weren't coming back."

Despite the situation, Stephen grinned. "That's OK, Ally, I didn't want it anyway. Listen, Mummy's not feeling well, so either play quietly in the nursery or outside, OK?"

"I'm too old to play in the nursery!" Alex declared indignantly.

"So am I," Pip echoed.

"And me," said Sam, not to be left out.

"Well, all right, let's call it the playroom from now on. Is that OK?" Stephen asked.

Pip and Sam looked at Alex, who nodded.

"Great! Go and clean your teeth, then, and off you go and play."

The phone rang. It was Dominic. "What are you going to do, Stephen?" he asked, his voice anxious.

"I don't know. Talk to Cell. What *can* I do? Just deny it. I won't talk to the press, I'll leave it to Cell. Charlie – Rob saw it. He's very upset. He might ring."

"You told him it wasn't true, didn't you?"

"Well, I was going to, but I must have looked guilty, I don't know. Oh, God, I couldn't tell him about Toni, but now he thinks I'm a complete bastard."

"He'll have to know about Toni, Steve."

"I can't," Stephen said despairingly. "He's so young, Charlie, it's not fair. It's all so complicated and not very savoury, any of it." He sighed. "He'll get over it, I suppose. I'll talk to him. Look, I'd better go and ring Cell. I'll speak to you later. Tell Harry not to worry."

He called Cell, Julian and Coral. Coral was out, so he left a message.

She returned his call a little later. "It's the premiere next week," she wailed. "Oh, Stevie! It'll be terrible; this is all they'll want to talk about! Listen, you and Toni don't have to come."

"I think it might be a good thing if we do," Stephen said slowly. "If we keep denying it, and if the three of us are there together and you and Toni are on friendly terms, it might help. It'll blow over, Coco."

But what about Robbie? he thought. And why did this have to happen now, just as me and Toni are getting our relationship back together again?

The morning wore on. He went into his study and stared out over the rose garden. He couldn't work, couldn't settle.

The phone rang. It was Harry. "Stevie, Rob's here. I'm going to drive him back to the Priory."

"Rob? With you?" Stephen was surprised.

"He was upset," Harry said, her voice steady and reassuring. "He decided not to go to Julia's, but to come and see us."

"Is he with you now?"

"Yes. Stevie, we'll talk when we get there. Is Toni OK?"

"She's fine," Stephen said. "At least one of us comes out of this well, thank God." He hung up and went to find her. She was upstairs in their bedroom, sitting on the window seat and staring unseeingly out of the window. She'd gone over and over it in her mind, feeling like a rat in a maze, wondering if it *had* been Callie. And if it had, then this was all her fault for not telling Callie the truth. She couldn't bear to think that. She realised she was never going to ask Callie either. If she didn't know for certain, she couldn't blame herself.

"Toni," Stephen sat on the edge of their bed. "Listen, I've been thinking. We've got to play this down, so when we go to the premiere, can you act as if you and Coral are friends?"

Toni stared at him. "We can't possibly go now!"

"We have to. We don't have to talk to the press, just show up, all good friends, and it'll blow over. It always does."

"Not going to the premiere was the only good thing to come out of this! I never wanted to go, I don't want to see that home wrecking tart's film! Certainly not now, with things being written about us. You can do what you like, but I'm not going."

Stephen got up. He'd gone white. The sun was shining through the windows, and as it fell on his face, it made his eyes look colourless. He was completely still.

"Stephen?" she said uncertainly.

"You bitch, you total, utter bitch!" He felt as if he'd just run a marathon, it was hard to breathe and his heart was racing. "All this is your fault, all of it. You've spent the whole of our married life mistrusting me and accusing me of infidelity without any reason whatsoever. I haven't had sex with another woman since the day I asked you to marry me, until Coral – and that wouldn't have happened if you hadn't been fucking someone else! And my God, Toni, I could have anyone, anyone I want, women offer themselves to me wherever I go, and not just groupies, either." He thought briefly of Malou Karlsson, the gorgeous Swedish pop star who had performed at one of their concerts in Scandinavia, and made it so obvious she wanted him. He'd found it very hard to resist her. "Anyone, younger women than you, Toni, prettier girls than you."

She stared at him, stunned.

"But I'm married and I love my wife, so I don't touch them. How many men did you sleep with before Leigh?"

"None!" she exclaimed angrily. She stood up, facing him. "None! How could you say something like that, you bastard?"

"Why should I believe you? You never believed me, and *you* had an affair!"

"So did you!" she yelled.

"To give you a taste of your own medicine!" He stopped and drew in a long breath.

"Yes, but if you hadn't there'd be none of this in the papers! At least I was discreet! Anyway, there were reports about you and her before you started the affair – or maybe you already had, maybe you fuck her every time you see her!"

Stephen grabbed her by the shoulders and shook her furiously. He wanted to kill her, wanted to put his hands round her neck and tighten them until there was no more life left in her. He let go of her, and she staggered backwards, hitting her head against the window frame. She was crying, wiping her face with her hand.

"Stop bloody crying and listen to me," he said, fighting to master his temper. "You're going to tell Rob that you had an affair."

She stared at him, shaking her head. "No, Stephen, oh no, I can't do that!" she whispered in horror.

"You can and you will. He knows I had this affair with Coral and he thinks you're the poor, innocent victim." He was shaking with emotion. "And you know what? I was going to let him think that, I was actually going to let *my* son think that because I didn't want him to think badly of you! I must be off my fucking head! So when Harry brings him back, you're going to tell him exactly what happened." He stopped and looked intently at her. "What *did* happen, by the way, Toni? How long did you know him for before… before…"

Toni stared at him defiantly. "About five minutes."

He screwed up his eyes as if the light was hurting them.

She realised he was trying not to cry. She felt dreadful, guilty and ashamed. She didn't want to be arguing with him like this, mistrusting him, resentful and unhappy. What had gone wrong with their marriage? "Stephen." She put her hand on his arm.

He shook it off. "Don't," he said, harshly. "I don't want anything to do with you. I don't want to be married to you any more, I don't even want to look at you!" He turned away and stumbled towards the door.

"Stephen! Stephen, please, I'm sorry! Please, Stephen, I'll tell Rob, I'll tell anyone, I'll do anything you want, please, please don't leave me, please, I love you!"

He turned back to her. "Not enough though. Not enough."

"I will – I do, I do, I promise, I *swear* things will be different! Oh, please Stephen, please give me one more chance, I've been so unhappy, please, I'll never ask you for anything again! I do love you, I do, please!" She was sobbing hard, and she paused to take a breath. Her eyes were swollen from crying. "Please, Stephen," she whispered.

They heard Harry calling. He grabbed her wrist. "Come on."

She pulled back. "No!" she said, horrified. "I can't go down like this! Harry will be there!"

"Two seconds ago you said you'd do anything I wanted. OK. I want you to come downstairs and tell Rob why I slept with Coral."

"Let me wash my face first?" she pleaded. "My head aches so much."

"So does mine," he said.

They stood and looked at each other.

"I'll go downstairs," Stephen said. "But Toni, if you don't come down, if I have to come and get you, this marriage is over. I really mean that."

He went slowly down to Harry and Rob.

Rob looked shocking, pale and ill.

"Dominic and I told him about Toni," Harry said.

Stephen gave a laugh of disbelief. "God, her luck! She's coming down to tell him herself when she's washed her face. Robbie, I'm so sorry. We're supposed to be the grown ups. You wouldn't believe how hard it is…" He couldn't go on.

Toni came down the stairs. "Robbie," she whispered, and started to cry again.

"Mum and Dom told me," Rob said stiffly. "I think you both behaved horribly!" he burst out. "You told me you loved each other!"

"Rob, love isn't fun!" Stephen said. "Love isn't romance and violins! It's hell, it's frightening and confusing, it's a mess, it's a painful, bloody mess! It's much worse than war, at least in war you know who your enemies are!"

"It's not always like that, Rob," Toni said, upset anew by the look on Rob's face. "Your dad feels like that now because things aren't right between us, and that's my fault, Rob, it's all my fault. Yes, maybe your Dad shouldn't have slept with Coral, but he was very angry with me, and he wanted me to know how it felt. He also thought, rightly or wrongly, that it would make us quits. In a skewed sort of way, Robbie, he was doing it for me. If he'd been unfaithful too, how he could he blame me? Do you understand?"

Rob nodded. "But, Toni, why did you do it?"

Toni swallowed. "Because I was stupid. I stuffed up so badly and I'm so, so sorry and I wish he could forgive me." Tears were running down her face.

"Harry!" Alex threw himself down the stairs, followed by Pip and Sam. "Where's Mab and Gus?"

"They didn't come today."

Pip stared at Toni, alarmed. "Mummy? Why are you crying?"

"Dad said you weren't feeling well," Alex said. "Are you seriously ill?" he asked, with interest.

"No, she's got a headache," Stephen said. "We're trying to talk, boys, so go away."

"Talking in the hall?" scoffed Alex. "That's stupid! Why don't you go and sit in the kitchen?"

"Because we're talking *here*!" Stephen shouted, making them all jump, "And if you don't do as you are told, Alexander, if I hear one more word from you, I will fetch a belt from my room and beat you with it, so hard you won't be able to sit down for a week. I am *fed* up with your bad behaviour. Now go, all of you!"

They went, Alex as fast as he could. As he reached the top of the stairs, he said, his voice carrying clearly, "Actually, it's against the law to hit little boys with a belt."

"Oh, no it's not," Stephen shouted after him, "as you will see if I hear one more word out of you!" He turned to the others. "He's right though. It is stupid to stand in the hall."

They went into the kitchen and Harry made them coffee.

"So, what are you going to do?" she asked. "That's what you want to know, isn't it, Rob?"

Stephen looked at Toni. "It depends. Toni, do you really want to stay married to me?"

She nodded.

"Why?" he asked. "I'm not trying to catch you out, I just want to know. I don't seem to make you very happy, you don't trust me, you wanted someone else."

"I didn't, I just wanted you to be different, and I'm so unhappy, I've been so unhappy for so long, but I love you. I can't imagine not living with you."

Stephen was shaken. "Why? Why aren't you happy with me?"

She shook her head. "I don't know." She looked at him. "Do you want to stay married to me?"

He hesitated. "I'm not sure. I love you, Toni, but I can't live like this much longer."

Harry put her hand on his arm. "Why don't you try counselling? Because you love each other, but there seem to be so many problems that you're both only half-aware of."

Stephen looked at Toni. She nodded.

"All right," he said. He reached over and took her hand. She clutched his tightly.

"Hi, Harry. Sorry I'm late." Lynn bent and kissed Harry's cheek. She sat down. "Have you ordered?"

Harry handed her the menu. "Only the wine. You're looking very pleased with yourself, Lynn, I must say! Is something going on? How's Paul?"

They were having lunch together. Lynn had been surprised and pleased when Harry had rung her a couple of years ago and suggested they meet. She and Harry had always got on so well, and she was so easy to talk to, full of common sense and never afraid to say exactly what she thought. They had both been wary to start with, but it hadn't taken them long to settle into an easy, affectionate friendship again. They never really talked about Stephen, but occasionally Harry would say something in passing, and from these tantalising little snippets, Lynn gathered his marriage was difficult, to say the least. It was also clear that neither Harry nor Dominic liked Toni much, which made Lynn glad, although she tried to suppress the feeling. These days, Harry was her only link with Stephen, as Sam no longer needed speech therapy. She was surprised by how much she missed him – not because he was Stephen's son, but because he was such a dear little boy. She missed the way he'd tell her all his news, the words pouring out in a torrent of excitement.

She smiled. "Paul's *lovely*! He's got a policeman's uniform and he's bringing it round tonight."

"A policeman's uniform? What on earth for?"

"To dress up in, of course. You know!" Lynn started to blush.

"Oh! Yes, I see. Lynn! You pervert! A policeman's uniform? The truncheon turns you on, eh?"

Lynn's blush deepened. "Shut up, Harry! Actually, it's the gloves I particularly like."

"The gloves? You're weird!"

"Well, I don't care! After all, you're always buying sexy underwear to dress up in for Charlie, I don't see the difference."

"Yes, that's true," Harry said thoughtfully. "Although, I must say, I can't really think of anything I'd like to see Dom in." She giggled. "Well, apart from his birthday suit."

"He'd look lovely in a Richard Sharpe uniform," Lynn said, thinking: God, so would Stephen!

"Lynn! What is it with you and uniforms?"

Lynn shrugged. "I've always been a sucker for a man in uniform."

"What, literally? That'll be nice for Paul!" Harry said, and they fell about laughing.

Lynn and Paul had been seeing each other for two years. They'd decided that they didn't want to get serious but Lynn could see that that they might easily drift into marriage later, they got on so well and they both wanted children eventually. The relationship was easy and uncomplicated, like Paul himself. He was never moody or difficult; they had rows occasionally, but only minor ones. The only real difference between them was that Paul wasn't much of a reader, preferring to play his Playstation or watch sport, but that was no problem. In every way, they were perfect together, and Lynn loved him very much. She just wasn't *in* love with him, that vital spark wasn't there.

"You need to be in love, don't you? I don't mean you, I mean people," she said to Harry, over dessert.

Harry smiled rather sadly. "You know, I'm not sure. Look at Stephen. He's in love with Toni – or was, I just don't know any more – but it doesn't seem to have made him happy. Are you saying you're not in love with Paul?"

"I *love* him, and I love being with him, but, no, I'm not *in* love with him."

"Love's hard to find, Lynn."

"You and Charlie did though," Lynn pointed out.

Harry beamed. "I know. We've been so incredibly lucky. But then, who could fail to love Dom?"

Lynn smiled at her affectionately. "Who indeed? Harry, I've got to go, I've got a patient in half an hour and I've got to get to the bank! Give Charlie and his bairns a kiss from me."

Her last patient had gone by four-thirty. She was on her way up to the shower when the phone rang. Thinking it was Paul, she ran to pick it up before the answer machine kicked in.

It was Tim.

"Hello," she said, surprised and pleased. "How are you?"

"Very well. How about you?"

"Me too."

"Yes, you sound in great form. Is something exciting happening?"

How well Tim still knows me, she thought. He's always been tuned in to my moods.

"Oh, you know, just things going well."

"I'm so glad. Lynn, remember when I said I was seeing someone? You said, "Invite me to the wedding" – did you really mean it?"

"Tim!" she squealed, with pleasure. "Yes, I did! Oh, Timmy, congratulations! When?"

"Next month. We'll send you an invitation, but I wanted to make sure you weren't just being polite. Sorry it's short notice, we weren't going to bother, we've been living together for a while but..." he paused for a fraction of a second, then continued, trying to sound casual, "...Kate's pregnant, so we decided to tie the knot."

"Oh, Tim!" Lynn's eyes filled with tears. "I am so very pleased. Oh, I can't tell you! You'll be a fantastic father! Oh, dear, I'm blubbing," she said, sniffing.

"Thank you, Lynn." She heard him take a breath. "Lynn..."

"Don't say anything, Tim, there's nothing to say. It was no one's fault we didn't work out. And we did have fun! And I'm so glad for you – for you both."

"What about you? Is there someone you'd like to bring?"

Lynn smiled, thinking of Paul. He'd be there in a couple of hours, with the uniform. "Yes, Tim. Yes, there is..."

Stephen and Toni went to London for the Verity Linden premiere in Stephen's new car, his pride and joy, a Porsche Boxster. It had literally only just been delivered and it was the first time he'd driven it. He was teaching Rob to drive and had him on his insurance, which made it astronomical, but he didn't care, he could afford it. He was actually teaching Rob in a Megane, but he planned to buy him a Boxster for his eighteenth birthday.

"Stephen, slow down! You've already got seven points on your licence!"

"Sorry." Stephen took his foot of the accelerator. "It just creeps up."

"Well, don't let it. You were really lucky last time they stopped you, just because that fat one's daughter had a crush on you, and he wanted an autograph for her. That's unlikely to happen again, you know."

"Well, you can always flutter your eyelashes and flirt," Stephen grinned.

The premiere was the following day. They were staying at the London house and going out to dinner with Callie and Fred that night. Toni wasn't sure now that she wanted to see Callie, she was afraid Callie would tell her that she had been the one who leaked the story about Stephen, but the dinner had been arranged weeks ago, and she couldn't see any way out of it.

She and Stephen arrived at the restaurant first. Looking round, she was glad she'd dressed up and put on her pearls. Stephen was looking very formal in a dark suit. She preferred him in casual clothes really, but she had to admit he did look very sexy in a suit. "You look like a pocket-sized James Bond," she said.

He grinned. "Why do your compliments always include a sting? I suppose it was growing up in Australia; all that poison you absorbed when you were a child."

Callie and Fred arrived. Callie kissed Toni warmly, but her lips merely brushed the air next to Stephen's cheek.

He was surprised, she usually kissed him properly. "How are you both?" he asked. "Nervous?"

Fred smiled. "I can't believe I'm committing to this maniac!"

"And how are you two?" Callie said. "How does it feel to be a love rat, Stephen?" She was smiling, but the smile didn't quite reach her eyes.

Stephen's smile froze.

"Callie!" Fred was rigid with embarrassment.

"Sorry! Just a joke! So, are you looking forward to the premiere?"

God, thought Toni, it *was* her! "Let's talk about your wedding," she said quickly.

Later, when the two of them were alone in the Ladies, she took a deep breath and said, in a rush, "Callie, Stephen was unfaithful because I had an affair with Gavin Leigh and he found out while he was in Fiji. He slept with Coral to get even with me."

Callie had been in the middle of applying lipstick. She paused and stared at Toni. "What did you say?"

"I had an affair with Gavin Leigh. Look, I'm really sorry I didn't tell you. I tried, that day Fred had his car crash, but you had to rush off, and then I realised I couldn't bear you to think badly of me, so I never mentioned it again." She bit her lip, trying to stop herself from crying.

Callie stared at her, horrified. "Oh! Oh, Toni, no! Oh, God, I've done Stephen such an injustice!"

Toni caught her arm. "Cal, I don't want to know. All this – it's my fault, and I can't stand any more guilt. Stephen and I, we're going for counselling. I have to forget it, does that make sense?"

Callie hugged her. "Yes, yes it does." She thought rapidly. "Look, this charity concert that Sid's Six are doing at Warwick Castle, maybe *Juliette* could do a feature on it, a really good one about the band – but particularly Stephen?"

"Maybe. He might not be too keen after the way you treated him this evening."

Callie had been very cold with him.

"I'll be wonderful over dessert, apologise, blame pre-wedding jitters."

Toni smiled. "Well, we could give it a burl!"

"Hey, Lynn, you know Stell and Lizzie are going to this concert at Warwick Castle? Well, I got us tickets too, I thought maybe we could all go together."

Lynn raised her eyebrows. "There's an 'and' at the end of that sentence."

Paul looked sheepish. "And, well, perhaps..."

"Spit it out, Paul!"

"I thought you might be able to introduce her to your ex. She's had a miserable time since David died."

"She does know he's married, doesn't she?"

Paul grinned. "She does. I think she has these fantasies though, where he sees her and falls instantly in love with her, you know, 'At last, the woman I've waited all my life for!'"

"I know the sort of thing," Lynn laughed, thinking: I was that woman once. "You know, I haven't been to a Sid's Six concert since they got famous."

He was surprised. "Good Lord, and you two get on so well!"

"You shouldn't have bought the tickets. Steve would have sent us a couple."

"I wanted to take you," he said simply.

Lynn was touched. "I tell you what though, I'll ring him up and make sure Stella definitely gets to meet him."

Paul's face lit up. "Oh, Lynn! She'll be over the moon." He kissed her. "You know, you're not such a bad old stick."

"Gosh, Paul, you certainly know how to compliment a girl!"

"Steve, this is Stella Adams."

"Hi, Stella. It's nice to meet you," Stephen said. "Who's this?" he asked, smiling down at Lizzie.

"My daughter, Lizzie."

"Hello, Lizzie. That's a pretty dress."

Lizzie smiled shyly. "Thank you. My mum's in love with you," she confided. "She's got pictures of you everywhere. Are you married?"

"Lizzie!" Stella exclaimed.

Stephen grinned. "I am. But look, I've got a programme here for your mum that we've all signed, even Rob and Dominic."

“Oh, wow, thank you!” Stella breathed. “Rob is so talented,” she said. “The music to ‘Bara Brith’ is beautiful!”

Stephen beamed with pride and pleasure. “I know!” He kissed her cheek. “Thanks for coming to see us.”

Stella looked as if she was going to faint. “We’re… we’re having a great time,” she managed to say. “Thank you for this!” She was holding the programme as if it was some sort of precious relic.

“Are you staying for the fireworks?” Stephen asked Lizzie.

She nodded. “That’ll be the best bit.”

He laughed. “Not another music critic! My little boys say the same. You’re quite right, Lizzie, it will be.”

“I’m taking Miss Big Mouth here away before she says anything worse!” Stella said. “Thank you again… Stephen.”

Stephen smiled. “Bye. What a sweet little girl,” he said to Lynn.

“Yes. I used to be her speech therapist.”

“That’s how you met…” He hesitated, trying to remember the name.

“Paul,” Lynn supplied.

“Paul, yeah.”

Lynn nodded. “I’d better go too, Stevie. Stella brought a picnic. Oh, Rob was amazingly good, by the way. Is he going to join the band when he leaves school?”

Stephen shook his head, grinning. “You will never guess what he wants to do!”

Lynn stared at him. “Oh, Stevie! Surely not?”

Stephen nodded. “Oxford University to study law!”

He held his arms out and she threw herself into them and hugged him. “That is *so* great! Oh, John would be so happy!”

“Wouldn’t he? Talk about full circle!”

“Yes, and apart from him being tall like John, he looks so like you.” Lynn moved out of his arms.

They felt impossibly empty without her. It’s where she belongs, he thought.

“I must go,” she said, “Paul and Stella will be wondering where I am.”

“Look, we’re having an after show party later. Why don’t you come along? With Paul and Stella and Lizzie,” he added quickly. “There’ll be loads of children there, Andy’s got three now – well, one of them isn’t born yet – and Fin’s got a little boy, and George has got twins…”

“All right, all right,” Lynn laughed. “That’d be lovely, Stephen. And I know Stella will be thrilled.”

“Hello, Lynn! I didn’t know you were here!”

“Andy! It’s lovely to see you! This is Paul and…” she looked around for Stella and saw her talking to someone. “Well, never mind, this is Paul.”

“Pleased to meet you, like. Come and meet the family,” Andy said proudly, leading them off.

Out of the corner of her eye, Toni saw them walk past. Her heart skipped a beat. *Lynn!* What the hell was *she* doing here? Furtively, Toni watched her chatting to Andy and Holly. She was wearing pedal-pushers and flat shoes with white ankle socks, and a tight, short-sleeved little powder-blue sweater. Her pale gold hair was swept up in a ponytail, and she looked as if she wasn’t wearing any make up apart from pink lipstick. She could have stepped off the set of *Happy Days*, and she made Toni feel overdone and old. She looked down at the dress she had changed into for the party. It was a rich red taffeta; strapless, a style that suited her, emphasising her shoulders, and the bodice was subtly boned, giving her not only plenty of cleavage but also plenty of support. Since having the boys, her breasts had changed, they were bigger – much to Stephen's satisfaction – and while not exactly saggy, she worried that they weren't as firm as they used to be. Something she doesn't need to be concerned about, she thought bitterly, looking at the other woman's obviously bra-less bust line. "How come Lynn is here?" she asked Stephen, frowning.

"I invited her, so don't start, Toni," he said, a warning note in his voice. "She's here with her boyfriend and his sister."

The previous week, he and Toni had had their first session with a counsellor, Madeleine, a pleasant woman in her forties, and they were supposed to be thinking about what they found good and bad in their marriage. Stephen could see that Lynn being invited to this party was likely to make Toni's list. On the bad side, obviously.

Harry and Dominic wandered over to them. "Brilliant concert," Harry said. "It must have raised a fair bit of money."

"Oh, God, that reminds me, did you see those poor children who'd lost limbs?" Toni shuddered. "How do they cope? I think I'd rather be dead, it creeps me out!"

Harry flashed her a contemptuous look, which she didn't notice. Stephen did. Oh, Toni, he thought, what happened to you? Or were you always like this, but I just didn't see it? He tried to remember back to when they'd first gone out. He recalled that she'd been a handful, but she'd always made him laugh, and she'd been happy and confident. Their marriage had diminished her in some way, eroded her personality. He wondered what would have happened if they hadn't had Sam. He might never have seen this side of her. He sighed. What was it Sian had said when they'd been talking about Rebecca being unhappy as a child? Something like: you can live with someone for years and not know them. He wondered suddenly if either of them knew the other at all. Was he a tremendous disappointment to Toni? He thrust the thought away.

"Don't you think, Stevo?" she was asking.

"Sorry," he grinned, "Gone a bit deaf. Some idiot's been playing loud music all day."

"Yes. Rather like a 'Disaster Area' concert," Dominic agreed. "God, there's Cherry!" He caught her up in his arms and whirled her round. "Come and dance with me, gorgeous!" he laughed.

Toni watched them sourly. How come Lynn, who had dumped Stephen when he'd been unfaithful, was so popular with everyone, when she, Toni, had forgiven him?

George sauntered over. He'd put on a lot of weight recently, in contrast to Andy, who seemed to get skinnier and more weasely every year. "Your Rob!" he said to Stephen and Harry. "He was brilliant! But Andy was telling me he's going to be a solicitor."

They nodded proudly.

"Aren't you disappointed, Steve?" George asked.

"Far from it!" Stephen replied.

George gave him a sceptical look. "Well, anyway, he's a chip off the old block, bonny lad," he went on. "Got all the girls after him, did you see the swarm of young lovelies buzzing round him today? Just like his old man! Especially on those tours of Scandinavia! Those lasses couldn't keep their hands off you! Mind, you weren't resisting!"

This was the last thing Toni wanted to hear. "Where's Kagami?"

George looked uncomfortable. "I may as well tell you, it'll be common knowledge soon enough. We're getting divorced, pet."

Stephen and Toni looked at each other. Stephen wasn't really surprised, he'd heard rumours that George was having an affair, but Toni was shocked. "George, why?"

"You must've heard the talk about my affair, man, Toni."

She shook her head.

George looked at Stephen. "Well, you must've!"

He nodded.

"Why didn't you tell me?" Toni demanded.

"*We* don't like it when people talk about *us*," he pointed out. "You know how they lie."

"There's been nothing in the papers," she said.

"No," George said with satisfaction. Then he looked gloomy. "There will be, now Kagami's found out. She's furious."

"Who..." Toni started. "I mean..." She didn't know how to ask.

"Alicia Bentinck."

"Oh." She was amazed. She remembered seeing them together at the charity modelling. Lady Alicia Bentinck was a wealthy socialite, daughter of a Tory peer, famous for being famous. She was only twenty-three, and Toni couldn't imagine what she could possibly see in George. Not that he was ugly in fact, she'd always found him rather attractive. He had regular, even features, and very nice, long-lashed, dark eyes – although he could stand to lose a bit of weight, she thought. Nor was he stupid, but he just wasn't the sort of man to appeal to someone like Alicia Bentinck. If it had been Stephen or Dominic, she could have understood it; both of them were very rich and very good looking, and Stephen was very middle class, while Dominic, of course, was tremendously posh. Perhaps that was it; maybe Alicia was fed up with those sorts of men. Maybe she wanted someone more earthy. The phrase 'a bit of rough' came into her head, and she thought of Gavin Leigh and blushed.

"It'll be difficult with the twins, won't it?" she asked.

George looked even gloomier. "Aye, man. Kagami wants to go back to Japan." He sighed, and put his arm around her. "I can't see why all wives can't be as understanding as you, pet! You're a lucky man, Stephen."

Stephen gave him a thin smile. "Thanks, George."

"You're a nice armful too, pet," George squeezed her tighter, staring down at her breasts.

This was more like it. Toni smiled with pleasure. Yes, she'd always liked George.

"Why thank you, George," she said, giving him a sideways look from under her lashes.

George's smile broadened. "Let's have a dance."

"Come and dance with me, Stevie," Harry said. "I hardly ever get the chance to put my arms round you these days!"

"We used to do that a lot, didn't we?"

Harry's lips curved into a smile of reminiscence. "We were good together, weren't we?"

"Yeah." He kissed her forehead. "You're the good one, lovely Hal. I should've made you marry me. Lovely, loyal, loving Hal."

Harry was very moved. "Oh, Stevie. It would never have worked. Dominic's the only one for me." The same as Lynn's the only one for you, she thought. The difference is, I got lucky. You didn't.

The song finished. Dominic and Lynn came over, hand in hand. Dominic caught

Harry round the waist. "Come and dance, my beautiful baby."

"I ought to be heading off," Lynn said, looking round for Paul, who was talking to Andy. She waved to him and he waved back.

"Have you got time for one more dance?" Stephen asked, as 'Don't Speak' came on.

Without a word, she went into his arms. She put her head in the hollow of his shoulder, and she could hear his heart beating.

"When did I last dance with you?" he murmured, his face buried in her hair. "Don't tell me; it was only yesterday."

Paul stood to one side, watching them. As the music stopped, and they moved reluctantly off the dance floor, he took Lynn's hand. "Have you seen Stella?" He pointed to his sister. She was dancing with a tall, well built man, both of them as oblivious to anyone else's presence as Stephen and Lynn had been. "They've spent all evening together, she could barely tear herself away from him long enough to introduce him to me!"

"That's Mitch!" Stephen exclaimed. "Dave Mitchell, our tour manager. He's had a rough time, lately, he and his wife split up, and his eldest daughter's very ill."

"Yeah, he said," Paul nodded. "It must be terrible."

"I can't imagine what it's like," Stephen said. "I mean, I know Sam's got some problems, but he's healthy."

Toni and George came over, laughing.

Toni was rosy from dancing, and tendrils of hair had escaped from her French plait. God, she's attractive, Lynn thought enviously, feeling underdressed and gauche.

Toni gave her a tight smile, and put her arm around Stephen, kissing him on the mouth.

"Hello, Lynn," she said carelessly, still holding tightly to Stephen, and looking as if she didn't have a care in the world, but her heart was pounding and her mouth was dry. His bloody women, how she loathed them, always there, always a threat. She didn't mind Harry so much, she was so obviously in love with Dominic, but Coral and Lynn, especially Lynn… Why couldn't they just stay away from him? And why did he encourage them, and flirt? He was always flirting with someone, even Holly, who flirted right back. Like they all did. If I didn't love him, I'd hate him, she thought suddenly.

Lynn smiled politely and took Paul's hand. "It's goodbye really, we've got to go. Thanks for inviting us, Stevie, we've had a great time." And, ignoring Toni, she reached up to kiss his cheek.

He untangled himself from Toni's arm and hugged her. "Take care," he said. He shook hands with Paul. "Nice to meet you." He wondered how he could stand there so calmly watching Lynn walk away, when all he wanted to do was run after her and hold her forever, never let her go. He heard Toni draw a breath to speak, but forestalled her by saying, "Well, I've been thinking; now the concert's over, how about inviting Swiggsy to stay?"

Swiggsy arrived two weeks later. He was a tall, very thin man, with a scrawny neck that always reminded Stephen of a chicken. He was actually English, his parents had emigrated to Brisbane when he was in his early teens, but his accent was far heavier than Toni's. He was perfectly pleasant, and if it hadn't been for his drinking, he would have been an amusing companion. Unfortunately, he drank copious amounts of alcohol and spent most of his time merry, to say the least. He was swaying slightly when he arrived.

"Grogging on already?" Toni asked.

He grabbed her and gave her a smacking kiss. "Just a few coldies, Tones. You're looking beaut, love! G'day, you old bastard." He shook Stephen's hand vigorously.

"Right, well, let's go then," Stephen said, trying to shepherd him out.

"Time for a cold one first, mate, surely? I'm hanging out for a beer!"

"Plenty of those at home," Toni said firmly. "Come on, Swigs, this way."

"Yeah, I s'pose you're right, Tones, they charge like a wounded bull here," he agreed, following her out and leaving Stephen to pick up his bags. He looked back. "Come on, Stevo! Stop standing around like a stunned mullet, and let's get home."

Home! Stephen thought despairingly. He's only been here five minutes and he's already calling my house home!

But the boys loved him. He was always ready to entertain them with tales of the time he wrestled crocodiles, or taught kangaroos to box, or de-venomised poisonous snakes. They swallowed them whole, and demanded more. Alex thought he was the bravest man he'd ever met and made him tell the same stories over and over again. As long as the beer was flowing, Swiggsy was perfectly amenable.

Stephen spent most of his time in his music room or the studio, on the perfectly truthful grounds that he was writing songs for the band's next album, 'The Argentinian'. It was thirty years since the death of Che Guevara, and he'd written a song about him.

'Do Let's!' was released at the end of the month to favourable reviews. There had been so much publicity surrounding Stephen and Coral that it sold like hot cakes. The first single released was the pair of them duetting on a version of Paul Simon's 'Song For The Asking', which was a song Stephen loved, and the plaintive tune suited Coral's voice perfectly.

It went to number two in the charts and Coral was delighted. "Everything I do with you always turns out brilliantly! I love you!" she said to him while they were waiting to appear on a daytime chat show, *Wake Up, Britain!* hosted by husband and wife team Patrick and Sally.

Stephen loathed these interviews. "For God's sake don't say that when we're being interviewed," he warned. "We don't want to fuel the gossip."

"But I do love you," she said naughtily. "You are so good in bed and…"

"Coral!"

"Don't you want me to say that either?" she asked, her voice innocent.

"Not in public," he grinned. "Course, if I ever need a reference you'll be the first girl I turn to."

Patrick and Sally asked the usual questions about recording the album, being very careful not to refer to the affair – not an easy task given the fact that Sally was obviously dying to and Patrick had to keep heading her off. Next they talked about *Hoodman Blind* and the notorious nude scene. Coral and Sally discussed clothes and cosmetics and Stephen was asked about being a vegetarian and anti-animal testing. When Sally asked him whether he was anti-fox hunting as well, he was tempted to say, 'Good Lord, no! Nothing more fun than seeing a fox being torn to pieces!' but simply nodded.

"Why?" Sally asked. "Surely it's just sport?"

"Well, not for the fox."

"But they say the fox enjoys the chase and after all, they are vermin."

"When you say they're vermin, do you mean the foxes or the hunters?" Stephen asked.

Sally smiled. "The foxes."

"Well, I'm afraid I don't agree, but as I'm not a politician, there's not much I can do about it, unfortunately! I tell you what though; most people would agree that politicians are vermin. Maybe we should start hunting them?" Stephen suggested.

Patrick laughed, but said, "Maybe we shouldn't continue with this topic. Stephen, you've got a fantastic career, but is there anything you wish you'd done differently? When Stanton Crawford died, you said you wished you could have worked with him earlier, so that you could've done more together. Are there any other missed opportunities you regret?"

Stephen thought about it. "Not really, no, no more than most people. It's a little like Frost and the road not taken, isn't it – I'm '*sorry I could not travel both and be one traveller*'."

There was a slight pause before Sally enquired, "Would that be *David* Frost?"

"Robert," Stephen said, trying not to laugh. He took a sip of water to give himself some time. "The poet."

"Oh." Sally had clearly never heard of him. "Of course, you studied literature at university – didn't you get a first?"

"Yes I did, but Robert Frost is a very well known poet."

"My God," he said to Coral afterwards in the green room. "Talk about the nadir of humanity! I can't believe she's never heard of Robert Frost."

Coral coughed apologetically. Sally was standing right behind him. "Fuck you, you adulterous little wanker," she hissed, and stalked away.

"Bravo, Stevie," Coral said. "You certainly have a way with the media!"

George rang him later. "What was that crack about politicians?" he asked indignantly. "Alicia's brother's an MP, man." Alicia's family were also vociferously pro-fox hunting.

"You have my commiserations, George, but if you will associate with riff-raff like that, what can you expect?"

There was a stunned silence. At last, George said, "You cunt!"

"Nice language," Stephen commented. "I bet that endears you to her mother."

"Next time I see you, man, I'll knock your fucking block off!" George shouted.

"Oh, yeah, I'd like to see you try, you fat git," Stephen said and hung up. The phone rang again instantly. He picked it up, and held it away from his ear as George shouted a string of obscenities. Finally, there was silence. "Did you want something, George?"

"Who the fuck do you think you are?" George demanded.

"Look, George, I'd entirely forgotten Alicia had a brother, but I'm damned if I'm going to refrain from giving my opinions just because the girl you're sleeping with doesn't like them."

"We're getting married when I'm divorced," George said truculently.

"Well, congratulations, but it makes no difference, George. You know how I feel about blood sports and I didn't mention Alicia or her family – I didn't even think about them, in fact – so it pisses me off when you ring here and start having a go."

"Well, it pisses me off when you shoot your fucking mouth off to the media, man!" George said, belligerently. "Everyone thinks you speak for the band, but you don't."

"Well, you talk to the press, then, tell them your side. I couldn't give a toss, George, it doesn't interest me."

"Right! Why aye, man, I'll do that!"

The day before they were due to start rehearsing the new album, an article about George and Alicia appeared in several newspapers. George was quoted as saying that Stephen didn't speak for the rest of the band, that they had no problem with playing in bullrings or eating meat, that he saw nothing wrong in hunting and it was a matter of personal choice. "*Stephen's very hard to work with,*" he'd said, "*he's very much a perfectionist and a hard taskmaster and tends to think he's always right, which is very wide of the mark. He's definitely a control freak, and his private life is chaotic, to say the least. His first wife left him because he was unfaithful, even though she was recovering from a miscarriage at the time, and his second marriage is struggling. In my opinion, he'd be better employed spending time with his wife rather than shooting his mouth off on TV.*"

Andy rang Stephen. "What are we going to do, like?"

"Ignore it," Stephen said. He was furious with George, but he knew if he rose to the bait it would only make more problems.

"I don't know, Steve. He said you don't speak for the band, but nor does he. Me and Holl have talked about it and we think I ought to say that George doesn't speak for me."

Stephen began to grin. "And then Fin can say that you don't speak for him, and then I'll say that Fin doesn't speak for me."

Andy laughed. "No, but seriously, Steve!"

"Seriously, I'd leave it, but I won't tell you what to do. And Andy, thanks. You and Holly are tremendous. It's great having my little brother looking out for me."

There was a long pause, and then Andy, obviously moved, said, "Anytime, Steve. And if you think leave it, if that's what you really want, like, that's what I'll do." His voice became even huskier. "Bye, Steve."

Nothing was said about either of the interviews when they started rehearsing. Stephen was determined not to give George the satisfaction of knowing he'd been upset. They went through the songs, Stephen being as laid back as he possibly could be without actually being unconscious, in order not to give George any excuse to complain. The two of them avoided eye contact.

One of the songs, 'The Evening Rain', had a difficult bass line and George just couldn't get it. Eventually, Stephen said, "Let's take a break, have a beer, everyone."

"Why don't you take your fucking beer and shove it up your fucking arse along with your fucking song, you fucking lass!" George yelled.

Stephen's temper snapped. "My God, I'm sick to fucking death of you, Ferguson!" he shouted back. "Just fucking well go home and either sort your fucking playing out or don't fucking bother to come back!"

Fin and Andy looked at each other in resignation.

"Are you sacking me?" George challenged.

"If you don't pull yourself together, yeah. Yes I am."

"Who said it was your band?"

"Don't be stupid, George, of course it's Steve's band," Fin put in.

George ignored him.

"It's always been my fucking band," Stephen said. "Right from the fucking start."

George pushed him. "That's fucking crap, it's always been fucking crap, we're a fucking team, man, we always have been. And it's not like you were the only one with experience of playing in a band!"

"Yeah, that's always rankled, hasn't it, George?" Stephen sneered. "Experience? A bunch of snotty nosed little kids doing covers in their local fucking youth club? You'd have been better off taking guitar lessons!" He pushed George in retaliation.

George, beside himself with fury, grabbed a handful of Stephen's tee shirt. "You fucking little twat!" he spluttered.

Stephen was even angrier. He wrenched George's hand from his shirt. "Take your fucking hands off me or I'll fucking kill you, you pathetic, talentless wanker!"

George howled with rage and leapt at him, knocking him to the floor.

Fin and Andy rushed over and tried to heave George off. George, busily punching at Stephen, struggled away from them, shouting obscenities.

"For God's sake, George, stop being a dickhead!" Andy yelled.

Stephen had rolled away and got painfully to his feet. His ribs and the side of his face hurt, but his back felt as if it was broken. "Get off my property, George, before I call the police and have you thrown off."

George stared at him.

"Just go, George," Fin advised.

"You'll not get a better bass player than me for your poncey band, man!" George said, glaring at Stephen.

"I know a *girl* who's better than you," Stephen jeered, thinking of Harry.

George lunged towards him.

Andy stepped between him and Stephen. "You'd start a row in an empty house, you would, George. Sling your hook."

George walked out without a backward glance.

Stephen half-fell against Andy.

"Are you all right, Steve?" Andy asked anxiously, supporting him.

"The bastard's crippled me," Stephen said, only half-joking. "My back's gone."

They got him over to the house, where Toni called Henry, their GP, who gave Stephen a steroid injection and told him to rest for a few days. "He'll be fine, Toni. What was it this time, surely not football again?"

Toni sidestepped the question and thanked him. "What's going on?" she asked, after he'd left.

"George went berserk, like, and attacked Stephen," Andy explained.

Toni sighed. "I knew this would happen! I told him to leave the rehearsals until everyone had cooled down, but does he ever listen? No, he bloody doesn't! Where's George?"

"Steve told him to get off his property," Fin said.

"Bloody men! You're worse than kids! Now I'll have to put up with endless hours of 'why didn't I just ignore him?' from Stephen. Great. I wish Swiggsy was still here!"

"Oh ey, I don't think you can blame Steve, like, Toni, George was behaving like a..." Andy broke off as Toni turned on him, glowering.

Fin shook his head at Andy. "Will we get out of your way then, Toni, or is there anything we can do?" he asked placatingly.

"No, there's nothing, thanks, Fin. I'd better go and make sure Mike Tyson's all right."

Stephen was propped up in bed looking despondent. "Why didn't I just ignore him?" he asked miserably.

She burst out laughing. "That's exactly what I said you'd say! Oh, Stevo, for God's sake, why do you have to be so stupid? Thank God the boys are at school, I'd hate them to see their father brawling. You're going to have a black eye too, you'll have to explain that to them somehow." She sighed. "Here's the phone and here's George's mobile number. Ring him up and apologise."

"Why should *I* apol—" Stephen started, but shut up at the look on her face. "Yeah, all right." He punched in the number. "George – don't hang up. Look, I'm sorry, OK? I know you're having a tough time at the moment... yeah... I don't know, I've done my back in... yes, it was... oh, well, forget it... Yeah, OK. I'll ring you. Bye." He put down the receiver.

"What did he say?" Toni asked.

Stephen shrugged and winced. "Oh, you know, he's sorry, he's got a lot on his plate. He's actually just a fucking wanker, he always has been."

"And yet, strangely, he never has these fights with Andy or Fin," Toni commented. She had become very fond of George since the concert at Warwick, he reminded her of her brother, Murray, who had moved back to Australia. She and Muzza had been very close as youngsters, and she missed him. She sometimes met George for coffee when she was in London, and they always made each other laugh. He liked exotic creatures too, and had an iguana, much to Alicia's disgust.

Stephen glared at her. "Well, he obviously has a problem with authority figures."

"It was our counselling this afternoon," Toni said.

"Shit! Can you rearrange it?"

"Stop swearing. I'll try." She went off to ring Madeleine.

Stephen privately thought the sessions a waste of time. This would be their fourth. They'd both made a list of what they considered to be their main problems and compared these, and also a list of what they thought was good and bad about the marriage. He couldn't see how this was supposed to help them.

He thought about the three sessions they'd had so far. Madeleine had asked for a brief overview of their problems. They explained that they'd both had affairs, and wanted to put things right, but didn't know how.

"Do you feel that there's a problem with sex between the two of you that might be partly responsible for the affairs?" she'd asked.

Toni blushed.

"Um…" Stephen looked at her. "Well, I like making love to Toni, and we make love quite a lot. I don't think it's that that's the problem."

"What about you, Toni?" Madeleine asked.

"I don't think so," Toni said quietly. "I like having sex with Steve," she added almost inaudibly.

"OK. Well, tell me a little more about yourselves."

There was a silence.

"Stephen?" Madeleine prompted.

He shifted uncomfortably. "I'm not very good at this," he said uneasily. "I hate talking about myself."

Madeleine opened her mouth to speak, but Toni got in first. "What on earth do you mean, Stephen? You're always talking about yourself! Think of all the interviews you give!"

Stephen stared at her. "I don't talk about myself! I talk about the songs, about my playing, not about *me*, not the *real* me, what I think about, and want, and all the rest of it."

Toni raised her eyebrows, unconvinced.

"Well, whatever," Madeleine said quickly. "Lots of people feel that way, Stephen, and it is difficult. Just tell me a bit about the problems you're both having."

At the end of the session, she'd turned to him. "As you are obviously such a private person, Stephen, these sessions are going to mean a lot of work for you. Do you think you're prepared for that?"

"Of course!" He was surprised. "I want Toni and me to get back to the way we used to be!"

Madeleine nodded. "OK."

The second session was the one where she'd asked them to make lists. At the third session they'd discussed these lists. Toni had gone first. She had a lot of grievances.

"OK, well, thank you, Toni," Madeleine said. "I think we'll have to prioritise those a little, but in the meantime, Stephen, what do you feel are the main problems?"

"Well, one, I know Toni doesn't trust me, she's never trusted me, even though I've never been unfaithful to her until now, and I think that has a tremendously negative effect on us both. I resent it, and she, obviously, is never at ease. Two, her attitude to Sam. He can't help being autistic. I know he can be very difficult, but no more difficult than Alex, and let's face it, Toni, let's be totally honest, Alex is your favourite."

Toni was stunned. "That's not true," she stammered. "I love them all the same."

"Three, the fact that Toni lies about Alex being her favourite."

"Stephen!" Madeleine said, warningly.

"Why would you say that, Stephen?" Toni asked, white faced.

"Oh, Toni, because it's true! I'm not saying you do it deliberately, or that you don't love the others, but you love Alex best."

"You love Rob best!" Toni said, defensively.

"Yes, in some ways I do," Stephen admitted. "I wasn't a full-time father to Rob, so I usually saw him at his best. Plus, as you yourself have said, he was a very good, very easy child. Very like Pip, really. If Pip didn't hero worship Alex, he'd be a dream, just like Rob."

"See, you don't like Alex!" Toni shot at him. "It's up to me to protect him."

Stephen stared at her. "Of course I like him! That is, well, sometimes I like him, as I said, he can be very difficult, but I always *love* him."

"You never liked him," Toni said, beginning to cry, "because he wasn't a girl, and you already had a son. You've always wanted a girl. When you said to me a couple of years ago you'd like another baby, you said you wanted a girl."

"That's not true, Toni! I honestly don't care. I thought you might like the idea of a little girl, you're always pointing out pretty little dresses for baby girls, in shops."

Madeleine had said, at the end of the session, that she thought they were getting somewhere, but he didn't see it. He and Toni had had that same discussion over and over again and never resolved it. And just as he couldn't make her believe he didn't mind if their children were boys or girls, which he genuinely didn't, he couldn't make her believe he wouldn't be unfaithful. And he suddenly realised why. *Because it isn't true.* He was unfaithful to her in his mind. He often thought about Lynn, thought about her body, thought about making love to her, being with her. And maybe Toni somehow sensed this. Which was why she was so insecure. What the fuck was he going to do?

"I rang her," Toni said, coming back into the room. "She said she could make a domiciliary visit."

"Oh."

"You don't sound very pleased. Don't you like her? I think she's brilliant. I love talking to her, she's such a good listener, isn't she?"

"Sorry, I was thinking about George," Stephen lied. "Yes, she is. Toni – you think it's helping, then?"

"Don't you?" Toni sat on the bed. "I've been thinking about my behaviour with the boys and trying to modify it. I think maybe I do favour Alex a bit, he's so funny and full of high spirits, sometimes he reminds me of Dad, and he's very like your mum to look at, and I do love her so much, but I can see it's not fair to the others. And I'm trying to be better with Sammy – I do love him, I really do, but he winds me up, and I just react to him before I think what I should do, and I find it so hard to make any connection with him; see, you have music, you both love music. But I really am trying. And I'm trying not to suspect you," she said quietly. "I don't know why I do, you're quite right, you've never been unfaithful, not till I was. It's just… well, you seem to have so many woman friends who you've been to bed with – Harry, Coral, Lynn – most men don't have these adoring ex-girlfriends hanging round, it's unnerving. And it's not like they're ugly. They're all gorgeous, and they're all younger than me. And you're so handsome and famous – what a combination! It's like you said, you could have anyone, younger or… or prettier than me. You could have them. I mean, God, look at George, he's fat and not spectacularly good looking like you, and he's got that pretty twenty-three-year-old interested in him."

Oh, my God, I am such a bastard! Stephen thought. He was racked with guilt. When I met her she was independent and strong-willed and confident. Now she's a nervous wreck and it's all my fault. I fucked up Lynn's life and now I've fucked up Toni's. There is no punishment harsh enough.

"Toni, when I said that – about girls prettier than you – we were right in the middle of the most terrible row." He took her hand. "You're much more beautiful than any of them. Look! I'll never see them again if you like. You say. Even Harry. Our marriage is far more important to me. I love you more than anything or anyone," he lied sincerely. "Pass me the phone. I'll ring them now and tell them I never want to see them again!"

Toni laughed. "Don't be silly!"

"I mean it, Toni. I'll never see any of them again." He was telling the truth and it was obvious to Toni that he meant it. She kissed him. He pulled her closer and french kissed her.

Eventually she broke away. "We can't do this, you're incapable of taking it any further at the moment! Thank you, Stevo, I appreciate the gesture. But Harry is married to Dom, anyway; he's your producer, apart from being your best friend."

Stephen was relieved. He couldn't bear the thought of not seeing Harry. She was more than his best friend; she was a part of him, he didn't actually think he could manage without seeing her, in fact, he thought, horrified, if it came to a choice between her and Toni… He pushed that thought away. Why did life have to be so impossibly difficult? Because he loved Toni, too. Yes, sometimes she made him angry or sad, sometimes he felt he could cheerfully strangle her, but she was the one he turned to when he was down, she was the one who took his side and fought his corner, and sexually, he still wanted her as much as ever. She knew how to push his buttons, how to turn him on, turn him off. And vice versa. They'd been married for ten years, and he couldn't imagine life without her. Harry was his best friend, but Toni was his wife. And his dreams of Lynn had to stop. Toni was his reality. "OK, Toni, but I promise you this. No more Coral. Or Lynn."

Her face lit up. "Do you mean that?"

He nodded. "I love you, Toni. I really want to be with you, and be like we used to be. Shall we try to get it back?"

Toni lay down next to him and buried her face in his shoulder. "Yes, please," she whispered.

Chapter Eighteen
Believe In Us

We bit into the apple and the gates are locked behind us,
Too late to cry, or find a way back in.
But if we try, we might just make it, here's my hand, if you'll just take it,
And believe in us and love, we might just win.

Alex was ten on New Year's Day. "I'm in double figures now," he boasted, after opening his presents. "*You* won't be for nearly a year, Pip, and as for you, you freak," he said to Sam, who was reading a book about Mozart that he'd got for Christmas, "*you* won't be for nearly *three* years."

Sam ignored him.

"Don't call your brother a freak," Toni said reprovingly.

"But Mum, look at him! He's only seven and he's reading a book on Mozart! He's wasting his youth!"

"It's a bloody pity you don't waste yours a bit more then," Stephen said. "Go and play, and leave us alone to cope with our hangovers."

"God, it's a bit much, isn't it?" Alex complained to Pip as they went out. "You'd think, seeing as it's my birthday today, they'd have made an effort not to get drunk last night!"

"You got your presents, you're having all your friends to your party this afternoon, what are you complaining about?" Stephen shouted after him.

"Don't shout, Stevo," Toni pleaded, wincing.

"You set of sissies!" Ray said. "You never could take your drink like a man, Markham."

Ray, Shannon, and their two children, Scott and Leanne, were staying with Stephen and Toni over the holiday. Stephen had been amazed by the change in Ray since he'd last seen him, two years ago. His accent had become very much more American, he'd put on a great deal of weight, and lost a great deal of hair. His character hadn't changed though. The day they arrived, he declared his intention to jam with Stephen.

"Shannie, fire up the camcorder and get some footage of me jamming with the world famous Stephen Markham. Don't worry," he reassured Stephen. "I won't show you up."

Stephen took them over to the studio. He'd moved most of his equipment from the music room in the attic, leaving a piano and a set of drums there for the boys, and, of course, there was a piano in his study and several of the other rooms, and there were guitars all over the house. Alex and Pip had guitars of their own and Sam had a piano in his room; he was a superb pianist, and was having lessons in Oxford.

"Look at all these awards!" Shannon said, in awe. Before he'd had the studio built, Stephen's awards had been scattered in cupboards and on shelves around the house.

Ray examined the Golden Globes. "What are these for?"

"*With Giants Fight,* " Stephen said.

"You won for best score and best song!"

"Mmm." Stephen was starting to feel a little embarrassed. "It's not like any of them are the Nobel Prize or anything."

Shannon was wandering around. "MTV, Brit Awards, Grammys – is there anything you haven't won?" she asked.

"If you hang around long enough, you're bound to win sometimes," Stephen shrugged.

Ray turned away from the awards and did a double take. "Fucking Christ, Markham, how many fucking guitars do you need?" he asked, looking round at them.

Stephen grinned. "I use them for different songs," he said, mildly.

"Why have you got so many Strats? One not enough for you?"

"I like Strats. And they all sound different," Stephen explained. "This one sounds very like my original Ocean Turquoise, which I don't usually take on tour." He picked up a Strat in Surf Green and started to play the introduction to 'Sweet Cherry'.

"You take all these with you when you tour?" Ray asked sceptically.

Stephen nodded. "Most of them."

"Bloody hell, it must take you years to tune them up before you go on stage! How early do you have to arrive to check them?"

Stephen's smile broadened. "I have guitar techs to do all that."

Ray gaped at him. "Guitar what?"

"Roadies."

"I thought roadies just fetched you groupies! You mean you don't even change a fucking string?"

"Part of the magic that is me, Raymond," Stephen grinned.

After Shannon had finished filming and gone to chat to Toni, Ray asked Stephen how his marriage was going.

"If *I'd* been fucking one of my ex-girls on a desert island somewhere, Shannon would've had my balls for breakfast."

"It was a bit more complicated than that. Toni had an affair first."

"Bloody hell, it's like *Hello!* or something – '*Lifestyles Of The Rich And Famous*'! Who did she shag?"

"Does it matter? She just did."

"Shannon'll ask, she likes hearing the dirt about celebs."

"Christ, I wish I hadn't mentioned it," Stephen groaned. "This is my life we're talking about, Ray, not a film. It bloody hurt!"

"Yeah, well, at least you got to bang that absolute little cracker. If Shannon cheated on me, my choices would be my secretary or Scotty's kindergarten teacher. Both double baggers."

Stephen laughed. "I wish you didn't live so far away, Ray, you're really good for my ego!"

Dominic and Harry arrived after lunch, bringing their children to Alex's party. Dominic liked Ray, he found him very amusing. The three of them sat in Stephen's study, drinking whisky and talking.

Andy came in. "Happy New Year, everyone."

Stephen poured him a drink. "Happy New Year, Andy. Where's Holl?"

"In the kitchen helping with the food. Hello, Ray, nice to see you again."

Ray leant over and shook hands. "Great to see you too, buddy."

"Shouldn't she be sitting down?" Stephen asked. "She's due in a few weeks, isn't she?"

"Beginning of February. She'll sit down if she wants to. She hates me fussing."

"So, how's it going, Andy?" Ray asked.

"Pretty good, thanks. What about you?"

"No, I'm terrific, it's going great," Ray nodded. He wandered around the room. "What's this?" he asked, picking up a bulky file.

"For God's sake, be careful!" Stephen exclaimed. "Oh, shit!"

Ray had turned it over, and all the papers inside fell out. "Oh, it's music," he said, rather dismissively.

"It's a soundtrack I'm working on. No, don't bother," Stephen sighed, as Ray started to pick the sheets up. "They were in order. I'll have to sort them out again." He got up.

"OK," Ray shrugged. "That reminds me, I hope you don't get pretentious when you get to forty, Steve. You have the potential."

"Why would you say that?" Stephen asked, stung.

Dominic grinned at Andy.

"Oh, you know, so many of you artistic types do. You know that guy, Snog, who was in The Silver Spiders? He reckons that to be a musician of his calibre you have to do more than just play the guitar, have a few licks – you have to be born with music in your very *soul*, luvvie!"

"Perhaps the poor sod was misquoted," Stephen said.

"No, he said it on TV."

Dominic knew Snog MacNaughton well; he was producing his solo album. "It sounds like something that tosser would say. He can't help it. He's all right when you get to know him."

"I tell you what, Ray," Stephen offered. "If I ever get pretentious, you have my permission to bring your gun over and shoot me."

"Deal!" Ray grinned.

"It's a bit pretentious still wearing red Kickers at his age, wouldn't you say, Ray?" Dominic drawled.

"Damn straight!" Ray said. He frowned. "Hey, hang on, you're a vegetarian, and into animal rights and all that. How come you wear leather?"

There was silence. The three of them stared at Stephen, who coloured guiltily.

"Oh ey, I never thought of that," Andy said.

"Nor me," agreed Dominic. "Well, Markham?"

"Um… well… Toni bought them for me," Stephen muttered.

"Bollocks, you hypocrite," Ray scoffed.

Stephen sighed. "I know, I know. It's just… they're so comfortable. It's the only thing I cheat over though. Honestly."

"Bring the gun next time, Ray," Dominic advised.

Andy chuckled. "Yeah, and you know what the next album's going to be called, Ray? The Argentinian. There's a song on it about Che Guevara – Steve knows the exact date he was killed. When was it, Steve?"

Stephen grinned. "See, the thing is, last year was thirty years since his death. If I hadn't hurt my back, the album would have been released before Christmas, so it would have fitted."

"When was he killed?" Ray asked. "And why the Argentinian? I thought he was from Cuba."

"No, that's why he was called Che, it's like calling someone… oh, I don't know, Taffy if they're Welsh."

"Wasn't that his name?"

"Oh, come on, Ray!"

"Ernesto," Dominic supplied.

"Oh, yeah, I remember. I did know that."

"Anyway, he was killed in Bolivia on the ninth of October 1967, by the Bolivian government – and the CIA knew about it," Stephen said.

"He was a bloody little Commie." Ray was dismissive. "Anyway, you're a Conservative, Steve, you voted for Margaret Thatcher! Why are you writing about him? You never supported Castro."

"Well, no, and I think he and Castro were bastards, all that persecution and torture of homosexuals and all the rest of it, but he interests me. He was a doctor – he had an upper class family. The song certainly doesn't glorify him; the opposite, if anything."

"Little red bastard. Hairy bugger too," Ray said, "I've seen pictures." He ran his hand across his balding head. "Deserved everything he got. What did you study at university, Dominic? History?"

"God forbid! Mathematics with philosophy."

"Jesus!" Andy stared at him. "I never knew that!"

"I only did it to piss my father off," Dominic explained. "He wanted me to study estate management or something at some sort of fucking agricultural college in the wilds of Wiltshire, or failing that, at least to go up to Oxford, so I picked the most bizarre fucking subject I had the grades for in an industrial fucking city he wouldn't be seen dead in. He had the last laugh though. I loathed it. And it was a four-year course, so I was stuck with it for four fucking years."

"Why didn't you drop it?" Andy queried.

"And give the fucker the satisfaction of being right? No fucking way!"

"That's your favourite song now, isn't it, Lynn?"

Lynn jumped. She hadn't heard him come back from the kitchen. "Um… I just like it," she shrugged.

Paul passed her a mug of tea and sat down next to her. "You've liked it tremendously since Stephen danced with you to it," he said quietly. "And if it's not 'Don't Speak', it's one of his CDs." He looked over at the VCR. The video of *Hoodman Blind* was lying beside it. "You're still in love with him, aren't you?"

She stared down into her drink. "Maybe a little."

"Maybe a lottle. I didn't realise. I mean, I could see *he* was still in love with you at Warwick – it was obvious, blimey, even Stella noticed – but I didn't realise you felt the same. Is that why it didn't work out with Tim?"

"In a way. Tim… he couldn't live with the situation."

"Well. The question is, what do we do?"

"Do we have to do anything? Can't we just keep on having fun?"

"Trouble is," Paul said, taking her hand, "I seem to have fallen in love with you."

"Oh."

"Oh, indeed. So, do we carry on as we are, with me hoping you'll fall in love with me, or do we call it a day before we get hurt?"

"Bloody love, I hate it, it spoils everything!" Lynn exclaimed. "The thing is, I do love you, Paul, I'm just not *in* love with you. But need that matter? Think of arranged marriages. They say they're often far happier than love matches because there are no preconceived expectations. And they say that love grows."

"Hmmm. I have a feeling that might be a myth."

Lynn sighed. "I don't know. I don't have any answers."

"Maybe we should just go on as we are. I mean, you could be right about love growing. Do you think it might?" he asked hopefully.

She sighed again. "I don't know. Paul, I can't get into the situation I was in with Tim, it wouldn't be fair to either of us. I tried so hard with him, but it all went wrong in the end. He was so jealous of Stephen and he did something I couldn't forgive because of it. You're right. I *am* still in love with Steve – I might always be, or I might get over him tomorrow, I just don't know. I can't make any promises, but I'm willing to try to make a go of a relationship with you. I mean, me having these… these feelings for Steve hasn't got in the way before now, has it?"

Paul shook his head.

"So it's up to you. I'll quite understand if you don't want to risk it."

Paul was silent. He was still holding her hand. He gave it a squeeze. "Let's give it a go," he said finally. "I love being with you, Lynn. Let's see what happens."

"And you won't start throwing wobblies if I listen to his music, or read articles about him or anything?"

"Look, as long as you don't want a cardboard cut-out of him in bed with us, I think I can cope."

That made her laugh. "And you know, I never think about him when I'm with you."

Paul smiled in relief. "Well then! I can't see we've got a problem!"

"Toni! Why are you doing that?"

Stephen had arrived home from a meeting with Alan, the band's solicitor, earlier than Toni had expected. She was in the kitchen, ironing. "Joanne isn't really up to it any more," she explained.

Stephen stared at her. "Then get someone who is! I don't expect to pay someone to do something and then find you doing it."

"No, you don't understand, Stevo, they depend on her money. Since her husband hurt his back…"

"Her husband spends all his time – and money – at the Rover." The Red Rover was the local pub.

"Well, that's not Joanne's fault, and with the new baby coming…"

"Yes, but Toni, it's not your fault, either. What's going to happen when she has the baby?"

Toni coloured.

"I see. We're giving her paid maternity leave and you'll be filling in."

"Well, kind of."

"In other words, yes. Do you want a cup of tea?"

"Yes, please. I got some more choccy biccies this morning."

"Great!" Stephen disappeared into the pantry and returned with the biscuit barrel. "Chocolate biscuits, the opiate of the masses!" He ate four before he put the barrel on the table.

"My God, you're such a pig, Stephen!" Toni exclaimed. "If the boys did that, you'd tell them off."

"That's different," he mumbled through a mouthful of biscuit.

"You're lucky I'm behind this ironing board, you know you're not allowed to talk with your mouth full."

He swallowed. "I'm not. And back to the ironing…"

"Stevo, I don't mind, really. And what else have I got to do anyway? I do my stuff for the conservation fund, and once a month I go to London to their meetings. I see Callie when she's not too busy, I go to coffee mornings, and I see the girls, but apart from that, I'm pretty redundant during the day."

Toni had a small group of female friends – 'the girls' – in the village. These were other mothers, not as close to her as Callie, but fun for gossiping with and chewing over their sex lives and their children's problems.

Stephen poured them both a mug of tea. "Well, you'll have to stop now, we've got our session with Madeleine in three quarters of an hour, and the traffic was quite heavy round Witney."

As he drove them in, he had an idea. "Why don't you write a book?" He hated the thought of Toni being so bored that she wanted to do the ironing. They'd discussed her going back to work, but she didn't like the idea of not being there when the boys got back from school or in their holidays, even though Stephen was at home more often. Sam had settled down very well at school, his routine never varied, and they tried to keep it that way. He was even starting to eat better, and they'd managed to cut his Fresubin down to one bottle (which he now drank from a cup) before bedtime.

"A book? Stephen, slow down! Just because you've got a sports car, you don't have to drive like Damon Hill!"

"Damon Hill sounds like a Ferengi."

"Trekkie! What do you mean, a book?"

"I heard you telling Pip and Sam those stories about Bunyip the other day. I meant to say something then, but I forgot."

Toni laughed. "They were just silly stories!"

"No, they were very good. I heard Sam – *Sam!* – ask you for more. A book about Bunyip the mischievous spider would be great. Why don't you?"

"Well," Toni said, thinking about it. The idea felt good. "I could give it a burl."

"I think you're ready to talk to each other about your affairs," Madeleine said.

Toni took a deep breath.

"Wait, Toni, you always go first. Let's let Stephen be the brave one for a change. Why did you have an affair with Coral, Stephen?"

Stephen was surprised, he thought Toni liked going first. "OK, well, basically, I found out Toni had had an affair. I thought if I slept with Coral, then we'd be even, neither of us could accuse the other, each affair cancelled the other one out."

Toni stared down at the floor.

"Yes," Madeleine said drily. "That's what you said before. Such a noble gesture. And such an amazing piece of reasoning for a man who's just discovered that the wife he loves and trusts has been unfaithful to him. I do congratulate you on your astounding generosity and self restraint."

Stephen stared at her, the blood draining from his face.

She smiled. "It's nearly six months since you began counselling. Don't you think it's about time you started attending these sessions, Stephen?"

Toni looked at her as if she was mad. "He's never missed one."

Neither Madeleine nor Stephen seemed to have heard her.

"Yes," he said, almost voicelessly.

"I told you at the beginning you were going to have to work, remember? So let's have the real reason," Madeleine said gently.

Stephen pushed his hair back off his forehead. "The real reason." He hesitated, pulling at the skin round his thumbnail. "OK. The real reason." He shrugged. "I was angry with Toni. I've been so angry with her since she made that scene, and Sam was born early. I blamed her for his autism. If he hadn't been premature, he might… he might be normal." He looked at Toni. "And then you handed me the perfect opportunity to hurt you, to pay you back for everything. I hated you when Coral told me about Leigh…"

"Coral told you?" Toni interrupted.

"Yes. That made it even better in a way. I hated you so much I wanted to kill you. But obviously, I couldn't do that, couldn't even think that, so I pushed it all, the hate and the hurt and the anger, right to the bottom of my mind, but the trouble was it wouldn't stay there, periodically it would surface, and then I'd be so angry, but of course I couldn't be angry with you because we're trying to get over it, so back down it'd have to go. But it's so hard to keep it there," he said despairingly.

Toni was staring at him, horrified.

"So what do you do?" Madeleine queried.

"I go to the studio and immerse myself in playing guitar, in music. I run, I swim." He paused. "Sex helps," he said quietly. "I used to go and meet Coral for lunch sometimes. Just lunch," he said quickly, at the look on Toni's face. "I haven't seen her since September, Toni, I swear."

"Absolutely just lunch?" Madeleine asked.

Stephen was silent.

"Stephen?"

"Well, a couple of times I went to her flat and... well, we kissed a bit."

"How much is a bit?" asked Madeleine.

"We didn't have sex," he said, evasively.

"So, quite a lot, then." Madeleine handed Toni a box of tissues.

"Do you want to be with Coral?" Toni sobbed.

"No, I want to be with you. I think. I don't know!" he burst out. "I don't know, Toni! Everything seems to be going fine, and then you mistrust me or do something spiteful, and I feel so angry and resentful."

"Do you think about your first wife?" Madeleine asked him.

"Yes. But I'm angry with her too."

Toni looked at him in amazement.

"Go on," Madeleine prompted.

"Why did she leave me? Why didn't she pull herself together, get medical help? I was as upset as she was, I wanted that baby, I'd have given up everything for her – for both of them! I'd have given up the band and got a real job; I worked so hard for my finals to get a good degree so that I could get a really good job and support them. And then when Dad died, when I needed her so much, she was with Franklin! How could she love someone else?" Hot tears stung his eyes and he brushed them impatiently away. "She said she'd love me till she died! She said she'd never leave me! And it's no good her hanging around at weddings and concerts making it obvious she still loves me, it's too bloody late now, and when we found out about Sam, what bloody help were you?" he shouted at Toni. "I held you and let you cry and rant and rave and blame me – and, God, *Dominic* held you and let you cry and rant and rave – where were you when I needed someone to hold *me*? I'm fed up with always being the strong one in my relationships, I'm *not* strong, sometimes all I want to do is get into bed and pull the covers over my head and never come out again!" He had to stop to draw a breath.

Toni had stopped crying. "I didn't know," she breathed. "Why didn't you say?"

"I thought, I just thought... I'd made my bed, I should pull myself together, suck it up. I hate whining, whining never gets you anywhere, just makes you feel worse, much better to pull yourself together and get on with it, I found that out when Dad kicked me out. I used to cry every night to start with, but I discovered I felt better if I stopped thinking about it. It usually works, I don't know what's happened."

"You've got too much anger. It's a bit like a computer using up all its memory," Madeleine said. "You've got no storage space left."

"Then I'll have to get rid of some of this anger."

"Very good, Stephen," she said approvingly. "It sometimes takes people a while to figure that out."

"Well, that bit was obvious." He wiped his face and poured himself some water from the carafe Madeleine kept on her desk. "But I haven't got a clue how to do it."

"I can help you," Madeleine said. She looked at Toni. "Are you up to telling us about your affair?"

Toni nodded. "I suppose it was much the same as Stephen. I was angry with you too, Stephen. I blamed you for Sam being born too early. You were dancing with her, everyone could see how you felt about her, Dominic and Harry tried to cover it up, but God, Stephen how could you do that to me? You said you were angry with me, but you had no excuse for that!"

"Oh, Toni, you'd been impossible to live with since you'd discovered that Sam wasn't a girl!" Stephen said defensively.

"That was no bloody excuse, and you know it! The way you behaved was just plain wrong whatever the state of our marriage! I was unhappy that the baby wasn't a girl because I felt insecure about you – and then you behaved like that! How did you expect me to react? How would you have felt if it'd been the other way round? And Sam; you were so patient and controlled, all that saintly stuff about we must face this calmly, we can cope because we love him! Yes, of course we do, but why should that make us able to cope? There was an advert around at the time, on billboards and things, for that charity – MIND, I think, or was it MENCAP? Anyway, it said something about special needs children aren't born with specially trained parents; I used to see it when I was driving to Waitrose. And that was so true, I still think about it sometimes. And, anyway, you always say, oh, he's not that difficult – no, he's not so bad, now, but you weren't there when he was, when he was always hurting Pip and himself, and having the most horrendous tantrums in shops, screaming and taking all his clothes off, *you* weren't coping, you were off rehearsing and recording and going on tour, *you* weren't the one lying with him for hours, trying to get him off to sleep, because if you didn't stay with him he'd scratch or bite himself till he bled, or tear down the wallpaper, or rip up his blankets, *you* didn't have to listen to him saying, 'Dr Venkman didn't come home again', over and over and not be able to comfort him!"

It was Stephen's turn to stare, ashen-faced.

"I know you lie with him now, and you think I used to whine about nothing, but he *is* easier these days, and anyway, he likes you better than he likes me, Stephen, he's always responded better to you, you sing to him, and calm him down, I've tried singing, but that's not what he wants, he wants you. And then, I had no one to talk to – all my friends were primarily your friends, and I don't have that good a relationship with my mum or Em. I have a great relationship with Sian, but I couldn't whinge to her about her favourite child."

"I'm not her—"

"Oh, Stevo! Even Kath and Becks know it! So I had no one to talk to, you wouldn't ever listen to my point of view, everything I said you twisted and wilfully misunderstood, and took the wrong way, and made out I was a bad mother to Sammy, and then I met Callie, and there was that show, and it was so exciting, and I went for the photos and someone from *Juliette* should have been there, but she wasn't, so it was just me and Gavin and he was so exciting, and… oh, I don't know, it was like, I seemed to have been making so many tough decisions about Sam, and, well, he just took charge and told me what to do, and I did it. And it was fun. I enjoyed it all so much. And I felt attractive and desired and like *I* was the most important woman in his life, *I* was one he wanted, not his ex wife, *me*. In fact, he was a bastard who treated women like dirt, but just at first…" She stopped and shook her head. "And to be honest, even then I thought, OK, so he's no better than Stephen, but he's no worse."

Stephen gasped, stunned and very hurt. "Toni! How could you think that? How *could* you? You just said he treats women like dirt!"

"I felt you treated me the same way," she said quietly. "With your obsession about Lynn, and your flirting. Have you any idea how humiliating it is when you flirt the way you do?"

"It's just a game, a bit of fun, it doesn't mean anything!" he protested.

"That's not how it seems to me. It's hurtful and demeaning."

Stephen opened his mouth, but she spoke first. "Do you still blame me for Sam?"

"Um, Sam – no." He shook his head. "No, I just needed someone to blame. And Al and Pip were early, maybe he would've been anyway. I'm so sorry I didn't listen to you, I didn't deliberately misunderstand you, really I didn't." He paused. "And you're right about the way I behaved at Sophy's wedding, it was unforgivable." He took another drink of water. "It was… well, when you kept going on and on about wanting a girl…" He stopped again.

"Go on, Stephen," Madeleine prompted as the silence lengthened.

"It brought it all back," he whispered, his voice shaking. "All the heartache when Lynn lost Sakura." He looked earnestly at Toni. "I honestly don't mind if we have boys or girls, Toni, really I don't, I love our boys so much, it wasn't that I wanted a girl, it was simply… I don't know…" He shrugged, trying to find the words. "It made me think of Lynn. It reminded me of those days in Manchester. And then there she was at the wedding. There's no excuse for what I did, and I'm not trying to weasel out, I'm just trying to explain." He took Toni's hand. "I'm sorry about the flirting, I don't do it to hurt you, it's just fun, but I'll try not to, and I'm sorry our life isn't more exciting and showbizzy. I don't know how I can make it better. I mean, those award ceremonies and what have you – they're so dull – you get stuck at a table with people like Patrick and Sally, and have to listen to endless speeches of thinly veiled self-congratulation. Maybe you should go to Cheyne Walk on a regular basis, go shopping, see Callie."

"Maybe," Toni said listlessly.

"Well, I think this is a good place to stop," Madeleine said. "You both look washed out, and we've made a lot of progress, especially you, Stephen. I'm proud of both of you. I want you to think about what was said today, try to see each other's viewpoint and think what you could do to help, OK?"

They usually went for lunch after the sessions, but today Toni wanted to go straight home. "I look like a fright."

"No, you don't. I don't mind what we do." Stephen replied. He wanted to touch her, but she seemed so distant. They drove home in silence and he went to the studio to play guitar when they got home. Despite the critics, 'Through The Bars' had been certified multi-platinum, and he'd won awards for it. He remembered writing 'With All My Heart' for Toni and dedicating the album to her. They'd been so happy then. He went to find her. "We've got to talk."

"We can't. I'm off to pick up Sam."

"I'll get him, he loves going in the Boxster."

Toni smiled, the first genuine smile he'd seen from her since they'd set off to counselling. "You love driving it!"

"Hmm. OK, we'll talk later then. When the boys are in bed. We used to be so happy, Toni."

"Did we?"

Stephen was shocked. "I thought so!"

"Go and get Sam. We'll talk later."

"So what do you want to talk about?" Toni asked. She was sitting on their bed, filing her nails.

"Us," he replied, sitting next to her. "Don't you?"

She moved up slightly. "I don't know."

"Do you remember when we first went out together, how you were seeing that other man?"

"Danny. We're not going to row about *him* now, are we?"

"No! Of course not! I was just thinking. I was the jealous one then, you were cool and confident and self-assured. You could read me like a book. What happened? What happened to us? We've got everything, Toni. Why aren't we happy?"

"I don't know. Do you still love me?"

"Yes. Yes, I do. Sometimes – sometimes I don't *like* you, sometimes you make me furious, or… or miserable, but, yes, I love you. Do you love me?"

"I don't know."

That hurt. "Why?"

"God, Stephen, I don't know, I don't know how I feel about anything."

"Do you love… him, Leigh?"

"I never loved him! I didn't even like him!"

This information made Stephen feel even more wretched. "Then why?"

"I told you. He took my mind off… well, off all those problems. And he was exciting."

"How can I be exciting?"

That made Toni laugh. "It's hard to be exciting when you've been married as long as we have."

"Harry and Charlie manage," he said quietly.

"Yes, they do. Perhaps we should ask them for the formula." She went into the ensuite to fetch her nail polish. "Oh, my God!"

"What's the matter?"

"Bunyip!"

Stephen imagined Bunyip lying stiff in the bottom of the tank, his legs in the air. Oh, please, oh, please! "What's up with him?"

"He's gone!"

"What?" He stared around the bedroom in horror. He felt like one of the girls in those old-fashioned horror films, all he wanted to do was stand on a chair and scream.

Toni came back into the bedroom, her face troubled. "Some imbo left the lid off!"

"Who would be *criminal* enough to do that?" Stephen demanded.

"Oh, Stevo! You're as worried as I am!" She threw her arms round him. "Of course I love you! You know how it is when you're as miserable as a bandicoot, you just don't think you feel anything! I know you don't like Bunyip much…"

Much? thought Stephen, hugging her.

"But you care because I do."

Stephen had never thought he'd feel grateful to Bunyip. "That's because I love you, my little Glaucus."

"You haven't called me that for ages!"

He kissed her. "Toni, is there anything I could... you know... do in bed to be more exciting?"

"We could have fun finding out!"

"Perhaps we ought to look for Bunyip first." He had visions of waking up in bed and finding the tarantula crawling across him, like in that James Bond film.

They searched the bedroom, dressing room and ensuite.

"He could be anywhere!" Toni wailed.

"I know," Stephen said grimly.

Eventually, they gave up and went to bed. They quietly checked the boys' rooms, and Stephen gingerly pulled back the covers of Rob's bed and his and Toni's. God! He wouldn't sleep a wink with that thing on the loose! And Toni was expecting him to be exciting!

In February, Rob passed his driving test, and he was surprised and delighted when Stephen told him that the Megane was now his. Wait till June, Stephen thought with excitement. He had ordered a red Boxster for Rob, and he and Toni and Harry and Dominic were buying it jointly.

Harry had been a little worried at first. "A Porsche, Steve? He's only eighteen, and he's only just passed his test. Isn't it a bit too powerful for him?"

Stephen and Dominic had convinced her that Rob was mature enough to handle it. "Now, if we were talking about *Alex*..." Stephen grinned. He couldn't wait to see his son's face when it was delivered.

'The Argentinian' was released the day after Holly gave birth to her second daughter. The single, 'The Evening Rain' was a huge hit, and the album went platinum within a week. Holly and Andy called the baby Marigold Platinum.

Bunyip was still missing. Toni had given up on ever finding him again.

One beautiful spring day, Mr Somers and Mr Trencher, the gardeners, came in for their mid morning cup of tea. "You'll never believe what we found this morning, Mrs M," Mr Somers said.

"What would that be?" Toni asked politely, steeling herself for a long, boring description of some plant neither of them remembered ever having seen in the garden before.

"A giant spider. Had the most peculiar colouration too."

"Looked like the sort of thing you'd find in the tropics," Mr Trencher added. He was a retired Army man.

"Bunyip!" Toni exclaimed joyfully. "What have you done with him?"

The two men looked at each other. "Knew about it, did you?" Mr Trencher asked.

"He's my tarantula! He's been missing for ages!" She noticed their expressions. "Stephen told you he was missing, didn't he?"

"Not as I recall," Mr Somers said, slowly. "What about you, Ralph?"

Mr Trencher shook his head. "I don't think so, Bert."

"What have you done with Bunyip?" Toni asked with trepidation.

"Well, you see, Mrs M, we thought it, that is, *he*, might be some kind of mutation."

"And?" Toni prompted.

"Well, we thought it was for the best..."

"What?" Toni practically screamed.

"We killed it... er... him, with a shovel."

Later, Stephen gave them both a large cash bonus for their bravery when tackling an unknown and possibly dangerous creature, and told them not to worry; it was an understandable mistake to make. "Probably best not to mention this conversation to Toni," he added casually, "it would only make her think about her loss."

Mr Somers and Mr Trencher, pocketing the money, agreed.

"I remember telling Mr Somers about Bunyip," he lied to Toni. "But you know how deaf he is. I should have told Mr Trencher." He hung his head in shame.

"Darling, it wasn't your fault!" She kissed him. "We can get another one. It won't be Bunyip, but we'll love him anyway."

Shit! thought Stephen. "I'm not sure that's a good idea, Toni. As you say, it'll never be Bunyip, and look how easily he got lost. I'm sure one of the boys left his tank open, you know how careless they are. If it happened again, it would be heartbreaking." He looked at her earnestly.

She sighed. "Yeah, you're right, mate. And I am very busy with my book. Maybe when the boys have grown up."

Stephen heaved a sigh of relief. "Good idea, Daisy."

They were getting on much better these days. He hadn't seen Coral alone since the previous September, when he'd rung her and explained that he was trying to make his marriage work. Lynn he tried not to think about. It seemed unbelievably cruel of fate that Dave Mitchell, Sid's Six's tour manager, was marrying her boyfriend's sister that September, and particularly ironic that they wouldn't have met if Stephen himself hadn't invited Lynn to the after show party at the Warwick concert. And he was glad for Dave, really glad, the man had had an abysmal time lately, but why couldn't he have fallen for someone else? He was determined not to do more than say hello to Lynn at the reception.

Toni often spent time at Cheyne Walk during the week, seeing Callie and other friends. She occasionally met up with George for coffee – she had rung him after Bunyip died, and he'd been very sympathetic, offering to buy a tarantula himself, which she could visit. Stephen thought the friendship between them rather bizarre, especially as George was now living with Alicia.

Toni liked Alicia, though she remarked to Stephen that she couldn't see the relationship lasting. "She can't stand it when he does things like mop up his gravy with his bread! He often reminds me very much of Dad."

Stephen was much struck by this. George *was* very like Jacko. He could imagine him as a policeman, and when George tried, he could be an amusing and perceptive companion. On reflection, he supposed Toni's relationship with George was no stranger than his own peculiarly antagonistic friendship with the man.

That night, as Toni sat in bed reading, Stephen went into the dressing room and began raking through her wardrobe.

"What are you doing, Stevo?"

"Looking at your frocks."

Toni put down her book. "It's kind of you to make the effort, but I honestly don't think I'd fancy you in one of them," she said, grinning.

"They won't do." Stephen came out of the dressing room. "You're going to need something far more expensive."

Toni was puzzled. "For what?"

"The premiere of *Matilda Street*." Stephen got into bed and picked up his book.

Toni stared at him. "What did you say?"

"Oh, don't say you don't want to go!"

"Stephen Markham! Are you telling me we're going to the premiere of *Matilda Street*? The actual premiere? The actual film with Trey Coughlin?"

Stephen grinned. Trey Coughlin was an Australian film star, one of Toni's favourite actors. She had been wanting to see *Matilda Street*, a film about the early settlers in Australia, since she'd first heard it was being made.

"Certainly are. And partying with him afterwards."

"Stevie!" Toni threw herself into his arms. "Oh, my God! I'm so excited!" She covered him with kisses. "Oh, you're so wonderful!"

"Mmm!" Stephen returned the kisses. "We'll have to go to more premieres!" He'd arranged this for two reasons, the first being that he genuinely was trying to make Toni's life more fun and exciting, the other that the band was flying out to the Caribbean to film the video for the single, 'The Argentinian', shortly, and he felt she'd be less inclined to be difficult if she had this premiere to look forward to.

Rob was amazed and delighted with his Boxster, even more so as he'd been under the impression that his main present was a trip to Hawaii with Julia. They gave it to him when he got home from school, Harry and Dominic and the children having driven over from London.

He stared at it, dazed. "This is for *me*? *This* is for *me*?"

Harry put her arm round him. "I can't believe my baby is eighteen!"

"Oh, for God's sake, cut the sentiment, Harriet, you'll have Stephen crying," Dominic warned. "Oh, too late."

Stephen wiped his eyes. "Shut up, Charlie! This is an emotional moment!"

"Can I drive it?" Rob asked, his voice full of awe.

"You can if you believe you can," Stephen grinned. "It's fully insured."

"Take me out in it!" Gus clamoured.

"No, take me, I'm the oldest!" Alex demanded.

"I'm *Sir* Gus and he's my brother!" Gus squared aggressively up to Alex.

"I'm Australian and he's *my* brother!" Alex retorted.

"Be quiet, the pair of you!" Dominic ordered. "Rob, you should take Stephen first."

Harry nodded. "This was his idea, and he taught you to drive."

Rob smiled happily. "Dad?"

Stephen hugged him. "I'd be honoured, Blue. You don't mind if I keep my eyes shut, do you?" he grinned.

"What do you mean?" Rob asked, stung. "I've passed my test now, you were never frightened when you were teaching me!"He paused. "Were you?"

"Frightened? Course not. I was bloody terrified!"

Rob stared at him, amazed. "But you were always so calm!" He looked at Harry. "He just sat there, his arms folded, looking completely unfazed."

"You should have seen the bruises round my ribs," Stephen said. "My arms weren't folded, I was clutching my sides in dread. I just didn't want to alarm you." He was only partly joking. It had been one of the scariest times of his life.

After the holiday in Hawaii, Rob went to work at Markham Cavendish for a month. He'd asked Julian if he could help out and learn something about the business, and Julian had been very encouraging, saying he'd be more than pleased to have him there. Rob drove off in his Boxster, looking very grown up. Stephen remembered the little boy he used to play rough-and-tumble with, and couldn't believe that so much time had passed. He went off on a tour of Europe with the band, but was back by the end of August, when Rob's results came out.

Stephen sat at the breakfast table, watching anxiously as Rob fumbled with the envelope. He had been offered a place at Merton College, provided he gained the grades he needed.

He looked up. "I got three As and two Bs!"

Stephen's face broke into a smile. "Oh, well done, Blue!"

Toni went round the table and kissed him. "We knew you'd do it, didn't we, Stevo?"

Rob was scarlet with pleasure and relief. "I've got to go and ring Mum and Dom," he said, getting up. "Then I'll see how Jules has done."

"Thank God for that!" Stephen said, after he'd gone out.

"Steve! You didn't doubt he'd pass, did you?" Toni was shocked by this lack of faith.

"Oh, not really, but you know how it is – suppose he'd been very nervous? He so wants to go, and you know how fate has this way of stabbing you in the back!"

Rob came bursting back in, his face clouded. "Julia only got a B and two Cs! She won't be able to get in!"

"Oh, Robbie, no!" Stephen said.

Rob nodded. "She was so upset. I'm going round."

"I'd get dressed first," Toni advised.

Rob looked down at himself. "I forgot I was in my pyjamas," he said, surprised.

"Was Harry pleased?" Stephen called, as he went out.

"What do you think?" Rob called back. "See you later."

"What was that you were saying about fate?" Toni asked.

"Oh, Lynn, I can't believe this is happening, and it's all because of you!"

"Rubbish!" Lynn smiled. She was helping Stella dress. "It's because Mitch fell in love with you because you're so lovely!" She kissed her cheek.

Stella, who was usually as calm and unflappable as Paul, was a bundle of nerves. "Mitch says there'll be press there."

"Bound to be, all the band are coming, and quite a few other celebs," Lynn pointed out. "I mean, think how famous Stephen alone is!"

Sid's Six was paying for the reception at the Dorchester.

"Yes. It's nerve racking enough getting married though, without that!"

"Just imagine you're Royalty." Lynn finally managed to get her ready, and they went downstairs to wait for the cars. Paul was in the sitting room with champagne for them all, even a small glass for Lizzie.

Lynn was jittery, keyed up at the thought of seeing Stephen again. Since Paul had told her he was in love with her, their relationship had continued in the same way as it had previously, but she was aware that he was subtly different. She couldn't exactly say how, but the difference was there. She didn't like it, it unsettled her and made her feel guilty because of the way she felt about Stephen. She had to be at the wedding, she had no choice, but she was scared. She'd managed to keep her craving for Stephen under control, and did she really want to stir up all those feelings again? And yet, could she turn down another chance to see him, talk to him, maybe dance with him? It was their only way of touching each other, and she desperately wanted to hold him again. Feeling disloyal and deceitful, and infuriated with herself for feeling that way – after all, it wasn't her fault Paul had fallen in love with her – she had bought a figure-hugging dress of wild silk, very beautiful and very expensive, in a deep cherry red. She thought it would stir and amuse Stephen, and she was aware that the colour, one he'd not seen her in before, suited her tremendously. She was only thirty-six, and knew she didn't even look thirty. Paul had done a double take and whistled appreciatively at the sight of her.

She stood alone by the buffet table, her mouth dry. The wedding itself had been a small private affair, only family and close friends, and throughout the ceremony, the knowledge that in a very short time she would be seeing Stephen, dancing with him, holding him, had driven her emotions to fever pitch.

And there he was! He was with Toni, who was laughing at something he was saying, and he smiled at her and took her hand, pulling her against him. She looked absolutely stunning in a moss green strapless dress that must have cost a fortune – had probably been designed for her – and she was flawlessly and beautifully made up, her hair styled so as to look artless and tousled. That doesn't come cheap, Lynn thought grimly, and she had no doubt that Toni was a valued client at one of the top salons. Her insides turned over with jealousy and fear. How could she compete with that? Suddenly the outfit she'd been so excited about, that had cost her more than she could really afford, seemed cheap and ordinary, just another mass-produced, high street dress. She felt panicky. Eight years ago at that wedding, she thought, he told me he loved me, ached for me, but nevertheless here he is still with Toni, who's looking more striking and glamorous and happy than ever. Her heart was pounding and her hands were clammy. What if Harry had been wrong about Stephen and Toni's relationship?

At that moment Stephen looked up and saw her. He caught his breath. She is spellbinding, he thought, so perfect, as sweet and luscious as the first time I saw her all those years ago. The vivid cherry red of her frock emphasised the smooth whiteness of her skin, and his heart lurched with longing. How could he spend the rest of the day acting as if she meant nothing to him, when all he wanted was be with her?

She gave him a wide, inviting smile, her eyes alight with expectation.

And suddenly it was easy. The longing was swept away by an abrupt and devastating surge of pain and bitterness. What right had she to expect anything of him? She'd broken her promises and broken his heart. He'd cried, he'd pleaded, he'd begged her not to leave him, but she'd thrown his love coldly back at him, had chosen another man over him, had betrayed and hurt him far more than Toni ever could. His face expressionless, he nodded to her, and turned his back on her, his arm tightly round Toni's waist.

She couldn't take it in. The room seemed to tilt. He'd snubbed her completely.

"Are you all right?" A pretty little girl she couldn't place had taken her elbow and was looking at her with concern. "Andy!" she called.

Andy joined them. "What is it, Holl? Oh, hello, Lynn. Are you OK, like?"

Of course, Havago Holly, Andy's wife. She hadn't seen her much at Warwick, she'd been pregnant and had been sitting down, but Lynn remembered thinking how nice she seemed.

"I'm fine. Yes, I'm fine." She managed to smile.

"No, you're not," Holly was concerned. "It was Steve wasn't it? I saw the way he looked at you."

"Oh. Oh, yeah," Andy said. "See, the thing is, Lynn, Steve's really trying with Toni…"

"You mean Toni's really trying, don't you?" muttered Holly.

"Holl!" Andy said warningly. "Lynn, Steve really wants to make the marriage work, they've had a tough time recently."

"I didn't expect… I mean, we always talk and – and dance…" Lynn felt as if she was bleeding to death. She had counted on seeing and holding Stephen, she couldn't be deprived of that now, she couldn't. She wanted to shout and scream and plunge a knife into Toni. The strength of her jealousy shocked her. "I'm going to go and say hello to him," she said, her face set.

Andy took her arm, his weasely little face troubled. "Please don't, Lynn, it's not fair to him. Toni… well, she hurt him very much and he's trying so hard with her. Don't make it more difficult for him than it already is. Please."

"Oh, I see, it was all right for him to have an affair with that French girl," Lynn said tightly. "But not to talk to me."

"He never sees Coral any more, and there was other stuff, anyway. It was much more complicated. And if I can just say, Lynn, *you* left him. He was gutted when you did, all he could talk about and think about was getting you back. The band making it and stuff – it didn't mean anything to him, he'd have given it all up for you. Then when his dad died and he found out you were remarried, like – well, he was practically suicidal. He'd looked forward so much to that first tour of the States, and it just turned to ashes for him. Because of you. And he's tried to make a life without you. So I really think you owe it to him to leave him alone, like."

Lynn stared at him, tears spilling down her face. "Oh, God, Andy, I've looked forward to this wedding for so long, it's all I've thought about. Holding Stevie again. I can't stand it if he isn't in my life, I can't stand it! I know I left him, and I can't believe I did." Her voice rose. "Seeing him now and again is all that keeps me going! I have to see him!" She felt as if her life was ending.

"Andy, I'm going to take her home," Holly said. "Keep your eye on Clif and Primmy. I won't be too long. It's all right, Lynn," she said, taking Lynn's hand.

They managed to get out of the hotel without anyone noticing that Lynn was crying. In Holly's car, she remembered she hadn't told Paul she was leaving. She asked Holly to tell him she'd had a migraine and to apologise to Stella and Mitch.

"No problem," Holly said.

"Why are you doing this?" Lynn asked. "Not that I'm not grateful," she added.

Holly smiled. "Well, Andy likes you a lot, which makes me favourably disposed. And I had an affair with a married man when I was younger – I really loved him, and it was shattering, so I kind of know how you feel. Also, I thought we hit it off at Warwick. I think we could be good friends. I sometimes get feelings about people, and I get a really good one about you."

"Is it Primmy or Clif that's your baby?" Lynn asked.

"Neither. The baby is Goldie, she's seven months. She's with my sister today."

"How old are Clif and Primmy?"

"Clif's eight-and-a-half, and Primmy's three."

"How old are you?" Lynn asked curiously. "If you don't mind my asking."

Holly shook her head, smiling. "It's OK. I'm thirty-eight."

Lynn was amazed. "God, I'm thirty-six, and people tell me I look in my twenties, but you look even younger! How do you do it?"

"I've not had any work done, I'm just really, really lucky. I can eat what I like and not put on weight too! Is this it?" She pulled up outside the house.

"Can you come in for a minute?" Lynn desperately didn't want to be alone.

"Course I can."

Lynn woke with a start. It was dark and someone was hammering at her front door. The last thing she remembered, she had been sitting on the sofa, crying. She must have drifted off to sleep. Disorientated, she stumbled into the hall, switched on the light, and answered the door.

It was Paul. "What happened?" he demanded. "You never had a migraine in your life!"

"Paul."

"It was something to do with him, wasn't it?" He peered at her. "You've been crying."

"Yes. Oh, Paul, it was awful—"

"Yes, it was," he interrupted. She realised he was very angry. "It *was* awful. Disgraceful. Couldn't you have had the good manners to stick it out for a couple of hours? Both Stella and Lizzie missed you, and I felt like... well, like a pork pie at a Jewish party! I don't think I want to see you any more, Lynn."

"Paul!"

"Will anything be different from now on?"

Slowly, she shook her head.

His shoulders slumped. "No. Well... goodbye, then, Lynn." He shut the door gently behind him.

Lynn turned off the light, so that the house was in darkness again. How could she ever have let Stephen go? She leant her head against the wall and wept.

"Daddy, can I have a pet starling?"

"A what?"

"A starling."

"I don't think you can get starlings as pets, Sammy. Why do you want one?"

"Mozart had one. He paid thirty four kreuzer for it. What's a kreuzer, Daddy?"

"Some sort of old-fashioned German money, I should think. We could look in a dictionary, or online on the computer. Would a budgie do instead?"

Sam gave him the withering look that he usually reserved for Alex. "I hardly think so! Never mind," he sighed and wandered off.

I'm sure I never looked at Dad like that, Stephen thought, going back to the soundtrack he was writing for a film based on the book *Pigeon Pie*, by Nancy Mitford. Joely Richardson, on whom he had a tremendous crush, was playing the lead role, and he'd spent as much time on set as he could, which had been great fun, but he really needed to get it finished, the band was due to start recording their new album, 'Beggars Can't Be Jesus', shortly.

At that moment the phone rang. Sighing with impatience, he picked it up. It was Cell. It had been brought to her notice that an ultra right wing group, the Albion Party, whose policy was ostensibly to 'get Britain back on her feet and restore the nation's pride' but whose real agenda was simply fascism, was using Stephen's song, 'Savages'.

The first line of the chorus went: *Hey, they're just a bunch of savages, Let them die!* followed by the words, *I think we all know who the savages are, That'd be you and I.*' and the Albion Party was using that first line, and lines from the verses, completely out of context to promote their policy on racial purity.

Stephen was outraged. He got hold of Alan, who dealt with the situation swiftly and competently, taking out an injunction to stop the Albion Party from using the lyrics, and suing for damages. Stephen was disgusted by the whole thing, and wrote a song, 'Dedicated Follower Of Fascism (With apologies to Ray Davies)'.

At the beginning of the recording, George declared his intention to play his fretless bass on one of the songs, 'Variations On a Theme'.

Stephen shook his head. "That's not the sound I want for this song."

"But listen, Steve, it's just what it needs!" George started to play.

"Forget it, George," Stephen said firmly.

George coloured. "What do you mean?"

"I mean you're not playing it on my song."

George glowered at him. "It's not *your* song. We all play on it, we make wor own contribution. It's the band's song, it belongs to all of us!"

Stephen sighed. "George, please can we not do this? Let's just get on with the recording."

"Aye, man, let's, and I'm playing this guitar!"

"No, you're not!"

"Come on, guys," Andy said soothingly. "Let's not fight about this. Listen, George, you haven't rehearsed with that guitar..."

"I don't need for to rehearse with it, I can play it fine!"

"No, you fucking can't!" Stephen interrupted, beginning to lose his temper. "I've already told you I don't want that sound on *my* song, George, but apart from that, you're not good enough anyway. End of discussion, now let's get on with the album."

George stared at him. "Who the fuck do you think you are? Of course I'm fucking good enough! I've been asked to play this guitar on the Jaco Pastorius tribute album!"

Stephen shrugged dismissively.

"Look, man, if I don't play this guitar, I'm not playing on any of *your* poxy fucking songs!" George shouted.

Stephen clenched his fists. "I don't suppose anyone would notice, to be honest, George. I heard a joke the other day; what do you say to the bass player in a famous band? What's your name?"

"For God's sake, Steve!" Fin interjected. "That was uncalled for, and fucking unhelpful!"

Stephen ignored him. "If you're not going to play, George, piss off."

George's face was scarlet with rage. "I'm playing this fucking guitar, and that's final!"

Stephen's temper exploded. He grabbed the guitar from George, and smashed it against the doorframe as hard as he could. "No, you're fucking not!"

"You'll pay for that, you cunt!" George roared, wrenching the battered guitar from Stephen. He swung it at him, hitting him across the back of the head and knocking him off balance.

"For Christ's sake, the two of you, fucking stop it!" Fin yelled. "I've had a bellyful of you both! Fuck you, fuck the album, fuck the bloody band, I've had enough!" He walked out of the studio.

Stephen got unsteadily to his feet. George put the guitar down, and reached for his cigarettes. His hands were shaking.

"Oh, brilliant, Steve, well done, like," Andy said sarcastically. "No bass and no keyboard. This is going to be a hell of an album."

Stephen rubbed the back of his head. "George..."

George glared at him. "I don't want to hear."

"George, just shut up!" Andy shouted. "What the fuck's the matter with you? Fin's right, there's no fucking point!"

Stephen sat down. His head was pounding. "Don't shout, Andy. George, I'm sorry I said you weren't good enough. And I'm sorry about your guitar. But I'd rather you didn't play it."

"Well, I can't play it now, can I, man? Look at it!"

"I've said I'm sorry."

"It was your fucking head that did it." George began to grin. "Look at that dent!"

Stephen smiled weakly. He held out his hand. "No hard feelings?"

George sighed. "Aye, well, I'm sorry I hit you. Mind, you were asking for it," he added, taking Stephen's hand.

Andy shook his head. "You're a pair of useless wankers. I'll go and get Fin."

Lynn and Holly had become firm friends. Although Lynn was very close to Harry, she had more in common with Holly. Apart from Tantony Pig, Harry didn't work outside the home and was very wrapped up in Dominic and her children, whereas Holly, much as she loved Andy and their children, was passionate about her career. She was still presenting *Not Just Kid's Stuff*, which was doing phenomenally well.

Lynn often met her after the show for lunch. One Saturday she was early, and wandered along to the canteen. As she made her way down the corridor, she saw Stephen walking towards her. Her heart stood still.

He saw her at the same moment and stopped dead.

"Stephen!" she breathed.

"Hello," he said warily.

"What are you doing here? Sorry, stupid question!"

He smiled. "Yeah, I'm being interviewed. Listen, Lynn…"

Someone started along the corridor towards them. Stephen's manner changed. He raised his voice slightly. "Yes, of course you can have an autograph." He fished a piece of paper out of his pocket and scribbled something on it. "OK, thanks. Take care," he said, smiling impersonally. "Hello, Patrick." He nodded to the man coming towards them, and walked off down the corridor.

Lynn waited until the presenter had gone, and then she looked at the paper. Stephen had written: *Cherry. Cariad, I'm not free and I can't live like this, it's tearing me in two. I've got to think of the boys. If you love me, let me go.* She blinked back tears, and started to fold it up. There was something on the other side. She smoothed it out again and read it. It was a shopping list, written in Stephen's untidy scrawl. It said:

Vets:
Turtle's tablets
Flea stuff
Town:
Toothpaste
Pasta
Beer
Crunchies
Sammy's book

Next to the last item was a big arrow, with the words *DON'T FORGET.* That list, even more than the words he'd written on the other side, told her all she needed to know. He would never be hers again. He was married, he had his children. She'd been wondering how Rob was enjoying Oxford, and had intended to ask Harry or Holly, but what was the point now? She'd lost Stephen completely. She realised how much she had relied on seeing him occasionally, and without him, she felt utterly alone. This is how he felt when I married Tim, she thought, remembering what Andy had said at Stella's wedding. She'd made her choice then, and he'd left her alone to live her life. He'd made his choice now, and she had to extend the same courtesy to him. How am I going to get through the rest of my life without him? she thought in despair. She folded up the paper, put it carefully away, and made her way to the canteen to wait for Holly.

Chapter Nineteen
Making It Look Easy

And I'm on a roll, I'm in control, but I'm faking it, making it look easy.

At the beginning of December, Dominic's father had a stroke. Harry took the children out of school, and asked Stephen and Toni to have them while she and Dominic went to Fenroth.

Stephen was reading *The Hobbit* and *The Christmas Mystery*, which had become a Markham Christmas tradition, to the boys. He started again for the Chaplin children. Fee sat on his lap, Gus leant against his right side, and Mab against his left, holding his hand. He loved all the Chaplin children, but Mab was his favourite. Fee and Gus both had Dominic's dark grey eyes, and looked very like him, even though Fee was dark-haired, but Mab was a mixture of him and Harry. Her full lips were Harry's and her hot brown eyes, even to the gold flecks in them, while the shape of her face was Dominic's and her hair was the same shade of gold as his.

"Will Grandpapa die, Uncle Stevie?" she asked, squeezing his hand.

He'd been primed by Harry. "He might, Mabs. But he'll go straight to heaven, like Bess." Bess, Angus's Labrador, had died that summer.

Fee took her thumb out of her mouth. "I don't want Grandpapa to die. I love him."

Stephen kissed her. "I know, darling, I know."

"Was he conscious?"

A muscle twitched in Dominic's jaw. "Oh, yes."

"Did he speak to you?" Harry asked, anxiously. She wanted to hold him, but something in his manner stopped her.

"Yes." His clear grey eyes were as bleak and cold as the North Sea in winter. "He's dead."

"Oh, Dom! I'm so sorry!"

"Do you know what he said to me?" Dominic continued as if she hadn't spoken. "He said, 'Try not to bugger up the estate too much.' That was all. The only time he ever showed any approval of anything I did was when we had Gus. He never said he loved me." His voice cracked. "Would it have been too hard for him to have said it now? I suppose he didn't. I'm going for a walk."

"I'll come with you."

"For Christ's sake!" he shouted.

Harry jumped.

"I'm not a child, I don't need someone to hold my hand every five minutes!" He walked out of the bedroom, slamming the door behind him.

Harry finished dressing and went down to breakfast. The only other person there was Oliver, Sophy's husband.

He made an expressive face at her. "Pretty glum, isn't it?"

She nodded. "How's Sophy taking it?"

"Devastated. I mean, she accepts that he was nearly eighty but you never think your parents will go, do you?"

"She got on well with Angus, didn't she?"

"Daddy's little girl," Oliver nodded. "Apple of his eye."

"Dominic didn't – or rather, Dominic would've but he was never given the chance."

Oliver looked sympathetic. "Yes. Old king-new king syndrome. Soph was telling me last night how he couldn't bear the thought of giving this place up."

"But Dom's his son!"

Oliver shrugged. "Pretty incomprehensible, isn't it?"

Harry reached for more toast. "You can say that again."

"Soph was saying how Angus couldn't bear having Dom around. Packed him off to school in Kent when he was only four or something, wasn't it?"

Harry stared at him. Dominic had never told her this, he'd always been vague about his childhood, never saying much about it apart from jocular remarks and his utter hatred of the public school system. She'd supposed it to be one of his humorous affectations. Angus had been gruff and offhand with him, and Susan treated him with a kind of amused disdain, but she'd thought it was just a way they had as a family; Dominic wasn't demonstrative in public, but she knew how very much he loved her, and he adored his children. Everything fell into place, particularly his attitude to his parents; it had often seemed to her that he went out of his way to provoke them, and yet he'd desperately wanted to name Gus after Angus and had been overjoyed by their approbation. She remembered him saying, when they first met, that it wouldn't matter if he became hooked on drugs, no one would care. She'd always found that strange, after all, she'd thought, he has his family. Now she understood completely. She felt the most intense hatred towards Angus and Susan but, "He hated school," was all she said.

Dominic and Susan came in, Dominic's face ruddy from being outside, Susan as perfectly groomed and composed as ever.

She's like an iceberg, Harry thought with a shudder. Dominic dropped a kiss on her head. She smiled up at him and looked at Susan. She wanted to kill her with her bare hands. "I'm sorry about Angus," she managed to lie.

Susan gave her a brief smile of acknowledgement. "You seem in good spirits, Dominic," she said coldly.

He helped himself to kippers. "Yes, I've just been wandering around my estate planning where I'll hold this massive pop concert I'm going to organise. Woodstock'll pale into insignificance beside it," he said, eating hungrily.

Susan went white. "I would have thought even *you* could have shown some respect!"

Harry was suddenly cold with fury. "Why should he?" she asked quietly. "I wouldn't have any respect for a father who sent me away to school when I was four, and never told me he loved me." She turned to Dominic. "Pop concert, Dom – great idea! Oh, and I know, let's turn the house into holiday flats, we could make a fortune!" She stood up. "Excuse us, Susan, but Dominic's going to ring up his children and tell them how much he loves them. Come on, Dom." She swept out of the room, ignoring the look on Susan's face.

Dominic got to his feet. "Don't worry, Mama. I'm sure she was joking about the flats." I hope, he thought as he followed her out.

She was halfway up the stairs.

"Harry, wait!" She ignored him and carried on walking. He caught up with her in the corridor. "Harry!"

She shook her head at him and opened the door to their room.

He could see she was trying not to cry. He shut the door behind them and took her in his arms. "What was all that about?"

She held him to her. "Why didn't you tell me they sent you away to school when you were four?"

"Why would you want to know? I take it Sophia has been blabbing to Oliver? What a meddlesome girl she is!"

"Why would I want to know? Because… because… I don't know, I just do."

"Harry, it was years ago. It's not important, it happens to lots of children, it's just school. I'd have gone at eight anyway, even if my parents had been besotted with me. It's what's done!"

"We won't be sending Gus."

"When have I ever done the done thing? Of course we won't be sending Gus away, it's a terrible thing to do to a child, I hated it, you know I did!"

"Well, there you are!"

"Yes, but the thing is, my darling, it's long over. I was upset when Papa died because… oh, because I'd always cherished a belief that deep down he did love me and we'd have this touching deathbed scene. How ridiculous! And, you know, I find it doesn't matter. When I was little I had Soph and Nanny, and now I have you and the children – and Stephen. And my parents always made sure that I was warm and well fed, I never lacked anything."

"Except affection."

He shrugged. "Yes, but I had Soph. And in the long run, it hasn't really affected me. Do you see what I'm saying?"

"Yes, I do see. But I don't understand why your father would feel that way. I mean, why have children at all, then?"

Dominic sighed. "I don't know. Maybe he didn't realise how he'd feel till I was born. Who knows? Anyway, when I came along, it must have dawned on him that one day he'd have to leave his precious estate to me. He never felt like that about Soph, she was never a threat."

Harry stared at him. "God, how awful! How terrible to feel like that about your own son! And what about Susan? How could she let her child be treated like that?"

"She was very young when she married Papa, and she was in love with him. I think after she had me she quickly realised it was him or me. She chose him. In some ways I can't blame her. After all, even if she'd made a stand, I'd have gone to school at eight, as I said, and she'd have been here with a man she loved who didn't care for her in return. She had a tough time of it as it was, he had affairs all the time. And she wasn't quite eighteen when I was born. If she'd been older, it might have been different." He took Harry's face between his hands. "I know you were only eighteen when you had Rob, but you… well, you could never behave like that. You're my miracle." He kissed her. "Forget it, Hat. I have. I've got you. Nothing else matters."

Harry hugged him. "Should I apologise to Susan?"

"God, no, let her fucking stew. Let's ring my bairns."

They spent Christmas quietly at Fenroth, with Stephen, Toni and their boys. Susan had moved out to Charnton, a Chaplin estate in Dorset.

Stephen hadn't known about this one. "Good God! Fenroth, Leezance, the estates in Norfolk and Leicestershire; how much room does one family need?" he teased.

"Fuck off, Markham, I've got bairns to provide for. Talking of which, where's Robert? I've barely seen him this holiday."

"Off somewhere with Julia," Harry shrugged. "Where else?"

Rob's first term at Oxford had surpassed his expectations. Apart from missing Julia, who'd been accepted by her second choice, Newcastle, he'd loved every minute of it. "There are loads of people like you there," he'd said to Dominic.

"What the fuck do you mean by that?" Dominic had been outraged. "There's no one else like me! I'm unique!"

"You know that song, I can't remember what it's called, anyway, there's a bit in it about guitarists might get a blister on their little finger?" Lynn hummed the tune.

"Yeah, I know the one."

"Look!" she said, bitterly. She held up her left hand. The tips of her index, middle and ring fingers were red and sore, with painful looking blisters.

Simon Elliott, her guitar teacher, grinned. "Don't worry, they'll go."

Lynn had decided to take guitar lessons as a way of being closer to Stephen. She often saw books in music shops: *The Guitar Style Of Stephen Markham* or *The Sid's Six Songbook – Play Their Hits*. She bought them for the pictures of Stephen, and played the songs on her flute, but then she began to think it would be fun to play them on the guitar. She could play the flute, how hard could it be? She bought a Fender Stratocaster, with a rosewood fingerboard, because she'd read that Stephen preferred them, and an amplifier. This had been difficult, she knew nothing about amps. She consulted her Stevie magazines and found that he mostly used Soldano and Fender amps; she vaguely remembered him having an old Fender amp in Manchester. Soldanos seemed to be incredibly expensive when she looked online, so she got the cheapest Fender with reverb she could find. Stephen liked echo; in Manchester he hadn't really used much else in the way of effects, and in his most recent interview he'd said it was still his favourite.

Next, she found a teacher. Simon Elliott was about her age, and good-looking in a thoroughly English way, with wishy-washy blue eyes, longish, ash blond hair and a lovely smile. He taught music at a local comprehensive, and gave piano and guitar lessons in the evenings and at weekends. He came from York, which pleased Lynn when she found out.

He whistled when he saw the Strat. "Unusual for a beginner."

She'd taken her Sid's Six songbook along to the first lesson. "I want to be able to play like this," she explained, "so I need the right kind of guitar."

Simon smiled. "We all want to play like Stephen Markham! And he doesn't only play a Strat."

"I know, but he loves Strats and that's the sound I want to make. I play the flute and read music. Does that help?"

"Well, it might," Simon said, cautiously. "Look, I'll show you some basic chords." He'd made her a chart, showing the fingering.

She found it much more difficult than she'd ever imagined it could be. She had no trouble tuning the guitar, and she could manage chords like A and E minor, but some of the shapes seemed impossible. She had a lot of trouble with G, but she loved the sound it made. For some reason, it reminded her of Stephen. "G is my favourite chord," she told Simon.

"That's nice," he said, amused. He found Lynn intriguing. She wasn't at all like his other pupils. The week before she'd told him she hated the snake chord.

"Which one is that?"

"D minor. Look." She'd taken a pen from her bag. "If you join up the dots, it looks like a snake."

"Is that why you hate it?"

"Oh, no, I like snakes. It just hurts my fingers."

Now he said, "Right, how have you been getting on with 'Johnny B Goode'?"

She made a face.

"Having trouble?" he grinned.

"Well, the chords aren't too bad, but I can't do the strum pattern. I'm crap! I'll never be able to play like Stevie!"

"Stevie?" Simon raised an eyebrow. "Big fan, aren't you?"

Lynn blushed. *Damn*, she thought. Now she'd either have to tell him she'd been married to Stephen, which would mean endless questions, or look like a total nerd. Which was worse? "Um, well, I used to be married to him," she said, finally, deciding she couldn't bear Simon to think her a nerd. "I still think of him as Stevie."

Simon stared at her. "You used to be married to Stephen Markham? *You're* Sweet Cherry?"

She blushed more deeply and nodded.

"Bloody hell! What happened, did he run off with that Australian woman he's married to now?"

"No, we split up long before he met her. We were at university together. We married while we were students."

"Well, there's a turn-up for the books! Never thought I'd be teaching Steve Markham's ex-wife! Why didn't he teach you?"

"I never thought about it then. He'd play guitar and sing, and I'd play my flute." God, those were the best days of my life! she thought.

"With the band?"

"Oh, no, I couldn't play in public, I'd be way too nervous! No, just in our flat."

"Why Cherry?"

"It's my name – my full name is Cherilynn."

"You know, I'd love to hear you play the flute sometime."

"Make a nice change from the strangled cat sound I make when I play the guitar!"

He grinned. "Lynn, would you like to come round for a meal on Saturday? You could bring your flute and we could play together. What do you say?"

Lynn hesitated. Did she want to get involved with anyone else? Look what had happened with Paul. But on the other hand, did she really want to end up an old maid? Stephen was out of her life forever, and she liked Simon. She smiled at him. "Thanks, Simon. I'd love to."

It was Dominic's fortieth birthday in January. Stephen and Toni offered to have the children for a few days so that Harry and Dominic could go away by themselves. Nanny Davies was still with them, but she was in her sixties and suffering badly from arthritis, and while she was marvellous with the children, and they loved her very much, Harry didn't feel it was fair to leave her to cope alone. "It would be different if the children were older," she said to Dominic.

He opened his mouth to speak, but she forestalled him. "I know there's the rest of the staff, but it's not the same. If only Nanny wasn't so resistant to having help," she added with a sigh.

Dominic grinned ruefully. "I know. That's the trouble with nannies. They're for life, not just for christenings."

Nanny Davies was enthusiastic about the idea when Harry tactfully consulted her. "No, of course I don't think it will be upsetting for them! I know Sir Angus has just died, but children adjust very quickly, and then Mr Markham is a *splendid* Daddy, I wish you could have seen him reading to them all while you were at Fenroth, dear, it was a picture, Fee on his lap, and little Gus leaning against him, and every one of them except Alex sucking their thumbs. I think they'll do very well there, and if you ask me, dear, Dominic could do with a break. He needs a bit of time alone with you. He's been very quiet since his father died. He was hoping for a reconciliation with him, wasn't he?"

"He didn't get it. Angus and Susan; well, they weren't kind to him."

Nanny Davies sighed. "Poor Dominic! Poor little boy! He had such a terrible time of it in that house. And you know, he was never jealous of Sophia, despite the fact that Sir Angus and Lady Susan doted on her." She patted Harry's hand. "I thank God every night that he found you, dear!"

Harry was tremendously moved, and very loving to Dominic, taking him to Paris for a romantic weekend. Dominic grinned and referred to it as a weekend of lust and debauchery.

'Beggars Can't Be Jesus' was due to be released in April, and Sid's Six were to tour England in June and July. In February, they flew to Los Angeles for the Grammy awards. They won for Best Album, 'The Argentinian', and Best Song, 'The Evening Rain'. They were jubilant. They had already won the Mercury Music Prize and a Q award for the album.

"How are you going to top this?" Shelagh asked.

"It'll be downhill all the way, now," Stephen declared. "We've peaked."

"Rubbish!" Toni said. "You'll just have to try harder!"

"Ah, we're too old now," Stephen said, mournfully. "We'll get asked to appear on the Identity Parade in *Never Mind The Buzzcocks* in a few years time. and no one will remember us."

"Speak for yourself, bonny lad!" George grinned. "We know better, don't we, pet?" He winked at Toni, who grinned back

Stephen suddenly felt cold. Something about the exchange, harmless and jocular as it had been, worried him. It reminded him of something, some other time, but he couldn't remember what. It was like a terrific sense of déjà vu. He shivered.

"More champagne, Steve?" Andy offered.

"Thanks, Andy. Well, here's to us, and what's like us?" he asked, raising his glass. It was a toast he and Toni used often.

"Damn few, and they're all dead," Toni replied.

"You two are seriously weird," Fin said.

"This is kind of a cigar moment," Stephen remarked.

Andy stared at him. "You don't smoke, like!"

"No, but some days I wander round the garden with a cigar."

Toni grinned. "He doesn't smoke it, he just likes the smell."

"Yeah, and the general cigar ambience," Stephen added.

"You're right, Fin," Andy nodded. "Steve, you're great and everything, but you're really not from this planet, are you?"

When 'Beggars Can't Be Jesus' was released, there was a torrent of criticism from Christian groups, who objected to the title. Stephen ignored them. As far as he could see, there was no blasphemy, and certainly none intended. The band appeared on TV and radio, saying the same thing over and over again; that Stephen's son had misheard his primary school teacher and thought that the phrase was beggars can't be Jesus. Stephen pointed out that Jesus was a popular name in Latin American culture, so how could it be blasphemous to use it?

"Simon, would you like to go out for a meal with Andy and Holly?"

Simon stared at her. "You don't seriously expect me to say no, do you?"

Lynn laughed. "They're just people, Simon."

He grinned. "I guess so. Yeah, I'd love to go."

Lynn and Simon were seeing a lot of each other, but on a casual basis. Lynn was wary of becoming too involved; she'd been very fond of Paul, and their break-up had upset her, particularly as she considered that he'd overreacted because he had feelings for her. She didn't want to get into the same situation with Simon. She'd made it clear from the outset that she'd just split up with someone and didn't want to get into a serious relationship. Simon had accepted this, and their dates had been light-hearted. They weren't sleeping together, and Lynn was determined to keep it under control. She hadn't been sure about this invitation to meet Holly and Andy, it smacked too much of meeting the family to her, but Holly had been so insistent that she'd given in.

She and Simon arrived at the restaurant first. "Posh, isn't it?" Simon whispered, slightly awed.

"Don't let it faze you," she said. As they started towards the bar, Andy and Holly arrived. "Sorry we're late." Holly kissed her. "Goldie woke up just as we were going out of the door."

Lynn smiled. "We've only just got here. This is Simon. Simon, Andy and Holly."

They ordered drinks and took them to their table.

"You're teaching Lynn to play the guitar, then?" Andy asked. "How's she getting on, like?"

"Kinder to draw a veil!" Lynn grinned.

Simon laughed. "You're not that bad."

"He's being tactful. I just can't get the hang of it, I sound like a cat in agony. You know that song, 'My Guitar Gently Weeps'? Well, when I play, it's not only the guitar that weeps, it's anyone within earshot!"

They all laughed.

"It takes time," Simon smiled.

"Well I hope you've got the next fifty years free!" she joked.

He took her hand. "I can't think of a nicer way to spend fifty years than with you."

She squeezed his hand, moved.

He turned to Andy. "Congratulations on the Grammys."

"Yeah, we were well chuffed, like. Steve reckons we've had it now, we'll never top 'The Argentinian' and we might as well stop while we're ahead."

"He's not serious?" Lynn asked, dismayed.

Andy shook his head, grinning. "He's already started writing for the next album. We're touring next month and he's got us rehearsing twenty five hours a day."

"He always was a bit of a slave driver," Lynn said, reminiscently.

"They're really nice," Simon said, on the way home. "Really easy to get on with."

"I told you, they're just people. Being famous doesn't make them any different."

As she was getting ready for bed, she thought about Stephen. Fame hadn't changed him, either. Suddenly she was sick of this obsession, fed up with dreaming her life away. She picked up the phone and dialled Simon's number.

"Hi. It's me. Can I come over?"

"I thought you'd never ask."

Chapter Twenty
The Evening Rain

Running by the river at the close of dismal day,
Cold breeze blows and makes me shiver,
Makes the water ebb and quiver,
Setting sun is just a sliver as it disappears.
The sky is full of pain, and the evening rain falls on my face like tears.

Touring was still Stephen's favourite thing. He loved the buzz he got from playing live, and the feedback from the audience made it seem as if they were performing every song for the first time. He'd always had a rapport with the crowd, even when he first started playing at the Angel; the fans were important to him, and it was with shame and guilt that he realised he'd never before paid attention to the prices charged for the Sid's Six merchandise sold at the venues.

He brought up the subject one night after a concert when the four of them were relaxing over drinks in his suite. There was a programme on the coffee table, and he picked it up. "Look at this! Ten quid, and it's really just a glossy ad for the band! It'd be expensive at a fiver." He refilled his whisky glass.

Fin shrugged. "It's what the fans want." He got up. "I'm off to use the facilities, I may be some time."

"Why don't you ever use your own sodding bathroom?" Stephen shouted after him.

"At least we don't have to worry about him shooting up in there any more," Andy grinned, stretching out on one of the sofas.

"Yeah, well, that didn't stink out my bathroom for the rest of the night," Stephen retorted.

George had been flicking through the programme. "This thing would be half the size if they cut out all these pictures of you, man, and edited the interview. They could easily charge five pounds for it then," he said sourly, irritated by the fact that there were far more pictures of Stephen than of the rest of them, and a much longer interview with him.

Stephen drained his glass and poured himself another. "They wanted the organ grinder rather than the monkey, George," he said annoyingly.

George frowned. "What the fuck do you mean by that? The rest of us are just as important to the band!"

"Oh, yeah? Written any award-winning songs recently, George? Well, any songs at all, really."

George reddened. "You wouldn't have got awards for your poxy songs if we hadn't played on them, man! And it's all very well talking about charging less for the merchandise; it's all right for you, you get more royalties than we do, and you make money from your soundtracks and your bloody films. The rest of us rely on the money we make from touring."

"Well, I don't see Andy and Fin complaining! For Christ's sake, George, it's not as if we're a struggling band just starting out. If that was the case, I might agree with you. You're not exactly short of money, why are you so bloody tight-fisted?"

"No, I'm not short of money, man, but I might be if you had your way, you two-faced fucking wanker. You're all, 'I'm a serious artist, couldn't exploit my fans', but I notice you never mind getting your shirt off for to sell posters and calendars and the rest of it!" He held up the programme, open at a large photo of Stephen wearing only a pair of jeans.

Stephen shrugged. "I *am* a serious artist, and it's not exploitation. The fans like it. I really would be happier if the merchandise was cheaper."

"Yeah, well, a serious artist like you would be. And you could always do another porn film to raise money, I suppose."

Stephen glared at him. "It wasn't a porn film."

"Course not, man, it was serious art."

Andy was starting to get uneasy. "Come on, youse two. Steve, put a zipper on it, and George, you'd jump at the chance of getting naked with Coral." He grinned. "Don't tell Holly, but so would I!"

They ignored him. "Look, George, the bottom line here is that the merchandise should be cheaper, and I think—"

"Turn the TV on, Steve, I want to see the footie results," Andy interrupted, trying to divert them.

"...we should do something about it," Stephen continued, picking up the remote.

George sneered. "Well, while you're at it, do something about the amount of exposure you get compared to the rest of us. I've never understood it, you're just part of the band."

Stephen lost his temper. "Why don't you stop kidding yourself, George? You know perfectly well why I get more exposure than you, it's because I'm far more talented and better looking," he taunted. "It's always pissed you off, hasn't it? You're so fucking jealous, you'd love the attention, you'd love it if they wanted to photograph you without your shirt, but that's hardly likely to happen, is it? And as you're very well aware, I've made several hit albums without your bumbling bass playing, so shut the fuck up!" He hit George across the side of the head with the remote.

George gave a bellow of rage and grabbed him by the throat. Stephen fought back and George dragged him to the ground. With his hands still round Stephen's throat, he started banging his head against the floor.

Andy leapt up. "Oh, not again, for fuck's sake!" He pulled at George's arm. George hit out at him, knocking him against the wall and dazing him.

Stephen took advantage of George's momentary lack of concentration to break free and land him a punch in the face. George punched him back as Fin came into the room.

Fin took one look at them hitting each other, grabbed a jug of iced water from the sideboard, and threw it over them. "Ah, Christ! I go out for ten minutes to take a dump and when I get back you two are beating the shit out of each other again! It's fucking tedious. Get up and help me with Andy."

Not long after Stephen got home, he and Toni found a litter of kittens abandoned in a ditch in the village. Only one of them was still alive and they took it in. It was just a few days old, and very weak. Their vet warned them not to become too attached to it, but they were determined it would live, and nursed it through, feeding it every few hours with a tiny syringe. It was a female, a pretty little thing, all black, apart from a blaze of white above her nose. The boys named her Savij, claiming hopefully that she was the offspring off a panther.

She was in the process of being weaned, which meant putting very small lumps of cat food into her mouth before each milk feed. It was a messy business, as she hadn't got the hang of chewing and tried to suck the food.

George's twins were staying with him for a few weeks and he took them to the Priory to see her.

Grace and Megumi were enchanted with her. "Can we have a kitten, Daddy?" Megumi begged.

"It's not up to me, Meg, pet, it's your mother's decision."

"Why can't we all live in England like we used to?" Grace demanded. "Tell Mummy she can't live in Japan any more!"

"You know I can't do that, Gracie!"

"Come and play on my Playstation," Alex invited, with rare tact.

The twins got up eagerly.

"Your Alex is a canny lad, Toni," George said.

Toni smiled warmly at him. "Thank you, George!"

"That was helpful of Alex," Stephen commented, after George and the twins had gone.

"Don't say it as if it was a miracle," Toni said, annoyed.

Stephen grinned. "Well, come on, Toni, it's not like him!"

Toni's lips tightened. "You've always got a downer on Alex!"

Stephen sighed. "No, I haven't, I'm just realistic."

"Of course, it's a different story when it's Rob. Look at that business in the holidays, you didn't say anything to *him*!"

"Yes, I did, I was cross!"

"Bollocks!"

The incident she was referring to had happened right at the end of the Easter holidays. Stephen and Toni had been woken at nearly three in the morning by a frantic Rob.

"Dad! Dad! Wake up!"

"What? Wossamatter?" Stephen groped for the light switch. "Rob! What is it?"

"What's going on?" Toni mumbled.

"We fell asleep!" Rob said, wringing his hands.

"Who did?" Stephen asked, mystified.

"Me and Julia. What will Mr and Mrs Moffatt say?"

"Don't they allow sleep at her house or something?" Toni asked crossly.

"They don't know we're sleeping together!"

"But you're both adults! And they know you went on holiday together," Stephen pointed out.

"Yeah, but we told them we had separate rooms. And it doesn't matter that we're adults, Jules's Dad is really strict. He'll kill me!"

"Well, why the fuck didn't you put your alarm on?" Stephen wasn't sure whether he was more angry with Rob and Julia or Mr Moffatt.

"We just didn't. Please, Dad, you've got to help!"

"How? I don't know what to do!"

Toni had been thinking. "I'll drive her home, apologise profusely and say we've been playing Risk and got carried away and didn't realise what the time was."

"Oh, Toni, thank you so much!" Rob was practically crying with gratitude.

"I think you should own up," Stephen said. "After all, Julia's nineteen, for God's sake! I mean, what's the worst that could happen? He can't stop you from seeing her."

"It would be an awkward situation, Steve," Toni said quietly.

"Anyway," Stephen said now, "what did you want me to do? And you were the one who came up with a solution and said forget it to Rob. And it's not his fault if Reginald Moffatt is a narrow-minded prig."

"You'd be just the same if we had daughters."

"I would not!"

"Anyway, my point is, it's always different for Rob as far as you're concerned. You just don't like Alex."

He was hurt. "Toni, that's not true, and you know it! I like them all!"

Her lips twisted into a sneer, and she turned contemptuously away. He was chilled by the look of near hatred on her face. Disturbed and upset, he stumped over to the studio, where he started to play a song that had been going round in his head since he'd heard it on the radio that morning.

The door burst open and Alex and Pip rushed in, carrying their guitars.

"Hi, Dad. We were just… what's that you're singing?" Alex asked in a suspicious tone.

" 'Angels'," Stephen answered, surprised. "You know, Alex, Robbie Williams."

"Course I *know* it, Dad! I just couldn't believe you were singing it! Robbie Williams is crap!"

"I thought you liked him, you're always singing 'Millennium'."

"Poor Dad, you're so square!" Alex said, pityingly. "It's not even like you're *that* old."

Pip looked concerned. "Poor Dad."

"I can't see what's wrong with Robbie Williams," Stephen said, exasperated.

"He used to be with a Boy Band, and besides, he's like, *so* last week! But if you can't see it, you can't see it!" Alex said, sadly.

"Blind as a bat," Pip agreed.

"Why can't you two be more like Rob?" Stephen asked, stung.

"*Rob?* Good old *Rob?* "Alex's voice was scathing. "He's just like you, only younger!"

"Younger, bigger, fitter, but just as square," Pip giggled.

"Go away, you're horrible," Stephen said.

"I'm going to have a band when I'm older," Alex said, ignoring him.

"Me too," said Pip.

"I'll play lead guitar and I'll be the greatest! I'll play really loud music, not the stuff Dad plays."

"Yeah." Pip's tone was uncertain. He liked Stephen's music.

"I'll be like Jimi Hendrix," Alex boasted.

"Oh, so will I," agreed Pip fervently. They both thought Jimi Hendrix was the greatest thing since sliced bread.

"I can play like Jimi Hendrix," Stephen said. "It's just not my style."

Alex stared at him. "You can't!"

"Yes, I can. Better, because he's dead and I'm not!"

"All right, show us!"

Stephen picked up a Strat. He adjusted the amp and played 'All Along The Watchtower'.

Alex and Pip stared at him, open-mouthed.

"That's my favourite, although it was actually written by Bob Dylan. I like Jimi, he was an amazing guitarist, and I like his music, I used to play it when I was a bit older than you, but it's not really my style. And I always thought he was an idiot to take drugs the way he did."

Alex groaned. "How square can you be? He was *so* cool! 'Move over, Rover, and let *Jimi* take over.' He was experimenting with *life*, Dad."

"Experimented himself to death!" Stephen retorted. "Sorry, I don't think that's cool. I'd rather be a live square than a dead…" He searched for a word, couldn't find one, and ended up lamely with "unsquare."

"If you don't get it, you don't get it. Can I have a go on a Strat?"

"What's wrong with your Yamaha?"

"Strats are cooler."

Stephen grinned at him. "Sorry, Alex, these are for squares."

"Dad! Don't be a git!"

"Clear off, the pair of you, I'm going to start working now."

As they went out, he heard Alex say, "Poor old Dad! First Robbie Williams, now Jimi. He's had it!"

Later, he felt mean; it wouldn't have hurt to have let Alex play a Strat. He went to find him. He was in his room, watching his TV.

"Hi, Ally! Listen, do you want to play one of my Strats?"

Alex looked up at him. His eyes were red. "Doesn't matter," he muttered.

Stephen was concerned. "Alex? What's wrong?"

Alex shook his head. "Nothing."

"Look, come on, Al. If you've got a problem, I might be able to help."

Alex looked down and shook his head again.

Stephen didn't know what to do. He patted Alex's shoulder. "OK. But please, Ally, if I can do anything, or if you just want to talk, come and get me."

He went straight to Pip's room. "Pipkin, what's up with Alex?"

Pip was playing with Rob's old Combat Force figures. "He told Mum you wouldn't let him play one of your Strats and Mum said it was because you didn't love him. You do though, don't you, Dad?"

"Of *course* I do, Pip. I love you all *so* much." He was having trouble with his breathing. How could Toni have done that? How *could* she?

"That's what I told Alex, but he didn't believe me. Dad!"

"Yes, Pip?"

"I like the stuff you play, I think you're better than Jimi."

Stephen felt tears well up in his eyes. He hugged Pip. "It doesn't matter if you like my stuff or not, I still love you!"

"Yeah, I know."

I'm going to kill her, thought Stephen. I'm going to fucking kill her.

He went back to Alex's room. "Alex, I love you so much, you won't know how much till you have children of your own. The only reason I wouldn't let you play a Strat was because you pissed me off, like sometimes you won't let Pip or Sam play with your toys, you know? I don't know why Mum said that. It must be nearly her period, she often says nasty things then without meaning them, doesn't she?"

Alex looked at the floor. "Do you love me as much as Rob?"

Stephen's heart turned cold with hatred of Toni. "Yes, Alex, I love you every bit as much, every bit, I *swear* it."

Alex flung his arms round him. "Pip said she was wrong!"

"And she was, she was so, *so* wrong!"

"Can I have a packet of crisps?" Alex asked hopefully.

"Gentleman's relish, eh?" Stephen grinned. "Alex, right now you can have anything you want."

"Wow! Thanks, Dad!"

Stephen went to find Toni. He was so angry he wasn't sure what he was going to do.

She was on the phone in the bedroom. He grabbed it from her, pulled the cord out of the wall, and threw it across the room. "How dare you?" he said, his voice unsteady. "How dare you tell Alex that I don't love him, that I love Rob best? How dare you?"

Toni had the grace to look embarrassed. She shrugged. "Sometimes that's what it seems like."

"So you hurt Alex because you're pissed off?"

"You wouldn't let him play your Strat."

"Because he burst into my studio, called me a square and a git and didn't have the manners to say please. *You'd* have sent him to his room without tea."

"Oh! Oh, he didn't tell me that!"

"So you instantly jumped to the conclusion that I don't love him. Jesus Christ, you bitch, if you ever do anything like that again I'll knock your fucking head off!"

Her eyes filled with tears. "I'm sorry, Stephen. I was wrong."

"Good. Well, go and tell Alex. And if he's got the entire contents of the pantry in his room, I said he could."

"But it'll be his teatime in a..." Her voice petered out at the look on his face. "Yes, all right, Stephen." She went out.

Stephen sank down onto the bed. He felt drained. Why did she do these things? Nothing, no amount of counselling, was going to make a difference. They'd had all those sessions, and what was the point? If Toni felt like being a bitch, she'd do it. He picked the phone up and plugged it in. He wondered who she'd been calling, and pressed the redial button. The phone rang, and almost immediately, George answered.

"Hello? Toni?"

Stephen hung up and unplugged it again. He faintly heard it begin to ring downstairs. Sian's face came into his head and instantly he knew what it was about Toni and George's friendship. It reminded him of his mother and Ted, the friendship, the bond they'd had, right from the start, even before his father died. He felt chilled. But Toni was nothing like Sian. And he was nothing like his father. He lay back on the bed and stared at the ceiling.

He and Toni patched the quarrel up. Toni seemed to make an effort, was warmer and more loving, but he couldn't shake the uneasy feeling that they were coasting towards the end of the line. He didn't want that to happen, but it seemed inevitable.

Lynn was very happy with Simon. In some ways he reminded her of Stephen, but quieter, more English, not so volatile. Stephen was the most lovable man she'd ever known, but he hadn't always been easy to live with; on occasions it had been like living with a whirlwind, there were times he was never still, either physically or emotionally. She'd never met another man with such vibrant intensity. Simon was much calmer, harder to ruffle, and, although, like Stephen, he was passionate about music, he was nowhere near as wrapped up in it as Stephen had always been. He sang too – not as much as Stephen, but then Stephen had always reminded Lynn of the dormouse from *Alice In Wonderland*, although in his case, of course, it was, 'I breathe when I sing is the same thing as I sing when I breathe'. Simon never sang when they were out, but he sang a fair bit around the house, and he was always playing guitar. He loved going into music shops, trying out various guitars and discussing them with the staff. Lynn remembered Stephen doing the same thing in Manchester, although when *he* played, the staff and other shoppers would often gather to listen.

Eventually they talked about getting married. Simon was in favour. She wasn't so sure.

"What about our children? We don't want them to be little b—"

"Yes, thank you, Si!"

He grinned. "You know what I mean though, Lynn."

"Who says we'll have children?"

"Well, I'd like at least one."

"But suppose I can't?"

"We'll cross that bridge when we come to it."

He didn't mind her talking about Stephen, in fact, he liked listening to her stories of the band playing gigs around Manchester. She told him far more about the marriage than she had Tim and Paul.

"It's weird," he grinned one day as they ate breakfast. "I mean, I've never even met the guy, and yet I even know he likes loganberry jam on his toast!"

She didn't feel that she had anything to hide from Simon, and consequently found that she was far more relaxed with him than she'd ever been with the other two, and was beginning to let go of her obsessive grasp on Stephen's memory.

Holly and Harry noticed the change.

"You're looking really blooming!" Holly said when they met for lunch. "I think you've even put on a little weight, you're looking nice and curvy."

Lynn smiled. "Thanks, Holl! I'm very happy, I must say, you can't think how nice it feels!"

Harry said much the same thing. "When are Dom and I going to meet this man who's put the sparkle back into your eyes?"

"Whenever you like."

"Bring him round for a meal on… let's see." Harry looked in her diary. "Not this Saturday, the Saturday after."

Toni invited Swiggsy to stay for Christmas. For once, Stephen was glad to see him; the visit created a buffer between him and Toni, and she was always more sparky, happier, when one of her countrymen was staying. It also meant that Stephen was able to spend the holiday finishing the soundtrack he was writing for a film about Catherine the Great, *The Winter Palace*, without Toni making a scene because of the amount of time he was working. He didn't want to be constantly rowing with her. Everything was fine between them when he spent large amounts of time with her, or if they were attending some glittering event, but as soon as he had to work, either recording, touring or writing, she became discontented and difficult, often complaining about him to the boys, which made him very angry. He found he was becoming less and less inclined to placate her.

While Swiggsy was there, Mick Ansty, who had been GI Joe's bass player, invited them to a costume party to celebrate the new millennium. The theme was video games.

Dominic rang Stephen. "You and your boys play these ludicrous games, Markham. What do you suggest?"

Stephen had been thinking about it. Mick gave fabulous parties, and Toni loved fancy dress. They'd been thinking of spending the New Year in Australia but Toni finally decided she'd rather go to the party. Stephen's first thought had been Lara Croft for Toni; he'd always thought she'd make a perfect Lara. She had the right build and colouring and her hair was long enough for the plait; indeed, when he'd first met her that's how she'd worn it. But he figured Lara would be a popular character.

"You could go as Sonic the Hedgehog," Toni grinned. "Just paint your body blue, mate, then all you'll need in the way of costume is sneakers and gloves. It'll be a real ice-breaker!"

Then Rob suggested *Metal Gear Solid*. It was one of his favourite games, and Stephen had played it a couple of times. He agreed with Rob immediately. He could go as Solid Snake, the good guy, Dominic could go as Liquid Snake, Snake's brother and bad guy, Harry would be stunning as Meryl Silverburgh, Solid Snake's girl, and Toni – well, he couldn't wait to see her in the evil Sniper Wolf's costume. Rob had had a book for Christmas on the art of *Metal Gear Solid*, and Stephen borrowed it and looked through it one night in bed. Toni put her own book down and moved up against him, looking at it with him. Solid Snake wore a dark blue combat suit with body armour – "That colour'll suit you, Steve," Toni approved – and Liquid wore military trousers and a long, rather kinky looking, leather coat. "Hmm," Toni grinned. "Dominic will look sexy in that."

"Hey!" Stephen protested.

When they found the pictures of Meryl Silverburgh, it was Stephen's turn to be interested. She wore a figure-hugging black vest top and green combat trousers. "Wow! I'm looking forward to seeing Hal in that top!"

"Look what I wear," Toni said, pointing. Sniper Wolf wore very tight combat trousers, and a short, even tighter leather jacket, which exposed a great deal of cleavage.

Stephen whistled. "Turns me on just looking at it!" He pushed Toni down on the bed, pulled up her nightgown and gazed at her body.

She smiled up at him provocatively. "Let's pretend you're Solid Snake and I'm Sniper Wolf, and you've caught me and you're going to do unspeakable things to me."

He grinned. "OK." He got up. "Stay exactly where you are," he said as she started to protest. "I'll be right back." He pulled on his robe. She raised herself on one elbow impatiently, but true to his word, he was back almost straight away. His eyes narrowed. "I thought I told you to stay where you were. This isn't going to do you any good, Sniper." He took a pair of handcuffs out of his pocket, grabbed her wrists and snapped them on.

Toni was tremendously aroused. "Where did you get them, Ste— er, Snake?"

"They were Alex's, we got them for him in that army set, years ago, remember? Sammy was playing with them earlier, he left them on the window seat. Anyway, enough of this idle chatter. Time for your punishment, Sniper!"

The next day, she remembered Swiggsy. "Who can he go as?"

They consulted Rob. "What about Revolver Ocelot?" he mused. "No too old, and anyway, he loses his hand at the beginning of the game."

"Yuck!" Toni shivered. "How gross!"

"No good for Swiggsy," Stephen grinned. "He needs both hands to hold his pints."

Rob thought for a minute. "Hal Emmerich would be perfect." He showed them the pictures. Hal Emmerich was a thin man with a scrawny neck. They agreed. Hal Emmerich it was.

"Simon, would we like to go to a fancy dress party?"

"Sure, I like you dressing up," Simon grinned.

"The theme is video games. Who could we go as?" She thought for a minute. Simon liked retro games and she sometimes played them. Her favourite was *Toy Story*. "What about Woody and Bo Peep? You'd look great in a cowboy suit."

"Why thank you kindly, ma'am, and you'd look mighty purdy as Bo Peep. Who's giving the party?"

"Mick Ansty. We'll be staying the night."

Simon goggled at her. "Mick Ansty? We're going to a party at *Mick Ansty's* and staying the night? Bloody hell!" He felt a spurt of pleasure. He really enjoyed this unexpected bonus to dating Lynn.

"Stephen, can I speak to you for a minute?" Dominic had been waiting for them to arrive.

"Sure. You go on through, Daisy, I'll be in in a minute. What, Charlie?"

Dominic was looking splendid as Liquid Snake. "I've got a bit of, shall we say, *disturbing* news, dear brother." Rob had given them each a character profile.

Stephen grinned. "What is it, Liquid?"

"Lynn's here."

Stephen's smile faded. "How come?"

"Holly asked Mick to invite her and her boyfriend. Apparently, she and Andy thought you weren't coming."

"Fuck! That's my fault. At Christmas, we weren't sure if we were going to spend New Year in Australia, do you remember? I haven't spoken to Andy since then, he and Holly were in Barbados. I didn't know they were so friendly with Lynn."

"Holly is."

Stephen sighed. "Oh well, what can't be cured must be endured, as Cell would say. We're all in costume, anyway. Let's go and find Meryl and Sniper."

Harry and Toni were having drinks with Mario and Princess Peach.

"Hi, Steve, hi, Dom."

"Hi, Mick, hi Tina."

"Great outfits, guys," Mick said.

"You too," Dominic replied, "although I haven't a clue who you're supposed to be."

"Come on, Charlie, even you must know Super Mario," Stephen protested.

"I don't play games, dear brother," Dominic grinned.

Andy joined them, his weasely face worried. He was dressed as Link from *The Legend Of Zelda*, and looked bizarre in a green elf hat, a long green tunic, white tights and leather calf length boots.

"I'm guessing Holly is Zelda?" Stephen queried, grinning at Andy's appearance. "Sam loves that game."

"Oh ey, Steve, we didn't know you were coming, like."

"Forget it. Lynn knows the score. It'll be fine." He was far from believing that. It was all very well to say it when he and Toni were getting along, but with things the way they were at the moment, he wasn't at all sure that he might not grab Lynn's hand and run. He decided not to mention that she was here to Toni. It was a huge house, everyone was in costume, and they might not even see each other.

Toni was dancing with George, who was dressed as the Terminator. It suited him. He'd lost his excess weight and was looking better than he'd done for a long time.

"Poor old George," Fin said. He and Shelagh were dressed as characters from one of the *Final Fantasy* games, Cloud and Tifa, Stephen thought, but he wasn't sure. Fin was wearing a purple sleeveless jumpsuit with a metallic shoulder pad and knee length black boots, and Shelagh was dressed in a white vest top which was little more than a sports bra, and a very short black denim skirt with braces which went either side of her breasts, emphasising them tremendously.

"Why?" Stephen asked. "You two look good," he added, trying not to stare at Shelagh's breasts.

"Thanks, Steve, so do you. He's given up smoking and spent months getting into shape, and Alicia's left him for some actor."

"Yeah, miserable tart!" Andy agreed.

Holly came over. She looked sweet as Zelda, in a long white dress with a purple bodice.

Stephen kissed her. "You look very pretty." He and Holly liked one another very much and flirted with each other outrageously

She hugged him. "I'm really sorry, Steve."

"Forget it. We didn't know if we were coming till the last minute."

Holly looked at Andy. "Have you told him yet?"

"Told me what?"

Andy grinned. "You know that house that's for sale about ten miles from Burford, Windrush Manor? Guess who's bought it." He put his arm around Holly, and she beamed up at Stephen.

"Oh, wow! That's great news! As they say in Yorkshire, I'm made up! Will your three be going to the same school as ours?"

Holly's smile got even wider. "Our four."

Stephen's eyebrows shot up. "Congratulations!" He hugged them both. "When's it due?"

"July."

George and Toni came over, laughing.

"I'm off for to get a drink," George said. "I'll be back!"

"Come on, Snake!" Toni grabbed Stephen. "Dance with me."

Stephen whisked her off. They were joined by Liquid and Meryl, and threw themselves energetically around the dance floor for a while before collapsing into easy chairs.

"I'm getting too old for this!" Dominic groaned.

"I'm going to find the food," Stephen said. "Hey, where's Swiggsy?" He realised he hadn't seen him since they arrived.

Toni grinned. "He'll be knocking back the grog somewhere. Get me something to eat, Stevo."

God! Poor Mick! thought Stephen. He wandered out to find the buffet and bumped into Lynn.

"Oh! Stephen!" she said, confused. "Holly said you were here. I didn't – that is, we thought…"

"Yes, I know, it's my fault, I didn't think we were coming, and then we did. Don't worry about it. I like your costume." He did, very much, the shepherdess style dress suited her figure to perfection. She looked like an exquisite piece of porcelain.

"I'm Bo Peep, from *Toy Story*. Who are you?"

"Solid Snake. From *Metal Gear Solid*."

She looked blank. "I don't know much about these games, but you look… you look good." She really wanted to say, 'You look incredibly handsome', but didn't dare.

Then he took her by surprise. "You look beautiful. Happy New Year, Lynn." He kissed her cheek and walked away without a backward glance.

He found the buffet and filled a plate for himself and Toni, but when he got back she wasn't there. "Where's Daisy?" he asked Harry and Dominic.

Harry shrugged. "She went after you. I expect she got sidetracked. Can I have one of those sausage rolls?"

To his surprise and annoyance, Toni ignored him pointedly for the rest of the evening, spending it dancing and flirting, mostly with George.

By one o clock, he'd had enough. He went up to their bedroom, sat in an armchair and waited. Eventually, he fell asleep.

He was woken by the door slamming. Toni didn't even glance at him. She went straight into the ensuite.

He looked at his watch. It was nearly five. He got to his feet and followed her in. "Enjoy yourself, did you?"

She ignored him and carried on removing her make up.

He could feel his temper rising. "Perhaps you'd care to explain your atrocious behaviour?"

She turned on him, her face a mask of fury. "My atrocious behaviour? What about *yours*? I saw you kissing her! How the fuck could you do that to me, you miserable little bastard? If you'd told me you'd invited her I would never have come! Am I the last to know? Are all your friends laughing about it? George couldn't believe you'd do that to me!"

"I wish George would keep his fucking opinions to himself!" Stephen said, furiously. "I didn't invite her, Andy did, because, if you remember, when we were first invited we weren't going to go. I didn't know she'd be here! I just gave her a peck on the cheek and said Happy New Year."

"It wasn't the New Year when you kissed her."

"Oh, don't be so fucking childish! Look, Toni, the bottom line here is I didn't know my ex-wife would be at the party but she was, so we exchanged impersonal pleasantries, and I gave her a happy New Year kiss on the cheek. After that I didn't see or speak to her for the rest of the evening, you know that."

"*How* would I know that?"

He caught her by the arm. "Yeah, that's right, how would you, you were too busy getting touched up on the dance floor! I'm fed up with your jealous behaviour and I'm sick to death of you making scenes!" He flung her away, and she staggered against the bath.

He went into the bedroom, and started to undress. What is the point? he asked himself despairingly.

Toni came out of the ensuite. She was naked, her skin smooth and creamy and inviting. She raised her eyebrows and smiled at him.

"What's this?" he asked, bewildered.

She shrugged. "Oh, you know, mate. Perhaps I was a bit hasty." She twined an arm round his neck and kissed him, guiding his hand to her breasts and moving impatiently against him.

He pushed her gently down onto the bed.

The following week, Dominic drove to the Priory. "Steve…"

"*Steve* is it, for all love? Whatever you want, you must be pretty desperate."

"Merely being fucking friendly, old chap. Although, now you come to mention it, I did rather hope you'd give me a hand."

"What is it?"

"I've written this song for our wedding anniversary…"

"Charlie, we're not actually married, we're just good friends."

"Shut up, Markham, you moron, and listen. I wondered if you'd play your Sellas on it."

Stephen had recently acquired an original seventeenth century guitar attributed to Matteo Sellas, a maker of guitars and lutes in Venice. It was a beautiful instrument; a five course guitar, made of ebony and ivory, with a foliate design on the fingerboard, and a three dimensional rose with a star design. He had played it on several of the songs on 'Beggars Can't Be Jesus'. He stared at Dominic. "Why me?"

"You're the best," Dominic said simply. "I want it to be as good as it can be."

Stephen was touched. "You want to record here?"

Dominic nodded.

"OK. When do you want to start?"

The song was called 'The Loving Cup'. "It's beautiful, Charlie," Stephen said, sincerely, when they'd finally got it done to Dominic's satisfaction. "Harry will be overwhelmed. Why the loving cup?" he asked, casually.

Dominic shrugged. "I don't know. I liked the symbolism; the two handled cup, the lovers sharing it." He finished his coffee. "Anyway, I must go, I've got some things to do this afternoon. Thanks again, Stephen."

"My pleasure." Stephen now knew exactly what to get them for their anniversary. That morning he'd been online checking some historical details for *The Winter Palace*, the soundtrack he was writing, and he'd come across a website that sold Russian silver. He knew Dominic and Harry had some pieces, Dominic had always liked it, and he'd introduced Harry to it. One of the items on the website had been an exquisite loving cup. Stephen went into his study and ordered it.

Turtle died at the beginning of February. He'd had heart problems for the past eighteen months, and had been on medication, and he collapsed early one morning. Stephen and Alex took him to the vet, where he was put to sleep. It was shocking; he wasn't even eleven. They rang Rob, who drove home, shaken and saddened, but in fact it was Alex who was the most upset. He had looked after Turtle while Rob was at university and during the summers when Rob was working at Markham Cavendish. It had been he who had given Turtle his tablets, and, in the last few months, he'd had Turtle's basket in his room at night. They had the little dog cremated the next day, and buried the ashes in the garden.

A week or so later, Stephen went to find Alex. He'd been very quiet and withdrawn since Turtle's death. He was lying on his bed, Turtle's collar and lead on the nightstand next to him.

"Can I come in, Ally?"

Alex looked up. "I'm not crying," he said defensively.

"I know. That happens to me, it's not that I cry, simply that my eyes water with sorrow."

Alex smiled weakly. "I know he was just a dog..."

Stephen sat on the bed next to him. "He wasn't just a dog, he was Turtle. He was a member of the family."

Alex leant against him. "Thanks, Dad."

"Al, you were wonderful with him. You made his last few months really happy, I've never seen a happier little dog. He loved you just as much as he loved Blue."

Alex sighed. "He wasn't my dog though."

"Well, that's the reason I wanted to talk to you. I was at the Rescue Centre yesterday. There's a lovely little puppy there. Would you like him?"

"Oh, Dad!" Alex stared at him, astounded. "Yes, please! He'll never take Turtle's place, of course," he added.

"Course he won't, he'll make his own place. Let's get our shoes on."

"Are we going now?" Alex asked excitedly.

"Certainly are!" Stephen ruffled his dark hair.

Alex flung his arms round him. "I love you Dad, even if you *are* mean to Mum."

Stephen was horrified. "What do you mean, Ally?" he asked, hugging him back.

"Oh, you know," Alex moved away and put on a pair of socks. "She's always crying because you go off on tour and have fun and leave her all alone and stuff. What kind of puppy is he?"

"Um, he's bigger than Turtle was," Stephen said. Whatever the state of their marriage at the moment, how could Toni let the boys think he was mean to her? The bitch, the absolute bitch. Surely she could see it hurt the boys as well as him? He stopped himself thinking about it. He'd talk to her later. Right now, he had to concentrate on Alex.

The puppy was an Irish wolfhound cross. No one knew what he was crossed with, but he was very appealing. He leapt at Alex and licked him frantically, squirming in his arms in an effort to get closer to him, and uttering high pitched little barks.

"What are you going to call him?" Stephen asked as they drove home.

"Cruncher Feet."

"Cruncher Feet! What a great name!" Stephen exclaimed, starting to laugh.

"Thanks, Dad." Alex sighed with pleasure. "This is the best day of my life!"

"Toni," Stephen said as he was getting ready for bed, "please don't cry and tell the boys that I bugger off and leave you to cope all on your own when I'm touring."

Toni was sitting in bed, reading. She stared at him. "Who said I do that?"

"One of the boys told me."

She flushed. "Which one?"

"Never mind. Just don't do it, all right?"

"I'll do what I want," she said hotly. "After all, it's true, you don't *have* to tour. Look at Pip's birth! Where were you? Touring! You'll be off again in a couple of months, having fun. Can you deny you have fun?"

"Yes I can, in the sense that *you* mean it." Stephen got into bed. "I do have fun, because I love touring. I love being up on that stage playing my music, I love the interaction, I love the audience reaction. Everything else about touring is crap. I do *not* have wild parties, as I tell you over and over. Not even George parties that much any more. And as for Pip's birth, he was nearly three weeks early."

"Even so, if you had a normal job, you'd have been there."

He lost his temper. She was wearing her black pearls, as she almost always did. He grabbed them and pulled hard. She jerked forward, and the necklace broke, sending the pearls flying off in all directions. "If I had a normal job, you wouldn't have those!"

She burst into tears. "That hurt! And my pearls! They're everywhere!"

"Tough." He turned off his bedside light. "Just don't tell the boys I treat you badly."

She'd got out of bed and was searching for her pearls. She leapt back onto the bed and thumped him hard. "You do! You bloody do, you bastard!"

He sat up, grabbed her arms and shook her viciously. Her head snapped backwards and forwards. She gave a terrified cry. He let go of her, horrified. "Toni!"

She collapsed into his arms, crying.

"God, Toni, we can't go on like this!" he said, shocked by the violence of his feelings towards her.

She leant against him, sobbing. "Don't you love me any more, Stevo?"

"Perhaps we ought to see Madeleine again." She nodded. "Although Toni – maybe we should split up. We're not making each other happy."

She stared at him, her eyes full of tears. "You want to dump me?" She began to wail loudly.

"No. Shush, shush." He stroked her hair. "I don't want to dump you, Toni. I just want to be happy again. Both of us to be happy. And I don't want the boys thinking bad things about me! They're our children and I don't want them disliking me because you're dissatisfied with me."

Toni sat back and reached for a tissue. "I'll ring Madeleine. We'll be right, Stevo, we will. Perhaps I'm just miserable because I'm going to be forty soon." It was her fortieth birthday on the twenty ninth of February, and she wasn't looking forward to it.

Stephen had worked out that it was the tenth twenty ninth of February since she'd been born, and he'd got cards for her that said 'Happy Tenth Birthday'. He'd also planned a trip to Japan, a place she loved, with a surprise visit to Tahiti afterwards.

"Maybe," he said. "OK, we'll talk to Madeleine." He helped her find her pearls. "I'm sorry. And I'm sorry I shook you, Toni. Did I hurt you very much?" How could he be violent to her? That was unforgivable.

"Not too much," she said pathetically, cuddling up to him.

He kissed her. "It can't be right, these scenes."

"Just make love to me."

She was touched by her birthday cards. One of them had a 'Ten Years Old Today' badge on it, and she wore it on the plane to Japan. Stephen had had her pearls restrung, and had bought her matching earrings and a bracelet for her birthday.

In Japan, they called in to see Kagami and the twins. By a strange coincidence, George was also visiting, although Stephen couldn't help wondering if it *was* coincidence, Toni and his surprise at seeing each other seemed a touch overdone. On the way home, he and Toni stopped off in Tahiti. Toni was overwhelmed by everything, and was very loving. If only it lasted, Stephen thought and was shocked by his cynicism. It was that, more than anything else, which made him wonder how much longer they could stay together.

"The alterations are finally finished! Would you and Simon like to spend next weekend at Windrush Manor with us, Lynn?" Holly asked when they met for lunch one Saturday in April. She smiled happily. "I love saying 'Windrush Manor', it sounds so posh!" She'd been born in a council house in Hereford and had a tremendous lack of self-confidence over this, which had amazed Lynn when she'd discovered it, Holly was always so confident in front of the cameras. "Oh, that's totally different," she'd laughed, when Lynn said this to her.

Lynn smiled at her fondly. "Holly, we'd love to."

"Great, I've got a load of catalogues and samples of furniture material and stuff."

"I can't wait to see what you're getting."

Holly looked crestfallen. "I hoped you'd help choose."

"God, Holl, I'm hopeless at that sort of thing! You've seen my house! Just get what you and Andy like."

"I'd rather you helped too," Holly said. "Oh, you know I had my scan? Well, it's a girl and Andy wants to call her Ivy. Can we give her Cherilynn as a second name?"

Lynn's eyes filled with tears.

Holly said, hastily, "Of course, you'll have children of your own, Lynn, you will."

"It's not that." Lynn scrabbled for a tissue. "I'm just really touched."

"Did you see Toni's book is out?" Holly tried to change the subject.

Lynn grinned. "Out of the frying pan into the fire, Holl! I'm just as likely to get emotional over that."

Holly was shocked. "B-but Simon!" she stammered.

"I know. I do love him."

"But you love Stephen more?" Holly asked gently.

Lynn nodded guiltily.

"Oh, Lynn! I'm really sorry."

"So am I," sighed Lynn.

She did love Simon. She spent most weekends at his house and she was happier than she'd been for a long time. He never minded her listening to Sid's Six, or buying magazines that contained interviews with Stephen, he often bought guitar and music magazines anyway, and she combed them for mention of Stephen and the band.

Simon had pupils on Saturday mornings, so she shopped for the weekend while he was teaching. Both of them were indifferent cooks, so she'd bought a cookbook and was determined to teach herself. She was still learning to play the guitar, and had become reasonably proficient. She was teaching Simon to play the flute; to her chagrin, he was very good. On Sundays, they spent the morning in bed, reading the papers and making love. They'd get up around midday, shower, and go to the pub for lunch. Simon put on weight easily, and Lynn usually made him go for a walk after lunch, unless the weather was appalling. This Sunday, it was pouring with rain. They ran home from the pub, and Lynn made them a cup of tea.

They sat on the sofa, cuddled up together.

"Did I tell you Holly and Andy want us to go and stay with them next weekend?"

"No!" Simon grinned. "I can't believe the way we hobnob with the rich and famous these days! Talking of Hobnobs?"

Lynn laughed. "Yes, I got some. I put them in the biscuit barrel."

When they arrived at Windrush Manor, Andy gave them a guided tour, and then Lynn and Holly settled down to look at decorating brochures while he and Simon played pool in his den.

At three thirty, to Holly's consternation, Stephen, Toni, and the boys arrived.

"Andy invited us to tea, to see the alterations," Stephen explained, following Holly into the sitting room. "Hello, Lynn." She looks lovelier every time I see her, he thought longingly.

Andy appeared in the doorway, with Simon, who was wearing a very old Sid's Six tee shirt, behind him. The tee shirt had the band's logo on it; a Strat resting against a bar stool, and the words 'Sid's Six' printed underneath.

"Erm… Steve, Toni, this is Simon, Lynn's boyfriend, like," Andy mumbled. He gave Holly an apologetic glance.

"I didn't know you were a fan," Stephen said, surprised. He peered at the faded tee shirt. "What tour is that?"

"Tabula Rasa. I'm not only a fan, I'm an old fan!"

"I think you know Lynn, Toni," Andy said, embarrassed.

"I think I do," Toni said grimly, her face thunderous.

Lynn's face was scarlet. "Perhaps we ought to go," she said imploringly to Simon.

Stephen and Simon had started a conversation about Stanton Crawford. "What?" Stephen said. "Oh, surely not?"

Toni shot him an evil look.

"I thought we were staying the night," Simon said. He very much wanted to stay and talk to Stephen.

"You are." Holly was even more embarrassed than Lynn. "This is your fault, Andrew!"

"Oh ey, I'm really sorry!" Andy's weasely face was mortified.

"Oh, well, no harm done," Stephen said. He liked Simon, he was the first of Lynn's partners with whom he felt any affinity. They chatted for a while, Toni making her displeasure obvious. Stephen ignored her. He entertained her friends on a regular basis, particularly Swiggsy. On the way home, she hardly spoke to him. He couldn't be bothered to try to cajole her. He found that the Beatles song, 'Girl', was playing in his head on a continual loop these days, as it had at the start of their relationship: *'When I think of all the times I've tried so hard to leave her, she would turn to me and start to cry, And she promises the earth to me and I believe her, after all this time I don't know why.'* It filled him with despair.

The following week, the band was touring Australia. It was the school holidays, and Toni and the boys flew over with them. Shelagh came, too, bringing Ben, who was nearly five.

Toni very pointedly ignored Stephen and spent her time talking to Shelagh or George. Since her book had come out, she'd been spending time in London. Stephen knew she saw a great deal of George, she was constantly saying, 'George says' or 'George thinks'. Somehow, though, he knew they weren't having an affair. Sometimes, their closeness worried him. Sometimes, he was glad she had someone she felt as close to as he did to Harry. He really didn't know what to think. He and Toni were seeing Madeleine again. He just hoped that was enough.

In August, they flew to Los Angeles as guests at Coral's wedding to the movie star Justin Page, who was playing the villain in the latest Verity Linden film, *Daybreak*, for which Stephen was once again writing the soundtrack.

Toni was torn between not wanting to see Coral and not wanting to miss out on the glamour and excitement. Justin was the latest big thing in Hollywood.

She had started a new book called *Albert's Watch*. It was the story of a boy who saved his mother and brother's lives during an air raid on the East End in 1940. *Bunyip The Brave* had been a huge success, particularly in the USA, and Toni had become something of a celebrity in her own right. She wallowed in the limelight and gave several interviews while they were in America.

In September, Harry and Dominic gave a dinner party at Leezance House. Like Andy and Holly, they'd had a lot of alterations done, and had only recently moved in.

Ted was overwhelmed by Harry being mistress of the place. He still hadn't got over the fact that his little princess was now Lady Chaplin. "I mean, it seems only yesterday you were doing gigs at the Angel!" he marvelled. He looked at Stephen. "I've got so much to thank you for, Steve," he said emotionally. "If it hadn't been for you forming that band, I've never have met Sian, and Harriet would never have met Dominic."

"Some people might say that would have been a good thing for Harry," Stephen joked.

"Fuck off, Markham." Dominic punched him on the shoulder.

Stephen grinned and, looking round for Sian, saw her sitting alone. There was something he wanted to know. "Mum?"

She jumped. "Stevie! I was miles away." She patted the sofa. "Come and talk to me, cariad."

Stephen sat down. "Mum, what made you fall in love with Ted?"

Sian looked at him quizzically. "What an odd question!"

"Yeah, I know, but what? He's so different to Dad, and I don't mean any of this in a derogatory way, I just want to know. There was such a connection between the two of you right from the first time you met."

Sian thought back. "Yes, there was," she said, smiling affectionately.

"Well, why?"

She shrugged. "Lots of reasons, really, but one of the main one was maternal."

Stephen stared at her. "You wanted his baby?"

She gave a peal of laughter. "No, you twit! He made me *feel* maternal. I wanted to look after him."

"Ted?" Stephen was amazed.

"Oh, yes." Sian was perfectly serious. "Your father never needed looking after; well, only in the way that all wives – in those days – looked after their husbands. He never needed me the way Ted does. His career always came first. He was very self-possessed. Like you. You're asking because of Toni's friendship with George, aren't you?"

"How did you know?"

"Because it *is* like me and Ted in lots of ways. There's nothing going on there except a mutual dependency. George needs looking after in a way you never did and never will. That maternal instinct, it's really the only thing Toni and I have in common."

This was too much for Stephen. He snorted. "Maternal instinct indeed!" He told her how Toni had told Alex he didn't love him.

Sian looked grave. "Yes, that was very wrong of her. But I don't think she meant to hurt Alex. She lashed out at you with whatever weapon came to hand. After all, how else can she hurt you? You've a very strong character, Stephen, you're much stronger than she is; when she has an affair, you don't go to pieces and beg her not to leave you, you simply go ahead and do the same, with a very attractive girl who is a real threat to her."

"How did you know about the affairs?" asked Stephen, aghast.

"Well, yours was splashed all over the papers," Sian said acerbically. "And Toni told me everything. She tells me a lot, we get on very well. I'm not blaming you, cariad. She shouldn't have had that affair. But in some ways, you can't blame her. You were working with pretty little Coral and she was stuck at home coping with Sam. And you were always so hard on her about Sammy, Stephen. She did her very best, and let's be honest, she was always there for him, she never left him to go off and do something she enjoyed. I never heard him asking where Janine had gone, only ever Doctor Venkman."

Stephen was stunned. He opened his mouth to speak, but she shook her head, putting her hand on his. "I'm not saying it's your fault, Stevie, I'm just pointing it out. It's a mess. So very sad, both of you hurt and unhappy. And you don't really need her, Stevie, not like she needs you. You're like John. How ironic! He always said you were! The only thing you really need is your career. Your music. Playing that damn guitar. Lynn always knew that, she always accepted that she was second best, but she didn't care. She knew she meant more to you than any woman ever could. When you first met Toni, you were lost and unhappy. You'd split up with Coral, you were afraid you'd never be able to sustain a relationship again, your life had no meaning. You *did* need her then. But that didn't last long, did it? You had your sons, and your career became phenomenal. Toni needs to be needed, and she needs someone who'll concentrate solely on her and her children. She can't cope with you – and she's not even second best, is she, Stephen? Lynn still is. Two mistresses Toni can never compete with. Your music and your memories."

He stared at her, ashen. He couldn't believe Sian – *Sian* – was saying these things to him in that calm and even voice. It was as if she was holding up a mirror and forcing him to confront a self he'd never acknowledged.

"But it's not your fault Toni is the person she is," Sian said, her eyes compassionate. "It's all such a terrible pity. And cariad, I know how much your boys mean to you, I wasn't talking about your relationship with them when I said all you needed was your music."

"What should I do?" Stephen asked. "What *can* I do?" he said, his voice anguished. "I don't want Toni and me to split up, but what we've got at the moment isn't worth holding on to!"

"Do you love her?"

Stephen sighed. "I don't know."

Sian shrugged. "That's something you have to sort out. If you do love her, you'll have to work incredibly hard to get the relationship straight. If you don't love her, what's the point?"

"The boys—" Stephen began, but Sian cut him off.

"No. Don't say 'the boys'. You've already told me how Toni used Alex as a pawn in the nasty little games you both play."

"Mum!" He was stricken. "I don't! I don't play games with her!"

"All those times you've bumped into Lynn accidentally?"

"They *were* accidents, and anyway…" He was about to say *it doesn't happen any more*, when he remembered how they'd met at Andy's. That *had* been an accident, but Toni had annoyed him and he'd been very attentive to Lynn. Deliberately. And then he'd asked Andy when she'd next be there, and had gone then too. God, Sian was right.

"Freud says there are no accidents," she was saying. "Hello, cariad!" Pip had come to sit with them. "Are you having fun?"

Stephen sat, not really listening to their conversation. He vaguely heard Pip telling Sian how much he was enjoying himself and what fun Mab Chaplin was. He didn't know what to do. He didn't know if he still loved Toni, but he was damn certain that a lot of the time he disliked her excessively. In two weeks, Sid's Six would be touring, and then recording 'Electric Playground', the new album. He decided not to do anything yet. He and Toni were still seeing Madeleine. He'd let things coast until the New Year. If they were no happier then, he'd leave.

On November the fourth he was forty. He was surprised by how undifferent he felt. Toni had loathed being forty and Harry was constantly bemoaning the fact that she'd be forty the following June. He'd expected to wake up and feel old.

Euterpe had arranged a surprise party for him. Toni, Harry and Dominic had planned it with the record company, who'd wanted a huge affair at the Ritz, all celebrity guests and glitter. Toni had been in favour, but Harry and Dominic argued that Stephen would hate it.

"It's his fucking birthday party, not a celebrity filled publicity event for Muse! He'll want his friends there," Dominic said, annoyed.

"His friends are celebrities!" Toni retorted.

Dominic frowned at her. "Yeah, but not all of them!" He picked up the list of guests. "Don't be stupid, Toni, he barely knows some of the people on here!" he fumed. "I mean, look at this – Li'l Bow Wow! For Christ's sake!" He scanned the list further. "Yes, and Steve can't stand Em…"

"I think what Dom means," Harry interrupted, putting a restraining hand on Dominic's arm, "is that Steve would want something less, well, showy, with people he knows and likes, whether they're famous or not. I mean, he's still sees friends from school and university – and you and he have got lots of friends in Oxford, Toni. I'm sure you'd both like them to be there."

Toni was forced to agree, and she added that Stephen would rather money was donated to the Markham Charitable Foundation, which he'd set up at the beginning of the nineties, than that presents were bought for him. Eventually, they agreed to hold the party at the Grosvenor House Hotel, and the guest list was amended.

"Are we inviting Coral?" Dominic asked, rather hesitantly.

They all looked at Toni.

She bit her lip. "OK. If Justin comes too." She quite fancied Justin. He was a bit young, only twenty eight, six years younger than Coral and twelve years younger than she was. But she didn't look her age, everyone said so. And he was pretty gorgeous. Although not as gorgeous as Stephen. She sighed. No one was. Why, then, was their marriage such a mess?

"And Simon and Lynn?" Dominic asked even more hesitantly.

"No fucking way!" Toni exclaimed.

"OK," Dominic said, meekly. "I only asked because I know you've all met up at Andy's a couple of times, and Steve likes Simon."

"No," Toni said again.

Dominic left it. He and Harry were seriously worried about Stephen and Toni's marriage. "For Christ's sake, you tactless git!" Harry said to him later. "For someone who comes home from producing this album at the Priory every day and tells me how awful the atmosphere is, you certainly know how to stir it!"

"It's Steve's birthday," Dominic pointed out. "If he wants Lynn, he should have her. At the party, I mean."

"You're not going to ask him, are you?" Harry was alarmed by the look on his face.

"I thought I might," he said, stubbornly.

"No, Dominic! We can't interfere, all we can do is be here for him. Anyway, it'd ruin the surprise."

Dominic sighed. "I guess you're right, baby. Poor bloody Markham! I can't believe he could've married you and didn't, the man must be mental!" He pulled her to him and kissed her, running his hands over her body. "You're still the sexiest girl I've ever seen! Let's go to bed."

Stephen was delighted with his party, utterly taken by surprise. He was also highly appreciative of the large donations Euterpe and the guests made to the Foundation. Harry, Ray and Graham, with Dominic on lead guitar and vocals, performed some of The Brigands' old sets. Stephen found this a peculiar experience; not to be playing, and watching Dominic take his place, was somehow unnerving, and it brought back so many memories.

When they'd finished, someone shouted, "Come on, Steve – play us something!"

Dominic handed him his guitar.

"OK." He looked at Toni. "For you, Daisy." He played 'With All My Heart'.

Toni started to cry, and George put his arm around her.

There was a hush afterwards, and then Harry said, "Come on, Stevie, let's do 'Kissing In The Crypt'!" This was a rockabilly number Stephen had written just before The Brigands broke up. It dispelled the mood and got everyone dancing.

When they finally got to bed in the early hours of the morning, Stephen made love to Toni very tenderly. "We have so much going for us, my Daisy," he said. "Let's try to hold on to it."

Toni clung to him. "I really want that, Stevo."

And yet somehow Stephen felt they were like two shipwreck victims. The wreck was all they had in common.

The recording was almost finished by Christmas. They were all tired, and decided to take a break over the holiday. The band was performing in a charity concert on the second Saturday in January in Newcastle, and they agreed to carry on recording afterwards.

Toni invited Swiggsy to stay for Christmas again. This time, Stephen wasn't pleased. "We need time to ourselves, Toni!"

"He's got nowhere else to go, Steve!"

"What about his fucking family? He's always going on about how wonderful they are!"

"That's only when he's a bit tanked. They're not very nice, and they don't really like him."

"That's one thing they and I have in common, then!"

Toni's face hardened. "Well, he's my friend, and I've invited him. This is my house too!"

Swiggsy turned up with another old friend from Brisbane, Frogeyes, so called because he'd had a squint at school, and had needed to wear thick glasses to correct it. Stephen had nothing against Frogeyes, he was an agreeable man, presentable and quietly spoken, and he did his best to restrain Swiggsy's alcoholic tendencies, unfortunately with little effect. Stephen grew to dread hearing 'Aw, no!', these being the words Frogeyes would utter when he found Swiggsy out cold somewhere. In retaliation, he held an impromptu cocktail party and invited Lynn and Simon.

Toni went mad. "How could you?" she screamed at him when he told her.

"Be quiet, you'll upset the boys," Stephen said coldly. "She's my friend and I've invited her. It's my house too." Suddenly, he couldn't believe how childish he'd been. "Toni, we've got to talk!"

"Fuck off! I'll make you sorry, you bastard!" she hissed and ran from the room.

Stephen marched over to the studio to play guitar. Eventually he cooled down and went back to the house to talk to her.

Rob was sitting in the kitchen, reading. He looked up and sighed. "If you're looking for Toni, she and Swiggs and Frogeyes have gone to London. She says they'll be back for Alex's birthday."

Stephen gritted his teeth. "Well, she needn't fucking bother."

"Oh, Dad, don't you be childish too! You two have got to sort yourselves out."

"Who the hell do you think you are?" Stephen demanded. "How dare you talk to me like that?"

Rob went back to his book.

"Robert! I'm talking to you!"

"You're ranting at me," Rob said quietly. "When you've calmed down, we'll talk."

Stephen stared at him. He burst out laughing. "My God! You sounded just like Dad! OK, OK, you're right. When she comes back, I'll talk to her."

Toni came back alone. Even Swiggsy, that most thoughtless of men, had realised he'd outstayed his welcome. "We've got to talk, Stephen."

"I know."

They looked at each other.

"Good party?" Toni asked eventually.

"Very," Stephen answered politely. "Everyone said it was fun. Except George, who, as you no doubt know, didn't come."

"No. He took me out."

Stephen licked his lips. "What are we going to do, Toni? Do you want to split up?"

She sank down onto the sofa. "Oh, Stephen, it seems wrong to let it go without a fight."

"Christ, we don't need any more fights!"

Toni smiled weakly. "No. Shall we give it one last try?"

He shrugged. "Do you want to? *Really* want to?"

"Was Lynn at the party?"

"Yep."

"Did... did anything happen?"

"Nope. I talked to her, that's all, in a group of people." He smiled. "I actually talked to Simon more. I like him very much."

"Oh, you approve?" Toni said sarcastically. "I'm sorry!" she added. "That's not trying, is it?"

"Fucking trying!" Stephen sat next to her and took her hand. "OK, Toni. Let's make our stand here."

"You mean like Custer?" she asked quietly.

A few days before the concert, Stephen came down with an ear infection. Henry prescribed antibiotics and he felt fine, but he couldn't fly, so he decided to drive up to Newcastle. Rob's term didn't start until the following week, but Julia, who had finally passed her driving test in the Christmas holidays, had started back to Newcastle the week before. Her parents had bought her a small car for her twenty first birthday, and she had driven it up to university. Rob had gone with her. Stephen was going to pick him up on the Sunday morning and drive him back down. Sam's piano teacher was putting on a concert that afternoon, with Sam as her star performer, and they aimed to be back in time for it.

On the Thursday before, after Stephen had read to Sam, he waited while Sam performed his nightly routine; putting his underwear out for the next day and arranging the socks carefully and symmetrically on the underpants, making sure his curtains met precisely in the middle, that his action figures were standing in a straight line, and lining up his torch, notebook and watch on his nightstand. He also arranged his music books in alphabetical order, and checked that his rug was at the correct angle to the wall.

Stephen frowned. They'd been encouraging him to loosen up on these inflexible rituals, and lately he'd managed to let those last two go.

Sam got into bed, and pulled the covers carefully round him. He glanced at Stephen out of the corners of his eyes, and then looked quickly away. "I wish you could come to my concert, Dr Venkman. Concert, concert, concert." He only avoided eye contact and repeated himself now when he was distressed, and he hadn't called Stephen Dr Venkman for years.

Stephen was very concerned. "I am coming to your concert, Sammy. You know that, cariad."

"Mummy said you were going to your concert. Your concert, to your concert."

"I am, but I'll be back in loads of time. I'm bringing Blue down to see you, remember?"

"Mummy says you'll be too busy having a party to come. Too busy having a party." Sam's mouth drooped and his gaze moved agitatedly round the room.

Something inside Stephen snapped. This was it. The last straw. They were both supposed to be at least trying to keep the marriage going. It was pointless. Toni would never change. And he didn't think he'd ever be able to forgive her for stressing Sam out like this.

"Mummy's silly!" he said lightly. "I'm much too old for late night parties now! I get way too tired, you'd think Mummy would remember that. Of course I'll be at your concert, Sammy! What I'll do is, I'll go a little earlier, drive up there tonight, and then I'm sure to be back in time. Nothing could stop me, I'll be clapping louder than anyone else at the end, they'll have to tell me to shut up."

Sam giggled. "Goodnight, Daddy."

"Goodnight, my little Mozart. I love you, and I'll see you on Sunday morning. You take care, and have a good day at school tomorrow." Stephen kissed his forehead very lightly; Sam still didn't like being touched. He lay rigid under Stephen's kiss. Stephen felt a wave of grief and pity wash over him, and had a desperate longing to take the tense little boy in his arms, but he knew that would freak him out totally. He turned on the night-light and, turning off the main light, went out, shutting the door behind him. He leant against the wall, his heart thudding.

Pip went past. "Are you OK, Dad?"

"Fine, Pip, um, a bit hungry."

Pip grinned. "Right!"

"Listen, little Pipkin, I've just found out I've got to be at the concert earlier than I thought, so I'm going tonight. I'll be back for Sam's concert, OK?"

Pip shrugged. "OK, Dad."

Stephen kissed him. "I love you."

Pip frowned. "Are you sure you're OK?"

Stephen nodded. "Hunger makes me weird. Where's Alex?"

"In his room."

Stephen said goodbye to Alex, kissed him, and told him he loved him. "Look after Mum when I'm gone, you're the man of the house! I'll definitely be back in time for Sammy's concert."

"Stephen? What are you doing?"

He went on furiously throwing clothes into the suitcase. "Packing."

"What on earth for?"

"Newcastle."

Toni came round the bed and took his arm. He shook her off.

"Stephen, will you stop doing that and talk to me! What do you mean, Newcastle?"

He turned to face her. "Newcastle, remember? The gig. That thing I do that brings the money into the house so that you can live in the manner to which you have become accustomed. Also, incidentally, according to you, the gig where I am going to piss off afterwards partying with the lads, ending up stoned out of my brain in bed with a couple of randy little groupies and forget all about picking Rob up and driving home for Sam's concert."

She sank down on the bed. "Oh."

"Yeah, 'oh'. Why do you do it, Toni? Why do you belittle me to the boys? I'd beg in the streets for them, you know that."

She stared down at her hands. "The concert isn't until Saturday."

"I'll stay at Cheyne Walk."

"So what's this, then? Our marriage is over because I exaggerated a little to the boys? That's a bit childish, don't you think?"

He was very angry now. "That wasn't exaggeration, Toni, that was pure, bloody malice. You deliberately hurt Sam to hurt me. Why? And we were supposed to be trying, remember? Our last stand? I don't understand why you'd do something like that to Sammy, anyway. How could you? You know he can't cope with stress. For Christ's sake, Toni, it's not as if it's something new, even before we found out he was autistic, we knew that!"

"Oh, spare me the moral lecture. I was pissed off over that party. It suddenly struck me, you invited *her* to *my* house!"

"Yes, I did. And it was childish of me, but it's over now, for Christ's sweet sake!"

"Is it?" she flashed up at him. "I've only got *your* word that nothing happened! After all, you were unfaithful to me – *and* to her!"

Stephen inhaled sharply. He grabbed her by the elbows and pulled her up. "You bitch! Yeah, all right, Toni, in front of all the other guests, I fucked Lynn senseless. You happy now?"

She yanked her arm free and slapped him hard across the face. He slapped her back.

She gasped and stared at him, her hand to her face.

His own cheek was stinging, and the chunky cocktail rings she wore had bitten into his skin, but he was stunned by what he'd done. He had never hit a woman before, ever. "*God*, Toni, I'm so sorry. Are you OK?"

To his amazement, she smiled slowly up at him. "I started it. You're bleeding, come here." She wound her arms round his neck and licked the beads of blood from the scratch her rings had left along his cheekbone.

He stared at her. "Don't tell me that turned you on!"

She pressed her body against his and rubbed her hands up and down his back. "You too, it seems."

"That's just a physiological reaction to your breasts." He held her away from him a little, thinking of other times he'd been angry with her and they'd had a scene, and she'd practically melted into his arms. She'd always wanted sex, and he'd always assumed that he'd frightened her and that she wanted him to soothe her, and he'd been ultra gentle, ultra loving. Was *this* what she'd wanted? For him to *hurt* her?

"Really, Toni. Did it turn you on?"

She nodded. "I guess I'm just a full blooded girl who likes her men macho, mate."

He pulled away from her.

She frowned. "What does it matter, Stephen? Right now, I find you incredibly attractive. You know, perhaps that's been the trouble with our marriage. I like it when you're… I don't know… *masterful*, but it only ever happens when you're really angry, doesn't it? Maybe I need a dominant man to keep me sweet, and you know what? I really want you, right this minute."

He shook his head. "Toni, you've just finished accusing me of having an illicit affair with Lynn, and I've just shocked the hell out of myself by doing something I didn't even know I was capable of. The last thing I feel like is sex."

She put her hand on his groin. "Liar." She began to unzip his jeans.

He pushed her backwards onto the bed and zipped himself up. "OK, you're right, from a purely physical point of view, I'd like to make love to you. And that is *not* because we've just had a violent scene, but because – from a purely physical point of view, remember – you're a very sexy woman with amazing tits which you've just been pressing against me. Mentally, I never felt less like it."

In one quick, lithe movement, she pulled off her dress. She wasn't wearing a bra and her knickers were just a scrap of lace.

He drew in a ragged breath.

"From a purely physical point of view, then. Pretend I'm one of your groupies if you like."

He groaned and cupped her breasts in his hands. Her nipples were hard. He bent his head and took one of them into his mouth.

She smiled and pulled him down on top of her.

Later, as they lay twined together, she ran her fingernails over his chest. "Stevo, I'm sorry."

"Hmm?" He was half-asleep.

"Steve, I'm sorry about all that with Sam."

He rolled onto his side and looked at her. "Please don't do it again, Toni," he said earnestly, brushing her hair off her face. "Why do you do it? How can we possibly stay together if you won't even try?"

"Sometimes I get so angry. I don't know why. I get so angry and jealous. I love you, Stephen, but sometimes I get so jealous, I hate you."

Two mistresses Toni can never compete with. Your music and your memories, he heard Sian say. He felt an overwhelming pity for Toni. He had to put things right, *had* to. He kissed her. "There's no need to be jealous. *You're* my wife. I chose *you*, remember?"

She gave him a half-smile. "Stevo, did you ever do that?"

"Do what?"

"Have threesomes with groupies?"

"Ah." He grinned. "Certainly did. They were twins. Blonde, eighteen-year-old Swedish twins, with huge tits and legs that went on and on. We got on the bed with me in the middle and one of them climbed on top of me…" He paused and looked at her. "And then I woke up."

She laughed and hit him with a pillow. "But you must have had more than your fair share of girls, right? So did you have threesomes?" she asked again after a moment.

He frowned. It was hopeless. "Yeah. I did all kinds of stuff. You know that. You know all about the drink and the drugs and the girls. And you know it all stopped when we got married." He climbed out of bed and started getting dressed. "I'm going to go, Toni. If I stay here we'll argue again. I can't see how we can go on like this. I don't know what else I can say to convince you. God knows I've had so many opportunities to be unfaithful to you since we got married, but apart from Coral, I never have and you know why that happened. I'll never do it again. If you don't believe me, there's nothing else I can say. I'll ring you tomorrow and I'll see you on Sunday in time for Sam's concert. We'll leave Newcastle early and we should back here by midday. If there's any delay on the road I'll go straight to the hall, but I *will* be there. And after the concert we'll talk about what we're going to do." He bent over and kissed her forehead. "Look after the boys for me."

She was silent until he got to the bedroom door, and then she said, "All that stuff about convincing me. You didn't say you wouldn't be unfaithful because you loved me."

He turned back and looked at her, an odd expression on his face, one she'd never seen before. "You never loved me enough to believe me," he said quietly. "I'm not sure you ever really loved me at all."

For once, he found the concert heavy going. He had his usual exchange with the audience before they started to play, but he was aware of having to work at it this time instead of it being spontaneous fun, as it usually was. As always, he lost himself in his playing, became part of the music, but when they did 'Sweet Cherry', he found he was starting to cry. He managed to get through it, thanking God it was the last song.

They were staying at the Gosforth Park Hotel. After the concert, he and Fin went to Andy's suite to unwind with a drink, and to his surprise, George was there, drinking Newcastle Brown. "It's just like the old days," he said, a wave of nostalgia sweeping over him. He wished he could crawl into bed and wake up twenty years ago. Who cared about luxury suites in swanky hotels? Twenty years ago he'd had the music and he'd had Cherry. He'd never needed anything else.

"What's wrong, Steve?" Andy asked sympathetically.

"Nothing. Tired. Antibiotics make me depressed."

Andy looked at him searchingly. "Is it worth it?"

"Gets rid of the ear infection," he said, trying to turn the direction of the conversation.

"Howay, man, when you start crying on stage, there's something seriously wrong," George said.

"Toni and I are just going through a rough patch," he shrugged, opening a can of lager.

"It's a fucking long rough patch," Fin commented.

"It's been going on for the last ten years, like," Andy added.

"Don't you think it might be time to call it quits?" George asked.

"What, so you can have her?" Stephen flashed at him.

George didn't rise to the bait. "Toni and me are friends, Steve," he said, mildly. "But I do know this, bonny lad, she's no happier than you are."

Stephen rubbed his eyes. "Sorry, George." He shook his head, wearily. "I don't know what to do." He finished his drink. "I need to get some sleep, I've got a long drive tomorrow." He tried to smile. "God, how things have changed! Fifteen years ago I could party all night; girls, booze, pot, and even get up the next morning and go for a run!" He sighed. "Oh, well. I'll see you all next week."

Chapter Twenty-One
Shattered

You left me shattered, battered,
Crushed and bruised and broken on the ground.

"Julia! Rob! Robert!" Stephen rapped harder on the door of Julia's room in her hall of residence.

It opened and Rob's bleary-eyed face looked out. "Dad! Come in. What's the time?"

"Ten past seven! I've been knocking for five minutes! You were supposed to have started breakfast by now!"

Rob grinned. "Sorry, Dad, heavy night. I'll grab a shower. Jules, wake up! Dad, do you want to get some toast? Jules'll show you where everything is."

Julia led the way to the kitchen. "I'm going back to bed," she yawned. "Have a safe journey. Look after my boy."

Stephen kissed her. "I will." He made several slices of toast and a cup of very strong coffee. As he ate, his annoyance evaporated. They had plenty of time, after all.

Twenty minutes later, Rob appeared, his hair still slightly damp. "Sorry, Dad."

"Forget it, Blue, you're only young once. Have you said goodbye to Jules?"

Rob nodded, picking up a couple of slices of toast. "Come on then, what are you waiting for?" he grinned.

The road from Newcastle to Leeds was pretty clear, but Stephen restrained himself, and averaged about eighty five miles an hour.

"What music have you been listening to?" Rob asked, turning the CD player on. It was GI Joe, and Dominic's voice, singing his first big hit, 'If I Should Lose My Heart', filled the car. " 'Class Act'? That's nice," he said approvingly.

"I think this is probably my favourite song of all time, it's superb," Stephen said. "I love this whole album. Don't tell Charlie," he added.

Rob smiled. "You two are weird."

"Yeah, well."

"So what's up, Dad?"

"Why should anything be up?"

Rob was watching his face. "What was it about this time? The row?"

Stephen sighed. "You know me too well."

"Bollocks! It's obvious, even Julia knew."

"Oh, bloody hell!" Stephen gave him the recorded highlights of his row with Toni. "It's not right to involve the boys – specially Sam – in our problems."

Rob was concerned. "Poor Toni. She must be very unhappy if she's doing that."

"What about me?" Stephen said, stung. "And it's not the first time she's done it either."

"Course I'm sorry for you too, Dad, and you wouldn't behave like that. But Toni can be very childish, usually when she's unhappy or feels that someone's being unfair to her."

"Namely me," Stephen sighed.

"Well, yes. I'm not saying she's right, but she *is* like a child; a 'that's not fair!' type of attitude. And, like a kid, she lashes out. She doesn't mean to hurt the boys. Oh, come on, Dad, you've known this for years."

"I *do* know," Stephen admitted. Rob was saying much the same as Sian had. "I'm just fed up with making allowances. Oh, Robbie, I think it's over."

Rob stared at him, appalled. Stephen and Toni were always rowing. It *couldn't* be over. He said as much.

"I don't know, Robbie, I just don't know. I don't want to give up on it – I feel we ought to keep trying – but on the other hand, I can't see us winning this. Not any more. But look, I'm very tired. Maybe I'm overreacting. Maybe you're right. Maybe we need space and time together, just me and Toni."

They stopped at Woolley Edge services to use the toilet.

"Better have a caffeine fix while we're here," Rob said.

"Yeah, and stock up on chocolate," Stephen added.

Back in the car, Rob rummaged through Stephen's CDs. "Let's have Madness on."

"Do you remember when you thought it was 'soap begins another weary day' instead of 'so begins'?"

"Yeah. I also thought it was 'an innocent speckled youth' not 'insolent speck of youth' and 'old man in a creepy suit', not 'three piece suit'."

Stephen laughed so much his eyes watered. "Why didn't you tell me?"

"Well, look at the reaction! I don't care now, but I used to hate it when you laughed at me."

"Why?"

Rob shrugged. "Your opinion of me was important."

"And now it's not?"

"You know it is, Dad, just not over that sort of thing."

They drove on, singing along until 'It Must Be Love' came on.

"You and Julia..." Stephen started.

"We want to get married when I'm qualified."

"I'm so pleased, Blue, she's a lovely girl. What will you do when her parents stay with you though?"

"What do you mean?" Rob frowned.

"Well, I suppose you'll have to sleep in the spare room. Bit awkward when she gets pregnant though. How are you going to explain that to Reg Moffatt?"

Rob thumped him. "Fuck off!"

"Don't hit the driver. Can I have a Crunchie please, Blue?"

"You can if you believe you can," Rob said annoyingly.

"Just open me a fucking Crunchie, you bastard."

"What did your last slave die of?"

"Answering back."

The M1 was much busier than Stephen had expected. "Where are all these bloody people going, it's a fucking Sunday, what's the matter with them?" he exclaimed in exasperation, much to Rob's amusement. By the time they reached the turn off onto the A43, it was eleven thirty. The traffic was very heavy and it took them over an hour to get to the M40.

"What time's his concert?"

"Half-past-one. That bloody road! We should have gone across at Birmingham."

"It might've been just as bad," Rob pointed out.

"I suppose. Oh, well, we'll have to go straight there, so shall we stop at those services just before we come off the motorway, have a cake or something and fill up with petrol, and then take everyone out for a meal after the concert's over?"

"That's a great idea, I'm starving," Rob said with feeling.

As they went into the cafe, Stephen heard a shriek of delight behind them. He sighed. They'd been lucky at Woolley Edge, no one had recognised him.

A large woman hurried up. "Oh, my God! It *is* you!" She turned to her husband. "See, honey? I told you it was him!" She fumbled in her bag for a pen. "Can I have your autograph, Steve? I'm one of your biggest fans!"

"In every way," Rob muttered into Stephen's ear.

Stephen shot him a warning look. He smiled warmly at the woman, who was waving a piece of paper and a pen at him. "Hi, I'd love to!" He took the paper. "What's your name?"

"Hildy Bergstrom."

"Is that Hildy with a Y or an IE?" Stephen asked, writing.

"Well, while you're doing that, honey, I'm gonna find me the restroom," Mr Bergstrom said, bored.

She took the autograph. "That's great! Wait till they'll see this back home!" She bustled off after her husband.

"She could have said thank you," Rob commented.

"You get used to it. And she must buy my records."

"I guess. Oh, look, Dad, they've got lovely roses! At this time of year! Get some for Toni. And I've been thinking," he said, as they bought coffee and cakes and sat down. "If you could survive that awful time she had the affair and you went off with Coral, you can get over this. You're the strong one, Dad. Help her."

How strange that everyone said that. "In what way? In what way am I strong?" he asked.

"You know what you want and you go for it. You left home rather than give up The Brigands, didn't you? And you make things work. Look at the band. You made that what it is, and you'd fight for it tooth and nail."

Stephen stared at him. "Yes, I would," he said slowly.

"And Sammy, with his speech therapy. You could've given in, not taken him to Lynn, found someone nearly as good. Did you really want to see Lynn every week? No. But you still took him. It's you that's kept your marriage to Toni together. Through all the difficult times you've had, when it really, really matters to you, you're strong."

Stephen rubbed his forehead. "Maybe you're right."

"You know I am. You and Toni are always having these terrible rows – you always make up. Tell you what, you get her the roses while I find me the restroom."

Stephen grinned. "OK. If I'm done first, I'll be in the car."

Toni's favourite roses were dark red. They didn't have any that colour, but they had some beautiful white ones. He bought four bunches despite the exorbitant price. It wasn't busy in the shop, a couple of lorry drivers, and a harassed mother with four boys who were swarming over everything. She was having trouble getting them back together. Stephen thought of Toni's method, which was simply to stand in the middle of the shop and shout 'Coo-ee!' at the top of her voice, like a Bushman. It never failed to work. The thought made him smile. Rob's right about me and Toni, he thought, we always make it up.

The girl at the till recognised him and, blushing, asked for his autograph. " 'China Rose' is my favourite song ever, the way you play the guitar is incredible," she mumbled, her blush deepening.

A real fan, Stephen thought. 'China Rose' had never been released as a single.

He took one of the roses and gave it to her along with the autograph, practically reducing her to tears of gratitude and devotion, and started out to the car. He and Rob had been listening to REM before they stopped, and he was singing 'Shiny, Happy People' as he walked to the edge of the pavement.

And then suddenly, from nowhere, a car rushed towards him and he stepped back, but it kept on coming, on and on, up onto the pavement, and someone was screaming in pain, and he realised it was him, and the pain was consuming him, it was everywhere, no way to be free of it, and he tried moving, tried keeping very still, but nothing worked, nothing helped, and there was noise and confusion, and someone shouting, and somewhere Rob's voice, terrified and crying, and *he* was terrified too, terrified that Rob was also suffering this unendurable agony, terrified of this unendurable agony, unendurable, but he was having to endure it, and he didn't think he could stand any more, but it never stopped, and he couldn't breathe, couldn't cry, could do nothing but endure.

Part Four
Through The Bars

Looking through the bars of my life,
The wind of reality cuts me like a knife,
And I'm stuck in this wasteland,
Time running through the fingers of my hand,
Looking at the mud, trying to see the stars.

Chapter Twenty-Two
Cry Havoc

Darkness spreading over me, blotting out the light, and I can't see.
All is fear and pain; cry Havoc! And mayhem reigns.

Sam was awake early, practising. Toni, who'd not been able to sleep, made him breakfast, and took it up to his room.

"What time will Daddy be home?"

"Depends on the traffic; I should think about twelve. Heaps of time, Sam." As she went downstairs, she heard the phone. She'd turned the answer machine on the night before in case Stephen rung very early. "…a bit late setting off," he was saying, "but we've made good time so far, so we should be with you by about half-past-twelve. Hope everyone's right. Love you."

Yeah, I bet you were late setting off, Toni thought, heavy night last night, no doubt. And Rob and Sam both waiting for you! So much for the 'I'd never do that to Sam' speech! You'd better be here in time, you bastard.

She woke Alex and Pip at ten thirty, much to Alex's disgust.

"How come we have to get up early just because Sam's playing the piano this afternoon?" he asked, when he finally dragged himself down to breakfast. "Bad enough we've got to go and watch," he added privately to Pip.

"Where's Dad?" Pip asked.

"Not back yet," Toni replied.

Half-an-hour later, Sam came down. "Where's Daddy?"

"Not back yet." Toni was reading the *Sunday Gazette*. She glanced up at the clock. "He should be here any time."

Ten minutes later, Alex asked, "Where's Dad?"

"He's gone mad and been shot!" she snapped. "How should I know? Come on, Alex, get dressed, we'll have to go soon!"

"We can't go without Daddy," Sam protested.

"Don't worry, little mate, he'll be here."

At quarter to one she said, reluctantly, "We'll have to go."

Sam was distressed. "Dr Venkman's not here! Not here, not here, not here."

"Why don't you ring him, Mum?" Pip asked.

"What for?" Toni demanded. "He knows what time it is. The traffic must be bad." I'll kill him, she thought, after the way he went on at me, I'll kill him! She smiled at Sam reassuringly. "Don't worry, Sammy, he'll go straight to the hall, he'll probably be there when we get there."

"Stephen, can you hear me?" The paramedics worked quickly, assessing his level of consciousness, giving him oxygen and putting him on something that looked like a giant surfboard.

"We're immobilising him in case he's injured his back," Annie, the young female technician, told Rob. "It's a spinal board."

To Rob's amazement, Stephen was still conscious. He'd responded to the paramedic and had clearly asked "Is Rob safe?" before they put the oxygen mask on him.

"I'm here, Dad!" he said, frantically, his heart breaking. "Why does he need that?" he asked. "Can't he breathe?"

"He's hurt his chest," they told him.

"He must be in terrible pain!" he said in anguish.

"It's all right, Rob," Annie said. "It's all being taken care of."

In the ambulance, they attached Stephen to drips and tubes. The journey to the James Radlett hospital in Oxford seemed to take forever. One of the crew called ahead, and Rob heard him relaying some sort of code.

"What's he saying?"

"He's telling the hospital your Dad's condition."

"He'll be all right, won't he? He asked about me."

Annie hesitated. "They'll do everything they can. They're really good, Rob." She leant forward and squeezed his hand. "Your Dad's great. I'm a big fan."

At the hospital, Stephen was rushed into the resuscitation room. Rob watched, terrified and shaking, as the doors shut behind the trolley. He'd never felt so alone. He had a terrible feeling he'd never see Stephen again. He wasn't able to tell them where Sam's concert was being held, so they rang Sian, and he asked them to ring Harry and Dominic. He told them Stephen had an ear infection and was on Penicillin, although he didn't know the dosage, and he gave them as much of his medical history as he could; as far as he knew, Stephen had never been in hospital, had never had anything worse than flu and a chronic bad back. He was aware he wasn't being much help, but everyone was very kind. And he kept asking, "How is he? What's happening?" but there was never any more news, apart from the fact that Stephen was in the operating theatre. Still. And then Harry and Dominic arrived and held him, but even as he hugged them thankfully, he realised he was finally grown up. For the first time, Harry couldn't make his troubles go away.

"God, my hands are freezing!" Simon grumbled as they arrived back at his house from their post lunch walk, glowing healthily from the exercise. The weather was miserable, cold and grey. It was only a couple of weeks into the new year, but it seemed ages since Christmas and even longer until spring. "Tell, you what, Sunshine," he went on, "you go and make us a cuppa while I light the fire. We can have chocolate biccies and dunk them."

"Not too many though," Lynn warned.

"Yes, miss," he grinned.

They sat companionably, eating the biscuits.

"Wouldn't it be great to be rich and jet off to the Caribbean at this time of year?" Simon sighed.

"Yes, it would. But I'm happy anyway," she smiled, kissing him.

He put his arm round her. "Lynn."

Somehow, she knew what he was going to say. And in that instant, she knew what her answer would be. She loved him, not like she loved Stephen, not rapturously, not to count the world well lost, but enough. She was happy with him, he made her laugh, and she was thirty eight. She wanted children.

"Will you marry me?" he asked. "I know we've only been seeing each other seriously for the last six months, but... well, I love you very much, Lynn."

She smiled at him." I love you too. I'd love to marry you, Si."

He was amazed. "I was sure you'd say no!"

She started to laugh. "Well, if you'd *rather* I said no..."

He shook his head, grinning. "I can't believe it!" he said, jubilant. He pulled her closer and kissed her. "I'm completely unprepared! No ring, no champagne – no, wait, just sit there, don't move!" He went into the kitchen. She heard the fridge open and close, and then the hiss of a can being opened. He came back in, beaming, carrying two cans of lager, one of them open. "Give me your hand."

She obligingly gave him her left hand. He slipped the ring pull on to her ring finger and handed her the lager. Opening the other one, he tapped it against hers. "Cheers!"

She laughed. "Cheers!"

"Let's go out at lunchtime tomorrow and get champagne, and I'll buy you a ring." He kissed her again. "I'm happier than… well, than a very happy thing!" They lay on the sofa cuddling, and chatting about the wedding.

"Will we be inviting Steve?" he asked. He hoped so, he liked Stephen very much. After the cocktail party he'd gone with him, Dominic and Andy to the studio, and they'd all played together, Stephen lending him his National steel.

"I'm not sure." Lynn was uncertain. "I'd like to, but I just don't know about his wife. I'll get Holly to ask him about it."

"Be great if he could come."

Lynn smiled at him. "I can't tell you how wonderful it is that you two get on so well! Tim was so jealous, and Paul couldn't really cope."

"I'd cope with anything to be with you."

Lynn's heart filled with love. "Oh, Si, I'm so happy!"

As he pulled her closer, the phone rang. "Bloody hell! Shall I ignore it?"

Lynn kissed his nose. "No, see who it is." She smiled at him suggestively. "But don't be long!"

He picked up the phone. "Holly! Hello! Yeah, wait a sec, I'll get her." He passed it to Lynn.

"Hi, Holl, how are—?" The blood drained from her face. "Yes. Right away. Thank you, Holl." She put the phone down.

"What is it?" Simon asked, alarmed.

"Will you drive me to Holly's?"

"Of course, but what is it, Lynn?" he repeated urgently.

Her eyes were wide with shock. "It's Stephen. He's been knocked down by a car. Holl said – she said – they're not sure if he'll live."

Stephen was barely hanging onto life. The doctor who came to talk to the family told them it was a miracle that he'd survived surgery. "His heart stopped twice," he said gravely, "and his condition is still critical. But he's made it this far, and that's something to hold onto."

They took a weeping Toni to intensive care to see him, but the sight of him, unconscious, on a ventilator, tubes everywhere, was more than she could stand, and she'd gone back to the Priory to be with the boys until her mother arrived from Chester.

Dominic, Harry and Rob stayed at the hospital, numb with shock.

Not long after Toni left, Andy arrived, and they told him what they knew.

He stared at them, devastated. "Jesus! Robbie, I'm so sorry," he said, rubbing Rob's shoulder. "Do you mind if I phone Holl, like? She wants to be here so much, but Sarah's mum's had a stroke, and we've no one to look after the kids." Sarah was their nanny.

"You go ahead," Dominic said.

Rob watched him walk down the corridor. He frowned. "Dom, why are the police still here?" he asked, looking past Andy. "Surely Dad's not in trouble?"

"In case – " Dominic swallowed. "In case he dies, Robbie." He took Rob's hand.

Rob stared at him. "He's not going to, is he, Dom?"

As Dominic opened his mouth to answer, Sian and Ted arrived.

"How is he?" Sian whispered.

"He's out of surgery, he's in intensive care," Harry said.

Sian collapsed onto a chair. "Oh, thank God," she said, beginning to cry. "Oh, thank God, thank God!"

Harry glanced up at Ted, who nodded at her. "It's OK, Princess," he said quietly. "Tell us what they say."

Harry swallowed. "He's really b-badly hurt, but, um, the worst thing – " Her lips trembled and she took a deep breath. "It's his hand, his left hand. It was trapped under the front wheel of the car. They had to cut it off."

The journey to Burford seemed to Lynn to take forever. She sat gripped with horror, staring out through the windscreen, seeing only Stephen. She remembered the first time she'd ever seen him, at the bar in Grosvenor Place. She was with that boy she'd been going out with, what was his name, Chris, that was it, and Pam and Caro and Pam's boyfriend, Mac, who was at Cambridge and had come to stay with Pam for the weekend. He was OK, but a bit of a hippy, and definitely a big head, and he'd taken his guitar over to the bar and was strumming 'Blowing In The Wind' rather badly.

Someone grabbed the guitar. "If we're going to have live music in here, for God's sake give the fucking thing to some bugger who can play it! Oi, Steve!"

Despite Mac's protests, the guitar was handed to the most gorgeous boy Lynn had ever seen. He was startlingly handsome, she thought, and his eyes were stunning, a marvellous pale aquamarine.

He passed the guitar back to Mac. "Sorry about that." He looked over at Lynn and smiled.

She smiled back, suddenly feeling breathlessly shy.

Mac had become surly. "If you're so bloody good, you play it."

The boy studied him with a kind of amused interest for a minute. He grinned. "OK." He started to play 'Blowing In The Wind.' He was amazing, absolutely phenomenal, and Mac went scarlet.

"God, he's fantastic!" Caro exclaimed. "Who is he?" she asked the boy who'd snatched the guitar from Mac.

"Stephen Markham. He usually plays a Strat. He sings too."

Lynn stared over at him. I'd give anything to go out with him, she thought, anything. She looked up at the girl he was with, she knew her very slightly, Virginia or something, very posh and a real bitch. She had her hand on Stephen's shoulder and she looked like the cat who'd swallowed the canary.

And then the memory faded and was replaced by that awful night she'd overheard Jean Pritchard talking about Stephen's infidelity. She saw his face as clearly as if he was standing in front of her, he was crying and begging her not to leave him. But she had. She'd left him and now he might die, she might never see him again, and she'd never be able to tell him how much she loved him, and how so, so sorry she was, and she began to cry hysterically, keening with grief.

"Lynn! Hold on, I'll pull over!" Simon began to slow down.

"No," she gasped. "No, Simon, keep going, please!" She pulled herself together. "I'm OK, honestly." She sat rigidly, digging her fingernails into her palms in an attempt to control herself until, to her relief, Simon pulled into Holly and Andy's driveway.

She was out of the car almost before it stopped, and Holly had the door open and they fell into each other's arms.

"How is he?" she gasped as Holly led them through to the kitchen.

"Sit down, Lynn," Holly said quietly.

There was a roaring in Lynn's ears. "Oh, my God, he's not dead, he can't be dead..."

Holly started to speak, but Lynn couldn't hear anything, the room was tilting and she swayed, and Simon caught her and sat her down, and squatted next to her, grasping her hand.

"No, Lynn, listen to Holly. He's not dead."

Holly sat next to her and took her other hand. "Andy just phoned. He isn't dead, Lynn. He's just come out of surgery. But..." She shut her eyes, trying to keep her voice steady. "Oh God, Lynn – they've cut off his left hand."

"Apparently the car hit him on the left side, so the worst injuries are on the left," Dominic had taken over from Harry. "But he was knocked sideways, and his face smashed into the kerb. He broke his right jaw and cheekbone."

Sian blanched. "Oh, my God! Is he... will he be...?"

"Scarred?" Dominic shrugged helplessly. "We don't know."

"His face was a terrible mess, terrible, it was all terrible, there was blood everywhere, so much blood," Rob said, his voice shaking. He clutched Dominic's hand. "He was conscious all the time," he went on, "all the time, he must have been in terrible pain, but he asked – he asked if I was OK." His voice cracked, and Dominic put his arms round him. He buried his face in Dominic's shoulder.

Holly had given Lynn a glass of brandy. She swallowed it down. "I'm OK, I'm OK, it was just the shock." She was shivering, and Holly fetched a shawl and wrapped it round her.

"At least he's alive, Lynn," Simon said.

She nodded. "What exactly did Andy tell you?" she asked, her eyes fixed on Holly's face.

Holly took a deep breath, trying to remember. "Um, well, the driver of the car was asleep and he just ploughed into Steve. He's really bad, Lynn. Apart from his... his poor hand, he's broken his ribs – what did Andy say? They were broken in more than one place and they punctured his lung, I think; damaged it anyway." She shook her head. "I can't remember exactly, but I know it's serious, and um, his," she gestured at her front, "his sternum's broken and his left knee and hip..."

"They had to take his spleen out," Harry faltered. Her face crumpled. "They said, the doctor we spoke to said he'd never seen anyone so badly injured before. His heart stopped twice, and he lost loads of blood. They had to give him a massive transfusion." She frowned despairingly. "Although apparently even that can cause problems." She looked at Dominic. "What was it they said?"

He shook his head. "I can't remember. There was so much to take in."

Fin, Shelagh and George came hurrying in with Kathy and Paul and Rebecca and Matthew, and Harry and Dominic went through it all again.

"Can we see him?" Rebecca asked.

Harry got up. "Yes, I'm sure you can. Let's go and find someone."

Lynn stood up. "I want to go to the hospital."

Simon shot a look at Holly, who frowned in concern. "Is that a good idea, Lynn?"

"Why not?" Lynn demanded. "I'm his... his friend." She grasped Simon's hand. "We both are."

"But Toni'll be there – I know, I know," Holly said, as Lynn started to speak. "I don't like her either, but she's his wife." She shrugged helplessly. "And Steve's family. They might not be too keen. Oh, Lynn, please don't cry! Look, I'll go and phone Andy."

Lynn sat down again, still gripping Simon's hand.

Holly came back in. "He says tomorrow would be better," she said apologetically. "Better for Steve too," she said quickly, at the look on Lynn's face. "Lynn, I'm sorry. Listen, you can stay here as long as you like, OK? And tomorrow we'll take you in to see him."

Stephen couldn't remember when they'd told him he no longer had a left hand. It was as if he'd always known; there was no past, no future, only the knowledge that he'd never play the guitar again. He remembered trying to get up, trying to see, and they'd given him something to make him sleep and he was drifting in a white room, with translucent walls, and Cherry was there somewhere, but he couldn't find her, and it hurt to move.

"Stephen. Stephen, can you hear me?"

His eyelids were so heavy. Just lifting them a fraction was *so* hard. "Yeah."

"Good. I want you to tell me how you're feeling. Do you have any pain?"

What a stupid question. Every bit of him hurt. He shut his eyes again and sank down into the white room. He wandered about, trying to find a door. If he could find it, he'd be able to get back into the flat where Lynn was waiting for him and they'd get into George's van and drive to Utopia and he'd play. But, like the door that wasn't there, he knew there was a reason why he couldn't play. He was suddenly cold and very scared. He had to find the door, he had to get out. "Cherry!" he shouted. "Cherry! Cherry! Cherry!"

"Stevie."

He opened his eyes. Harry was sitting by the bed. By the bed in the hospital in Oxford where they'd cut off his hand. Hot tears welled up in his eyes and rolled silently down his face, while Harry held his right hand, his only hand, and cried with him.

He'd always been very fit, had run and swum every day, and despite his listlessness and despair, his body healed fast. Within forty eight hours he was off the critical list and, far sooner than the staff had predicted, he was well enough to be transferred out of intensive care. To everyone's relief, his face, once the swelling and bruising had gone down, wasn't badly marked; he would have a scar under his right eye and a longer one along his right jaw, but the doctors said they would fade.

The boys went to see him regularly. They had been stunned and horrified when Sian told them about his hand. "Oh, poor Dad!" Pip had exclaimed. "How will he play the guitar?"

"He won't," Alex said slowly. He looked at Sian. "He won't be able to stand that."

Sian tried to smile. "He'll have to, Ally." That was when the absolute enormity of it hit her. She'd spent the past few days being strong and sensible, for the boys, for Toni, and most of all for Stephen, but she couldn't cope with it any more. She loved Stephen more than anything on earth and she couldn't bear to see him suffering like this. “Why couldn’t it have been me?” she raged to Ted. “Why him? He’s such a good boy, how could this have happened to him?”

Ted held her and murmured soothing words. There was nothing else he could do.

While Stephen was in intensive care, Dominic discovered, with horror, that someone who had been at the scene of the accident had picked up one of the roses Stephen had bought for Toni at the service station shop, and was selling it on an internet auction site. Stephen’s family and friends had been prepared to deal with the swarm of reporters who were everywhere, asking inane, insensitive, and sometimes macabre questions, but this was different. “Look at this,” he said grimly to Harry.

She looked. ‘*World Exclusive!*’ she read. ‘*Ultimate collectors item for any serious Sid’s Six/Steve Markham fan! You are bidding on a rose stained with Steve’s blood! He was holding a bunch of roses when he was knocked down last weekend and this is the only undamaged one! It’s probably the last thing he touched with his left hand! Beautifully preserved in an airtight container.*” Next to the description were two photographs, the first a grainy picture of the scene outside the service station after the accident. Roses were scattered on the ground, crushed and broken, apart from one, which had been ringed in black marker pen. The second photo was a clear close up of the same rose, its delicate white petals splashed a vivid crimson.

She stared at Dominic, her eyes wide with shock and disbelief. “Oh, Dom! Oh, my God! How could anyone do that?”

Dominic’s face was taut with anger. “I don’t know. It’s incomprehensible. My God, I’d like to get my hands on the bastard!”

“What are we going to do?” Harry asked, her voice shaking.

“Buy it ourselves and destroy it,” Dominic said. “I’m going to put in an colossal bid, and make sure no one tops it. And keep an eye out for anything else some fucking ghoul might have picked up.”

“B-but that means whoever is selling it will get the money!”

Dominic sighed. “There’s nothing else we can do. It’s the price of fame, darling. Everyone wants a piece.”

Later, he got George, Fin and Andy together. “Listen, this business with the rose started me thinking. If the fans want something of Steve’s, he might as well get the benefit. We should finish the album.”

“How can we?” Fin demanded.

“Steve’s recorded all the vocals. Even the harmonies.”

“Yeah, but we haven’t finished ‘Caught In Your Headlights’ and ‘Trademark’, and some of the others need work.”

“I’ll play on them.”

“Oh ey. I’m not sure, like.” Andy looked at the other two. “What do you think?”

“Look,” Dominic said. “You know my sister, Sophy, is a surgeon? Well, I was talking to her about Stephen last night. She said a high percentage of post op patients in intensive care die.”

They stared at him, aghast.

“Splenectomy in particular, carries a high risk of post op sepsis.”

“Post op what, like?”

“Going gammy,” George explained.

“B-but they said he was doing well last time we were there,” Fin stammered. In truth, he’d been shocked by Stephen’s appearance. “Although he looked dreadful,” he added.

"Yes, well, I hope to God I'm just scare mongering. But the thing is, if he did, well, you know, not make it, the money from this album will be helpful for Toni and the boys. And if, please God, he's OK, well..." He stopped.

"Well?" Fin prompted.

"Well, I can't really see him and Toni staying together. That means him paying for two establishments. He can still write, he can still sing. But Christ knows whether he'll be prepared to do either. And supposing he needs help when he comes out of hospital? You know, like equipment, apparatus, that sort of thing." He paused. "And one thing is certain. Toni knows how to spend money."

George looked as if he was going to object to this, so Andy said quickly, "OK, Dom. I'm in." He looked at Fin and George. They nodded.

Harry, meanwhile, had been worried about Stephen coping after he came out of hospital, and had given it a lot of thought. She'd practiced having a bath and washing using only one hand, and had devised several strategies. To wash her hair, she'd poured shampoo into the crook of her left arm and scooped it into her right hand. Washing her right arm and underarm was the only thing that defeated her. The next day, she went out and bought a wash mitt, clenched her left fist and put it on. She then lathered it up and washed with it. It was a good idea in theory, but it kept slipping off. Undeterred, she made one of her own, with an elasticated wristband.

Dominic sat in the bathroom, watching her trying out the prototype. "It works splendidly," she said, pleased. "And if he uses an all-in-one shower gel and shampoo, it'll be even better. Thank goodness he doesn't have to shave under his arms though. God, if it was me, I'd not be able to manage half my beauty routine!"

"I'd do it for you," Dominic said. "We could have a go now." He stripped off and climbed into the bath with her, displacing what looked like a gallon of water over the floor.

"Dominic! Be careful!" she giggled.

He started to wash her back.

"Yes, but imagine having to ask *Toni* for help," she said seriously. "She'd be all condescending and martyred."

"Yes," he agreed. He sighed. "Poor Steve!" He kissed the nape of Harry's neck and slid his hands round her breasts.

"You were supposed to be helping me wash," she reminded him sternly.

"Oh, yes; oh dear, I seem to have dropped the soap!" He groped around. "Is this it?"

"Dominic!" Harry squealed.

"No, it isn't, what the fuck can it be?" Dominic explored with his fingers, and Harry gasped. "Hmm, it feels nice," he grinned.

She twisted round and kissed him, and the prototype wash mitt fell unheeded to the floor.

She bought shower gels for Stephen from Penhaligon's and Cyclax, neither of whom tested on animals – and Cyclax had the added benefit of being made in Wales – and made seven wash mitts for him, all in different colours.

Simon had to go back to work, but Lynn arranged a locum for her patients and stayed with Andy and Holly. She went to the hospital with Holly as often as she could, keeping out of the family's way.

Ray had flown in from Boston after the accident and stayed for several days, and Coral had been a frequent visitor. George and Fin made regular trips to the hospital and often stayed the night at Andy's. Lynn was touched by the fact that neither they nor Andy cared about the effect the accident would have on the band except where it pertained to Stephen. "He's lucky to have such good friends," she said one evening.

"Much bloody good that'll do him!" Andy said. "Sorry, Lynn. I didn't mean…"

"It's OK," Lynn sighed. "I know what you meant. And it's no good, is it, all this talk of poor Steve, what's he going to do? I'm not being heartless, but he's lost his left hand. He's going to have to come to terms with it."

"Well, fucking Toni's not going to be any fucking use," Fin said savagely. " 'I hate disability, I hate illness!'" he mimicked. "Why the fuck he ever married her…"

"She's doing her best!" George cut in. "Leave her alone! Running her down won't help Steve, man."

Holly couldn't stand this championship of Toni any longer. "She's an absolute bitch," she said tightly. "When I think of all the grief she caused Steve with her affair!"

"Holly!" Andy warned.

"No!" Holly insisted. "It's about time George knew."

George frowned. "It was Stephen who had the affair," he said slowly.

"Yes – because he found out she'd had one with that bloody photographer, Gavin Leigh!" Holly flashed back.

Fin was astounded. "How do you know this? Not that I'm surprised," he added.

"Coral phoned Andy when she found out," Holly explained. "None of us knew what to do, so we told Harry. She thought we ought to wait and see what happened, but then Coral told Steve when they were in Fiji."

George got up.

"Where are you going?" Andy asked.

"Home," George said heavily. He went out to his car. He couldn't believe Toni had never told him. He started to drive home, but changed his mind and headed to the Priory.

Toni opened the door. Her face lit up. "George! Come in."

"Can we talk?" he asked abruptly.

Toni was taken aback by his tone. "Come into the kitchen. The boys are in bed and so's my Mum. I was just going to ring the hospital, then I was going to bed. I suppose you don't know when Lynn's going back to London, do you?"

"Why didn't you tell me you had an affair?" George demanded.

Toni went white. "Who told you?" she breathed.

"Holly."

Toni looked away. "I didn't want you to think badly of me," she said, blinking back tears. "I was so unhappy with Steve, and Gavin seemed as if he wanted me, and I didn't feel like he was always thinking about his ex wife." She laughed bitterly. "He was just thinking about the next girl he was going to fuck!" She looked at George, the tears making her eyes intensely green. "I love you, George," she whispered, huskily. "I couldn't bear it if you weren't my friend."

George gathered her into his arms. He held her against him, kissing her hair. "I'll always be your friend, Toni. I love you too, I've never loved anyone like I love you."

"What are we going to do?" Toni asked her voice full of despair. "I couldn't possibly leave Stephen now, he needs me, for the first time in our marriage." She stared up at George. "I can't believe this has happened."

"We can't do anything, man. Steve comes first, poor bastard." George sighed deeply. "We'll always be friends, Toni. I'll always be here for you. And look at Harry's Dad. He waited for Steve's mum."

"But… her husband died!" Toni was horrified. "I don't want Steve to die!"

"Well, no, nor do I," George said, embarrassed. "That wasn't what I meant. I just meant he might get self-sufficient in time." He held her tighter. "By, you're a canny lass, Toni!"

"You'd better go, George, or I don't think I'll be able to trust myself!" She gave him a weak smile.

He bent his head and kissed her. "I'll see you tomorrow, pet."

Simon rang Lynn every day. A couple of weeks after Stephen came out of intensive care he asked, hesitantly, "How's he doing these days?"

"Much better, physically. He should be able to go home soon." She hesitated. "Mentally; well, he's very depressed."

"I'm not surprised, so would I be! Point is, Lynn, I'm missing you like crazy! I don't want to sound selfish, but when are you coming home? We want to go and buy the ring, remember?"

"Yes, of course," Lynn lied. In truth, she had no desire to do anything except be with Stephen. Which was foolish, because he'd soon be back home with Toni and the boys. Her heart had leapt at the news of Toni's infidelity, but she'd realised straight away that it had happened a long time ago. Despite everything, they were still together. Still in love. "Next week," she said, her heart heavy.

"Phone me as soon as you get back. The very minute!"

"I will," she promised, but the first thing she did when she arrived home was find a videotape containing a recording of a Sid's Six concert from the previous summer. She fast forwarded to the end, and watched, numb with grief, as the band played the finale, 'The Hooded Stars', the instrumental theme to the TV series *Cambria's Chieftain*, for which Stephen had written the soundtrack.

It was a beautiful piece of music, and the crowd were still and silent as Stephen played and went on playing, and one by one the rest of the band left the stage and the house lights came up and the roadies came on and began packing away the equipment and instruments, and still Stephen played on, wholly absorbed, oblivious to the world, lost in his music.

Chapter Twenty-Three
From The Brink

Rage and pain and unforgiving,
Not dead, not living,
One step from the brink.

The Priory looked totally different to Stephen when he got home. Everything had changed, it was as if he'd gone through the looking glass, like Alice. He was in an alien world that was the same, yet not the same. He couldn't bear to look at the studio. Day followed weary day, and everything was futile, eating, sleeping, living. What was the point of waking each morning to a new day of misery? What was a day anyway? Empty monochrome hours of pain between sleep. And even sleep was fraught with dreams. When he slept, in his dreams, he was whole. He could play, and make the sweetest music.

He discovered that if he took his painkillers with a couple of shots of whisky, he slept without dreaming. But he was finding he needed more and more of them to do that, and the sleep didn't refresh him, he was always tired. Why did his body continue to function, to hurt, to feel hot or cold or hungry? What was the rest of his life? Time dragging on and on, no meaning, nothing left. He looked at his sons, he knew how much they loved him, but they'd become strangers to him, strangers with two hands. Even Harry couldn't break through. People came to see him, people he felt he no longer knew, had never known. They mouthed platitudes at him and left, the words 'so sorry' hanging in the air after they'd gone, back to their safe, happy, whole lives, where they could forget the scarred, damaged man, and comfort themselves with phrases like, 'It takes a while to come to terms', 'He's facing it so bravely', 'He's got his family', 'At least he wasn't killed'. None of them knew that that was what he regretted most of all. He wished he'd never woken up in that hospital, had just died by the roadside. He knew he was standing on the very edge of suicide and every day he fully intended to end it, but something, some rage at the way life had treated him, some urge to be able to shout at God, 'See! You couldn't beat me, you bastard!' stopped him. And yet, he couldn't seem to draw back, to move away from the brink.

Time passed endlessly, and he, who had always so delighted in the changing seasons, found delight in nothing. He sat morosely in the drawing room, or lay in bed, Mardi curled up at his feet and Savij lying on his legs.

"She really missed you when you were in hospital, Dad." Pip sat on the bed, stroking the little cat.

"Yeah?" Stephen said indifferently.

"Are you going to get a hook, Dad?" Alex asked hopefully. "That'd be great!"

"Great for whom? I'd rather have my hand."

"Yeah, but think, Dad," Pip exclaimed, his imagination fired by the idea. "You're so rich you could probably get the hook of a real pirate, you know, like Bluebeard or someone. Bet you could get it on eBay!"

Stephen sighed. "I don't want one."

"Come on, Dad, it'd be way cool!"

"Not for me, so shut up, OK? Go away, boys, I'm tired."

Toni came in and caught the end of the exchange. Her lips tightened. "They won't come at all soon. Why don't you get up, Steve? You've been home for weeks now, there's nothing wrong with you!"

Stephen stared at her. "What the fuck do you mean? I nearly died! I've only got one fucking hand!"

"Yes, but you're not ill! Come on, get up, it's ridiculous to be lying in bed. I know you're still convalescent, but you could sit out, it's a lovely day, the garden's a riot of blossom and the candles are out on the chestnut trees. Or you could go for a nice walk in the bluebell wood."

"I don't want to. I'm staying here with Savij and Mardi, they're the only ones who don't make stupid remarks. Anyway, I'm tired. They said at the hospital I should rest."

"They also said gentle exercise and fresh air," Toni pointed out.

"Stuff them."

"Stephen…"

"Fuck off, Toni! I said I'm tired! All this, 'get up, Stephen, there's nothing wrong with you' – how the hell would you know what it's like?" His voice rose. "Just leave me the fuck alone!"

Toni left without another word.

He shut his eyes. He was so tired, always so tired. He reached for his painkillers. He had a whisky bottle in his nightstand. He got it out and washed down a handful of the pills.

Toni went to the kitchen and wept. She didn't know what to do. She'd moved into one of the guest bedrooms on the pretext of not wanting to disturb him, but it was really because she couldn't bear the sight of his stump. It revolted her. Suppose it brushed against her in the night? She shuddered. And she couldn't cope with his moods, he'd never been like this before.

When Stephen woke, he got up and ran a bath. At the hospital, they'd recommended getting an electric shaver, but he had no difficulty shaving. It was everything else. He used a bathrobe as well as a towel, so it was easier to dry his back and right arm, and he had the wash mitts that Harry had made him. These had touched him very much, it had moved him tremendously to think of her trying to manage with one hand and then making something to help him. But everything was still so hard, and even the most basic tasks, things he'd taken for granted all his life took forever. Cleaning his teeth, just getting the toothpaste on the brush, was extraordinarily difficult. Some things were impossible to manage on his own, and he had to ask for help. He loathed that.

The wounds from the accident and subsequent surgery were still very painful, and it took him a long, long time to bath and dress. When he'd finally finished, he was in a foul mood. He went downstairs to the kitchen.

Alex was eating a sandwich. "Hi, Dad," he exclaimed, eagerly. "Can I get you something?"

"I might be a fucking cripple," Stephen scowled, switching the kettle on, "but I can get myself a cup of coffee."

Alex stared down at his plate.

Stephen put coffee and sugar in his mug, and went to the fridge for the milk. It was a unopened carton. He stared at it. It would be impossible for him to open it without help. Rage and sadness and self pity rose in him like a tidal wave. With a yell, he picked the carton up and chucked it across the room. It hit a row of glasses, smashing them, and burst open, spilling everywhere.

Toni, Pip and Sam came running in.
"What happened?" Toni gasped.
"Dad couldn't open the m-milk," Alex stuttered, pale and scared.
Stephen was crying with sorrow and frustration. He walked upstairs to his room and sat on the bed.
Sam followed him in and sat looking at him.
Stephen found it was impossible to keep on crying when someone was staring at him. He wiped his face with the back of his hand.
"You're like me, now, aren't you, Daddy?"
"What do you mean?"
"Different."
"Too bloody right I'm different!" Stephen tried to smile.
"You always told me it didn't matter and not to worry about it."
"It's not being different I mind, Sammy, it's not being able to do stuff – all the stuff I used to do." Tears of self pity filled his eyes again.
"I can't do stuff, either," Sam pointed out. "I can't do creative writing, I got into trouble till Al helped me. And I haven't got any friends. Everyone thinks I'm a freak, but I don't understand why."
Tears were pouring down Stephen's face again, not for himself, but for Sam. How could he complain? He'd had forty years of being normal; Sam had never had that and never would. How *awful* that he had no friends, that he could calmly say, 'They think I'm a freak.' He pulled Sam towards him and hugged him. "I'm so sorry for being so selfish, Sammy!"
Sam stood it for as long as he could. He hated being touched. Eventually, he wriggled away.
"Sorry," Stephen said again. "I know you don't like that, Sammy. I'm not myself." He made an effort. "What's this about creative writing?"
"It's, you know, stories. Like '*A Trip To The Moon.*' I wrote about what kind of rocket you'd need and what kind of fuel and how far it was. But Miss Johnstone didn't like that, she said, 'How would they feel?' I said, 'They wouldn't, they'd be wearing gloves'. She said not to be rude, but I don't see how I was."
Fucking bloody teachers, I'd like to drown the fucking lot of them, Stephen thought viciously. "Which one is Miss Johnstone?"
"She's new. She's our teacher while Mrs Hopcroft has her baby. I'll be glad when she comes back."
"What about Mrs Brayfield?" This was Sam's special needs helper.
"Oh, she wasn't there. She was having her legs waxed."
"Having her *legs waxed?*"
"Yeah, they're lumpy and green at the back and she went to hospital to have them waxed."
"Oh, stripped! Varicose veins! Yes, I see. And how is Alex helping you?"
"Well, now, when Miss Johnstone gives us a title, Alex talks to me about it. Like for the one last week when it was about Pharoahs, he made me think what I'd do if I had unlimited power. And then we talk about it, and then he sees what I've written, and if it's not going to be creative enough for Miss Johnstone, he helps me work out why. It's fun!"
Stephen felt ashamed. All this had been going on under his nose, and all he'd done was sworn and sulked and felt sorry for himself. What a good boy Alex was! He'd have to remember to thank him. He looked at Sam, and his heart turned over with love. How could he have wished he was dead? Imagine never seeing his sons

again! The thought was a revelation, he felt like Paul on the road to Damascus, but instead of being blinded, the scales had dropped from his eyes. He suddenly felt euphoric. I didn't die, he thought, I beat death and I'm still here with these people I love! It was as if he'd woken from a long nightmare.

He got up. "Thank you, Sammy," he said, his heart full of gratitude. "Come on, let's go back downstairs, there's something I need to tell you all."

Toni had just finished clearing up the mess he'd made. "What is it now, Stephen?" she asked, wearily.

"Hang on." Stephen called Alex and Pip, and smiled earnestly round at them all. "Everyone, I'm sorry. I've been behaving like a complete wanker..."

"Stephen!"

"What's a wanker?" Sam asked with interest.

Pip and Alex were giggling. Toni had gone scarlet.

"Um, sorry. I'll explain later, Sammy. Anyway, I won't act like that any more, OK? At least, I'll try not to. I'm very..." He swallowed, blinking back tears. "I'm very, *very* sad about my hand, I often feel tired and in pain, so there'll be times when I'll be crabby and mean, but I'll try not to be. Will you help me?"

Alex and Pip threw themselves at him and hugged him.

"Ow! Careful of my scars!" He looked at Toni. "Daisy?"

She pushed her hair behind her ears and tried to smile. "OK, Stephen."

Gradually, he began to feel less tired and listless. He tried very hard to keep his promise to his family, although after the first euphoria had worn off, he often felt the depression creeping over him; the knowledge that he would never play guitar again would hit him anew, and he would feel rage and pain and anguish.

To his dismay, he realised he'd become terrified of being in a car. He could no longer drive, and wouldn't discuss alternatives, claiming it depressed him too much, but secretly he was relieved. He was ashamed, and despised himself, but he couldn't help it, and he hated being driven anywhere, hated the sight of the oncoming traffic, had panic attacks at the thought of something happening – to him, but especially to his children. Anything could happen at any time, it seemed to him, random acts of God that could maim or kill any one of them. He became obsessive about their whereabouts, insisting on checking that their mobile phones were always fully charged, phoning them several times when they were out to make sure they were all right, and demanding full and precise details of where they would be going and when they would be back.

The boys bore this for as long as they could, but eventually Alex rebelled and turned his mobile off the next time he went out.

Stephen was frantic with worry and furiously angry. When Alex came in, he shoved him against the wall. "What the hell did you think you were doing?" he yelled. "How dare you turn your phone off?"

Alex was tall for his age, as tall as Stephen, and very fit. He pushed Stephen back. "For fuck's sake, leave me alone, Dad! You're being mental! We're fucking fed up with you!"

Stephen had never smacked his children, he was totally opposed to it, but at that moment he wanted to hit Alex and go on hitting him. The feeling shocked him. He stepped back. "Don't you dare swear at me like that. Get up to your room, you're grounded for the rest of the month."

Toni had run into the hall when she heard them shouting. After Alex had marched angrily upstairs, she turned despairingly to Stephen. "You've got to stop this, Stevo."

He stared at her. He felt as if he was standing in a deep, black pit, no way to climb out, no way to ever regain his old self. I'm going to feel like this for the rest of my life, he thought, the panic mounting. "Butt out, Toni," he said, and walked out of the house.

Dominic and Harry tried to talk to him. Rob tried. He wouldn't listen. Finally, Fin drove over to the Priory.

"Fin! Come and have a drink." Stephen led him into his study. "Coffee or a Coke?"

Fin had given up alcohol after his near fatal overdose twelve years ago. "Coke, please, Steve." He waited until Stephen had fetched him a Coke and poured himself a neat whisky – an extremely large one, Fin noticed. He sipped his Coke. "Steve, you can't go on like this." Stephen opened his mouth to protest, but Fin ignored him. "I can't pretend to know what you're going through, but I do know what it's like when your life's out of control. When I was doing drugs I would have sold my mother's soul to get my fix. I denied it to myself and to all of you, but I loathed myself. Towards the end, I started to think I'd be better off dead."

Stephen stared at him. "Is that why you—?"

"No, it was an accident," Fin interrupted. "At least, I think it was. I really don't know, I only know I couldn't have gone on like that much longer. And the point is, nor can you. You can't do this to your boys. They can't cope with much more. You nearly died, they nearly lost you, and now you're back home you're a stranger to them, a violent, frightening stranger."

"You don't understand," Stephen whispered. "You don't know what it's like. Anything could happen to them, anything, Fin, one minute you're just walking along, and the next – the next..." To his horror, he found he was starting to cry. He got up and walked to the window.

Fin followed him, and put his arm round his shoulder. "Life's always been like that, Steve, always," he said, gently. "The only thing that's changed is your perception of it."

"I can't stand the thought of losing them, Fin, I can't stand it. And I hate being like this," he burst out. "I'm like an old woman. I hate myself, I hate my life!"

Fin put both arms round him. "I know," he soothed. "I know. You've just got to let it go, Steve. Just let it go. And try to trust your boys. They're good, sensible kids."

Stephen leant against him for a moment. Why aren't I Fin? he thought. Why aren't I anyone but me, I don't want to be me, it's too hard, I can't cope. He pulled away and wiped his face. "Thanks, Fin. I will try, I do try. But it's so hard."

"Do you think it would help to talk to someone?" Fin suggested, looking at him with compassion. The light from the window falling on his face emphasised the livid scar along his right jaw. "I found counselling very useful."

Stephen's mouth twisted. "No. I don't want to talk about the accident. No," he said again, as Fin started to speak. "No. It won't help."

Fin sighed. "Well, Steve – you can talk to me anytime. To any of us."

Stephen managed to smile. "Thanks, Fin."

The following weekend, Harry and Dominic stayed, as they often did. "How's it going?" Harry asked Toni.

"A bit better, I think," Toni said cautiously. "He's been better with the boys, explained a little of how he feels, and asked them if they'll keep their phones on as a favour to him. He's promised to try and stop phoning them all the time, and he's mostly managed to over the last few days." She sighed. "He went for a check-up at the hospital yesterday, and he was in a foul mood afterwards. He wouldn't tell me why. It's nothing to do with his health, they say he's healing nicely."

Harry shook her head. "At least that's something. God, Toni, I wish there was something someone could do!"

"So do I," muttered Toni.

Dominic, meanwhile, unaware of this conversation, broached the subject of the album with Stephen.

"We can't finish it," Stephen shrugged. "Is it worth releasing what we've done?"

"We finished it." Dominic watched his face carefully. "It's due to be released soon."

"How?" Stephen demanded, guessing the answer.

"I played."

Stephen exploded. They'd talked to him about artificial hands again at the hospital. He didn't want to know, he'd told them that, but they wouldn't listen, just kept on and on about the advances in prosthetics, how there was so much on offer these days, and why didn't he have a look? He wasn't ready and he didn't see why they couldn't accept that. Maybe sometime in the future, but not now. And they kept saying, 'think about it', but he didn't want to, he wanted to forget the accident, forget his disability. Why couldn't they leave him alone?

"Who the fuck gave you permission to do that?" he yelled at Dominic. "They're *my* songs, it's *my* fucking band!"

"I talked to the others. They agreed. Stephen, be sensible. You might have needed the money."

"I'm a fucking multi-millionaire!"

"And if you'd died?" Dominic asked quietly.

Stephen stared at him. "There'd have been enough," he said, but without heat.

"You've got a wife and four boys. And as you've found out, life is a fucking bitch."

"Yes. Yes, I know. I'm sorry, Charlie." He sighed heavily. "They were on at me about false hands again today. I just want my own hand back." He looked at Dominic and tried to grin. "I can't even say I was just venting spleen any more."

Lynn and Simon chose a ring and Simon put it carefully on her finger. He hugged her. "I never thought I could be so happy!" He felt as if he was going to burst with joy. "I love you so very, very much, Lynn!"

What had she done? Again! All she could think of was Stephen. The sight of him in intensive care, so helpless and vulnerable, more like he was Rob's age than forty. But then, he didn't look forty anyway. Forty! She'd missed so many years of him. But what was the point in dwelling on that? He was out of her life, swallowed up by his home and family.

She smiled at Simon. "Sorry, what did you say?"

"I said, when do you want to tie the knot?"

"Well, we'll have to sort out who we're going to invite, and give them plenty of time, so that they're free," she said, thinking of Holly. "How about sometime in the autumn – say October?"

"Let's get the date fixed." Simon grinned happily. "Then we can send out the invites."

When 'Electric Playground ' was released, it shot to the top of the charts. This was the last album Stephen Markham would ever play guitar on, and demand for it was intense.

Stephen listened to it feeling as if his heart would break. I wish that bastard had just killed me, he thought again. He could tell where his playing ended and Dominic's began, but he didn't think many people would be able to. He told Dominic this.

"Course they will, don't be so fucking stupid, Markham," Dominic said, colouring.

"For God's sake, Dominic, why can't you just say 'thank you' when someone compliments you?" Harry demanded.

In June, it was Rob's twenty first birthday and Harry's fortieth and they had a joint party at Fenroth.

Stephen was feeling completely well again, apart from his knee. It hadn't healed properly, and he was having physiotherapy for it. And his amputated hand, which felt as if it was still there. He could actually feel it, it itched, sometimes it hurt. He could make the chord shapes with his fingers. But he didn't have any fingers. It was horrific.

Toni blanched when he told her. "Don't, Stephen! I can't bear to think about it!"

She was still sleeping apart from him. He appreciated the thought, but he was better now. And she'd been so careful of him, so kind, since he'd come out of hospital. It's been tough on her too, he thought.

The night after the party, he said to her, "Darling Daisy, I feel so well now. Come to bed with me, I want your beautiful body so much. I've really missed holding you."

She stared at him. She didn't know what to do. She'd hoped that the revulsion would go, but it had got worse. "I… I've got a splitting headache," she mumbled.

He was all concern. "My poor darling! Never mind, we'll just cuddle." He took her hand and they went upstairs together.

Toni's mind was racing. What the hell was she going to do? Maybe she could just shut her eyes, pretend he still had both his hands, but suppose *it* touched her? She shuddered.

In bed, she stared at his left arm in horror, jumping convulsively when he reached out for her. "I can't!" she screamed. "I can't, Stephen, I can't!"

He frowned anxiously. "Is your head very bad, darling? Do you think we should get Harry to call the doctor?"

"I don't have a headache! It's your… your… I can't stand your…" She stared at his arm.

Realisation dawned on Stephen. "My stump," he said tonelessly. "You can't stand my stump."

"Stop *saying* that word! Yes! I can't stand it! I'm sorry, Stephen." She was crying hysterically. "Perhaps there's someone I could see who could help me, but right now, I can't be in here. Not with… with *that*!"

After she'd gone, he sat on his bed, shaking with emotion. Did everyone feel like Toni? He looked down at his arm. He *was* deformed. It *was* repulsive. He'd bought a bottle of painkillers with him, in case he had any problems. Well, this certainly qualified. He opened the tub with difficulty, as his hand was still shaking, and swallowed several of the pills. He needed a glass of whisky. Downstairs, he heard voices in Dominic's study. Composing himself, he went in. Dominic, Andy, Mick Ansty, and Snog MacNaughton, who had been the frontman for the hugely popular Seventies band, The Silver Spiders, were drinking whisky, and laughing at something Snog was saying.

Dominic smiled at Stephen. "Markham! We were wondering where you were! Glass of whisky?" He poured Stephen a drink. "Sit down."

"Where's that bonny lass of yours?" Snog asked.

Stephen drained his glass. "Bed. Can I have another, Charlie?"

Dominic raised his eyebrows. "Of course." He passed Stephen the bottle.

Snog dug Stephen in the ribs. "She's away in bed and you're down here drinking whisky? Aye, that's marriage, all right! Will I go and tuck her in for you, Steve?" he leered.

Stephen swallowed his whisky and forced himself to smile. "In your dreams, Snog! Anyway, she's not feeling very well. Actually, I'm feeling a bit iffy myself. I thought the whisky might help, but I think I'll go on up too. Goodnight."

He managed to get to his room and collapsed, fully clothed, on the bed.

"Toni, you'll have to see someone, talk to someone about this!" Callie was aghast. Toni had arrived at her door in a terrible state, and told her what had happened at Fenroth, the words tumbling out, sometimes almost unintelligible, for she was crying at the same time.

"I know, I know, but I just kept hoping it would go away, that I'd stop feeling like this, and, oh, Callie, I feel so awful, but I don't love him any more!"

Callie put her arms round her. "You just feel that way now," she soothed. "If you see someone, sort it out, you'll be fine, I know you will."

"No." Toni shook her head. "I'm in love with George."

Callie stared at her. "Oh, Toni, Oh, my God. What are you going to do? Are you and George, you know, lovers?"

"Oh, no! No, we're not having an affair, neither of us could do that! He loves me too, but we can't do anything about it, not with Stephen… the way he is. I just don't know what to do!"

Neither did Callie. She didn't know what she could say or do to help. "You'll have to talk to Stephen."

"No," Toni said again. "I can't." She stood up abruptly, startling Callie. "I must go, Cal." She bent and kissed her. "Thank you for listening. I'll ring you." She left, leaving Callie staring after her.

Stephen became morose and withdrawn again. He wasn't unpleasant to the boys, but he avoided them. He made Toni ask people not to visit him and went back to drugging himself into unconsciousness. When he ran out of pills, he went to see Henry, telling him he had phantom limb pain. Henry was very sympathetic, prescribing him three months' supply. Stephen knew he'd go through them in a couple of weeks. He wasn't sure how he'd get more after that. Maybe the Internet.

To Rob's joy, he gained a first class degree. Julia got a 2.1, and Harry and Dominic arranged to throw them a party at Leezance after they graduated.

"What's the matter, Stevie?" Harry asked. She'd driven to the Priory unexpectedly after Rob's excellent result, on the pretext of discussing the party.

"Nothing," Stephen said. He wouldn't talk to her.

In the end she left. "I don't know what we can do," she said despairingly to Dominic.

"Absolutely nothing," Dominic said sadly.

On the first Friday in July, Stephen's case came to court. The driver, who had been asleep at the wheel, had been charged with dangerous driving, but had pleaded not guilty. Julian went with Stephen and Rob, and they met Alan and Cell there.

Cell, who was the least demonstrative woman Stephen knew, astonished him by giving him a brief, fierce hug. Her familiar scent of patchouli oil and cigarettes filled his nostrils, taking him back to the first time he'd met her, in the dressing room at Utopia. He wanted to break down and cry, but he knew if he started, he wouldn't be able to stop. They made their way into the courtroom, and he and Rob gave evidence, along with several other witnesses eager to have their fifteen minutes of fame with the papers afterwards.

The jury found the driver guilty of careless driving. He was fined five hundred pounds, and his licence was endorsed. Julian had spoken to Stephen and Rob about the case earlier, warning them that the courts often took falling asleep at the wheel leniently. Stephen, staring down at his left arm as the sentence was passed, was aware of the excited buzz in the public gallery.

Afterwards, despite Cell advising him to say nothing, when the reporters asked him if he thought the driver should have been convicted of dangerous driving and imprisoned, he said no, it had been an accident, the driver had pulled into the service station because he knew he was too tired to be driving.

"Why ruin his life as well?" he asked wearily.

"So do you forgive him then, Steve?" one of the reporters queried.

"No," Stephen replied.

Rob drove him home. His graduation ceremony was at the end of the following week. "You are going to be there, aren't you, Dad?"

Stephen smiled, a smile that didn't quite reach his eyes. "I wouldn't miss it for worlds, Blue."

Rob relaxed. "You'll feel better, soon, Dad," he said, hopefully.

"Sure," Stephen agreed, dully. Rob drove off and Stephen walked wearily into the house.

His knee was hurting. The constant nagging pain tired him and made him irritable. He fetched a bottle of whisky and started drinking.

Toni watched anxiously as he downed three large glasses in rapid succession. She had asked to go to court with him, but he hadn't wanted her. "Is that a good idea, mate?"

"Mate! That's a laugh! Tell me, Toni, are we ever going to make love again? Because if we're not, what's the point of our staying together? After all, it's not as if you have a lovely personality, is it?" He finished his drink and poured himself another. The whisky felt good, warm and sustaining.

Toni was staring at him.

"Well, come on, Toni, you're a miserable bitch. The only thing in your favour is that you're a good fuck, but I don't even get that any more."

"Stephen! How can you say that?" She was having difficulty breathing.

"Yeah, I guess you're right. You weren't that good," he said reflectively. He finished the bottle. "Lynn was much better."

Toni was shaking violently. "You bastard! You utter, utter bastard!"

"Do me a favour? Fuck off back to Australia where you belong, with the rest of the venomous creatures."

She left the room. He heard her run upstairs. He fetched another bottle of whisky and poured himself a glass.

When he woke, the house was in darkness. He looked round, disorientated. It had been light when he got back from court. He got up, and the room tilted. He managed to stumble to the window. It was late, the sun had set and there was just a faint afterglow in the deep, dark blue sky. Bron came wagging up to him. He stroked her and started up the stairs. His missing hand was hurting, a gnawing pain. He flexed his nonexistent fingers, and it felt slightly better.

Into the bedroom. He turned the light on; instant sunrise. It hurt his eyes. There was a pink square on his pillow. He weaved across the room and picked it up. A notelet and Toni's bold, clear handwriting, jerky, and blotted with tears. *Stephen,* it said. *I have taken the boys and we've gone to Australia as you suggested.* As he suggested? When? He read on. *I've had enough, Stephen. I want a divorce. I'm sorry, but I can't live with you any more, you're horrible to me, you're horrible to the boys. Toni.*

He sat on the bed and looked at the bedside clock. The hands pointed at five to twelve. He spent some time wondering if that was in the morning or at night, before he remembered it was dark outside. He felt that that was important but wasn't sure why, something to do with time zones. His head was starting to ache, and he lay down. He was on the point of sleep when he remembered Toni's note. Time zones. Toni was in Australia, and if it was night here, in Australia it would be… He couldn't remember the time difference, but daytime, anyway. He dialled Jacko's number.

"G'day?"

"Jacko. It's Stephen. Can I speak to Toni?"

"Toni? She's not here, Taddie."

"Oh." He didn't know what to say. "Her note says she is."

"Stephen." Jacko realised he was drunk. "When did Toni write the note?"

"Um." He tried to concentrate. "Earlier."

"She wouldn't be here yet, then, son, it's a long way. She might not even be on a plane."

Stephen clutched the receiver tightly. "What am I going to do?" he whispered. "I want to speak to her and the boys. What am I going to do, Jacko?" He began to cry. "I don't know how to get hold of her."

"Have you tried her mobile, mate?"

"Um, I can't, um, the number, I can't remember…"

"It's OK, son," Jacko interrupted. "Listen, Stephen, is anyone else there?"

Stephen glanced round the room. "I can't see anyone. They say the house is haunted," he whispered.

"No, son, I mean people. Real people. Friends, staff."

"Well, the thing is, Toni would normally be here, but she's gone to Australia with the boys. Is she there, Jacko?"

"Look, Stephen, you go to bed. That's what Toni's done, she and the boys were very tired. You have a good sleep, and I'll get her to phone you as soon as you wake up, OK?"

"I don't want to do that, Jacko. I can't stand it when I wake up and remember. In my dreams I'm playing my guitar and then I wake up – and then I wake up – there's really no point to it is there? No point to ever waking up."

Jacko was seriously worried. "Stephen," he said, urgently. "Look, son, don't go to sleep, then. Just lie on the bed for a little while, OK? For a rest—"

The line went dead. "Christ!" he said to Kay. "That was Stephen. Toni's left him and taken the boys. He sounded shocking! Get me Robbie's mum's number, love."

"Who the fuck could that be?" Dominic asked blearily, as Harry turned on the light. He picked up the phone. "Dominic Chaplin?"

"Mate, look, it's Toni's father here, Jacko. I've just had a call from Stephen, and I'm really worried. Toni's taken the boys and left him – apparently she's coming here. He was in a shocking state, pissed to the eyeballs."

Dominic was already out of bed. "OK, thanks, Jacko, we'll take care of it…yes, thank you…Yes, of course, I'll let you know." He hung up, and started to pull on his clothes.

"What?" Harry asked, scared.

"Stephen's in a bad way, Toni's left him, he's drunk, Jacko's very worried. I'm going over there."

Harry picked up the phone.

"What are you doing?" Dominic demanded.

"Phoning Andy. He can go round. Stop faffing about, Dominic! Holl? It's Harry." She spoke into the phone for a few minutes. "Yes, OK, Holly, thanks. Bye. Come on, Dominic! Aren't you dressed yet?"

After she'd left, Toni had picked up Alex and Pip and told them they were fetching Sam and going to Australia.

"But why? What about Dad?" Alex had asked, bewildered. "He needs someone to help him with stuff, Mum. We can't leave him alone!"

"I don't want to go without Dad," Pip agreed. "I don't think he's very well, Mum, he was crying yesterday."

"Your Dad is fine. He said – he said we ought to go."

"Let's go home and ask him," Alex suggested.

"No!" Toni shouted, making them both jump. "Now shut up, the pair of you."

There was a brief silence, and then Pip asked, "How long will we be away, Mum? I'm in the swimming team, you know I am, and we've got the tournament next week."

"Well don't ask your Dad to come and see it, he can't afford to lose his other hand," Toni said bitterly.

The boys were incredibly shocked. "That is *so* not funny, Mum," Alex said, finally.

"You're horrible!" Pip said, his voice choked. "I don't want to talk to you!"

"Good!" Toni retorted. They drove in silence for a while. She couldn't bear it any longer, and pulled up just before they got to Sam's school. "Your Dad and I have split up."

They were even more horrified. "He'll be so sad!" Pip said.

"We've got to go back!" Alex said urgently. "And what about Cruncher Feet? He's my dog!" They began to wail dismally.

"For God's sake, shut up!" Toni started the car. "You've got to be helpful with Sam, it'll be hardest for him."

Alex pulled himself together. "She's right, Pip. But we want to speak to Dad, Mum."

"Later," Toni said. "I promise."

She took them to their favourite pizza restaurant for tea, where she explained the situation to Sam. He sat, huddled in his school jersey, staring up at the ceiling out of the corner of his eyes. "I want Dr Venkman, Venkman, Venkman."

"Oh God, don't, Sam," Toni implored. She was immensely sorry for him, but she couldn't cope with this now.

Alex cast her a look of loathing. "Don't worry, Sammy. We're going to ring him up soon. Tell me about Mozart's starling."

That worked. They got in the car and Toni drove them to Cheyne Walk. She was too unhappy to attempt anything else. When they got in, she rang Stephen. There was no answer. "There! He's taken Crunchy and Bron for their run." She left a message, asking him to ring the boys. Alex looked at his watch. It was about the time he and Stephen usually took the dogs out, although Stephen hadn't gone of late. But he'd be there alone tonight, he'd have to.

"Go and play in your rooms, or watch TV or something, boys," Toni said. They went reluctantly off and in relief, with shaking fingers, she rang George.

"I'm coming round," was all he said. When he got there, he took her in his arms. "You're never going back to him."

Toni fell against him. "No. But you don't understand, George. It's not really his fault. I couldn't bear his… his… where they cut his hand off. I couldn't go to bed with him. I could barely look at him. Poor Stephen. But I couldn't."

George held her. "God, Toni, man, what a mess," he muttered, kissing her head. "What about Steve? Is he all right?"

"He's taken the dogs out. I left a message for him to ring."

Lynn and Simon were staying with Holly and Andy, and they went with him to the Priory. He knocked at the front door. A deep and thunderous barking answered him.

"Jesus Christ, it's the hound of the Baskervilles!" exclaimed Simon. He wasn't too keen on dogs.

"That's Crunchy, Alex's dog. He's lovely," Andy said.

Simon looked unconvinced.

They tried all the doors, but couldn't find any that were unlocked.

"Oh, well, nothing else for it," Andy shrugged. He carefully broke a pane of glass in the french window in Stephen's study, and reached in to unlock it. "Thank God the alarm system's off!" he said, with relief.

"Have you done this before?" Lynn joked, and was taken aback when he said, "Oh, yeah, all the time when I was a kid, like."

Crunchy bounced up to them, followed by Bron. Andy patted them quickly. "Come on, you two, out of the way."

They found Stephen in his bedroom, stretched out on the bed. "Do you think he's overdosed?" whispered Simon, with a kind of horrified fascination.

"No need to whisper," Andy said. "He's just pissed, I've seen him like this loads of times. Well, occasionally," he added, at the look on Lynn's face. He wrinkled his nose. "He stinks of booze! What we need to do is get him into the shower and then into bed, and make him drink some water. Simon, give me a hand. Lynn, you find him some pyjamas. Steve! Come on, Steve, wake up."

"Leave me alone," Stephen mumbled, trying to roll away from them.

Andy and Simon got him into the ensuite and stripped him off.

"Jesus, look at those scars!" Simon exclaimed, shocked. Stephen had a long scar reaching from his breastbone to below his navel where the surgeons had done the exploratory laparotomy, and one at the bottom of his ribcage where they'd taken out his spleen, and the accident had left him with scars of varying sizes all over his body.

Andy nodded. "Yeah, poor sod. It's all right, Steve," he went on, reassuringly as Stephen mumbled something. "You can get into a nice warm bed in a minute, and have an aspirin and a drink of water. Just get into this shower first."

Stephen gasped and spluttered as the water cascaded over him. They helped him out and into a bathrobe.

"Andy? What's happening? How are you here?"

"It's all right, Steve, we've come to help. Lynn! Pee jays!"

"Cherry!"

She smiled at him. "I'm here, Stevie."

He grasped her hand. "Please stay with me, Cherry, I love you so much. Please don't go!"

Lynn pulled him to her. She felt his arms go round her and she buried her face against his chest, feeling the warmth of him. She was home, and she'd forgotten Simon as if he'd never existed.

"I'm not going anywhere, my darling," she whispered unsteadily.

Stephen bent his head and kissed her. 'I'm Alive' started to play in his head, and the past twenty years was nothing, and all that mattered was Cherry, there was only him and Cherry, and she was in his arms. He was never going to let her go again.

Simon stared at them, thunderstruck. He couldn't believe what he was seeing. How could Lynn do this to him?

Andy put his hand on his shoulder, and led him out of the room.

"But… but she's my fiancée!" Simon gasped. "I love her, Andy, we're in love, you know we are, she wants to marry me, she promised to marry me! We're getting married in a few months, it's all arranged!"

"She's Stephen's wife," Andy shrugged. "She's never really been anything else, like. I'm sorry, Simon," he said sympathetically. "I'll make sure Steve's all right, then I'll run you home."

"I'll get a taxi to the station," Simon said stiffly. "Tell her, will you? If she ever notices I've gone," he added bitterly. He shook Andy's hand. "It was nice knowing you, Andy. Thank Holly for me."

Andy went back into the bathroom where Stephen and Lynn were still holding each other. Lynn smiled at him, her eyes like purple stars. Andy had never seen her look so beautiful.

"You two'll be all right, then?" he asked, smiling at them.

"I'll look after him, Andy," Lynn nodded. She gasped. "Oh! Simon!"

"He understood. He told me to say goodbye," Andy said, embroidering the truth somewhat. He patted Stephen on the shoulder. "I'll be off, like."

Stephen smiled at him gratefully. "Thanks, bro."

"Shall we go to bed?" Lynn suggested after Andy had gone. "It's cold in here."

As Stephen lay in bed watching her undress, a chilling thought struck him. His stump. Supposing Lynn felt like Toni? Supposing everyone did? It *was* repulsive, a deformed arm.

Lynn jumped into bed and snuggled up to him. "Brrr! Cuddle me, Stevie, I'm freezing! What is it?" she asked, alarmed by his expression.

"You know I'm – I'm deformed, don't you, Cherry? I mean, can you bear it?"

"What's wrong with you?" she asked anxiously.

"Well, my arm."

"Yes, of course I know. It's not deformed, it just hasn't got a hand on the end." She took it and stroked it gently. "Oh, that doesn't hurt, does it?" she asked, at the look on his face.

He shook his head, wordlessly. "It's just… Toni didn't… she couldn't… she was repulsed."

Bitch! Fucking bloody bitch! Lynn thought. "Well, I'm not. Oh, Stevie, darling, darling Stevie, make love to me, I've wanted you for nearly twenty years."

He grinned. "God! Let's hope I come up to expectations! Bloody hell, I wish I hadn't had all that whisky." The thought of it made him wince. "Oh! Wait!" He leapt up and crossed to a chest of drawers, where he rummaged around. He came back with a little box and handed it to Lynn.

Intrigued, she opened it. It contained her antique rose diamond engagement ring and the wedding rings she and Stephen had bought for one another. Her eyes filled with tears.

"You might want a better one now I can afford it."

"No! Oh, no! I want these!" She pulled off Simon's ring. "I'll have to send this back to him," she muttered. She felt terrible about him, but she pushed it aside. She was here with Stevie, and nothing else mattered. She slipped his rings onto her finger. They still fitted perfectly.

"Are you wearing them both now? I thought we were just engaged."

"As far as I'm concerned, we're married right this minute!" Lynn said, kissing him. She helped him try to get his ring on the third finger of his right hand, but it was too small.

"Never mind," he shrugged. "I'll get it altered tomorrow. Now then – where were we?"

Chapter Twenty-Four
Right To Love

I know it's right to love you,
It's all I want to do,
Give me the right to stay with you.

The phone woke him from a deep and refreshing sleep. For the first time since the accident, he didn't wish he was dead, in fact he was filled with joy. Lynn was still asleep next to him, making little snoring noises. He picked up the phone. "Hello?" he whispered.

There was a silence at the other end. "Dad?" Alex whispered back finally.

"Alex?"

"Why are we whispering?" Alex inquired.

"So I don't wake – Savij."

"Oh." Alex stopped whispering. "Dad, we're in London. Why didn't you ring us?"

"I didn't know where you were. Mum left me a note to say you were going to Australia, and I couldn't find her mobile number." Too drunk, he thought, but didn't say that.

"But we rang and left a message. You were out with the dogs."

"Was I?"

"Dad, are you all right? You're acting weird."

"Yes, sorry. Look, Ally, what's Mum doing?"

"Well," Alex said, his voice dripping with disapproval, "George was here at breakfast time, so Pip and I can only speculate."

Stephen grinned. "Is Sammy all right?"

"He is now. Mum was no fucking good at all."

"Alex, you know you shouldn't swear like that," Stephen whispered weakly.

"Sorry, Dad. But, you know, sometimes! Anyway, I got him to tell me all about Mozart." He lowered his voice "It was very boring, but he was OK after that."

"Alex, I am so proud of you," Stephen said, forgetting to whisper.

Lynn stirred and opened her eyes. She smiled at him.

He leant forward and kissed her nose. "Hello. Sleep well?"

"Is she awake now?" Alex asked.

"Yes. I was kissing her nose."

"Mind she doesn't scratch you."

"I was hoping she might scratch my back later," Stephen said, naughtily.

"I think Mum running away has made you a bit odd. I'll tell her she's got to get back with you."

God, no! thought Stephen. "Well," he said, carefully, "the thing is, Al, me and Mum do still love each other, just not in the marrying way any more. But you boys have got to come home, you've got school for the next two weeks. And hasn't Pipkin got his Swimming Tournament? Could I have a word with Mum?"

While Alex went to get her, Sam talked to him. "I miss you, Dr Venkman. Miss you, miss you."

Stephen's heart contracted with pity. "I miss you too, my little pianist. Listen, you'll be home soon."

"Here's Janine. And the Stay Puft Marshmallow Man."

Stephen laughed delightedly. What an excellent name for George!

"Steve?" It was the Marshmallow Man!

"George."

"Now listen, Steve, you can't blame Toni for anything, man. Blame me, if you like."

"I don't blame you, George, I thank you. I know you'll look after her."

"What?"

"Cherry's here," Stephen explained.

"Oh! Oh, well, congratulations, bonny lad." George sounded relieved.

"Thanks. Look, don't say anything to the boys, I want to tell them properly myself. George – please don't let Toni tell them. She sometimes does that – to get even with me."

There was a silence at the other end of the phone. Stephen thought George had taken his comments the wrong way. Then George said, his voice a little grim, "Divn't fret, man, there'll be none of that from now on. I'll put her on."

"Toni." He couldn't think what to say. "I can't remember much of yesterday, but I'm sorry. I wasn't very nice."

"Nor me." She sounded very subdued. "I'm sorry too. I have to be with George, Stephen."

"That's OK, Toni," he said cheerfully. "Lynn's here. We spent last night together. We're getting married as soon as you and I are divorced."

"Lynn? In my bed? My sheets?" Her voice scaled upwards.

Stephen heard George's voice. Toni said something in reply, and then George raised his voice. "Not if you know what's good for you, pet!" Toni came back on the phone. "Sorry, Stephen. I – I'm glad you're happy. George and I will be getting married too. Won't we, George?"

"Give me the phone, man!" Stephen heard George say. "Steve?"

"Yeah?"

"We'll be back later with your boys."

Stephen hung up. He kissed Lynn. "You've got to scratch my back now."

"What?"

"Can I make love to you?"

"Oh, yes, please!"

Much later, when they were lying curled up together, Lynn touched his earlobe. "What happened to your earring?"

"God! I took that out years ago! You can't wear an earring much over thirty five, and even that's pushing it."

"I still wear earrings," she giggled.

"If you're a man. You know perfectly well what I meant."

"What happened to it?" She'd loved him in his earring. And he barely looked thirty five now.

"I gave it to the boys to play pirates with."

To his dismay, he received letters from outraged families whose relatives had been killed or seriously injured by negligent drivers only to see the driver walk away from court with a fine. He got Cell to issue a statement to the effect that he was only talking about his own accident when he'd said he thought the sentence was just. He replied to the letters himself. He also had letters from religious crackpots saying that the loss of his hand was God's punishment for his blasphemy over 'Beggars Can't Be Jesus'.

"How can people be so horrible?" he asked Lynn, distressed.

"Burn the fucking lot of them," she advised.

He grinned at her. "You never ever used to swear! What happened to my innocent little girl?"

She grinned back. "I joined the real world."

Julian was handling the divorce. In the meantime, Toni was living in George's flat during the week, while Stephen and Lynn lived at the Priory with the boys. At the weekend, Stephen and Lynn moved to Cheyne Walk, and Toni and George went to the Priory. It meant that the boys stayed at the Priory full-time, which was far less disruptive for them. Of course, when the divorce was final, this would no longer happen, but that was a way down the line yet, and by then, the boys would be used to the situation. George and Toni were looking for a house, and Toni's new book, *Albert's Watch*, had just been published.

Lynn had given up her practice. She simply wanted to be a full-time wife to Stephen and look after him and the boys.

Sam, who was finding the situation extremely stressful, was delighted to see her again. "Lynn! I missed you! Missed you, missed you, missed you."

"I missed you, Sammy," she replied, smiling at him. "Do you remember when you used to call me Win?"

He nodded. "But that was a long time ago, I was only a baby, then. Only a baby, only a baby."

Pip and Alex were a little more wary. They liked George, but they'd known him ever since they could remember. Lynn was unknown territory. She didn't try to win them round with bribery or promises, simply treated them as she did Sam, with affection and interest.

At the end of the month there was a huge article in one of the tabloids, *Dumped For Love Rat Markham!* Simon, hurting very badly, had sold his story to the press. He'd said spiteful things about Lynn, and repeated many of the stories she'd told him about her and Stephen from their Manchester days. She felt terrible, very guilty. She felt she'd driven Simon to it, and she desperately wished she hadn't talked to him about Stephen.

There was tremendous interest in everything to do with Stephen and Lynn, and articles with titles like *Steve Takes Another Bite Of The Cherry*, *Rock Star's Retro Romance*, *Off With The Old And On With The Even Older*, appeared in the papers. When the press found out that Toni was living with George, their jubilation knew no bounds. Reporters clustered around the gates of the Priory, and Stephen thanked God it was the school holidays. "By September it should all be over," he said wearily to Rob, when he and Julia came to stay for a weekend.

Rob thought he was looking terrible. "He looks done in," he said to Lynn.

"I know. Bloody Simon and those bloody reporters, I'd like to boil them in oil!" She felt awful for talking so freely to Simon about Stephen, he seemed to have remembered and regurgitated everything she'd ever told him.

Rob grinned. "Even the Spanish Inquisition stopped short of boiling people alive. Apparently they tried it but it was so terrible they couldn't carry on with it."

Lynn smiled at him fondly. "You're just like Stevie! You know something about almost everything."

Stephen came in. "For God's sake, don't feed his ego!"

"Can't stand the competition, can you, Dad?" Rob grinned.

"Competition, Blue? In your dreams! Cherry, I'm going for a lie down. Will you give me a shout if Julian rings?"

Lynn looked at him anxiously. "Are you OK, Stevie?"

"Oh, fine, just a bit tired," he said, breezily.

After he'd gone, Lynn bit her lip. "That's not like him."

"He was having trouble getting upstairs earlier," Julia said hesitantly.

Rob turned to her in amazement. "Why didn't you tell us?"

"Well, he asked me not to," she said apologetically.

"Yes, he would," Lynn said grimly. "What was hurting, did he say?"

"Well, his knee, but I think his chest too; he was kind of hunched over."

"God, I hope he's OK!" Lynn was scared. "What should I do, do you think? I mean, he's not a child, I can't just take him to the doctor!"

"I'd phone Henry and see what he thinks; he'll understand and he won't say anything to Dad. But I tell you what I think he needs," Rob said. "A bloody good holiday, far away from all this hassle. Take him to the lake house, Cherry."

They had an idyllic time in Massachusetts.

Ray and Shannon had bought a small house a few doors away and spent several weekends there. The first evening they were all together, Lynn and Ray spent most of the time saying 'Do you remember?' to each other.

Lynn had persuaded Stephen to see Henry before they travelled, and Henry had referred him back to the James Radlett, where he had been X–rayed and scanned and generally pulled and prodded about. "Your body had a very hard time, a great deal of trauma. It's not uncommon for it to have twinges of pain from time to time. It's still sensitive," his consultant told him. "The accident was only six months ago; it takes a while for everything to get back to the way it used to be. And you're over forty now." He grinned at Stephen over his half-moon glasses. "Just take it easy; gentle exercise. Swimming's excellent. But build it up slowly."

Stephen took his advice. He swam in the lake every day, gradually going further and further. Lynn came in sometimes, but preferred the heated pool. They sat up on the deck after a swim and Stephen told her about the first time they'd come to the house, not long after he'd made *Hoodman Blind*, and how tactless Ray had been about Coral and the nude scene, and how he'd told Ray the lake was heated.

"And he believed you?" Lynn grinned.

"I told him I was so rich I could have anything I wanted and he jumped right in! It was April and way colder than this."

"Poor Ray!" Lynn smiled fondly.

"Poor Ray, my foot! Stirring it as usual! Although if Toni hadn't always been ready to believe the worst it wouldn't have mattered. *You* wouldn't have been jealous, would you?"

Lynn made a face. "I'm not sure, it's pretty steamy stuff! And I read all the newspaper reports about you and Coral sharing a joint, and the dot-to-dot on her bottom."

"It was a 'herbal cigarette'," he grinned, "and the freckles were on her back!" His face changed. "Pass me my robe, Cherry."

Someone went past in a small boat and waved. Stephen waved back. Lynn noticed how he hated anyone seeing his stump. Bloody Toni! she thought. It was the only thing that marred the holiday. Despite the heat, he wore a jacket whenever they went out.

"How long do you want to stay?" Stephen asked when they had been there for a month.

"Forever! Is there any reason for going home yet?" You're still not looking right, she thought, anxiously. He'd been much happier since they'd come to Massachusetts, much more his old self, but he was still very thin and drawn, and, although he never said anything, she was pretty sure he was often in pain.

"Only the boys."

"Darling, I'm sure the boys won't mind you staying as long as you want, and I'm happy to be wherever you are," she smiled.

"Let's stay a little longer then. It's like a dream being here with you. I keep thinking I'll wake up and you'll be gone."

"Oh, darling Stevie!" She felt terrible. "If I hadn't left you…"

"Ssh!" He put his arm round her. "That was then, this is now. We're here, Cherry, we're together. That's all that matters. This day alone is ours."

She shivered. "What do you mean?"

"Anything could happen at any time. When I was in hospital I thought how amazing it was that one minute you're thinking you're invincible, you'll live forever, and the next, your life is hanging in the balance. This day alone is ours. Let's make love."

The next time she went shopping, she bought a pregnancy testing kit. Her period was nearly a week late, and while she was sure she couldn't possibly be pregnant, she'd started to feel a little sick in the mornings. The kits were so different from the ones that were available when she got pregnant with Sakura. In those days you had to collect the urine and wait at least eight hours for the result. She went home took the test and waited for the required minute. A minute! she thought. It's nothing! And yet the seconds dragged.

She couldn't believe it when the indicator turned blue, she stared at it, held it up to the light. She rushed out, waving it like some kind of trophy. "Stevie! Stevie, where are you?"

He came running upstairs. He was only wearing shorts and he looked absolutely gorgeous, she didn't even notice his missing hand any more, she realised. She wished he would believe her when she said it wasn't repulsive.

"I'm pregnant!" she shouted in delight.

He stared at her, stunned. "What?"

"Well, I suppose it's not surprising, is it, we've been at it like knives since that night at the Priory," she grinned.

His face broke into a smile of pure joy. "My beautiful, brilliant, beloved Cherry! This is all we need to make our life perfect!"

Before they went home, he took her to New York to buy some new clothes. They went to Serendipity 3, the funny little restaurant that Dominic had introduced him to in the Eighties. That was when I discovered Charlie still had groupies even though he was married to Hal, he remembered. God, I can't believe the way I worried about their marriage, he thought ruefully. How ironic!

He'd taken the boys to the restaurant several times, and he thought, correctly, that Lynn would enjoy the ambience. He hadn't booked, and he used his stardom to get seated right away, something he didn't like doing and usually avoided, but he didn't want Lynn standing around in her condition.

As usual, he pigged out, having three puddings and two helpings of their delicious Frrrozen Hot Chocolate drink. "Do you suppose it would be OK to undo the top button of my jeans?" he groaned, as Lynn finished her sundae.

"Certainly not!" she said. She grinned. "Suppose someone saw? You'd never live it down! Let's go back to the hotel, then you can take them off."

Stephen shook his head. "Sex! That's all you think about!"

When they got home, Lynn went to see Heather Donaldson, who examined her very carefully. "You do realise you're going to feel like a specimen under a microscope during this pregnancy, don't you?" she smiled.

Lynn smiled back. "I don't care, I really want this baby."

Heather told her she'd need a stitch in her cervix at about fourteen weeks. "That'll be done under a general anaesthetic, and you'll need to rest all the time. And no sex. We'll take the stitch out at around thirty eight weeks."

"No sex for how long?" Lynn inquired.

"Until the baby's born."

"Until the baby's born?" Lynn repeated, stunned. "Poor Stephen!"

Heather grinned. "Well, you can satisfy each other in other ways."

Lynn blushed.

"No sex! God, that'll be so difficult," Stephen groaned. "Look at you, standing there provocatively like that, I want to ravish you right here!" he whispered.

They were in the waiting room and Lynn was making another appointment. She giggled. "If you're good, I'll do something to you when we get home. Heather said we could satisfy each other in other ways. It's terrible though, because I've just got reacquainted with your great big, beautiful w—"

"Lynn!" Stephen exclaimed.

"Warm heart, I was going to say! Oh, Stephen, you surely didn't think I was going to say willy?"

Stephen turned scarlet and hurried her out of the room.

She noticed, with some misgiving, that he didn't seem so happy now they were home. Being in America had been a bit like being at university – now they were back in the real world. He wouldn't go near the studio, wouldn't look at it, talked about pulling it down. She and Dominic persuaded him not to. But he was adamant that he was getting rid of his guitars.

"Even your first Strat? And your National that your grandfather gave you?" Lynn asked, stunned.

"What fucking good are they to me now?" he shouted.

She turned away.

"Cherry!" He caught her arm. "Sorry."

She rang Harry and asked her to come and take the guitars. "Look after them," she begged.

Harry kissed her. "Of course I will! He'll want them one day, even if only to give them to the boys." She fingered his Matteo Sellas guitar. "He played this on our anniversary song." Her eyes filled with tears. "How can life be so cruel? He was simply the best I ever heard. And that's not just because I love him; according to Stanton Crawford – oh, not just him, *everyone* said it – he was exceptional, one of the greats. Oh, God, Lynn!"

"Can I hear your anniversary song?"

"Of course. It's in the car. Dominic wrote it for our fifteenth anniversary last year. It's called 'The Loving Cup'." She brought the CD in, and they listened to it together. It was a superb song, with lovely lyrics, and Dominic sang it beautifully. But Stephen's playing was sublime.

Lynn put it on again. "Can I have a copy?"

"No," said Stephen from the door.

They both jumped and turned to look at him. The expression on his face was almost frightening. "I don't want to hear anything I've ever played guitar on being played in this house."

"But Stevie—"

"No!" he shouted. "I mean it, Lynn. If you do, I'll be very angry."

"She's not Toni, Steve," Harry said, perturbed.

"Butt out, Harriet," Stephen said, his eyes on Lynn. "I mean it, Lynn." He turned and left the room.

Lynn sat down. To her humiliation, she found she was shaking.

"Are you all right?" Harry asked anxiously.

She managed to nod.

"Perhaps you ought to lie down," Harry suggested.

She nodded again, trying to hold back tears.

Harry helped her to the bedroom. "Has he been like this before?"

Lynn swallowed. "No. He was so happy in America, except he couldn't bear anyone to see his stump."

"Really?" Harry was surprised. "He didn't used to care."

"No, he said he didn't until June. Then he felt up to having sex with that bitch again and she wouldn't because she said he was deformed and his stump revolted her. He reckons that's when he realised how hideous it was."

Harry stared, horror-stricken. "Oh, Lynn, no!"

Lynn nodded. "Yes. So in America, he wouldn't wear a tee shirt if we went anywhere, even though the weather was boiling."

"My God, I'd like to kill her!" Harry exclaimed.

"She really was a wrecker, wasn't she?"

"And then some," Harry said, grimly. "Hanging, drawing and quartering is too good for her. Dominic will go ballistic."

He did. He called Toni every name under the sun.

"You should have heard Steve shout at poor little Lynn too," Harry said. "In her condition." She told Dominic what had happened.

Dominic sighed. "It's not good, is it? I tried to talk to him about singing. I was talking to Cell, she says Jenny Coleman, amongst others, wants to do another album with him, and she's had requests for him to do soundtracks, but he's turned them all down. He nearly bit my head off. And you know what else, Hats? He doesn't sing any more. I haven't heard him sing since before the accident."

Harry stared at him. "My God, you're right! I knew there was something odd about him. Oh, Dom, what can we do?"

"Not a fucking thing."

Harry mentioned the absence of singing to Lynn.

"He does occasionally," she replied. "More when the boys are home from school. I keep hoping he'll get back to normal. It's been a terrible shock to him, every bit as bad mentally as physically. No, worse. Physically he's more or less fine, but mentally, well…" She shrugged. "But think of shell shock cases. They took ages to get better. And it's not been a year yet."

Harry sighed. "I pray you're right."

Lynn didn't repeat this conversation to Stephen, and neither of them mentioned his music again. He seemed to be his usual cheerful self, very caring and careful of her. Heather had told her at her last antenatal appointment not even to carry a handbag and to spend as much time as possible sitting or lying down, and he made sure she rested all the time. He gave her an eternity ring made from Welsh gold, with the word 'cariad' designed into the pattern, and 'Only Ever You' engraved on the inside, and earrings and a pendant to match. He wrote poems for her, some of them rude limericks, some of them romantic, some just plain silly, and bought her presents, sometimes something expensive, sometimes some little thing he thought she'd like. She'd always loved Christmas crackers, and he went online and ordered boxes and boxes of them, which they and the boys pulled after meals, amid general hilarity.

The boys were very excited at the prospect of a little brother or sister, and as it grew, they loved feeling it kick.

Neither Lynn nor Stephen wanted to know the baby's sex. "Doesn't matter what it is, we love it," Stephen said. He realised, that, with Lynn laid up for the duration of her pregnancy, he'd either have to get a driver, or face up to getting his cars modified. He'd more or less overcome his phobia about driving, and anyway, he had no choice. He rang the DVLA and sorted out an assessment. He was surprised by how little he had to change, really. He needed to have a steering knob fixed to the steering wheel, a parking brake that was foot operated, and automatic transmission. He found that it was possible to have a stump operated switch pad that accessed several different functions – horn, indicators, windscreen wipers, the music system and so on. He simply bought new cars, all automatics, and had them modified before delivery, selling his geared cars on eBay for charity. "At least that way, someone gets the benefit," he said to Lynn. He loathed automatics; one of the things he liked best about driving was the throaty roar of the engine when he changed gear, and the satisfaction of pushing it into top.

His success with the cars inspired him to turn his attention to the house. He enjoyed cooking, and had the kitchen subtly adapted so that he could manage everything with one hand. "You wouldn't think a cripple lived here, would you?" he said to Rob one weekend.

"Dad! You're not a cripple!" Rob exclaimed, shocked at the bitterness in his voice.

Stephen shrugged and turned away. "Whatever."

He kept the house full of flowers, most of them from the garden. The weather was lovely, and stayed that way long into the autumn, and he and Lynn sat out, Lynn tucked up in a reclining garden chair. When it got too cold, he turned the winter parlour into a private boudoir for her. It was a bright and cheerful room, the walls were hung with buttercup yellow paper and the curtains were gold silk. "It looks as if the sun got in here and never got out again!" Lynn had said, the first time she'd seen it, but Toni had favoured heavy ornate furniture, which rather swamped it. Stephen moved it all out, and installed pretty little Chippendale side tables, deep, cosy armchairs, and an elegant and supremely comfortable chaise longue. The fire was lit every morning, and he and Lynn spent most of the day there, reading, watching TV, listening to music, and talking.

"It's amazing, all this luxury, I'll never get used to being this rich!" she exclaimed.

Stephen smiled at her fondly. "When you've had junior, I'll really show you rich!" he promised. "We'll buy you fabulous jewellery and beautiful clothes and we'll travel the world. I want you to have everything!"

Lynn took his hand and put it on her bump, where the baby was turning cartwheels. She put her hand on his and smiled. "I've got everything."

In February, Stephen's divorce came through. He and Lynn had a very quiet wedding in York on the fourteenth of March, the same date as their first. When they'd originally discussed it, Stephen had talked about maybe holding it in Manchester again, at the Register Office on Jackson's Row.

Lynn hadn't been sure. "I don't know, Stevie. It would never be the same, and perhaps we shouldn't try to go back," she said doubtfully. But, to her dismay, he seemed to become obsessed with recreating their first wedding. When he suggested buying a house in Whalley Range for the reception, she really began to worry.

"We'll get caterers in, of course, but we could maybe have it decorated in a sort of grungy way, kind of give it the feeling of George's old house. We'll have to get you a dress similar to the one you had, no good hoping you'll fit into the original," he smiled, stroking her bump.

"It's as if he's trying to wipe out the past twenty years," she said to Harry and Dominic, feeling rather disloyal to be talking about him behind his back, but too anxious not to discuss it.

They were concerned. "Couldn't you simply tell him you don't want to get married in Manchester again?" Dominic asked.

Lynn sighed. "I suppose I could, but, I don't know, he's so set on it, it's almost frightening." She realised with shock and horror that she was slightly scared of his reaction if she disagreed.

Dominic looked gravely at Harry, who sighed. "Yes. He's been, well, difficult since the accident, although I suppose it's understandable. He's been so very unhappy. But he's got you back, now, Lynn," she said, brightening. "He keeps saying it's like a miracle, he can't wait till you two are married again, and things are just like they used to be." She stopped and stared at Lynn. "Oh, my God."

"Things *aren't* going to be just like they used to be," Lynn said despairingly. She was close to tears. "He's never going to be able to play the guitar again, I can't wave a magic wand and make things right!"

Dominic put his arm round her and she started to cry. "It'll be all right, sweetie," he said, giving her a large, beautifully ironed handkerchief, which made her smile despite herself, it was so typical of him. "I'll try talking to him, shall I?"

"Oh God, no, I don't want him to think I've been talking about him behind his back!" she exclaimed, alarmed. "Although I have." She cried harder.

"Darling, only to us," Dominic said. "Hatty and I don't count, we love him like you do. Anyway, I won't say we've spoken to you, I'll just get him talking about the wedding. I want you to go home and stop worrying. You concentrate on Markham minor in there." He patted her bump. "I'll sort out Markham major."

How lovely he is, and how uncomplicated – how easy it would be to be married to him, Lynn thought, with a rush of envy for Harry, which stunned her. She loved Stephen so much, how could she possibly think that? And yet, as Harry had said, he was difficult these days. She suddenly felt panicky. He'd always been a private person, but in the old days he'd always confided in her, and even if he'd sometimes kept his deepest feelings to himself, she'd usually had some inkling of what he was thinking. She realised that now she had no idea. And he'd always had a temper, but she'd never dreamed that a day would come when she'd be unsure of him, even, much as she hated to admit it to herself, slightly scared of him. How was she going to cope?

She swallowed the fear down. "Thank you, Charlie," she said gratefully, kissing him and reaching out to take Harry's hand. "I don't know what I'd do without you two."

However, to her huge relief, when he started to organise the wedding, Stephen discovered that the Register Office in Manchester had been moved from Jackson's Row and the building had become a restaurant.

"I don't know what's happening to Manchester," he said, angrily. "If it's not broke, why fix it? What are we going to do? It'll have to be Oxford, I suppose, or London. It won't be the same."

Lynn sighed thankfully. "Oh, well, it wouldn't be the same, anyway. You can't turn back time, Stevie. And would you really want to?" He opened his mouth to speak, and she rushed on. "Think of the boys. You'd hate to be without them."

He gave her a stony look. "But if you and I had stayed together we'd have had children of our own. And I would never have known the boys, they wouldn't have existed. You can't miss what you haven't got," he said, his face set and his mouth a straight, hard line.

Her heart sank. "Yes, but Stephen – you *have* got them," she faltered. "You wouldn't want to undo all you've shared with them, surely? You love them so much! Can you really bear to think of them not existing?"

His face changed. He stared at her. "No." He swallowed. "No, of course not. Oh, Cherry, I'm sorry, I've been behaving like an idiot. You're right, I love the boys, I'd never want to be without them. And you can't go back. It's just... I so wanted..." His eyes filled with tears.

"I know, my darling, I know," Lynn took his hand, overcome with pity for him. "But we've got so much to look forward to, Stevie. Hey," she said suddenly. "How about we hold the wedding in York? That's where you proposed, where we got engaged. It's got so many memories, and it'd be much easier for Sian and Ted."

He hugged her. "You're brilliant, Cherry. York'll be perfect."

It was a very small wedding, only family and close friends. They didn't invite George and Toni, who were planning a huge celebrity studded wedding later in the year; George loved glamour every bit as much as Toni did. Stephen had discussed the weddings with him beforehand, and had been relieved when George said he thought it might be awkward. They agreed it would be better if neither of them attended the other's wedding. It wasn't that Stephen didn't want George to be there, or that he didn't want to go to George and Toni's; despite the fact that he and George often disagreed – sometimes violently – they had known each other for more than twenty years and were good friends. It was Toni that Stephen didn't want at his and Lynn's wedding. Apart from it being a potentially embarrassing situation anyway, he was afraid Toni might say or do something to cause mischief, and he was also very angry at the way her lawyers had handled the divorce. He would have been more than happy to have made the settlement that was finally agreed without the nasty and aggressive tactics that had been employed.

Toni had made sure they'd been reasonable about the boys though. She'd readily agreed to joint custody and to let the boys continue living with Stephen during term time. He hadn't been surprised. She could be a scheming, manipulative bitch in his opinion, but she'd never been petty, and she loved the boys very much. "And I wasn't blameless," he said to Lynn. "I never loved her like I loved you, and I could never forget you."

George sent them a case of Veuve Clicquot champagne as a wedding present. He and Fin and Andy had bought the drink for their first marriage. "I thought I'd stick with the same theme," he laughed. "Just a bit posher, this time, bonny lad!"

Stephen and Lynn's daughter was born on the fifth of May. Lynn had a long and painful labour, and she was exhausted at the end of it. Exhausted but euphoric. The baby weighed six pounds two ounces, and they called her Lucinda Cherry Frances. Her soft, wispy hair was so blonde it was almost white, she had Lynn's English rose complexion and her eyes were exactly the same colour as Stephen's.

He was elated by Lucinda's birth. He held her for hours while Lynn slept. "Lulu, that's what you are," he whispered, "a Lulu of a baby." He started to sing softly to her in Welsh.

Lynn stirred, and heard him. She kept her eyes shut, hardly daring to breathe. Thank you, God, she thought.

Lucinda was an intensely difficult baby. She had colic and cried all evening, every evening. She hardly slept and wanted to be held the whole time. Lynn was breastfeeding and desperately tired, but she didn't want a nanny.

"This is ridiculous!" Stephen said. "You're no good to her like this, Cherry, you can barely drag yourself out of bed to use the lavatory!"

"I want to look after all the children myself," Lynn sobbed.

"That's bollocks! I'm phoning Harry and getting a full-time nanny."

Nanny Davies was able to recommend a very good one, Norland trained, and just leaving the family she was with, as their youngest had started school. Lynn was terrified of meeting her. "I'm lower middle class at best," she said pleadingly to Stephen. "I didn't grow up in that sort of family."

"Neither did I," he retorted. "Neither did Harry, or Holl and Andy! They've got nannies!"

Barbara Kendrick was nothing like the nanny Lynn had been expecting. She was young, in her late twenties, small and plump. Lynn took to her straight away. They hired her immediately, and Stephen heaved a sigh of relief.

Dominic and Harry came to stay for the weekend, to see how Barbara was working out. "Nanny wants a full report," Harry told Lynn.

"Yes, and Nanny always gets what she wants," Dominic added.

"How long will you be keeping her?" Stephen wanted to know. "Fee is eight-and-a-half."

"Until one of my bairns marries," Dominic said gloomily.

"Won't she be too old by then?" Lynn asked doubtfully. Nanny Davies looked ancient.

"Not her, she's sold her soul to the devil," Dominic grinned. "Actually, I think the devil might have sold his soul to her!"

"Cherry, can I tell you something?"

The Chaplins had gone and Lynn was making the boys' tea. "Course you can, Pipkin." Secretly, although she loved them all, Pip was her favourite. He was the most like Stephen, both in looks and personality. He tended to stay very much in Alex's shadow, and as Alex was so full of energy and high spirits, he often got overlooked. Which was a great shame, Lynn thought, he had a wonderful personality, very caring, and a great sense of humour. His hair was exactly like Stephen's, the same thick, silky black. She brushed it off his forehead.

"I'm in love with Amabel Sian Chaplin."

"Are you? I'm not surprised, Pip, she's such a pretty girl."

"Oh, yes, I know, but it's her *mind* that's really important."

"Well, yes it is, that's quite true. But it's nice if it comes in a pretty package."

"Yes, I suppose so. The thing is, can we get married?"

"Well, one day."

"Yes, but when? When is it allowed by law?"

"When you're both sixteen, but that's a little young, really."

Pip's face fell. "*Sixteen*? That's *years* away!"

Lynn smiled. "Only two."

"Two-and-a-half," he corrected. "Nearly three for Mab!"

Lynn gave him a kiss. "Why are you in such a hurry?"

"Because we love each other so much, look." He showed her a small scab on his arm. "We've united our blood, but we hardly ever see each other."

"Hmm." Lynn stirred the beans. "Damn, these aren't supposed to boil, it impairs the flavour. I'm a crap cook, can't even do beans on toast! Look, Pip, how about if Mab comes to stay in the summer holidays?"

Pip's eyes widened. "That'd be great! How long for?"

Lynn shrugged. "As long as you both want."

"Cherry, you're so cool!"

Stephen walked in at the end of this exchange. "She is, but why specifically?" He sniffed. "Is something burning?"

"Oh, hell, it's the toast!" There was a wail from upstairs. "I've got to feed that bitch now, and the toast is ruined!"

"Don't call my daughter a bitch!" Stephen said. "Go and feed her and I'll sort this out. Honestly, women!" he said to Pip.

Rob and Julia were married at Burford Church on the third Saturday in August. Stephen and Lynn, holding hands, sat with Alex, Pip and Sam, all looking very grown up in suits, waiting for the bride to arrive.

"This wedding's not a moment too soon," Stephen whispered to Lynn. "Julia's pregnant; Rob told me as we were leaving the house."

Lynn stared at him. "Stevie!"

He nodded. "Kids today, huh? No one else knows."

"It's great how you and Rob get on. Why not tell Harry though? She, of all people, would understand."

"You know, I think she'd be cross with him. She's got tremendously 'pillar of the community'-ish since she became Lady Chaplin. Charlie wouldn't care."

"No, dear old Charlie, he wouldn't. Amazing to think that little Rob is getting married, and a daddy!"

"Oh, my God, I've just realised! I'm going to be a grandfather!"

Chapter Twenty Five
Such A Crying Shame

Such a crying shame, and is the game worth the candle?
Accusations, recriminations, and no one willing to take the blame
For a life too hard to handle.

Miles Tindall was making a film. *Ali And Nino* was the story of Ali Khan Shirvanshir, a Muslim boy, and Nino Kipiani, a Christian girl, growing up and falling in love in Azerbaijan just before the First World War. He'd wanted to make this film for a long time, and finally he had the backing and the actors. All he needed now was Stephen to write the music.

Stephen refused. He couldn't bear the thought of writing when he was unable to play the guitar, even though he didn't use it when he wrote soundtracks. As Dominic had noticed, he no longer sang spontaneously – what Dominic didn't know, indeed, what no one knew, was that this was deliberate. Just as he'd trained himself not to sing at school, so he forced himself not to sing now. He sang to Lucy, and sometimes with the boys, but that was all. He didn't want to think about music, it was over, finished with. He was desperately trying to come to terms with his loss; he'd looked into the possibilities of a false hand and was cheered by the information that the way his hand had been taken off, wrist disarticulation, where the hand is taken off at the wrist rather than further up the arm, made for greater mobility when wearing a prosthesis. He was actually in the process of having a hook made. He hadn't even told Lynn this; he was going to claim that it had belonged to a Welsh pirate and tell the boys that it was reputed to be possessed by his evil spirit. It made him grin every time he thought about it.

"Cell, I told you, no… I don't care what you think, I'm not doing it and that's final… You've been talking to Charlie… Because he said that to me once before… No my fucking vocal chords didn't get cut, it's personal choice… Yeah, and the same to you."

"Miles… I told Cell… Look, I'm sorry, but I'm retired… There's no law against it… Well, I'm sorry… Really, I am… Take care, Miles."

The front door bell rang.

"OK, Mrs Dean," Stephen called to the housekeeper, "I'll go." He opened the door. "Miles!"

"Hello, dear boy." Miles kissed his cheek. "I've come to discuss this soundtrack you're writing for me."

"It's no good, Miles, I'm not doing it," Stephen said, showing him into the study.

It was a gloomy autumnal day, and Miles moved appreciatively to the fireplace where a log fire was spluttering cheerfully. "Well, you could at least offer me a drink since I've come so far."

"Fifty miles? Wow." Stephen poured him a gin and tonic. "Ice? Lemon?"

"Please. Actually, I was in LA."

Stephen stared at him. "You've come from LA?"

"Well, via Heathrow, yes. I've brought you a copy of the script, and the book."

"I've read it."

Miles smiled. "I knew you were interested."

"I read it twenty years ago." Stephen crossed to the bookshelves and found a slim, battered volume. "Whoever Kurban Said was, he tells a great story."

Miles was taken aback. "You're the only person I know who's read it."

"Yeah, well, I'm a man of parts."

"Yes, I've seen them, very nice, dear. It *is* a great story, and it needs a great composer to handle the score."

"Better go and find one then."

Miles sat down. "I'm looking at him."

Stephen gave an exasperated laugh. "Miles, I'm enormously flattered, but the answer is no!"

"Why?"

"What?"

"Why?"

Stephen looked down at his stump, hidden by his shirtsleeve. The hand was still there, he could feel it, he just couldn't see it or use it. "Because."

"You can still write," Miles said gently.

"No, I fucking can't!" Stephen got up to hide his distress, and poured himself another whisky.

Miles sipped his drink. "I'm glad this is such a nice house."

Stephen was thrown. "What? Why?"

"Well, dear boy, do you know, I like to be comfortable. I'm staying here till you agree."

"You'll be here till hell freezes over, then," Stephen said desperately. He had to get rid of Miles, he could feel his resolve beginning to weaken.

"Stephen, this film is very, very important to me. I've wanted to do it for a long time, it's going to be my last film, my crowning glory, if you will."

Stephen hadn't known this. He frowned.

Miles leant forward. "The music is vital. It's one of the key ingredients; well, you've read the book, you know how almost *delicately* it's written. The wrong music would kill it. You're the only one who could do it – and work with me." He smiled. "You might not believe it, but apparently I have a reputation as a bit of a bastard."

"Surely not!" Stephen grinned.

Miles stood up. "Stephen, if you don't do the music, I can't do the film."

"That's blackmail!"

"Dear boy, do you know, it is."

"No, that's not fair! I'm not doing it!"

"Well, this is no use to me now, then." Miles took the script and made as if to throw it in the fire. "So much for my crowning glory."

"Miles, no! Oh, for God's sake! All right, I'll do your bloody film! But I'll do it my way and it'll cost you an arm and a leg."

Miles raised an eyebrow. "Your rates gone up?"

"Certainly have! I want £1.5 million for the Foundation." He stared challengingly at Miles.

"Agreed!" Miles grasped his hand. "Well done, Stephen. Now then, where's this beautiful Lynn I've heard so much about?"

Three days later, Stephen's hook arrived. He tried it on. It was odd, but not uncomfortable. He showed Lynn.

She recoiled from it. "Stephen! You can't wear that!"

"Well, not out, no." He told her his plan; he needed her help.

She frowned. "I'm not sure I should, it's a bit mean. Anyway, they'll never believe you."

"They might." He couldn't wait for them to get home.

Sam had joined his brothers at the Grammar school that term, and seemed to be enjoying it. He'd become friendly with a very intelligent boy called Marcus Erskine. Alex and Pip referred to him as Marcus the Nerd, but Stephen and Lynn thought him an extremely polite, interesting boy, and encouraged the friendship.

Stephen had read *Ali And Nino* again, and then the script that Miles had given him, and he'd been impressed at how well the book had been adapted. He already had a fragment of music playing in his head, which scared him. He didn't want to write music he couldn't play. He wished he hadn't agreed to do it. While he waited for the boys, he played around with the tune.

When they got in, he wandered casually into the kitchen where they'd congregated to scoff chocolate biscuits, as usual. "Hi, boys. How did it go today?"

"Great!" Pip said enthusiastically. "We had rugby and I – Dad! Where did you get that from?"

They all stared at the hook.

"This? Oh, eBay. One of you suggested it ages ago, remember? It used to belong to Howell Davis, a notorious Welsh pirate, he was actually one of our ancestors, which is why it fits me so well." He twitched violently and screwed up his face. "Yes, he was really evil," he went on, as though nothing had happened. "He used to rip his victims' throats open with this very hook!" He slashed it at them and they jumped back. He twitched and grimaced again.

"Are you all right, Dad?" Alex asked.

"Fine. Why?"

"You keep screwing up your face and jerking."

"Do I?" Stephen looked alarmed. "Cherry!" This was Lynn's cue to get Sam out of the room. She and Stephen were afraid Sam would be scared of the possession story.

Lynn came in. "I can't stop, I'm busy with Lucy. Hook looks good, Stevie. Sammy, could you give me a hand?" Sam followed her out.

"Cherry didn't notice anything," Stephen shrugged.

"Well, you didn't do it," Pip said. "Oh! You did just then! Can't you feel it?"

"No. God, boys, you know what this means, don't you?"

"What?"

"I'm being possessed by his evil spirit!" He lowered his voice. "At any time in the night, I might creep into your rooms…and rip your throats out!" he yelled, lunging at them.

"Oh, God!" Pip exclaimed, falling against Alex in an attempt to get away. Alex had gone pale.

"I'd better take it off," Stephen said, giving one last tremendous twitch. "Listen, don't tell Sam about this possession thing. Lucky Cherry needed him."

Alex had recovered. "It's just a trick," he said to Pip. "You set it up, didn't you Dad? That's why Lynn took Sam away!"

Pip was looking relieved.

"Certainly not!" Stephen said, innocently. "You can ask her!"

"Nice try, Dad," Alex grinned.

"Yeah," Pip echoed. "Nice try."

That night, the door to Stephen and Lynn's room was flung open, waking Stephen. The room felt cold and his heart thumped. "Who's that?" he managed to say, fumbling with his bedside light.

Pip stood in the doorway.

"Pip!" he hissed angrily. "You stupid bloody little idiot, what the hell do you think you're doing?"

Lynn sat up. "What is it, Pipkin?"

Pip was in a terrible state, white and shaking. "I had an a-a-a-awful dream about Dad in the h-h-h-hook, slashing my throat," he sobbed. His glance fell on the hook, lying on the writing desk, and he shuddered.

Lynn moved up, making a space between her and Stephen. Pip scrambled gratefully in, and clung to her. He was as tall as she was, and looked ridiculous sitting in between them.

"It's not true about the hook," she said, rubbing his back. "Your naughty father made it up. The hook's not even from eBay, he had it specially made."

"I did," Stephen admitted. He took Pip's hand, and Pip began to relax. "But honestly, Pip, how old are you?" he asked.

"Nearly fourteen."

"Exactly! God, I'd never have gone into my mum and dad's room after a nightmare at your age, they'd have killed me!"

"Not Gran!" Pip protested.

"Huh! Don't let that sweet little old lady act fool you. She used to be really strict, we were always getting our legs slapped."

"Did she really smack you?"

"Certainly did. Hard."

"Is that why you don't smack us?"

"Yes, I hated it, and it didn't stop me misbehaving, I just made sure I didn't get caught."

"Did your dad ever smack you?"

"No. Well, once, when I was so naughty Mum made him spank me. No, he was strict in another way, he used to talk to me."

"*Torture* you?" Pip said, his eyes popping.

"*Talk* to me, you idiot! Talk!"

"How was that strict?"

"You had to be there."

"What did you do that was so naughty?" Lynn wondered.

"Mum had this horrible friend, she always used to find fault with me and go on about my behaviour to Mum, so I gave her something to complain about. She came round for tea, and Mum had made these delicate little fish pastey sandwiches. I scraped the paste out and put cat food in instead."

"Stephen!"

Pip was delighted. "How old were you?"

"Seven."

"Did the horrible woman eat them?"

"Certainly did," Stephen grinned. "It was worth the spanking to see the look on her face. She had to go and be sick, then go home and lie down, it made her feel so ill." He gave Pip a hug. "Feeling better now?"

"Yes, thanks, Dad."

"Come on, then, let's get you back to bed." He tucked Pip in and kissed him.

"Sorry I scared you, Pipkin."

He tiptoed back to his bedroom. "Jesus!" he said to Lynn. "I nearly had a bloody heart attack when he came in, I thought it was the fucking ghost!"

Lynn rolled around the bed, laughing. "How old are you, Stephen?" she managed to gasp.

He grinned sheepishly.

"I *thought* you were harsh with him at first," she added.

"Harsh with him! He was bloody lucky I didn't beat him to death with my shoe!"

"You know what I'd like to do?" Lynn said one morning over a late breakfast.

"What?" Stephen looked up from scribbling some lyrics into his book.

She smiled. "You can't think how wonderful it is to see you writing in your lyrics book. It's one of my strongest memories of Manchester. That and watching you stuff down the Othello Gateau!"

"You can't get that any more," Stephen said, regretfully. "That Danish shop is gone."

Lynn sighed. "I suppose it's a good thing in a way. It used to put pounds on me and I've still got so much weight to lose!"

"You're gorgeously voluptuous. Anyway, what was it you wanted to do?"

"Go riding. It's just the weather for it!"

He stared at her. "I didn't know you could ride."

"I grew up in the New Forest! I love riding!"

"I lived with you for over two years and never knew," Stephen marvelled. "You keep unfolding like a flower, Cherry! Why don't we buy you a horse?"

"What?" She was taken aback.

"Why don't we buy you a horse? I can get the stable block sorted out and we can employ someone to muck out and exercise it for you when you don't want to."

Lynn shook her head. "It's like… oh, like being royalty! My every whim catered for!" She leant over and kissed him. "Thank you, darling, I can't tell you how much I'd love that."

He got up. "Right! I'll go and see about these stables, then!"

Lynn finished her toast, and wished she could sort him out as easily. He wasn't happy. He'd been unhappy before he'd taken on this soundtrack, but now he was much worse. In some ways, doing the film might be a good thing, a catharsis, but it was going to be very difficult for him.

After making some phone calls, Stephen sat in his study and looked at what he'd written. It was rubbish, he thought, tearing the page out with difficulty. He knew he ought to be in the studio, he had everything he needed there, but he was very reluctant to go. The last time he'd been, he'd still had both his hands, he'd been able to play. But he'd told Miles he'd do the soundtrack, he hadn't had to, he could have been adamant in his refusal. He couldn't let Miles down. Could he?

He'd forgotten he'd got rid of his guitars. Their absence struck him like a blow. What the fuck had he been thinking? He stared round. It was like losing his hand all over again. There was no way he could do this soundtrack. No way. And Miles shouldn't have asked him. He felt resentment growing in him. Miles *shouldn't* have asked him, why couldn't people leave him alone, how dare they treat him as if nothing had happened, as if he still had both hands? He felt anger and sadness in equal measure. He'd thought at first that losing his hand was a small price to pay for getting Lynn back, but he was used to her being there now, and it seemed so incredibly unfair. He'd just swapped one sorrow for another. Dominic hadn't had to pay a price in order to marry Harry, Toni was in love with George and hadn't been penalised. He sat on the floor, his back against the wall, and cried until he had no more tears. His throat hurt and his eyes were sore.

He went outside and whistled for Cruncher Feet, and walked until even Crunchy gave in. Finally, he headed back to the house. Lynn ran out to meet him. "Where have you been? I've been out of my mind with worry!"

"I took Crunchy out," he said curtly, pushing past her.

"All this time? Look at him, he's knackered!"

The big dog flopped on the floor and lay there, looking boneless.

"Oh, for God's sake, he's fine, he's a fucking wolfhound, for Christ's sake, they used to go out hunting for hours! He'd move fast enough if you offered him a choc drop! Anyway, what is this? Do I have to get your permission to leave the fucking house?"

Lynn was hurt. "I was worried."

"Oh, get a life!" Stephen snapped. He went into his study and slammed the door. Before the boys came home, he apologised to her and kissed her contritely, but there was a slight constraint between them.

Lynn's horse was an Akhal Teke, a light bay, with a star on his face, and four white socks. He was a hardy, intelligent horse, spirited and sensitive, with masses of stamina. He stood fifteen hands high, and had a small, pretty head, large eyes, and long, narrow, highly set ears. Lynn named him Daroslav, which was Russian for Glorious Gift, but shortened it to Dasha. He was a joy to ride, and she spent as much time with him as possible. She loved riding, and was looking forward to teaching Lucy, and getting her her first pony.

She always took Dasha out after breakfast, while Stephen ran and swam, and then she and Stephen showered together before he went off to work on his soundtrack, although she was beginning to suspect he wasn't doing much with it at all. "Blimey, we're both so fit," she said, one morning before Christmas.

Stephen was sitting on the bed in his boxer shorts, putting his socks on. "Bloody hell!" he snapped, trying with difficulty to wriggle his foot in.

She knew better than to offer to help. "Are you going to be working all morning?"

He looked shifty. "Why do you ask?"

"I wondered whether you wanted to come to the garden centre and choose a Christmas tree. We can all decorate it when we get back from the concert."

The boys' school was giving a Carol Concert that evening. Alex, Pip and Sam were in the choir, and Sam would not only be singing a solo, but also playing the piano in the orchestra.

Stephen's face lit up. "Oh, what a great idea! Course I'll come. Let's get some of their homemade mince pies too."

"Oh." Lynn was disappointed. "I hoped we could make some at the weekend."

Stephen bit his lip. She was still an appalling cook. He couldn't imagine what her mince pies would taste like, but if they were anything like the vegetarian shepherd's pie she'd made for him the other day, he'd sooner starve. It had been like eating mouldy cardboard. Last year, she hadn't had this desire to cook, she'd been pregnant and resting, and then she'd been tied up with Lucy, but recently she'd apologised for neglecting him, and had promised to make it up to him. "It's time I started behaving like a real wife again, not only in the bedroom, but in the kitchen too!" she'd said, kissing him. The thought filled him with horror. "It's like living with Crippen," he'd remarked privately to Dominic and Harry. "I never know which meal will kill me."

He'd bought her an apron with 'Burnt To Perfection' printed on it; she hadn't been amused.

"Yes, OK. But we could buy some anyway, in case we don't get time."

Lynn wasn't deceived. "Hmm."

"What time do you want to leave?" he asked.

"Whenever you've finished working. How's it coming along?"

"Oh, you know," he said evasively. " Look, we can go now and I can work later."

"Seriously, Stevie, you don't seem to be spending much time on it. How's it coming along?"

"Seriously, Lynn, it's none of your fucking business." He felt rage welling up inside him. Who the fuck did she think she was, questioning him like a fucking teacher? He wanted to grab her by the hair and hurt her, hit her. The feeling frightened him. "I'll go and get the car," he said, and moved quickly out of the room.

Rob and Julia were spending Christmas at the Priory. They arrived mid afternoon. Julia was nearly six months pregnant, and looked absolutely exhausted.

"She doesn't look well, Blue," Stephen commented, pouring him a drink. He found, to his amazement, that he was looking at Rob and remembering him not being ready in Newcastle before the accident. Your fault, you bastard, all your fault.

"No. She's very anaemic. I'm glad she's given up work."

"Yes, she ought to be taking it easy. Why don't you take her over to see Heather?"

Rob smiled. "The guy she's seeing is fine, Dad, very competent."

"Yes, but Rob, Heather is so good, and she knows us all and she's had children herself, so she knows what it's like. This man Julia's seeing – who recommended him?"

"Our GP."

"It wasn't a personal recommendation?"

"No. It didn't have to be. He knows what he's doing. Look, Dad, she's my wife. I can look after of her."

"But are you?" Stephen asked, contemptuously. Can't even take care of your fucking wife, he thought.

"What do you mean?"

"Well, she doesn't look very well at all. I think she'd be far better off with Heather, or someone Heather recommends in York."

"Dad, leave it, OK?"

"Why don't you ring Heather? She'd see Jules while you're here."

"I said, leave it!" Rob glared at Stephen. "Like I said, Dad, she's my wife, and it's my child."

"I feel bloody sorry for them, then."

"What do you mean by that?" Rob was beginning to get angry.

"I mean you're not doing them any favours by standing on your pride." Christ knows what you've got to be proud of, chucking up a career in music and ignoring the income from the trust fund I set up for you. You could give your wife the world, you selfish little shit. Like I would have done for that bitch Lynn if she hadn't fucking left me. He wanted to cry and throw things. He wanted to hurt someone.

"Dad, the way I live my life is none of your business," Rob said tightly.

"Oh, don't be so bloody stupid. I'm your father—"

"Yes, you're my father, you're not God! Stop trying to run my life! I'm a grown up, I can look after my wife and child myself!"

Stephen looked him up and down. "*You? You*, Robert?" His tone was vitriolic. "I hardly think so. Julia's ill and suffering, and, as usual, all you're thinking about is yourself." He stalked from the room leaving Rob staring after him, stunned.

He went up to the nursery to see if Lucinda had woken from her afternoon nap. She was nearly eight months old and very bright. She was awake and out of her cot, and she chuckled gleefully when she saw him.

Barbara was sewing a button onto a tiny pair of pink dungarees. "I was just about to bring her down," she smiled, biting off the thread.

He smiled back. "I thought I'd come and spend some time up here. Hello, Lulu," he said to the baby.

She crawled over and tried to pull herself up, grasping his jeans. He sat on the floor and she climbed into his lap. He hugged her to him. He'd written a song for her; at least, he'd written the lyrics. He couldn't think about the music. He'd never be able to play the guitar to her, like he had to the others, to Rob. And here was Rob, who hadn't been ready, Rob, who was a jerk, given everything on a plate, and not just turning it down, but chucking it back at him. Well, fine. Let the little fucker find out the hard way.

"Shall we read a book, Lulu?" he offered. He settled her on his lap, and looked at a picture book of baby animals with her, telling her what each one was and making up silly stories. She put her thumb in her mouth and curled up against him, her other hand tugging at the hair at the nape of his neck. Later, he helped Barbara bath her, thinking bitterly that if he had two hands he could've done it alone. After her bath, he played with her until Lynn came looking for him.

"We wondered where you were. It's nearly time to go." She picked Lucy up and kissed her. "Hello, darling."

Stephen gave Lucy a kiss. "See you later, Lulu."

The baby didn't want to be put down. She screamed imperiously.

"Stop that, you little madam!" Barbara took her from Lynn. "Go on, you two, she'll shut up when you've gone."

"What happened between you and Rob?" Lynn asked. "He's really subdued."

"Good. I suggested Jules see Heather. He says the man she's seeing is 'competent', and told me not to interfere. She's his wife, it's his child, and, apparently, he's looking after them. It doesn't seem like it to me."

Lynn was concerned. "Well, but Stevie – I can see his point."

"Oh, can you really, Lynn?" he said sarcastically. "I'm *so* glad." Of course she could see his point, she was as selfish as he was. He ran on down the stairs ahead of her.

The boys performed admirably, Sam bursting with pride. Afterwards, they had mulled wine and mince pies, and the headmaster congratulated Stephen on Sam's playing. "It's nothing to do with me," Stephen said, his hand on Sam's shoulder. "Sam's the one with the talent."

Throughout the holiday, the atmosphere between Stephen and Rob stayed the same. Stephen was also remote from Lynn, although she couldn't exactly say how. It was as if part of him had withdrawn from her. She was glad when Christmas was over and Rob and Julia went home and the boys went to spend New Year and the rest of the school holidays with Toni and George. Stephen had been tetchy with them, and she hated seeing the hurt, puzzled looks on their faces. He'd been so much better since Lucy's birth that she'd almost forgotten how difficult he'd been after they got back from America. Almost, but not quite, and over these last few days the sense of unease and the fear of saying or doing something to anger him had returned, but she didn't know what to do about it. She could only hope that once he really started to work on the soundtrack, it would pass.

"Stephen! Miles is on the phone. Stephen? Where are you?"

Stephen came out of the morning room, a small reception room off the entrance hall, which was very rarely used by the family.

Lynn frowned. "Whatever are you doing in there?"

"Thinking."

Lynn was taken aback. "Oh. Well, Miles wants to talk to you. You must have heard the phone ringing! Here." She held it out to him.

He recoiled. "Make an excuse."

Lynn frowned. "I can't keep making excuses!"

"Why not?" he asked contemptuously. "It's not as if you do anything else around here."

She stared at him, stunned. "Make your own bloody excuses!" She went upstairs and sat on the bed, her mind racing. How *could* he have said that? She felt cold at the memory of the scorn in his voice. What was she going to do? She didn't think she could cope with him much longer.

Downstairs, he stared at the phone. He carefully replaced the receiver and then took it off the hook, putting a cushion over it. He went back into the morning room, where he'd been, not *hiding*, exactly, but keeping out of everyone's way, and poured himself a whisky. Fuck them all. He wasn't doing the soundtrack, Miles could whistle for it. Let them all fucking drop dead and leave him alone. He drained his glass and poured himself another.

Half an hour later, he heard Andy and Holly arrive. He'd finished the bottle and was lying on the sofa. He wondered vaguely what they wanted, but couldn't be bothered to get up and see. What was the point? What was the point in anything?

"Is everything all right?" he heard Andy ask, as Lynn let them in.

"Of course," Lynn answered, surprised. "It's lovely to see you both. You're so tanned! Did you have a good holiday?"

"Brilliant, thanks," Holly replied.

"I've just had Miles on the phone, like," Andy said. "He can't get through to you."

Stephen tensed, and clenched his fists; well, technically, fist, but he could feel them both.

"How odd!" Lynn was saying. "He spoke to Stephen a little while ago." There was a silence, and then Stephen heard her exclaim, "Oh, my God, look at this! Who would..." Her voice changed. "Oh." He heard footsteps cross the hall, and the door opened. He stared up at the ceiling.

"Why's the phone off the hook?" Lynn demanded.

"Go away," he said, without looking at her.

"Andy, you talk to him."

"Erm, Steve, Miles wants you to phone him, like."

"Does he? Well, want will have to be his master."

"Don't be stupid, Steve. He wants to know how it's coming along, and talk to you about some changes to the script."

Stephen sat up. "It's not coming along. I'm not doing it."

"You have to, Stephen," Lynn said, startled.

Holly spoke for the first time. "Why, Steve?" she asked quietly, sitting beside him and taking his hand.

"I can't." He shook his head. "I can't do it, Holl, it's too hard, I don't want to write, I want to play, I can feel my hand making the chord shapes, but there's no hand there, I'll never be able to play again and without that I'm nothing, nothing!

That was who I was, what made me *me*!" He looked up at Lynn. "It's all your fault!"

Lynn gasped. "What? Mine? Why?"

"If you hadn't left me, if you'd pulled yourself together and seen a doctor after the miscarriage, I'd never have been in that bloody service station! All those wasted years, all that longing for you, eating my heart out and saying I'd give up everything to have you back. And I did, and I have." He stopped and stared down at his stump. "But I can't cope without it. All I want to do is play the guitar. It's all I'm good at."

"Stephen..." Lynn was shocked beyond belief, but Andy interrupted her. "I never thought I'd ever hear you saying something like that, Steve! It was a tragedy what happened to you, none of us can imagine what it feels like, but you've got to pull yourself together."

"Why? Why have I?"

"Because you have to move on, Stevie," Lynn said gently.

"How can I move on? And what's the point? What am I going to do for the rest of my life? It's all very well for you to preach, you didn't move on after you lost Sakura!"

Lynn was crying. "No, I didn't," she said in a low voice, "and I've blamed myself for what I did to you every day since then. But don't you see, Stevie, I know what I'm talking about. I didn't move on and I regretted it for twenty years."

Stephen stared at her. "I can't. I *can't*!"

"Of course you can, Steve," Andy said.

"How the hell would you know?" Stephen demanded. "You've got Holly and your children and everything you ever dreamed of, and you didn't have to lose your hand to get any of it!"

Andy frowned. "There are lots of people worse off than you, like, Steve."

"Oh, and that's supposed to be a fucking comfort to me, is it?" Stephen shouted. How dare Andy stand there and presume to tell him that? What the fuck did he know about suffering? He stood up and squared aggressively up to him. "Yes, of course, I feel so much better knowing that, I'll just fall on my knees and thank God for ruining my fucking life! Why don't you fuck off and become a fucking priest, Andy, you fucking little ray of sunshine?"

He pushed Andy, trying to provoke him into a fight, but Andy stepped back unsteadily, and stared at him. "You know what, Steve?" he said, finally. "I'm ashamed to have you for a brother, like. I used to admire you so much, always thought, Steve, he's really great, copes with adversity, faces up to his responsibilities. How wrong I was! When the chips are down, you're just a loser. Go on then, Steve, let everybody down – Lynn, your kids, Miles. But you know who you're really letting down, like, don't you? Yourself. I'm going home. Are you coming, Holl?"

Holly shook her head. "You go on, Andy."

He nodded. "OK, sweetheart. Bye, Lynn. Good luck." He looked at Stephen. "You're going to need it." He shut the door quietly behind him, and there was silence in the room, broken only by the deep and regular ticking of the old Grandfather clock.

Stephen sat back down on the sofa, his hand over his eyes.

"I never told you about my friend in Africa, Kentice, did I, Steve?" Lynn asked.

He shook his head. He wasn't sure he wanted to hear. Andy's words were echoing in his brain. You're just a loser. Let everybody down. Loser, loser, loser.

"She was a refugee, not much older than me. She and her husband, Gideon, had been lecturers before the civil war. When it started, they lost their home, they lost everything. Gideon lost a leg, and their only son was killed. They and their two little girls came to the camp. Kentice started a school. Then she had a baby, another little girl. A year later, a load of refugees showed up with cholera, and despite all we did, it spread round the camp. All Kentice's daughters died. And the next day she was back teaching. When I asked her how she could, she just shrugged and said, 'Someone has to give these children education, or how will my country ever be free?'"

"Oh, Lynn," Holly whispered, tears rolling down her cheeks.

"See, my point is," Lynn went on, "she realised, no matter how bad her grief, she had to move on, for her husband, for all those other children – for her sanity. *You* have to move on, Stephen. You said you're a guitarist, but is that all you are? You're my best friend, my lover, my husband. You're a father, a son, a brother. But more than any of those things, you're a musician. Music is your lifeblood, Stevie and it's killing you to be deprived of it. OK, you can't play any more. Andy was right, it *is* a tragedy. But you can write and you can sing. Loads of people rate your voice as highly as your playing, they buy your albums to hear you sing. I know playing was your first love and I don't know how bereaved you feel, I can only guess, and I can't tell you how so, *so* sorry I am. And you're in denial. But you can't deny the music that lives in you. Sing! Write! To thine own self be true!" She gazed at him. "I'm leaving, Stephen."

"No, Lynn!" Holly exclaimed, aghast.

Lynn shook her head at her.

Stephen had gone white. "Oh, God, Cherry, no, not again, don't leave me again, please, *please*! I can't live without you, Cherry, I didn't mean those things I said—"

"Yes, you did. Stevie, don't cry. I'm leaving for six months. You need time on your own to sort out these feelings. You're angry at the whole world. That's what a lot of it was with Rob, wasn't it? And you need to work. I'll go to Cheyne Walk, I'll enrol on a full-time cookery course, then at least I'll be some use here if you have me back – shh, don't speak – I'll leave Lucy here during the week and Barbara can bring her over at weekends. If you get yourself back together, if you work, I'll come back – if you want me to, Stevie. You've not let yourself get over the accident. It happened, and six months later we were together and I was pregnant. You need space." She sat down and put her arms around him. "Maybe you won't be able to get over your resentment of me. Didn't you say you knew a very good counsellor? Why don't you see him?"

"Her," Stephen murmured. His anger had gone, and he was swamped by misery and pain. "Cherry, don't go, *please*. Come with me and see her."

Lynn shook her head, trying not to cry. "I'm going to pack. I love you, Stevie. I'll ring." She kissed him and stumbled from the room.

He stared despairingly after her. He was stunned, unable to speak, unable to think, barely able to breathe. He couldn't believe this was happening. Not again, God, not again. It was like having the same bad dream and being unable to wake. He was falling down into a deep, black pit, lost and alone, nothing to hold onto. He shut his eyes.

Holly put her arms round him and he leant against her. He couldn't cry, there were no tears, just the knowledge that he was more alone, more afraid, than he'd ever been in his life. Everything had gone, he'd lost it all.

The front door slammed. No hand, no Lynn. Nothing. Nothing left. How utterly pointless life was.

"Steve?" Holly stroked his face.

He opened his eyes. "Holl."

"Is there anything I can do, anything I can get you?"

He shook his head wearily. "No. Shall I run you home?"

"I'll phone Andy. Steve, the things he said…"

He tried to smile. "I know, Holl. I know why he said them. I know he cares. And you too." He took a deep breath. "I don't know what to do, Holl," he whispered.

"She'll come back, Steve," Holly said with certainty. "She will. You two were made for each other and she loves you so much." She kissed him. "You look exhausted. Why don't you have a lie down for a while? I'll phone you this evening, see how you are. And if you want anything, anything at all, phone us. You mean so very much to us, Steve. I wish there was something I could do! I'd give anything to help you."

"God, don't say that!" he said, alarmed. "I said I'd give anything once." He drew in a ragged breath. "Thanks, Holl."

She rang Andy, and Stephen went upstairs and lay on the bed. He was lost, lost. Eventually, he fell asleep.

Chapter Twenty-Six
Getting It Together

I'm getting it together and I know I'm winning through,
I'm going to hit the jackpot and the prize I want is you.

He woke from a dream so vivid that, at first, he didn't know where he was. In seconds, it had faded; all he could remember was a feeling of peace. Strange to feel so tranquil when his life was in a worse mess than ever. It was very dark in the bedroom, but looking at the clock, he discovered it was only six thirty. Lynn had been gone for three hours. He got up and went into the dressing room. She'd left a reassuring number of clothes. Next, he went to the nursery, where he found Barbara bathing Lucy, who shouted and hit the water with the palms of her hands when she saw him.

Barbara regarded him with sympathetic eyes.

"You saw Lynn." It was a statement, rather than a question.

She nodded. "I did. She explained you both need a little time alone. I'm going to take Lucy to London tomorrow, and I'll be back on Sunday."

The boys would also be back on Sunday; term started the following Tuesday. He played with Lucy, read to her after her bath, and put her to bed. Then he went over to the studio, but it was pointless. The familiar feeling of hopelessness and despair swept over him as soon as he opened the door. He shuddered, and turned back to the house. It was silhouetted against a sky so dark blue it was almost black, studded with stars. It was very, very cold and he had the same feeling of peace he'd had earlier, as if he'd made a momentous decision, taken a first step down a long and impossibly difficult road. It was done, there was no turning back.

The next morning, Barbara left with Lucy. He waved them off with desolation, watching the car disappear down the drive. He went back into the house and rang Madeleine, who said she would see him that afternoon. He thanked her, hung up, took a deep breath and dialled Miles's number. His secretary answered and told him she'd get Miles to return his call. He didn't know what to do. He didn't want to do anything.

The staff arrived and he explained to Mrs Dean, the housekeeper, that Lynn had gone to London to take a full-time cookery course and would be away for a few weeks. He could see from her expression that she thought this was a good idea. All the staff had learned very quickly to decline if Lynn offered them homemade cakes or biscuits with their mid-morning tea.

He left her to her work and wandered round the house. It was enormous when it was empty. Mardi was asleep on Alex's bed. That was all he did, these days, eat and sleep. He woke, and stared up at Stephen. Stephen sat on the bed and stroked him. The cat purred and shut his eyes again. Savij stalked in and jumped up onto the bed. Stephen lay down and she climbed onto his chest and curled up, as she had when she was a kitten. She didn't seem to realise how much bigger she was now, or maybe she just didn't care. Stephen felt overwhelmingly tired. He shut his eyes and was asleep in seconds.

Mrs Dean woke him. "I'll be off then, Mr Markham, I'm taking our Ryan to the hospital for his leg this afternoon. Joanne and Madge are here, and Mr Trencher and

Mr Somers have had their lunch." She peered at him. "Are you all right? You don't look well."

"No, I'm fine. I just seem to be very tired all the time."

"Well, you take care," Mrs Dean said, unconvinced.

He went down to the kitchen and made himself a cup of tea and a sandwich. It wasn't long until his appointment with Madeleine. He was surprised by his faith that she would be able to do something. After all, what could she do? What could anyone do? He'd lost his hand, he could never make music again. It was all pointless. He wandered into the sitting room, turned on the TV and flicked. Dozens of channels and nothing decent on. MTV was showing the video of 'She's Mine'. He watched it with a mixture of fascination and despair. God, and he'd thought he had problems then! He watched himself playing. He'd taken it completely for granted, his left hand. Why hadn't he married Coral? She'd wanted to go to Hollywood, to break into acting, but he knew that if he'd asked her to marry him, she would have stayed. What a fool he'd been. But then, why had he let Lynn go in the first place? He turned off the TV. It was time to see Madeleine.

"I didn't think there was a problem. I thought I was over it. I mean, it was two years ago! It was – it was, oh, *devastating* when it happened, horrific, I wished I'd died, but then I got Cherry back – that's what I call Lynn," he added.

Madeleine nodded. "I know."

"Well, it almost seemed, um, not worth it, but like it had balanced out, do you see what I mean? But now – I don't get it, I feel so angry, so resentful with everyone. I look around at my friends, they all have partners they love – Harry and Charlie, they're more in love than ever, neither of them had to lose a body part. Toni and George, apparently ecstatic – why the hell should they be? All I ever wanted was Cherry and to play guitar in a band. It's great being rich and all that, but I never cared about the money or fame." He took a deep breath. "I'm angry with Lynn – if she hadn't left me this would never have happened. I'm angry with Rob – if he'd been ready that morning we'd have been able to get home without stopping again. I'm angry with everyone who's got two hands," he finished quietly. He looked at Madeleine. "I'm just so angry and so unhappy. I want things to be like they were, I want to have my hand back. I don't want to have to cope. I can't cope any more."

"You said on the phone that you can't write or sing any more. Did you mean can't or won't?"

"I don't want to – what's the point?"

"Why do you feel like that?"

"I don't know! That's why I've come here!"

"Stephen, I can't say to you, this is what's happening, and this is how you sort it out! What counselling did you have directly after the accident?"

"None. I didn't want any. They kept on at me, but I just wanted to be left alone, I wanted to forget it, to get on with my life. But I can't!"

"Do you remember anything about the accident?"

He hesitated. "I remember the car hitting me, and the pain – not being able to stand the pain. I remember being terrified that Rob might have been hurt. That's about all, really, until, well, I don't remember them telling me about my hand, exactly, I just remember knowing."

"Do you have nightmares about it?"

He stared at her. "How strange you should ask that! I hadn't for ages, but lately I have been having some. I mostly have frustrating dreams though – I want to play the guitar, but all the strings are missing, or the amp won't work, that kind of thing."

"Do you tell Lynn, or anyone, when you have the nightmares?"

He shook his head. "I just try to forget them."

"Hmm. Tell me a typical one."

He went pale. "I'd rather not."

"That's why you're here, Stephen," she said, gently.

He felt tears springing to his eyes, tears of fear. His pulse started to race. "I'm playing my Strat," he whispered, "and then suddenly it's dark, and I can hear the car, but I can't see it. I try to run, but I can't move..." He stopped and stared at her, his eyes haunted.

"Go on," she encouraged.

"I can't move, um, and then I know it's not a car at all, it's a chain saw, and I'm in an operating theatre, and the surgeon's going to cut off my hand, and I'm begging him not to, but he can't hear me over the noise of the saw, and I'm frantic, desperate to get away, but I still can't move, and I know how much it's going to hurt, but there's nothing I can do, absolutely nothing, I can't move, and it's cutting into my wrist, I can hear it, I can feel it biting into the bone..." He stopped. He was shaking, and his mouth was dry. Madeleine passed him a glass of water. "That's about it," he gasped, swallowing a mouthful of it. " I usually wake up crying."

"It's all right, Stephen," Madeleine said soothingly. "Take some deep breaths, slow deep breaths."

He nodded, breathing deeply. "In some ways, the powerlessness is the worst part, knowing what's going to happen and not being able to stop it."

"What do you do when you wake up?"

"Get up, get a drink. Several drinks."

"And Lynn doesn't disturb?"

"Sometimes, when I get up. I just say I can't sleep."

"Doesn't she notice you're crying?"

He shook his head. "She's a heavy sleeper, and it's not like I'm hysterical or anything. And it hasn't happened that much. It happened a lot after the accident, but Toni wasn't sleeping in the same room, and anyway I did say I was having them then, the doctors said it was normal and they'd go. They kept saying I should have counselling, but I didn't – I couldn't – I just wanted to forget."

"That doesn't work though, does it?"

"No."

She smiled at him fondly. "If you were a little boy, I'd ruffle your hair in exasperation at this point!"

He grinned weakly. "Sorry."

"Don't be sorry. You're doing enormously well. This is so hard for you, and it's so unfair. That sense of powerlessness that you feel in the nightmare, that's what's happening in your life at the moment. We'll work on it, I promise you. How well have you come to terms with the loss of your hand in other areas of your life?"

"Oh, fine."

"So no aspect of it is difficult? You're not self-conscious about it?"

There was a long silence.

"Stephen?"

"I hate it!" he burst out. "I hate having to have my cars 'modified'! I hate not being able to tie my own shoelaces, having to ask people to do the simplest things for me! I'd rather go without! I can't even cut up my food! I hate being a cripple, can't bear it! And I hate the look of it, it's repulsive!"

"Repulsive to whom?"

"Well, everyone, I should think. Toni couldn't stand to be near me."

"What about Lynn?"

"Oh, well, Cherry loves me. She puts up with it."

"I see. So if you never bothered to wash, or change your clothes, Lynn would put up with it because she loves you?"

"Well, no…"

"What about your children? And your friends' children? They aren't usually bothered about saying the right thing, even if they've been told to."

He thought about it. "Well, Sam would like me to have a lizard's hand grafted onto my wrist like Doctor Connors in *Spiderman*."

That made Madeleine laugh. "Any other comments?"

He thought some more. "Nothing adverse," he admitted. "The Chaplin children were interested, but they thought my scars were more exciting. Only Mab really said anything, she was tremendously sympathetic, made a terrific fuss of me." He smiled fondly at the memory of Mab's sympathy. He'd been surprised and very touched by how concerned she was. "But apart from feeling sorry for me, her main worry was how I managed to give Mardi his thyroid tablets. Mardi's the cat," he explained.

"So, no horror or revulsion there. Just Toni really, then. And you know she can't stand any medical condition that makes the sufferer different. People who don't know you are always going to be embarrassed, Stephen. Some may well be horrified, even revolted. But that's really their problem, isn't it? You've been through so much stress in the last two years. You split up with Toni, you remarried Lynn, and had a new baby. All this takes a tremendous toll on anyone, and, on top of that, you nearly died and you've had to cope with a life changing disability, compounded by the fact that you can no longer play the guitar, which was not only part of your job, but a huge part of your life. Of course you're angry! It's perfectly normal that you should be! You're angry, you're sad, you're frightened. A terrible thing happened to you, Stephen, and no one was made to pay, no one was held accountable. It's OK to be angry; you're bereaved, you're mourning for an incredibly important part of your life that's died. And it's perfectly normal to want someone to blame. One of the most common forms of grief when a husband or wife dies is for the survivor to feel angry with their dead partner for leaving them! How logical is that? Grief isn't logical, and there's no set time for it. You can't say, oh, I had my accident two years ago, I can't possibly be grieving now. You can and you are. You've pushed everything down again, and your subconscious can't cope, it's pushing all these memories back up in your dreams, and it's saying to you: face them, deal with them, take them away. You want to get better, Stephen, and this is your way of doing it."

He thought about this. "But I don't understand. Why now? Why not earlier? I was tremendously unhappy before I got Cherry back, but then I was fine, so happy, and we had Lulu, our little girl, and everything was fantastic! Everything *is* fantastic."

"But you're not writing and singing?"

"Well, no, not as such."

"Not as such?"

"Um." He paused. "Well, not at all."

"Why? You always sing, I remember that being a huge grievance of Toni's; she didn't mind you singing at home, but it really embarrassed her when she went anywhere with you because you sang all the time. If you're not singing, you're not happy, everything isn't fine. I remember you saying when you first came here, that to you, singing isn't to do with whether or not you're happy, it just happens, you sing regardless of how you're feeling. This absence of music, of singing, in your life is very indicative of the disturbed state you're in."

"I know, I know, but I *can't*. It feels so wrong," he said reluctantly, "such a betrayal of who I was."

"In what way?"

"If I can't play the guitar, I can't do anything! The guitar wasn't like a musical instrument, it was part of me, like my voice – no, much more so! If I wanted to say anything musically, I always used the guitar first. I'd hear something, some scrap of music in my head, and play it and keep on playing it, keep working it out on the guitar until I got what I wanted. That's how I work. So now if I was to write songs or soundtracks, or sing, it's as if…" He stopped.

"Go on."

"It's as if I'm saying it wasn't that important, I can still do the stuff I did and the guitar wasn't that important. It's like, why am I making so much fuss?"

"So if you move on, you're belittling your loss?"

He stared at her. "Yes! That's it exactly!" He took a deep breath. "And I'm supposed to be writing a soundtrack for a new film. But I can't," he whispered. "It's not that I'm trying to be difficult, I just can't do it."

"But you have to, Stephen, you *have* to come to terms with it. You've got the rest of your life to live. You said earlier you hate being a cripple, but if you don't move on, you're crippling yourself emotionally. You want Lynn back, you want to get on with your life. The soundtrack is the reason for this crisis; you're being forced to return to your old life and it's so hard, but you're powerless to stop it happening because time moves on." She gave him a sympathetic smile. "And *you* have to, as well."

"Yes, I see. I do see that. I just don't see how."

"I'll help you. As we've said before, you're very strong, Stephen, you can get through this. I want you to think about what you *have* got—"

"That doesn't work!" he interrupted. He gave a despairing sigh. "Andy said that, that there are loads of people worse off than me. I know that! But all that happens is I feel guilty about being depressed, and then I feel resentful. There are loads of people *better* off than me. Andy for a start," he muttered.

"I don't want you to think that there are loads of people worse off than you. I just want you to think what's good in *your* life. What you like about it. That's important, and there *are* good things – your children, your love for Lynn – and you need to be able to focus on something positive. Think about how much they mean to you. And when you feel strong enough, think about what's bad about your life, even the most trivial things. Don't pretend some things aren't bad because you feel you shouldn't be complaining about them. Then we can start to work on how you can change the bad things, or at least the way they affect you. For instance, you can't play the guitar. Is there any instrument you *can* play with one hand? What about prosthetics? I imagine they talked about that to you at the hospital; were you not ready?"

He shook his head.

"OK, well, you could start thinking about it. Just to help you out at home if nothing else. I've got some website addresses for you. And here's something else. You probably won't want to think about this yet, and I know it would never be the same, but just to sow the seeds – you could learn to play the guitar with your left hand. I understand that lots of left handed people play the guitar with their right hand."

He thought about this. "I wouldn't be able to finger pick," he said finally.

"No, you wouldn't. And it would be for you to decide if you ever wanted to do it.

But with a prosthesis, you could strum, and it might be better than nothing. Like I said, I'm just sowing the seeds. You can see if anything grows. And if you want to sing, sing. You have such a superb voice and it's part of you, a part of you they couldn't take away. Think about it, Stephen, about everything I've said." She smiled at him. "Don't think for a minute that I don't sympathise. But you've probably had a bucketful of people being sorry for you. Now you need someone to help you get back your self esteem."

He smiled at her. "Yes. I hate people being sorry for me."

"I know. You can do it, Stephen. I know you can. And Stephen – it's your life. You don't owe anyone a thing."

"This is nice!"

It was the middle of February, and Toni and Harry were having tea at Claridges. It had been Toni's idea to meet, Harry hadn't been keen, but when Toni had said, 'Fancy Lynn and Stephen splitting up already', she felt she ought to go and see what Toni knew, or thought she knew.

"Mmm." Harry sipped her tea. "How are you, Toni?"

"Wonderful! George is a little ripper!"

"Great." Harry's smile was nailed to her face.

"So! Steve and Lynn?"

Harry could see that Toni was watching her like a hawk. "Yes, fancy Lynn – of all people – taking a cookery course!" She forced herself to laugh, determined not to let Toni know there was any problem whatsoever. "Mind you, she did tell me that Steve was beginning to lose weight and she was afraid she'd end up killing him! And Stevie told me none of the staff will touch anything she's made! So she took the opportunity to enrol on this course while he's working so hard on the film. Give him some peace and quiet to work. When she's there all they want to do is make love, apparently. It's sweet, don't you think?"

"Very." Toni didn't sound as if she meant it. "Course, it's like that with me and George," she added.

"How did you know Lynn was here?" Harry asked casually. She was sure neither Andy nor Holly would have told her.

"I bumped into her coming out of Harvey Nicks. She had Lucinda with her, she'd been buying her some new clothes. So I asked George if Stephen was in London, and he said he didn't think so, and he asked Andy, who told him that Lynn was living at Cheyne Walk taking some course. It just sounded a bit sus to me. I must say, Lucy's a gorgeous baby, her eyes! There are exactly like Steve's! If anything would convince me to have another baby, it's her."

"Are you thinking of having another one?"

"George wants one. I think I'm too old."

"Rubbish! Look at Madonna."

"Hmm. If I could have a little girl like Lucy, I would. Steve wanted another one a while ago. I wish I had."

I bet, Harry thought. She made a noncommittal noise.

"Anyway, how are things with you?" Toni asked.

"Fine. Dominic's very busy and Mab's become a Mosher, although you no doubt know all about the band!"

Toni sighed. "Isn't it horrible? I couldn't believe it when Alex and Pip announced they were Moshers and that they and Mab had formed a band. Thank God Sam isn't interested, he thinks they're morons! Have you heard their songs?"

"I try not to listen," Harry sighed.

"Yes, and your Mab has got such a pretty face, and a lovely singing voice too, and when you hear her screaming out, *'You are a duck, but we don't give a fuck!'*"

"She didn't!" Harry was shocked. "She'd better not sing that sort of thing at home!"

"I told the boys off and told her I didn't think you'd approve. They all groaned and made faces at each other, you know the sort of thing."

"I'm sure we weren't like that when we were their age. Although that's the constant cry of the older generation, isn't it? I wonder what Stephen thinks of it?"

"Encourages them, I expect," Toni said darkly. "Pip informs me that he's become a vegetarian. I'm not having that. I shall speak to Stephen about it tomorrow when we take them back."

The boys had been spending the weekend in London. Pip went as often as he could to see Mab. It was the tragedy of their lives that they weren't allowed to go to the same school; Pip would have happily lived in London all week, much as he loved the Priory, if he could have been with Mab.

God, good luck, Stevie! Harry thought. She made up her mind to ring him and alert him to Toni's intentions as soon as she got home.

As it happened, Stephen was in complete agreement with Toni. He'd heard about the band, RhymeNReason, over the Christmas holidays and hadn't liked what he'd heard. Since then, he liked it even less. He hadn't heard any of the more explicit lyrics, but the ones he had heard were bad enough. There was 'Lucifer's Son': *'You're Lucifer's son, you're Lucifer's son, in a dead end job AND YOU DON'T HAVE A CAR!'*

Then there was 'Bearded Guy': *'Bearded guy has no life, in the unemployment line, BEATING UP HIS WIFE!'*

And 'Van Gogh'. All he'd heard of that was: *'Back down, Van Gogh, back down, Van Gogh, I'LL CUT OFF MY EAR BEFORE I BACK DOWN!'*

Apparently, they were still working on that one. All the songs seemed to have the same tune, with the last line screamed out at the top of Mab's voice. When he objected to the Van Gogh song on the grounds that it was rubbish, Alex groaned, "Oh, come on, Dad, even an old square like you should be pleased that we can write something with a bit of culture in it."

Then Pip informed him that he and Mab were becoming vegans.

"Over my dead body!"

"Don't be a drag, Dad."

"You're not even becoming a vegetarian, let alone a vegan. Your mother would have kittens! We agreed; when you're sixteen you can be a vegetarian – when you're eighteen you can go on hunger strike if you like, but until then you'll do what you're told!"

Pip and Mab stared defiantly at him, both of them wearing their peculiar Mosher clothes and Mab's skirt so short it left very little to the imagination. She was very, very pretty, and reminded him tremendously of Harry, although, apart from Harry's eyes and full, rather sensuous lips, she looked exactly like a female version of Dominic. She had Harry's insouciance and way of cutting straight through to the heart of the matter. He could definitely see the attraction for Pip.

When George and Toni arrived at the Priory with the boys, Toni was beside herself with rage. While she'd been having tea with Harry, Pip and Mab had somehow managed to convince the staff at a body piercing shop that they were eighteen and had had their tongues pierced. George had driven Mab straight home. Toni had made Pip take his out then and there.

He was furious. "Dad would let me keep it!"

"I couldn't care less what he'd let you do! You are not having any part of your body pierced until you're eighteen. Then you can do what you want."

"Dad had an earring!" Pip retaliated.

"Aye, man, but that wasn't until he was in his twenties," George said, coming in in the middle of the row. "Andy did it."

Toni and Pip, their anger forgotten, stared at him. "Andy?"

"Aye, we were all pissed, it was late at night, and the lass decides he wants an earring. So we say, they'll be closed, bonny lad, get it done tomorrow. So he says, no, we'll be recording tomorrow. So Andy freezes his ear with some ice, although we didn't leave it long enough, anyway, Andy gets this fu – flaming great needle and jabs it through Steve's ear. But then he remembers he hasn't got an earring to put in the hole. We had to get these two lasses from across the corridor to lend us one."

"Wow, that's *so* cool!" Pip exclaimed, and hurried off to tell Alex.

"The piercing was bad enough," Toni said now. "I'm not standing for this vegetarianism, Stephen."

Stephen had made her a cup of coffee and given George a beer. He sighed. "I don't see what we can do, Toni. He really believes in it. I can't force him to eat meat when I don't. If we let him be a vegetarian, I think he'll drop the vegan idea."

"That's blackmail," Toni said, annoyed. She turned to George. "I knew he wouldn't do anything. You'll just have to knock some sense into Pip, George."

Stephen went pale. "You lay a finger on my son, George, and you'll be sorry."

"George has my consent to discipline the boys," Toni declared.

"Well, he doesn't have mine!" Stephen retorted. He was furious. "I mean it, George."

"And how would you stop me, man?" George asked lazily.

"I'll beat you to a bloody pulp!" Stephen's temper rose. "I can take you any time, George!"

"I'll say this for you, you're no coward, bonny lad. Howay, I wouldn't touch your boys! Not that they'd need it, they're canny lads, the lot of them. I'd like a son like them."

Stephen was taken aback. "Thanks, George," he said awkwardly.

George looked at Toni. "Stop stirring it, pet, Steve's right. You can't force a man to drop his principles. We'll just have to make sure that Pip gets the right food. It doesn't seem to have done the lass here any harm."

"Don't push it, George," Stephen grinned.

"Now we're here, man," George went on, "I might as well ask. What's happening with the band? I mean, there's not much point us staying together, is there? I know the papers made a big deal of it when we released wor greatest hits album last year, but we never confirmed or denied it."

"I don't know, George," Stephen said, slowly. "I've been thinking about it. Can we let things ride a little longer?"

George shrugged. "It's all the same to me, man. Come on, then, Toni, we better be getting back."

After they'd gone, Stephen went to see Pip. He found him in his bathroom, staring despondently at his tongue in the mirror. "I read tongue piercing can be fatal," Stephen said, mildly.

"Anything can be fatal! I might get knocked down by a bus tomorrow!" Pip realised what he'd said, and coloured. "Sorry, Dad," he stammered.

Stephen shrugged. "Why? I'm living proof that it happens. Listen, I've been talking to your mother. We've agreed that you can be a vegetarian – but not a vegan."

Pip's face lit up. "Dad! Oh, you're great! I knew you'd let me! I must ring Mab!"

"Can I talk to you first? To all three of you?"

Pip stared at him. "Is something wrong?"

"No. But you know I've been seeing Madeleine?"

"Yeah?"

"Well – look, get the others and I'll explain."

Madeleine had suggested that he do something symbolic to mourn the loss of his hand. "You need closure, Stephen. You need to be able to say to yourself, OK, that's it, I'm starting a new life, not worse than before, just different. It's entirely up to you how you do it, but I'd suggest something symbolic. That's the point of funerals, really, they're for the living."

Stephen saw the logic of this, but he couldn't think what to do. He asked the boys for their advice.

"We could have a memorial service," Alex suggested. "You know, like when we buried Turtle."

"Yeah, but we had his ashes," Pip pointed out.

"Well, we could find an old photo of Dad and cut the hand off and bury that. If we did it at the weekend, Mab could come over, and RhymeNReason could perform a song. Something like, '*You don't have a hand, You don't have a hand, It's made you real sad BUT WE UNDERSTAND!*'"

"Hmm," Stephen said. "That's not exactly what I was thinking of, Alex, but I'll bear it in mind."

"What about balloons?" Sam asked.

"What are you on about, you freak?" Alex demanded.

"At least I've got a *reason* to be a freak," Sam retorted. "You just make yourself a freak, you Mosher."

"Well, I'd rather be a Mosher than…"

"Boys! Please! What about balloons, Sam?"

"Well, I thought you could get some helium balloons and release them, as a sign your hand isn't there any more."

"That's actually a good idea, you could tie them round your left arm," Pip said, warming to the idea, "then cut the strings with a pair of scissors. Or a knife," he added. "A knife would be way cooler."

"You know, that *is* a good idea," Stephen said. "Thanks, Sam!"

"It was my idea to tie them to your arm," Pip put in.

"Yes, well, thank you too."

"And what about the song?" Alex asked.

"Um – not sure about the song."

Alex was crestfallen.

"Because I think it should be a private thing, just us men," Stephen added quickly.

"Oh, yeah, right," Alex nodded. "Oh, well, we don't need Mab. I'll sing."

Stephen had found the sessions with Madeleine enormously helpful. He'd had a look at the website addresses she'd given him, and found that one of them was about car modifications. He'd followed this up, and bought himself a new Boxster S with gear change paddles which he could operate with his stump; the upper paddle changed up, and the lower paddle changed down. He'd loathed driving an automatic. I feel like a human being again, he told Madeleine, gratefully. And he hadn't attempted to work in the studio again, but had gone up to the music room in the attic. There was a piano there, and he'd got Alex to carry a desk up. He had started to work on *Ali And Nino* in earnest.

He picked up the boys from school the next day and they drove into Witney and bought six balloons, one for each finger, one for his thumb and one for the rest of his hand. At home, they tied them carefully to his arm and filed out into the garden. It was cold and wet out there.

"We'll do the song in the house, afterwards," Alex shivered.

They stood huddled in their coats. Stephen took the knife from Pip and cut the ribbons as Sam held them taut. The balloons drifted lazily up into the darkening sky. They watched them till they could no longer see them.

"That's that, then," Stephen said. He felt terrible, old and sad. But he no longer felt angry.

That night, as he was lying on the sofa flicking through the channels, Savij draped over his chest like a tiny fur rug, he came across a documentary about Leon Theramin. He watched, fascinated. Theramin was a Russian scientist who'd been born at the end of the nineteenth century. He invented the world's first electronic musical instrument, a kind of wooden box on a stand, with antennae, which made its sound not by being touched, but by movements in the air around it. Stephen knew, with absolute certainty, that he could play a Theramin. He went online and ordered one from Big Briar, the company formed by Robert Moog in the late seventies. It was a mesmerizing instrument, much harder to play than he had visualised, but tremendously satisfying. He discovered that it was possible to make it produce a sound very like a violin. He started to write music for it. He was determined to get good enough at it that he could play it in the band.

The boys found it intriguing. "Can we use it in *our* band?" Alex asked when they came up to the music room to play and found him practising on it.

"You learn to play it properly and I'll get you one of your own," Stephen promised.

Sam enjoyed experimenting with it, but preferred the piano. He read the music Stephen had written the night before, and began to play it. "This is nice."

Stephen smiled. "Thanks, Sam. My God, you play well!" He was awed by Sam's talent. A wave of joy swept through him. This child, these boys, and Rob and Lucy, were *his*, flesh of his flesh. How lucky he was! Madeleine had been right, there was still so much in his life that was good. He thought, with love, of his family; Lynn, Sian and Ted, his sisters, Harry and Dominic, and his friends.

By the beginning of March, he was not only working on the soundtrack, he was writing songs for the band, songs he would never be able to play. But he could sing them. Someone else would have to play.

Andy and Holly had been frequent visitors since Lynn left. They'd spent time with Stephen, had him over for meals when the boys were away, and had unobtrusively made it clear that they were there for him. Now he had an idea that he wanted to discuss with Andy before he spoke to anyone else. He rang him after breakfast, but the answer machine was on. He left a message. Almost as soon as he replaced the receiver, the phone rang. He picked it up, expecting it to be Andy, but it was Rob. Stephen had driven up to see him after his first counselling session and explained, and apologised for the row at Christmas, and Rob had said, no, he was sorry, he knew Stephen had been trying to help, and he, Rob, had behaved like an idiot, and they'd hugged each other and discussed the way Stephen was feeling, and were as close again as ever, but Rob had been very busy at work, and they hadn't seen each other since.

Now though, Rob was crying. "Dad?"

"Robbie, what's the matter?"

"It's Julia. She's having the baby, we're at the hospital."

"God, Rob, no! What happened?"

"She fell. They're examining her at the moment, I've got to get back to her, but I… I wanted you."

"OK, Robbie, look, you go back to Julia and try not to worry, cariad," Stephen said, doing his best to sound reassuring. "I'm sure it'll be OK. I'll get up to you as fast as I can. Give her my love."

He rang Andy and left another message. Then he found Barbara and explained the situation to her. "I may have to stay overnight, but I'll ring and let you know."

The drive to York usually took him about three-and-a-half hours. This time he made it in just over two. He found Rob in the maternity wing. "Dad! I didn't expect you yet!"

"I drove very fast. What's happened? Are they all right?"

Rob beamed. "They're fine. Jules is sleeping – my *son* is in the special care baby unit."

Stephen sagged with relief. "God, Rob, I can't tell you how pleased I am! Can we see him?"

He was tiny. All Stephen's children had been small, but nothing like little Rhys. He was over six weeks early, and weighed three pounds.

"He's amazing!" Stephen gazed at the little boy. "God, he's my grandson! I can't believe I'm a grandfather! Have you told Harry?"

Rob shook his head. "She and Dom are out, and neither of them have got their mobiles on. I left a message."

"Oh, yes, of course, her dogs," Stephen said dismissively. Harry was picking up two German spitz klein puppies from a breeder in Hereford, and he didn't approve.

After he and Rob had been in to see a sleepy Julia, they went to the hospital restaurant and Rob told him what had happened. "She kept getting these dizzy spells, they said it was probably because she was anaemic, but she didn't have high blood pressure – the opposite, in fact – or anything else, so they said she was fine, that she should keep taking the iron tablets and take things easy. Anyway, this morning she, well, she kind of crumpled at the top of the stairs and fell down them." He stared at Stephen, his face wretched. "If I hadn't been there, if it'd been a working day, she and Rhys could both have died. If I'd just listened to you and taken her to Heather…"

Stephen put his arm round him. "Stop it, Robbie. If I've learnt anything over the last few years, it's that accidents happen, things go wrong, and wishing you'd done something differently just makes you ill. Whatever happened, you can't change it now. When Julia and Rhys badly needed help, they got it and they're both fine. You can't blame yourself, you did nothing wrong, none of this is your fault."

"It is! It was my stupid pride! I put my pride before their welfare! All my life people have said, 'Oh, it's all right for you, your dad is Stephen Markham and your stepfather is Dominic Chaplin'. Nobody ever thought I'd got anywhere because I was me. That's why I want to work, to bring in the money myself. I know you've never understood why I don't use the trust fund money – and it's not that I don't want it, or that I'm not grateful; I am, but I want to feel that *I'm* taking care of my family. When I say to you, 'You worked for your money', you always say, 'No I didn't,

I just got lucky' – well, whatever way you look at it, whether it was work or luck, you did it yourself, you knew it was down to you that you could buy pearls for Toni, or diamonds for Lynn, or a huge house in the country for your children. I'd like to feel that way, to have the satisfaction of saying: *I* did that for my family. If I give Jules a piece of jewellery, I want to feel that I bought it, but if I use the trust fund money, I feel you're really the one who's buying it. Do you understand?" he asked imploringly. "See, Dad, I just wanted to be normal, just an average husband, who works and takes care of his family."

"But, Robbie, you could never be average, it's not in your nature! And of course people are going to think you got everything handed to you on a plate, because in a way, you did! I know how hard you worked at school and at Oxford, but you never had to hold down a job while you studied, did you, or worry about your tuition fees, and how you were going to pay the loan back. You and your brothers and sisters are the children of very famous parents. It always strikes me as so ridiculous when celebrities say they didn't do anything to influence the start of their children's careers! Of course they did, just by being who they are! It would be naïve to think otherwise. It's like this band of Alex, Pip and Mab's. It's obviously going to make a difference to them who their fathers are; they'll never have to struggle for a recording deal like Sid's Six and GI Joe did! Mind you, if their music doesn't improve, they'll never sell any records," he added with a grin. "The thing is, Rob, it's what you do with what you've been given that counts. What you make of your career now, and how successful you are, is down to you. And life has given you me and Charlie – both of us would do anything for you. Charlie loves you every bit as much as his other three. He told Harry once he wished he could leave Fenroth and his title to you. We're here for you, whenever you need anything. But I do understand, Robbie. We're very alike. I want to give my children everything too, and it doesn't matter how old you are, to me you'll always be my child. I'm sorry I never looked at it from your point of view before. The trust fund is yours to do what you want with. Use it or not, Blue, it's entirely up to you."

Rob hugged him, tears in his eyes. "Thanks, Dad. Dad, did Dom really say that?"

"He really did."

Stephen stayed until late afternoon, when Julia was completely awake, and then he left, promising to bring the boys up at the weekend. He drove down to Cheyne Walk. "Cherry!"

She came running down the stairs, and he caught her in his arms.

"What are you doing here?" she asked, hugging him.

"You, in a minute. It's our anniversary next week, and I'm fed up with this separation bollocks. I'm going to make love to you, and then I'm taking you home. Don't interrupt," he added as she opened her mouth to speak. "I'm working on the soundtrack, and I'm writing songs for the new album."

"Songs? B-but who's going to play them?"

"You'll see. Come on, Gran, up to bed."

"Gran?"

"Julia's had the baby early."

"Oh, Stevie! Why didn't you say straight away? What happened? Are they all right? What is it?"

Later, as Lynn lay sleeping, Stephen rang Andy and asked him if he would agree to Dominic joining the band. "See, I've written all these songs. We're going to have to do another album, Andy. I'll sing, Charlie'll play lead guitar. At least, I hope he will, I haven't asked him yet."

"Better ask him, then!"

"What about George and Fin?"

"They'll be OK with it. Fin said to me a little while ago we ought to find a new lead guitar, like, but we didn't know what to say to you. And George is raring to go. I think he's missing his groupies."

A smile of pure pleasure slid across Stephen's face. Lynn was coming home. If Dominic agreed, Sid's Six would be back together. And Toni would have to contend with groupies. Could life get any better? He woke Lynn. "Come on, get up, lazy bones. I've run you a bath. Then we'll go and see if Hal and Charlie are in."

Dominic and Harry had only just got home when Stephen and Lynn arrived.

"Stephen! I'm a grandmother!" Harry was laughing and crying at the same time.

"I know and I've seen him!" Stephen smirked.

"Yes, Robbie told me. Poor things, what a time they had! I can't wait to see him!"

Stephen kissed her on the mouth. "He's a little beauty, like his glamorous Grandmama."

They went into the drawing room, where Mab, Gus and Fee were lying on the floor squealing with laughter as two fluffy, cream coloured puffballs licked their faces.

"You got your puppies then, I see," Stephen said, disapprovingly.

"Oh, my God! They're adorable!" Lynn exclaimed.

"Here." Amabel gave a puppy to Lynn. "She's called Magda, it's short for Magdeburg, that's a place in Germany. Mama and Papa! It's your turn to be licked! Come on Gus, give Brandenburg to Papa!"

Dominic raised his eyebrows. "My turn to be licked by a smelly little dog?" he asked, disdainfully. "No thank you. Yes, we did," he said to Stephen. "And yes, they were very expensive, and no, they haven't had their tails docked, although I don't suppose it's any of your business."

They already had two black Labradors, Pegswood and Cambo, named for towns near Fenroth, and the previous year, Harry had bought a pair of wire haired fox terriers, which she named Rushy Knowe and Longframlington, again after places in Northumberland. Stephen was against dogs being bred for money, and totally opposed to tail docking, and had subjected Harry and Dominic to a long tirade when they'd bought the fox terriers, eventually ending up with the words, 'although I don't suppose it's any of my business.'

"Yeah – these aren't the kind of dogs that have their tails docked!" he retorted now. He sighed. "Well, you know my feelings on the subject…"

"Only too well," Dominic interrupted.

Stephen ignored him. "So I won't say any more, except that I don't see why you just can't go to a rescue centre and get a dog! Breeding dogs for money is wrong and unnecessary, when so many are abandoned every day."

"Yes, well, thanks for not saying any more, Markham."

"Oh, Stevie, don't be cross," Harry pleaded. "I wanted German spitz kleins."

"Although I can't think why," Dominic remarked, looking at the puppies. "They're not dogs, they're powder puffs, the others will probably eat them. Run along, now, children," he said to Mab, Gus and Fee, "the grown ups want to talk." He rang the bell, ordered champagne and despatched the puppies off to the kitchens to be fed.

Watching him opening the champagne, Stephen felt a pang of misery. He couldn't do that any more.

"There are so many things you *can* do though," Dominic said, sympathetically.

Stephen jumped. "How the hell did you know what I was thinking?"

"You have a very expressive face. I can read it like a book."

"Well, here's something you won't have read. I've written buckets of new songs and someone's going to have to play them. Will you? Will you join the band and play lead guitar?"

They all stared at him.

"M-me?" Dominic stammered. "Take your place?"

Stephen pushed him. "Fuck off, Charlie, you won't be taking my place! Jesus, jump into my grave that quickly? *I'll* be doing the vocals, and it'll still be *my* band."

Dominic was grinning foolishly at him. "My God, Steve, I can't believe this! Yes, of course I will, it'll be tremendous!"

Lynn and Harry were crying, and Dominic had tears in his eyes. For once, only Stephen was dry eyed. He relished it. He said, "God, you feeble English! Emotional bloody set, aren't you?"

He and Lynn stayed the night at Leezance, they'd drunk far too much champagne to drive anywhere. They discussed the children and shook their heads over RhymeNReason.

"I wouldn't mind if the songs had either rhyme or reason, but as far as I can see they're utterly fucking devoid of both!" Dominic commented.

The conversation became more general, and they had an animated discussion about the European Union. Eventually, they decided they weren't in favour of it, although Dominic had taken this stance from the beginning. He was vitriolic in his condemnation of it. Stephen hadn't seen him so drunk for a long time.

"I loathe the fucking Europeans, particularly the French," he said, enunciating every word with drunken emphasis. "One of the fucking masters at school was French, he was the most sadistic fucking bastard I've ever met."

"But, Charlie, you're French," Stephen teased.

Dominic's eyes widened in fury and he glared at Stephen. "How dare you, how fucking dare you? You take that back, you fucker, Markham!"

"You're always telling us your family came over with the Normans," Stephen pointed out reasonably.

"For Christ's sake, Markham, you fucking moron, the Normans weren't fucking French, they were fucking Vikings!" Dominic retorted. "That's why I'm tall and blond – unlike you, you fucking Welsh troll," he added.

"Yes, well, OK, that explains your hatred of the French," Harry put in. "What about the rest of them?"

"Scum. In fact all foreigners are scum. So are most of the British."

"Is there *any* nation you like?" Stephen asked, amused.

Dominic was silent for such a long time that Stephen thought he hadn't heard, and repeated the question.

"I heard you the first fucking time! I'm not fucking deaf, I'm thinking. Norway. The Norwegians are OK, fucking brave in the war, and they all wore those yellow stars, so the fucking Krauts didn't know who was Jewish."

"Hmm, well, that's true, and it's got a Viking connection. They whale though," Stephen said.

Dominic stared at him. "Are you fucking sure, Markham? I've been to Norway, I've never heard them."

Part Five
Only Ever You

It's you who floods my world with grace,
Only you can make me whole, you wrap me in your warm embrace,
Your loving fills my soul, you it is who shapes my life,
You make my dreams come true, you're all I ever wanted, only ever you.

Chapter Twenty-Seven
Bright New Day

Dark was the night and narrow the way
And a bitter furrow to plough,
But we're standing in the light of a bright new day,
And I think we're going to make it now.

Stephen was more involved in his work than Lynn had ever seen him. She spent most of her time with Lucy, relishing every moment, and practising her cooking, which hadn't got much better, as she'd only completed half a term of her course.

"I think we'll have to face it," Stephen said gently one evening, after another disastrous meal. "Cooking is never going to be your thing."

"I know," Lynn sighed. She looked at him uncertainly.

"Come on then, out with it."

"Well, ever since I saw Rhys… oh, Stevie, I'd love another baby!"

"Why ever? Lulu's not even a year old yet! And you're having one of Frammie's puppies."

Harry's fox terrier, Longframlington, known as Frammie, was pregnant, and Harry had promised Lynn one of the pups. As the father was Harry's other fox terrier, Rushy Knowe, Stephen didn't feel he could really object, although he'd told Harry rather aggressively they didn't want its tail docked.

"I'm not having any of the puppies' tails docked," she'd replied calmly, taking the wind out of his sails. They were due the following month.

"A puppy's not quite the same," Lynn laughed. "Yes, I know Lucy's not a year yet, but it would be nice for them to grow up together, and I'd so love a little boy; ever since I first saw Rob I've wanted your little boy, and I was forty last birthday, and with my cervix… well, I don't want to run out of time."

"It would mean no sex for months, cariad!" Stephen groaned. "And I've only just got you back!" He took her hand. "I was thinking we might book ourselves a holiday on that island Coco's gone to with Justin. It sounds perfect – no phones, no email, no interruptions, just the two of us. We wouldn't be able to go if you were pregnant. And, you know, it could just as easily be another girl." He recalled Toni's obsession with having a girl. "You wouldn't get like that about having a boy, would you, Cherry?" he asked anxiously.

She shook her head. "No. I'd love another daughter just as much. And it's such fun making them! If I don't get pregnant, we can go away, and if I do, we can go after the baby's born." She gave him a kiss. "Let's start now."

By the end of the Easter holidays, Rob and Julia were able to take Rhys home.

Stephen had taken to calling him Buttercup, because of Reese's Peanut Butter Cups, which infuriated Harry. "Whatever's the matter with you?" she asked crossly. "Why must everyone always have a nickname?"

"It's my way," Stephen grinned. They were in York, visiting the happy parents for a few days and he and Harry had gone for a nostalgic walk. It was a beautiful spring day. "Let's go and look at my old house," he suggested.

Harry tucked her hand into his arm. "This is just like old times."

The house was for sale. Stephen stared at it, gripped by powerful memories. "I'm buying it." He looked at his watch. "Come on, or they'll be closed." They went into the estate agents on High Petergate.

"I want to buy this house," he said, showing the girl the brochure.

She gave him an odd look and sneezed at him. "Sorry." She blew her nose. Her eyes were streaming and she coughed.

He moved back. "I'll pay the asking price in cash," he went on.

"I wish people wouldn't come to work when they've got colds as bad as that," Harry muttered to him. "Suppose we get it and give it to Rhys? It could be really dangerous for him."

Stephen had decided to offer the house to Rob and Julia. If they didn't want it, he'd keep it until the others were older. It would be handy to have a house up here, anyway, he thought. But they fell over themselves to accept.

"I love that house!" Julia exclaimed. "It's the perfect family house!"

Rob stared at Stephen, a faraway look in his eyes. "It reminds me of Grandpa," was all he said.

"Full circle," Stephen said, hugging him.

Back at the Priory the following week, he rang the others and told them he'd finished writing the songs for the new album, 'From The Brink'. "So we can start rehearsing."

He was feeling tired and out of sorts, and the next morning he didn't want any breakfast. Lynn raised her eyebrows. "That's not like you."

He felt the same at lunchtime. "I just don't feel like eating," he shrugged.

"Are you dying or something, Stephen?" Lynn joked. "You're never off your food!"

That evening, he started to feel ill, complaining of stomach pain and headache.

"Can't be anything you ate," Lynn grinned. "Perhaps you're coming down with a cold."

He shivered. "I do feel all achy."

She put her hand on his forehead. "God, Stevie, you're burning up! You go up to bed, I'll get you some iced water and ibuprofen."

By the early hours of the morning he was having difficulty breathing and was so ill that she called Henry, who had him admitted to hospital immediately. "It's OPSI," he told her.

OPSI, as Lynn knew only too well, stood for overwhelming post splenectomy infection, a potentially fatal condition attacking the immune system. Because Stephen's spleen had been ruptured in the accident and subsequently removed, he was unable to make antibodies against any bacteria new to him. It was something Lynn had dreaded, but as time went on, she'd thought that he was no longer at risk. "But surely that's impossible – he's had all the vaccinations," she breathed, dazed.

"Sometimes they fail," Henry said. "I wish I could say 'Don't worry, Lynn, he'll be fine'." The death rate from OPSI was very high.

"I asked him yesterday, when he didn't want any lunch, if he was d-dying," Lynn stammered, tears spilling down her cheeks. "It was just a joke, I didn't even think, didn't even *consider* this." Stunned, feeling as if she was dreaming, she rang Sian, Kathy and Rebecca, got hold of Rob and Harry, and drove the boys to the hospital.

Harry and Dominic were there within the hour. Harry hugged Lynn. "I bet he got it from that wretched girl in the Estate Agents! I said to him, if we caught it, it might be dangerous for Rhys, I never thought of this!" She started to cry.

Sam stared at her. "Dad's going to be all right though, isn't he? Isn't he, isn't he, isn't he."

Dominic put his arm around him. "Don't you worry, Sammy. Women are always blubbing."

Harry pulled herself together. "Take no notice, Sam, I'm just tired."

Lynn was allowed in to see Stephen. He was on a ventilator, hooked up to drips and monitors, flushed and ill, his lips cracked and blistered from the very high fever he was running. His thick, black hair was rumpled like a child's, and he looked young and vulnerable. She wanted to hold him and never let him go, but she just kissed her fingers and touched them gently to his head. He stirred slightly. She tiptoed out.

His family and friends haunted the hospital as his life hung in the balance, and the infection rampaged through his body. Harry was a tower of strength, comforting Lynn and Sian and the boys, but inside she was numb. She had known Stephen for longer than any of them except, of course, Sian: nearly thirty years. He was her best friend, and she loved him more than she loved anyone, even her children. Only Dominic meant more to her than Stephen, and only in front of Dominic did she break down.

"I was so crabby with him about Rhys," she sobbed. "I told him he was so annoying, always giving everyone a nickname. How could I have been so mean, what does it matter? If he… if he dies, I'll never be able to tell him I'm sorry…" She couldn't go on.

"Darling, he knew, he understood, he knows how much you love him."

"Oh, Dom, how can this be happening again? I couldn't bear to be without him, I just couldn't *bear* it!"

Dominic held her against him, kissing her hair while she cried. There was nothing he could say to comfort her, nothing anyone could say. All they could do was wait.

Ray flew over from Boston, as he had when Stephen had been knocked down. He held Lynn for a long moment. "He'll be all right," he said, trying to smile, trying to believe it. "He's always been stubborn as a mule, he beat the odds last time, he'll do it again!"

Miles came to Oxford and booked into an hotel, despite Lynn's protestations that he could stay at the Priory. "You've got enough on your plate without entertaining guests," he said adamantly. "If you need anything, anything at all, I'm here."

The press besieged them, and Cell issued a statement, asking them to respect the family's privacy and be supportive of them during this traumatic time. As far as Lynn could see, it didn't make much difference. She didn't mind the fans, who were genuinely worried and sympathetic, but she found the sensation seekers impossible to forgive. His sons were having a hard enough time as it was.

One evening at the hospital, after Harry had taken the boys home, she broke down. "I couldn't live without him, Charlie," she sobbed to Dominic. "And the boys – Sam – how would they cope without him? I can't believe this is happening. He's had so much pain and heartbreak and come through; he can't die now, he *can't*!"

Dominic took her in his arms. "I know." His voice wasn't steady. Like Andy, he thought of Stephen as his brother. He couldn't believe that, for the second time in two years, he was facing the possibility of a world without him.

But the following morning, Stephen began to respond to the treatment. Eventually, he was allowed home, weak and tired. He was prescribed penicillin twice a day for the rest of his life, told to continue with the vaccinations, wear a medic alert necklace, and see his GP at the slightest sign of ill health.

Lynn couldn't believe it. The pregnancy test was positive. She must have conceived in York, just before Stephen had got so ill. Ironically, because of his illness, she hadn't realised she'd missed her period until now, it was only when she had began to feel very sick every morning that she'd checked her dates. She rang Heather and booked an appointment.

Stephen smiled weakly when she gave him the news. "Oh, well, I can't really complain about the no sex rule, can I? I'm hardly Casanova at the moment." He was working on his soundtrack, in short bursts, as he got tired very easily, finishing the theme song, 'This Day Alone Is Ours'. He had once said those words to Lynn, and although he was writing it for the film, it was really for her.

He rang Miles. "It's finished."

"Splendid, dear boy – and how are you?"

"Better, thanks, Miles. I just don't seem to have any energy."

"What you need is a long holiday somewhere hot."

"That'll have to wait. Lynn's pregnant and she has problems. She'll have to stay in bed for most of her pregnancy."

"Oh." Miles was taken aback. "Well – congratulations! You never cease to amaze me, Stephen."

Sid's Six started to rehearse 'From The Brink'. Stephen hadn't been prepared for the devastation he felt, watching Dominic playing lead guitar in his place, in his band, on his songs. He'd thought he was over all that, had accepted it, but he realised, with dismay, that he wasn't anywhere near being over it. The most he could hope for was that the ache would become dulled by time, and that he would become used to not playing. He tried to stay cheerful, and the others were tremendously supportive, but not even Lynn knew the depths of his despair during those first days.

Dominic had some inkling of the way he was feeling. "I feel terrible, as if I'm flaunting the fact that I can play and he can't," he said to Harry, the first evening. "If you could see the look in his eyes, Hat! It nearly made me cry."

"God! I'm glad I can't! I'd break down, and that'd be no help to him at all. He's been through so much, Dom. I don't know how he does it."

"No," Dominic agreed. "There's nothing anyone can do, either. He's got to do this all on his own."

Lynn was pleased to see Heather. "I'm so excited! I really think it's a boy! I've been feeling completely different from how I felt with Lucy, or my first one – incredibly sick."

Heather smiled and examined her. Her smile faded. "Are you sure of your dates, Lynn?"

"Yes, why? What's wrong?"

"How far along do you think you are?"

Lynn swallowed. "Um, about ten weeks. What's wrong, Heather?"

"Maybe nothing." Heather smiled at her, a smile that didn't quite reach her eyes. "Your uterus is bigger than it should be."

"What would cause that?"

"Let's do a scan. I'm sure there's nothing to worry about."

Lynn immediately started to worry. They went down to ultrasound, and she lay on the bed, gripping Stephen's hand.

Heather looked at the screen. A huge grin spread across her face. "You'd be extremely unlucky *not* to have a wee boy, Lynn. You're expecting triplets!"

They went home, punch-drunk. "Triplets!" Stephen said. "Triplets! I don't believe it!" He kissed her. "You are the most amazing woman!"

Toni couldn't believe the news, either. She hadn't really believed Harry when Harry had assured her that Lynn and Stephen hadn't split up, and even when Lynn went back, she'd heard via Shelagh that Stephen spent all the time he wasn't resting working, and felt that the reconciliation was all show. But this news, that Lynn was pregnant and expecting triplets, was a blow.

"George, you know you wanted to have a baby? I think I'd like that too," she said to George when he came in one evening from rehearsal. They had never got around to moving. They hadn't seen a house they liked, and George's mansion flat in Battersea, overlooking the park, was big enough for the boys when they stayed. Toni was still looking on and off, but she was in no hurry.

George gave her a shrewd look. He knew perfectly well what was going on in her mind. "OK, pet." He leered at her. "We could start now, if you like."

She grinned at him. "I'm easy."

"Aye, that's one of the things I like about you."

Toni wasn't completely happy. She found George much easier to live with than Stephen, she knew where she was with him. She'd said to Stephen once that George reminded her of her father, and that was true. To George, everything was black and white, there were no grey areas. He had certain lines and she was learning not to cross them. In bed, he was perfect for her, with a roughness she'd always found lacking in Stephen, but also an unexpected tenderness. And he loved her devotedly.

But her life was very much the same as it had been when she was married to Stephen. She'd thought living in London would be more exciting than living in Oxford, but it wasn't. She and George went to more events, but somehow even these didn't quite come up to her expectations. George wasn't anywhere near as famous as Stephen, and Toni missed the perks that went with Stephen's fame. Last Christmas, Harrods had opened early to let Lynn do her shopping undisturbed, which had driven Toni mad with jealousy, and she hated the fact that Lynn was now the hostess at the lavish parties Stephen delighted in holding at the Priory. Unlike George, who preferred to be entertained, Toni loved throwing parties. And she and Stephen had always had tremendous fun planning them too, and she missed that very much. George would grudgingly agree to a dinner party occasionally, but his favourite way of spending an evening was to go out, and he often went to the pub with friends. He was quite happy for her to go with him, but she got bored.

She saw a lot more of Callie now she was living in London, meeting her a couple of times a week for lunch and shopping, and going out with her in the evenings, sometimes with a group, sometimes with George and Fred, sometimes on their own, but somehow, it wasn't enough. She'd had Swiggsy over to stay, but he and George got on very well, and George took him to the pub. She sighed. Perhaps if she had a baby, she'd feel more fulfilled. She imagined herself shopping in Harvey Nichols with a little girl who looked like Lucinda. Bloody Lynn, how she hated her. She must be a bit of a freak to want to sleep with a deformed cripple. She said this to George after they'd made love and was startled by his reaction.

"I don't ever want to hear you saying that again, Toni!" he roared at her. "If you do, I'll belt you!"

She knew he meant it. "Yes, George," she said meekly.

"There's a good lass." He put his arm round her.

"But I thought you didn't like Stephen."

"Whatever made you think that, man, Toni?" he asked, astonished.

"You're always calling him a lass and fighting with him!"

"Why aye, he's a lass all right, and an annoying little lass at that. I like him fine though. I admire him too. It's been really hard for him since the accident, but, by, you should hear some of the songs he's written, they're crackin'!"

"Oh. It seems a bit odd, letting Dominic play lead guitar."

"Well, who else would he ask? He can't play himself, and Dom's his best friend and a canny player. Not as good as Steve, but who is? No, Steve's been very sensible. This new album's been really tough for him, watching Dominic play instead of him, but he's never once complained or taken it out on anyone. So I don't want to hear any of that stuff about him being a cripple. Now be a good girl and fetch me a drink." He slapped her bottom and she went off to get him a beer. He thought of her as being like a nervy, highly strung, but plucky little horse that had only been partially broken; the lass had been far too soft with her, he thought. She was beginning to learn, but it was a slow process.

She brought in his beer.

"Thanks, pet. When we've finished recording, how about we go and see Jacko? Maybe go on somewhere afterwards; Tahiti, or maybe Japan?"

"Oh, George, yes!" She covered him with kisses.

George smiled to himself. It was simply a matter of checks and balances.

Ali And Nino premiered at the beginning of July. Stephen wanted to go, but not without Lynn. "I can say I'm not up to it, Cherry. It's not such a lie, I certainly won't be up to more than just watching the film."

"Think how hurt Miles will be if you don't go," Lynn pointed out. She was lying on the bed, her fox terrier puppy curled up next to her. She'd called him Snowdrop, after an endearingly stupid criminal played by Bernard Bresslaw in a Terry Thomas, film *Too Many Crooks*. "If you really don't feel well enough, don't go, but don't not go just because of me. I honestly don't mind not going, there'll be loads of others. I definitely want to go to the next Verity one." Stephen had started work on the new Verity Linden film, *Black Moon*.

He kissed her. "You are such a darling. Yes, I would like to see this film."

She returned the kiss. "Good. You go and have a lovely time."

She'd been given the usual advice about resting. This was especially important as she was expecting triplets. She'd had the stitch put into her cervix and it was just a matter of waiting. She'd made up her mind that, if one of the babies was a boy, they should call it after Stephen.

Stephen was dubious. "I thought we'd decided on David Alistair."

"Well, Lucy's got three names. How about Stephen David Alistair?"

Stephen shook his head. "It would be too confusing to have two Stephens around the place."

Lynn thought for a minute. "What about Esteban? That's Spanish for Stephen. Esteban David Alistair."

"Well, if we were Spanish, it'd be perfect, but as we're not..."

"Oh, Stevie, it's a lovely name!" Lynn said, warming to the idea. "If we have three boys – and you know, I feel sure they *are* boys – they'd be Andrew, Dominic and Esteban." She sighed happily. "It's perfect!"

They'd decided that if they had more than one boy, they'd call the others after Andy and Dominic. "They're like my brothers," Stephen had said. "Actually, I honestly think Andy thinks he *is* my brother. And," he'd added, looking uncertainly at Lynn, not too sure of her reaction, "I'd like to name a girl, if we have one, after Harry. She's been so good to me – she's so very special to me, Cherry."

Lynn smiled. "I know, and I think it's a lovely idea. Although I have to say, Stevie, I'm not awfully keen on the name Harriet. I mean, I love her and everything, but..." She shrugged. "We both like the name Eleanor – how about Eleanor Harriet? That's not too bad."

"Well, actually, I've been thinking. What about Arabella?"

She stared at him. "Yes, Arabella is a beautiful name, but how does that help?"

"Sorry, of course you wouldn't know! Arabella is Harry's middle name. Her mother loved the name and it was actually going to be Hal's first name, but then she died, and Ted felt he had to name the baby after her. So Arabella became her middle name. That's why Charlie sometimes calls her Hat or Hatty, her initials used to be H.A.T."

"'My Beautiful Hat'! I finally understand that song!"

She was referring to a song on GI Joe's fourth album, 'It's Nice, But Is It Art?', which Dominic had written when he was first dating Harry.

Stephen grinned. "Yeah. He'd never explain it when interviewers asked him, either, it gave him tremendous satisfaction to be able to write a love song for her that meant nothing to anyone else."

"Andrew, Dominic and Esteban," he repeated now. "You're serious, aren't you?"

She nodded. "It's a lovely name! Oh, come on, darling Stevie, why not?"

"Lynn, we cannot in all conscience land our poor kid with the name Esteban!"

"But I really want to call him after you!"

Stephen sighed. "Middle name only, and that's my final offer."

Lynn pouted. "Who says you're in charge?"

"I do." He went off to get her a drink, singing, 'First they had triplets and then they had twins...' He was singing all the time again, and he'd got his guitars back from Harry. He might not be able to play them, but he couldn't bear them not to be there. He let the boys play them if they were careful. They were very cheerful, amazed at the thought that Lynn had three babies inside her. "How will they all get out?" Sam had asked.

"Well, one at a time," Stephen said.

"Oh." Sam was relieved. "I thought they all came out together!"

"Dear God, that would kill me," Lynn said faintly.

Alex and Pip were still adamant that when they were older they would be playing in RhymeNReason. "We need a bass player and a drummer, of course," Alex had said, "and maybe a keyboard player. Sam would do."

"I will not!" Sam had retorted. "I'm not playing in your rubbish band!"

They were working on a new song. It had been inspired by the song Alex had written when Stephen had released the balloons to symbolise the loss of his hand. He'd heard them practising and had been horrified. It was called 'Sad Man' and it went: *You're a real sad man, you lost your hand, then your wife left home, now you're all alone, SAD MAN! SAD MAN!*

He hadn't waited around to hear any more.

The pair of them came racing down the stairs, singing '*RhymeNReason at the top of their game!*'

Stephen was in the kitchen, making Lynn drinking chocolate and singing 'This Is How You Remind Me'.

Alex was wearing a hoody with 'Slipknot' printed on it. He stopped singing

'RhymeNReason' and stared at Stephen. "God, Dad, don't sing *Nickelback*!"

"Why not? I would have thought you'd like them, you're a Mosher."

"Exactly! They're crap!"

"Crap on a plate," Pip agreed. He was busy with Stephen's cook's blowtorch, trying to singe the fur of an old teddy bear for Mab. She'd given him one of her soft toys, a fluffy dog, with its eyes gouged out and a stab wound in its back.

"Nickelback are great, I really like some of their stuff," Stephen said. " 'Breathe', for instance. I can't see why – Pip! What the fuck are you doing? Put the tea towel over it, quick!"

"Sorry, Dad." Pip had gone white. "I was just trying to singe its fur a bit!"

"What the hell for? No, don't tell me, I don't want to know. Just please, please, boys, promise me, the pair of you, you won't try to singe anything else. Look!" He held up his left arm.

"What?" Alex asked, bemused.

"My stump. Have you any idea how much it hurt being knocked down?"

They stared at him. He'd never asked them anything like this before.

"Were you awake?" Pip asked in awe.

"Yes. I remember being hit and the terrible pain. I don't ever want to be involved in any sort of accident again, and that includes a fire. OK?"

"Yes, Dad. We promise."

Stephen woke early the next morning with a bad back. He got up, took some pain killers, and decided to go and play the Theramin. He headed up to the music room. As he got to the door, he heard a guitar; his Sellas – someone was playing 'The Loving Cup', the song Dominic had written for his and Harry's anniversary. And playing it very well. He suddenly felt cold. Supposing he'd slipped into a parallel universe? Supposing he went in and it was himself in there? He wanted to run. He gritted his teeth. You watch too much fucking *Star Trek*, he told himself, and went into the room. His heart thumped. A black haired boy was bent over the guitar, engrossed in the music. And then he looked up, and the spell was broken. Black eyes – Pip's eyes – smiled into his. "Hello, Dad."

"You play superbly, Pip!" Stephen was amazed. All he'd heard Pip do up till now was torture his guitar and shout out RhymeNReason songs.

Pip flushed. "Not as well as you."

"Every bit as well. Why don't you play like that more often?"

"It's not cool."

"Of course it is!"

"Maybe I will when I'm older. But I couldn't play like this in RhymeNReason."

"No. But as you say, maybe in the future. And Mab could sing in your band. She's got a terrific voice."

Pip flushed again. "I know. She's amazing. I'm going to marry her."

"When her legs are longer?"

"What do you mean?" Pip asked, puzzled.

"Don't you remember how Sammy always said he was going to marry the cat at Fenroth when her legs were longer?"

"So he did! I'd forgotten all about that!"

"Yes, well, he's so much better now, isn't he? Do you remember when we used to have to explain what characters in films were thinking? Whenever we watched a film we had to put it on pause every five minutes to explain what they were thinking and why they were behaving the way they were."

"Yeah," Pip said, soberly. "Poor old Sam! I'm going to be nicer to him from now on."

Stephen turned on the Theramin. "That's a good idea, no more calling him a nerd."

Pip stared at him. "God, Dad, I just said I'd be nicer to him! I didn't say I was going to lie!"

Recording 'From The Brink' hadn't been as bad as Stephen had feared. The initial feelings of desolation had receded slightly during the rehearsals, so that by the time they started recording he could keep his feelings separate, and concentrate on what he was doing. And, in fact, it'd had been fun, and he was pleased with how well they were all working together. With the addition of Dominic to the line up, their sound and style was starting to change; Stephen had preferred to play using his bare fingers, but Dominic favoured picks, particularly thumb picks. When they'd first started rehearsing he'd tried to replicate Stephen's sound, however, by the time they begun recording, he'd relaxed and was playing more like himself. Stephen didn't mind, he was pretty sure that by the next album he and Dominic would be writing together – the only reason he hadn't said as much to Dominic was because he'd been worried that the other three might resent Dominic having so much say in the band. Dominic, for his part, had always been very aware that his addition to the line up might cause problems, and had behaved with great tact and diplomacy, so much so that even George, who was the one most likely to object to his involvement, had no difficulty working with him.

After every session, they'd gone into the house and had a drink and something to eat. Lynn was usually lying on her chaise longue in the winter parlour, and they'd go and talk to her. One of them would say 'Do you remember?' and that would lead to reminiscences which would often have them roaring with laughter.

Sometimes Harry, Holly and Shelagh joined them, and very occasionally, Toni, although this was rare and she and George would leave soon afterwards. She didn't like the way Lynn and Stephen had redecorated the Priory; once, after she'd used the bathroom, she'd crept along to the bedroom she and Stephen had shared. It was totally different, completely redecorated, and the furniture had been moved around. A chest she'd liked very much had gone, and there was an exquisite marquetry writing desk in its place. Stephen's lyrics book was on it, which meant he worked there. He had never worked in the bedroom when she was married to him, had never shared what he was writing, or discussed it with her. The fact that he obviously did with Lynn upset her very much. Also, she hated seeing Lynn lying around – like Lady Muck, she thought, visibly swelling. Lynn often wore her cariad pendant, and she always wore the cariad eternity ring. The sight of them made Toni's heart contract with hatred of Stephen. He'd never called her cariad, not even when they were first married. She wanted to rip the pendant from Lynn's neck, and the ring from her finger and shove them down Stephen's throat.

And, on top of all this, she still wasn't pregnant. Because she'd always conceived so quickly and easily when she was married to Stephen, she'd considered herself to be very fertile. Now she realised it must have been more to do with him, which added to her annoyance. And then George had always been very fond of Lynn, ever since they were at university, and Toni often felt out of it when they were talking. She could have been like Holly and Shelagh and asked interested questions, but she didn't want to, she was too jealous.

"For God's sake, pet, lighten up a bit!" George said as they were going home one evening. "You stick out like a spare prick at a wedding."

"Don't be so coarse," she said primly.

"Oh, it's don't be coarse now, is it? You don't mind how fucking coarse I am when I'm giving you one," George retorted.

Toni lips tightened, but she didn't reply.

When they got home, she said goodnight in a cold little voice.

"I'll be in later for a shag," George said. He watched her flounce along the corridor, displeasure emanating from her. "And you can stop behaving like that, man, else you'll be in trouble!" He fetched a bottle of Newcastle Brown from the fridge and drank it down while he watched an episode of *The Sweeney*. Then he went to the bedroom. It was in darkness. He turned the light on.

Toni sat up indignantly. "I'm trying to sleep."

"Well, that's tough, pet, because I want a shag. Come on, get your kit off, man."

She stared at him. "I want to go to sleep, George."

He sighed. "Look, Toni, you're married to me now, not the lass. It's about time we got that straight. Those tricks you got up to with him don't work with me. Now stop messing about, and get naked."

"Make me!" she challenged.

George smiled broadly. "I knew you wanted it, pet!" He got into bed and straddled her, catching her wrists and pinning them above her head as he pulled up her nightgown. She wriggled unconvincingly. He let go of her wrists and she wrapped her arms round his neck, pulling him closer. "I don't like it," she murmured.

George tweaked her erect nipples, making her squeal. "I think you do!"

"No, I mean the fact that you know me so well."

"Bad luck, man. Now shut up, and let's get on with it!"

It was Lynn's birthday at the end of August. Stephen held an impromptu party.

At one point, Dominic turned to George. "You and I have got quite a bit in common, haven't we, George?"

"Oh aye, and what would that be?" George had never been quite sure of Dominic; was he a lass like Stephen or not?

"We're both Geordies, we're both in Markham's band, and we're both married to his cast offs."

Toni had gravitated over to Lynn, who was holding Lucinda. The noise had woken her, and Stephen had brought her downstairs. Her hair had darkened slightly and was now the same pale gold as Lynn's; her eyes were Stephen's. She was fifteen months old, and talking in sentences. Like Stephen as a baby, she sang even more than she talked.

"She's very beautiful," Toni said reluctantly.

"She's very like Stephen," Lynn smiled.

"She's like both of you. I envy you," Toni said in a rush. "I'd love a little girl."

"I envy you your boys. They're lovely, such lovely manners. You must be very proud of them."

Toni gave her a genuine smile. "I am." She sat next to her. "I used to hate you."

"That's such a shame," Lynn sighed. "I tried not to hate you, but I was beside myself with jealousy."

Toni stared. "*You* were jealous of *me*?"

"God, yes! I had Stephen for less than three years, you had him for fifteen! And you had your lovely boys. Listen, Toni, we might not be friends, but we could be – civil to each other. I don't know about you, but I'd like that. I loved *Bunyip The*

Brave. You really had a Bunyip, Alex was telling me. He showed me the photos. He looked like a sweet little spider."

"I didn't know you liked tarantulas."

"Oh, yes," Lynn lied, hoping she'd never be put to the test. And she *had* liked Toni's book. She had started to read it to please Sam; she had finished it because she wanted to.

"He *was* lovely," Toni sighed.

"You ought to write another book about him."

"Well, you know," Toni was pleased, "I have been toying with the idea. I thought I might call it 'Bunyip Bounces Back'."

"Go for it," Lynn encouraged.

"Thanks, mate, I will!"

Stephen had put some music on, and Dominic came over. "Come on, Toni, come and dance with me." He'd been alarmed to see her talking to Lynn, he knew what a barbed tongue she had, so he nearly fell over when she said, "I never realised how nice she is. I hope she and Stephen are happy."

He kissed her on the mouth. "Toni, you never cease to amaze me!"

Chapter Twenty-Eight
World Without End.

And the beat of my heart, and the sweet, sweet scent of you,
And the touch of your skin and the heat of the earth, and I worship you.
And the freewheeling birds flying up high,
Above the restless sea and the bold, flushed sky
Bear witness to our love. And the secrets of our hearts are told,
World without end in a circle of gold.

Heather removed Lynn's stitch at the beginning of December. "I think you may well go into labour soon," she said. "I'd like you to come into hospital, Lynn."

She was right. Lynn went into labour four days later, on Monday the eighth of December. The first two babies were born quickly and, for Lynn, fairly easily. They were both boys, one of them very like Lucy, his fine, wispy hair a white blond, but with Lynn's violet eyes. The other was the image of Stephen.

"God, he's exactly like Robbie was!" Stephen exclaimed.

"Esteban," Lynn murmured happily.

"David Esteban Alistair," Stephen reminded her. "And this little one's Andrew."

"Andrew Dominic James," Lynn said proudly.

"I wonder whether number three will be Arabella or Felix?" Stephen smiled, but his face changed as she clutched his hand. A fierce pain, much worse than the earlier contractions, gripped her. Beads of sweat formed on her brow. As the pain receded, she managed to smile at Stephen. "I think we're going to find out any minute!"

But nothing happened, she seemed to be stuck, and the contractions became stronger and longer, until there was no gap between them, just wave after wave of excruciating pain surging over her, she was drowning in it, despite the gas and air, and the baby seemed no nearer to being born. She was vaguely aware of Stephen's concerned face, and more people in the room, a lot of bustle, and then Heather was examining her, which was almost unbearable. She began to cry – why didn't they do something, make it stop? Maybe they couldn't, maybe it was never going to stop, it was pulling her under, and she was exhausted, and terrified for the baby.

As if she'd read her mind, Heather said, her voice calm and soothing, "This last wee soul seems to be having a bit of a problem, Lynn, so we're going to give it a hand. This is Adrian Clarke, he's going to give you an epidural. Just relax now, there's absolutely nothing to worry about, you're both going to be fine."

They turned her on her side, and the anaesthetist inserted the needle into her back, and to her immense relief, the pain drained away. She was wheeled into theatre, where Heather, scrubbed and gowned, was waiting, with rather a bewildering amount of staff, to perform the caesarean.

A screen was placed across Lynn's stomach, so that neither she nor Stephen could see what was going on. She was feeling better, the pain had gone, but she was very frightened, scared for the baby, despite Heather's assurances. She could see from Stephen's face he felt the same way.

"Now then, are you ready to say hello to your baby, Lynn?" Heather was asking.

"You'll feel some pressure, and maybe a little tugging," she went on, "and then – yes, out she comes!" The room filled with the sound of the baby wailing and the smell of warm, fresh blood.

Heather cut the cord and passed the squirming little girl to Lynn. "She is super, Lynn, well done! You have a look at her, while we get you all sorted."

Lynn and Stephen were looking at her. She was tiny, even smaller than the two boys, and she had a shock of jet black hair that stood up from her head. She stopped crying and opened her eyes, gazing around the room.

Lynn gasped. "Oh, Stevie, her eyes are just like yours! This is how I always dreamed Sakura would look! We've got her back!" Tears were streaming down her face.

Stephen stared at the little girl, his heart full. He felt about twenty, full of energy. He wanted to turn cartwheels and kiss everyone in the room, but contented himself with kissing Lynn and the baby. "You know we're going to have Eleanor as a middle name? Well, how do you feel about calling her Arabella Sakura Eleanor?"

Lynn nodded, unable to speak.

The paediatrician took Arabella off to weigh her, and one of the nurses wiped Lynn's face. "All these tears! You're worse than the baby!"

Heather finished closing the incision. "You've got dissolving stitches, Lynn, and I've put a drain in. Are you feeling all right?"

Lynn nodded, smiling, the pain and fear forgotten. "I'm feeling fantastic!"

Stephen stroked her hair back from her face. "You are fantastic, my sweet, sweet Cherry."

Harry cried at Arabella being named after her, and Dominic shook Stephen's hand vigorously and patted his shoulder. For Dominic, this was quite a demonstration.

Andy was very moved. "I can't tell you how much this means to me, Steve," he said, his voice unsteady.

Sian couldn't get over them. "They're so beautiful!" She kissed Lynn, who had been reading to Lucy. "Thank you, Cherry."

"Whatever for?" Lynn asked, surprised.

Lucy climbed over onto Sian's lap. Sian kissed her. "Hello, cariad. For Stephen. He's his old self again. I never thought he would be. And he's got over that phobia with his stump."

Lynn smiled. "I knew he was finally over it when we were at an ante-natal appointment recently and a child asked him if he'd been born without a hand, and he wasn't upset." She thought back to the incident. The little boy must have been about four. He'd been glancing at Stephen for a while, and finally said, "Was you borned without a hand, Mister?"

His mother had been mortified, but Stephen had just smiled and said, "No, a naughty man ran me over with his car and my hand came off. So be very careful of cars, won't you?"

Ted joined them. "Three generations of Markhams. Pity Rhys isn't here."

Stephen nodded. "It's weird to think he's their nephew!"

"You know how David Beckham has his children's names tattooed on his body?" Dominic said. "It's a good thing Markham didn't start that when Rob was born."

Andy laughed. "Yeah, he'd be a bit pushed for space, now! We've got to be off, Steve," he went on, patting Stephen on the shoulder. "Congrats again, bro."

Holly smiled at Stephen. "I'm so happy for you," she said. She kissed Lynn. "For you all."

'From The Brink' was released to a storm of publicity and Sid's Six was in huge demand for interviews. One of the first they gave was to the enormously popular daytime TV programme, *Wake Up, Britain!* The band did a set first, and then went over to the couch.

"We're more than pleased to see you, aren't we, Patrick?" Sally gushed.

"We certainly are, Sally!" Patrick nodded. "It's wonderful to know that the band is staying together, after the tragedy and uncertainty of the last few years." He turned to Stephen. "And congratulations on the birth of your triplets."

Stephen smiled. "Thank you."

"So, there are five of you now. You only need one more and the band would live up to its name," Sally went on.

"Only if the new member was called Sid," Stephen pointed out.

She gave him a hard look and turned to Dominic. "So what's it like, stepping into Stephen's shoes?"

Dominic took a sip of water. "It's a little nerve-racking. I have my own style of playing; I like to use picks, whereas Stephen preferred to play with his bare fingers, so I'm always conscious of trying to modify my playing to fit in with the band's sound."

Sally nodded. "And how do you feel about Dominic taking your place, Stephen?" She'd moved closer to Dominic while she was speaking. He, in turn, moved away slightly.

What a stupid question, Stephen thought. He tried not to sound or look as though he thought that. "Well, obviously, I'd love to be playing, but I can't, so I'm glad Charlie is."

Sally did a double take. "Charlie?"

"Charlie Chaplin," Stephen explained.

"Oh!" Sally laughed. She moved round towards Dominic, who shifted again, until he was right next to Stephen and could go no further. She smiled triumphantly.

"But he doesn't have to worry too much about changing the sound of the band," Stephen continued. "It's natural to evolve, and I imagine he and I will be writing songs together for future albums."

Dominic's eyebrows shot up, and the other three stared at Stephen.

"Really?" Dominic stammered.

Stephen shrugged and grinned at him. "I think it's inevitable."

"Can I ask you the question I think all your fans would ask if they were here?" Patrick said. "You've been through a tremendously traumatic three years; the title song from the new album, 'From The Brink', is a very hard song to listen to, and offers an insight into the despair you obviously – and understandably – felt after the accident. How are you?"

Stephen considered the question. "Well, I suppose I'm like everyone. I have good days and bad days. I won't ever get used to the loss of my hand and I can't bear the fact that I'll never play guitar again. But I wake up every day and revel in the knowledge that I didn't die in the accident, I lost my hand instead of my life, and I'm still here with my family and friends. I feel very lucky."

"Are the lyrics exaggerated for the song?"

"No, not at all, they're toned down, if anything. I did actually wish after the accident that I'd died. I can't believe now that I felt that, but I did. I was tremendously depressed. They tried to get me to have counselling at the hospital, but I didn't want to know. I didn't want any help. It was a mistake, but I just… I didn't…" He stopped and shrugged, unable to explain the complex welter of emotions. "I just wanted to forget it, thought I could do it on my own. I couldn't, and I'm so grateful to my family and friends. They helped me see how incredibly lucky I was to cheat death." He smiled. "And when I was so ill earlier this year, it really brought home how much I've got to live for. I desperately wanted to live."

Fin patted his shoulder.

"That's how we all felt," George said quietly.

"You dedicated the album to your wife, but you've thanked, by name, the paramedic crew who came out when you were knocked down, and also the staff at the James Radlett hospital, along with family and friends," Patrick said.

Stephen nodded. "Without them, especially the ambulance crew, I wouldn't be alive. I'll never forget what they did for me."

"Have you considered any sort of reconstructive surgery?" Sally asked. "I understand there are a lot of things happening in that direction in the USA."

"You mean like the Bionic Man? Better, stronger, faster than I was before?"

Sally laughed.

"Seriously though, Stephen," Patrick said. "There have been several hand transplants performed in the last few years."

"Seriously, I don't know. As you say, there is a lot happening, a lot of stuff to look into. As far as the hand transplants go, it wouldn't really be an option for me at the moment. I'd have to take drugs to suppress my immune system in order not to reject the hand, and not having a spleen, I couldn't do that. Maybe in the future they'll find a way round it." He smiled. "And anyway, I've spent more than enough time in hospital over the last few years."

"And you've been asked to do some adverts for the National Blood Service," Sally said.

"Yes, I had to have a massive transfusion after the accident. Without all that blood from all those donors, I wouldn't have made it. It's nice to be able to give something back."

"Although I understand you're a blood donor yourself – or used to be?"

"I was, but ironically, I can't donate now, there's a tiny risk that there might have been variant CJD in the blood I was given."

"Oh." Sally was alarmed. "Doesn't that worry you?"

Stephen shrugged. "I'm alive now, without the blood I wouldn't be. What's the point of worrying?"

Sally looked unconvinced, but before she could say anything else, Patrick cut in. "The new album. I understand there's definitely going to be a tour to promote it. How do you feel about touring these days?"

Andy answered. "Well, I think we're all raring to go, like. It's been a while."

"Yeah, there's nothing better than touring, that's what it's all about," Fin added.

"Dominic." Sally turned to him. While Patrick had been talking she'd moved up again so that she was pressed against him.

"Sally," he said, smiling charmingly.

"What about fan reaction to you being in the band?"

"It's very positive. They're all for it on the website."

"Do you all keep up with the website?" Patrick asked.

"Oh, definitely," George said. "The website and the fan club. It's great to know what wor fans are thinking, they're really important to us. Without them, we wouldn't exist."

Stephen nodded. "We get so many lovely letters from fans who have been with us since we first started – who've grown up with us, as it were – telling us how important our music has been to them over the years. It's enormously rewarding."

"What's your earliest memory of each other?" Sally asked.

Stephen rolled his eyes at Dominic.

"My first memory of Steve is being amazed by his having brought four guitars with him to university," Fin laughed.

Stephen grinned. "Yeah, you made me play my Strat. Do you remember meeting George, Fin? It was in that pub, it was packed, but he cleared a path to the bar without any problem."

Fin nodded. "Yeah, well, that's why we asked him to be in the band – we hadn't even heard him play!"

"Do you remember auditioning Andy?" George put in.

"Oh ey, I was dead nervous! I didn't think I'd get in, like, and I was dead pleased when I did, and then you lot told me you were calling it Gay Boys In Bondage."

"Gay Boys In Bondage?" Sally was shocked.

"It was a joke," Fin explained.

"What about Dominic?" Sally put her hand on his knee.

"What are you implying?" Dominic raised an eyebrow.

Sally blushed slightly. "I mean, what does everyone remember about meeting you?"

"We've entirely wiped that from our minds," Stephen grinned.

"You were being a little swot when I first met you," Dominic drawled. "Sitting in the library studying. You always were a creep, Markham."

"Yeah, and you were being an obnoxious, bigheaded, upper class twit," Stephen retorted. "As usual."

"I met Andy long before I joined the band," Dominic went on, ignoring him.

"Yeah, that's right, in the fishmongers where I worked."

"I remember Dominic being very stand-offish," Fin said. "I didn't like him much then."

Dominic stared at him. "Really?"

"Aye," George agreed. "Very arrogant."

Dominic was stunned.

"We liked you when we got to know you." Andy assured him.

"Aye, we like you fine, now, bonny lad."

"Do we?" Stephen asked, still grinning.

"Moving on," Patrick said. "Stephen, I understand you play a new instrument, the Theramin."

Stephen was astonished. "Who told you that?"

Patrick smiled. "What is a Theramin?"

Stephen sat back and rubbed his chin. "It's a little difficult to explain unless you've seen one. It's an electronic instrument, and it's like a wooden box on a leg. It's got two antennae and you don't touch it to play it, the sound comes from movements you make in the air around it. It works by electricity, and it needs an amp. It makes all kinds of sounds, you can get it to sound like a violin or a cello, but I think the sound it's best known for is that science fiction, horror sound, a bit like the theme to the original *Star Trek*. A Theramin was played on the soundtrack of *Ed Wood*."

"And will you play this with the band?"

"Not yet, I'm nowhere near good enough. I just play it at home, I couldn't stand not being able to play an instrument. But I'm using it on the new Verity Linden soundtrack, and I hope eventually to play it in the band."

"There's huge interest in the band at the moment, especially since Dominic joined," Sally said, stroking Dominic's leg. "Is there anyone you can see yourselves working with?"

"I don't know about the rest of you," Stephen said, "but I've been thinking about Shakira a lot, recently."

The others made approving noises.

"Aye, but who do you see us working with, bonny lad?" George asked, grinning.

"Oh, I haven't a clue," Stephen grinned back.

Sally was bemused. "I thought you said Shakira?"

"Let's talk some more about the album," Patrick said, ignoring her. "You've written all the songs, as usual, Stephen, except for the last track, 'What A Wonderful World'. What's going on there?"

"Well, while I was recovering in hospital a few months ago, Toni, George's wife…"

"Your ex-wife!" Sally exclaimed. Six pairs of eyes turned on her furiously. She blushed.

"Well," Stephen went on, "Toni brought me a huge bunch of red roses, and that immediately made me think of the song. It just summed up the way I was feeling – it *is* a wonderful world and I'm so lucky."

"As usual, there are a couple of controversial songs on the album," Patrick said. "'Keeping Mum', for instance, is about the lack of care for the elderly, and 'New Technology' seems like a jokey song, but in fact, you have a go at Tony Blair, there's a line about Leo and the MMR."

Stephen nodded. "I think the government has behaved appallingly over it. My son, Sam, is autistic; I couldn't say it was down to the MMR, but he was terribly ill just after he had the injection, Toni and I were afraid he was going to die, he was so ill. And all my boys had mumps after having it. And a few years later, parents were told that there was going to be a measles epidemic and all the children were given another dose of the measles vaccine; surely the first one should have worked? So it's not even very good as far as I can see, and then we're not even given the choice of having each injection separately. They keep telling us that experts are sure it's safe, but they said that about thalidomide! My four youngest certainly won't be having it. And as for 'Keeping Mum'; again, it's something I feel needs addressing. There are far too many people in this country quietly struggling to care for their elderly and infirm parents at home, because there's no other alternative."

Sally had lost interest and was smiling up at Dominic.

"You've never fought shy of being controversial, have you?" Patrick said. 'Blown Away', which you wrote after John Lennon was shot, is a call to tighten gun laws, and there's 'Please God', which is a bit of an attack on the catholic religion."

"Well, only in the way it actively tries to stop the use of contraceptives in third world countries."

"Then there's 'Dedicated Follower of Fascism'; you wrote 'Fat Girls' about anorexia, 'Savages' about the third world countries and the profits drug companies and arms dealers are making there – you don't hold back. You probably aren't on anyone's list for an honour."

"What, like an OBE, you mean?"

Patrick nodded.

"I wouldn't really be comfortable with one, to be honest; I mean, what have I ever done to deserve an honour?"

"You do a tremendous amount of charity work," Patrick interrupted.

Stephen shook his head impatiently. "When you make the kind of money I do, you have to try to give something back. Setting up the Foundation, doing a few runs, and playing charity concerts is hardly the same as devoting my life to a cause, is it? Someone was quoted recently as saying you used to get a knighthood for discovering Sydney, now you get one for playing Sydney, and that's so true! Honours should go to people who really deserve them, not actors and pop stars! And it seems to me that song writing is like; well, you've got a soapbox if there's something you want to say. And there are these things that I feel strongly about. I'd much rather be able to say what I feel than worry will I offend anyone?" He smiled. "Anyway, I wouldn't want to compete with Charlie's baronetcy!"

"Of course, you're *Sir* Dominic," Sally put in, fluttering her eyelashes at Dominic.

"Yes, and my wife is Lady Chaplin," Dominic agreed.

"So it looks like Sid's Six will be around for a while then," said Patrick.

"We certainly hope so!" Andy said.

"Well, thank you very much, Andy, Fin, George, Dominic – or should that be Charlie? – and Stephen." Patrick turned to the camera. "We'd like to wish the band all the best with their new album, 'From The Brink', available in shops now. Join us after the break for – "

Lynn turned the TV off.

"God, poor Dominic!" Alex said. "That woman was like a shark!"

Lynn smiled. "Yes, isn't she awful!" She sat and thought about the first song the band had performed on the show. She'd said to Stephen, when he'd been so depressed about losing his hand, 'A guitarist – is that all you are?', and he'd written 'All I Am' for her. It was a hauntingly beautiful song, finishing up with the words 'All I am is yours.' He'd dedicated the album to her: 'To my wife, my only love, Lynn; sweet, sweet Cherry.'

Oh, Stevie, she thought. I love you so much.

'What A Wonderful World' was released as a single and became Sid's Six's first ever Christmas number one, much to their delight.

Stephen, Lynn and the children spent Christmas at Fenroth with the Chaplins. Stephen took Lynn to Bamburgh. The beach was spectacular, and they walked hand in hand along the shore. An RAF fighter plane screamed over, making them jump and temporarily deafening them.

"It's just like *Local Hero*," Lynn smiled.

"I'll take you to Ben's Beach next year," Stephen promised. "You need a long holiday. Would you like to go to that island that Coco and Justin went to? She said it was paradise."

Lynn wrinkled her nose. "I'm not sure, Stevie. I don't like the idea of not having access to a phone; suppose something happened to one of the children?"

"Yes, that's true. Well, OK, where would you like to go?"

Lynn leant against him. "Your lake house."

"It's your house too." He kissed her hair. "Don't you want to go somewhere exotic? Cherry, start spending my money!"

"If I think of somewhere I really want to go, I'll tell you. I just want to be wherever you are. Helmsley," she added. "I'd like to go there."

Stephen laughed. "Exotic North Yorkshire!"

They sat in the sand dunes and watched the white horses on the storm grey sea.

"Do you remember when we took Ray and Robbie to Nunnington Hall?" Lynn asked. "We said we'd buy a house there when you were rich and famous."

Stephen felt the familiar pang at the thought of all the years together they'd missed. He repressed it. They were together now, that was all that mattered. "In the spring, we'll go to Nunnington Hall again," he said.

It was Alex's sixteenth birthday on January the first. After consultation with Pip, they bought him a white Fender Strat, like the one Jimi Hendrix played at Woodstock. He was amazed and delighted. "Oh, wow, this is *sooo* cool! Move over, Rover, let *Alex* take over. Come on, Pip and Mab, let's give them 'Manga Plot'." Manga was a form of Japanese graphic novel, of which the boys were inordinately fond.

The adults sat politely through the bizarre song the group had written, wincing at the guitar solo (Alex) and Mab's screamed vocals. When the song had obviously finished, they applauded.

"Well, that was money well spent," Dominic commented.

"Guys, what can we say?" Stephen asked. "Good isn't the word!"

Alex beamed. "Thanks! OK, for our encore, we're going to do 'Join Me On The Dark Side'."

A low moan went round the breakfast table.

"Did I hear Barbara calling me?" Lynn asked hopefully, getting up.

Stephen pulled her back down. "If we have to stay, so do you," he hissed. They sat and listened to Mab screeching.

Alex and Pip went into the instrumental, which was mostly the theme from *Star Wars*.

Alex stopped playing. "No, Pip! Stop it! You're spoiling it!"

"Could it get any worse?" Dominic muttered.

"I wasn't!" Pip denied hotly.

"You were playing the wrong tune! That's not how *Star Wars* goes!"

"It is! I was playing the right tune, wasn't I, Dad?"

"God, I don't know! I don't listen to that music, I hate those films and that bastard George Lucas."

"I forgot he was a *Star Trek* nerd," Pip said.

"I am not! I just hate *Star Wars*."

"*Star Wars* versus *Star Trek* – it's a huge theme in nerddom," Alex nodded.

Stephen spent January quietly at home with Lynn and the children. Lucy was twenty months old now, old enough to choose her bedtime stories, and Stephen was enjoying rediscovering the books he'd read to the boys. He still read to Sam, not because Sam had difficulty reading, far from it; he was always top of his class at school, particularly in science, but although he read plenty of textbooks and manuals, he never read fiction. This worried Stephen, who felt that, because of Sam's Aspergers Syndrome, he tended to lead a rather blinkered life, obsessing over his hobbies. He thought it was important for Sam to broaden his interests, although it was often hard to find books that he liked.

While he was browsing on Amazon early in the New Year, he came across a book called *The Obsidian Key*, by a writer he hadn't heard of before, Eleanor J Cramphorn. It looked as if it would be perfect for Sam; it had several enthusiastic reviews, and was described as *Manga style swords and sorcery for young adults*. All three boys loved Manga. He bought it, and not only did Sam enjoy it immensely, but Alex and Pip also sat and listened.

It finished on a cliffhanger, much to the boys' consternation.

"Why didn't you get the sequel, Dad?" Sam demanded.

"I didn't know there was one, Sammy."

"Let's go and order it," Pip urged.

However, they found that the sequel, *The Lock Of Animus*, wouldn't be out for several months.

"Damn!" Alex said. "Oh, well, pre order it, Dad."

"It was just like the old days, all three of them avidly listening," Stephen remarked to Lynn afterwards. "I love reading to the children."

Lynn smiled at him fondly. "Don't forget the trips. You've got years of reading ahead of you!"

At the end of the month, *Ali And Nino* was nominated for several Oscars, including best song and best score. Stephen was staggered, and took Lynn to bed to celebrate. "I really can't believe I've been nominated," he said, as they lay in each other's arms.

"I can," Lynn said, looking at him with love. "I'm just surprised you've never been nominated before! Oh, my God, Stephen, we'll be going to the ceremony! I'll have to get something to wear! I'll have to lose weight, I'm so fat! Oh, my God!"

When Toni heard about the Oscar nominations, she was furious. It seemed so unfair, all those years she had been married to Stephen, and he got nominated now. "I can't believe it!" she said to Callie over lunch. "I don't hate Lynn any more, but I'm not happy about this. And if there's heaps of stuff about 'Stephen Markham's lovely wife', I probably will."

"Calm down, it's not good for your blood pressure in your condition," Callie said. Toni was three months pregnant. "It's terribly unfair," she sympathised.

"I know!" Toni fumed. "I mean, I love George to bits, you know I do, much more than I loved Stephen, but let's face it, he's never going to be nominated for an Oscar, is he? Course, you know what it is," she went on, "Miles Tindall. He always liked Stephen, and I expect they felt sorry for him being deformed and crippled and everything." She couldn't say this in front of George, and she didn't really believe it herself, but she was so upset, she wanted to be mean.

Callie understood and went along with it. "I'm sure you're right."

When Toni got home, she was still feeling miserable.

"Hello, pet," George shouted from the sitting room, where he was watching Newcastle playing.

Toni went in. The room was a pigsty; it reeked of curry, and there were several beer bottles and a plate covered with congealing remains on the floor. George was wearing jeans and an old tee shirt. Since they'd married he'd put on weight, and had a bit of a beer belly.

"This room is disgusting!" She burst into tears.

"Toni, man, what is it?" George exclaimed, jumping up.

"Why are you such a slob?" she sobbed.

He looked down at his stained tee shirt. "A man can be a slob in his own home," he said, but without conviction.

"Stephen was never a slob!" Toni stormed. "He takes care of himself! *And* he could always get it up! *He* never left me unsatisfied!" This was a reference to the night before, when George had had slightly too much to drink and had not been able to make love to her.

He went white. "You bitch! If you weren't pregnant I'd take the skin off your arse with my belt!" He strode to the door.

"Where are you going?" Toni demanded, alarmed by the look on his face.

"Out."

She followed him into the hall.

He pulled on a sweatshirt and reached for his jacket.

"George, don't go!" she wept. "I'm sorry, I didn't mean it! I *am* a bitch, I was upset because Lynn is going to the Oscars."

George looked at her, an odd expression on his face. "I told you before, Toni, you're married to me now. I'm going out, whether you like it or not. And if you don't, maybe you'll think twice before making that sort of remark again."

"George, I'm pregnant!" she wailed.

"Have an early night then. You keep telling me how worn out it's making you." He left her staring at the door, sobbing.

Stephen had to perform his song, 'This Day Alone Is Ours', at the ceremony, so he had to be in Los Angeles beforehand to rehearse. When he and Lynn got there, they went out to lunch with Coral, who was going to be presenting the Oscar for Best Song.

Lynn had never met her, and Stephen hadn't seen her properly since before the accident. She'd visited him in hospital, but he'd been so sunk in pain and depression that he only had a hazy memory of it. Since then, they'd spoken on the phone frequently, and exchanged birthday and Christmas presents, but she'd been tremendously caught up in her career, and they hadn't managed to get together. She'd been away on holiday with Justin when Stephen had been so ill earlier in the year, and after that he'd been busy with the band. He was looking forward to seeing her very much.

Lynn had had a dress made in palest rose-coloured silk for the occasion. It was based on a wiggle dress from the fifties, very Marilyn Monroe, with a square neckline and a very low cut back, and it was completely covered with row upon row of fringes that swayed and shimmered with every movement she made. When she put it on to show Stephen, he gave a low whistle. "Talk about a weapon of mass destruction! You'll knock them dead!"

Coral was waiting at the restaurant. She hugged Stephen, and turned to Lynn. "That dress is beautiful and so are you," she smiled, her French accent very much in evidence. "Well done, Stevie!"

Stephen sat between them at lunch, Coral on his left side. She took his arm, and gently kissed his wrist. "My poor little Stephen," she said, tears in her eyes.

Lynn could have kissed her.

Coral looked over at her and smiled. "I hope you don't mind me kissing your husband! He is so adorable, I can't help myself!"

Lynn smiled back. "I have that trouble too."

"Stop it you two, you're making me blush," Stephen said, but he looked smug rather than embarrassed.

"You're loving it!" Lynn accused.

"Oh, all right, yes I am! Come on, the two most beautiful women in the world saying I'm irresistible? Of course I love it! I just don't want to appear big headed," he grinned.

"How about a threesome: you, me and Lynn?" Coral whispered to him.

He made a yelping noise. "Coral!" he managed to say. "Stop it!" He shifted uncomfortably in his seat, almost unbearably aroused at the thought of being in bed with both of them.

"What did you say?" Lynn asked her, intrigued.

Coral leant across Stephen, her perfumed breasts in her low cut frock inches from his face. "I suggested we all three go to bed together," she said, smiling mischievously.

Lynn looked at Stephen's flushed face and grinned. "Perhaps we ought to order," she merely said, thinking that she might almost consider it. Coral was so sweet and very, very pretty.

The Oscars were to take place on the twenty ninth of February. As the day approached, Stephen became more and more nervous.

Lynn was astounded. She'd never seen him like this before. "Why are you so nervous?" she asked as they got ready.

"I don't know."

She helped him dress. Normally, he didn't need much help, he'd got marvellous at coping, but on the day, after his bath, he pulled on his boxers and sank down on the bed. "Lynn," he said, his face anxious, "please don't despise me, but I don't think I'll be able to manage on my own. My hand is shaking so much."

She hugged him. "Stephen John Markham, I'd dress you every day if you wanted me to. Although I like undressing you best!"

Miles rang before they set off. "Dear boy, don't worry about a thing. I'll see you both there. Give Cherry a kiss from me." He was the only person Stephen knew outside his family – and that included Harry and Dominic – who called Lynn Cherry. Even Andy didn't. He liked Miles very much because of it.

By the time they arrived at the Kodak Theatre in their limousine, he was feeling better. He'd become fatalistic. They were there. What was he nervous about? He wasn't going to win, he was absolutely sure of that, so he could relax and enjoy showing Cherry off. She was wearing an exquisite dress which had been made for her by Chanel. It had a bodice in pale celestial blue, and a full, full skirt, not quite floor length and slightly higher in front, made from layers of tulle in shades of violet. He'd bought her a delicate necklace of amethysts and diamonds, with earrings to match, and she looked breathtaking, he thought.

They met Miles and went into the auditorium together.

His nerves came back when he went up on stage to perform 'This Day Alone Is Ours'; he felt the same way he'd done before The Brigands played their first ever gig at the Angel all those years ago. He wished Harry was with him, playing bass. He got through it, and collapsed thankfully into his seat. Lynn squeezed his hand.

And then Coral came on, looking very elegant in a vintage Schiaparelli evening gown. She read out the nominations for best song, and tore the envelope open. "And the Oscar goes to… Stephen Markham for *Ali And Nino*, 'This Day Alone Is Ours'." She smiled happily.

Stephen was absolutely stunned. He sat paralysed.

Lynn elbowed him. "Go on!"

It seemed like miles to the podium. Coral threw her arms around him and kissed him on the mouth. He'd prepared a short speech when he'd been nominated; every word of it escaped him. He managed to stammer out his thanks, and stumbled back to Lynn, clutching the Oscar.

Lynn couldn't speak. She smiled up at him, her eyes bright with unshed tears. Miles leant across her and patted his knee.

Several other nominations and presentations followed. Stephen kept looking down at the Oscar in his hand, almost afraid he might have imagined it. They came to the nomination for best score. The actor presenting the award, Palmer Black, introduced the nominations, opened the envelope, joking that it was very well sealed, smiled and said, "The Oscar goes to Stephen Markham for *Ali And Nino*."

Stephen's heart turned a somersault of delight. On the podium, he shook Palmer's hand and took the Oscar. "Thank you so much, I'm overwhelmed." He thought of his children, how much they'd helped and supported him since the accident, how very much they meant to him. "Rob, Alex, Pip and Sam – thank you for everything." He walked back to his seat. Lynn hugged him, breathless with pride and excitement.

They came to the nominations for Best Director. Stephen could feel the tension emanating from Miles. They had won, besides Stephen's two, the Oscar for best actress, best supporting actor, best cinematography and best adapted script.

"And the Oscar goes to… Miles Tindall for *Ali And Nino*!"

The audience were obviously pleased. They clapped hard as Miles strolled breezily up to the podium and accepted the Oscar gracefully, kissing the pretty actress who awarded it to him. He made a speech full of thank yous and witty remarks, and then he said, "Finally, I'd like to pay tribute to a remarkable man. You have honoured him twice tonight, as his exceptional musical ability deserves." Stephen, who had been staring down at his Oscars, lost in thought, looked up. Miles went on, "Three years ago, he was fighting for his life in an intensive care unit after being hit by a car. He overcame crippling injuries, and, despite being close to death last year as a direct result of that accident, still managed to finish the soundtrack to *Ali and Nino*. Ladies and gentlemen, I would like you to put your hands together for Stephen Markham. His music lifted *Ali And Nino* from excellent to sublime. Come on, Stephen," he beckoned, "come on up here."

Stephen stared at him, astounded by this speech. Lynn gave him a little shove, and he got up and walked to the podium. Miles grabbed his left arm and held it up in a salute. He kissed the pretty little actress again and marched Stephen back to their seats.

The Academy agreed that *Ali And Nino* was sublime. They awarded it the Oscar for Best Picture. Everyone went up, Miles made another acceptance speech, and Stephen stood at the back feeling rather numb. "Brilliant way to retire," he said quietly to Miles.

"Ah, dear boy." Miles sounded slightly embarrassed. "I decided to postpone the retirement. There were some exciting projects on the horizon."

"You utter bastard!" Stephen grinned.

They went to a party afterwards. Stephen never found out who was hosting it. He liked to think it was Al and Betty.

Miles was elated. "I'm walking on air, dear boy," he remarked to Stephen, drinking his champagne as if it was lemonade. "Your wife is a little beauty," he said, looking over at Lynn, who was talking to Palmer Black and Justin Page, and blushing prettily at something Palmer was saying to her. "Yes, I could eat her," Miles continued.

Coral came over and wound her arm round Stephen's waist, pulling him against her.

"Here's another," Miles smiled. "Make an old man happy," he said to Coral, and whispered in her ear.

She smiled secretively. "Maybe."

Miles went to talk to Lynn.

"He's very taken with her," Coral commented.

"What did he say to you?" Stephen asked curiously.

"He wants me to spend the night with him."

Stephen was stunned. "B-but you're married to Justin," he stammered.

Coral made a face. "That's over."

"I'm so sorry!"

"Don't be, it was fun while it lasted. I don't feel bad, I tried my best to save it – that's why we went away last year." She shrugged. "C'est la vie. And there are always men around. If I pushed hard enough I could probably get Miles to marry me, I think he's about ready to settle down."

"I always wondered – don't tell him, Coco – if he was gay."

Coral went into peals of laughter. "He knows. It makes him laugh. He's far from gay, Stephen! I had the most glorious affair with him right through *Hoodman Blind*. He got rather a kick out of seeing us together."

Stephen digested this. "Oh. Well, how come he's never married?" he wondered.

Coral shrugged. "He's never needed to, there have always been women. And he's a very private person. But I think he's getting a little lonely now he's older." She gave Stephen a lascivious smile. "He'd like to have Lynn, you know; what do you say to you and me and Miles and Lynn tonight?"

Stephen was utterly shocked. He'd always considered himself to be very broadminded, but he realised that by Hollywood standards he was about as broadminded as Mother Theresa. It didn't make him dislike Miles or Coral, but he knew without a doubt that he could never live in their world. Before he could answer, Miles brought Lynn back over to them, holding her hand. "You know, I'm going to call it a night. I'm too old for all this partying till dawn lark. Coral?"

Coral smiled. She kissed Stephen and turned to Lynn, taking her face between her hands. "I'm hoping to see a lot more of you!" She kissed her, wiggling her tongue against Lynn's lips. To her surprise and delight, Lynn, who had drunk considerably more champagne than she'd intended to, opened her mouth.

Miles watched them contentedly for as long as the brief kiss lasted. "Hollywood!" he said happily to Stephen, and left with Coral.

"That was fun," Lynn said. "Let's see if we can find Johnny Depp."

"No fucking way! I'm taking you back to the hotel *right* now!"

"Oh, good," Lynn smiled. "You're much more gorgeous than him, anyway."

Toni and George had been watching the Oscars.

Toni could hardly believe this was happening. Stephen had not only been nominated, but had won two Oscars, and *Lynn* was at that most glittering, important, prestigious of ceremonies! She was beside herself with rage and disappointment.

"It's not fair, it's not bloody fair! I did so much for the flaming little ratbag! *I* was the one who stayed home and ran the house and cared for his children when he was out touring and recording! *I* should be there, not her, not that – that stupid bitch! She can't even cook!" She was crying, her mascara running down her face.

George got up and turned the TV off.

"Why did you do that? I was watching!"

"It's not agreeing with you, you're getting hysterical. Howay, pet, it'll be in all the papers tomorrow. I'm taking you off to bed, and I'm going to rub that oil onto your tummy and your periscope or whatever it's called, and then we'll make love and you can drift off to sleep."

"Perineum," Toni sobbed. "It's called the perineum."

George picked her up as easily as if she'd been a child and carried her to their bedroom, where he tenderly undressed her, cleansed her face with her facial wipes – "desperate things, these, pet!" – and massaged her perineum, her growing bump, and her nipples with sweet almond oil.

"George, you're so kind to me, I don't deserve you," she sighed gratefully. She'd had quite a scare when he'd stormed out the night she'd been so angry about the

Oscar nominations. He hadn't come in until late the next morning, and he'd been with a woman, she could tell that straight away. He smelt of Rive Gauche, which wasn't a scent she wore, and there was something about him, a look of the cat who got the cream. Later, she'd asked him and he said, straight out, "Aye, I was, she was a canny little thing too, lovely tits and arse on her." Toni had started to be angry and he'd shouted at her, telling her that if she didn't pull herself together and stop behaving like a spoilt little girl, next time he wouldn't come back. She didn't want him to leave her and she'd found herself apologising and wheedling him into a good mood, even to the extent of giving him a very good time in bed, doing all the things he liked. She'd never been the one cajoling a partner before and she realised how badly she'd sometimes behaved to Stephen.

She never guessed that George had spent the night at Fin's and gone into Boots on the way home the next morning and sprayed himself from a tester with a scent he didn't recognise as one of hers. He'd got some very odd looks too, and on the way out, he'd made a kissing noise at a weedy youth who was with his very overweight girlfriend. The youth had looked as if he might expire.

George was very satisfied with his marriage to Toni. She was turning into a decent little wife, she was a good cook, and she was cracking in bed.

He was right about the newspapers. They decided that Stephen and Lynn were the hit of the Oscars, and a picture of Miles and Stephen on the podium, Miles holding Stephen's left arm up in a victory salute, was on the front page of several of the tabloids. *Juliette*, Callie's magazine, wanted to do a feature on Lynn and Stephen, and the *Sunday Gazette* had a big Oscar edition in the following week's magazine, with a leading feature on Miles, and Stephen appearing in three of their regular articles; an interview with him for *Tears And Laughter*, documenting a time in his life when something good and something bad was happening simultaneously to him, one with him and Rob for the section *Blood Ties*; and *Twenty Four Hours*, featuring a day with Sid's Six as they rehearsed for their autumn tour.

Callie waved her copy at Toni when they met for lunch after the magazine came out. "You'll have seen this of course, your George is in it. It's a good photo of him."

Toni agreed, it was a good picture of George. "I didn't really read the rest of it," she admitted.

"I love the article with Stephen and his son," Callie went on. "I know it all went wrong for the two of you at the end, but he's really very sweet, isn't he? I mean, listen to this: *Rob was the best thing that had ever happened to me,* the article started. *I can't describe the way I felt when I first held him. I was nineteen, I was in enormous trouble with Ted, Harry's (Harriet Chaplin, Rob's mother) dad, for being Rob's father, I had a dead-end job in a tailors shop and couldn't imagine how I was going to support a wife and child, and I was terrified of telling my own father he had an illegitimate grandson – I was already a bitter disappointment to him – but as soon as I held Rob, nothing else mattered, I'd have walked over hot coals for him. As it happened, Harry chose not to marry me, but I saw Rob all the time. He was an incredibly bright child. He was always good tempered, but he always wanted his own way – and he's still like that now. It makes him sound dull and priggish to say that he never gave Harry nor I cause to worry about him – he is neither, he was capable of some breathtakingly bad behaviour on occasions – but he's always been mature and sensible. We had tremendous fun appearing in Miles's (director Miles Tindall) film,* With Giants Fight, *together, and he is enormously talented musically; he wrote the music for the song 'Bara Brith' which he plays on my album 'Through The Bars', when he was only eleven. He is also very intelligent, and when he told me he wanted to go to Oxford and study law, like my father, I was delighted. It was the proudest day of my life when he graduated with a first-class degree.*

'He's married, and lives with his wife and their son in the house I used to live in as a child in York. He and I talk on the phone every day. I don't know what I'd do without him.

"Rob *is* a lovely boy," Toni said. "We still keep in touch. Rhys is gorgeous too, very like Steve and Rob. What did Robbie put?"

Callie gave her the magazine.

'There's only nineteen years between us, Rob had written, *'so Dad's often more like a brother to me than a father. He was never very strict and he doesn't believe in hitting children, so the worst that ever happened to any of us was being sent to our rooms. Also, because he and my mother weren't married and he didn't live with us, it was always a tremendous treat to see him. I saw him frequently, he made sure of that, but when I was little, I never knew when he would be coming, and it seemed like magic to me. All of a sudden he'd be there, and all his time would be devoted to me. It was great, because he always had this unflagging energy and enormous capacity for fun – well, he still does – and he'd play fighting games with me and always let me win. I remember jumping up and down on him regularly and thinking I was invincible! He taught me to play the guitar and piano when I was really young. One of my earliest memories is sitting on his lap at the piano, thumping away on it with my right hand, while he filled in with his left and made up funny lyrics. It's unbearable to think he hasn't got his left hand any more, just because of someone's stupidity.*

'I didn't live with Dad full-time till I was eleven, when I went to secondary school in Oxford, where he lives. We had great fun, he got me a puppy from a Rescue Centre, and I had a Strat, and we used to play together all the time. My brothers and I knew he was famous, but he never made a big deal of it; he and Toni (novelist Antonia Standish, Markham's second wife) always made sure we had a normal, stable, family life, they weren't forever dashing off to glittering events and parties, and leaving us with a succession of nannies and so on. That's not to say that they didn't enjoy parties, they did; they were always giving them, some of them really spectacular affairs. I remember once they had this huge party, and loads of the guests stayed for the weekend, and on the Sunday, I'd invited a couple of my friends round for the day and just as they arrived, Alec Guinness was leaving and I said goodbye to him and it was all round school the next day – Rob Chaplin's on first name terms with Obi-Wan Kenobi! But, to us, Dad was just an ordinary dad, who happened to be rich, and know famous people. He's always been there for me, he was really pleased when I said I wanted to go to Oxford and study law, but he'd have been supportive no matter what I'd wanted to do, because he's always said, as long as his children are happy, he is.

I was with him when that car hit him. I feel really guilty about it, because he'd arranged to pick me up in Newcastle at seven that morning and I wasn't ready, so we didn't leave on time. If I'd been ready, we probably wouldn't even have been in that service station. And while he was lying waiting for the ambulance, with all those terrible injuries, he was still worrying about me, in case I'd been hurt too. He managed to ask if I was OK. That's typical of Dad. He never puts himself first.

Toni stared down at the magazine. I never knew that, that Rob was late, she thought, Stephen never said. I assumed that he'd stayed up the night before with the band and overslept. How could I have been so mean? She felt devastated.

"*Tears And Laughter* is really touching," Callie was saying, "about when Sid's Six had just made it and they were due to go off on a tour of America, and Steve's dad died, and he found out that Lynn had remarried. It made me cry. I thought he'd do about losing his hand when he was at the peak of his career."

"Hmm," Toni said. "I always said Lynn was a bitch, but no one ever listened." She was thoroughly put out by all the media attention Lynn had attracted. Coral had been interviewed and said that Lynn had been the most beautiful woman at the Oscars in the most beautiful dress. The guilt Toni felt over Stephen made no difference to her annoyance with Lynn, especially since there seemed to be pictures of Lynn in every paper and magazine she opened, and articles with titles like *Lynn Markham – Get The Look!* Toni and George didn't take the *Gazette*, both of them preferring a tabloid, and their paper had an interview with Lynn, entitled *Sweet Cherry – A Peach Of A Girl!*

"Girl!" Toni snorted. "She's over forty!"

"She doesn't look it," George said, taking the magazine. "She was always a canny looking lass – crackin' legs."

Chapter Twenty-Nine
Sons And Lovers

Sons and lovers, watching others making my mistakes,
All the fun of being young, all the joys and heartaches.

In the Easter holidays, the entire family, plus Barbara and Christianne, their French au pair, went to Massachusetts, taking Mab with them. This had nearly been the cause of a serious rift between Dominic and Stephen.

A month or so before the holidays, the Chaplins were spending the weekend at the Priory. After lunch, everyone went in the pool except Dominic, who lounged on an easy chair, sipping a large whisky. Lynn and Harry took the triplets in, and after splashing around for a while with the boys, Mab joined them.

Stephen spent some time teaching Lucy to dive, and then played an energetic chasing game with her and Sam, before climbing out and sinking down next to Dominic. "God, I'm getting old! They wear me out these days!" He took a small pot from the pocket of his bathrobe, opened it, and began to slather the contents onto his face.

Dominic stared at him. "What the fuck are you doing?"

"Moisturising."

"Moisturising? *Moisturising*? What the fuck is wrong with you?"

"Don't worry, it's not tested on animals."

"That's not what I meant, as well you know! I used to think George was hard on you, but he's quite right, you're a big lass. Christ, it'll be a 'man's bag', next!"

Stephen grinned. "Well…"

"I'm warning you, Markham, you say you've got one and you'll be discovered drowned in this pool tomorrow morning."

Harry joined them. "You smell delicious, Stevie."

"It's his moisturiser," Dominic said distastefully. "No doubt he'll be changing into his ball gown and putting on full make up for dinner."

Stephen grinned. "A thing of beauty is a joy forever, Charlie. You're just jealous of my boyish good looks."

"If that's how you keep them, I think I'd rather look like an old prune!"

"That's lucky," Stephen remarked.

"Yes, thank you, very funny, Markham."

"Look at those two," Harry smiled. Pip had joined Mab, and was holding Bell, his arm round Mab's shoulders as she cuddled Davy. "I think Mab's pretending they're hers and Pip's!"

Dominic's eyes widened. He stared at Mab and Pip.

"Well, you know, Cherry and I have been thinking," Stephen said. "It would be nice if Mabs came with us to America. What do you think?"

"What a lovely idea…" Harry started, but Dominic cut in. "Nice for whom?"

"Well, all of us, but specially Pip," Stephen said, rather taken aback by Dominic's tone. At that moment, Lynn, Mab and Pip came over with the triplets. "Here," Lynn said, dumping Andrew unceremoniously into Stephen's lap. "Time these three had their naps. Carry Drew up to the nursery for me, Stevie."

After dinner, Lynn took Harry to see a dress she'd had made, the boys and Mab drifted off to listen to music, and Stephen and Dominic wandered into the drawing room.

Stephen poured them both a large glass of brandy. "So, what about this holiday, then, Charlie?"

Dominic drank his brandy. "I can't say I'm keen, Markham."

Stephen stared at him. "Why?"

Dominic stared back. "Frankly, I'm not happy at the thought of Pip and Mab being in such close proximity unsupervised."

Stephen frowned. "That's a bloody insulting thing to say! Both to me and Pip!"

Dominic shrugged. "I didn't mean to insult you, but it's the way I feel. I don't want Mab and Pip…" He hesitated, trying to find the words. "I don't want there to be any possibility of Mab being, uh – compromised."

"Compromised? *Compromised?* What the fuck do you mean by that? I'm fucking fed up with your attitude to Pip, Dominic!" Stephen said, exasperated. "Why are you so suspicious of him? He's a good, sensible, trustworthy boy. And let's face it, Mabs is… well, the clothes she wears! Last time she was here, she was wearing one of those skirts of hers, which are so short they're really belts, and she bent over to pick something up, and she was wearing a *thong*. I can only imagine what the sight did to Pip, I know what it did to me!" He grinned at the memory of Pip's stunned face.

Dominic assumed he was leering at the thought of Mab, and leapt at him, shoving him against the wall. He pinned him there by the neck. "How *dare* you think about her like that?"

Stephen tried to push him off, but Dominic's hands were tightening around his throat, and in desperation, he brought his knee up into Dominic's groin. Dominic shouted and doubled up in pain as Lynn and Harry came into the room.

Harry helped Dominic up. "Have you two gone mad?"

"What the hell's going on?" Lynn asked, astonished. "Are you all right, Stevie?"

Stephen nodded, rubbing his bruised neck.

"Well, what's going on?" Lynn asked again

"He tried to kill me…"

"The bastard was lusting after Amabel…" they both said at once.

"I bloody well wasn't!" Stephen said angrily. "I was remembering the look on Pip's face when Mab bent over!"

Dominic frowned. "Oh." Lynn poured him a glass of brandy, and he swallowed it gratefully. "I thought you…"

"Yes, I know," Stephen answered coldly. "How could you think that, Dominic? What is this with you and Mab and Pip, anyway?"

"Yes, what *is* wrong with you, Dominic?" Harry demanded.

Dominic refilled his brandy glass. "Pip is so like you, Stephen, and Mab is – in character – very like Harry," he said slowly. He downed the brandy and looked at Stephen. "They remind me of you two being together."

Stephen stared at him blankly.

"Oh, for fuck's sake, don't be dim! I'm jealous, OK, I've always been jealous, I just didn't realise how jealous until Pip and Mab started seeing each other."

Stephen was astounded. He could see from Harry's face that she felt the same.

"You told me that you the two of you only had sex that once, Harry," Dominic continued, "when Rob was conceived, but Stephen's said things occasionally that made me wonder, and then on his birthday last year I overheard Rebecca telling

Kathy and Paul how she once walked in on you two making love."

"Shit," Harry muttered.

"God, I'd forgotten that!" Stephen grinned. "Poor Becks was so embarrassed! It was that time she took Rob to the fair, do you remember, Hal, and they came back early because Robbie had won a goldfish, and he leapt into bed with us and spilled it out." He started to laugh. "Yes, and you said it was like the bit in the book you were reading, what was it called, where some prince put a goldfish up his girlfriend's—"

"For Christ's sake, Stephen, you bloody big mouth, SHUT UP!" Harry screeched furiously, her face scarlet.

"Well, why didn't you just tell him, Harriet?" Stephen asked crossly. "What did it matter? It's not like either of us was going out with anyone else. It was before she even met you, Charlie," he said to Dominic, but couldn't resist adding, "And we didn't do anything with the goldfish."

"Stephen!" Lynn exclaimed, and Harry thumped him

"I didn't say it was logical, did I?" Dominic stared down at his glass. "Mostly, I can turn it into a joke. But you mean so much to Harry, Stephen, you two have such a long and complex relationship, you're so very, very close – seeing Pip kissing Mab, and – and *touching* her, I could simply see you two. I'm sorry, Stephen."

"What are we going to do?" Stephen asked. "I mean, they're only young, but as you say, Pip's very like me, and Mab is tremendously like Harry; they might well stay together and maybe even marry."

"I'll just have to pull myself together," Dominic shrugged.

"Dom, I love you so much." Harry was close to tears. "I *was* in love with Steve for a very long time, but I'd fallen out of love with him well before you and I met. I didn't tell you we made love more than once because, well, when we first talked about it, you assumed that it had been just that once, and you seemed, well, a little uncomfortable with the thought of me and him, so it was easier not to go into it, oh, I don't know, it was really stupid, and I do love Steve, better than anyone except you, Dom, but it's nothing like the way I love you, I love you more than I could ever love anyone, I love you a hundred times more than I loved him, oh, there's no comparison! Sorry, Stephen," she added apologetically.

"No, don't be sorry. I always knew that, and it's exactly as it should be. Charlie, I really don't know what to do."

Dominic shook his head. "You don't need to do anything. This is just me being childish. You're my best friend, Steve. And Hatty – I love you too. Too much, I think! Can we just forget this? Mab is still my little girl, but I'll lighten up on Pip. I'm sorry about your neck, Markham."

"Sorry about your balls," Stephen grinned, "but I thought you were going to kill me. Have you no sense of honour, Charlie?" he added. "Attacking a cripple!"

"Don't fucking push it, Markham."

The weather in Massachusetts was glorious. Pip and Mab took to going for long walks together.

"Did we ought to let them?" Lynn worried. "I know Charlie said he'd ease up, but he didn't want them left alone together."

"Well, we're not *leaving* them," Stephen pointed out. "And how do we know that Alex isn't with them right now?"

Right then, Pip and Mab were lying entwined in a cornfield, in varying states of undress. "I don't know how long I can stand this," Mab groaned, " I don't think I can wait till we're sixteen."

"We have to," Pip said seriously. "I promised Dad I wouldn't let it get out of hand."

"Papa tried to make me promise I wouldn't let you make love to me till I was eighteen! Eighteen! I ask you! I said no. It was really full on, he was so cross, I was almost frightened, but luckily Mama came in and told him to shut up." She giggled. "You should have seen his face!"

"I can't imagine anyone telling Dom to shut up," Pip said, with feeling. Since he'd been seeing Mab he'd discovered that Dominic wasn't nearly as laid back as he appeared. "Hey, did you know that Cherry hadn't done it before she met Dad? He was her first!"

"God, that's sweet!" Mab rolled over onto her stomach. "You'll be my first and my last."

"You're my first, my last, my everything," Pip sang. He was very like Stephen. He stroked Mab's bottom, and slipped his hand down into her knickers. She shivered with pleasure. He stopped singing and kissed her.

Sam had taken his laptop, and he emailed Marcus every day.

"The nerds are netting again," Alex commented over breakfast one morning. "I think they're gay over each other."

Stephen hit him with a tea towel.

He got up and loomed over Stephen. He was nearly six foot tall. "Don't make me have to hurt you, little man," he grinned.

"My God, you've got no fucking respect for me at all, have you?" Stephen demanded.

"Dad," Alex said, making a good attempt at mimicking Bart Simpson's voice, "I have as much respect for you now as I ever have or ever will!"

He was in great spirits. There were several very pretty girls at the lake and he was much in demand, being tall, extremely good looking and Stephen Markham's son. He'd lost his virginity to a pretty little redhead the night they arrived, and there had been several others since. He was always careful to wear a condom; he didn't want to end up a father at his age. He couldn't understand how Pip could want to get tied down so young.

"Are you fucking mental?" he'd asked him. "There are so many sexy girls here! They'll drop their knickers as soon as look at you. I mean, Mab's pretty, and she's got a great figure and everything, but she's a bossy little bitch! I bet Dad wouldn't mind if you just wanted to screw an American girl."

"I'm sure he would!" Pip was shocked. "You can be horrible sometimes, Alex."

"Thanks," grinned Alex, "but I don't need your permission. Come on, let's go for a swim. I'll tell you who I really fancy though," he said, after they had raced each other to the other side of the lake, Pip beating him easily, much to his chagrin.

"Yeah? Who?" Pip was lying on his back, staring up at the cloudless sky, and thinking about Mab's breasts.

"Christianne. I bet she's a real goer."

Pip propped himself up on an elbow and stared at his brother. "Dad would seriously kill you."

"Not if he didn't find out. Come on, Pip, think about her, her tits are huge, imagine them naked!"

"Yeah," Pip said, imagining. "But I don't advise it, Alex."

"Bollocks! I'm going to ask her to go out with me tonight after the trips are in bed." He hung around the house that evening, and watched Christianne. After she had finished clearing the triplets' things away, and was putting some washing in the machine in the basement, he asked her if she'd like to go for a walk with him.

She smiled. "You are very nice boy, Alex," she said, in her heavily accented English, "but I am going to keep in this house and write some letter to my boyfriend." She patted his cheek and turned the washing machine on.

He flushed with humiliation.

Later, Pip wanted to know how he'd got on. "I didn't ask her," he shrugged, nonchalantly. "When I got up close I could see she had a bit of a moustache and that put me off. And she doesn't shave her legs or under her arms. I gave her a kiss though, out of pity," he lied. "She begged me to do more – 'have your way wiz me, Alex, right 'ere on zees floor', she said, but I just didn't fancy her."

Pip regarded him with awe. "Wow, you're really experienced, Alex! It must be because you're so tall." He was only five foot nine inches; he had grown a great deal the year before, but he seemed to have slowed down, if not actually stopped, whereas Alex was still growing.

"Oh, well, you might grow a bit more, Pip, and at least you're taller than Dad."

"God, I should hope so! Only midgets are shorter than Dad!"

Stephen and Lynn took them to see Mark Twain's house in Hartford, Connecticut. They enjoyed it, and Mab bought a huge soft toy frog modelled on Daniel Webster, a frog from one of Twain's stories, at the gift shop.

"Are you calling him Dan'l Webster?" Lynn asked, admiring the frog.

"I'm calling him Pip," Mab said, kissing Pip's hand.

"Yeah, it looks just like him," Sam agreed.

When they got home, Stephen bought a house near Helmsley in North Yorkshire, for Lynn and himself. It was an old vicarage dating from around 1880 and had five reception rooms, a kitchen, utility and breakfast room, six bedrooms, and a huge playroom on the second floor. Outside, there was a walled garden, a double garage, stables and a paddock. The front garden was full of rose bushes, and the scent was divine. Roses always reminded Stephen of his childhood, the summers spent on the Isle of Wight with Mam and Dada. "I know it's not very big…" he started apologetically when he took Lynn to see it.

"Not very big!" Lynn interrupted, staring round. "God, Stevie, you live in another world!"

They took the triplets and Lucy, who had been two at the beginning of the month, to stay there for a few weeks, and went to Nunnington Hall.

"It's just the same!" Lynn exclaimed happily. "Last time we were here Robbie was only a baby, remember?"

"Yes, I took him in the baby sling, didn't I?" Stephen said. "My back was terrible the next day!"

"Yeah, and Ray was pissed off because you were getting all those girls looking at you," Lynn giggled. "He wanted to wear the baby sling."

"And we talked about having babies that we didn't have to give back at the end of the day," Stephen smiled.

Lynn laughed. "We've got those in spades!"

Toni's baby, another boy, was born at the end of July.

George was overjoyed. "I don't know how to thank you, pet," he said, tears in his eyes. He showered her with presents; a diamond and emerald necklace with earrings to match; scent; beautiful, delicate silk and lace underwear in palest pastel colours; an exquisite hand embroidered kimono; a magnum of vintage Krug champagne;

dozens of fragrant, long stemmed red roses, and a tiny fluffy white Birman kitten.

"Oh, George, she's adorable," Toni exclaimed when she opened the box. Her room in the Lindo wing was beginning to look like a very sophisticated Santa's grotto, the floor awash with tissue paper.

In the middle of all this, Stephen arrived, bringing the boys to meet their new brother. He shook hands with George, kissed Toni and peered at the baby in his cot. "Congratulations! He's very pretty."

He was. What hair he had was chestnut, like Toni's, and he had beautiful colouring, a creamy complexion with a rosy blush to it.

"He's big too, isn't he?" Stephen added.

"Aye," George said proudly. "He weighed over twelve pounds!"

"Twelve pounds!" Stephen said, awed. "Was it a hard labour?"

"No," Toni smiled. "Heather says I'm amazing."

Stephen thought of Harry and Lynn, both of whom had long and difficult labours. "Yes, you are." He looked around the room. "I bought you champagne and body lotion," he said, handing the lotion to Toni and the bottle to George, "but it looks as if George has got it all sewn up! What are you calling him?"

"Anthony George," George said. "Ant for short."

The baby woke up and started to cry. George lifted him out and gave him to Toni.

Sam was playing with the kitten. "What's your kitten called, Mum?"

"I haven't named her yet." Toni smiled at him. "Would you like to?"

Sam was pleased. "Can she be mine, then? We can't have a kitten because of Savij."

"No, Savij wouldn't like that at all," Toni agreed, busily feeding Ant, who was sucking greedily.

Alex and Pip looked away, making expressive faces at each other.

"I think I'll call her Mozart," Sam said.

"Mozart's a boys name, you crapweasel!" Pip groaned.

Sam looked at him witheringly. "Tell that to Mrs Mozart."

"It's a lovely name," Toni said quickly. "And the new house in Hampstead's got a great big garden, so you can have a puppy too, if you want."

"What's it like?" Stephen had known they'd bought it, but he hadn't had any of the details.

"Just what we wanted. It's got a lower ground floor flat our boys can have, and there's an enormous bedroom on the top floor for me and George, and the nursery's on the floor below, a lovely sunny room."

"Which I'm decorating," put in George with satisfaction.

"Why don't you get someone in to do that?" Stephen asked, surprised.

"We've been through this," Toni sighed.

"Get someone in?" George mocked, scornfully. "I'm not a lass, man. My dad's a builder. I think I can manage to decorate a nursery for my own son!"

The next day he fell from the ladder while painting the ceiling and broke his right arm.

"Bloody hell!" Stephen said with exasperation when Fin rang up with the news. "How long will he be out of action?"

"He's not sure. A couple of months, certainly."

"Well that's the tour out of the window," Stephen sighed. "God, honestly – all that bloody crap about, 'I'm not a lass, I can decorate a nursery'! Oh, well, we'll have to try to sort out new tour dates. I'll get on to Cell."

The Fender Stratocaster was fifty years old in September, and there was to be a big celebration, the Miller Strat Pack Concert, at Wembley Arena, which would also be a fund raising event for the Nordoff-Robbins Music Therapy charity. Stephen had been tentatively approached, and asked if he would like to attend. The Strat was so very much his instrument. All his big hits; Lost Souls, This Northern Sky, Postmodern Romance, She's Mine, The Evening Rain, All I Am and, of course, Sweet Cherry and The Sound Of One Hand Clapping, which he now privately thought of as his theme song, had been played on it. He couldn't possibly go, and he'd immediately said no. He had come to terms with his loss to an extent, but to attend an event like that would be sheer madness. He didn't mention it to Lynn, merely made a large donation to the charity and tried to put it out of his mind. As the date drew near, however, he realised he couldn't bear to be at home on the night it was taking place, he wouldn't be able to behave normally and pretend it wasn't happening. He'd expected to be out of England in September, away from it all, up on stage somewhere; the band should have been touring, but George's arm wasn't healing as fast as his doctors had hoped, and the tour had had to be cancelled. They all felt bad about it; they'd had to cancel the 'Electric Playground' tour after Stephen's accident, and they hated letting their fans down.

He booked a table for himself and Lynn at a restaurant that had recently opened in Oxford, Le Grand Seize. They had been there once before and had enjoyed it very much; it was discreet, exclusive and the food was terrific. "Get yourself a posh new frock," he told Lynn, "and maybe we'll go on somewhere afterwards."

She looked at him shrewdly. Dominic had told her about the Strat party, but, "Painting the town red, are we?" was all she asked.

He forced a smile. "Certainly are!"

He was dressed and ready before she was, and he lay on the bed, trying to read, while she sat at the dressing table putting on her make up. He wished he hadn't booked this meal, all he wanted to do was drink copious amounts of whisky and pass out, blot out all knowledge of the concert, his disability, everything.

"This reminds me of getting ready to go out when we were at university," Lynn was saying reminiscently, as she applied her mascara. "I'd put my make up on, and you'd sit and read." She smiled. "Do you remember the time you were reading *Charlie And The Chocolate Factory*, and you told me it was part of your course work, and I believed you?"

He didn't answer. She glanced over at him. To her dismay, he was crying silently, tears coursing down his face.

"Stephen!" She hurried over and got onto the bed next to him. "Darling Stevie, what is it?"

"All that time without you, all those lost, wasted, empty years!" he sobbed.

"But – but we're together now!" She put her arms around him. "I'll never leave you again, Stevie, not ever."

"One day you will – or I'll leave you."

She started to deny this, but he interrupted. "Whoever dies first."

She was shocked into silence. What a horrific thought. She stroked his hand, looking down at the raised scar across the back of it. Poor, poor Stevie, she thought, none of him escaped unscathed. He had a scar under his right eye, and a longer one along his jawbone. Neither of them were disfiguring, the one under his eye barely noticeable, but they were there. "It's the concert isn't it? That's why you're so depressed."

"How did you know?"

"Charlie told me."

He looked at his left arm. "God, Cherry, oh, God, I miss it so much. I thought it would get better, it was so terrible when we first started rehearsing 'From The Brink' but it kind of became a dull ache, and I thought, well, OK, that's it, I'm more or less over it, but I'm not, and I don't think I ever will be." He sat up. "I must get a tissue."

Lynn passed him the tissue box and he blew his nose.

"I don't know what to say," she said, her heart aching with pity. "I don't know what I can do to help you."

He took her hand. "You do help. I don't know how I'd manage without you. You and the children, sometimes you're the only things that make sense in this senseless, bloody world." He gave her a tiny smile. "I'll get over this, and it'll hurt less as time goes by."

"But you must talk to me about it. When it hurts, when you're feeling sad. I'm always here, Stevie, I'll always listen."

"I know." He took a deep breath. "You'd better finish getting ready or we'll be late."

"Are you sure you want to go?" Lynn asked, looking at him with concern.

"Yes. I feel better now. Thank you, cariad." He put his arms round her and held her for a minute. Then he pulled himself together. "Come on. Let's go and drink gallons of champagne and eat till we burst. And if we're able to stand afterwards, I'll take you dancing!"

Black Moon premiered at the beginning of October. Stephen and Lynn went with Miles and Coral to the party afterwards, and later Miles suggested the four of them went back to his house for something to eat.

He showed them into his minimalist sitting room. It was all white, with huge windows framed by blond linen curtains. There were vases of fresh mimosa everywhere, but apart from a glass coffee table and the most enormous leather sofa Lynn had ever seen, there was very little else in the room. It's like some sort of celestial waiting room, she thought, any minute now an angel will come in with a clipboard and take our names.

They sat on the sofa, and Miles went to get the food. He came back with caviar – 'The most delicious you ever tasted, dear boy!' he told Stephen – and vodka so cold it was smoking, like liquid nitrogen. He was crestfallen when Stephen explained he was a vegetarian. "You could have told me," he reproached Coral.

"I forgot," she shrugged. "Anyway, I thought you knew."

"What can I get you, dear boy?" Miles asked.

Stephen shook his head. "I ate at the party, I'm not very hungry. But I'd love some of that vodka!"

"Are you a vegetarian, Cherry?" Miles looked at her anxiously.

She smiled guiltily. "No. I should be, I know."

He brightened. "Do you like caviar?"

She hesitated. "I've never tried it," she admitted.

Miles smiled broadly. "You're in for a treat!" He poured the vodka and passed round the food.

They started to talk about Coral's latest film, *Royal Velvet*, which was about Charles the Second, and for which Stephen had been asked to write the soundtrack. It was very Hollywood, but reasonably historically accurate, and, despite Miles's objections that it was absolute rubbish, Coral had wanted very much to do it.

"It's just a bit of Hollywood fluff," Miles said, rather contemptuously

"But I get to wear such fabulous costumes!" Coral fluttered her eyelashes at him. "Wait till you see me in them, Miles, they're very sexy! And Stevie's music will lend it gravitas." She was playing Barbara Palmer, Lady Castlemaine, Charles's very beautiful mistress, and a friend of hers, a relatively unknown actress, Carenza Douglas, was playing a young girl, Lady Jane, with whom Charles becomes romantically involved, much to the fury of Barbara. Carenza had to do a nude scene in the film, and Coral had very much taken her under her wing.

"I know exactly how she feels. She's only twenty three, the same age I was when we did *Hoodman Blind*, and she doesn't have you to look after her," she said to Stephen. "She's been living with Peter Ingram for the last two years, he's been 'directing' her career."

Peter Ingram was a director, around Miles's age but without Miles's talent. He, however, considered Miles to simply have been lucky, and thought he had sold out.

"I wouldn't have thought he would have approved of this film," Miles said.

"He didn't! She finally woke up and left him."

The subject turned to the situation in the Middle East. Miles's nephew was a reporter currently working in Tel Aviv. Stephen had never really talked to Miles about anything other than films, and became engrossed in the conversation.

"Stevie," Coral whispered.

He looked round and shook his head. Lynn was fast asleep, her head on Coral's shoulder. He grinned. "Drunk again! I can't take her anywhere!"

"She is tremendously sweet, your little wife," Coral said. "If such things were allowed, I would marry Miles, and have her as my concubine."

Stephen grinned. "You do know my little wife is four years older than you, don't you?"

"I am an old soul, I have lived many times before."

"Yes," Stephen said slowly. "I think that might be true."

"You have been here maybe once or twice before, Stevie. Miles is like me, but this little girl is brand new."

"I better get this brand new baby back home," Stephen smiled.

Coral moved carefully. "Don't wake her yet. I'll go and phone for a taxi."

"You know, it was a lucky day when I asked you to write the soundtrack for *With Giants Fight*, Stephen," Miles said after she'd gone. "I think of you as the son I'll never have."

Stephen was inordinately touched. "I'm sure you and Coral will have a son."

Miles shook his head. "I can't have children. I caught mumps in my early twenties, and one of the side effects in adult men is often sterility. That was one of the reasons I never married. There seemed little point."

"I'm so sorry." Stephen was stunned by this revelation.

Miles shrugged. "I tell very few people, but I felt you would understand."

Coral came back in, and Miles took her hand, pulling her against him. "Coral told me what she said at the Oscars. She's a very naughty girl. I might find Cherry… desirable, but the wish for the four of us to share a bed came from Coral's wayward little head alone."

Coral dimpled at Stephen. The doorbell rang.

"That'll be the taxi," Miles said. He kissed Lynn, who had been woken by the bell, and also Stephen.

"Miles." Stephen grasped his hand, very moved, "We would love to have you stay at the Priory, both of you. Any time."

He helped Lynn into the taxi and put her to bed when they got home. He sat up for a long time, imagining how he'd feel if he couldn't have children. He'd said to Madeleine, 'There are loads of people better off than me.' He would have put Miles in that bracket then. You can never take anyone at face value, he thought.

Chapter Thirty
Sea Change

Bright new morning, new day's dawning rich and strange for you and me.
Going to be a sea change, has to be change sets us free.

At half-term, the boys went to stay with Toni and George. Sam's friend, Marcus, had also been invited, and Stephen drove them over to Hampstead. Lynn went too; she wanted to see Ant, who, according to Harry, was a gorgeous baby, the image of George, and very good-natured. "He's adorable," she said, "smiles all the time! And he's *huge*!"

In the car, the boys were talking about university. Pip would be taking his GCSEs the following year and was studying hard.

Alex had finished with school. He'd done well in his GCSEs, but, like all Stephen's children, he would always have money, and since he'd never liked school anyway, he didn't see the point in wasting any more time on studying. Pip, however, enjoyed school, and he was hoping to be allowed to move in with Toni and George and take his 'A' Levels at the same school as Mab. He wasn't sure whether he'd bother with further education, he really wanted to concentrate on his and Alex's band, although he was toying with the idea of The Royal Northern College Of Music in Manchester.

Sam was set on Geology, and he and Marcus were keen to go to Oxford. Marcus, who was very intelligent, wanted to study Biochemistry. "When I graduate, I'll pioneer a way to grow you a new hand, Mr Markham," he said earnestly to Stephen, pushing his glasses up his nose.

"I'll hold you to that," Stephen said.

"Oh, Toni, he's lovely!"

"Here, you can hold him," Toni said, as if she was conferring a huge favour on Lynn.

"Gosh, he's so big!"

George smiled proudly. "Takes after his dad, pet."

"How's the arm, George?" Stephen asked.

"It's a pain in the arse," George replied, gloomily.

"I brought you a crate of Newcastle Brown."

George brightened. "Champion, bonny lad! Let's get some down wor necks!"

"I'd better not, I'm driving," Stephen said quickly. He'd never been very keen on it.

"I will," Lynn said, "I love Newcastle Brown."

"Aye, so you do. Come on then, pet, and we'll get the lass a cup of tea. What about you, Toni?" he asked.

"Tea, please."

"I'll come and help you," Pip offered. "I'd like some Coke."

"How's the saving going?" George asked him in the kitchen. He fished around in his pocket. "Here's a fiver for the cause."

"I didn't know you were saving, Pip." Lynn was surprised.

Pip took the money. "Thanks, George. Don't tell Dad, Cherry."

"What's it for?" Lynn asked.

"Um, a motorbike," he said reluctantly. "Dad's really against them, he thinks they're dangerous. But so are cars – one nearly killed him, and he wasn't even in it."

Lynn sighed. "You ought to tell him, Pip."

Pip gave her a charming smile. "I'm sure you're right."

Lynn was touched by how much like Stephen he looked. "Listen, I won't tell him, but will you promise me you will?

Pip nodded. "Thanks, Cherry."

They took the drinks through.

"Swiggsy's coming for Christmas, isn't he, George?" Toni said.

God! Poor George! Stephen thought.

"Aye, canny lad," George nodded.

Stephen stared at him. Was he being sarcastic?

"You should see him put away the beer," George went on. "He really appreciates it!"

"Don't you find he tends to, well, to hang around a bit?" Stephen asked.

"Not at all, man. I just say to Toni, time for to get shot of him, pet, and off she packs him, no trouble at all. No, he's a canny lad."

It was Pip's sixteenth birthday on December the fifteenth. He wanted a guitar, but not a Stratocaster; he wanted one like Stephen's Matteo Sellas.

"Why do you want one like that?" Alex asked in amazement. "You can't play that in the band."

"I don't care. I just want one."

Stephen found him a guitar attributed to Andreas Oth, who had trained in the Sellas workshops. It was very similar in style to his Matteo Sellas, with a rosewood vaulted back, a foliate design on the fingerboard, and a spectacular rosette in six deep tiers. He and Lynn gave it to Pip at Toni and George's house in London, where he was celebrating his birthday.

Pip was speechless when he saw it, tracing the rosette with his fingers in wordless delight. He began to play, hesitantly at first, but gaining in confidence until the guitar was almost singing in his hands.

George put his hand on Stephen's shoulder.

Stephen was breathless; spellbound by Pip's playing, touched by George's gesture, almost overcome by the desperate longing to be playing himself. He pressed George's hand, and smiled at Pip.

Pip stopped playing and hugged him. "Thanks, Dad."

"Happy birthday, Pip," he said

For several months, Stephen had been trying to teach himself to play the guitar left handed. That meant he'd had to get a prosthesis. He loathed it. It was uncomfortable to wear and hurt his non existent left hand. And his right hand didn't seem to grasp the chord shapes like his left hand had. It should be easy, he couldn't see why it was so hard. He hadn't even told Lynn what he was doing, he didn't want people asking him how it was going. He wasn't sure he was doing the right thing, in some ways it was like opening an old wound; every attempt reinforced how much he had lost. And yet, he thought, many left handed people played the guitar right handed – Paul Simon and Mark Knopfler, for instance – and in schools up to the mid fifties and sometimes later, left handed children were taught to do everything with their right hand, writing, and holding a tennis racquet included. On the other hand (ironic phrase, he thought) children learn much more easily than adults, and he wasn't even a young adult. And he'd never be able to finger pick, so really, what was the point? He put the guitar away and went downstairs. It was nearly Christmas. He, Lynn, Pip, and Mab, who had arrived to spend the weekend before Christmas with them, were going carol singing that night. Miles and Coral, who had married quietly a few weeks previously, were arriving on Boxing Day and staying for a week, and Sian and Ted, and Rob, Julia and Rhys were coming for the holiday and staying until after the New Year.

He glanced out of the window. It looked as if it might snow. Lynn was making her way back to the house from the stables, dressed in her hacking jacket and jodhpurs. He loved her in those clothes, thought she looked so sexy. He went out to meet her.

Sam and Alex joined them for the carol singing. It didn't snow while they were out, but it was bitterly cold. Despite gloves and warm socks, their hands and feet were frozen by the time they got home. They took hot drinks up to bed with them, and Pip made Mab a hot water bottle.

"Mab and Pip are very sweet together," Lynn said, getting into bed.

Stephen put down his book. "They remind me of us," he said, kissing her.

"Yes." Lynn sighed heavily.

He raised his eyebrows. "That was a big sigh!"

"I was just thinking. If only if I hadn't left you after I lost Sakura!"

"Oh, Cherry." He shook his head impatiently.

"But if I hadn't—"

"But you did," Stephen interrupted. "And it's over, done with, and there's no use crying for it, so where's the sense in keep talking about it?" he asked sharply.

Lynn's eyes filled with tears. "I'm sorry. It's just... I feel so sad and angry sometimes."

Stephen could feel annoyance welling up inside him. Well, why didn't you see a doctor when I begged you to, and then we wouldn't have spent all those years apart, he thought. He pushed it down, and shrugged. "It's over," he said again. "It's the present and the future that are important, cariad, not the past."

"Don't be cross," she pleaded.

He gave her a small smile. "OK. But Lynn, please let's not talk about it. It doesn't do any good, and it makes both of us miserable."

She bit her lip, and looked away.

He felt mean. She'd been so kind to him when he'd been depressed about the Strat concert. He put his arm round her. "Sorry, cariad. I didn't mean to snap, I just hate thinking about it. And I'm sorry you feel sad and angry. Do you think it might help to talk to Madeleine? She's very good."

Lynn moved away from him, shaking her head. "I know why I'm angry. It's all those years we were apart." She paused and he started to say, 'I know', but she interrupted him, bursting out with, "Oh, why did you have to marry Toni?"

He stared at her, stunned almost into speechlessness. "Why did *I* have to marry *Toni?*" he managed to say. "Why did *I* have to – why the bloody hell did *you* have to marry *Tim?* If you hadn't, we could have got back together again after Dad died!"

"I tried to get in touch with you!" she retorted hotly. "It's hardly my fault you were in London, how the hell was I supposed to know?"

"Oh, yeah, you tried so hard! Two lousy phone calls!" he shouted, rage and grief sweeping over him. How dare she imply it was his fault they'd spent twenty years apart? "Why the fuck didn't you phone Mum? She'd have told you where I was – unlike *your* mother, when I phoned her! But, no, nothing had changed for you, had it, Lynn? I didn't answer your messages, did I, when you were finally ready to have me graciously back, ready to forgive me for my past crimes; once again I was the evil bastard who ruined your life, so you ran off to Tim. And how long was it before you dumped that poor sod? At least Toni and I tried to make a go of it! None of your relationships have lasted, have they? Why's that, do you suppose? Maybe because you're a selfish, self-centred bitch, and the only person you ever really loved was yourself!"

Lynn was staring at him, ashen-faced. She got out of bed and walked unsteadily into the ensuite.

He was shaking. How the hell had this happened? They'd had such a lovely evening; this row had blown up from nowhere. Had Lynn always felt like this? He had to find out. He got up and tapped on the bathroom door. "Lynn."

There was a pause and then she answered, her voice muffled. "What?"

"Come out. We have to talk about this."

Another pause, and the door slowly opened. Her eyes and nose were red and swollen, and her face was blotchy. "What is there to say?" she asked, finishing on a sob.

He opened his mouth to apologise, but couldn't bring himself to do it. How was this his fault? "Sit down," he said instead.

She sat rigidly on the bed, and stared at her hands. A teardrop fell on them and his heart filled with pity and remorse. "Lynn…"

"Did you mean all that?" she interrupted in a low voice.

"Did you?" he countered.

She stared up at him. "I didn't say anything!"

"You did! You as good as said it was my fault we were apart because I married Toni, but what did you expect me to do? You were gone, you were lost to me…" His voice cracked, and he swallowed hard. "I wanted someone to love me, someone to love. I wanted children; Rob was living with Harry and Charlie and they were great about access, but obviously he was with them ninety per cent of the time, and I wanted children who were always there, and I was sick of longing for you! I wanted to forget you, Lynn and never let you hurt me again!"

"Well, how do you think I felt? How do you think it felt to hear that the man who'd said he'd die for me had run out and slept with someone else the minute we had a problem?"

He drew in a sharp breath. "Don't you *dare*! Don't you *dare* start that! I loved you more than anything in the world, but for Christ's sake, I'm not a saint! You calmly informed me – after *months* of treating me like crap, punishing *me* because *you* couldn't carry a baby to term – that you didn't want me, and you didn't love me! What the fuck did you expect me to do?"

"I expected you to honour your marriage vows!"

He recoiled from her. "God, you bitch! Well maybe I was just sick to death of you! Maybe I just wanted someone who didn't whine and nag and think of herself the whole time!"

Lynn raised her eyebrows. "So you married Toni! Good choice, Stephen!"

He stared at her and the absurdity of it suddenly hit him. He started to laugh. "You're right," he gasped. "Talk about out of the frying pan into the fire!"

Lynn was looking at him as if he'd gone mad.

"Cherry." He managed to control himself. "This is a ridiculous argument! We sorted all this out years ago, why the hell are we beating each other up about it now?"

She couldn't see the funny side. "I don't know, Stephen, but I don't think it's a laughing matter. You're obviously very bitter."

"Yes." He took her hand. "Yes, sometimes I am. But I don't think I'm any more so than you." He looked at her questioningly, and she turned her face away. "See, here's the thing, Cherry. We loved each other so much, and we let each other down. That's very hard to forgive – and even harder to forget. I think we *have* forgiven each other – I hope we have – but we haven't forgotten, and I don't suppose we ever will. Yes, I think you're selfish sometimes – for Christ's sake, so am I; so is everyone. We're only human! Come on, I don't believe you don't ever think I'm a selfish, bad tempered git!"

She shrugged.

"Exactly! Oh, come on, Cherry, don't sulk! It's like sitting here with Lulu!"

"Oh, I see, I'm selfish *and* childish!"

"Yep."

She frowned at him. "It's not a joke, Stephen!"

He sighed. "I know. But, Cherry, what can we do? Do you want to split up? I don't."

She started to cry again. "No. Oh, no, Stevie, I don't, I don't want to split up!" She threw her arms round him and buried her face in his chest.

He held her, tears in his own eyes. The thought of losing her again was appalling.

"I'm sorry," she was saying, "I'm so sorry, Stevie, you're right, I'm a miserable, selfish bitch!"

He kissed her head. "Yes, I know," he said, soothingly.

She laughed shakily.

"Cherry. I forgive you. Will you forgive me?"

"There's nothing to forgive you for, it was all my fault," she began, but he put his finger on her lips.

"No, Cherry, that's no good. You say that now – you *think* that now, but later, you'll start to feel resentful again. We were both at fault; what I did, sleeping with Miyuki, was very wrong, whatever the provocation. Listen. Don't say anything now. Let's get into bed and hold each other, and sleep on it, and see how you feel tomorrow."

Lynn woke before him the next morning. She sat up and watched him as he slept. He looked like Davy; young and vulnerable and innocent, his black hair tousled. She felt her heart contract with love, but at the same time, she knew that, deep down, she did blame him: for sleeping with Miyuki, for not finding her again before she married Tim, and for not only marrying Toni, but for staying with her, even when it started to go wrong. But far more than any of those things, she blamed him for ruining their life together by getting her pregnant in the first place. She knew it was unfair, but it was the way she felt. And yet she loved him more than anything or anyone, and she knew that she could never give him up. Which meant that her only option was to forgive him. As he'd forgiven her. A thought struck her and took her breath away. It took two to make a baby. What had she done to prevent the pregnancy? She'd shown up at that gig, driven Stephen to a fever pitch of desire and then blamed him when she fell pregnant. And throughout their entire relationship, he'd never moaned about using condoms, had never suggested that she shoulder any of the responsibility for contraception. All these years, and that had never occured to her until now. She was stunned by the realisation, overwhelmed with guilt and remorse. And the way she'd treated Paul and Simon, too, particularly Simon, she thought, sick with shame. She'd never loved him the way he'd loved her and then she'd dumped him for Stephen, without even a word of explanation – she'd forgotten him the moment she was in Stephen's arms. How could I ever have behaved like that? she thought in horror. Maybe compassion and the ability to know oneself and accept one's faults and those of others are the compensations for growing old, she mused. *Forgive us our trespasses as we forgive those who trespass against us*. She'd made her peace with Tim. There was nothing she could do about Paul and Simon. Except maybe learn from her mistakes, become more tolerant, less selfish. Perhaps I'm finally beginning to grow up, she thought. She leant over and kissed Stephen.

He stirred, and smiled sleepily up at her. "Come here, sexy."

She snuggled into his arms. "Stevie, thank you for forgiving me. I forgive you."

His arms tightened round her. "Thank God! I didn't get a wink of sleep last night, worrying about it!"

The outrageousness of this took her breath away. "You lying toad! You were snoring within two minutes of us getting into bed!"

The triplets were a year old, and beginning to walk and talk. They and Lucy were a formidable gang.

Miles was enchanted with them. "My God, Stephen, you are a lucky man!"

They were sitting on the sofa in the drawing room, watching Coral, who was on the floor with the babies. She'd given them her handbag and they were busily rummaging through the contents. David had found a mirror and was staring at himself in it. Arabella wanted it, and was pulling at it.

Davy hit her and she started to howl.

Coral picked her up. "Daddy!" she shouted imperiously, wriggling in Coral's arms. Coral gave her to Stephen.

She climbed from Stephen's lap onto Miles's, and looked up at him under her lashes, smiling shyly.

"What a terrible flirt!" Miles shook his head. "She's worse than you, Coral!"

"Takes after her father," Coral said, smiling intimately at Stephen.

Mab looked in. She had begged to be allowed to spend the rest of the holidays at the Priory. In the end, Dominic and Harry, worn down by her continual clamouring, had given in. "Where's Pip?"

"In his room?" guessed Stephen. "I haven't seen him, Mabs."

"Is she one of yours?" Miles asked, confused.

"No, that's Amabel Chaplin, Dominic and Harry Chaplin's eldest."

"Why does such a pretty girl want to make herself look so hideous?" Miles wondered. He looked down at Arabella. "You'll never dress like that will you, Bell?"

She poked him in the eye.

Mab found Pip in the music room. "I go to the lavatory for two minutes and when I come back you're gone!"

"Sorry. I just wanted to play my new guitar in peace – I don't mean from you, I mean Alex. Listen." He played her an exquisite piece of music.

"Yes, I see what you mean, Alex would go mad. It's lovely, but it's not exactly RhymeNReason, is it?"

"I wrote it for you. It's called 'Beautiful Beloved'. There's lyrics too," Pip told her, blushing.

"Sing it!" Mab demanded.

He sang, and Mab sat on the floor, leaning against his legs. The song made her cry. "I can't wait till we're eighteen!" she sighed.

Stephen had also been writing songs. It had dawned on him that next year it would be twenty five years since he first formed Sid's Six. It was their silver anniversary. He wrote a song called Quicksilver. That was going to be the name of the album, he decided. The last report on George's arm was that it was finally healing, and he thought he'd be able to start playing again soon. The band was due to tour Britain, Europe and the Far East from July, which would give them time to record the new album beforehand.

He was in his study one evening just before the New Year, ostensibly working, but in fact dozing on the sofa, in front of the blazing log fire, when Miles rapped apologetically on the door. "Could I speak to you on a rather delicate matter, Stephen?"

Stephen was intrigued. He gave Miles a glass of whisky and poured one for himself.

Miles stared into his glass. "Stephen," he began and stopped.

"What is it, Miles? Have I offended you in some way?"

"Oh, my dear boy, far from it!"

There was another pause. Stephen began to feel nervous. He drank his whisky and poured himself another, passing the bottle to Miles, who topped up his drink, drained the glass and cleared his throat. "Coral very much wants a baby. She doesn't say anything, but before I told her about my infertility, she talked about children. I considered adoption, but I know she'd like a child of her own." He shrugged. "And maybe I'm vain, but I don't want to make public the fact that I'm infertile. So then I looked into the possibility of artificial insemination by donor, but I wasn't altogether happy with that idea, it seems so – so impersonal, somehow." He looked earnestly at Stephen. "As I told you, Stephen, I think of you as a son, which is why I'm asking you for this favour. I'm aware that it's the most tremendous impertinence, but would you donate your sperm?"

Stephen was staggered, and also very moved, not only by the request, but also by the effort it must have cost Miles to make it. "Miles. I – I'm really touched." He wasn't sure how to go on. "I understand completely, but, well, I don't know what to say. I'll need to think about it."

He saw the older man hide his disappointment. "Of course, of course. Needless to say, I haven't discussed the matter with anyone except Coral."

"I'll have to talk to Lynn; as I say, it's not that I don't understand completely your point of view, but if it worked, it would be my child, and I'd have absolutely no say in his or her upbringing. I mean – and this may seem trivial to you – I'm totally opposed to smacking children. I don't know how you or Coral feel about that, many people still have a 'spare the rod and spoil the child' mentality. I'm a very paternal man, Miles. My children mean more to me than anything else, and I'm not sure I could I could cope with having a child I didn't share. It was very hard when Rob was little, I missed him all the time he was living with Harry and Charlie. But, then again, I know how desolate I would feel if I couldn't have a child of my own, and I feel very close to you and Coco. So. I'm in a bit of a quandary."

Miles was contrite. "Dear boy, I'm so sorry. I didn't look at this from your point of view at all." He stood up. "Please forget it. It was thoughtless and selfish of me."

"Sit down and shut up! Have another drink. I need to think about this. If I decide to go ahead, which I very well might, we'll need to talk, the four of us. For instance, suppose the child – if it did work – looked exactly like me, as Rob, Davy and Bell do. And all my children are tremendously like me, even Sammy and Drew, who don't have my colouring or eyes. People would automatically assume that Coco and I have had an affair. Are you prepared to live with that? Or would you want to tell people the truth?"

"Yes, I do see. Again, I hadn't thought of any of this."

"Well, these are the kind of things we'd have to sort out, decide what we'd do. Can I think about it for a while?"

"Stephen, of course, of course. I'm profoundly grateful that you would consider it at all."

Stephen found Lynn and told her. She stared at him. "What are you going to do?"

"God knows. My first instinct was to say no, but you should have seen the look on his face!"

"I know. It was the same with Coral and the triplets; she couldn't get enough of them."

Stephen sighed. "I don't know what to do."

"When do you have to give them your answer?"

"Oh, whenever, there's no time limit. But obviously I'll have to let them know sooner rather than later."

They held a cocktail party on New Year's Eve.

"Can Swiggsy come?" Toni asked when Stephen rang and invited her and George.

"I'd forgotten he was here. I suppose so, although I imagine the closest he's ever come to a cocktail is a paper parasol in his pint!"

He could hear the laughter in her voice when she replied. "Don't be an imbo, Stephen!"

The boys and Mab had been invited, provided they wore something decent.

"What do you mean, decent?" Alex demanded.

"Like normal people," Stephen replied.

"Normal by whose standards?"

"By my fucking standards! If you don't like them, stay in your room!"

"OK, OK, keep your teeth in, Grandpa! I just think it's misleading saying 'normal' when you're talking about yourself!" Alex went off to give the others the bad news.

"I haven't got a frock or anything with me," Mab worried.

"Tell Cherry, she'll sort you out," Pip reassured her.

Lynn and Mab were much the same size and height, and she lent Mab her wiggle dress. Mab looked tremendous in it; it was tighter on her, emphasising her breasts and showing off her figure to perfection. The colour suited her, and Lynn helped her with her make up, applying it very lightly, so that it merely enhanced her already long dark lashes and English rose complexion. She plaited Mab's golden hair, coiling it up around her head like a shining crown.

Dominic raised his eyebrows appreciatively at the sight of her. "And who is this beauty?" he asked, kissing her hand. "You look very familiar, do I know you?"

Mab giggled. "Don't be silly, Papa!"

Pip caught his breath when he saw her, awed by this transformation. "Amabel, you're *so* beautiful!"

The Chaplins, the Fergusons and the Harpers stayed the night, and breakfast the following morning was an informal affair. Sam and Alex, whose birthday they'd celebrated at midnight, were still in bed, but Pip and Mab, who wanted to spend as much time as possible in each other's company, had got up early and were cooking bacon and eggs.

When Shelagh and Fin came down, Toni and George were sitting at the table with Stephen, Lynn and Rob. Dominic was lounging on the window seat reading the paper, and Harry was making some sort of high energy drink in the blender.

"Bacon and eggs?" Pip asked.

"Please, Pip," Fin nodded, but Shelagh winced slightly. "I'll just get some coffee, thanks."

Pip grinned. "Over indulged last night, eh? Seconds, George?"

George held out his plate.

"You should've had breakfast in bed like Jules, Shelagh," Lynn said sympathetically.

"Yes, she was feeling very fragile," Rob grinned. "I took her up a tray, but she couldn't even look at it!"

Toni sniffed. "You let her walk all over you, Blue! I always cook George's breakfast, and I used to get yours too, didn't I, Stevo?"

"Aye, that's true, you do, pet," George mumbled, his mouth full of bacon.

Stephen didn't answer her. He stared at George, incensed. "How come George can talk with his mouth full in front of the boys? I never could!"

Before Toni could answer, George swallowed and said, "Howay, man, Steve, you lass, because I'm master in my own home!"

"So was I!" Stephen declared, hurt.

Rob and Pip burst out laughing. "In your dreams, Dad!" Pip said, kissing him on the head.

"I am now though, aren't I, Cherry?" Stephen asked in a pathetic voice.

"Course you are, Stevie," she said, soothingly.

Rob finished his coffee and got up. "Well, if the master of the house will excuse me, I'm going to see how Jules is feeling. I'll see you all later."

Fin was leafing through a copy of a new celebrity magazine, *Scene*, that Mab had brought with her. "You're in here, Steve."

"Oh, yeah?" Stephen said, warily.

"Yeah," Fin grinned. "They reckon you should get your hair cut! Listen: '*Why does rock star Stephen Markham insist on wearing his hair the same way he did twenty years ago? Someone ought to tell him that at nearly fifty*'..."

"Hey! I'm only forty four!" Stephen protested.

" ...'*he's far too old to wear a floppy fringe*,' " Fin continued. " '*It looks ridiculous, and doesn't fool anyone. Act your age, Markham, not your shoe size!*' "

"Oh, Stephen, don't get it cut!" Mab exclaimed.

"You wouldn't be you if you did," Shelagh said.

"It hides your wrinkles too, Stevo," Toni laughed.

"Take no notice," Harry said. "You look gorgeous with your hair falling into your eyes like that, and you always have!"

"You do," Lynn agreed, kissing him.

"And this," Stephen grinned, "is why I act my shoe size."

"What is your shoe size?" Fin inquired.

"Six."

"Explains the Robosapien you got for Christmas," Dominic said, going back to the paper.

"Did you get that Kylie calendar that's in the studio for Christmas as well?" Fin asked, glancing at Shelagh.

"No, that's Alex's."

"Shelagh wouldn't let me have one," Fin said.

"I agree, Shelagh," Toni said, emphatically. "Sexist, isn't it?"

"Oh, it's not that," Shelagh laughed. "I just don't want him staring at some other woman's bottom!"

"You needn't have worried," Stephen said. "There are no shots of her in shorts, and, let's face it, that's why you want it, to see her bottom. If you're going to do calendars, you ought to think what your fans will want. Before the accident, I always took my shirt off."

"You slut, Markham," Dominic drawled.

Fin got up. "Well, I suppose we'd better be off, we've got Shelagh's family arriving later, and I haven't hidden the silver yet."

"God, you're an awful wee eejit sometimes, Finbar Harper," Shelagh said crushingly. She kissed Lynn. "Thanks for the party, Steve and Lynn, it was great fun."

"We'd better go too," Toni said. "Come on, George, finish your brekkie, we have to check in by two o'clock, and we've got to get Swiggs up." They were flying out to Australia that afternoon. She smiled over at Stephen. "Shelagh's right, it was a good party."

Stephen smiled back. "We've had some amazing parties in this house, haven't we? Do you remember the Egyptian one?"

Toni laughed. "I do, but my favourite was that pagan summer solstice one."

"Would that be the one where Dom and Brad went off in search of sacrificial virgins and got arrested for being drunk and disorderly?" Fin grinned.

"Don't remind me!" Harry groaned.

Dominic glared at him. "Yes, thank you, Fin. Didn't you say you were leaving?"

After the four of them had gone, Pip grinned. "George was telling me last night that he's writing his autobiography and – wait for this – launching his own perfume!"

They goggled at him.

Stephen began to laugh. "What's it called? Eau de Geordie?"

"How about A Night On The Tyne?" Dominic put in.

"Daisy," Pip said.

"Daisy? That's my name for Toni! If I'd known the bugger was going to make money out of it, I'd have trademarked it!" Stephen exclaimed.

"Actually, you know, there's a lot of money in cosmetics," Dominic said.

"Yeah, that's what George said," Pip nodded.

"Well, in fact," Stephen said, "Cherry and I were thinking about it the other day. I was saying it's really hard to find an ordinary shampoo that just washes your hair without giving it bounce, or volume, or taming its frizz and all the rest of it, and isn't tested on animals, and she said it's the same with face and body creams, and we were half-thinking about doing our own. I mean, Penhaligon's and The Body Shop and what have you, are great, but it would be nice to find a range that you could pick up in your local shop. We even got as far as thinking up names. It's a niche that needs filling, we might look into it."

"Make the stuff smell like food," Dominic advised. "Harry's got this delicious body stuff that smells like crème brulée. She puts it on before we go to bed, it's like making love in a restaurant! The best of both worlds!"

"You lot are deeply mental," Pip said disapprovingly. He'd expected them to greet George's perfume with the derisive disbelief that he'd felt, but not only had they taken it seriously, they'd actually been thinking along the same lines themselves. He sincerely hoped he would never become middle aged.

"What about George's autobiography?" Lynn asked.

"Yeah," said Stephen. "Come on, Pip, tell all. What's he calling that?"

"Pretentious Geordie Twat?" Dominic suggested.

"Dominic!" Harry exclaimed.

"Well, come on, Harry, he is. I like him, but you can't deny the man's pretentious."

"He is," Stephen agreed. "He always has been. That's the point about liking someone, I suppose, you can see their faults, but you don't mind them. So what is he calling it, Pipkin?"

"Um – oh, yeah – *Touching Bass* – that's b-a-s-s, not b-a-s-e."

"God, how cheesy!" Stephen groaned.

"It's definitely an autobiography is it?" Harry asked. "It's not about fish?"

They stared at her. "Fish? Have you gone mad, woman?" Dominic demanded.

"No, you know, bass is a type of fish. Touching bass. It might be like tickling trout."

Stephen laughed delightedly. "Or maybe George is coming out. He's a fishophile and this is his story. He goes online when Toni's asleep and trawls the internet for pictures of fish."

"'Trawls' the internet!" Lynn gasped, crying with laughter.

"Mind you," Stephen said, getting himself under control, "although I'd never write one myself, I don't really blame him. It's so bloody annoying when some moron writes an unauthorised biography about you. People never seem to realise that unauthorised means exactly that, and take the rubbish they print as gospel."

"Well, yes, in your case I'd agree," Dominic said. "But how many biographies have been written about George, authorised or otherwise?"

Stephen thought about it. "I can't say I've actually heard of any."

"Exactly. Pretentious."

"Oh, well. Maybe when he's written Feeling Fish, he'll get it out of his system."

Pip stared round at them all, doubled up over their breakfasts. This was how he'd expected them to react to George's perfume venture – the autobiography seemed perfectly acceptable to him, all aging celebs did it. He sighed and took Mab's hand. "Come on, let's leave them to it."

She shot him a conspiratorial look. "Let's go for a swim. Alex and Sam and Gus and Fee are still in bed and this lot'll be in here talking for hours." She squeezed his hand. "We'll be all alone."

The Chaplins went back to London late that evening. Pip and Mab didn't want to be parted. They clung to one another and Mab started to cry.

"Come along, Amabel," Dominic said, impatiently, holding the back door of his Jaguar open for her. She slouched despondently over, casting longing glances at Pip. All the way back to Leezance she sulked, and snapped at anyone who spoke to her.

By the time they got in, Dominic had had enough. "For Christ's sake, Amabel, grow up!" he shouted. "I am sick of you behaving like this! You spent your entire holiday with Pip, you'll be seeing him again next weekend when he's at Toni and George's, stop behaving like a silly little girl!"

"I'm in love with Pip!"

"You don't know the first thing about love!" Dominic said, with disgust. "And I'd be inclined to take you a little more seriously if you stopped behaving like a toddler whose doll has been taken away! We had to put up with all those tantrums before Christmas, and now this! I'm seriously thinking of sending you to boarding school."

Mab turned white. "You wouldn't!"

"Try me!" he retorted.

Mab turned and ran upstairs.

Dominic went into the drawing room and poured himself a whisky.

Harry followed him in. "Saying you'd send her to boarding school was a bit harsh."

"I'd like to send her to a fucking convent! Oh, Harry, I'm fed up with her. You were about her age when you were in love with bloody Markham – honestly, he and fucking Philip have got a lot to answer for! Did you behave like this?"

"No," Harry admitted. "Dad would have killed me."

"Exactly. We're too fucking soft with them!"

Gus peered round the door. "What's wrong with Mab? She's in hysterics upstairs."

"Oh, for fuck's sake!" Dominic went to the bottom of the stairs and yelled. "Amabel! Get down here!"

Mab appeared at the top of the stairs, crying, her chin quivering pathetically.

Dominic couldn't stand seeing his children miserable. He held out his arms. "Come here."

Mab hurtled down the stairs into them.

"Let's go and see what we can find to eat. Would you like some ice cream?"

Mab shook her head. They went down to the kitchens and Dominic sat her at the table while he looked in the freezer. "What about these doughnuts?"

"Yes, please."

He read the label. "Hmm, they take an hour to defrost."

"I eat them frozen," Mab said, taking one.

Dominic sat next to her. "I'm sorry I shouted, and I'm sorry I said I'd send you to boarding school. But, my darling, you can't behave like this. Sometimes you have to be separated from the person you love, and then you have to be sensible about it."

Mab nibbled at the doughnut. "Can me and Pip go to the same school to do our A Levels?"

"Toni doesn't want Pip to move from his school, Mama and I were talking to her and Stephen about it last night."

"Well, can't I live at the Priory and go to Pip's school?"

Dominic rubbed his chin. "Frankly, I don't really like that idea, nor does Mama."

"Why not?" Mab demanded.

"Because you're doing so well at St. Luke's, and we'd never see you if you were at the Priory. You might not believe it, but we love you very much, you know!"

"Oh, Papa, of course I believe it!"

"And you'll have the rest of your life to spend with Pip, or whoever you eventually choose."

"What do you mean?"

Harry had joined them. "He means that you're madly in love with Pip now, but in five years time you might not be," she explained gently.

"I'll always love Pip!" Mab cried passionately.

"When I was your age, I was in love with Stephen."

Mab nodded. "I know."

"I felt like you do now, that's why I had Rob," Harry continued. "It was the next best thing to having Stephen. But within six years I was out of love with him, and a year later, I met Papa and realised he was the only man for me. But supposing I'd married Stephen and then met Dominic?"

"You could have got a divorce," Mab pointed out.

Harry was taken aback. "Well, yes, I suppose I could've."

"You got a divorce from your first husband, and you were hardly married to him for any time."

"Mab, divorce isn't fun," Harry said. "Nobody wants to go through it. It's not something you take lightly."

Mab nodded. "I know. And what you're saying is that Pip and I might not stay in love. But that's a risk that everyone who ever gets married takes. Look at Stephen and Lynn. She was only a couple of years older than I am when she met Stephen.

She knew she'd never love anyone else. And she didn't, and neither did he, and they're back together." Although, in fact, Mab didn't approve of the way Lynn had treated Stephen, and thought she was exceedingly lucky that he'd taken her back. Before she'd fallen in love with Pip, she'd had a secret, fierce, and all consuming crush on Stephen, and still felt slightly proprietorial about him.

"This is nothing to do with that, anyway, Mab," Dominic said. "All we're really saying is that you can't be with Pip full-time for several years yet, so you'll have to be grown up about it. Could you try?"

Mab sighed. "I suppose. But it would be easier to be grown up about it if I was treated more like one!"

"You went to a fucking cocktail party last night, for Christ's sake!" Dominic was starting to get angry again. "When I was your age, I *was* at boarding school, a school I loathed, and during the holidays I wasn't pampered and petted and invited to cocktail parties, I spent my time keeping out of my father's way!"

Mab stared at him. "Why?"

"He hated me."

Mab's eyes widened. "Grandpapa? Grandpapa hated you? But why?"

Dominic shrugged. "I was a living reminder that one day he'd have to give up his beloved estate."

"That's horrible!"

"Yes, it wasn't much fun. So Mab, please don't complain. Mama and I do our best to make your life as happy as we can, so do us a favour and start thinking about people besides yourself and Pip." He got up. "Come, it's very late, and you were up till three last night. You ought to be in bed."

Mab's lips trembled. "You're right, Papa, I'm sorry. I *have* been childish. And I'm sorry that Grandpapa was horrible to you. But I love Pip so much I can't think about anything else!"

Dominic put his arms around her. "Don't think I don't understand, that's how I feel about Mama. I suppose it's easier to control yourself when you're older."

Mab went to her room and rang Pip.

He answered on the first ring.

"They're not going to let us go to the same school," she said despairingly. "Your mother wants you to stay where you are, and my parents don't want me to move to Oxford."

"So Dad would let me move?" Pip asked.

"I suppose. Papa just said Toni didn't want you to."

"I'll just have to try working on Dad. If he's on our side already, it shouldn't be too hard."

"I wouldn't count on it," Mab said grimly. "The rest of them are pretty determined."

Stephen hadn't given up trying to play the guitar. He got slowly better at it, and slowly more reconciled to the false hand.

Lynn was on her way out to a dental appointment on a cold, wet afternoon in January, when she remembered she hadn't told him that the vet was coming to look at Mardi. She ran back into the house. He'd been working in his study before she went out, but now it was empty. Puzzled, she went into the kitchen. He wasn't there, and he wouldn't have gone outside, it was pouring with rain. She looked in the library, the drawing room, the morning room and the small sitting room. "Stephen!" she shouted. The house was like the Marie Celeste, although she could faintly hear the whine of the vacuum cleaner. She went upstairs, but he was nowhere to be seen.

Finally, completely baffled, she started up the small flight of stairs leading to the attic. Someone was in the music room, strumming 'Sweet Cherry' on an acoustic guitar. It wouldn't be Alex, he never played acoustic, and although Pip was home from school with a sinus infection, she'd heard him singing in his room. She peered in through the open door. Stephen was bent over a guitar, absorbed in what he was doing. As though he sensed she was there, he looked up.

"Stephen!" she breathed. "How are you doing that?"

"I'm trying to teach myself to play the chords with my right hand. Of course, I can only strum. I wasn't going to tell you until I was any good. If I ever am!"

"You are good!"

He shook his head. "No. No, I'm crap. I used to be able to – to make the guitar talk, to, oh, I can't explain – to *express* the way I felt. I can play tunes now, but that's all. I don't really know why I'm bothering. I just couldn't bear not being able to play." He took off the prosthesis, and gave her a weak smile. "I wonder how long it'll take Marcus to grow me that new hand?"

They went downstairs.

"Take care," Stephen whispered, holding her tightly to him.

Lynn kissed him. "I'm only going to the dentist," she smiled, but with understanding.

Pip came hurtling down the stairs, and followed Stephen into the kitchen. "Do you want a cup of coffee, Dad?" he asked.

Stephen nodded. "Please, Pip."

Pip made the coffee and brought it over. He fetched the chocolate biscuits.

Stephen sipped his coffee. "This is delicious, Pip!"

"I put some cinnamon in, I know you like it and you were looking sad." He reached out and patted Stephen's left arm, stroking the stump. "I love you, Dad." Although he was doing his best to get into Stephen's good books, he genuinely meant this, and he'd put the cinnamon into the coffee in the hope of cheering him up. He didn't know why Stephen was sad, but he couldn't bear to see the look of desolation in his eyes.

Stephen put his hand on Pip's. "Oh, Pipkin, I love you too. You and your brothers and sisters mean more to me than anything in the world."

After he'd finished his coffee, he rang Miles. "The answer's yes, Miles. Whenever you and Coral are ready."

Chapter Thirty-One
This Day Alone is Ours

This love, this now, is all, before the darkness falls,
Time devours flesh and bone, this day alone is ours.

At the end of January, Stephen started recording 'Only Ever You', a collection of songs he'd written over the years, for each of his children, for Lynn, for Sian, for Harry and Dominic. He'd never meant to record them, feeling they were too private, but since his accident he had realised he wanted a permanent monument to them all, so that there would never be any doubt about how much he loved them. He wanted the whole world to know how much they meant to him. He asked Dominic and Harry to play on it, and also Pip, who was overwhelmed. "You don't really want *me*, do you, Dad? I mean, I'm nowhere near good enough!"

"Course you are! You're a seriously talented musician, Pip."

Royal Velvet, Coral's movie, for which Stephen had written the music, premiered in March. It was Stephen and Lynn's wedding anniversary on the fourteenth, and they spent several days at Cheyne Walk.

Coral and Miles, who had moved into a large, opulent house in Belgravia, gave a dinner party to celebrate the premiere. To Stephen's amusement, Coral had arranged the seating in the French manner, with she and Miles, the hosts, seated opposite each other at the centre of the long, rosewood table in their elegant dining room. He was on Coral's right, and he found, with pleasure, that the actress Carenza Douglas, who played Lady Jane, Coral's rival in the film, was seated on his other side. She was very pretty, small and slender, with delicate bones, long, thick hair the colour of ripe corn, and bright green eyes. He was delighted to discover, as they chatted during the first course, a delicious chilled watercress soup, that her mother came from York.

"It's a beautiful place," she enthused, "although I don't know it very well, I was born in Birmingham, but I was in *After The Fair* at the Theatre Royal last year, so I spent some of my time exploring. I'm thinking of buying a house in the area."

Stephen laughingly gave her the telephone number of Markham Cavendish. "They'll handle the legal work for you. I can recommend them wholeheartedly," he grinned. "Just ask for Rob Chaplin! Although Coco tells me you're making another film right now – about witchcraft, isn't it?"

"Yes, it's a romantic comedy. I play a fortune teller who gets caught up in a satanic cult."

The caterers brought round the main course. Because Stephen was a vegetarian, Coral had had them prepare a vegetarian meal; griddled aubergine stacks, comprising layers of sliced aubergine, beef tomatoes, and a mixture of herbs, onions and peppers, covered in a rich red wine sauce, and accompanied by a mange-tout and avocado salad. Stephen stared down at his plate and started to grin. It looked and smelt delicious, but there was no way he could eat it unless it was cut up. He nudged Coral. "Sorry about this, Coco, but would you cut this up? Cherry usually does it for me."

Coral was stricken. "Stevie! I'm so sorry! I remembered about the food, but I didn't think – I forgot about your hand." She bit her lip, and took his plate.

"Don't worry about it," he smiled. "I'm not an easy person to feed, am I? A one-handed vegetarian!"

He noticed Carenza's look of appalled sympathy as Coral cut up his food. "It's OK, I'm used to it," he assured her. "I tell myself I'm the Sultan of Brunei, beautiful handmaidens to cater to my every whim!" He winked at Coral, who smiled back. "The sweet is a syllabub, so you should be all right with that," she said, as she gave him his plate.

"Thanks, Mum," he joked.

"It must have been very difficult to come to terms with," Carenza said, seriously.

"Yeah, certainly was. Still is, sometimes." He shrugged. "But it's done now, and no amount of whining can change it. Of course," he added, grinning, "that's not to say I don't whine! I do, frequently." He caught Lynn's eye and she smiled at him across the table. "Grumpy old man, that's you!" she laughed.

Carenza began to talk to him about the band's forthcoming tour. "Will you be going to Latvia?" she asked.

He'd always enjoyed the company of women, and the more attractive they were, the more he enjoyed it. He had a way of concentrating on a woman that made her feel special, as if she was the only woman in the room, and he found it very hard to resist flirting. He'd always thought, when he was married to Toni, that if he was with Lynn he wouldn't be interested in other women, but he realised guiltily that that wasn't so. When he and Lynn had first met, he'd been intoxicated with her, had never felt like that before, and had been so completely in love with her that he'd barely noticed other girls, but after she left him he toughened up, was determined that no one would ever hurt him like that again, and by the time he married Toni, he'd become used to being able to have any woman he wanted, and flirted as a matter of course. He glanced over at Lynn. To his relief, she was absorbed in a conversation with Miles. He smiled at Carenza. "We will, we've got three nights at the Kipsala Hall in Riga. Why do you ask?"

"My sister works there. It's a beautiful place. Last time I went to stay, she took me to Sigulda, and we went on the cable car over the valley. It was amazing! Have you been there?"

"We don't get to see much of the places where we play," Stephen sighed. "But maybe we'll be able to sneak in some sightseeing this time."

She gave him a sideways glance from under her long, curving lashes. "How about I read your palm and find out?" she offered. "I've become a bit of an expert on this fortune telling stuff."

He held out his hand, and she took it, leaning towards him so that her shoulder was touching his, exposing, very provocatively, a good deal of cleavage. She held his hand until dessert was placed in front of them.

Lynn had actually noticed immediately, and was upset and annoyed. For the first time, she felt a tiny flicker of understanding for Toni. If I wasn't completely confident in his love for me, I'd be worried and unhappy, she thought. She mentioned it to Coral later, when they were in the large drawing room having coffee. Miles had taken Stephen to look at a painting he had recently bought. Carenza had expressed an interest in seeing it too, and had gone along with them, holding Stephen's arm.

Coral smiled reminiscently. "He simply can't resist a pretty woman. That's what most of our rows were about: one – or both of us – flirting with someone else!" She giggled. "I wanted so much to marry him, but it's a good thing I didn't, it would certainly have ended in a crime of passion!"

Lynn was surprised. "He never did it at university. And not since we've been remarried. Well, only with Holly, but he always did, and I put that down to them being such friends."

Coral shrugged. "Over the years he's got used to women throwing themselves at him. And the loss of his hand affected his confidence badly; well, you yourself said he was very sensitive about the way the stump looked. In a way, this is a good thing, yes? It means he's his old self again, confident and happy. And Carenza is a very attractive girl. It's not as if he'd ever act on it," she added. "He just likes to flirt, Cherie." She had taken to calling Lynn this rather ambiguous version of Cherry, ambiguous in that it was also the French word for darling. "They make it so obvious they want him, you can't really blame him. Or Carenza, either, for that matter." She smiled at the look on Lynn's face. "You can't, Lynn. He's so… oh, what's the word?" She frowned impatiently. "Charismatic, I suppose, although that's very overworked these days. But he is. When he performs, even now he can't play his guitar, it's him you look at, always; it always was, whatever he's doing. That's why Miles wanted him for *Hoodman Blind*. With that… that magnetic quality, and his looks, and the fact that he genuinely likes the company of women… well, it's a lethal combination! Don't ever let it bother you, it's just a game he likes to play, but it's you he loves, so very much, and always will be, you're his world." She kissed Lynn's cheek.

Back at Cheyne Walk, Stephen lay in bed reading, while Lynn took her make up off. She glanced at him in the mirror. "You and Carenza seemed to get on very well," she said, idly, watching him.

He coloured guiltily.

Bastard! she thought, but without real acrimony.

"She's nice," he said casually.

Lynn turned to face him. "And very pretty. With an incredible figure, and that dress left nothing to the imagination. And so young."

"Sorry." He was contrite. "Please don't be jealous, Cherry, it was just a bit of flirting. It doesn't mean anything."

She got into bed and hugged him. "What would Toni have said?"

"Jesus! I wouldn't even have dared to *look* at her if I'd still been married to Toni!"

Lynn grinned.

"And she *is* nice. She was sorry for me having to have Coral cut up my food, and I told her how I used to have that phobia about my stump, but now it doesn't bother me so much, and she said she thought that me having only one hand was dashing and James Bondish. I'd forgotten that Felix Leiter lost his hand. She said I'd be a really good James Bond." He smiled smugly.

"God! Talk about don't feed the ego!" Lynn groaned. She must really have fallen for him, she thought. "No doubt she'd be your Bond girl."

He slid his hand over her breasts. "No way! That'd be you!"

She reached up and kissed him. Coral had been right; the flirtation had done him a lot of good. "OK, Markham, I'll forgive you – but just this once!"

March was also Harry and Dominic's wedding anniversary, their twentieth. They held a rather posh party at Leezance. It was black tie, very formal.

Alex, Pip and Mab were invited, Mab looking lovely in a white velvet ball gown embroidered with rosebuds.

Pip stared at her. "You look so beautiful in ordinary clothes, Amabel. Let's stop being Moshers, I was never that keen, anyway, and the clothes are so ugly."

"What about the band?"

"Well, we can wear them in the band, I suppose, although I've been thinking about that. I think we should tone the Mosherism down a bit."

"Yes," Mab agreed, "I'd like to sing songs like 'Beautiful Beloved', but what about Alex? He'll go mad!"

"I can deal with Alex. I've got plans for the band, Mab. Since I played on 'Only Ever You', I've been thinking about the way we ought to go. Dad's music is incredibly good, and he and Dom expect such a high standard. It has to be the best, or they're not interested, and that goes double for their own work. I want to be like that – I want *us* to be like that. Don't worry about Alex, it'll be cool." He took her hand. "Less than a month till you're sixteen! I've got something for you."

"What?" Mab's eyes were alight with excitement and anticipation.

"We've got to go somewhere private."

Mab led him down to the cellar stairs. "Now show me!"

Pip took a small, leather box out of his pocket and gave it to her.

She opened it carefully. A tiny solitaire diamond, surrounded by little emeralds, winked up at her. "Oh!" she gasped. "Oh, Pip!"

"Will you marry me, cariad?"

"Oh, yes, you know I will! It's all I want!"

Pip slipped the ring onto her finger. "It fits," he said, with satisfaction. "But you won't be able to wear it, so I got you this as well." It was a thin gold chain. He took the ring off her finger and put it on the chain, which he fastened around her neck. "No that's no good, not with that neckline. I'll wear it for tonight, and give it to you just before we go."

Mab leaned against him. "Just think – soon you'll never have to go!"

At the end of March, just before Easter, the band started recording 'Quicksilver.'

"This'll be your first ever tour without groupies, then, George," Stephen said to him when they were taking a break. "How will you cope?"

"What are you talking about, man?" George asked, opening a bottle of Newcastle Brown.

"Well, you're married to Toni now!"

"So what?"

Stephen stared at him. "You mean you're still going to have groupies?"

"Why aye, man, a groupie is nature's way of dealing with stress!"

"Supposing Toni finds out?"

"She knows."

"She knows?" Stephen was dumbfounded.

"You were always far too soft with her, Steve; you can't treat women as equals, bonny lad, they need a firm hand! I simply said; pet, a man's essential juice has to flow freely."

"And she swallowed that?"

"Erm – I think you might want to rephrase that, like, Steve," Andy grinned.

That night, Coral rang him up. "Miles and I thought you might like to know, Stevie. I am pregnant."

His heart thumped. It was done, whatever happened in the future. There was no going back now for any of them. "Congratulations, Coco! I'm so very pleased. Would you like to come and stay for Easter weekend?"

"Thank you," Coral said. "We would like that very much."

Sam and Pip were going on a school trip to Hadrian's Wall over Easter. Pip hadn't originally been going, but Stephen and Lynn were worried about Sam.

"Dad! There'll be teachers there, and Marcus'll be going," Pip pointed out when Stephen talked to him about it.

"Yeah, teachers." Stephen was dismissive. He'd never lost his dislike of them. "And Marcus going doesn't exactly fill me with confidence. I like him very much, but in a lot of ways, he's worse than Sam! It's only five days, Pip, please would you go? I'll owe you," he promised.

"Mab's going to stay with a friend in the Lake District, so OK," Pip sighed reluctantly, "but Dad, could we meet at Fenroth and travel down on the train together? Sam'll be OK on the minibus."

"That's fair. I'll sort it out with the school."

They set off early on the Sunday morning, and arrived at the youth hostel just after lunch. Sam and Marcus were both very excited, Pip was bored already. He was counting the days until he saw Mab. He went on long walks to the wall and around the beautiful countryside with the rest of the group, but all he could see was Mab's smiling face. She was his only reality.

At last it was Friday morning. As arranged, the school coach dropped him off at Central Station in Newcastle, so that he could get a train to Morpeth. It was Mab's birthday the following Monday, and Dominic had reluctantly agreed to let him meet her at the Manor, and for them both to stay there overnight on Friday, travelling down to London on the Saturday. The Morpeth train came and went. Pip didn't even attempt to catch it. Minutes later he was on a train taking him to Mab in Scotland.

While he'd been at Hadrian's Wall, Mab had been in Gretna Green. Under Scottish law, one person must attend the Register office in the seven days before a wedding, and she and Pip were getting married at ten thirty on the morning of her birthday. Pip had planned the whole thing with an attention to detail worthy of Wellington. He'd never had any intention of buying a motorbike, simply used it to account for the fact that he was saving hard, and it was he who had cunningly and unobtrusively sown the seeds of doubt about Sam in Lynn's mind; she, as he'd known she would, had shared them with Stephen, who, as Pip had also known he would, asked Pip to go on the trip. The only tricky part had been in making sure that Lynn hadn't been around when Stephen had spoken to him.

Mab's friend in the Lake District had not exactly been fictitious, she was supposed to be staying with a girl from school, Jane, at her aunt's home in Penrith. The aunt really existed and really lived in Penrith, where she ran a teashop. The letter of invitation, however, *was* fictitious and had been written by Mab's best friend, Emily, the only other person who knew about the elopement. On Saturday, Mab was going to ring Harry and say that she and Pip had missed the train, but had got their tickets changed for the train on Monday. Harry and Dominic would be angry, but neither Mab nor Pip were going to let that stop them. They were terrified but determined.

Mab met him off the train and fell into his arms. "Oh, God, Pip! I was so afraid something would go wrong!"

Pip grinned. "I told you!"

"Yes, but it's April Fools Day!"

"They're the fools! Amabel, in three days, you'll be my wife!"

When Stephen had decided to help Miles and Coral, they'd got together and talked the situation through. Lynn had mostly stayed silent, feeling that it wasn't really her business.

"You are very quiet, Cherie," Coral had said.

"It's not really much to do with me," she smiled.

"Of course it is!" Miles said. "If Coral becomes pregnant, the child would be your children's half-brother or sister, and you, as much as Stephen, will have to bear the brunt of media intrusion if it looks like him."

They'd decided that, should this happen, they would issue a statement explaining what they had done.

"With any luck, it will have red hair," Lynn said. "And, hopefully, navy blue eyes like yours, Coral, not Stephen's eyes."

"Yes, they are very distinctive," Miles agreed.

Coral sighed but said nothing.

When they arrived at the Priory for Easter, Coral hugged Stephen and Lynn. "Isn't it good news!" she exclaimed. "We're so happy!" She was looking more beautiful than Stephen had ever seen her, glowing with joy.

Miles kissed Lynn, and took Stephen's hand in both of his. "I don't think I need to tell you that this baby will be very much loved and cherished."

"Do you mind what sex it is?" Lynn asked.

Coral and Miles smiled at each other. "No," Coral said. "It's our child. That is all that matters."

Dominic and Harry had bought Mab a ruby coloured Cavalier King Charles Spaniel puppy for her sixteenth birthday. She was tiny, only eight weeks old, and Dominic and Harry were hoping that Mab would find her irresistible. They were very much looking forward to giving her to Mab, feeling that it might help her to get over her obsession with Pip if she had something small and dependent to look after at home, so it was with considerable annoyance that Harry took the phone call from Mab, who explained that she and Pip had missed the train. "But if you don't get a train until Monday, we'll miss most of your birthday! And term starts again on Tuesday!"

"Oh, well, never mind, Mama, it can't be helped now."

"I'll drive up and fetch them," Dominic said, when Harry gave him the news. "I'll give her a ring and tell them to be ready to leave this afternoon." He dialled the number and spoke to the housekeeper. "Hello, Mrs Fletcher, I'd like to speak to Miss Amabel… what? Not at all? Are you sure? Yes, of course you are… no, it's obviously my mistake… Wrong dates, yes, thank you, Mrs Fletcher." He hung up and stared at Harry. "They're not there!"

"Where are they, then?"

"God knows!"

"It was Fenroth, wasn't it? She didn't say Pip was meeting her in Penrith? Penrith, Fenroth, they sound pretty similar when you say them fast."

Dominic gave her an exasperated look. "Don't be stupid, Harry. Where the fuck are they?" He called Gus and Fee down from their rooms. They so obviously didn't know anything that there was no point worrying them.

"I'm going to ring up Stephen, he might have heard from Pip."

Stephen picked up the phone. "Stephen Markham."

"Markham, it's me. Do you have any idea of the whereabouts of your number three son?"

"Pip? Fenroth, isn't he? They're coming back on Monday, aren't they?"

"Is that what he told you?"

"Yes, he rang half an hour ago, said they'd missed the train and Mabs was phoning Harry."

"They're not there."

"Perhaps they've gone for a walk."

"No, you don't understand, they've not been there at all. I was going to drive up and collect them, but Mrs Fletcher tells me they were never there!"

Stephen was stunned. "Well, where are they? Sam's here, they dropped Pip off as arranged. I don't understand."

"Look, could you speak to Alex? He might know something. Neither Gus nor Fee do."

"Yes, of course. I'll get back to you."

Alex didn't know anything. "All I can tell you, Dad, is that he borrowed four hundred pounds from me. He wanted to buy a motor bike."

Stephen stared at him. "God! You don't think the idiot bought a bike and drove to Penrith or something, do you?"

Alex shrugged. "I wouldn't put it past him. Sorry, Dad, I should have told you. But he begged me not to and I didn't think he'd do anything freaky."

Stephen rang Toni. There was no answer. He remembered that she and George were in Australia, so she wouldn't know anything. He rang Dominic and told him about the motorbike, then walked slowly back to the sitting room.

"What is it?" Lynn asked, concerned by his expression.

Briefly, he explained. "I'm really worried that they might have had an accident," he said. He was consumed with fear; the thought of Pip being involved in a traffic accident, in unbearable pain somewhere…it was his worst nightmare. He took a deep breath.

Lynn was stricken. "I knew he was saving for a motorbike," she admitted. "I found out when we took them to George and Toni last autumn. I was under the impression that he was going to tell you, then I forgot all about it."

"I wish you'd told me, Cherry."

"Darling, I'm so sorry." She took his hand. "Perhaps you ought to ring the police."

"I've just thought of something!" Gus burst into the drawing room. "Ezza might know, Mab tells her everything."

"*Ezza? Ezza*? Who the fuck is *Ezza?*" Dominic demanded.

Harry frowned at him. "Don't swear, Dominic. You know Ezza; Emily Rochford-Percy."

"What, that pretty little girl who used to go to ballet with Mab? I haven't seen her for years."

Harry gave him a surprised look. "She was here just before Easter, she and Mab went out shopping together. You bumped into her when you were coming in from rehearsal."

Dominic stared. "The scarecrow with the orange hair? That was Emily? A boy in a leather jacket and tartan trousers was picking her up. Come to think of it, he had a motorbike." He and Harry exchanged despairing looks.

"Yeah, that was Duddo," Gus said. "He's way cool!"

"Duddo?" Dominic asked.

"John Dudley," Harry said.

"Of course, the Hon John Dudley, I should have known," Dominic said, sarcastically.

"I'll ring Emily's mother," Harry said. She came back a few minutes later. "Emily's away – no, not with our two," she said in answer to the look of hope on Dominic's face. "She's with her father in France."

"Well, what about this girl Mab was staying with in Penrith?"

"Jane Arundel. Oh, Dom, what a good idea! I'll go and find her number." She returned looking grim. "Mab was never there, either; Jane has been at home all over the holiday. She didn't invite Mab anywhere."

Dominic stared at her, white faced. "Where the hell are they?"

Mab had booked Pip into the Bed and Breakfast where she was staying. They had single rooms on different floors.

"Two more nights apart then we'll never be separated again," Pip said. He'd booked a four poster room at the Moffat House Hotel in Moffat for their wedding night.

"How much is all this costing?" Mab wanted to know.

He wouldn't tell her. "I'm paying. I've got plenty of money. Don't worry!"

He'd booked them both taxis to leave at slightly different times on Monday morning. His left first. He thought he'd be nervous, but he wasn't in the least. His heart was singing as he waited at the Register Office for her.

She arrived ten minutes later, looking stunning in a green silk dress that matched the emeralds in her engagement ring. He thought he'd never seen anyone so beautiful. Afterwards, he could remember nothing of the ceremony except Mab smiling at him, her dark eyes full of love.

When they came out of the Register Office, hand in hand, a young woman approached them.

"Hello, I'm Isobel Murray from the *Listener*. I wonder if I could, first of all, congratulate you on your marriage, and then ask you a few questions and take some pictures?"

"How did you know we were here?" Pip asked, warily.

"I write up the wedding column," Isobel smiled. "I couldn't believe it when I saw your names!"

"Does anyone else know?" Mab was anxious.

"No fear! This is my big story! So I take it you're eloping?"

Pip and Mab exchanged looks. "Yes, we are," Mab admitted. "No one else knows, except my best friend, Lady Emily Rochford-Percy. Pip and I love each other, we've been in love for years, but our families won't even let us go to the same schools to take our 'A' Levels. Now they'll have to!"

"Well, actually, my Dad would've let us," Pip put in. "It was just my Mum and Amabel's parents."

Isobel was writing it all down. "And you are sixteen today – Mrs Markham?"

Mab smiled with delight at being called Mrs Markham. "Yes, I am!"

"Happy birthday! May I take some photos?"

They posed for several photos, and then Isobel, barely able to contain her glee, hurried off to write up her story.

Mr and Mrs Markham took a taxi to the Moffat House Hotel and went straight to bed.

"Amabel! Where the fuck have you been? Mama and I have been sick with – what? You are WHAT?... I'll kill him! And you! Amabel? Amabel!" He stared at Harry. "She rang off. She and Philip are at Gretna Green. They got married this morning."

Stephen was having much the same conversation with Pip. "God, Philip, I thought you'd had an accident, I've been out of my mind with worry!"

"Dad, I'm *so* sorry!" He felt terrible, he should have remembered that this was what Stephen always thought if any of them were so much as five minutes late. He'd been so wrapped up in Mab, he hadn't spared a thought for anyone. "You see, Dad, I just didn't think. We couldn't risk Dom finding out."

Stephen sighed. "He and Harry will go insane! How could you do this, Pip?"

"Dad, we're in love! There was no chance that we were going to be allowed to take our 'A' Levels together. Now they won't be able to stop us!"

"I wish you'd talked to me first."

"What would you have said? Bless you, my son, you may get married? You'd have said the same as everyone else – wait. But Dad, if Cherry had only been sixteen, would you have waited two years? Would you have thought, oh yeah, we might feel different then? You didn't hold onto her, and you spent twenty years being miserable because of it."

Stephen was silent. When he spoke again, he simply said, "Congratulations, Pip. Kiss Mabs for me." He hung up and rang Dominic and Harry.

Harry answered the phone. "Dominic's so angry he can hardly speak."

"That's pointless, Hal."

"Well, do you think it'll last?" Harry challenged. "They're barely sixteen!"

"No, of course I don't, but that's not the point, Harry. Pip just said to me that I wouldn't have waited two years to marry Lynn, and he's quite right. If they fall out of love they can get divorced, like you did, like I did. It's far from ideal, but what can we do? They'll have consummated the wedding by now, where's the sense in making a fuss? All that will do is destroy our relationship with them. Does Charlie really want to be estranged from his daughter? Harry, you remember what happened between me and Dad. Look, Cherry and I are coming to Cheyne Walk. We'll see you in a couple of hours."

By the time they arrived, Dominic had calmed down a little, but he was still very angry. He gave Stephen a bleak look.

"There's no point in looking at me like that," Stephen said, as he and Lynn followed him into the drawing room. "If you and Toni hadn't been so adamant about them not changing school, this wouldn't have happened."

Dominic glowered at him. "How do you know? Were you in on it?"

"Don't be stupid, Charlie, of course I wasn't. Pip said on the phone this morning they couldn't stand another two years like this and, to be honest, I'm not entirely sure I blame them. All it needed was a bit of flexibility. If Pip had been living with George and Toni, he and Mab would have seen each other every day. They might even have got tired of each other!"

Dominic started towards the door. "I can't discuss it. It makes me too angry."

"They probably wouldn't even have slept together."

Dominic stopped and clenched his fists. He turned slowly. "Are you doing this deliberately?"

"Mmmhmm. You've got to face this and get over it, Dominic, before they come home tomorrow. You know I was estranged from my father because I didn't conform to his wishes. It was bad for both of us, and although we patched it up before he died, I've never stopped regretting it, and I know he didn't. Come on, Charlie, suck it up. You love Mabs. Don't lose her because of your pride and anger."

Dominic's shoulders sagged. He sat down and put his head in his hands. "You're right, damn you."

"Think of it this way," Stephen said, patting his back. "You're not just gaining a son, you're getting rid of Nanny Davies."

He and Dominic picked Mab and Pip up from Euston station the following afternoon. He kissed the pair of them, but Dominic merely grunted at them and led the way to the car. Stephen saw Mab clutch Pip's hand tightly. They drove to Leezance House in silence, Stephen's attempts to make conversation failing miserably in the strained atmosphere. The fact that the story of the marriage had been splashed all over the tabloids that morning, and that there were reporters camped outside the gates of Leezance hadn't helped.

"Well, what have you got to say for yourselves?" Dominic demanded, after they had dumped their tiny amount of luggage and followed him into the drawing room where Harry and Lynn were waiting.

"Congratulations!" Lynn said warmly.

Dominic shot her a furious look.

"Oh, Mab!" Harry said.

Mab burst into tears.

Pip put his arm around her shoulders. "It's all right, cariad." He looked up. "You're upsetting my wife."

Stephen's lips twitched. He opened his mouth to speak, when the door opened and Dominic's butler announced Lady Susan.

She swept disdainfully into the room. "They're home, then." She glared at Mab and Pip. "I suppose you have an explanation, Amabel?"

"What are you doing here, Mama?" Dominic asked coldly.

"Trying to sort this mess out!" Susan snapped.

"We've had a very long journey and my wife is tired and hungry," Pip interrupted.

"She's got a name, for fuck's sake!"

"Stop swearing, Dominic, and do something!" Susan exclaimed.

"What do you suggest I do?" Dominic rang the bell and a maid came in. "Could you bring us some tea, Claire, please? Amabel and Philip, sit down!" He looked over at his mother. "They're married. It's a fait accompli."

Susan perched on the edge of a chair. "Oh well, what can you expect?" She looked at Stephen. "I mean no offence, Stephen, but Philip probably knows no better! All those children by all those different women!"

Stephen leant towards Lynn. "Would now be a good time to mention Coral and Miles?" he whispered in her ear.

She elbowed him in the ribs. "Shh!"

"Philip's great grandfather was a miner, I understand," Susan went on. She looked at Harry. "And, of course, your father ran a public house. Bad blood will out!"

"How dare you?" Harry spluttered, incensed.

Dominic shook his head at her and turned to Susan. "I presume you're talking about the Chaplin Roxburgh bad blood?" he inquired politely. "Papa always took great pains to point out that the first Chaplin came over with William the Conqueror. Licked William's arse to get the land. Then the baronetcy. Didn't a Chaplin help that fat German, George the Fourth, cheat someone at cards? And the Roxburghs don't bear too close a scrutiny, do they? Wasn't the first Earl the bastard son of Louise de Kerouaille? Of course, the Roxburghs say that Charles the Second was his father, but Charles wasn't so sure, was he, that's why the son was only given an earldom. So, not even a royal bastard, then. And Papa wasn't much better, either, all those affairs. Yes, I'm descended from an arse licker, a cheat, a whore and an adulterer. I'd much prefer the miner and the innkeeper, frankly."

Susan was scarlet with rage. She stood up. "You always were a disappointment, Dominic, but I never expected you to be quite such an appalling parent. You've spoilt those children beyond—"

"Be quiet!" Dominic interrupted. He'd gone white, and his eyes were arctic. Neither Harry nor Stephen had ever seen him so angry. "How dare you? How dare you call me an appalling parent? You and my father were, without doubt, the worst parents I ever encountered! Between you, you made me feel like a leper! If it hadn't been for Sophy and Nanny Davies, I don't honestly know how I would have survived. As it was, I grew up feeling completely worthless. School, however loathsome, was preferable to living with you two. I'd like you to leave, Mama. Oh, and I'd like you to leave Charnton too, I intend to settle it on Amabel and Philip."

She stared at him. "Where do you expect me to live?"

"You have your own house here in London, as well as the cottage on the estate in Norfolk. Frankly, I could never see why you wanted to be at Charnton, you always told Papa you hated the place." He rang the bell for the butler. "Show Lady Susan out, please, Barlow. Good day, Mama." He waited until the door shut behind her. Turning to Pip, he held out his hand and grinned ruefully. "Welcome to the family, Pip!"

Late that night, after an amicable dinner, when Pip and Mab had told about the wedding, and Harry had cried at missing it, and everyone had got rather tipsy, Harry was sitting at her dressing table, smoothing night cream onto her face

Dominic came in from the bathroom. "Ah, slapping on the old mortician's wax," he remarked, getting into bed.

"At least I bother to try and stay young looking," she retorted, nettled. "You're getting wrinkled, Dominic."

"I'm nicely weathered," he said, picking up his book. "Girls like the craggy look, think of Sean Connery."

Harry sighed. "It is unfair. Susan was looking old, I thought." She turned to face him. "That reminds me; Stevie didn't seem surprised at the things you said. Does he know how your parents treated you?"

"Steve? Yes, of course."

Harry stared at him. "When did you tell him?"

"Years ago. Why?"

"Before you told me?"

"Before I met you."

"I see. So you tell *Stephen* really private things about your life, but not me. If Angus was still alive, I probably wouldn't have known until now!"

"That's true."

"I thought you loved me!"

"I do, and that's why I didn't tell you, my darling. I told Steve years ago, on that tour when I first met you. It was after a concert, we were high or drunk..."

"Probably both," Harry put in.

He grinned. "Yes, well, anyway, he was saying how success didn't mean as much to him as he'd thought it would without Cherry, how you need someone to love you, and I said at least he had his family and he asked what I meant. John and Sian had been to one of the concerts a few days before, and had come backstage and fussed over him, and I was feeling, oh, I don't know, fucking miserable, I suppose; my parents never came to watch me perform, and so..." He shrugged. "Well, I used him as a shoulder to cry on. And then he brought me you, and after that, nothing else mattered,

Hats, you were all I needed." He smiled. "I think that's why he introduced us. He's a good friend."

"Yes," Harry agreed. Very occasionally, if he was extremely moved, she'd seen Dominic with tears in his eyes, but she'd never seen him actually cry. She couldn't imagine how terrible he must have been feeling to have broken down in front of someone, no matter how much alcohol or cocaine he'd imbibed. How very lucky it had been Stephen. She blinked back tears of her own, and took him in her arms. "I love you, Dom."

He kissed her. "I love you too, beautiful baby. And, you know, much as I wish they'd waited, I'm glad Mab's got Pip. He's so very like Stephen."

It wasn't all plain sailing after that. Toni and George cut their holiday short, and arrived at Leezance the next day. Toni was furious, demanding to know how Stephen could have let the marriage happen.

"Calm down, pet!" George soothed. "Remember your condition! She's got a bun in the oven," he told Stephen.

"Again?" Stephen exclaimed, earning himself a tongue lashing from Toni. Finally he said, "For God's sake, Toni, put a sock in it! I only meant you haven't given yourself much time to get over Ant's birth, but to be honest, I couldn't give a toss! Churn them out every nine months! And as for Pip and Mab, as I already said to Charlie, if you and he had been a bit more understanding about the 'A' Levels, I doubt this would have happened!"

George surprised him by agreeing. "I said that, man, but you knew better," he said to Toni.

"Oh, shut up, George, shut up both of you!" She burst into tears.

Eventually, it was agreed that Pip and Mab would live with Stephen and Lynn, and Mab would transfer to Pip's school. They'd insisted that they had to be available to write and rehearse songs with Alex. They'd renamed the band The Borders Reivers and were determined to make a go of it.

"Oh, and we've talked it over with Alex and decided we're not taking 'A' Levels. We want to get the band together and start playing gigs," Pip declared, provoking a fresh storm of outrage.

"Why the fuck did you have to say that now?" Stephen asked him. "Why didn't you just wait till all the fuss had died down?"

"Sorry," he muttered. "Didn't think."

"Can I beg you not to say anything else? And the same goes for you, Mabs."

Harry and Dominic had given the puppy to Mab and she was sitting on the floor, playing with her. She'd named her Lady Poppleton The First, following in the Chaplin family tradition of giving their pets place names – Poppleton was just outside York – but she was calling her Poppy for short. She looked up. "It's not me! I told him not to say anything, but he said we should start as we mean to go on."

Stephen sighed. "Sometimes it's best to do things – not sneakily, exactly, more *artfully*," he said.

He took them back to the Priory a week later, installing them in the guest suite for the time being. He was having a house built in the grounds for Sian and Ted. Ted had recently had a hip replacement and Stephen was trying to convince Sian to move to Oxford. He'd bought a large flat in the centre of York, which she and Ted could use whenever they wanted, and he thought a house in the Priory grounds with easy access to his heated indoor pool, which would help Ted's arthritis, might swing it. It would be a simple matter to alter the main house so that Pip and Mab had their own self contained wing. When they left, it could be used as guest accommodation.

Their elopement had started him thinking about his and Lynn's first wedding. True, they hadn't exactly eloped, but it was a similar sort of occasion. Rather impulsively, he booked the two of them a suite at the Midland Hotel in Manchester.

"Are you sure this is a good idea, Stephen?" Lynn asked anxiously. "You got really peculiar about Manchester when we were sorting out our second wedding."

Stephen smiled. "That was different, I was very depressed then. Don't worry, Cherry, we'll have a great time. Manchester has changed a lot in some ways, but in others it's exactly the same – it's still got that buzz and excitement – and some of our old haunts are pretty unscathed. When were you last there?"

"Nineteen eighty three."

He stared at her. "Seriously?"

She nodded. "Why would I go back and torture myself?"

He took her hand and kissed it. "We'll have a great time," he repeated.

He was right, Manchester had changed, enough to blunt her longing for the old days, but not enough to eradicate it completely, so she found herself feeling a pleasant nostalgia, which only very occasionally became sharp enough to hurt. They went to Platt Fields; to her dismay, the Pet's Corner had gone, but they hired a boat and went on the lake, sharing the rowing, and they went to the City Art Gallery and the museum on Oxford Road, and Stephen had booked them a meal at the restaurant that had formerly been the Register Office in Jackson's Row.

"It was a lovely meal, but I preferred it when it was a Register Office," Lynn said as they walked back to the hotel.

"Yes, me too," Stephen agreed.

"But we have had a lovely time, haven't we?" she smiled.

He smiled back, tenderly. "Certainly have, and you haven't changed at all, my darling girl. You're still as beautiful as you were the day I first met you."

That night he wrote a song, for Lynn and for Manchester, 'City Of Dreams'.

'Quicksilver' was released at the end of June. The band had filmed videos for the singles 'City Of Dreams' and 'Sea Change', and were concentrating on rehearsing for the tour, which was due to start at the beginning of July, after they'd appeared at Live 8. They would be touring Europe, the Far East, and Britain, finishing with a concert at the Royal Albert Hall in aid of charities for the physically disabled on the second of December, the anniversary of their very first gig twenty five years earlier in the bar at Grosvenor Place.

"Will you be all right while I'm away?" Stephen asked Lynn, the night before the tour, after they'd made love and were lying in each other's arms. "It's more than five months – it's a long time."

"Of course I will! I'll have all the children here, and Sian and Ted and Barbara, and Coral seems to be popping in more and more frequently, and Harry and Holly and I see each other all the time, and I was thinking of starting up my practice again – oh, but Stevie, I'm going to miss you so very, very much!"

He kissed her. "I'm going to miss you too, my Cherry."

"Will *you* be all right?" she asked anxiously. "You'll be doing so many shows! A hundred and twenty six! It's a punishing schedule, Stevie!"

"And I'm not as young as I used to be," he grinned.

"I didn't mean – it's just, well, this is your first tour for how long?"

"Five years," Stephen replied. "Five years!" he repeated. "It can't be!"

"And you won't be playing guitar," Lynn went on. She stroked his left arm. "I'll be worrying about you!"

Stephen smiled. "Don't be. I've come to terms with the accident, Cherry. It was…" He swallowed. "It was horrible, unspeakably horrible, but it wasn't the worst thing that ever happened to me. Losing you was. And getting you back was the best thing. If I had to pay a price for it, so be it. If I had to choose you or my hand, I'd choose you."

Lynn was crying. "Oh, Stevie, I love you so much."

"There's a song that Dada used to sing; I've been thinking about it a lot, recently. It sums up everything I feel." He started singing:

"*Mine's the old, sweet story,*
Full of shining glory,
About the girl I'm proud to call my wife,
Who stands here right beside me,
Whose sweet love helps and guides me,
The girl who is the best thing in my life."

He held her tightly to him. "The very best thing. Cherry, you *are* my life."